A MILLION TEARS

'The summer's best holiday read . . .'
Scottish and Universal Newspapers

'An unquenchable thirst for daring and creativity . . .'
The Sunday Times

'As a literary publicist we receive over 50 books a week
to evaluate – we knew instantly that *A Million Tears* was
a classic.'   Tony Cowell, *PressGroup UK*

'Henke has written a gripping story . . .'
Corgi Books

'I smelt the coal dust in Wales and felt the dust in my
eyes as I fought alongside Evan.'   Dr Peter Claydon

'Henke tells interesting and exciting stories. He doesn't
use bad language and writes good English. A joy to read.'
The Sun

Visit Paul Henke on his website
for current titles and future novels at:

www.henke.co.uk

or email Paul at

henke@sol.co.uk

A MILLION TEARS

Paul Henke

To Sarah,

A million thanks!

Paul Henke

GOOD READ PUBLISHING

First published in 1998 by Good Read Publishing
A Good Read Publishing paperback
Reprinted in 2006 by Good Read Publishing

10 9 8 7 6 5 4 3

A CIP catalogue record for this title is available
from the British Library

ISBN 1 902483 08 1

Typeset by Palimpsest Book Production Limited,
Polmont, Stirlingshire
Printed and bound in Great Britain by
Antony Rowe Ltd, Chippenham, Wilts

Good Read Publishing Ltd
Balfron
G63 0RL

This book is dedicated to Richard and Louise

A MILLION TEARS

Prologue

David Evan Griffiths stood next to the large bay window, looking out over the rolling grounds of the Sussex estate. He was 87 years old, stood with a stoop, was still slim and had a shock of white hair, his vanity in old age. He was waiting for a reporter from Time magazine who wanted to write the story of the Griffiths family. A wry grin cracked his lips as events and people flashed through his mind like a kaleidoscope.

He glanced away from the vista and towards the open door of the walk-in safe, where the journals, diaries, letters and the other papers he had acquired over the last seven decades resided. The history of the Griffiths family in one location. The loss didn't bear thinking about should something happen to it all. The information contained in the safe was a microcosm of the twentieth century. Hardly an event of any importance that had impacted on the world in the last fifty years or more hadn't been influenced or in some cases caused by a member of his family. In many cases, indeed, he had been the prime mover of events. He looked back out of the window, enjoying the sight of the deep frost sparkling in the sunlight, the sea, his ruling passion, was a dark blue in the distance.

There was a noise behind him and the door swung open. A young man stood in the doorway, a briefcase in his hand.

'Come in, come in,' Griffiths repeated. 'Good of you to come all this way.' As always, in spite of the fact that the interview was taking place at the request of the magazine, Sir David made it appear as though the favour was for him. The young man walked purposefully across the wide expanse of carpet, his hand outstretched.

'It's very good of you to see me, Sir,' he said in a soft east coast American accent which Sir David placed immediately as Bostonian. The reporter tried hard not to be overpowered by the wealth surrounding him nor by the sheer presence of the man standing in front of him. He realised that he was shaking hands with a legend of the twentieth century. Sir David's achievements sprang to mind and in spite of himself the young man cringed inwardly. He's just another man he thought.

They settled opposite each other in leather wing-backed chairs and the reporter took out his tape recorder and asked permission to switch it on. With a gleam in his eyes Sir David nodded his acquiescence. Coffee was served by a butler who then silently withdrew.

'I've been thinking how to start,' Sir David said. 'It's easy to say I'll begin at the beginning but it's difficult to know where that is precisely. In retrospect and believe me, young man, at my age you spend a great deal of time in retrospection, it was the events of 1890 that changed our lives irrevocably. I've been looking through the files and papers of the period, reminding myself about the early years. It's strange how in our arrogance we think that we have total control over our destinies. We haven't. Destiny controls us. Decisions we make play a part, but each tiny event builds on the last and affects the next. This goes on until we have lived out our lives, for better or for worse. For many of us, we hope it is for the better. I have outlived my contemporaries, friends and, thankfully, my foes. My family is still around me. That has always been the source of our strength, the family.' He lapsed into a meditative silence for a few seconds and then focused his considerable intellect on the man opposite.

'When I look back on the early days, I think what a

pretentious and precocious ten year old I must have been. But there again, in those days we grew up a lot faster than children do nowadays. It was not unusual for a twelve year old to be working down a coal mine, as most of my friends did, and at fifteen you were a man. I think it gave me an insight into the adult world. Childhood should last as long as possible. Naturally, no child agrees with me but most octogenarians do!' Sir David gave a chuckle which turned into a mild coughing fit. 'Blasted bronchitis. The wretched doctors said it'll be another fortnight at least before I can get out. That's why I agreed to the story. You wanted a short, sharp interview.' The reporter nodded. 'Instead, I'm offering you a chance to use that lot,' Sir David waved his hand in the general direction of the room safe, 'to put together the full story. It'll take time but I think you'll find it worth your while.' Before the reporter could say anything Sir David went on. 'I estimate that interviewing me will take the next two weeks at least. The papers are yours to browse through whenever you want but they must not,' he emphasised his words with a shake of his right index finger, 'be taken from here. If you put together the story to my satisfaction I will arrange publication. I have read some of your work and I think it's good. You show an insight into events that is sadly lacking with most journalists nowadays.'

The reporter was surprised and excited at the same time. Publication of a book or a series of books about the Griffiths family would make him famous, even wealthy. Knowing some of the history of the man sitting before him he knew that he was being offered a ringside seat at the story of events and people that had shaped and changed the century.

'What if you don't like what I find?'

Sir David chuckled. 'Twenty years ago I would have reserved the right to edit anything I didn't like. Now I am only interested in the truth being told, warts and all.' He held up his hand. 'Don't misunderstand me, as far as

the family is concerned there are few warts. I believe that
we have acted as honourably and decently as we could.
We've cut a few corners, trod on a few toes and made a
few enemies, but on the whole I think history will judge
us favourably. So, in answer to your question, you can
use anything you find.'

'Fair enough, and I must say that's mighty generous
of you.' The reporter sipped at his coffee, giving himself
time to think the matter through. 'I'll need to clear it with
my editor.'

Sir David looked at the young man and tapped his
steepled fingers together before saying, 'I've already
agreed with your editor. He says you can stay as long
as it takes.'

The reporter grinned warily. The cunning old fox, he
thought, still as sharp as a tack even at his age. 'Where
will I stay?'

'Here, of course. There are twenty bedrooms and we
have better facilities than a five star hotel.'

At that moment the door opened and a beautiful
black-haired girl entered the room, smiling sweetly. Sir
David's heart stopped beating for a second as it seemed
that his beloved sister had walked into the room. He
collected himself and made the introductions.

The reporter was tongue-tied. The girl was slim, had
a vivacious if cheeky smile and was perfectly at home in
her jodhpurs and hacking jacket.

'Gramps, I've been told to tell you that we'll be out for
dinner and don't forget that the Foreign Secretary will be
here for tea.'

Sir David nodded. He hadn't forgotten. In April Dr.
David Owen, Foreign Secretary to the Wilson government would be visiting South Africa to hold talks with
Ian Smith on the future of Rhodesia. Sir David had a great
deal to contribute to those talks. His granddaughter waved
the riding crop she was holding by way of farewell and
breezed out of the room.

'My granddaughter,' he said by way of explanation. 'Sian.'

'How's that again? Did you say Sharn?'

'That's how it's pronounced but we spell it S. I. A. N. She's named after my sister.' A faraway look came into Sir David's eyes and then he pulled himself together. 'Why don't you rewind that contraption,' he pointed at the tape recorder, 'and let's begin. I think we need to start in early 1890 . . .'

BOOK 1

Dai's Story

1890

1

It was a typical wet autumn day. I was in the front room with my nose pressed to the window looking up the road trying to see my father. In spite of the heavy rain and fading light I could see still the glow from the colliery furnaces, a constant reminder of the hell on earth the people of Llanbeddas endured in order to extract a meagre living, digging into its bowels.

Long streets, six deep, stretched along the valley and up the hillside. On the other side of the river, a mile away, was the colliery, the reason for the existence of our village and many more like it. They ran into each other, one house in one village, the next door house in another.

I was ten in 1890 and I had never been further than five villages to the north although once I went as far south as Pontypridd, the market town where the rivers Taff and Rhondda meet. I had bought a small present for myself at one of the market stalls, a little tin soldier in a red jacket and black breeches. I carried it in my pocket or took it to bed with me, a constant reminder of that wonderful day.

Today I heard my brother and sister squabbling in the living room. They were twins and always fighting. I wanted to tell them to be quiet; they were disturbing my concentration as I willed Da to come into sight. If I did not wish him to come home now, I knew he would do a double shift, and I would not see him for at least another twenty-four hours.

I turned from the window to shout and as I did they fell silent. I let out a deep breath and turned back to my vigil. I was in the front room, not used much except when the vicar called which was not often, or at birthdays and Christmas. It was small with a settee along one wall and a chair either side of the fireplace. Recessed either side of the chimney were shelves, one with Mam's best china, the other with the family Bible and brass ornaments she had acquired in ten years of marriage. Their eleventh wedding anniversary was next month, the twelfth of November. The room would be in use then; everybody would be there. Sion, Sian and myself were more excited at the prospect than our parents were.

I pressed my nose harder against the window and strained my eyes looking along the road, wishing with all my heart for him to come. It was a week since I had last seen him – he was working double shifts to make extra money – but he had promised to come home early tonight. I knew he would be tired but he would play with us for a while, ask us about school and in a stern voice tell us to finish our greens.

For a few seconds I sensed rather than saw the two figures coming along the street through the dusk. There was no mistaking his big frame and the way he walked. His heavy, determined tread distinguished him from the shuffling gait of his friends. His stubborn pride prevented him from showing how tired he was. I was told by most of my relations, Grandmother in particular, that I had inherited the same pride as my father. I rushed from the room into the short passageway and threw open the front door. He was only a few yards away when I ran out into the rain and threw my arms around him. He ruffled my hair as we stepped back into the house.

'Mam will be angry with you, Dai,' he smiled, his teeth gleaming white in his coal black face. 'You've got dust all down your side.'

'That's okay Da, I put my old clothes on so it won't

matter. I knew you'd come and I wanted, eh . . .' I trailed off, embarrassed at my show of affection.

He realised how I felt and said: 'Well then, it won't matter, will it? Come on, let's go and see what's for tea.' He opened the door into the living room, off which was our small kitchen. This room was the same size as the room in front. It had a table and five chairs, an open fire with an oven on one side, Da's easy chair and Mam's dresser along one wall. It was warm and clean.

'I'm home Meg,' he called upstairs.

'I realised that love, when I heard Dai rushing out. I'll be down in a minute. Your water's in the kitchen. I'll come and scrub your back when you're ready.'

The twins grinned at Da but did not rush to him; he was too dirty for them, covered as he was from head to foot in coal dust and white streaked where the rain had washed the black away. I followed him when he went out the back, into the small yard and stripped off, shaking as much dust from his clothes as possible before he came back, wet from the rain. I had lifted the bath from its hook on the wall in the yard and put it down in the kitchen. I poured hot water from the first of our large saucepans, heating over the fire. While I went for another saucepan, Da added cold water from the tap. He quickly washed, climbed out of the bath, carried it outside and poured the black water down the drain. He brought the bath back, ready for the next lot of water.

'That's better, eh Dai? I'm white after all. I was beginning to doubt it for a while back.' Mam came in just then, bent over the bath and kissed him.

'Dai, go and see what your brother and sister are up to.' She turned back to Da. 'Now where's the soap?' She put her hand in the water and Da grabbed her arm. 'Stop it Evan, the children,' I heard her say as I closed the door.

In the living room Sion was starting to build another kite from bits of sticks and paper while Sian played with her doll. I sat in Da's chair and waited for him to come in. I heard my Mam squeal and say: 'Evan, you've splashed me, look you. This is the last time I scrub your back, just you wait and see!' She was always making the same threat.

The door to the room we were in opened and he came in, a towel wrapped around him. 'I'll go and dress Meg while you lay the table.' He gave us a merry wink and went up the narrow stairs to the front bedroom.

I helped lay the table and Mam put a pot of stew in the middle. The smell made my mouth water. The twins were already at the table waiting for Da to come down, impatient to eat.

'Hurry up, Da,' called Sian, always the greedy one. 'I'm hungry.'

'All right, all right, miss; I'll be there in a minute.'

I leant forward, lifted the lid and sniffed. 'Hmmmm, that's good. Have a smell, Sian,' I teased her.

She knew what I was up to and poked her tongue out at me, a cheeky smile on her face. She had black hair like Mam's and the same blue eyes. She was very pretty and one day she would be as beautiful as our mother. She was precocious, cheeky and adorable. We spoilt her even if there was little to spoil her with.

By the time the colliery had deducted the rent from Da's pay and we paid for the food and other necessities, there was not much left over. Mam and Da were determined we should have an education and they wanted to send us to the big school down the valley. They saved every penny they could to pay for it. By the rules of life as far as they applied to our valley I should start in the colliery next year, at the old age of eleven. The thought filled me with dread. I'd seen the effects on other children . . . old men by the time they were twenty. Through Mam, Da had learnt the benefit of a good education and was as determined as she that we had one.

Mam had been a teacher in the local school until a few years earlier. Her best friend, Sian after whom our Sian was named, had given up teaching to have a baby. Six months after the baby was born Sian's husband was killed in a pit accident. Knowing the dire straits she was in, Mam gave up her job to let Sian have it. This was Mam all over. Although we had needed the money at the time – when was there a time we did not need money? – Mam had not hesitated to help.

Mam devoted her time to teaching the twins and me. She had shown me pictures of other countries, firing my imagination with tales of America, South Africa and Australia.

Now every spare penny went into a little box hidden in their bedroom, ready for when I was old enough to go "down the valley". Next year, instead of crawling down the smaller, stinking, rat infested wet holes of the colliery I would be going to school; normally this was limited to the rich. To get there, I needed excellent marks in the entrance examination. If I did not get them I would lose my place to someone whose father was rich and influential. When I protested, Da had shrugged and said it was the way of the world. Thanks to Mam, though, I was a long way ahead of my classmates and because I worked hard I stayed ahead. I didn't enjoy it and would have preferred to be out with my friends but my fear of going down the mines and my dreams not coming true stopped me.

Mam often said that education produced dreams, but it was hard work that would bring them to reality.

Da came down and sat at his usual place. We bent our heads and he said a quick grace in Welsh. Mam lifted the top off the pot and the rich aroma filled the room. Sian pounced on the serving spoon, had her fingers gently rapped by Da, pouted and let Mam serve.

After the dishes were washed we sat around the table with our slates and chalk. Even the games we played were educational. For instance, we were each given a letter and then had to write down the names of places, birds, flowers, rivers, kings, historic battles and so on. We had played this game so often even the twins, though only eight, did well. Somehow Da always came last.

The next morning I was up at six thirty. By that time Da had been in work an hour and Mam, after seeing him off, was back in bed. I stoked the fire and got some coal from the back shed. I put on half a bucket, emptied the remainder in the polished coalscuttle alongside the grate, grabbed the other tin bucket and let myself out the front door.

It had stopped raining though the sky was overcast, the threat of rain still heavy in the air. I hurried along the street in the direction of the colliery. At the corner shop I turned left and ran down the steep hill towards the river. I exchanged 'Good mornings' with the people I met, speaking Welsh. Welsh was our natural language, English was foreign to us. At home we spoke English and like some others we were bilingual; most spoke only Welsh and refused to learn English, in spite of the fact that thousands of immigrants from England came into the valley looking for work. Some of the older Welsh families even moved further west, where the English seldom came. The immigrants were not wanted in our valleys; the men said, 'they are stealing our jobs, yes Bach, and the very food from our mouths!'

I hurried along the bank of the river, the filthy water swirling only a foot below my feet. There had been a lot of rain recently and the river was swollen to nearly twice its usual depth. Granddad said that when he was a boy the water had been clean enough to swim in and the fish caught in half a day could feed a family for a week. But nowadays, the only things living in the water were the rats, as big as kittens. For many years the water had been used to wash the coal from the colliery. As a consequence it was as black as night with a peculiar, horrible smell.

What it gave us though was as much coal as we needed . . . free.

I reached the part of the river where the bank had collapsed and the water had spread over a larger area. With the rain more coal than ever would be washed down. It would reach this spot and the widening of the river would deposit coal near the sides of the banks. I slipped off my socks and shoes and stepped into the cold water.

Twenty minutes later, my feet numb and black, I had both buckets full. Rather than dirty my socks and get my shoes wet, I walked back bare footed. I was so used to this that I did not feel the stones and cinders underfoot. I stopped every few hundred yards to rest and threw stones at any rats I saw. I arrived home as the rain started again. I was annoyed because I had hoped for another load before breakfast. Instead, I washed my feet and sat drying them in front of the fire, Mam's old school atlas on my knees.

I opened it to the map of America and as I followed the rivers and towns my dreams took over once more – New York, Pittsburgh, and west to Denver and San Francisco. One day I promised myself, one day. Unlike my parents and the twins, my friends laughed at my daydreams. What they were not aware of was that Mam and Da shared a similar dream. Why didn't we go? Why didn't we pack up and go? – the family, that was why. The Welsh older generations had a tight grip on the children, which was why we wandered less than other nationalities.

Granddad had now turned to God, trying hard to save his soul before the dust in his lungs killed him. Ours was a typical close knit Welsh family, with our grandparents and uncles living within a mile of our house.

'Dreaming again, Dai?' Mam interrupted my thoughts.

I closed the atlas guiltily. 'Only a bit Mam. I was thinking about us – all the family I mean.' I paused, uncertain how much I could say. 'I mean, why don't we

just go? You want to, Da wants to, and I want to. You
keep saying there's a whole world out there. Couldn't we
go and find it? Find a better life. Not' I added hastily,
'that life isn't good here. It's just . . .' I hesitated, not
knowing how to go on.

'I know, Dai,' she knelt beside my chair. 'I know
what you mean. But just think. There's all the family,
our friends. Grandmother especially has only got Aunt
Olive and me.' She paused. 'And there's Grandma and
Granddad. What will they do without us?'

'Mam, Mam, Mam, you know they'll do very well.
They've got four others besides Da and look how many
grandchildren they've got. No Mam, we'll rot and die
here, strangled by our family.'

There was a sadness in her eyes as she laid her hand
on my arm. 'You're too wise for your age and your own
good,' she said softly. 'You may be right,' she sighed
and then smiled sadly. 'Who would have thought such
insight in a child of ten?'

'I'm not a child Mam. If it wasn't for you and Da I'd
be going down the mine in a year's time. Instead I'll
be staying in school, costing you both more than you
can afford, with Da killing himself working doubles to
make enough money.' I could not help the bitterness in
my voice. I loved my parents and wanted them to have
a better life before it was too late.

'You may be right, Dai,' she repeated, 'but for now
there's nothing we can do. We have your schooling to
think about and then there's the twins. Until that's all
finished we can't think of going anywhere. So let's have
no more talk about it.' She stood up.

'Mam, use the money you've saved for our education.
It's enough to get us out of here, and before the dust gets
Da, like it gets everybody eventually.'

Without a word she went into the kitchen and a
few moments later returned with half a loaf and some
dripping. She placed them on the table and looked at me

thoughtfully. 'Did you mean what you said? About the money I mean.'

'Yes, Mam.' I nodded and lowered my eyes to the atlas. Did I mean it? All my dreams about school, getting on in life, revolved around the money and my education. If we spent it emigrating what would happen to my schooling then? I was annoyed at my selfish thoughts. Why think about it? Nothing would ever happen.

We were doomed to stay here for the rest of our lives, living our dreams in our heads and not striving for the reality, at least, not until I was grown up. Then, no matter how much I loved my parents I was going to move on in the world. I would make my fortune and return to take them away to live in a fine house with servants and everything. Sion and Sian would come as well. I wandered into my dream world once more, the atlas still showing the continent of America.

After breakfast I helped the twins with their school-work. Neither of them appreciated it. They only wanted to go out and play even though it was still raining. Not so long ago I felt the same way, until one of my friends, three years older than me, started in the mine. He drowned six days later when one of the smaller shafts had been flooded after heavy rain and a pump had failed. After that I spent weeks dreading the thought of my eleventh birthday. Finally, I realised the only way out was as Mam kept saying; I had to work harder than anyone else and continue my education.

The rain stopped about midday and I repeated my earlier trip to the river, returning with another two buckets of coal. Sion and Sian were in the street playing with their friends, a gang of ragamuffins together and always up to mischief. As I staggered around the corner I was in time to see Sian knocking on the door of old Mr Price and then running pell-mell past me. I grinned as I walked towards the old man's house knowing the explosion that was to follow. Sure enough his door slammed open and there he stood, angrily shaking a stick at no one in particular.

This was the first time I had been nearby when his door had been knocked. As he stood there shaking his stick and yelling after the kids I saw there was something wrong but could not work out what for a few seconds.

'You rascals,' he called in Welsh, hopping from foot to foot, looking up and down the road, not knowing which way they had gone. 'Just you wait. I'll catch you and when I do I'll give you all the leathering of your lives, look you. Just you wait and see if I don't.'

He was a sprightly old boy in spite of the years he had worked in the mine. As I took in the darned cardigan, the patched trousers and the grey hair, I realised what was wrong. He was not angry. He was smiling under his fierceness. I was so surprised I stopped and gaped at him.

'After all these years Dai Griffiths and you caught me out. Heh, heh but I had you fooled for long enough didn't I boyo? Heh, heh.'

I smiled back. For the first time I was unafraid of him. I saw a friendly, lonely old man. How did I, a mere ten-year-old boy, see that? I suddenly realised what old age meant and why families stayed together.

'Well, Dai Griffiths, are you going to come in for a cup of tea or are you going to tell your young friends that I'm not really angry at all? Mind you, if you do, then you'll spoil not only their game but mine too. And you must admit I make them run just a little bit faster and give them more spice in the game than anybody else, even that old biddy at twenty one.' Again he laughed. 'And just think young Griffiths, if you come inside with me for a cup of tea you'll be a hero in no time. Ha, ha, especially when you leave and tell them all about the live bats and frogs I keep. Don't look so alarmed it's not true. But just think of the stories we can make up to tell them. Well then, are you coming or aren't you?'

I put the buckets of coal on his doorstep and followed him inside. His house was identical to ours, not quite as clean perhaps and certainly shabbier, but there was a friendly air about the place that somehow went well with its smell.

2

'MAM, GUESS WHERE I've been,' I said as I tipped the coal into the back shed.

'Apart from down to the river, I've no idea,' she replied, scrubbing Da's clothes on a wash board.

'I went in to old Mr Price's for tea. You know Mam he's a nice man, only a bit lonely I think.'

'I think so too, Bach. That's why I go and visit him from time to time, just to have a chat see.'

I looked at her in surprise. 'I didn't know you'd been in his house.'

'Oh, not often like, but now and again, when you're at school usually. What did you talk about?'

'Um . . . nothing much. Mostly about school and working down the mines. He said I should work hard and go to grammar school and do well and perhaps get to university in Cardiff. He said if I did and other folks hereabouts saw how much of an advantage there was in it then they'd try harder perhaps for their children, like you and Da are doing. He said that education was . . . was the working man's way out of s . . . sludgery, I think he said.'

Mam chuckled. 'Aye Dai, that's what he probably did say. I persuaded him ages ago that was the best way for us. I had the devil's own job, a lot of nonsense he kept calling it, but he changed his mind and now tells everybody how important schooling is for the working class. You never know Dai, perhaps one day they'll learn, and then we'll have a decent education system available to everybody.'

I nodded, struck by the idea. After all, was it fair my parents had to work hard, deny themselves so much to put us through school? So many rich people made sure their children had a proper education without any effort or hardship. Life, I reflected for the umpteenth time, was unfair. I got out the atlas and wandered back into my daydreams of adventure, exploration and fortune.

After the twins came in and washed I had an idea.

'Sian,' I asked seriously, 'do you think you're brave?'

'Of course,' she replied, scornfully. She was a proper tomboy, which was not surprising with a twin brother as well as an older brother to influence her.

'Good. Well you saw me going into old Mr Prices's didn't you?'

'Gosh, yes, Dai. That was awfully brave of you. What was it like? Is he really a man witch like old Mrs Jenkins is a woman witch?'

'Don't be daft, Sian. He's just a nice old man who's very lonely. So' I paused, 'you and me and Sion are going to visit him before tea, all right?'

They both gasped. 'I'm not,' said Sion. 'He eats little boys,' he voiced the fear of the myth that had been in existence for as long as I could remember.

'Tell me,' I said craftily, 'name one little boy he's eaten, ever.'

They screwed up their faces in concentration and finally admitted they could think of none.

'Right, because it's not true. He's really very nice and we're going in to see him.' Who could have possibly foreseen the consequences of such a simple decision?

They looked at one another uncertainly, then Sian said, in a timorous voice, 'All right then, Dai, but you must come too.'

'Of course, that's the whole idea. You wouldn't go alone, anyway.'

I told Mam where we were going and we left the house. Reluctantly, they followed me along the pavement.

I reached for the knocker and as I did I realised the twins were edging away.

'Come here, both of you. It'll be all right, I promise you.'

They nodded, wariness mirrored in each other's eyes.

I rapped a couple of times and stepped back. The two of them were poised for flight and as the door swung open I thought they would run before I could stop them.

Mr Price's scowl was replaced by a smile when he saw me. 'Back so soon, boyo? What can I do you for?' He used English for the first time.

'I hope you don't mind but we've come to visit.'

'We? Who's we?'

He could not see the twins tucked down by the side of the wall. I pulled them into view. 'Me and Sion and Sian,' I replied.

His smile broadened. 'Come in, look you. Come on in.'

He ushered us through the door, the twins shuffling their feet so slowly it was maddening, but he didn't seem to mind. We went into the living room and sat awkwardly at the table while he went into the kitchen to make a cup of tea.

'It's just like ours,' whispered Sian. 'Where do you think he keeps the bats and things?'

'Shshsh and don't be silly,' I whispered back, 'he'll hear you.' Her eyes opened in fright and her hand flew to her mouth. 'I told you, he's just a nice old man.'

He came back in with four cups and the tea pot. The twins fidgeted as he looked at them, still with the same broad smile on his face.

'And so you're the young lady that takes such pleasure in knocking my door and running away, are you?'

Sian looked at him in horror. 'Please, sir . . .' she began.

'Tut, tut, don't apologise. I used to do the same when I was a little boy,' he admitted.

'You did?' asked Sion.

'Of course I did. You don't think you children invented the game do you? Why I can even remember your mother doing the very same thing,' he chuckled. 'She thought she was being original too. Now let's see about this tea.'

For an hour we listened to his stories about the old days and about mining when he was a boy. Suddenly I realised it was past time to meet Da in the allotment and I got up to go.

The twins were about to follow, but Mr Price said: 'I have a biscuit or two . . . .' They decided to stay. Biscuits were a little known luxury.

The allotment was further up the hill, behind the last row of houses. The land, like most of the valley, belonged to the mine owners but because it was unsuitable for any-thing else they allowed the villagers to grow vegetables there. The soil was tough, rocky and unyielding, at first. Hard work, tons of good soil brought up from the river and a lot of time had finally given us land, which was productive. It was Da's greatest pleasure, even after a hard shift, to work in the allotment and watch things grow.

I ran past the last house, badly winded but determined to run all the way as a test. Out of breath I gasped my apologies for being late and explained why.

'What made you do that?' He stood stretched, his hands in the small of his back. He was still covered with coal dust from the mine; he had not yet been home.

I shrugged. 'I'm not sure. I suppose I just felt sorry for him. No one ever seems to visit him much. I thought he must be pretty lonely, that was all. Sion and Sian are still there. At least they were when I left. He persuaded them to stay with some biscuits.'

Da chuckled. 'I don't suppose our Sian could resist that, could she boyo?'

'You're right Da, she couldn't. What do you want me to do?'

For an hour I helped. I dug, lifted out the smallest

stones and pulled up weeds. Although I did not mind the work I did not get the same pleasure from it as Da. I had told him so once and he had said that was because I had not been underground and so I wasn't able to appreciate the joy of something green growing in fresh air, the sun on my back.

Although it had stopped raining earlier in the afternoon the sky was threatening again and so we packed up early. Just as we reached home, the rain started again.

Da looked up and frowned. 'That's too much,' he murmured, 'too much.'

The twins had not yet returned and by the time supper was ready I was sent to fetch them. They were in high spirits and came home reluctantly. They had promised Mr Price that they would visit him again soon.

After supper Sion started building a new kite, the previous one having failed to fly. This unusual hobby had started six months earlier when Mam had shown us pictures of Chinese children playing with kites. From three or four illustrations and descriptions he had managed to make a couple that had flown reasonably well. Now he was designing his own, so far with little success, but he was far from discouraged; his hobby was a ruling passion with him. The setbacks he claimed always told him something; he could then try to correct them. He was often to be found up, past the allotment near the top of the hill, trying to get a kite into the air.

Just before the twins' bedtime we got out the slates for a game.

I was trying to think of a river beginning with Z, Sian's choice, when she said unexpectedly: 'You know what? I like Mr Price. He's very nice. I don't know why I haven't spoken to him before.'

We looked at her in surprise and burst into laughter. It was not what she had said, it was the way she had said it . . . solemn and somehow cute at the same time. The crash of thunder overhead startled us into silence. Sian took Da's hand and I must admit, it was so loud I was frightened too for a moment. Da looked worried.

'What is it Evan? The rain's been worrying you, hasn't it?' Ma saw his expression and wanted to find out what was troubling him.

He said nothing for a moment and then sighed. 'Yes, love, it has. There's too much. You know what happened last time and nothing's changed. Those new pumps we were promised haven't turned up and they're still skimping on the shoring materials. They argue they aren't making enough money to pay for it, in spite of the extra output we achieved. All the time they demand more and more and give us nothing in return.' He shook his head slowly. 'Where I am, it won't affect me,' he put his hand on Mam's, 'so don't look so worried. The problem is at the lower level where Ivan, Ted, Gareth, the two Jones boys and a lot more besides are working. If anything goes wrong I don't see how we'll get them out.' He shrugged and forced a smile. 'What am I worrying about? I don't expect it will happen, see. I'm just being a pessimist. Come on, let's play. After this game it's bed for you two,' he said to the twins. 'It's already past time.'

It was half past seven. On Saturdays I was allowed to stay up until eight.

We had no way of knowing Da was right. The mine was safe. The disaster was going to strike somewhere else and be much worse.

On Sunday we attended early morning chapel. Da made one of his rare appearances because the vicar had been to the house a week earlier and shamed him into coming. For the rest of us it was a weekly habit that none of us wished to break.

When we left the house, dressed in our best clothes, it had stopped raining but was still very windy, the sun occasionally breaking through the clouds. The chapel was always filled to capacity. It was a solid, large building on the hill with a graveyard stretching behind.

As we approached the bells became louder, summoning us to pay homage to a god most of us did not believe in nor, we felt, need. That was the way I had heard Da describe it once. At my age I was not so sure, though I did have my doubts which I kept to myself. The one time I had been brave enough to voice them I received a rap over the knuckles from the teacher and another one from the vicar the following Sunday. After that I never trusted my teacher with any of my ideas or thoughts. Furthermore, I took a hearty dislike to him. Unfortunately, I could not hide my feelings and pretty soon he heartily disliked me too. That had the effect of making me work harder. On more than one occasion he let me know he resented the extra work I did at home.

His attitude was common. Working class people only needed to read, write and do simple sums. Anything more was reserved for the sons of the rich who would become the future rulers of Britain. The advantage of education had been so drummed into me that neither his jibes nor the taunts of some of my classmates could deter me. I was going to leave the valley at all costs.

As we filed into the chapel the vicar greeted us at the door. He knew all his parish, their attitudes to the church and the way they treated their families. In his opinion the latter was a direct reflection of the former. Da he described as an enigma, the exception that proved the rule.

Inside we children were herded to one side. I could see my father talking with a group of men in the back. From their worried looks I guessed they were discussing the weather and safety in the mine, or rather, lack of it.

We fooled around as usual, and I was asked to show my toy soldier. A couple of the other boys tried to barter for it, but they soon realised it was not for swaps.

Before the service started I gave a mighty sneeze

and before long I could not stop. I was now shivering continuously and guessed I was in for a bad cold. It meant at least two days off from school, in bed. I felt like smiling at my good fortune but thought it prudent not to, especially as I saw my teacher glaring across at me after one of my louder explosions.

The service was in Welsh, although some of the English congregation did not understand the vicar nor the hymns we sang.

When it was over I found Mam talking to aunt Maud and asked her if I could go home, as I was feeling ill.

'I was going to send you home,' she said. 'I'll bring you something up when we get home. Go on, I'll tell the vicar you won't be here this afternoon. Off you go.'

When I got back I went to bed and tried to read. Quite soon my eyes began to ache and I gave up. I must have fallen asleep and did not hear the others returning. I woke sometime in the afternoon and realised nobody was in the house. I dozed, just below the surface of awareness, able to dream but controlling my thoughts at the same time. It was my favourite state, like just before falling asleep. As usual I dreamed I had made a fortune, though how I did so always seemed slightly different in different dreams, the details hazy. I never regretted leaving my dream world for the real one, which I saw as a challenge. It was my goal, the object of my existence.

I came awake finally when Mam came in to see me. 'How're you feeling, Dai?'

'Okay, I guess. I'm a bit shivery like, but otherwise I'm fine.'

'I'll bring you up some hot broth. Do you want anything else?'

I shook my head, no mean feat with it resting on a pillow. 'Oh yes,' I changed my mind. 'Could I have the atlas please? Just to look at because my eyes ache if I read.'

'I'll bring it up but don't go straining your eyesight

mind you. If I think you are now, I'll come and take
it away.'

'Okay Mam.' I hid a smile. She often made threats but
never carried them out, not even the mildest. Even so we
never needed telling more than once . . . well, perhaps
twice. With Da it was never, ever, more than once.

The door flew open. 'Here's your atlas,' said Sian,
throwing it onto the bed. 'I can't stop. I'm going to
have tea with Uncle James.' It took me a second or two
to realise we did not have an Uncle James.

She grinned. 'Mr Price. He told us to call him Uncle
James. He's going to build me a doll's house. He said if
we went over today we could talk about it. And he told
Sion he had some, – what is it? Bamboo? – Something like
that. So I must rush. Sion's waiting for me.' She slammed
the door behind her, earning a rebuke from Mam, but still
she slammed the front door. Sian was convinced doors
only closed properly when slammed.

I picked up the atlas. It fell open at America. Uncle
James . . . they were becoming very friendly. They were
getting a dolls house and I guessed the bamboo was for a
kite. I decided to call on him as soon as I was better. There
might be something he could get me, though I wasn't sure.
Apart from my books I had no other real interest.

I concentrated on the atlas, losing myself as I wandered
across the American prairies.

The plate by the bed was empty now and when the door
opened I thought it was Mam to take it away. Instead it
was Da. He sat on the edge of the bed.

'How're you feeling son?'

'I'm all right, Da. I'll be up and about in no time'. In
those days concern over a simple cold was not unusual.
Colds easily became pneumonia or pleurisy, or whatever
it was called. To die was not uncommon from such
illnesses, which was why Mam had sent me straight to
bed.

'Well, keep warm and if there's anything you want just

yell. Do you want any more soup? I can fetch it for you, if you like.'

'No thanks, Da.' I propped myself up against the pillows. 'I was talking to Mam the other day about leaving here and going to some other country. Do you and Mam talk about it?'

'Sometimes. Why do you ask?'

'Don't get me wrong but don't you think there's a chance of a better life somewhere else? I've read about America and Africa. It all sounds too good to be true. Is it? I mean, is it true?' I paused and added hastily. 'Da, I'm really grateful for all you and Mam are doing for me and I'm sure the twins'll be grateful too when they understand better. But what's going to happen? I go to school and I'll work hard and try and make you proud of me. But what about you and Mam? What are you going to be doing? Working double shifts for the next ten years or so? Da, I know I'm only ten but I can see what it's doing to you. I know how hard it must be and how tired you must be.' I trailed off. I had never spoken to him like that before and I was unsure how he would react. I was taking advantage of not being well, hoping that instead of becoming angry he would talk. I wanted to persuade him to leave.

He was silent for a few seconds, looking at his hands, perhaps seeing the ingrained grime no amount of scrubbing would remove properly, or the calluses as hard as the lumps of coal they dug out of the ground.

'I know what you mean son and I suppose one of the reasons Mam and me are doing what we are doing for you is because we know you appreciate it. If we thought you were ungrateful then perhaps we'd send you down the mine like the rest of the kids. And don't forget that may still happen. We don't know how much it will all cost yet, not until we try it. And how will we pay for Sion?' He shrugged. 'And don't you get me wrong. We aren't asking for gratitude. You are the way you are and

Mam and me are the way we are. Together we make a family which, I hope, cares for one another.' He paused. 'I don't even know what I'm trying to say. Except maybe we feel your education is as important to us as it is to you, and that it's worth trying for. So why don't we get that over with first and then think of a future somewhere else? At least, see, we know the system here. If you can get to school and down the valley then you've a chance of getting to university, like Mam explained it to you. I know you'll still need a scholarship and all but there's a chance for you, son; a chance I never had.' He smiled. 'Your Mam would have done better if she had been a boy. As it is . . . and she taught me the importance of schooling. It's a chance not only for you but for us too. Why,' his eyes glowed, 'you could even become a doctor. Mam said and she should know. Just think of that Dai. A doctor in the family. Why, Granddad and Grandma will be tickled pink, look you.'

'I know, Da,' I interrupted, 'but Mam could teach us for a year or two,' the words came in a rush. I had thought of it so often. 'And by then we could be established in a new place, where there'd be a school and college. Look at America. They've got colleges there. It said so in that book Mam brought home. I wouldn't lose any time that mattered and if I had to stay an extra year or two, well,' I shrugged, 'it won't matter, see?'

He leaned forward and ruffled my hair. 'Aye, Dai, I do see. And look you, I'll give it some thought. But I don't think it's possible just yet. Don't forget that all the money we saved for school will be used. Then what? How will we pay for it in America? It isn't as simple as you think. I know,' he held up his hand to forestall my interruption, 'the amount of money paid in the mines there. But I hear things are worse there than they are here for safety and unions and things like that. So things aren't all greener over there, or whatever that saying of your Mam's is.'

'The grass isn't always greener on the other side of the hill,' I quoted.

'Exactly. Look you, Mam and me do talk about it sometimes like I said and I think hard about it. I'll think some more but I don't know . . .' he trailed off.

After he went downstairs I picked up the atlas again and compared South Africa with America. I had thought of Australia at one time but for some reason I forget now, I had discounted it. No, it had to be Africa or America and I knew which had my vote, if we ever got as far as voting on it. I paused. Maybe Da would go but Mam put so much store by our education she would probably be the stumbling block. My heart sank. Mam was a formidable person if you tried to get her to change her mind.

I heard Sion and Sian arriving downstairs, from the way the door slammed Sian was obviously last. I could hear their excited chatter and then they came bounding up the stairs. The door flew open and they bust into the room, talking at the same time.

'Uncle James . . .'

'He gave me some bamboo . . .'

'When he finishes the house . . .'

'I'll have the best kite I've ever . . .'

'All my friends will eat their hearts out . . .'

'I bet I could make it fly for . . .'

'And they all said we were silly to bother with an old man . . .'

'Hey, take it easy,' I said. 'You had a nice time, did you?'

'He's really very nice,' said Sian solemnly. 'I mean, not just because he's going to make me a doll's house. He just is. Do you know he cooks his own biscuits? And they're very nice too.'

'Yeah, I had four of them,' said Sion proudly, grinning at the memory.

'Yes, the piggy. He would have taken a fifth if I hadn't kicked him.' Coming from Sian that was about the funniest thing I had heard in a long time. It probably meant she could eat no more and so Sion was not allowed to either.

'Huh, you didn't do so badly,' said Sion more or less confirming what I thought.

After I sneezed a few more times they left. Not so much from an understanding of spreading germs as a desire to go and play a while longer before bed. I felt a bit lonely by myself but soon Mam came up with the supper. There was boiled cabbage, green beans and potatoes from the allotment. We had our main Sunday meal in the evening, not at midday, because Mam had more time to cook, as she never went to evening chapel. Prayers twice a day was sufficient for her.

On Monday morning I felt better, which would mean I had to go to school the next day. I thought idly about pretending to be worse than I actually was but then remembered the last time. Mam had fed me a dose of cod liver oil every hour until I announced I was much better. I thought so, had been her reply.

Sian made jokes about me being lazy, spending my life in bed, and missing school. I just scowled because they were exactly the words I had used a few months earlier when the twins had been down with flu. Sian had been a terrible patient, always demanding something, from a drink, a pencil or her potty emptied. When we were ill, we were not allowed out to the back toilet. Instead we used the chamber pot as Sian insisted on calling it when she learned those were the "posh" words for it.

I read for a while and must have dozed. The next thing I knew was Mam bringing in some broth. As she handed it to me the bells started ringing. We looked at each other, puzzled for a few seconds. The bells only rang on Sundays and . . . and 'Oh God, no,' said Mam, the blood draining from her face, leaving it chalk white.

We waited for the siren from the mine, telling us there had been an accident. It was a strict community rule. The bells only rang on Sundays. There was something wrong though. We usually heard the siren first and then the bells. Where was the siren? Perhaps there had not been an accident after all, but then what? The vicar knew better than to ring them for any other reason. Any other reason . . .

I jumped out of bed and began pulling on my clothes. 'Come on Mam, something's happened. We must find out what.'

3

THE STREET WAS filling with people stumbling hastily from their homes. Night shift miners were wiping
the sleep from their eyes, women were drying hands,
tying scarves around their heads or struggling into coats.
Nobody moved. The villagers were like statues, standing
looking at each other, wondering. Then Mam pushed
past me and headed for the chapel. The villagers started
walking in the same direction. God help the vicar if the
bells had been sounded for no good reason.

God help him perhaps, but there was not a person there
who did not hope and pray it was only a stupid mistake.
There would be harsh words spoken but they would be an
outlet for the real, deep-rooted fear the noise created.

Around the corner, where the street ended, by the road
to the river, people stopped to look down the valley
towards the mine. The fires were still throwing their
heat, their smoke and their orange flame into the sky.
It looked peaceful. The heavy morning rain had abated
and now a steady wind blew down the valley, the clouds
occasionally breaking up and shafts of sunlight streaming
through. The scene was firmly implanted in my mind. A
woman standing next to me pointed. 'Look,' she yelled,
above the noise of the bells.

I could see nothing. Just the black slag on the other
side, gleaming from the rain. Then, with a sickening
feeling I knew why the bells were ringing. Somebody
screamed the words.

'Where's the school? Where's it gone?'

From where we stood looking across the valley it was usually possible to see the school, the caretaker's house and a few sheds higher up dotted around some allotments. Now there was virtually nothing. The black mass of slag had slid across the allotments and swept like a towering wave over the school, burying it up to the roof. The caretaker's house was only partly buried, the school wall helping to hold the slag back.

As one, the people of the village began running along the road going for the footbridge over the Taff. I ran directly down to the river, keeping away from the crowd, aware they would slow me down.

I could hear the screams and yells from behind. People shouting the names of their children. Gareth, Llewelyn, Gwyneth, Myvanwi, Allan, Huw, Beatrice . . . the names flashed through my mind, forced there by the screams of the grown-ups. Above them all came Sion and Sian: Sion and Sian. 'God please. God please. Not my little brother and sister. Please. Not Sion and Sian. I'll go to chapel God, honest I will. Every Sunday God, only please spare them. Please,' I screamed the last word aloud.

I reached the riverbank. A few others were following; grown-ups, miners. I was winded but I still ran. Some of the men passed me. I recognised Mr Williams from two doors down. He had three children at the school, all younger than me. I was just behind when we got to where we collected coal. There were stepping stones a short distance further but nobody bothered with them. I could hear others behind splashing through the dirty, cold river. In the middle the water reached my waist and many of the men waded past. Hughes the shop, the owner of the village small general store, forced his short plump body along, gasping for breath, tears streaming down his face.

I was almost at the school and by now hundreds of people from the nearest villages were pouring down the hill, still a couple of hundred yards away, as they were slowed by the bottleneck of the bridge. The effort of running and my concentration to cross the river had prevented me from looking closely at what I had expected. Expected? My imagination, even coupled with the distant sighting had not prepared me for the sheer, mind bending horror of what was before us.

The thick, oozing slag was like quick silver under our feet. It still flowed, albeit slowly, through the school gates; a river of black mud moving down the road. We could see the roof of the school and about three feet of wall. Neither the tops of the windows nor doors were visible. As they reached us everybody fell silent, too shocked to say anything, unable to move. I felt the tears rise in my eyes . . . Sion . . . Sian.

Suddenly the whole crowd, as one, threw themselves at that hill of black obscenity. We used our hands to pull at the mud, trying to shove it to one side, trying to get inside . . . to the children.

I was sure that in the lull before we attacked the mud the others had noticed what I had. The silence. There was not even a whimper from inside the building. Nothing.

After a few minutes of useless scrabbling at slag I was pushed aside and one of the miners took my place. Unable to help I stood and watched sickened by the hopelessness of what they were trying to do. There was hardly a person without a tear-stained face. This was all the more shocking in a community hardened to mine accidents and sudden death. People normally grieved in private.

In every situation I suppose someone rises to the occasion and this was no exception. It was surprising who it was – the vicar! Suddenly he was among us screaming at us to stop.

'Get back, get back, all of you,' he yelled in a stentorian voice. He took hold of men and women alike and pushed them to one side. Slowly they began to take notice, all except one or two, too distraught to heed the vicar and still clawing at the slag. With a furious gesture he pointed at Lewis Lewis, the acknowledged leader of our community.

'You man, get to the mine. Tell them what's happened and tell them we need all the men down here. Tell them we want shovels, axes, picks, buckets. The Devil take it, Lewis Lewis, you know better than I do what we need. Take Llewelyn and Thomas with you,' he pointed at the two men. 'Thomas, when you reach the mine, get to the shaft and tell them what's happened. They'll get the cages ready and spread the word. Llewelyn go to the time shack. Get them to sound the alarm. If they refuse . . .' his voice trailed off. If they refused? It was unthinkable, but the rules were explicit. Nobody less than a foreman could sound the alarm, certainly not the timekeepers. And how long would it take to find a foreman? The alarm would bring the whole mine out and production would stop. What would the owners' reaction be to that?

'I'll ring the alarm vicar, don't you worry none.' Llewelyn was over 6′ 6″ tall and as wide across. The walking mountain he was often called (behind his back).

'Away with you and quickly,' said the vicar. 'In the meantime you women run home and bring back all the shovels and buckets you have. You men . . . Away with you, you women.' he screamed at them. They scurried as though the dogs of Hell were yapping at their heels. 'You men concentrate on getting a passage into the doorway and then through to the classrooms. Davis Jones, Lloyd, Huw Jones, go and find planking. Tear down the wooden fence by the river, the one on this side. We need to hold back the rest of this Devil's concoction from filling in where we dig.'

Six of the men formed into a squad using their hands to drag the mud to one side. It was soul-destroying work. As they pulled the black sludge away more oozed down to take its place. They were up to their waists in the filth, the one in front pushing the slag to the one behind. It looked ineffective but after a few minutes I thought I could see that they were making slow progress. They inched towards the door, over fifty yards away across the playground.

I had no idea what to do. I just stood there, the only non-grown up on the scene. All I could think of was Sion and Sian. They had to be alive, I told myself, they just had to be. The silence was because they were all sitting quietly, preserving their air, waiting for us to rescue them. It had to be that way. It had to be.

Some of the women returned carrying buckets and shovels. Some had brought blankets, to keep the survivors warm I heard. Mam was back with our coalscuttle and the grate shovel. I think it was the futility of this that suddenly came home to me the fact that the rescue attempt was pathetic, and it was the hope on the faces of the villagers that brought me to tears. I felt a hand on my shoulder and looked up to see old Mr Price.

'Have a good cry Dai, but don't give up praying. There's always,' he stumbled over the word, 'there's always hope. If the windows on the other side didn't break then most . . . at least a lot of the sludge will have been kept out.' He said the words in a rush and somehow I got the feeling he did not believe them either.

'Why isn't there any calls from within then Mr. Price?' The vicar yelled at the top of his voice and didn't get any reply. I wiped my tears and nose on my sleeve.

'You must remember this is pretty thick stuff and we're quite a way from the school yet, look you. It's impossible for sound to get through that lot so don't give up hope yet boy . . . not yet.'

I saw him wipe his eyes with his fingers and then he blew his nose in a handkerchief. His words comforted me a little.

Mam came over just then, her hair blowing across her face, slag streaks across her brow, her hands and arms black to the elbows. I noticed the white rivulets down her cheeks where she had been crying but her eyes were dry now – dry, and harder than I had ever seen them before.

'Dai, are you all right?'

'I'm fine, Mam,' a shiver ran through me, belying my words.

'You'd better go home and go to bed,' she said softly. 'You're wet through. I don't want you catching pneumonia not . . .' her voice broke and then recovered harshly, 'not now. Go on Dai.'

'I can't, Mam. Please don't try and make me. Please Mam.' Perhaps she understood that no matter what she said, I would stay.

At that moment we heard the intermittent hooting of the mine alarm. Immediately it seemed to put new life into the villagers. We knew that within minutes the men would be there, the gangs would form up and dig into that hell hill of blackness. Those who were already trying to get to the door attacked the slag with renewed vigour, passing the buckets down the lines. Helped by the women, the heavy ooze was tipped on the other side of the road.

I saw a few of the men coming round the corner dragging the riverside fencing and I ran to help, relieved to have something to do.

The sea of blackness stretched down the road out of sight. It was dangerously slippery with people continually falling over. It was hard to tell who was who. The piece of fencing was taken from us and the vicar ordered us to bring more. A crowd of us ran sliding and falling down the road towards the riverbank to fetch it. The few villagers in front of me suddenly stopped and seconds later I saw why. Hurrying down the hill towards us, spurred on by the sound of the alarm came a beautiful sight . . . a disorganised crocodile of children. We gaped at them, those behind jostling past me to see why we had stopped. The children, seeing us black and wet slowed, a little afraid. Then we were running towards them, Ma Grimes the schoolteacher hurrying towards us and the children following. I saw Sion and the same time he recognised me and he came running. I looked for Sian, never far from him as a rule but did not see her. My heart sank and fresh tears stung my eyes. I did not see the other reunions going on around me, I saw only my brother.

I hugged him. 'Where's Sian?' I asked, expecting her to jump on me any second. His words brought bile to my mouth I felt so sickened.

'She's in school Dai. Why? What's happening? Why are you all here and look at you – all of you so dirty. We heard the alarm and came quickly. What's happened? Is it the mine? Is Da . . . ?'

'It's not the mine. It's the school.' I turned, unable to go on, trying to fight back my grief. At first sight of the children I had hoped. I had seen Sion and known some were safe. Now . . . now Sian, my lovely sister . . . I choked on my thoughts.

Some of us went to get the fencing though a few of the women stayed where they were, their arms protectively around their children.

'Sion, Mam's at the school. Hurry and find her and let her know about Sian. Why isn't she with you anyway?'

'We all came out for a nature ramble. Ma Grimes thought we needed fresh air and so we went to look at some trees or something. I didn't take much notice. Sian . . . Sian was sniffling. Teacher thought she might be going down with a cold see. So . . . so she stayed behind to . . . to sew or something.'

I said nothing. All I managed was to nod for him to follow the others. A cold. My cold. All mine. I was blinded by tears as I stumbled to the side of the road and sat down, sobbing. I suppose the whole event, the original fear, the joy at knowing they were all right and the unspeakable sickness of discovering that Sian was still in there, was too much emotion for me to handle. I only stopped when Mr Price came and sat besides me.

'I saw Sion,' he said quietly. 'I thought . . . I thought

Sian was there too. When I found she wasn't I felt like you.' He put his arm around my shoulders. 'But I can't cry, not properly. I guess I've seen too much suffering in my time. Been through too much myself. You're shivering. Come on, let's go and see how they're getting on. The men from the mine have arrived. Come on.' He pulled me to my feet and I stumbled along behind him.

Now the scene was different. The mine foremen had taken charge. Six teams were steadily digging their way across the playground, not far short of the school walls. As they went they put up side timbers, brought with them, holding back the black ooze like Moses' passage across the Red Sea. The women had been pushed to one side and now they stood with the children, a silent crowd watching the men.

I did not recognise Da for some time, the men looking so alike, wet and filthy covered with sludge. Then I saw him briefly in front of the gang going for the door. Hurry Da, I told him silently, hurry. Go straight to the last classroom Da, the last one. That's where she is – in the last one.

The one storey building was of grey stone, thick and solid. Inside the main door was the cloakroom where we hung our raincoats. Through swing doors was the corridor. Three classrooms on the furthest side had taken the brunt of the collapsed slagheap, and Sian was in the end one. On this side were the assembly hall, another classroom and the headmaster's study. Two classes had gone on the nature ramble. My class had gone with the younger children because our teacher was home ill.

I imagined Sian sitting at her desk, alone, when the darkness enveloped her. Sewing. My cold. I bit my lip, trying not to think, concentrating on the men's progress. Da's gang reached the door. I heard them shouting but did not understand what was said. Then the door was pulled open. The darkness inside, the overcast gloom of the day and the surrounding slag made it impossible to see whether the way in was clear or not. Everyone was breathless, watching. If the men walked in then there was a chance. All other work stopped. Da began digging. Moans and sighs escaped the men and women and we knew what we all thought but had been afraid to admit even to ourselves.

Another shiver ran through me, and Mr Price took off his jacket and put it over my shoulders. It hung to my knees, filthy from the slag but not too wet. His arm was around my shoulders and when I shivered again he pressed me close to him. I knew I should go home to bed, he knew it too. But he never even suggested it, for which I was grateful.

There were further shouts as two of the gangs reached the walls and started breaking windows. The setting sun broke through the clouds and lighted up the scene for a brief second. I thought I could see the slag, as high inside the building as it was out. Hope dropped to a mere flicker, though it was not completely extinguished. Human nature, I learned that day, never gave up until the bitter end.

In those days we went to school at the age of six and stayed until eleven. Even though the school was used by three villages and there were only four classes, thankfully they were not big classes. There were twenty-four children in mine, about the same in the others. Two classes were safe. Forty-eight children plus Sian could be in there, I thought. Why did it happen? How could it have happened? Forty-eight little children dead, just like that. No, not dead, not yet, I persuaded myself. We don't know they're dead. There's always hope. The corridor was full but that did not mean the classrooms were affected too. I latched on to the idea, excited by the thought. Why not? If it was only the corridor it would explain why we had heard no noise. The slag in the corridor would prevent the children getting out and stop any noise they made. Possibly they were keeping silent to preserve their air –

except Sian of course. She had plenty, being alone. She would be frightened; very, very frightened. Don't worry I told her, Da will be through soon Sian, very soon.

Da and his team were through the doors. More of the men attached themselves to his gang as they burrowed deeper through the filth. Those at the windows were digging into the nearer classroom and the furthest team had reached the headmaster's study. Word was passed back. The study was filled with slag.

At what point did hope die? It's impossible to say but I think for me it was about then. I knew she was dead, along with all the others. I prayed I was wrong. There was still a tiny part of me that refused to acknowledge in the weirdest way imaginable, the reality of the sludge, the evidence of the men digging through every filthy, stinking, heart rendering inch.

I was surprised to realise it was nearly dark. The men were lighting their helmet lamps, the flames flickering yellow in the gloom and against the black background of the slag. Mr Price and I sat in a corner, his arm around me while I shivered from time to time.

Two of the bosses from the mine appeared with offer of help. Luckily for them they caught our mood and left before the scene became too ugly. They were the focal point of the people's hate, anger and frustration. They were blamed for what had happened. After all, it was their slag; they ordered it to be dumped there. If they had not the men would not be crawling through that filth, trying to rescue their children.

In the days that were to follow they would argue they were not responsible for the rain which caused the accident and that the slag had been dumped there for years without danger, or even a hint of danger. Even so our dislike of the mine owners turned to hatred that was to persist for a long time and lead to further deaths.

The men organised themselves into shifts after the initial frantic digging. One hour in, one hour out, they

worked like demons, like men possessed. When they
came out the women gave them hot snacks and drinks.
Hardly a word was spoken and as time went on and as
hope died even those few words dried up. Pathetic. That
was the word that came to mind when they got into the
headmaster's study and found his body. They said he was
still at his desk. Old man Williams had been a dry stick
of a man with a sour outlook on life but he had been a
person. Now he was nothing. That was what struck me
most deeply as the body was wrapped in a blanket. It
was nothing. A lump of flesh and bones covered with
black slag and now hidden from view by a grey blanket.
His wife kneeled by his side and wept. His? No, it was
no longer his, it was its. A nothing. The vicar ordered the
body be taken to the chapel.

I was shivering again, whether from the cold or my
thoughts, I was not sure. Da was out now and with Mam
and Sion came to find me.

'Are you all right?' he asked in a voice I barely
recognised.

'Yes, Da,' I replied as he knelt beside me; putting his
hand under the coat to feel my body.

'You're like ice, son. I think you ought to go home.
Mam will take you and give you a hot bath and put you
to bed. Sion will go with you as well.'

'Not now, please, Da. Not now we're so close to . . .
to getting in there.' I had been about to say so close to
finding Sian's body but stopped myself in time. We might
all have thought so but nobody was going to say it.

Surprisingly it was Mam who intervened on my behalf.
'I'll get him a blanket, Evan, and some hot tea. He may
as well stay now he's been here this long. It can't be long
now . . .' she tailed off, looking towards the school, now
lighted by dozens of miners lamps and oil fired wall lamps
from the mine. The blackness, pierced with the flickering
yellow lamps casting deeper shadows in the slag, was like
a scene from hell. The slag blackened men and women

making then look like insubstantial ghosts as they worked in silence.

The quiet came to a shattering end when the first child's body was brought out. Someone screamed and then they all started, crying, moaning, cursing.

Each small form was identified, covered with a blanket and taken by the family to the chapel.

Da was kneeling alongside me and with a sense of shock I realised he was shaking with silent sobs, the tears washing white streaks on his blackened face. Mam bent down, took his hand and pulled him to his feet. With her arm around him I watched as they walked away. I called Sion back in time as he made to follow them, knowing somehow that they needed to be alone.

Sometime during that period I had begun to call Mr Price Uncle James and as I sat there his arm was a comfort. Sion sat on the other side and I put my arm around his shoulders. Like me he appeared to have cried all the tears he had in him. We sat like that for God knows how long. Time passed slowly as we watched the small bodies being carried out from the first classroom.

Husbands and wives stood side by side, some holding hands and trying to find comfort in their contact. Some families had lost one, some two children. One family had lost three. In silent procession once the bodies had been claimed, the families made their way to the river, across the bridge and up the hill to the chapel. A million tears were shed that night.

Twenty-two bodies were brought out from the first classroom. After that there was a lull as the men carried on towards the next room of death. The gang which had entered the study had now worked their way into the classroom opposite. It was the empty one, apart from Sian, the children having been for a walk. Mam and Da went to meet the miner who brought her out and handed her still form silently to Da. We got to our feet and followed as they put her in a blanket and started towards the Chapel. I was incapable of crying but Sion sobbed his heart out as we stumbled along in the dark. Uncle James swept Sion up in his arms and carried him.

I walked besides Da, Mam on the other side. Sian was completely hidden by the blanket, a shapeless bundle of grey. I would no longer hear her high pitched squeal, whether of delight or anger, or hear her telling us to hurry because she was hungry. I realised what my parents were going through and with the realisation came more tears. This time they were not for Sian. They were for Mam and Da.

At the chapel Mam and Da went inside with the others but Sion and I were told in no uncertain terms to go home. This time there was no argument. Uncle James took us.

Sion went directly to bed but I had to wait and have a hot bath. It was four thirty in the morning and by then I was shivering continuously.

4

WHEN I WOKE it was to find the doctor with his hand on my forehead. Mam was behind him looking drawn and worried, her eyes red rimmed. Da stood at the foot of the bed, his face haggard, his mouth set in a grim line. I gave a harsh, dry cough, accidentally spitting out phlegm.

'Sorry Mam,' I said hoarsely, as the three of them looked at the rusty coloured sputum. Mam quickly wiped it away.

'Hush Dai,' Mam soothed, 'it's nothing. Here, let me prop you up.' She fussed with my pillow and then gave me the one from Sian's bed.

'Now Dai,' said the doctor, 'tell me, do you have any pain across here?' he indicated my chest.

I nodded. 'A bit,' I admitted. I found it difficult to breathe comfortably but I did not say anything.

The doctor took my pulse. 'You're going to have to stay in bed for a while, my boy. And I mean in bed. You must keep warm. Even though you've got a temperature and feel too hot, never mind, you keep those blankets around you. All right?'

I gave another harsh cough by way of answer, this time catching the phlegm in my hand. Mam stepped forward and wiped it away.

'Your Mam will give you a hot water bottle to keep on your chest to help the pain. And stay propped up on your pillows; it'll help your breathing and your chest, look you. Now you go back to sleep while I have a talk with your parents.'

I sighed and closed my eyes.

I am unsure how long I was ill. I do remember whenever I awoke Mam or one of my aunts was there. I remembered being given sweet drinks almost continuously. I had periods of delirium and periods of clarity. My temperature dropped and I started eating. No one needed to tell me I was getting over a bout of pneumonia. The doctor visited regularly though I was not always fully aware of him.

During that time thoughts of Sian and the nightmare of the school kept returning. Sometimes I believed it had not happened, at other times I knew it was all too real.

It was the day after the funeral. I was upset because I had not been able to attend. When I awoke I found Aunt Nancy with me. She was one of my favourite aunts, Uncle William's wife. Da and Uncle William probably got on better with each other than they did with their other brothers, and so inevitably Mam and Aunt Nancy did too. She had two sons, both older than me, one working in the mine, the other on the railway. Between them, with the wages they took home, they lived well compared to other families. Whenever we called there was a glass of home-made lemonade and biscuits for us.

She smiled. 'Take some of this,' she held out a cup of her lemonade. 'How do you feel?'

'Not so bad. At least the pain in my chest isn't as bad as it was.' I coughed, but this time it was not a harsh dry cough, nor was there any phlegm.

'Good boy. The doctor says your temperature is nearly normal and after a few weeks rest you should be all right. You didn't half give us a scare, I can tell you. Though the doctor said you weren't as ill as some he's seen. Still boy, it's nice to have you on the road to recovery. It'll be a load off your Mam's mind.'

'How is she? I'm real sorry see, if I've upset her, especially after . . . after Sian.'

'Now don't you fret none. She'll be fine in a little while, as soon as she gets over the funeral like. That was yesterday,' she added.

I nodded miserably. I felt the tears welling in my eyes.

'Hush now Dai,' she said, sitting on the edge of the bed and stroking my forehead. 'Don't upset yourself. The Good Lord giveth and the Good Lord taketh away. Sian is probably up there in heaven looking down on you right now, telling you not to cry. So don't take on so, there's a good boy. She had a lovely funeral, they all did. They all went to their maker knowing how much we all loved them.'

I nodded, clinging to her words for comfort but not believing them. 'Why did God take her away then? She was a good girl, never did anybody any harm . . . at least nothing serious, only childish games. Why take her from us?'

'I don't know Dai and I suppose nobody really knows though all the vicars and preachers have some reason for it. Perhaps God looked down and saw what a lovely girl she was and wanted her in heaven with him.'

As she paused I leaped in: 'But we wanted her down here with us, as did all the other families. The Bible says if we're good we'll go to heaven forever and ever – that's a long time. So why couldn't the children stay with us until it was time to die? . . . Like in old age.'

'I don't really know,' she had the honesty to admit. 'It does say in the Bible that our God is a selfish God and it says, "Suffer the little children to come unto me". Perhaps that had something to do with the reason.'

'Well I don't care for our God anymore and I'm not going to chapel ever again and if he wants to strike me dead with lightning for saying so he can,' I said defiantly.

'You shouldn't talk like that, Dai. It's not nice. And of course you'll go to the chapel as soon as you're better again. You have to thank God for making you better.'

'Tell me, auntie,' I said slyly, 'is God responsible for everything that happens on earth? I mean, he's all-powerful, right? So when he sees something is going to happen that isn't right he could use his power to change it, right? So he probably gave me pneumonia in the first place, so why should I thank him for curing me? It was the doctor who cured me, not God.'

She looked a bit dubious, whether this was at my logic, or because she did not understand my argument, I was unsure. 'Well, never mind that now,' she fussed over me, straightening my blankets and pillows. 'All I do know is you'll be in chapel with the rest of us in no time at all,' she said cheerfully.

A short while later Sion came into the room. He was sleeping downstairs until I was better.

'I was hoping you'd be awake,' he said. 'Can you play yet? Or do you have to stay in bed still?'

'I've got to stay in bed. It's a pity but I'm going to be here for a bit longer.'

He nodded. 'You know it's lonely without Sian. I know . . . I know we used to fight and things but at least there was someone to talk to.' He looked sadly at the bits and pieces he was holding, the beginning of a new kite. 'I wish she was here now. I'd never tease her again, or get angry with her. I'd let her do anything she wanted, even fly my kite. And I'd play with her dolly if she wanted me to, instead of me always telling her I was too busy.' I could see his lower lip trembling. 'I wish I hadn't been so nasty to her now'.

'You weren't nasty to her,' I said. 'She's gone to heaven and is probably looking down on us, telling us not to worry about her.' I hoped the difference in our ages would let Sion believe me, even if I had not believed my aunt, who was smiling encouragement at me. 'I'll soon be well and then I'll play with you, all right?'

'All right, Dai. I guess you're right. Uncle James said the same thing to me a couple of days ago. And Mam and Da did, so I suppose it's right. Do you want anything? The atlas or a book maybe?'

Before I could reply Aunt Nancy answered. 'No he doesn't, thank you Sion. It's time he rested again, before the doctor gets here. So off with you now.'

He gave me an uncertain smile and left. 'I feel much better now. Couldn't I just have the atlas to look at for a bit?' I pleaded.

'No, you close your eyes and try and rest,' she said firmly.

'But . . .' then I stopped, to keep her happy. I was asleep within seconds.

The next few days were a procession of relatives, uncles, aunts, boy cousins, girl cousins, Grandmother Osborne, Granddad and Grandma Griffiths. They all brought me little gifts like a packet of biscuits or the loan of a book. On the fourth day, the doctor said I could get out of bed for an hour and sit in a chair. He emphasised that it did not mean I could walk around or go out of the room.

'You've been pretty ill, Dai, and you've got a lot of strength building to do yet. So you just take it easy and do what I tell you, and we'll have you on your feet again in no time.'

I nodded. We were alone and I took the opportunity to ask him something that still bothered me. 'Doctor, do you believe in God?'

'Why do you want to know? Having doubts yourself are you?' he asked kindly.

'Sort of,' I replied cautiously. 'What with Sian and the other little kids and me getting ill like this. I just can't make what's happened and what we're taught

about God make any sense. If you see what I mean,'
I finished lamely.

'Aye, Dai, I see what you mean all right. I've seen
death in most of its forms I reckon; from disease to mine
accidents and from war to suicides and each time I see it
I wonder. I go to chapel like everybody else and I say
the words like everybody else but when I come down
to it I guess I only do it to keep my wife happy.' He
looked over his shoulder at the door and then dropped
his voice to a whisper. 'If I was honest, and you're not to
tell anyone this mind, coming right down to it, I suppose I
don't believe. You're old enough now, and been through
enough to realise that we aren't all God-fearing, and
worshipping believers. We all have our doubts, some
more than others I guess.'

'If that's so why do all the men and women go to
chapel then?'

'Not all do. Your Da for one goes only when he's made
to but I know what you mean in general. They all have
their own reasons but on the whole I'd say it was fear
that drove them. You know what life is like in the mines
– all the accidents down there. The railways aren't much
better, nor the iron and steel works. I suppose the men
are trying to make sure that if something does happen to
them then they may not be quite as frightened of dying as
otherwise they would be.' He shrugged. 'That's as good
a reason as any for going. Now don't you say I said that,
mind, or else I'll get a reputation for being an atheist.'

'I won't,' I said solemnly. What he had said gave me
food for thought though I was convinced more than ever
that if there was a God then he did not give twopence
what happened to us, or what we did.

During the next week I was allowed to sit longer in the
chair though not to walk around or do anything else. My
aunts and Mam had stopped their vigil by the side of my

bed and Sion was back sleeping in the bedroom. He now used Sian's bed, instead of sharing with me.

A regular visitor was Uncle James Price. Perhaps it was my imagination but he looked as though he had aged since Sian's death. I was aware that they had quickly become close to each other but had not realised how close. Sian had obviously meant a lot to him.

'How come you're always looking in that there atlas?' he asked me once.

'I like to imagine what it would be like to leave this place and travel – not around the world, but to go where there's something other than rows of houses and mines – a place where there's open land and fields, I suppose. One day,' I began to get excited, 'I'll go to these places. Here we are in Europe and I can't even get to Cardiff, never mind such places as Paris or Rome say.'

'Where's that Dai? Those places I mean.'

'Paris is the capital of France,' I began importantly.

'Oh, them,' he interrupted contemptuously. 'Why, God Bless him, the Duke of Wellington defeated them at Waterloo. Sent them no good Frenchies running he did. What do you want to go there for?'

I shrugged. 'I dunno, just to see it I suppose. Anyway, Waterloo was eighty years ago.'

'It doesn't matter see. We beat them then and we'd beat them again. Why, we freed all of Europe from Napoleon . . . was that his name?'

'Aye, Uncle James it was. But that doesn't mean I shouldn't go and see what it's like today, does it? I mean, it must have changed an awful lot like. Like we've changed here in Britain and especially here in Wales.'

'I guess,' he said, looking unsure.

Mam came in with cups of tea. 'Here you are Dai, and one for you too, Mr Price.'

'Thank you, Meg. We're just talking about Dai's ideas to travel. I reckon he's been bitten by some bug that gives him the urge to move. What do you think?'

'I think you're right. He's been on about nothing else since I can remember. Or at least since I showed him that atlas and taught him what it means. Mind you, he's not the only one in this family. Oh well,' she turned to the door, 'I suppose we'll see what we shall see.'

I wondered what she meant, but I put it down to her usual brush off whenever I mentioned leaving Wales.

Though I felt weak, I was allowed downstairs and to walk around a little. The doctor explained I was not to overdo it because pneumonia leaves the heart and lungs weak and I had to take care. If I did, then I would be back to normal, more or less, in two months time. It had been three weeks since I fell ill; since Sian's death. The village was still in mourning, though the people, used to tragedy, were beginning to put it behind them. I heard the vicar was preaching the goodness of God, quoting often, 'Suffer the little children to come unto me'. Perhaps for many it offered consolation but for me, and I suspected for Da as well, it offered nothing. There were eight days to go to the wedding anniversary when Grandmother Osborne called in.

'But Megan,' she said plaintively, 'you can't have a party. Not so soon after the little one's burial. It's not nice.' Grandmother thought of everything in terms of whether it was nice or not. She was dressed in her habitual black dress, as shapeless as she was. 'What will the village think and say? Thank you,' she added taking another biscuit and promptly dunking it in her tea.

'Never mind what the village thinks or says,' Mam emphasised the word says. 'Evan and I have decided that that's what we want. Mourning for our little girl doesn't help anyone, least of all us.'

Grandmother Osborne looked put out for the moment. 'Well, I don't think it's right. Her only just in her grave and all.'

'Listen Mam,' she replied, 'it's a quiet get together of the family. It'll do us all good. We need to talk about the accident if it helps clear people's feelings. We can't ignore it and pretend it didn't happen, worried we'll say the wrong thing and upset the others. It'll be good for Huw and Mair as well, if we can persuade them to come. They said they'd think about it. Perhaps the sight of all the other children will be too much now they've lost Johnny. It might be. I know how I'll be feeling about Sian and I know how Evan will feel and Dai and Sion. But we must still . . .' she faltered a moment, 'still make the effort and get back to normal as quickly as we can. Life goes on, Mam, and we have to go on with it.' There was a sort of defiance as she poured more tea for the three of us. Sion was out playing or else round visiting Uncle James and Da was at work. The school was still closed and looked as though it would not be opened for some time, if ever. There was talk of using the chapel vestry for classes for some of the older children but so far nothing had come of it. There was also talk of getting the mine owners to build a new school away from the danger areas of the slagheaps. Somebody was supposed to investigate what had happened but what good would come of that we all knew only too well – nothing.

The Union was making its usual noises but its only definite offer of help was to contribute towards the memorial for the children. The mine owners had also offered a contribution but I had not heard whether it was accepted or not. The owners were insisting what had happened was nothing to do with them, but had been an Act of God. Bitterness against the owners was rising. There was a threat of serious trouble in the offing.

I cannot say I liked my Grandmother very much. She was too fussy, always telling me what I should or should not do. Like 'don't play in the river, Dai,' 'don't climb trees, Dai,' 'don't go over to the quarry with the other children, Dai,' 'you'll get into trouble, Dai' . . . and so on all the time. She had never believed Da was good enough for Mam but I had heard uncle Albert tell Da that was usual – no man was ever good enough for any woman's daughter.

With an air of finality Grandmother replaced her cup and stood up. 'I must be going.' Both Mam and I remained silent. 'All I can say, Megan, is I hope you know what you're doing, that's all. That's my last words on the subject, see, but mark my words, people won't like it. They'll think it not nice. Fetch my coat, Dai,' she ordered.

'Yes, Grandmother,' please, I said, under my breath.

'What did you say?' she asked sharply.

'Nothing Grandmother,' I rushed to get her coat. She could hear an asthmatic flea cough at fifty paces.

As I helped her on with her coat she went on: 'Now you mark my words Megan Griffiths . . .' I switched off, knowing we would not hear the end of it before, during or for a long time after the event. From Mam's sigh I guessed she realised it as well.

After Grandmother left, Mam made me get out my schoolbooks and we went through some arithmetic. I still tired quickly so after an hour I went to bed. I slept until late the next morning.

Through the curtains, partly drawn, I watched the clouds scudding past and amused myself seeing them as animals and funny faces. My Grandmother Osborne's voice – she had come back – brought me back to earth and I tried to listen. After a few minutes I realised she was still on about the party and tried to ignore her. She saying, 'I told you on that day you were marrying below your station', brought me back to listening to her.

'Now this trouble. I've never heard of anything like it. The men holding meetings, talking about striking and for what? Tell me that. For what? Compensation for the children? That won't bring them back, will it? Nor will it put clothes on your backs or food on your table. I expect your Evan is mixed up in this as usual?' Her voice had a hint of bitterness as she said Da's name.

'Yes, he is,' Mam retorted, 'but not in the way you think.' Before she could go on Grandmother interrupted.

'I thought so. I knew it,' she said with a good deal of satisfaction. It was then that I realised how much she disliked Da. I had never liked her very much but knowing how she felt about Da I liked her a lot less. I poked my tongue out at her, safe in the knowledge that a door and ceiling separated us.

'You mark my words. There's going to be trouble unless someone persuades the men not to be so stupid.'

'Evan is trying to,' Mam said loudly, immediately bringing her voice back to normal. 'Sorry, Mam but I couldn't get a word in edgeways. If you'd listened you'd have heard me try to say that Evan is against it. He agrees with you about the food and clothes, or whatever you said. He doesn't think any good will come of it but the men, and the women too come to that, are so angry they won't listen to reason. It's not as though they're asking for much . . .'

Again Grandmother interrupted. 'What are they asking for then? Do they even know? Or is it the usual sheep-like instinct of the herd? All following without knowing why or where they're going?'

'No, Mam,' I could almost hear Mam sigh. By now, intrigued, I climbed out of bed and sat at the top of the stairs. This was all new to me and I wanted to know what was going on. 'All they want is a new school built over this side of the river and up behind the Powis place,' I knew where she meant. It was a stretch of waste ground near the chapel and a bit further along. 'They also want the mine owners to admit it was their fault. I don't know much more than you so why ask me? We won't know any more until tomorrow's meeting. You'll know then, Mam.'

'Yes, well I just thought you could enlighten me some more, seeing how Evan always knows what's going on.' I heard the rattle of cups. 'Thank you.'

'Hullo, Meg, and where's my boy then? Oh, hullo, Mrs Osborne,' Grandad said in a stentorian voice, breezing through the front door, as usual.

'Upstairs, Dad,' Mam replied.

'I must be off, now you've got,' Grandmother paused, 'other company.' I could imagine the loud sniff she affected when she was annoyed, and Grandad turning up would certainly annoy her.

'Well, look you, don't let me keep you,' Grandad emphasised the "me."

'You won't,' Grandmother stressed the "you" and I heard her close the door, not quite slamming it.

'I don't know how she had such a lovely daughter.' I knew he was fond of Mam, and I always thought she was his favourite of his sons' wives. Mind you, that may have been wishful thinking because I thought such a lot of Grandad.

'Now, Dad, she's not that bad. You know all the trouble she's been through since my father died. We have to make allowances.'

'Huh,' he snorted, 'most of her troubles I reckon she's brought on herself or else imagined them. Never mind her now, how's the boy?'

'Not too bad. The doctor says if he rests and we keep him in most of the time he'll be all right in a month or two. He said we were lucky it was such a mild dose. Go on up and see him. He may be awake by now.'

I scrambled for my bed as Grandad parted the curtain at the foot of the stairs. When he came in he was grinning.

'Now, Dai, you shouldn't be listening at keyholes. You might hear something bad about yourself, see, and you won't like that will you?'

'No, Grandad,' I grinned back. 'Only I wasn't listening at a keyhole but at the top of the stairs.'

'Cheeky monkey,' he ruffled my hair like Da did. 'You're lucky you're ill, that's all I can tell you. But don't go taking advantage of the fact or else I might forget and put you over my knee, by mistake like.'

'Okay, I won't forget,' I replied solemnly and then we both laughed.

'I can see there's very little wrong with you lad and that's a fact.'

'Grandad,' I said, suddenly serious, 'what's going on in the village? With the mine owners, I mean.'

'Why do you ask?'

'Nothing much. I'm just interested that's all. I heard Mam and Grandmother talking about it earlier. And if anybody knows it's you, after all.'

Grandad was one of the most important men in the community. He was one of the mine leaders and sat on the committee that dealt with the owners; and he was a member of the union. He was a big man with a shock of white hair and a seamed face. His nose was hooked where it had been broken in a fight years before, and his eyes were piercing like Da's. He was heavily built though not fat.

'Aye lad I guess I can tell you, though it's not much. We'll know more after the meeting tomorrow. What it comes down to is the people of the three villages want the owners to admit responsibility for what happened. Then they want compensation and a memorial for the . . . the kids,' he paused.

'That's reasonable, after all it was their fault. We didn't ask them to put their rotten slag there, did we?'

'No, Dai, we didn't. But I remember when the school was built. We picked the site and there was already a slagheap then. Not so high, maybe, but it was there. And again there's the rain, which was hardly the owners' fault, was it?'

'I suppose not,' I said quietly, wishing I could kill the owners like Sian had been killed.

'But that isn't all the problem. The owners are worried that if they admit it was their fault we could take them to court. And then we could get a lot more than we're asking for right now. Do you see, Dai?'

'Aye, Grandad, I see. But,' I went on bitterly, 'the courts will side with the owners, they always do.'

'Give me one example of a court case the owners have won against us then, clever clogs,' Grandad smiled wanly.

I pulled a face as I thought. 'I don't really know one,' I began slowly, 'but everybody knows the courts are always on the side of the owners.'

'The reason you can't think of one is because in my living memory I've never known it to happen. That doesn't mean if we did go to court we'd automatically lose. We'd definitely win, though, if they admitted it was their fault and agreed to what we're asking for. See, I reckon with the way things are in this country now, if we've got a just grievance the courts will decide fairly.'

'What's the meeting for, then?'

'Me and the others are going to try and persuade the owners that if they agree to our demands – that's the wrong word – I should say requests, then I'll assure them and so will the rest of the committee that there'll be no action in court. After all Dai, what do we know about court cases and such like, eh boy?' He coughed into a big handkerchief. 'Mustn't give you my germs, must I?' He smiled, kidding us both he had a simple cough and not miners "dust".

'And if you don't persuade them, what will happen then?'

He thought for a few minutes, as though he had not considered the idea before that moment. 'I can't rightly say, Dai,' he shook his shaggy head slowly. 'The villagers don't have much faith in courts either. They reckon they're rich men's tools, letting them get away with blue murder if it suits them. Even if the owners agree there's no telling if we could keep our promises. It's all very difficult. The men are talking about strikes and pickets.' He sighed heavily. 'I can remember the last time and it wasn't very pleasant, I can tell you. Nobody won. We went hungry and the mines lost a lot of money. That's all I seem to remember about it. I think it was in the year your Mam and Dad married. It wasn't nice at all,' his eyes became hooded as he thought of the past. 'We almost had the militia here. 'Twas lucky we went back when we did. The day after, we heard the militia turned out and cleared the men from the mine in Bedwas, killed a few, too. Mind you, the miners had been trying to damage the owners' property at the time. Still, I don't reckon the militia should have done what they did. There'd been talk that they were to come here but we'd gone back by then. Six weeks, Dai. Six weeks of hunger, trying to find food where we could. Even eating rotten potatoes and cabbage heads if we could get them. The parents starved so the children could eat. It was a bad time and I don't want to see it happen again.'

'Grandad,' I hesitated, not sure how to go on. He waited patiently. 'Grandad,' I began again, 'it's not like you, I mean you don't, I mean . . .' I trailed off in confusion.

'You mean it's not like me not to fight the owners. Nor the rest of the committee either.'

I nodded. 'Yes, that's it exactly. You've always said that if something is worth fighting for . . .'

'Yes, that's true. But this time I don't think it is.'

'Grandad,' I said shocked, 'how can you say that? Sian . . . and the others . . . aren't they worth fighting for?'

He winced at Sian's name, the pain evident and I wished I had kept silent.

'Dai, Dai, Dai,' he shook his head sadly, 'of course they'd be worth fighting for, even dying for, if it would have saved them. I'm not talking about that. I'm talking about what we're trying to achieve. If the courts decide in our favour, all well and good; if they don't, then I'll be sadder than anybody in the villages. But if we fight in the way the men are talking about, what then? Hunger at least, possibly deaths? For a monument to the dead?' He shook his head again. 'Don't get me wrong. Let's use the union funds if they'll let us and do this thing properly, through the courts. It probably won't come to that anyway, if we can persuade the owners to give a large contribution to the new school and persuade them the act will not be looked on as an admission of guilt. I know a few of the hotheads are demanding that the owners must admit it's their fault, particularly blaming Sir Clifford. If the owners realise how deep those feelings are then they'll agree to our terms, I'm sure. After all, they aren't daft are they?'

I shook my head, dubious about the point.

Grandad cheered up. 'Look you, that's not what I'm here for. It's about the get together next week. We've got a few small things for them but is there anything Mam and Da need, particular like?'

I pulled a few puzzled faces as I thought, and then shrugged. 'I dunno Grandad, honest I don't. I guess they've got everything they need.'

He laughed. 'Everything . . . that's a good one, Dai, but,' he added hastily seeing my hurt look, 'I know what you mean. You, Sion and Si . . . you and Sion think about it and let me or your Gran know. Tell us Wednesday or Thursday, whichever it is we're coming over. I don't know,' he grumbled with good humour, 'she never tells me what's going on until the last minute and wonders why I'm not ready. I'll be off before Gran comes looking.' He ruffled my hair and stood up.

'So long, Grandad,' I smiled at him. He waved and left.

I thought about what I had learned. I hoped Grandad could persuade the owners, the swine, my fists clenched as I thought of them. I hated them irrationally. There was hardly a person in the valleys who felt differently. To hate them was as natural as breathing. They were the haves, we the have-nots.

5

THE NEXT DAY dragged by. I sat at the window watching the clouds, wishing I were as free, able to travel the world. I wanted to see India, the Antarctic, Australia. I shook my head sadly and sighed. Perhaps one day, perhaps never, I thought.

I looked along the sad, depressing street, watching the few people that were around, hurrying about their business. I thought briefly about the workers' meeting. I hoped it would be successful.

Mam was as concerned as I – more so I suppose. There was a tension to the village; though perhaps it was my imagination, my own tension distorting my view of things. Whatever the reason, the village appeared to brood and wonder.

During the afternoon I tried to settle down to some homework but ended up staring sightlessly at my books. Da would be waiting at the mine for Grandad to finish with the owners. They would return with the committee and go to the Wheatsheaf, the local pub, to meet the other men.

I had been to one or two of their earlier meetings. One was the safety meeting, which had ended in bitter denunciation of the committee. It had taken a further two meetings with the owners before the men had been satisfied. Like Grandad said, though, as long as the talking went on then the less likelihood there was of other action being taken, and that was an achievement in itself. It was when the talking stopped that intelligent men worried.

The shadows lengthened as another early night closed in. The sky was overcast and rain was in the air, bringing the darkness with it. Sion was out with friends near the river, building a raft from scraps of wood. I would have helped if I could because it was the sort of thing I enjoyed, but I had to stay in. It was the doctor's orders. I was fed up and bored.

The evening wore on. Sion was in bed. I was ready to go but Mam let me wait up for Da. I guessed she wanted my company as much as anything else. At last we heard the door open and slow footsteps in the passage. To our surprise Grandad came in with Da.

'Get us a cuppa, lass, will you?' asked Grandad. 'My throat is that parched with all that talking.'

'Was it that bad?' asked Mam. 'You both look sick at something. Shouldn't you go home to Mam?' she said to Grandad. 'She'll be worrying where you are and wondering what happened.'

'I'll be off in a bit, Meg. I told her I'd probably stop off here on the way home. Well then, the meeting was as difficult as we feared and perhaps even more so, see. They wouldn't admit responsibility for the accident nor talk in terms of compensation of any kind. They will, however,' Grandad became bitter, 'contribute towards a monument. They emphasised how generous they were going to be, helping towards a new school by paying for the foundations. The rest we have to get from the Government. They assured us that was more than possible, especially after they drop words in the right ears. Lewis Lewis exploded when he heard them. I had difficulty at one stage calming him down. God, Meg,' Grandad rubbed his eyes, wearily. 'You should have heard the arguments.'

'Didn't they budge? Didn't they offer anything more?' Mam asked, rigid with anger.

'No,' he said softly. 'Not a bloody thing. They were adamant that the accident was nothing to do with them. They said the mine was dumping there before the school was built . . . exactly as we expected. They said they couldn't be held responsible for too much rain falling. Oh, so it went on, back and forth, back and forth. They did say how terribly sorry they were and all that pious claptrap, but nothing further. They just aren't prepared to accept responsibility. They had some bigwig law man from London with them who did most of the talking. Christ! Talking to that man was like talking to a brick wall. Lewis Lewis started in on him by asking what he knew about mining community life and he haughtily said that was irr . . . irreverent? Whatever that means.'

'Irrelevant,' said Mam absently as she poured tea.

'Yes, that's the word. Well anyway, he said he was only concerned with the letter of the law and as far as he and his clients were concerned there was no question in law that they were responsible. I guess that means if we bother going to court we don't stand a chance of winning.'

'Nonsense,' said Mam, 'he's trying to bluff you, that's all. How do we know what'll happen in court unless we try? More importantly, ask a solicitor and let him advise us. Did you threaten to take them to court?'

He nodded slowly. 'Lewis Lewis did. But see Meg, all the man did then was quote other cases that had been taken to court under similar circumstances. He said that all law in this land was based on previous decisions and so the law builds up,' he finished lamely.

'Of course, Dad,' said Mam, pausing to sip her tea. 'Our law is, I think, called Common Law. Once a decision is taken by a High Court Judge it becomes the standard for further decisions. These decisions aren't irreversible though, just guide lines. That way every case is judged on its own merits. Do you see?'

'I think so. Anyway Meg, it don't matter now. We told the men what happened and they're up in arms about it. Hell, I can't remember when they were so angry.'

'I don't blame them,' said Da, cutting into the conversation at last, after staring moodily at his cup. 'I don't blame them but they're wrong to do it.'

'Do what, Da?' I asked.

'They're talking about striking, son. Holding meetings, picketing, preventing mine safety. You name it and they're talking about doing it.' He shuddered. 'It doesn't bear thinking about. Especially if they prevent mine safety. It's not as though we've got that much as it is. What we have though is better than nothing.'

'What'll happen now, Da?' I asked.

'Well, the worst that'll happen,' answered Grandad, 'is the lower shafts will probably flood, because nobody will be checking the water levels and using the pumps when they're needed. That in itself is daft, I can tell you, because when we do start back we'll have to clear the shafts and that will mean lost production and more work before we start earning any money worth talking about, let alone bonuses. There's a greater risk of fire by spont . . . spont . . . bursting into flames.'

'Spontaneous combustion.'

'Thank you, Meg,' said Grandad with a little smile. 'I'd be tongue tied without your help. Anyway Dai, the fire risk is that much greater. There's more gas leaking than it should be, and when the time comes for us to go back into the shafts it'll be all the more dangerous. Mines are a bit like women, son, he said to me, ignore them at your peril. Don't look so puzzled, you'll understand one day. In the meantime . . .' he trailed off.

'In the meantime we could be out on strike within days, with the possibility the union won't make it official,' added Da.

'What . . . ?' I began.

'What'll that mean?' asked Da and I nodded. 'That'll mean no money for rent, food, gas . . . nothing.'

We sat in silence, each of us looking at the picture presented before us. It was not a pretty one.

The talk became desultory and I was sent to bed. I could not fully understand what it would all mean because I had nothing to measure it against. Like Sian's death, it was something different. I didn't want to understand it.

The next day it was Grandmother Osborne who woke me, her voice penetrating my sleep. I lay for a few minutes listening to her going on about the trouble. In some cack-handed, twisted way only she could see, she was trying to put the blame on Da.

'You mark my words,' she said loudly. 'You, Megan Griffiths, just mark my words. There's going to be trouble. Before we know it they'll have the militia up from Cardiff and then what? Somebody will be killed before this is over and for what? Nothing. I know, I've seen it all before.'

'I know you have, Mam. Evan and I dread it as much as you do but what can we do? Evan's father . . .'

'Bosh,' interrupted Grandmother, 'Evan's father is no better than your husband is . . .'

Reluctantly, I dressed. With me downstairs Grandmother tended not to say so much and at least that would spare Mam a little bit. I guessed she was sick and tired of hearing her mother going on about Da. It seemed to be getting worse, too, not better.

'You'll see my girl. They'll have more meetings and nothing will come of it. Then they'll try and persuade the men not to strike and promise more meetings. When one side is fed up then something will happen. Then . . . oh, good morning Dai,' she broke off as I came through the curtain.

'Morning,' I said shortly.

'Would you like something for breakfast, Dai?' Mam asked, relieved to change the subject.

'Yes, please. Where's Sion?'

'Gone to visit Uncle James. He said something about a new type of kite, which I must admit I didn't fully understand. A boiled egg?'

'That'll be fine,' I replied appreciating it. A boiled egg for breakfast was a luxury.

From Grandmother's sniff she thought so too.

'More tea, Mam? It won't be long brewing.'

'Eh, I don't think so. I've said all I came to say and ought to be on my way. I've some shopping to do. Take care of yourself, Dai,' she added as she left.

Both Mam and I heaved sighs of relief.

'What are you looking at me like that for, Dai?' Mam asked, making me jump, breaking into my thoughts.

'Nothing, Mam,' I felt myself blush.

'Come on, out with it. What were you thinking?'

'Well,' I hesitated, coughed. 'Er, er, well, nothing really. It's just I was thinking that's all. Eh, what Da said to you once. He eh, said eh,' I paused. 'He said he'd drown you if you turned out like your mother and you said not to worry because you'd do it yourself. And then he said, I guess this is one time when instead of looking at the mother to see how her daughter will turn out one should look at the father. Something about that being against all the rules or something.' I ended with another cough to cover my embarrassment.

She laughed. 'You've got an excellent memory. He was only joking but I have to admit that if I did become like your Grandmother I'd think about it.' She became serious again. 'She hasn't been the same since Grandfather died. I suppose we ought to make allowances for her, but after two years the allowances get to be too much. I don't know, I sometimes think she's getting worse.' With a shrug she went back to the kitchen to bake bread and cakes for the get together. I went back to dipping a piece of bread in my egg.

It rained most of the day and I sat in front of the fire dreaming over my atlas. I was not in the mood to do any schoolwork and Mam was too busy to set me any, so I just sat and thought. About Sian mostly and I wondered for the millionth time if there really was such a place as heaven. I wanted to believe there was, if only for Sian's sake, but no matter how I tried I found it impossible to reconcile my intelligence to the idea. And now with more problems coming . . . It was impossible for there to be some Supreme Being looking after our interests on earth.

Sion came back for lunch. He talked of nothing else except his new design for a kite that he and Uncle James were building together.

By now I was fed up with staying in and not being able to do anything. It was all the more galling because I felt much stronger. Mam was being over cautious, just in case. But even I knew that a relapse could be very serious.

I woke with a start, the smell of Mam's cooking filling my nostrils. My mouth watered when I thought of her pikelets and Welsh cakes, cooking by the hot plate. I went to see if she needed any help, like someone to test the texture and flavour of her baking. Unfortunately, she assured me my help was not wanted so I returned to my seat to think up another ploy. I was not above pinching a cake if she turned her back, even for a second. I pondered a strategy, thinking about diversions, sneak attacks and help from Sion. But there was a problem because Sion was not there and I could not go out to get him. It was certainly a ticklish campaign to wage but I easily fell into the roll of general, planning to outwit my clever and implacable enemy. As usual I had been outmanoeuvred and outthought on every point. I sighed as Mam came in with a cup of tea and a Welsh cake.

'Just one Dai, to make sure they're all right, see' she said, putting them on the table.

I grabbed it, the spoils no less sweet because I had done nothing to earn them. Only after I finished did I remember Welsh cakes had been Sian's favourite and the edge was taken from my enjoyment.

Nothing of consequence happened that day nor for

a few days afterwards. Meeting followed meeting. We were left on tenterhooks, the whole village wondering. On Wednesday, Da came home late. There had been another meeting at the Wheatsheaf and the men had voted to strike. The night shift, due to finish at five the next morning, would be the last before they came out.

A short while later there was a knock at the door. Da answered. I heard voices and then Da came in followed by some of the men.

'Your father will be along soon,' said Lewis Lewis to Da. 'Hullo Dai, feeling better boyo?' he asked. He was a short, red-faced man running to fat. He was always pleasant and cheerful, but now his usually smiling face was uncommonly grave. With him were Huw Shepherd, and Peter Lloyd. I suppose they and Grandad were the village leaders. The committee. Nothing important happened at the mine or village without their involvement.

'You know what happened today, Evan,' began Peter Lloyd without preamble. 'We realise the vote was carried by the younger men. Hullo, Meg,' he broke off as Mam came in.

'Hullo Peter, Lewis, Huw. What are you all doing here?'

'I'm just coming to that Meg,' continued Peter. 'The three of us and Evan's dad had a long talk and we want Evan to go round to the men, individually like, and try to persuade them to change their minds about the strike. Goodness Meg, you know Evan is virtually the spokesman for the younger men,' he nearly smiled but didn't quite manage it, 'now that you've taught him to read and write better, aye and talk proper like. Well, they respect that and we thought he might be able to do something.'

'That's no good,' said Da. 'First of all I don't think they'll listen to me and secondly as soon as they get together again Thomas or Williams will bully them back to supporting the strike. I don't think it'll do any good at all, look you.'

'Hold it a second, Evan,' said Lewis Lewis. 'There's no doubt in my mind that I'd like to smash the bloody owners financially and physically. I hated them before and now I feel . . . I just don't know how to put it into words. I thought hate was the strongest feeling I could have and I thought I hated the owners. But by God the feelings I once had are nothing compared to now. Hell man, I wouldn't walk across the street and piss on them if they were on fire . . . Sorry Meg, my feelings got the better of me.'

'That's all right Lewis. I'll just go and make some tea while you men talk.' She went into the kitchen, leaving the door ajar.

'What I'm trying to say, Evan, is despite how strongly we feel we don't think what the men are doing will do any good. Our only hope is to try our luck with the courts. I know we might not win, but anything else is utter madness. Christ Almighty, you know how they're talking. What was it one of them said? Something about tightening the belts for a long fight. And for what, for God's sake? Some sort of bloody principle they aren't too sure of anyway,' he leaned back on his chair, looking worn out. 'I think I'm getting too old for this.'

'There's years left in you yet, Lewis Lewis, so don't talk daft, man,' said Huw Shepherd. 'But I know how you feel. The point is Evan, we can't afford a strike and you know it. I don't mind admitting I'm frightened what might happen, see. I remember the past only too well. We'll spend what little savings we have, eat like . . . like animals, too hungry to waste even rotted food . . . Remember, Peter?'

The old man nodded sadly. 'It'll get to the stage when our pride won't let us give in. We'll lose any ideas of being reasonable and stick it out for everything we demand. You know what'll happen then, boyo?' Peter was addressing me, much to my surprise.

I shook my head, fascinated and horrified at the same time.

'Then the strikebreakers will come. The owners know that if they don't do something quick then it'll not only take a hell of a lot of money to put right but some shafts may even be beyond saving. Before they bring in the scabs they'll let us know what they're doing and give us one more chance to go back. The men will get angrier and angrier, an anger fed by their families' hunger and they'll be more determined not to return like whipped dogs with their tails between their legs. There'll be fights with the scabs, splintering amongst the villagers as some will try and get the men back to work. There might even be killing. The stinking militia will be with the scabs, with their guns and batons. And do you know what'll happen in the end?'

I shook my head again. The others knew what was coming. They had not only heard it all before but had seen it too.

'I'll tell you, boyo,' went on Peter Lloyd, 'we'll end up going back, some time, God knows when. And the strikebreakers will return to their homes. And the village will be bitter, counting the cost. Some men will be sent to Coventry, neighbour not speaking to neighbour. There'll be more fights, all the more frightening because instead of being a fight with strangers it will be friend against friend, family against family. Actions and attitudes during the strike will be remembered forever, and for what? Tell me that, for what? Nothing. Less than nothing if there's such a thing.' He broke off as Mam returned with tea and cakes. The curtain by the stairs moved and Sion put his head through, his eyes heavy with sleep.

'Oh, hullo,' he said sheepishly. 'I heard voices and wondered who was here.'

'Well, now you know off you go! Back up the wooden hill,' said Da. 'And go to sleep.'

Sion pushed out his bottom lip in a pout. 'Can't I have

a cake, like Dai?' he said, suddenly smiling as all heads turned to me as I bit into my second Welsh cake. I paused and looked guiltily at Mam.

'All right. Take it up to bed with you,' she said. 'And try not to make a mess with it, there's a good boy.' He nipped in, grabbed the cake and was back up the stairs in a twinkling of an eye.

There was a further interruption as Grandad arrived fresh from talking to a few of the other miners.

'Still up, Dai?' he greeted me. 'Thanks, Meg.' He took the cup Mam offered, sipped, grimaced and added a teaspoon of sugar. 'It wasn't good,' he shook his head. 'Not good at all. I spoke to Evan Evans, look you, Robert Jones, the two Jones brothers and Henry Wilks. I dunno, look you, what the hell they think they're playing at. Evan Evans started in on me by claiming I didn't understand how they all felt because I hadn't lost anybody myself. Even after I reminded him about my grandchildren, God bless their little souls, he didn't have the decency to apologise. Just said it wasn't the same thing as I was their grandfather and not a father. I could have killed the bastard.' His hands clenched into large fists, the whites of his knuckles showing. 'How I wanted to hammer some sense into him! Anyway,' he went on, sounding tired, 'I couldn't persuade him it was a pointless strike and that we had to find a better way. He as good as called me a scab. The Jones brothers were worse. Clive Jones suggested that perhaps I was in the pay of the owners.' The others exchanged glances. 'Luckily for him, his brother intervened and played it down or else I would have hit him.'

'What about Henry? He usually sees good sense when it's put before him,' said Da.

Grandad made a rocking motion with his hand. 'He'll sway either way. He didn't have anybody killed,' Grandad said bluntly, his bitterness emphasising the word killed, 'so he'll follow the majority which at the moment is for the strike.' He looked at the clock on the mantelpiece, the clock that was the wedding present to Mam and Da from him and Grandma. 'Which will start in exactly eight hours when the night shift comes up.'

'Look,' said Lewis Lewis, 'this mine employs men from what? Seven villages? Our three villages make up most of the work force. Perhaps with those that's wavering here and with the men from the other four we can get a majority to remain in work. After all, not all the men have voted by a long way.' He paused as the others nodded or shrugged. 'If we do that, then the strikers may agree to go back and we'll get a chance to use the courts.'

'What then?' asked Da. 'And anyway, it's too late now. We couldn't get organised before tomorrow morning. It would take too long.'

'There's no doubt about that,' went on Lewis Lewis. 'We can't stop it from starting, but if we got organised . . . perhaps in a day or two we can get them back.'

'What are you suggesting?' asked Grandad. He smiled at Mam as he said, 'We could draw up a list of the men we think want to work. We'll get more names as we go along and visit them one by one. Or perhaps we could get small groups together and talk; we could save time that way. I'm sure many of them don't want to go through the hardships we can see. Just for this. I know what we all lost. There isn't a family in the village that wasn't affected by the accident but this won't get us anywhere.'

'We know that, Lewis,' said Peter Lloyd, 'who're you trying to convince man?'

'Um, sorry like. I forgot for a minute. What do you think?'

There was silence for a few moments. The patter of rain outside and the crackling hiss of the fire gave a background homeliness out of place with the serious issues at hand.

'I'm not sure,' said Da, hesitatingly. 'It'll cause an

awful lot of bad feeling and possibly add to the problem, not help.'

'I can't help feeling my son's right, but what alternative is there? Apart from backing the strike one hundred percent I can't see another answer.' Grandad was anxious to agree with the others, but knew he couldn't really do so.

'Couldn't we try the men who are all for the strike? If we persuade them the others may follow . . .' Huw Shepherd's voice trailed off.

'No good, Huw,' said Peter Lloyd, 'you know what they're like. My God, I don't really blame them, see. Both Thomas and Williams lost two kids. Perhaps I'd feel different if they'd been my kids, I don't know. Sorry Evan,' he broke off, seeing my father's pinched, white face, 'that's the wrong thing to say. No, I do understand their anger and frustration, we all do. But they're going about it the wrong way.'

It seemed to me the talk had gone round in more than one circle and they were getting nowhere fast.

6

THE FIRST TWO days of the strike passed peacefully.
Of course, as I was not allowed out, I saw nothing but
Da or Grandad told me what was happening. The mine
was effectively sealed: nobody and nothing was allowed
to move in or out. The owners protested strongly about
the need for mine safety supervision but got nowhere
with the men. When one of the managers tried to talk to
the pickets they threw mud at him, making him duck and
run. There was no further attempt on the owners' part to
reason with the men; instead they tried talking through
Grandad, Lewis Lewis and the others who thought the
same way. This was all to no avail. Another problem was
already arising according to Da. The men were beginning
to reject out of hand anything the leaders said. Yet for
all that it was relatively quiet, no one attempted to go
to work and the owners did not attempt strike breaking
tactics . . . not yet.

The committee and some of the others visited the men
in the surrounding villages, talking to as many would
listen. By the third day they were hopeful. ey had
names of more people who wanted to go b to work
than wanted to be out. The committee decid n a mass
meeting. A proper show of hands and the could b
back within a few days. The committee tened t
and worked hard whenever any incident
out of hand.   that
Unfortunately there was one incidam
mittee had no control over, and a

...tly it started pleasantly enough when two of the ...s' wives were out riding in their carriage and a ...en of the men stopped them. The men tried to explain ...ow they felt about the loss of their children and asked them to talk to their husbands on the villagers' behalf. One of the men asked how they would feel if it had been their children and one of the women replied she would feel proper human feelings of grief, not the animal reactions of the workers. The women were nearly hanged for that remark and it was only Granddad's timely arrival on the scene that prevented serious trouble. By the time the story did the rounds, feeling amongst the villagers was hardened, and the ditherers sided with the strikers as a result.

Even so there was enough common sense left that the committee thought they could end the strike. A meeting was called for Monday.

Saturday dawned bright and fair. The wind had inexplicably dropped and the clouds disappeared. The day promised to be mild and sunny for the twelfth of November, Mam and Da's anniversary.

Sion and I burst into their bedroom sometime between seven and eight, not long after first light. With cries of 'Happy Anniversary' we gave each a present – a scarf for Mam and a tobacco pouch for Da.

'Where on earth did you get the money for these?' asked Mam. Her smile held a hint of worry.

Sio...nd I squirmed. 'Ask no questions and we'll tell no lies,' I said. 'Would you like a cup of tea? Sion can make ...hile I light the fire.' I was halfway through the door be...' they replied.

'No, ...it Dai,' said Da. 'Come on, tell us, there's a good boy...,'d like to know. Not that it will lessen the gift any.'

I looked...

...cause we...on and he shrugged. 'We can't really say ...can't ve...sed not to tell,' I said hesitatingly, 'and ...' break a promise now, can we?'

'I suppose not,' said Mam dubiously. 'All right then tell us, was it Grandad you promised?'

We both shook our heads.

'Uncle William? Uncle Huw? Uncle David? Uncle Albert?' Da went through the family, to which we shook our heads in each case.

'Then who . . .' he began.

'I know,' interrupted Mam. 'It was very nice of old Mr Price to have done so, but you shouldn't have let him.'

'We couldn't stop him, Mam,' blurted Sion.

'Idiot,' I hissed at him as Mam and Da laughed.

'Oh,' Sion looked sheepish, realising Mam had tricked him.

'It's all right,' I said, 'we'll be delivering coal and doing things for him so we can pay him back. We drew up a list of jobs and prices and Mr Price will keep count until it's all square.'

'And how long will that take?' asked Da.

'About a year,' replied Sion, skipping out of the room to make tea.

Mam and Da laughed but abruptly stopped. 'It seems wrong somehow to be happy,' said Mam, sadly. 'I think, boyo,' she turned to Da, 'that I wish we'd never agreed to the party but celebrated some other way.'

'Hush, love,' Da put his arm around her, pulling her down besides him. There was no need to tell me to leave, nor that the tea could wait. I wandered downstairs, thinking. Were they wrong to laugh? Was Sion or I to enjoy ourselves or not? I knew Sian had been dead only a matter of weeks. We still thought of her often, most when something made us laugh, something we knew would have enjoyed. There would be an instant's sad and then it would pass, to be replaced by an empty f The emptiness came, I thought, because we were Sian would never enjoy the occurrence, would ne in demanding to know what was funny, being she did not understand and making us laugh n the sense of loss, the absolute and permanent loss, which was hardest to live with.

Sion was standing in the middle of the kitchen, the kettle in his hands. 'I don't feel like doing this, it was Sian's job,' he said, tears rolling down his cheeks. 'I wish God hadn't taken her away,' he paused. 'I don't think I like God anymore.'

'Me neither,' I felt my own tears rising. I realised because they had been twins Sion might feel Sian's death more than any of us. 'I'll just light the fire,' I said taking the kettle from him. 'We can't make tea until then.'

In the middle of the afternoon Grandad and Grandma arrived, quickly followed by Da's four brothers, their wives and their nine children. Grandmother Osborne came last, with her sister, Great Aunt Olive. The grown ups were in the front room while we kids were banished to the living room and no chairs. We had no objections; we were nearer the food.

I think that for the grown ups it was not a particularly happy affair. We were aware of Sian and Johnny not being with us but we still played games and laughed at blind man's bluff and tailing the donkey. But in the front room it was different, especially as Grandmother Osborne kept making remarks about how tasteless it all was. I could see she was upsetting Mam and Aunt Mair. I went into the room to listen, tired of play-ং games.

'What's going to happen do you think, Dad?' Uncle ɱm asked.

'r guess is as good as mine William, better prob- know what some of these hotheads are like . . .'

'not hotheads,' interrupted Uncle Huw . . .

'ordinary people like us. They are friends ol ll our lives.'

few upted by Grandad, who said, 'Come party. Let's forget the strike for a

The others nodded their agreement and the conve
sation turned to happier matters. The laughter was forced
an underlying sadness pervaded the room but at least for
a while the strike was ignored, if not forgotten.

Then Grandad said, 'I guess this wasn't such a good
idea after all. Perhaps we ought to try again next year.'
He looked around at the others who appeared to agree
with him.

Before anyone made a move to leave Da spoke. 'Wait
a second. Meg and me spent ages trying to decide what
to do about today. I know it's our anniversary, but to
be honest neither of us wanted this – though we didn't
expect it to be quite as bad,' he paused. 'The thing is we
wanted to tell you something. We've,' he paused again
and then the words came in a rush, 'we've decided to go
to America as soon as we can.'

I was sitting on the floor next to the door and my mouth
dropped open as I heard what Da said. I could not believe
it . . . America!

It was Grandmother Osborne who protested first and
loudest. 'Megan, you can't,' she wailed. 'You can't just
go off to the other side of the world like that. What'll I
do without you? You're the only flesh and blood I have
except for Olive. What'll I do without you?' she repeated.

'Don't cry, Mam,' Mam kneeled at her mother's side
and took her hand. 'We'll write often and who knows?
Once we're settled perhaps you could come and visit us,
even live with us.'

'What?' Grandmother pulled her hand away in horror.
'And who will look after your father's grave? Why,' the
thought dawned on her, 'who's to look after Sian's? You
can't just leave your daughter's grave unattended,' she
said, hurtfully.

The others joined in the protest. They did not want to
see the family split up.

'Are you serious?' asked Uncle David. 'Do you mean
you're really going?'

'But what will you do there?' asked Aunt Maud, David's wife. 'How will you support yourselves?'

'We aren't sure yet,' replied Da, 'but I can always work in the mines in Philadelphia or somewhere, if I have to.'

'What about the boys' schooling? Dai is going to grammar school next year. At least,' amended Uncle Albert, 'he ought to get there with all the help you've given him, Meg.'

'I'm sure he would,' said Mam, 'and that was probably the hardest decision to make. We think there'll be good schools in America. In the meantime I can keep them on top of their work. After the effort we've put in and all the saving we've done to pay for their education it was heart breaking to decide to go to but after all that's happened . . .'

'But where will you live?' asked Uncle David. 'Where will you go? Do you know yet?'

Da shook his head. 'We've a few places in mind but we're keeping it sort of open for now, look you. We'll decide later.' He shrugged his shoulders.

'I've never heard such rot,' said Grandmother Osborne furiously. 'I absolutely forbid it, Megan, do you hear? Absolutely forbid it. You can't just go off and leave me like that. What on earth will your poor father think?' Her comment was greeted with silence and then Grandad spoke.

'Never mind what he'll think,' he said brusquely. 'He's dead. It's the living we have to concern ourselves with. I guess your mind is made up, son?'

Da nodded. 'Yes, Dad. I'm sorry, Mam, but we both feel that it's the best thing for us and the boys.'

Grandma gave a tremulous smile. 'I understand, Evan, both of us do. We'll be heart broken to see you go but you must do what you think's best for Meg and the boys.'

'That's right son, what your Mam says. We don't want you to go, not for all the tea in China but we certainly won't try and stop you.' Grandad was quick to accept the plan.

Grandma blew her nose. 'It's come as a bit of a shock, that's all,' she forced a smile.

'When do you intend leaving?' asked Uncle William.

'Not until the spring,' replied Mam. 'That'll give us plenty of time to find a place before the winter settles in.'

'You've obviously thought a lot about it and I can't say I'm exactly surprised,' said Uncle Huw. 'Not after all the nagging Dai's done to emigrate. All I can say is "good luck". Great good luck.'

The others nodded except Grandmother and great Aunt Olive. In the silence Sion put his head around the door. 'Come and play, Dai,' he said.

'Hey, little brother,' I replied, 'we're going to America.'

'Eh? What are you on about, Dai?' he asked exasperated.

'Like I said. We're going to America in the spring.' The news still left me with a sense of shock. After all the dreaming it seemed wrong somehow that it should happen just like that.

Shortly afterwards everybody went home. The exodus was started by Grandmother Osborne and Great Aunt Olive who as usual had said nothing worth noting.

We were washing and clearing up when Sion said: 'Mam, what about Sian? What are we going to do about her? We can't take her grave with us can we? And who's going to put flowers on and sort of look after it if we aren't here?' He was close to crying.

'Don't worry, son,' said Da. 'Grandad and Grandma will look after it for us. She'll have flowers on her birthday and things.'

'And anyway, Sion,' said Mam, 'she'll always be wi us. In our hearts and our thoughts, and that's what's re important you know. Not where she's buried, but in memories.'

He shook his head and burst into tears. 'I don't want to go to rotten America,' he announced. 'I don't want to leave Sian.' He ran up the stairs.

'I'll go and talk to him,' said Mam. 'You two finish these dishes.'

Da washed and I dried, silence between us for a while and then: 'What do you think Dai? Do you want to go?'

'Yes, Da, I want to go all right. You know I've always wanted to.'

'You don't mind about school?'

There was the nub of it. Did I mind about school? 'To be honest Da, I'm not sure. Part of me minds, I think, but most of me is glad we're going. Gosh,' I began to get excited, 'just think of seeing all those places. And seeing the sea. Gosh, I can't wait. I hope Sion comes round soon, it'll be terrible if he doesn't want to go. Will we leave him behind Da?' I paused. 'If we're going to, I'd better stay as well.'

He looked at me in surprise for a moment and then laughed briefly. 'No Dai, we won't be leaving him behind. Where we go he goes and so do you. So no more talk of staying behind, right?'

'Right Da, I just wondered, that's all.' Pensively I dried another plate. Mam came back a little later, as we were finishing. She pulled a face at Da and took the towel from me. 'Go and see if there's any more dishes in the other room,' she ordered.

Things seemed to be getting back to normal.

7

THE WEATHER STAYED fine, with no wind, blue sky and sunlight that gave a tepid warmth. The doctor came on Monday when I was becoming frustrated and beginning to pace around, getting on Mam's nerves with my whining to be allowed out.

'You can go for a walk for an hour or so,' the doctor said, 'but make sure you're back after that. And no getting wet and also, young man, no exerting yourself.'

'That doesn't leave me with much to do, does it?' I complained.

'Maybe not Dai,' he sighed, 'but try and understand you've had a nasty illness, which could have been worse . . . a lot worse. Now, if you do more than just walk in the fresh air and I hear about it, or your Mam hears about it for that matter, then you won't go out for another week. Give me your word you'll behave.' He spoke sternly.

'I promise,' I said solemnly, my hands behind my back, fingers crossed. I grabbed my coat and made for the door. The last thing I heard was the doctor asking: 'What's all this I hear about you emigrating, Meg?'

After being cooped up for so long I felt a special excitement at being out and started to run along the street when I remembered I had to walk. I got to number twenty-three and called for Cliff, my closest friend. He was out, down watching the pickets his mother thought.

tried a few more doors – same story. I hesitated, fighting with my conscience and finally told myself that if I walked quickly I could say hullo to the gang and come straight back. It would be a tight hour but I could make it. Just.

It was not the sort of scenery poets wrote about and though daffodils were supposed to be the Welsh national flower, even in spring there were only a few of them waving their golden heads along the route I took. The endless streets of houses were roofed with grey slate and built from local grey stone. Curling trails of smoke covered the sky with their own greyness and the hills, sparsely covered with grass had a few grey looking sheep wandering over them. The sunlight did nothing to alleviate the bleakness of the valley.

My illness had taken more out of me that I had realised. Soon I was more breathless and tired than I had been in a long while. I slowed and finally stopped. I hesitated, wondering whether I should go back. I was over half way to the mine. It was only down the road and round the corner, just past Devil's Elbow where the road almost doubles back on itself. After that another few hundred yards . . . that was okay, but returning? Most of the way would be uphill. Reluctantly I turned around.

I had looked away from the school, still half covered with slag. Workmen were slowly clearing it but they would be a long time yet. When I had a clear view I paused, but there was not a great deal to see. A black forlorn building, the roof and half the walls were showing through the sea of slag. The playground and road outside were still covered, a river of black running down to the banks of the Taff. I shivered, whether from the cold or the bleakness of the view I was unsure. I thought of Sian and knew where I could go for a short while.

I stood by her grave and read the stone.

Sian
Dearly beloved
Daughter of
Evan and Megan Griffiths
Born 29th July 1882
Died tragically 14th October 1890
"Suffer the little children to come unto me."

The engraving was in old-fashioned Welsh. I tried to imagine her lying almost under my feet. Her arms would be crossed, her eyes closed and she would look as though she was sleeping. I felt the tears coming to my eyes. I looked around to see if I could find any flowers, feeling guilty that I had not brought anything now that I was there for the first time. Of course there was nothing to be found in November but I promised her that the next time I returned I would bring a plant.

The hand on my shoulder made me jump.

'Sorry Dai, I didn't mean to startle you,' said Da. 'I was passing and thought I saw you standing here.' He looked at the grave, silent for a few moments. 'Just after the accident I couldn't walk past without stopping for a few minutes, even if it meant leaving for the mine a bit earlier and getting home later,' he paused and shook his head sadly. 'Now I come once a day, usually on my way home. Today I'd just persuaded myself to go straight home when I saw you. In a little while I'll be going every other day, then once a week, on a Sunday because we'll already be here and it'll be less inconvenient. Do you know what I'm trying to tell you, son?'

'I dunno, Da. I'm not sure.'

'I suppose I'm trying to say that life goes on, see. We have to go on living, eating, breathing, laughing. Time, Mam tells me, is the great healer. We'll go to America and . . . although we'll never forget Sian . . . no, that would be impossible, we'll just remember her less and less.'

'Even Sion, Da?'

'Even Sion. Come on, let's go home.' He put his arm across my shoulders.

'What happened at the meeting?'

'It was postponed for another two days. Damn them. I don't know how they did it but the strikers got it called off. The fools.'

I went to bed for a nap and slept until suppertime. The strike was beginning to be felt. For supper that evening we had bread and cheese. The latter was green in places but buried between two pieces of toast (to hide how stale the bread was). It was not too bad.

'We need to keep our savings for as long as possible,' explained Mam to Sion and me. 'So we'll have to make do with what we've got in the allotment and what I've got here. Evan, how long is this going to go on? Do you have any idea?'

Da shook his head. 'We still have to wait for the meeting. If we got a shift back now it could cause more problems than it's worth. A proper show of hands will do the trick, though God knows what'll happen now. I thought we'd persuaded them to go back but if the ringleaders got a postponement so easily I don't know . . . I just don't know. I tell you, Meg, I'm sick of it, sick of it all,' he burst out bitterly. 'Those swine of owners sitting in their big houses, screwing us down like they do. All we want is what's right. I know, I know, we're trying to do it the right way, through the courts. And where will that get us? Meg, you know as well as I do . . . nowhere, no damn where. I don't like it. Something's wrong, but I can't place my finger on it.' He shrugged. 'We say we ought to go back to work. Then we lose in court. It'll be impossible to get the same sort of bitter, soul aching anger back into the people – the sort needed to sustain a strike. Something to help them through the cold and hunger. And it's not their hunger, that's easy to live with, but the children and babies. I hate those people up there. Meg, I don't know yet what I'm going to do in America but on one thing I'm certain I won't go back into the mines. I'll find something else, anything else, but not the mines.' He suddenly fell silent.

Mam placed her hand on his arm and squeezed. 'I'm glad, Evan. We'll find some way to live, I know we will. I don't want you to go into the mines either and I always hoped that one day you'd decide to stop. I don't want you coughing your lungs out with silicosis. In America there'll be something better for you. Aye, and good schools for Dai and Sion too.'

'I'm not going,' said Sion defiantly.

Da clouted him across the back of his head. It had never happened before; Mam and I were startled and Sion was too shocked to cry at first. It had not been a hard blow but as Sion lifted his hand to his head he started to sob. Da seemed as surprised as us.

He looked at the palm of his hand. 'God Almighty, I'm sorry, Sion. I didn't mean it son. But you're coming with us whether you want to or not and don't let me hear another word from you saying otherwise. Understand?'

Sion sniffled, not speaking.

'Understand?' Da barked in a harsh voice. Sion nodded and began crying again. 'Damn! First of all it's my brothers and now I've hit my son. I'm going to the Wheatsheaf Meg,' he pushed back his chair and stalked out of the room.

Mam closed her eyes and leaned back in her chair. 'Come here, Sion,' she said after a while. 'Come on,' she coaxed him. Sion slid off his seat. She pulled him on to her lap and stroked his hair. 'I don't suppose you understand but Da is under a great strain at the moment. Not only with the strike making him worry about feeding and clothing us but also with your Uncles. Uncle Huw and Uncle David are for the strike and bitter at Da for ιot supporting them. They don't see things the way Da and Grandad do. The trouble is Da also agrees with them, but he knows it's pointless to do what they want. That's what's tearing Da up. He sees America as a solution for the ones he loves most in the world: us. So you see Sion, you must come with us. Do you remember what the vicar said to you on Sunday? About Sian always being with us because we love her so?' Sion nodded. 'Well then, it's true. As long as she's in our thoughts she's with us. And she's in heaven too of course, with God. Her grave is just a symbol, meaningless in itself, because she's not in it but up there looking down on us. Do you see?'

'But how will she know where we've gone? She'll never find us in America,' he sniffed.

'Of course she will, silly,' Mam comforted him. 'God knows everything and if she did happen to lose us He'd tell her where we are, wouldn't He? Besides, if you say your prayers every night you can tell her where we are, can't you? So don't worry about that. Now,' she smiled, 'if I know Da he'll be back in about ten minutes having walked as far as the pub and back. He'll be sorry. He's said he's sorry. Now you have to tell him too. All right?'

'Yes, Mam,' Sion said in a small voice.

As Mam predicted Da came straight back. When he came through the door Sion gave a tremulous smile. Da smiled back, and it was all right again.

Soon afterwards Sion went to bed.

'Have you seen Mair or Maud?' asked Da, as he settled into the chair by the fire. He coughed and phlegmed into the flames. 'Sorry Meg,' he wiped his mouth in his handkerchief.

'No, I haven't. What's happening at the mine?'

'At the moment, nothing,' he replied, stretching his legs in front of the fire. 'Not a damned thing. Nobody goes in or out. There must be twenty or more there all the time and a lot more close by in the old hall where we were going to have the meeting. They've set themselves up in there with the women supplying tea and any food they can spare. There's a determination about it all that's frightening. I tried to talk to Huw this afternoon. All he said was that I was a scab and walked away. This was in spite of the fact I was doing my stint at the gate along with the others.' He sighed heavily, coughed and used his handkerchief. 'David came and talked to me. Wanted to know if it was true that we'd been around to the men, trying to persuade them the strike was a waste of time. I argued that there was a better way. He stalked away. Now neither of them will speak to me. Although William's against the strike he's not for us either, just sitting in the middle as usual. I suppose it's just as well Albert works for the railways. He's against the strike, but his opinion doesn't count for much with the other two. God, Meg, what a lousy stinking mess. It'll get worse before it gets better.' He sat staring at the fire for a few moments. 'I'd better go down to the river tomorrow and find some coal if there's any left. At least we can try and stay warm even if we do go hungry. I heard number eight shaft was already flooded to about twelve feet. That'll take some shifting already and each day it gets worse. I reckon the owners will be in with the militia and scabs the day after our meeting if we vote to continue with the strike.'

'So soon?' I asked.

'They're all ready son, so Grandad told me, and he's never been wrong yet.'

'What'll happen do you think, Evan? Will the men go back?'

He sucked in on his cheeks, a sign of indecision. 'I just don't know, Meg. I think it'll be touch and go. When they got the meeting postponed it was an important victory for them and they know it.'

'Why's that?' I asked.

'Well, because I suppose the longer the men are out the more determined they become to carry on fighting.'

'Will it be very bad if the militia comes?' I asked.

'It'll be worse than very bad,' answered Mam. 'The militia will force entry for the scabs who will do our men's work. Any resistance will surely lead to fighting and possibly killing. When the villagers see what's happening some of the men will go back to work realising there would be nothing to gain by staying out. It'll earn them the enmity of people they once thought of as friends. Then more will return and the die-hards, the leaders, will be sacked and thrown out of their houses. And for years to come there will be bad feeling between friends and families. And when it comes to a court case, if it ever does, the strike will count against us because judges don't like strikers.' Mam paused. 'That's the best it'll be. I'm going to make a cup of tea.'

On the day of the meeting Mam had wanted to go but Da had been adamant she stayed at home in case of trouble. She had protested but finally agreed. It was rare Da insisted she do anything but when he did it was even rarer for her to disagree. This, I supposed, was one of the rarer occasions.

'Don't tell Da,' she said as she left.

'I won't need to, he'll see you anyway, Mam.'

'Yes, well, never mind that. Just don't say anything – unless he does, see.'

Mam told me later that Da scowling was the first person she saw. However, he agreed to let her stay and they went into the hall together. It was nearly packed yet there were still many more coming down the hill and from the other villages further up the valley.

'There's David and Maud,' Mam waved and was disconcerted when they pointedly ignored her.

'Dear God, you did warn me. Is this what we've come to?'

'I'm afraid so, Meg,' said Da grimly. 'We'll get the same from Huw and Mair too, if we see them.'

More and more people crowded in. The hall was a

ramshackle place, old and musty, smelling from disuse.
It had been a warehouse for the mine but was disused
for years. When a group of travelling players had visited
the valley years before, a rude stage had been built at the
far end.

Many of the villagers wore their best clothes. The
men all wore suits and caps and many had white scarves
at their throats. The women wore gaily coloured head
scarves though a few could afford a hat.

More people pushed their way in. The noise, heat and
closeness was getting worse. A few men climbed onto
the stage, Grandad amongst them. Slowly but surely
silence descended until finally you could have heard a
pin drop.

Peter Lloyd stepped forward. 'You all know me and
I know most if not all of you. Those who don't know
me, ask a neighbour what I'm like. I'm a plain speaker,
see. Always been for looking after the men, women and
children in my village and those around us. You all know
that. You all know I'll stick by you through thick and thin,
no matter what. That's always been my way and always
will be, look you. No doubt many of you have heard
stories, rumours about what's going on. Well now I'm
going to give it to you straight. From the horse's mouth
like, as they say. I believe, along with the other men here
on this stage that the strike is wrong.'

Someone called from the crowd, too indistinctly to
understand. Then someone else yelled and then there
were cat calls and booing from all over the hall, calling
them silly old buggers, raving fools and other words I
would not have understood. After a few minutes Grandad
came forward and in his powerful voice yelled for silence.
It took a while but the noise subsided. Some of the crowd
badgered the louder ones to be quiet and eventually Mam
could make out what Grandad was saying.

'Now we'll have no more of that. If you have anything
to say come up on the stage and say it. That way anybody

with anything worth saying can tell all of us. Now, look you, let Peter finish what he was going to say.'

'All of the committee, your committee, who have worked for the villages for years are against the strike.' There were more yells. 'Please let me finish.' Peter was quietly determined.

'Yes, shut up,' said a voice in the crowd, 'and let him have his say.' The heckling stopped.

'I want to tell you why we think it's wrong. Because we can't win, that's why.'

'Who said we can't?' came a familiar voice.

'Huw,' said Da to Mam.

'Because we can't. We're fighting a dubious principle. We say the owners are responsible for what happened to our children. They say they're not. Now they'll contribute to the memorial we plan and towards the new school. They're afraid if they do more it'll be seen as an admission of guilt once the case goes to court and we could easily win the case. They say they are taking a risk giving us so much, but to show good faith are willing to do so. But they will only do that much if we go back to work.' There was a general booing and hissing from the crowd. Peter Lloyd took out a handkerchief and wiped his forehead. Eventually after another intervention by Grandad there was quiet again.

'Now, listen to me, please. I know what I'm talking about. Unless we agree to go back to work tomorrow then the owners will bring in the scabs and militia. You all know what that'll mean.'

The silence showed that the crowd knew what it would mean only too well. They began to fidget and whisper to each other. It looked as if it might be possible that the men would vote to return to work.

The men on stage exchanged glances and Mam wondered if they too sensed victory. As the word came to her mind she realised it was a hollow sort of victory. The winners and the losers came from the same side . . . the people of the village. Grandad stepped forward and held up his hand for quiet.

'I just want to add what I think about this matter and I hope most of you here will see it my way too. Nearly all of us lost a child near to us. I lost two grandchildren and the thought will haunt me all my days. My heart bleeds not only for my two sons and their wives but for the rest of you. I know the anguish you must be suffering. You heard what Peter had to say will happen if we stay on strike. The hardships will be that much greater. Hunger will feed our sorrow. And it'll do no good because it won't bring the children back. Most of you here know we'll end up going back. We'll have to. There's no way we can win. And the next time we want a pay rise or an added safety feature in the mines, and all you coal face workers know we've got plenty of ideas, the owners will remember. They'll know many of us will have spent a lot of our savings, if we have any, and they'll know we wouldn't be able to last long the next time. On the other hand if we go back now, with our dignity and savings intact, then next time we'll stand a better chance of getting what we want.'

'Why should we get something then and not now?' a voice asked.

'That, friend, is a good question. When we say we want increased safety, and say so again and again, they'll know it's as much in their interest as ours to see that we get it. Greater safety often leads to greater production which puts more money in our pockets as well as theirs. They know this as well as we do. It just sometimes takes a little bit of persuasion on our part to make them realise it. And you all know they have often come round to our way of thinking. I know and so do the committee who've been at the meetings. We can't win by striking but we have a chance through the courts. Remember the saying, he who fights and runs away,' he paused. 'The younger ones are better educated than me, and they know these things.' The crowd laughed.

Peter Lloyd took over again. 'I suggest we have a vote to decide whether or not we return to . . .'

'Wait a minute. Wait a minute. Not so fast.' A group of men pushed their way to the stage. Amongst them were Uncle Huw and Uncle David. About eight of them clambered onto the stage.

'Before we have any vote I've got a few words to say.' It was Ivan Thomas. He was a short, bald man who was renowned for his fiery temper.

'We've heard what the old men of the villages have to say. Well, now it's our turn, see. I'm sick of being told to think with my brain and not my heart. It wasn't my brain that loved my children, it was my heart. I lost two good boys down there in that black shit as did many of you here. If you didn't, then I suspect you at least lost a nephew, a niece or a grandchild. Remember what is was like. A black sea engulfing them, choking them to death. Our children died horribly. And do you know who's fault it was? The owners, that's who. They put the slag there. Sir Clifford and his cronies killed our little ones. I say we hurt them as hard as possible and that means we strike. Force them to acknowledge they were in the wrong and that they are responsible. Only then will we see justice done and get the compensation we deserve. And don't get me wrong. I don't want the money. I want to rub their faces in their crime. I want them to wake at night, plagued by their consciences, like I wake and think of my two sons, choking in that slag. That is what I want and the only way we'll get it is by staying on strike and fighting the bastards every inch of the way.' He stopped speaking and stepped back.

Immediately Uncle Huw stepped forward. 'I say we fight to the bitter end. Let them send their militia. Let them send their scabs. We'll get organised and fight in such a way they won't be able to see us, never mind hit back. I lost a son that day and I want him to know I'd die avenging him rather than slink back to work with my tail between my legs. I'd rather die a man knowing I'd done what was right. I say *strike*,' he screamed the word.

A group of men began to chant the word and more joined in. Almost the whole hall screamed '*strike, strike, strike.*'

There was no point in waiting for a show of hands.

Grandad joined Mam and Da as they made their way home. They were a silent group, full of worry and fear.

8

I WAS AWAKE IN time to see the grey dawn nibbling at the edge of night. I sneaked downstairs, so as not to disturb Sion, sure I was the first up. The fire in the grate proved me wrong. Da must have been up for some time and had gone out already. I stoked the fire with our dwindling coal supply and put the kettle on. While I waited for it to boil I went into the front room and sat in the half light, watching my small part of the world come to life. I could see men coming and going outside. If it had been a normal working day activity would have reached an early morning peak and would die down again, waiting for the wives to send the children to school or out to play. Today, though, was not a normal day.

Late the previous night, after the meeting, we had received word that a gang of scabs, protected by the militia, were already mustered and coming from Cardiff. We expected them to arrive sometime in the afternoon. The committee had been staggered by the speed of the owners' response. None of the committee had told the owners of the outcome of the meeting but, as Grandad said, it was naïve of the committee not to expect a spy in their midst.

At the window I became more aware of the undercurrents pulling at the village. It showed in the way people rushed about their business as if they were frightened of being caught in the streets; it showed in the lack of name calling and greetings; it showed in the slight movement of curtains as the occupants watched and waited. After a while the slightest noise, like the meowing of a cat, made me jump. I found myself gripping the curtains tightly with one hand, my toy soldier in the other.

I suddenly started out of my tension and left the vantage point of the window to make tea. I was pouring a second cup when Mam came down and joined me. Her own tension showed in the way she fidgeted with the spoon in her saucer, and turned the cup, round and round.

'I'm going down to the mine later, Mam,' I announced.

She looked at me steadily for a few minutes before replying: 'I expected you would. I don't suppose there's anything I can do or say to stop you. You're a big boy now, not a child any more. Just keep out of the way, and if any trouble comes, leave. Run home. Hide. I don't care what you do as long as you get out of there. Understand?'

It took me a second or two to reply but it was long enough for her to repeat harshly: 'Understand, Dai?'

'Yes, Mam, I understand.' I left a few minutes later, before Sion was out of bed. Mam intended keeping him at home all day.

A watery sun was half a diameter below the hillside, the sky was cloudless and there was hardly a breath of air moving. There had been a heavy frost, the day was bracing and made me feel it was good to be alive.

I felt guilty when I passed the cemetery and looked up at what I thought was Sian's grave. I had still not taken her flowers or a plant, and I promised to do so as soon as possible. Further along the road the feeling of excitement returned. I walked at a steady pace, feeling better than I had done for a long time. I felt almost recovered from the effects of the pneumonia.

There was quite a crowd at the mine gates, mostly men but a few women too. The boys of my age were on the outskirts; just about all the gang was there. I found Cliff, and we hung around watching what was going on and keeping out of the way.

From time to time one of the strike leaders like Ivan Thomas or Uncle Huw got on a box and spoke to the gathering. They said nothing new or interesting. They only spoke of the need for solidarity, keeping the scabs out and said that the strikers should not use force unless the militia did first. Some of the men were armed with sticks and staves, poor weapons against guns.

One of the men said, 'Don't worry, the scabs won't be here today and perhaps not tomorrow either, even though they're on the way.' Some of the crowd laughed. Shortly after this Cliff nudged me and nodded to the edge of the crowd.

In dribs and drabs men were sneaking away. My initial thought was that they were a cowardly lot who did not want to stay and fight. But then I realised they were the die-hards, as Grandad called them, Thomas, Williams, Uncle Huw, Stevens, Pratt and a dozen or so others.

'Come on,' whispered Cliff. 'Let's follow and see where they're going.'

'I shouldn't,' I whispered back. 'I promised Mam I'd stay out of trouble.'

'I promised mine as well. But we aren't going into trouble are we? We're just going to see what's going on. We can stay in the background, hidden like, and just watch.' He snorted, 'course if you're a scaredy cat . . .'

'I'm not. It's just that . . . Oh well,' I sighed. 'Let's go.'

Carefully we edged away. With only two of us there was little chance of being seen. The men were at the river bank, going downstream, when we followed.

My heart was hammering, my nerves stretched as tight as bow strings when somebody yelled, 'Hey you.' We looked back to see a man gesturing for us to come back. We turned, slipped, skidded and half fell down the steep incline. We ran and within seconds were hidden from the top by a turn in the Taff and high leafless bramble bushes. We hurried along but soon I was out of breath and sweating.

'Got to stop,' I gasped. I took some deep breaths. 'Sorry Cliff, the pneumonia, look you.' I got my breath back and we continued. Cliff was frowning in frustration.

'You go on if you want to and I'll follow,' I suggested. 'I don't want to hold you back.'

'Naw, it's all right, I don't mind. Honest I don't. It's just if you could walk a bit faster we might see where they go, like.'

I stepped up my pace. We carried on for about twenty minutes. I kept silent, saving my breath. We passed a few hundred yards away from the school, the slag now hidden from view. Spurred on by memories of the place, I found the breath and energy to run the next quarter of a mile. We passed the shallows where I went for coal and reached the road leading up the hill near where we lived. We paused.

'Which way do you reckon?' asked Cliff.

'I dunno. I guess we can't be far behind. If they'd gone up there or crossed the river we'd see them.' I frowned. 'And why come along the river bank if they wanted to go up either way? They must have gone straight on.'

We followed the river further, hoping for a glimpse of someone soon. Although we hurried and occasionally ran, we saw nobody. Excitement at what we might see wore off a mile past our houses, and though I was not out of breath or tired, I felt like stopping.

We had left the last of the houses behind and were in an area about two miles long. The next place would be Eglwsarn and then continuous streets of houses like ours all the way to Pontypridd. The floor of the valley broadened out a little; the area was overgrown with brambles and other bushes. Many had shed their leaves, stripped by the heavy rain and approach of winter but others still retained some, brown and red, curling and dying. The ground was damp underfoot, soggy after

absorbing so much water in the previous weeks. I was
glad I wore gum boots and thick socks.

Another mile and we could see Eglwsarn. We stopped,
hesitant about going further.

'What do you think, Dai?' Cliff asked.

'I dunno. What do you think?' I responded.

'I dunno. There's nowhere else they could have gone,
is there?'

I pulled a face. 'I guess not. We've come a long way
haven't we? What time do you think it is?'

He shrugged. 'I guess it's well after dinner time. Mam
will be getting worried.'

'I think you're right. Should we go back now or go on
a bit further?'

Again the shrug and the pensive frown. 'I guess we
ought to but we've come this far . . .'

I nodded. 'I know we have, but how much further do
we have to go? The scabs might have already got here
by now and we might be missing it all.'

'Look you, I heard they were coming up from Cardiff
by train and getting here this afternoon. And we haven't
heard a train yet, have we? We wouldn't have missed
it.'

I nodded in agreement. I was sure the men had gone
this way but how far had they gone?

'I tell you what, Cliff. Let's go as far as Eglwsarn and
no further. If we don't see them we'll go up to the road
and walk home. What do you say?'

He nodded. 'That's fine with me. What about you? Do
you think you can make it?'

I nodded that I could. So far the river had been partially
hidden by bushes still bearing some leaves in spite of the
time of year, but now they thinned out and the path went
closer to the bank; the water, black and uninviting, gur-
gled at our feet. Across the river we saw the railway bank
and from time to time as the rails dipped or the river bank
went higher we could see the gleaming ribbons of track.

Cliff suddenly grabbed my arm and pointed. We had found the men. We were so surprised for a moment or two we stood still and then ducked behind a thick, leafless bush. At first their actions puzzled us.

We could see some of them shoving posts into the ground and hanging sacking or something like sacking between them. We started to move carefully along the bank, hidden by the bushes. Finally we were close enough to read the crudely painted sacks. "Scabs go back." "Scabs go home." "Death to scabs." "Down with the militia."

I felt disappointed we had come so far only to see that. But why come so far down river just to put up a few signs?

'You know when that man said something about the scabs not getting here today I thought something really exciting was going to happen. This isn't going to stop them is it, Cliff?'

'I don't think so, look you.'

I sighed, thinking of the walk back. I looked up at the sun and guessed it was the middle of the afternoon. 'Should we go home now?'

'I dunno. Let's wait and see if anything else happens.'

Where the men stood the track curved, following the river about twenty yards from the water's edge. There were two signs on the curve and two immediately before it. Further back, now hidden by the bend, we had passed four men. They had not been putting up signs. We went back to take another look at what they were doing. 'I think they're doing something to the track,' I said.

'It looks like it, bach. What's that they're pushing and pulling on do you think?'

'I dunno,' I replied, not daring to suggest a crow bar in case Cliff laughed at me.

'Remember what the man said back at the mine?'

I nodded. 'And why come all this way down river just to stick up a few stupid signs?'

'Do you think,' Cliff hesitated. 'Do you think they're going to . . . to stop the train?'

The idea was so staggering it took my breath away. Excitement gripped me. The men did not take much longer. They removed their boots, rolled up their trousers and recrossed the river. Silently, with odd looks on their faces, they replaced their boots and left. I wondered if they felt the awfulness of what they were doing. Sabotage of this sort carried a heavy penalty.

We stayed hidden until they passed out of sight. Then I followed Cliff down to the water's edge. I removed my boots but then remembered I was not to wade in the river. 'I'd better not go,' I said with a disappointed sigh. 'Not after what happened.'

'Aw, come on man, you can't back out now, not at this stage.'

I hesitated, tempted. Reluctantly I shook my head. The memory of my illness was too fresh in my mind. 'I better not, see. Just in case.'

'I'll carry you if you like.'

I was tempted further but one look at the racing current and I knew he could never manage to carry me. 'I'd better not, Cliff. You go on and I'll stay here and keep watch. I'll whistle if I see or hear anything.'

He shrugged and turned away. I watched him cross, stumbling and nearly falling more than once. I cursed my illness for not letting me see our adventure through to the end. This was likely to be the most exciting thing that ever happened to me.

On the other side, Cliff followed the track, reading every sign, and then turned the bend. He knelt, looked at me, jumped up and began running back to the river. He was half way across when he started talking.

'It's like we thought. It's like we thought,' he repeated. 'You should see it Dai.' He pulled on his boots as fast as he could.

'Tell me then,' I said, annoyed.

'Hurry boyo, we gotta go. I heard the train sort of vibrating on the line . . .' As he spoke we heard the whistle and knew it was at the Treces tunnel, less than a mile away.

'Come on, up to the road,' I suggested. 'Once we get there we can see what happens.' We had started away from the river when Cliff grabbed my arm excitedly and pointed.

'The track Dai, the track. It's been forced off to one side and down like. Golly, there's the train.'

We paused to look back at the smoking train. We began to run as fast as we could, the brambles and stinging nettles whipped at our legs. We were halfway to the road when we stopped again. The train was approaching the bend about five hundred yards from us. We saw the packed carriages, the first four coaches with men in ordinary working clothes, the last four with men in uniform. We saw the guns. The train slowed for the bend. When the men saw the signs a great jeering and booing went up and the train driver blew his whistle. Suddenly there was a screech which built up to a scream of locked wheels sliding on metal. The men fell silent as the train slowed rapidly but could not stop in time.

The engine lurched, bounced and stopped. It angled over slightly, paused and slowly turned onto its side. Steam escaped with a loud hissing noise, but was quickly masked by the screams of the men inside the carriages as one after the other they overturned. Three went onto their sides, the fourth went half way, but the last four stayed upright, though one jumped the track. Screams mingled with loud curses as the militia tried to get their men into some semblance of order. We watched them line up, face outwards, rifles at the ready. Some civilians crawled out of the carriages and staggered away from the train. The screams died down to moans and shouts for help. The militia began to break into the carriages to help those trapped.

I felt no sympathy for the injured, in spite of one or two being covered in blood and needing help to reach the ground. These men had come to break the strike. They deserved anything they got as far as I was concerned.

I did not realise what was happening at first when some of the militiamen broke into small groups and spread out. With a shock I saw they were starting search parties. Without a word we turned and left quickly.

The hillside became steeper and the bushes thinner the closer we got to the road and finally we had to stop. Any further and there was a good chance that we'd be seen. Disconcerted we looked at each other in dismay.

'They'll see us,' I whispered to Cliff. The nearest search party now began to cross the river, about seven hundred yards away. 'We could make a dash for it. They might not see us. And anyway, what if they did? They'll never catch us from there.'

'Maybe not,' said Cliff, 'but they might try and shoot us.' It was a terrifying thought. 'Or they might see us and then search all the houses, find us and blame us for what happened.'

I looked back. It was impossible to recognise anybody at that distance until Cliff suggested they might have a spy glass. With a sigh, no further answer available, we began crawling and shuffling along just below the road and still hidden by bushes. The sodden ground wet our knees and hands, stones and sticks scraped and hurt but we kept at it for about three hundred yards until we reached a bend. Out of sight we stood up and darted onto the road, crossing to the other side. From there it was impossible to see the river or railway.

'I'm going to have a look,' I said. 'We won't stay long and once we know what's happening we can go home. What do you say?'

He grimaced. 'All right, but we mustn't be long. It's getting late.'

I looked at the sun. It was late afternoon. Mam would

be beginning to wonder where I was. She would not bother about me missing a meal, that was fairly common. And anyway, with things the way they were, it would not have been much of a meal.

Once round the bend we got onto our stomachs and crawled to the edge of the road. The scene around the train was unchanged but the search parties had moved quite a distance. Two had crossed the river and came slowly and surely towards us. Four other groups followed the river banks north and south. The civilians sat in huddled groups around the wreckage. After about ten minutes we wormed our way backwards, got to our feet, dusted ourselves down and started up the valley. We were dirty, scratched and sweating. A light breeze picked up as the sun dropped behind the valleys' side and the shadows crept inexorably towards us.

Here the hill was at its steepest: there were no houses and nobody passed us.

I felt worn out and my body ached but luckily I did not feel cold or shivery and had no desire to sneeze. I thought if I sneezed it would mean I was getting another dose of pneumonia. 'Cliff, I know what we thought before but I think we'd better not say anything to anybody. Just in case, like. It's got awfully serious, somehow.'

'You're right, Dai. Know something? I'm kind of scared.'

'Me too, Cliff. So it's a deal then? We'll say nothing?'

'Sure Dai. You can count on me.'

I knew that. We had been in enough scrapes together. We pressed on and at last the first of the houses came into view.

I paused outside my door and waved to Cliff. I went in.

'Where on earth have you been?' Mam greeted me. 'Just look at you.' She was more annoyed than I had seen her for a long time. Sion told me later that for about two hours before I arrived Mam had been to the door about every five minutes to look for me.

She made me bath and sent me to bed early. I was grateful to snuggle under the blankets, absolutely worn out. I thought my day was over but I was in for a rude awakening.

9

'WAKE UP, DAI. Wake up, boyo. Come on.' Da shook my shoulder. Slowly the message got through to my tired brain and with difficulty I forced open my eyes. I felt languid and heavy with sleep, ready to drop off again immediately. 'Dai you've got to get up and come downstairs. I must talk to you. Come on, boy.' Da threw back the bed clothes and the cold brought some action in my mind. Awkwardly I got out of bed and fumbled for my clothes. 'It's okay son, you don't need to get dressed. Just put your dressing gown on.'

I followed him downstairs. Uncle Huw was sitting by the fire. My heart started pounding and I became more alert. I went into the kitchen and washed my face in cold water. It had to be important to get me out of bed and in my guilt-ridden mind I had no doubt what it was.

'Hullo, Uncle Huw,' I greeted him warily. He nodded and grunted something. I looked at Da, waiting for somebody to say something.

'Are you going to ask him, or am I?' my uncle spoke to Da.

'It's your mess, but as he's my son I'd better ask. Now listen Dai and please don't lie. Did you and another boy follow some of the men today?'

'I . . . eh . . . We . . . eh . . .' I was about to deny it. After all I had made a promise to Cliff. The trouble was I had never really lied to my parents. I realised how serious it was and while I wrestled with my conscience I suddenly remembered we had been seen sneaking away from the meeting. I gave an embarrassed, little cough and nodded.

'What did you see, Dai?' asked Uncle Huw.

He disconcerted me for a moment and when I replied, my anger at his tone turned to defiance. 'I saw you and some of the others putting up those signs. And I saw four of the men do something to the track. I saw the train crash as well . . .'

'My God,' he interrupted, 'did anybody see you, you little fool?'

'No. We were too careful.'

All this time Mam was sitting quietly, her hand to her throat, her face white. 'But you can't be sure, can you Dai?' she asked.

I thought about it. I was pretty sure but how sure was that? 'I guess not,' I said finally, in a low voice.

'Goddamn it, Dai. What the hell did you want to follow us like that for anyway? What business did you have doing so? I've got a good mind to tan the hide off you.' My uncle jumped to his feet in agitation. So did I, ready to dart upstairs if he took a step in my direction.

'Don't talk foolishly, Huw. What's done is done. The boys had no idea what they were going to see. How could they? Nobody in their right mind would dream of doing what you fools did. So don't blame the boy. Who was with you Dai? Was it Cliff? You may as well tell me so I can have a word with him and his father.'

I nodded miserably.

'Christ, what a mess,' my uncle sank back into the chair, his hands to his face.

'I'll make a cup of tea,' Mam said. 'You'll feel better then.' She had a strong belief in the therapeutic powers of tea. Mam went into the kitchen and returned a few seconds later with the kettle. We sat in silence watching her. Finally she said: 'What are we going to do, Evan?'

Da shrugged. 'I think there's only one way out of this mess and I want to add the mess has nothing to do with

Cliff and Dai seeing what happened. God, Huw, what on earth were you thinking of when you and the others did this? You must have been out of your minds.'

Uncle Huw's face was drawn and haggard: 'It seemed like a good idea at the time. We thought if we stopped the train and kept them away for a day or two then they'd know we meant business and perhaps be more willing to give in. Or at least give us more compensation. All the men were for it, and it worked a treat. Didn't it Dai?'

I was so surprised by his change of tone and attitude I could think of nothing to say. I had no need. Da answered for me.

'Never mind that, you bloody idiot. Don't you realise what you've done? They aren't going to be content until they've got the men who did it and unless I'm very much mistaken they won't care how they find them either. How many people knew you were going to do something? And how many more will put two and two together and know who was responsible? God man, it's as plain as the nose on your face.' He paused.

Mam got up and made the tea. There was silence while it brewed.

Finally, Da said heavily: 'What you did can get you deported for at least five years. Just think what's going to happen next. The militia will arrest different men from all the villages. They'll accuse the men of derailing the train. The men will be told they won't have a chance at the trial and their only hope will be to give a name, the name of one of the men involved. And they'll give that name, believe me. I would say within a week . . . no, that's too generous, I'd say four days till you're arrested. So don't blame the boys. In fact thank your lucky stars you came here tonight to see Dai. At least we may be able to do something before it's too late.'

'Nonsense,' said Uncle Huw fiercely, 'utter bloody nonsense. Nobody will give us away. We're all in this together. The whole village will stick by us – all the

villages. There'll be a wall of silence that they won't
be able to break. You and your ideas for solving the
problem! I don't need your ideas nor your help. I just
came here to tell you that your bloody kid had better not
utter one word of what he saw today or else it will be
the worse for him – and that other boy, Cliff, too.' He
got to his feet, shaking with anger.

'Sit down and shut up, Huw,' said Da in his most
commanding voice. 'We've got a problem and unless
we come up with an answer damned quick you and the
others are going to be in terrible trouble. Huw, you're
my brother; we've been through a lot together. I know
how the death of Johnny upset you. Sian's death upset
us just as much, believe me. What you've done is worse
than wrong. It's criminal. What good will you be to Mair
and the kids if you're in jail? I'll help you in every way
I can but you must listen to reason Huw. Please, bach,
while there's still time.'

Uncle Huw seemed to shrink into the chair. 'I'm sorry,
Evan. The stupid thing is I know you're right. It won't be
the kids. No one will think of them. It'll be like you said.
One of the villagers will crack, and I can't say I'd blame
them either. God, it was such a stupid thing to do. But it
seemed such a good idea at the time.'

'I know, so you keep saying,' Da said wryly. 'When
I heard it had happened I didn't think that even you'd
be stupid enough to be a part of it. Sorry, recriminations
aren't the order of the moment. Meg love, go and fetch
the rest of the family – don't forget Albert. Tell them it's
a family crisis, and we need them. Warn them they'll be
up most of the night. That's assuming they haven't got a
better idea than mine.'

'What do you have in mind?' asked my uncle.

'I intend getting a shift down that mine in time for the
first hooter tomorrow,' he announced calmly.

We looked at him, our mouths agape.

'What good will that do?' Uncle Huw asked bitterly.

'All it'll mean is us giving in without a struggle.' He flicked his wrist as though sweeping the idea away. 'And I thought you had a good idea,' he said even more bitterly.

'I never said it was a good idea, only that I had one. Which is a damned sight more than you can offer at the moment, so don't knock it. Come on Meg, off with you, there's a girl.'

Mam put on her coat. 'I'll be as quick as I can. Is there anybody else you want me to bring? Like Lewis Lewis and Peter?'

'Damn, I should have thought of that myself. Yes, and stress the importance of the meeting. Peter will probably be in bed by now, it's past nine o'clock, and he won't take kindly to being woken up. But if you can bear with his curses and stress how much we need him, you might be able to persuade him to come.'

'I'll try,' Mam promised and left

'Dai, take these chairs into the front room, bring the trolley in here and push the other chairs back against the wall to make more space.'

I went to do as he ordered, still listening to Da and Uncle Huw as they argued.

'What good will this do, Evan? I ask you, man. It's bloody ridiculous.'

'Huw, Huw, Huw,' Da said sadly. 'Think about it. At the moment we have everything to lose. If they find out it was you, and I've no doubt they will damned quickly, you and the others will be arrested. Once you're all gone, the rest of the men who are for the strike will give in. We'll all end up back in work and at least a dozen good men will go to prison or worse. What I'm hoping is if we all go back to work, we may be able to persuade the owners . . .' He paused. 'Look, the owners will make a lot of money sooner than they expected because the strike will be over. We can try and get them to pay for the damage to the railway and get the charges dropped. If

they can't or won't then we'll fight them with everything
we've got and by God they won't get coal from that mine
inside a year. And this time boyo we'll do it properly and
really hurt them. I've got a few ideas on that score too,
only pray to God we don't have to use them.' He broke
off for a moment and then he added, 'Do you fancy a
whisky? I think I've got a dram left from last Christmas
which I was keeping for the right moment. I guess this is
as good a time as any. Come on, get this down,' I heard
the clink of bottle on glass.

I went back into the living room.

'Dai, put the blinds up in there will you? I don't want
any nosy parker seeing what's going on.'

'I already did, Da.' I was pleased with myself when
he said 'Good boy.' I was becoming tired but when Da
suggested I went to bed, I protested. 'Aw Da, can't I stay
up now? I want to hear what's going to happen. Please,
Da? I'll be quiet, honest I will.'

'All right, you can stay. But don't say a word.'

'Right Da.'

Not long afterwards the front door opened and Grandad
came in. 'What in hell's name is so important to bring me
out at this time? Meg didn't . . . You needn't look at me
like that Evan, I can guess now I see our Huw is here.'

'Look Dad,' Uncle Huw jumped to his feet, bristling
with indignation.

'Shut up, Huw for God's sake,' said Da sharply. 'And
stop taking offence so easily. You were involved. You are
involved I should say and everybody will know it when
they get here . . . I just thought. What about David? Did
he go with you?'

'No,' he replied shortly.

'Thank the Lord for small mercies,' said Grandad.
'What the hell are we going to do about it? Perhaps we
can get Huw away somewhere tonight. Get him north or
as far as Scotland.'

'I've thought of that,' said Da. 'And I reckon we plan

on it just in case my other idea doesn't work. After all, it isn't only Huw that's involved. There's all the others too. If the worse happens they'll have to look to themselves and we'll take care of Huw. But in the meantime there's something else we can try.'

'I wouldn't go anyway. I'm not leaving Mair and Sally for anything or anybody.'

'Huw, this is one time you'll do as you're told and like it,' said Grandad. 'We'll get Mair and Sal to you as quickly as we can manage. Maybe it'll even have to be abroad. God knows we haven't much money but I've got enough for you to get away and I may as well use it to save your stupid hide. I'm sorry son, I didn't mean that. It's just that . . . .'

'I know, Dad,' Uncle Huw said quietly. 'I'm sorry too. I'll do whatever you think is best.'

'Me? It isn't me, bach. It's Evan here. Okay brains, what are you suggesting? I'm damned if I can see an answer.'

Da explained it all to him. Grandad's initial scepticism turned to half hearted agreement by the time Da finished.

'It's possible I suppose. The combination of the carrot and the heavy stick might work, especially if the owners believe we'll all fight as hard as possible. It's true to say with us against the strike the owners were hoping it would collapse that much easier. Which is true. There's only one snag. What would you do if you were the owners, Evan?'

Da grunted. 'That's easy, Dad. I'd insist that part of the deal would be an agreement from us not to take them to court over the accident.'

'Yeah, that's the way I see it too,' said Grandad heavily.

'No!' Uncle Huw said vehemently. 'We can't allow that after all we've been fighting for. I'd rather run and take a chance on getting away than say we've been beaten.'

'Huw, don't talk wet! How are we going to spirit away ten or twelve families? Tell me that.' Grandad frowned. 'Now stop thinking with your bloody feelings and start thinking with your brains. Bloody Sir Clifford has us by the short and curlies and the sooner you realise it the better. Tell me something. What do you think they're doing up there in their fine houses right now? I've no doubt they're celebrating the near end of the strike because you've played us right into their hands. They aren't stupid.' We heard a knock on the door. 'That'll be William,' he said.

Within minutes of each other Uncles William, David and Albert arrived. Da said little until they were all there. Mam returned a few minutes later. She told us that Aunts Nancy, Maud and Gwyneth had gone for the committee. She had not bothered Aunt Mair, Uncle Huw's wife. We went into the front room to sit.

Lewis and Shepherd arrived soon after, but though we waited ten minutes for Peter he did not turn up.

'All right,' said Grandad. 'I think we'll start without him. It's now ten to ten and we don't have much time and a hell of a lot to do. You all know what happened to the train. Does anyone have anything to add?'

We looked at each other and then Uncle William shrugged. 'I heard from the vicar that nobody was killed and that he reckoned it was a miracle. A few were hurt, he said, but he didn't say how badly.'

'That's good,' said Mam. 'It'll help at any rate.'

'I agree,' said Lewis Lewis. 'If anyone had died it would have been murder.'

Uncle Huw began to protest.

'Oh, I don't mean planned murder or whatever it is they call it,' Lewis paused. 'The charge would probably be reduced to manslaughter at the trial, but until then they'd treat it like murder and use the extra police and resources they'd have. Anyway it doesn't matter because no-one died.'

'Did he say anything else, William?' asked Uncle David.

'He said a few things about how angry the militia were and that they wanted to shoot the men responsible.'

'That's the militia's usual response,' said Huw Shepherd bitterly.

'Maybe so,' replied Uncle William, 'but according to the vicar they were ready to come and take the villages by storm. The scabs were of a slightly different mind,' he grinned unexpectedly, 'because they just wanted to go home. According to the vicar they said they hadn't signed up to be attacked like that and had been promised there'd be no trouble. And if this was the way the militia were suppose to guard them then they wanted to go back to Cardiff. Quite a few have already left.'

'That's an added bonus I hadn't counted on,' said Da. 'It means we have something to argue with.'

'How about telling us this idea of yours, Evan,' said Uncle Albert. 'Meg said something about getting the men back but how will that help?'

'Hang on and I'll tell you. William, was there anything else from the vicar?'

'Not really. The militia are staying where they are for tonight, sleeping in their tents. They're probably coming on here tomorrow or the next day. I expect they're waiting for orders from Cardiff to tell them which is more important, the railway incident or the mine being reopened.'

'Good. All right, look you, I tell you what I have in mind. We get a shift into the mine first thing and start as normally as we can. The committee go and see the owners. Our conditions for staying in work are as follows. One, no prosecution of the men responsible for the crash. Two, no intimidation and no sackings. Three, we continue negotiations about compensation with a view to going to court if we can't get what we want. That last point I don't think will even be considered. They'll insist

on an agreement from us not to go to court unless I'm
very much mistaken. But it can't be helped now. This is
far more important. If they don't agree then you tell them
that we'll fight with everything we've got. It'll become so
expensive that even if we do lose in the long run, which
we will, they'll lose a hell of a lot. We can only go hungry.
They'll lose a lot of money and by the time we do give in,
probably a few shafts as well. Remind them about safety,
water pumping, gas and stuff like that. I think that with
a little luck they'll see reason.'

'What about plans for getting the men away, in case it
doesn't work?' asked Grandad. 'I think we ought to have
something ready.'

'Yes,' said Uncle David. 'I have one or two suggestions
to make about that.'

'What are they?' Huw Shepherd asked. 'We don't have
much time.'

My head fell forward and I dozed. The next thing I
heard was Grandad saying: 'It's now quarter past eleven.
We've only got a night to get organised. We need at least
two hundred men for a shift. There's eight of us . . .'

'Nine,' interrupted Mam.

'No, Meg,' half a dozen voices said together.

'You've done enough for one night, love. It's not right
for you to be out in the streets until the early hours of
the morning. And,' Da added, 'especially in case some
of that militia swine are wandering about.'

'Look you,' said Uncle David, 'we can just about get
two hundred from here.'

'No good,' replied Da, 'because it'll seem like we've
gone back and left the other villages out of it.' He nodded
as the others started to murmur. 'Ridiculous maybe
but we don't want to antagonise anybody needlessly.
Everybody must be involved. Huw, this is important.
You've got to persuade Ivan Thomas, Williams . . .
who else? Pratt? Gordon? All those who were for the
strike. Make them understand. If you can't do that then

we may still fail in what we're trying to do . . . In
fact . . .'

'In fact,' interrupted Grandad, 'maybe it would be
better to see them first. If we can persuade them to go
back then we can take one of them with us. That way
perhaps less explaining will be needed. Is that what you
were going so say, son?'

'In a nutshell, Dad. The more I think about it the better
it gets.'

I must have dozed again because I saw that they were
leaving and I had not heard anybody suggest it. Da put
on his coat, kissed Mam and said: 'I don't know what
time I'll be back but it should be before daylight.'

Mam smiled. 'Good luck. Right, Dai, time you were
in bed.'

Mam emptied the ashtrays into the dying fire and I
asked: 'What do you think will happen Mam? Will they
go back? And if they do will it save the men from going
to prison? Or being deported or whatever?'

She shrugged. 'I just don't know. I suppose we'll
manage to get some of them away. We'll certainly get
Uncle Huw away, you can rest assured about that. Some
of the others will be caught but some'll make it. The best
thing, I'm sure, is this scheme of Da's. If it doesn't work
then the men will be hunted like criminals and that's
a pretty unpleasant thought. Now off with you, up the
wooden hill.'

I went to bed thinking about what was going on in the
streets. Though I did not think for long, I was asleep
almost as soon as my head touched the pillow.

10

THE NEXT MORNING Sion was up and out by the time I went downstairs. I guessed he was with Uncle James, who was taking a real interest in kites and flying. He and Sion were often on top of the hill trying to get one of their designs into the air.

Mam looked happier than she had done for ages and I heard her humming. She said: 'Da came in about five o'clock and said they'd filled the shift. The others are now going round the rest of the villages explaining the situation to everybody. He said they'd had difficulty with Ivan Thomas but all Ivan could suggest was getting the men away.' She laughed, but there was only a touch of humour in the sound. 'Ivan Thomas said that as leader of the strikers he ought to stay and fight for the people, whatever that means, look you. If all the others ran for it he'd be in the clear. The worm! Fight for the people! Huh! Grandad promised Ivan the authorities would know of his involvement; he'd make sure of it. Da said that was when Ivan gave in, calling Grandad quite a number of nasty names. But, like Da said, names don't matter, as long as the men started work.'

'Is that why you're so happy, Mam?' I asked, sipping my tea.

'It's all part of it. Da and I were worried about using up all our savings especially now we need every penny to get to America. If the strike went on for too long we could end up using more than we could afford. It may have meant putting off going for another year, who knows? But now with the men back and if Da is successful in trying to persuade the owners to leave things alone . . .'

'Da,' I interrupted. 'What's he got to do with it? I thought the committee was dealing with the owners.'

'It is. But Grandad insisted that Da went along as well, to help them. Especially as it was all his idea. The rest of the committee agreed. They were keen on the idea. Da was reluctant to go at first because he wanted to go down the mine. Like he said, he doesn't get anything for going to the meeting. Grandad persuaded him it was for the best, just this once. Finally he agreed to go. So at this moment he's with the owners and Sir Clifford at their offices.'

'I see, and when will they be finished?'

'They don't know. Grandad said it could take all day. We'll just have to wait and see, won't we?' Her mood changed. 'I hope they do manage it. We'll never get to America if we have to make a fight of it.'

With that sombre thought in mind I went to find Cliff. He told me Da had been there in the middle of the night to get his father and left a message for Cliff not to say anything to anybody and to see me. I would explain everything. I did.

The day dragged. I went in early to sit and stare at my atlas, thinking of America. About three o'clock I remembered my promise to Sian but the problem was finding flowers or a suitable plant in the last week in November. I ended up taking a bunch of holly from a tree down by the river and placing it on her grave.

As I looked at her headstone I tried to conjure up a picture of her while I told her what had happened. I found her image was blurred and fuzzy. Though I knew it was Sian, her face wasn't clear. It upset me, but by the time I arrived home my grief had faded. I sat in the solitude of the front room and tried to bring back my feeling of grief but failed. Time was doing its work well.

At five there was still no sign of Da. I wondered if the argument was so bitter they were making no headway.

Mam sat nervously strumming her fingers on the table; I looked unseeing at the atlas.

When the door opened Da's voice startled us both and we jumped to our feet. He came rushing in, a huge grin across his face and grabbed Mam in a hug until she squealed.

'Put me down, Evan. Put me down, you clown,' she laughed. 'What happened? Come on tell us. What happened?'

'Get me a cuppa first and then I'll tell you. I'm parched after all that damned talking. Oh, and one for Dad, he'll be in shortly as well. He's just seeing the committee about something, private like.' Grandad walked through the door as Da spoke.

'Did he tell you Meg?' Grandad was smiling.

'No, he's insisting on a cup of tea first. You tell me while I make a fresh pot.'

'You should have seen him Meg. Evan I mean. You'd have been proud, I can tell you. Anyone would think he'd been dealing with bosses all his life. The way he neg . . . neg . . .'

'Negotiated,' supplied Mam.

'What about compensation for the children?' asked Mam.

Grandad pulled a face. 'It was exactly like Evan said. There's not a hope of getting anything. They'll drop the charges against the men if we sign an agreement not to take them to court. You know, that in itself convinced me we'd have had a good chance if we'd gone to court. The stupid fools really cocked things up for us, didn't they?' Grandad sighed and added, 'There was one complication that made our position all the more difficult.'

'What was that?' asked Mam.

Da answered. 'At the front of the train one of the younger militiamen was playing cards with the scabs. He wasn't supposed to be there, but he was. He was killed when the train went over.'

'Oh my God,' said Mam sitting down heavily. 'But the vicar said . . . Was anybody else hurt?'

'A few broken limbs and nasty cuts. The boy died when a piece of glass from the window stabbed him in the neck.' Da said. 'I did get them to agree to have the militia moved back to Cardiff as soon as possible. Hell Meg, think what would happen if they took the law into their own hands and went on the rampage here. And though it sounds incredible we've all heard enough stories not to discount such a thing. Don't you agree, Dad?'

'Aye son, I do. I don't know why but I got this feeling in my bones that there's going to be trouble. Let's pray I'm wrong. Ah, well,' he got to his feet, 'I must go. Don't bother with tea for me Meg,' he said as Mam went into the kitchen.

'If you're sure, Dad,' she replied, returning with the kettle.

'I'm sure. I want to get home and tell Mam about it. You know how she worries.' He chuckled, a rich throaty sound and said something I did not understand but made Mam blush. 'I think I'll go and celebrate with some of her dandelion wine and pretend it's her birthday or Christmas,' he winked at Mam.

'You,' said Mam, pushing him towards the door, 'are incorrigible.'

'No doubt, and no doubt I'd be the first to admit it if I knew what it meant. Goodnight to you all. And thanks, Evan, for what you did today,' he became serious. 'The village will never appreciate it properly, but me and the others do.'

When Sion came we played word games for the first time since Sian died. I guess it was still too soon because the evening fell flat and Sion and I went to bed early.

Once more I was rudely woken. This time dawn had broken. Mam shook me with news far worse than when Da had called me.

'Wasermarra, Mam? Wasermarra?' I asked groggily trying to wake up.

'Get dressed and come downstairs,' she whispered, 'and try not to wake Sion.'

'Okay Mam,' I nearly put my head back on the pillow when with a shock I saw she was crying. I came awake with a start as she turned and left. I grabbed my clothes and followed her. She was sitting at the table, a half empty cup of tea in front of her. Her eyes were bright with tears.

'What is it Mam? What is it? Is it Da?' The words tumbled out and irrationally I felt the tears rising.

She shook her head. 'No, it isn't Da,' she said in a small voice.

Relief flooded over me. Her next words sent grief through me so that I felt sick to the stomach.

'It's Grandma and Grandad,' she said, having to bite her lip to keep back the tears. 'They were both killed last night. A fire in the house or something. Da's there now. He's been there for hours since they came to get him. We both went to see if . . . if there was anything we could do. There was nothing.'

I threw off my pyjamas, forgetting the newly found bashfulness I now had in front of Mam and pulled on my underpants. 'Are . . . are you sure . . . ?' my voice quivered, but I held back the tears. 'They . . . they're d . . . d . . .' I could not bring myself to say the word.

Mam nodded. 'I didn't want you waking to an empty house so I came back. I'll wait for Sion but go and see what's happening and come back to tell me.'

I nodded and rushed from the house. My heart was like lead. First Sian and now Grandad and Grandma. It was too much. Grandad had only been with us a few hours earlier, laughing and joking and talking about it going to be Grandma's birthday or something.

I ran. Their place was further up and two streets back. After a few hundred yards I had to walk to get my breath

back. The house was at the end of the street, just before
the allotments. There was a group of people standing in
the road, mostly the family but a few others too.

All that was left was a smoking, blackened ruin. The
house next door was also damaged, the roof half gone
and the wall demolished. I felt the tears starting afresh
as I saw the ruin. Through the blur of my tears I saw the
blackened figures of Da and my uncles picking amongst
the rubble. Aunts Maud and Gwyneth were standing on
the road crying, a few of my cousins with them.

All that was left of the house was the outside wall
and the chimney. The front, back and roof had collapsed,
taking the second floor with it. Charred remains of the
rafters stuck out, black, jagged daggers against the blue
sky. The top of the sun appeared over the valley edge,
adding warmth to the day, melting the white frost of
the night. I stood alone, watching, not wanting to talk
to anyone.

I knew our family had been Granddad's favourite. He
had loved us just a little bit more than he loved the others.
Mam had been the special one among his sons' wives.
I choked on the thought. I remembered why I was there
and went across to Da. I noticed the bundle wrapped
in blankets near my aunts. It took a few moments to
remember what it reminded me of and when I did I was
nearly sick. I thought of Sian and knew without doubt
what was under there. I turned my head, trying not to
look, and picked my way across the rubble to Da.

He was too busy picking around in the black, soot
covered bricks to notice, me until I was right next to
him. I had to call him twice before he looked up. His
blackened face was tear stained. I burst into tears and
threw my arms around his waist.

'Easy, Dai, easy,' he muttered. 'I suppose Mam sent
you, did she?'

I nodded.

'Go home, bach, and tell her that I'll be home shortly.

Tell her everyone knows so there's not a lot she can do. I want to get hold of Dai Coffin before I come, ok?'

Again I nodded. When I turned to go I saw my cousins were also crying but the grown ups, though their faces were tearstained, had stopped. We were a forlorn and dishevelled group. I hurried back, sure Mam would want to be there too, in spite of what Da said.

I literally bumped into her at the door. 'I'm on my way up. Sion's having breakfast. I haven't had the heart to tell him yet. What did Da say?'

'He said he's going to find Dai Coffin before he comes home.' I paused, a picture of the house came to my mind. 'It's horrible Mam, really horrible. There's nothing left and . . . and there's a bundle in a blanket just by the road. Like Sian was,' I bit my lower lip trying to fight back the tears.

'They could only have just found them then, I suppose that's something. It must have been awful for your Da and your uncles. Stay with Sion and don't let him go out until I get back. I won't be long.'

I put on a brave face for Sion and when he asked what all the excitement was about I told him nothing. I did not have the heart to tell him the truth; besides, it wasn't up to me. It was difficult waiting for Mam to return and I was annoyed at her for not having told him. Sion was disgusted because he could not go out and play with his friends. Finally the front door opened and Mam and Da came in. Da was streaked in black, Mam dirty handed and with a smudged face. Gently Mam explained to Sion what had happened. He nodded, appearing not to understand properly. They he asked: 'Have they gone to be with Sian?'

'You could put it that way' said Mam.

'That's good. Now there'll be somebody to look after her. But I'm going to miss them,' he added. 'Mam, why didn't they come and say goodbye?'

Mam forced the ghost of a smile. 'I don't think

they knew God was going to call them away when He did son.'

He began crying and put his arms around Mam's waist, squeezing tightly. 'I don't think I like God any more,' he said, using the same words he had used after Sian's death. 'He shouldn't have taken them from us like that.'

David Jones was known as Dai Coffin and had been for as long as Da could remember. He had developed the art of burial to a fine degree, and Grandad had always said when he died he was to be buried by Dai. He used to joke about booking up with him in advance, just in case. We used to laugh, assuring Grandad he would be around for a long time yet. The laughter that used to greet Granddad's description of his own funeral was missing on the day, a week later. The weather had changed and the day started grey, with a fine drizzle soaking the land.

Before Dai arrived we paid our last respects. Both Grandad and Grandma were being buried together in one coffin. Da was the last to go through and he slid the lid into place.

After the death of the children there had been no wake. Today was different. In his will Grandad had put aside ten pounds to be spent on beer and whisky. Grandad had written "So my sons and their families can see me off in fine style."

'Here's to the old souls,' Uncle David announced. 'Perhaps not so old but they had a good innings. God rest them.'

They raised their glasses in a toast, the men with whisky, the women with sweet sherry. As the drink flowed the merrier they became, cracking ribald jokes and laughing. I realised a lot later when I thought back on that day the reason behind the fun. Death was no stranger. But it was still difficult to become accustomed to, if we ever did. Turning it into a wake, laughing at death hid, if not actually removed, the fear we felt at its proximity.

The women had spent days preparing sandwiches and cakes for those who came to pay their last respects. Each person was given a glass of ale and something to eat and all toasted my grandparents' memory.

'He was a good man,' said Lewis Lewis, 'and he's going to be sorely missed in the years ahead. He did a lot for us and the village, always with our interests at heart. God bless his soul.' Another toast.

BOOK 2

The Story of Evan

11

EVAN MATTHEW GRIFFITHS stood in the middle of his front room after the wake, and proudly, through his drunken haze, watched his son grimace over the ale he had been given. Aye, he thought, he's a good lad and no doubt. Tall for his age. With his black hair and good looks he will be a lady-killer one day, no doubt of that. Damnation . . . no doubt . . . no doubt . . . there was plenty of doubt. Evan felt the tears rising and quickly drank more whisky, spluttering on the sharp taste.

He looked at the others, and said to Dai, the only one awake. 'I don't think . . . think they're going to be very well in the morning,' Evan managed to say with difficulty. 'But then I . . . I don . . . don't think I am either. Dai, how about a cup of tea?' he slumped into a chair . . . 'Please.'

'Okay, Da,' Dai replied but he doubted whether his father heard because he was already asleep.

When Evan woke, the grey dawn lit the room. For a few seconds he stayed slumped in the chair, wondering how he had got there, where the blanket had come from and who had removed his shoes.

He groaned. His head was splitting and he had a foul taste in his mouth. He half noticed the room had been cleaned, the ashtrays emptied, glasses removed and spilt ale cleaned up. He still felt giddy as he went to the kitchen and drank about a gallon of water to cure his raging thirst. He sat at the table, his head in his arms, closed his eyes for a moment and was next aware of his surroundings when Meg shook his shoulder.

He lifted his head with difficulty and groaned. 'Roll on, death.'

She smiled. 'Suffering are we? And serves you right. I thought you and your brothers were planning to drink the valley dry, bach.' She felt sorry for him. 'Do you want the hair of the dog?'

'No, Meg,' he gagged. 'The thought makes me feel ill. Just give me some love and kindness in the form of a cup of tea with plenty of peace and quiet.'

'Poor Evan,' she bent and kissed his cheek. 'Aren't you going to work today?'

'No, love. William and me have got things to see about. We have to talk to the others as well. We thought today would be a good time to do it, under the circumstances.'

Meg frowned. It was so unlike Evan she was about to ask what was so important and then thought better of it. Evan rarely took a day off. He worked as hard as possible, too hard in her opinion, with his double shifts, to make extra money, first for the children's schooling and now for their emigration.

Evan spent the morning in bed, recovering. With the children out of the house Meg went to wake him. She stood smiling down at Evan and thought how lucky she was to have him. She would never love another man, and she was sure Evan would never love another woman. After eleven years of marriage they still found each other exciting. Slowly she pulled back the sheet and blankets, not to disturb him . . . yet. She slipped off her blouse and skirt and sat on the edge of the bed.

Later she lay by his side, her arms around him. 'You know how much I love you, don't you, Evan?' she said softly.

He pulled her closer still, if that was possible. 'Aye, love and I love you, more than you'll ever know. I guess we're two of the lucky ones.' He paused. 'Like my parents were I suppose. They seemed to have had a good life together. Not an easy one but a good one. In a way it was just as well they went together, though I wish it had been in twenty years time and not now. I'm going to miss them.'

'I know, so shall I. They were pretty wonderful people. I only wish my parents had been so happy. But with a mother like mine how could any man have been happy? God, she told me that, after I was born, she permitted my father to "have his dirty way" as she put it, only once a month. If she wasn't my mother I would dislike her intensely.'

Later Evan's brothers arrived at the house.

'William and I have learned some good news,' said Evan. 'At least, I suppose you could call it that if you think it took Dad and Mam's deaths to bring it about.' He paused. 'The fact is, Dad had one of those life policy things that Meg was telling us about. Remember?' They nodded. 'It seems that Dad contacted some sort of office in Pontypridd. I understand he paid every week through the post office and well, it seems we are due to receive some money from them.'

'How much?' asked Albert. 'Are we talking about a few pounds or more?'

'Oh more, a lot more. Exactly how much we don't know yet until we hear from them. But I think we can expect a few hundred at least.'

They gasped. A few hundred? That was a fortune! Eighty pounds would buy them a house, a few hundred . . . Good grief!

For Evan, it meant that they now had enough money to emigrate to America.

The following day Evan was up at four thirty. He lit the fire, put the kettle on and went into the kitchen to wash and shave in cold water. He shivered with the shock and quickly dried himself, rubbing his cheeks hard for warmth, then put his head out the back door to check the weather. It was bitterly cold. A cloudless night after the rain had resulted in a heavy hoar frost, bathing the back with a silver white, gleaming in the half moon now setting behind the hill. The moon would set soon and then it was going to be pitch dark before the dawn but for Evan it was going to be dark for a long time, for most of the winter in fact. A double shift today and most other days would mean being down in that hell hole of a mine for a least eighteen hours every day, longer by the time he had caught the lift to the surface. He shuddered again, but this time not with the cold, but with the thought of being entombed down there for so long. He remembered just before he and Meg had married. He had worked doublers all summer long, including Sundays. People spoke of it as the best summer in years, warm sunshine and balmy days with gentle breezes and picnics in the country – for some, but not for him.

This was his winter underground. When he got to America he would never go down a mine again, not as long as he lived. With a few sacrifices during these last few months, plus their savings and his father's money he was sure they would be all right in America. While he sipped his tea and ate a bread and dripping sandwich he thought about 'sacrifices'. What the hell was there to be sacrificed? He and Meg had talked about it without mentioning details because they knew there was little more they could sacrifice. He looked at his sandwich in disgust. Christ, he was going to start on a double shift on bread and dripping. His stomach contracted and he had to force himself to chew and swallow. He knew he would be glad of it later.

He shrugged on his heavy work coat, put the sandwiches Meg had made the night before into his pocket and left. Huddled inside his jacket, shoulders hunched, he walked quickly in the direction of the mine, grunting good mornings to the other miners he met.

Evan went straight to number three shaft and crowded

into the lift with the others. When they stepped onto the
open cage the old man told them to mind their hands and
with his usual cry of 'Hell first Stop' they descended.
Evan craned his neck for a last glimpse of the stars,
pinpricks of light against the black sky. He hated going
down, where there was insufficient air, where the sweat
never dried on your back and where the dust settled into
everything, filling every hole in his body starting with his
nostrils. Some of the men lit the lamps on the front of their
helmets, the flickering yellow flame giving their faces an
eerie, ghostly appearance. With a bone-jarring jerk the lift
stopped: they cursed the lift attendant fluently while they
stepped off the platform and let those going off shift climb
on. There were no greetings, no laughter; this was a place
to work and eke out a livelihood, a place hated and feared
by the men. This was the place where the men toiled to
help Victoria's England in its great industrial revolution,
creating massive wealth but not sharing in one quarter of
one percent of it.

Evan walked away, along one of the mine's many
branches that followed the seams of coal. The farther
from the entrance he went the muggier it became and
sweat soon formed on his forehead. He was weary before
he started, with a tiredness which came from the spirit. He
followed the bright rail tracks as they sloped gently down,
gradually becoming steeper. He was thankful there were
no ponies in his part of the mine. He hated the sight of
the ponies, blind from being so long in the dark.

Every few yards an oil lamp flickered, throwing shadows across the walls of the tunnel. As he trudged along
heavy boots echoed in the quiet.

He felt a vibration through his feet and stepped off the
track, pressing himself against the side. A few moments
later a half dozen empty trucks, with the lone brakeman on
the last one, rattled into view. Seeing him, the brakeman
slowed and Evan jumped on board, nodding his thanks.
Over the next four hundred yards the train of trucks picked

up a dozen men. It rounded the last bend, screeched to a halt and the men jumped off, forming themselves into small groups to start digging at the coalface.

It was like a scene from Dante's Hell, half naked men swinging pick axes, using shovels and, where the seam narrowed too much, crawling on their hands and knees to chip at the chunks of coal, pushing them back where one of the others would carry it to the trucks.

Evan put his mind into a kind of stupor, not thinking about the work but dreaming. One day, he thought to himself, I shall tell Dai how I dream. He thinks he's the only one, sitting with his atlas on his knees, in a land of his own. He does not, he cannot, know I am there as well, away from this hell, in a world of sunshine and light. He does not realise why I could never condemn him to a life down here, where he would surely go without an education. Evan shook his head. That was the dream before America – Dai a doctor or solicitor. Now the dream included them all. America. Evan shuddered. It had taken little Sian's death to convince them they should go. God, how often had he and Meg discussed it? Meg, my strength, my love. We'll have that life we talked of so often, I promise you.

He hacked at the coal with a pick, sweat pouring down his body, making rivulets of white which quickly covered over with dust to be washed away again. All around him men laboured silently, their breath needed for work, none to spare to talk. Besides, the shift overseer would have been on them like a ton of bricks if they slackened. The poor bastard was hated by them all, irrationally really, because he was given a quota by the engineers, and it was the overseer who had to ensure the men achieved it. Sometimes it was not difficult but at other times, like now, they had to work extra hard. The only respite came when the trucks were winched along the track, but even that was only for a few minutes because the next one was already empty and waiting to be brought down. Time was non-existent, life a limbo of sweat, aching muscles and continual thudding as the picks and shovels dug deep into the soft seam.

A whistle blew and with a sigh the men threw down their tools and moved into the main shaft from the short, narrow holes where they were digging. They sat down, opened their sandwiches and with coal black hands picked out the white bread, eating the dust along with the food. Normally they would have brought bottles of cold tea or water but here there was a small run of water which soaked through the ground into a natural catchment area and then escaped through the tunnel. By the time it filtered through the overhead rock it was as clean as anyone could wish and, more importantly, cold.

Evan ate just two sandwiches, knowing the danger of cramp if he took too many at one time. While he sat there, still half lost in his thoughts, he looked at the other miners. Between young Raymond, only fourteen years old, and old Clifford at fifty-eight, they spanned three generations. Three generations who had been treated like animals, worked like slaves with no hope of the system ever changing. The whistle blew; with an inward groan he started working again, lifting, swinging, dropping and levering his pick into the coal, gnawing at the small area assigned to him. His mind was in neutral or away with Meg, or off to America, or back again to Meg, or with the boys as they made good in college in America. It was funny, wasn't it, how his dream had already changed from school in Pontypridd to college in America . . . and back to a warm, cosy evening with Meg, always Meg and their love. It sustained him as he dug into the never-ending seam of coal, the monotony going on for ever . . . until the next whistle, a life time away.

And so it went on . . . and on. Evan worked double shifts six days of the week but Meg insisted he take Sundays off to recharge his strength. Sometimes he did, but more often than not he would work a single shift, which let him have the evening at home.

He had no time for the committee and could not care less what was going to happen now. He had laid the groundwork, and now it was left to his brother and friends to sort matters out. William was already a member of the committee, so all was going according to plan.

Meg wanted to find a job even if it meant scrubbing floors. She would do anything rather than see Evan work so hard. Evan was adamant. She was not to take a job. The reason was not male pride but because he felt that Meg was better employed amassing information about the best way to get to America. What was the difference in cost if they went from, say, London or Liverpool? Where was it best to land? What part of the States would give them the best opportunities? Meg was kept busy between trips to the new public library in Pontypridd and borrowing books from her school teacher friends.

The new school would be ready about the second week in February. It would be better than the old place, with no chance of a repetition of the accident which had killed the children. A commemorative plaque was to be placed over the main entrance, listing the names of those who had died. Evan was glad he was leaving the area. He could not bear the thought of seeing Sian's name every time he walked into the school, and he hated the thought of Sion and Dai seeing it there every day. No, it was better for them all to get away, to leave the sad memories behind and take the happy ones with them.

Christmas Eve was a Friday night and Evan had finished his double shift. He was not working Christmas day nor Boxing day, the latter at the insistence of Meg. He came out of the lift into the cold night air, the sweat drying on him instantly, causing him to shiver violently. By the time he reached the gate it was snowing, the flakes wafting gently down with no wind driving them. As he trudged homewards they intensified, and soon the visibility was only a matter of yards. Near to home he passed a neighbour he could not recognise and exchanged a 'Merry Christmas' with him. The streets and houses were already covered in a white mantle, his feet crunching the snow as he walked. Evan found his spirits lightening as he opened the door. For the first time he was looking forward to the holiday, albeit with mixed feelings. This would be the first Christmas without Sian and his parents.

12

CHRISTMAS HAD BEEN and gone and the new year had followed quickly. The snow, once a pleasing background to the festivities, had now become a dangerous nuisance. Trudging through the drifts meant leaving home earlier to get to work on time, arriving wet and cold, and returning home even more tired, if that was possible, after sliding and cursing up the slippery road. The Taff had also flooded, but down near Pontypridd, causing damage to low-lying houses and shops. The snow turned to sleet, the sleet to rain and melted into ugly lumps of blackened slush and ice. Paths were worn and walking became easier. Only the children regretted the change in weather.

It was a Sunday evening in February and they were gathered together to discuss the move to America in some detail.

'There are three places to sail from,' Megan began, 'Southampton, Tilbury and Cardiff. Not Liverpool as I originally thought. Though the fare is slightly cheaper from Southampton by the time we get there and stay in a hotel and so on it'll be more expensive than going from Cardiff. So I think Cardiff is the cheapest by about ten pounds.'

'Ten pounds,' Sion whistled, an impressed expression on his face, though he had no real understanding of the value of money yet. Even so, he expressed what Evan thought.

'This is a new route and the ships don't sail as often

as they do from the other two places. In fact, there's only one sailing a month. The one in March is due on the fifteenth. There was still room yesterday, according to the booking agent.'

'Where will we land?' asked Evan.

'It stops at Boston and then New York. After that it comes back to Cardiff. The journey takes eighteen days in one of the new type of steam ships. This one is very new apparently, and very luxurious.'

'How much will it cost altogether, Meg?'

She grimaced. 'Let me put it this way. We'll arrive with about two hundred pounds left.'

'Hmmm, not too bad, I suppose,' said Evan. 'Then what?'

'Well, look you,' in her excitement Meg's Welsh accent strengthened. 'We can take a train from New York all the way to Kansas City if we wish,' her finger traced a line across the atlas. 'Apparently there's still a lot of land there nobody has claimed. It's real cowboy country where people travel on horseback and carry guns and things.'

'Gosh,' said Dai, 'cowboys. Are there Indians too, Mam?'

'Some but . . .'

'Wild ones?' interrupted Sion gleefully.

'No, not wild ones. At least, not very wild, just a little bit,' she added seeing the disappointment on Sion's face.

'The point is, how far do we wish to go?' Evan asked.

Meg sighed. 'I just don't know, I really don't. Of one thing there's no doubt, you aren't going mining, right?' The question was rhetorical, but Evan nodded. 'We still haven't decided exactly what we're going to do, have we? I mean, we've talked about being there and having a nice life and so on, but what are we going to do? Farming? A small shop of some sort? What?'

Evan shrugged and the two children copied him.

Meg smiled. 'We plan in great depth how we're going to get there, we have money to ensure a better start than many other immigrants yet we can't . . .' she trailed off. 'You're hopeless, all three of you.'

Evan nodded. 'True, but that's why we have you.'

'True,' echoed the boys solemnly.

Meg suppressed her urge to laugh. 'All right. Well, while we think about it, you two get ready for bed.'

With many groans they left.

'What are you going to do, Evan?'

He grimaced. 'I'm not sure Meg, and that's a fact. I wouldn't mind trying my hand at farming or something. After all, I like working in the allotment. On the other had I don't think I know enough about it to be able to cope with a farm. But then what do I know about? Nothing,' his voice grew bitter, 'except mining and I'm not going to do that.'

'We'll find something, you'll see. A shop wouldn't be a bad idea. We could stop off at David and Maud's and talk to them. I know they haven't had the shop for long but there must be something they can tell us that'll be of help.'

'I agree. We'll stay over night the day before we leave,' said Evan.

At last, it was Evan's final day in the mine. In four days time they would be on their way. They would have one night in Cardiff with David and Maud and then join the ship in time to depart at eight o'clock.

He trudged along the mineshaft, his mind turning to the family. Now he was in the mine, he could no longer believe it was his last double shift; he could only think he had to get through the day in the same way as he always did; Dream . . . Plan . . . Revenge? No, he did not want to think of that.

He lifted, swung, dropped and levered in his mechanical, never ending rhythm. The trucks clanged up and down, moving away even as the last lump of coal was thrown into them. The men sweated silently, the whistle blew, they ate their coal dust and sandwiches, the whistle blew, they drank the cold water thankfully. They dug, the whistle blew again . . . and they drank and sweated. To Evan it was the longest shift he could remember. The accident happened two hours before he was due to finish.

He heard the trucks returning, their noise an unnoticed background to the hell of the mine. The noise surfaced to his conscious level a few moments before the shouts. He looked up to see the trucks moving far too quickly, rolling unchecked along the rails. The brakeman was ineffectively hauling back on his lever but to no avail. It was fifty feet away and going to come off the rails at a tremendous force exactly where Evan was standing. The brakeman jumped, hit his head on the roof and collapsed unconscious. The trucks were thirty feet away and swaying from side to side.

Evan stood at the bottom of a narrow tunnel, barely wide enough to allow him to face the coal seam and swing a pick. The last truck rocked too far, tottered and fell, taking the other trucks with it. The leading truck came off the rails only feet before it reached the tunnel in which Evan stood. The truck then slewed slightly; still moving quickly it caught the side of the wall and spun round. The back of the truck hit the other side of the tunnel and dug into the soft coal. The noise was horrendous, sparks flew as metal screeched on metal and the truck dug deeper into the coal. Evan pushed so hard against the coal face that the irregular wall bruised his back. The trucks stopped inches from his legs.

The noise subsided and the men rushed to see if he was all right. Evan found himself trembling. He had never been so close to serious injury or death before. The miners shouted for joy when they discovered he was safe.

Someone remembered the brakeman and they went to find him. Evan clambered over the trucks, picked up his shirt and coat, and started up the tunnel. He edged wordlessly past the men clustered around the inert body of the brakeman and without a backward glance continued to the lift. Ten minutes later he was outside the gates walking quickly to hide the tremors that still coursed through his body.

It was a beautiful, early spring night. The three quarters full moon was just coming over the edge of the valley. It was a splendid sight, the white light bathing the scene. Evan looked back at the mine then up at the sky and said: 'Almost, but not quite. You'll never find me down there again. I promise you.'

Meg was surprised but pleased to see him home early. When he told her what had happened she was moved to tears. Their love making that night was extra special.

Monday dawned bright and early. They had packed eight wooden crates, put together by Evan, William and Uncle James. Two men could lift one crate with a little difficulty. They had hired Dai Coffin's horse and cart – not the hearse – but the one he used in his capacity as local furniture remover. The packed cart was outside the door, the children sitting on it while Meg and Evan took one last look around.

'I'll miss our lovely little house,' Meg said, tears in her eyes.

'Aye, me too, love,' replied Evan softly. 'We had some good times here, didn't we?' He put his arm around her shoulders and hugged.

'Will we be as happy in America?'

Evan laughed. 'Much, much happier, I promise you. You'll see. Come on, the horse and cart will wait all day but the train won't.'

The farewell to the family was tearful, especially Sion's

as he paid his last visit to Uncle James. When the horse
and cart were about to move Uncle James slipped Sion
a small, neat package.

'See you don't open it until you're on the ship,' he
whispered. 'It's for all of you. Goodbye and God bless.'
He turned away quickly, determined no one should see
his tears.

'Uncle James, Uncle James.' Sion jumped down and
ran back, throwing his arms around the old man's waist.
'I love you, Uncle James.'

'I love you too, Sion,' he said with difficulty, a lump
in his throat.

Sion returned to the cart and scrambled on board,
standing on the back waving to Uncle James until the
cart turned a corner and was out of sight.

David and Maud met them at the station in Cardiff.
Meg, Maud and the children took a hansom home while
Evan and David went directly to the docks. There they
arranged to have the cases stowed in the hold.

'Before we return,' said Evan, 'show me the coaling
yards will you?'

'What on earth for?'

'Em, never mind. But there's something I want you
to do tomorrow. I know you'll find it unusual but let
me explain. Incidentally, don't say anything to Maud
or Meg.'

'Excuse the mess,' said Maud to Evan when they
arrived. 'Like I told Meg we've only just finished the
alterations a week age.'

'Come on Evan, I'll show you around,' said David.
The shop was larger than Evan had expected, the shelves
behind the counter stacked high with different goods.
David sold everything from food to lengths of cotton to
steel nibbed pens.

Evan shook his head. 'How on earth did you manage
all this? Surely you didn't have enough money . . .' he
trailed off.

'No,' laughed his brother, 'of course not. It was the banks man, the banks. I got a new suit, told the bankers I was a merchant from North Wales and was thinking of settling down in this area. In the second bank I went to I opened an account, deposited a hundred and ten pounds and kept fifty in my pocket. Evan . . . Ha, here's the sherry. I propose a toast to a happy voyage and a good life in America.' They drank. 'Now, where was I? Oh yes, well, I borrowed five hundred pounds and came home and got blind drunk.' He shook his head in wonderment. 'Look,' David held out his hands to his brother. 'See how the hard skin and the cuts are going? Do you know what I had to do when I went to the bank? I wore gloves and told them I had a skin disorder. Evan boyo, if business stays like it was for the first week then I'll pay back the money I borrowed plus interest in four years. God, think of all that slaving down the mine and it's here to pick like . . . like apples from a tree.'

'I'm impressed, David. I really am,' said Evan.

'Come on and I'll show you the rest of the house. I suppose you've already seen it, Meg?'

She nodded.

'I'll tell you a few of my ideas, Evan. By the way, what are you going to do in America? Have you decided yet?'

'I hadn't, but you've certainly given me food for thought.'

Later that night, after they were all in bed, Evan spoke to his wife. 'Listen, there's something I must do. I'll be away all night but . . . .'

Meg sat up in alarm. 'What do you mean?' Her voice was loud in the quiet of the house.

'Shshsh, keep your voice down. I don't want you to wake the household. Listen love, you know I love you and I love the children,' Evan paused. 'Just believe me when I say if I don't go and do this I'll . . . I'll never be able to live with myself.'

'Tell me what you're going to do then I'll be able to understand. At least I . . . I suppose I will. I mean, I can't imagine where you want to go at this time of night.'

'Meg, I've got to go back for a few hours, that's all.'

'Back where? You mean . . . home?' She was incredulous.

'Yes. I've got something to do and nothing is going to stop me.' He spoke more harshly then he had intended.

Meg curled her knees up to her chin and hugged herself, deeply hurt. 'Nothing Evan? Is that what I am? Nothing? Is the family nothing?' She felt the tears rising and angrily wiped her eyes.

'Don't talk daft,' Evan was becoming angry. 'You're everything to me, everything. And the children too. And you know it, don't you, love?' Awkwardly he tried to put his arms around her.

'Evan, please tell me why you're going back. Anyway,' she suddenly brightened, 'how can you? There's no trains now. How would you get there and back in time?'

'There are trains Meg. Coal trains. I know an empty train leaves the yards at the docks at midnight and another arrives back at six thirty. I can easily manage both. If I go now,' he added, taking his arms from around her.

'Please tell me why first. Evan, after all this time surely we aren't going to start having secrets from one another, are we? What's so important back there?'

'Meg, I have to see a man. I'll tell you everything when I return. I promise I will,' he spoke gently while he reached for his clothes. Meg noticed he dressed in his old working clothes and realised what the brown parcel had been in his bag.

'I thought you'd thrown those away. What do you want with them for? My God what am I saying? Why are you going Evan?'

'Meg, when I return I'll tell you and perhaps you'll understand why I won't say now. Don't you trust me?'

'It's not a question of that,' she replied more in sorrow than anger.

'Well then. Look, it's eleven now. I've an hour to get to the docks and find the train. I'll be back shortly after seven at the latest and I'll meet you at the ship. David'll have some clothes for me and . . .'

'He knows?'

'No, only that I'm going up on the train, nothing more.' He bent and kissed her lips. They were like marble. 'I love you Meg and always will, please believe that and trust me. Try and get some sleep while I'm away, all right?'

'Try and sleep? Don't be daft. How will I be able to sleep?'

He grimaced. 'See you later,' Evan whispered and left.

Meg lay back, tears welling in her eyes and trickling down the sides of her face. Evan, Evan, she said to herself. Take care, please take care. She thrust her hand to her mouth to stop herself from crying out loud in her anguish.

Evan closed the front door behind him and hurried along the street. He had known it would be difficult to leave her. How could he tell his wife he was going to kill a man, and burn his house to the ground?

13

THE STREETS WERE cold and dark and Evan hurried to reach the marshalling yards at the docks. The image of Meg kept recurring and nearly made him give up.

The road he was on was long, straight and still busy, the pubs doing a roaring trade. Evan glanced into one as he walked quickly past, the door opening when a drunk reeled out. Through the haze of smoke he saw hard faced seamen and equally hard prostitutes appearing to enjoy themselves.

Evan paused at the gates to the yards, looked to see there was no guard and dashed through. He moved as quickly as he dared in the moonlight. He had found the main line. As Evan darted along the side of the train, two things happened simultaneously. A man appeared in front of him and the train started to move.

'Oi, you. What do you think you're doing, hey?' The man clutched Evan's arm.

Without thinking Evan hit him on the jaw and the man staggered back, more surprised than hurt. Evan steadied himself, waited for the centre of the next truck and leapt for the truck's side. With a mighty effort he pulled himself up and over and lay still for a few moments. Then, with a sigh, Evan huddled into a corner, out of the wind.

After a few minutes Evan began to shiver and cursed the cold. Haunted by his thoughts of Meg, cold to his core, for the first time he had doubts about what he was going to do.

At long last he was past Pontypridd and close to Llanbeddas. The village came into sight and was soon behind the train, which slowed as it approached the bend Evan was looking for. Evan stood, paused and jumped, landing on the bank. He lay still for a few minutes to regain his breath, frightened to move in case he found he had broken a bone. Finally he staggered to his feet; painfully, he climbed the fence, dropped down on the other side and made his way to the Taff. He followed the river's banks until he was past the mine and then climbed up to the road. A quarter of a mile along the road Evan came to the large, ornate gates he was looking for.

He had often walked past them with Meg, trying to see through and get a view of the mansion. The wall surrounding the grounds was eight feet high and topped with broken glass. The gates were locked at that time in the morning and Evan followed the wall for about fifty yards until he came to the big old oak tree. It grew inside the grounds but its lower branches spread wide; one hung over the wall five feet above Evan's head. Two weeks earlier Evan had acquired a length of rope from the mine and had hidden it near the wall. At the second attempt he got it over the branch, tied the ends and climbed up. He sat astride the branch, pulled the rope up and edged his way to the trunk of the tree. He fixed the rope and lowered himself to the ground. He stood in a small copse of trees dominated by the oak. Across a wide sweep of lawn Evan could see the house. With a hammering heart he waited in the shadows to see if there was a watchman or dog loose. There appeared to be neither. He decided to approach from the furthest corner, so if anybody did happen to be looking through a window there was less chance of being seen. The moon came from behind a cloud and, in the light, the lawn looked like a black sea stretching in front of him. Crossing it he would be completely exposed, even in his dark work clothes and with his face covered in coal dust.He waited patiently for a cloud to cut down the light, conscious as never before of how wrong this was. God, he thought, looking up, you say an eye for an eye and then that vengeance will be yours. Which is it? I want my vengeance now Lord, not in some nebulous hereafter. This man ordered the deaths of my parents so what should I do? His indecision angered him and the anger resolved into determination to go on.

He crept forward to the side door, every sense alert to the noises of the night. When he reached the door he paused, straining his ears. So far nothing. He tried the door only to find it locked. He used the jemmy he had brought to force open the door; he found himself in the kitchen. Quickly, he made his way to the hall and finally to a large ornate room.

He pulled together the furniture and ripped open the cushions, making a pile in the centre of the room. He went back to the kitchen and filled a jug with oil from the store, returning to the hall. Though it was difficult to see properly, Evan had no doubt of the opulence of the house and the enormity of what he was about to do swept through him. He wavered, but then he thought of his parents. Had they died in their sleep? Or had they woken to find themselves surrounded by smoke and flames, knowing for horrific moments that they were about to die?

Back in the drawing room he poured the oil over the pile he had created and then threw more oil over the curtains and walls. Finally, he stood with a box of matches in his hands and looked around at the mess. Evan thought about the murder he was about to commit. It was the first time the word had come to his mind. Murder. It had a ring about it, so unlike revenge. An eye for an eye, avenging his parents' horrible death. Murder was what it was and he couldn't do it. Slowly he put the matches in his pocket and with tears in his eyes said softly: 'I'm sorry Dad, Mam. I can't. It isn't in me. Please forgive me, please.' He walked towards the door, the heavy fumes of oil nauseating in the back of his throat. He reached the door but stopped when he heard footsteps.

Evan stepped to the side, pressed himself against the wall and waited. The door swung open soundlessly to reveal a cocked pistol held in a white hand. Evan grabbed the pistol jamming the hammer, pulled the man into the room and smashed the man's face with his fist. Evan recognised Sir Clifford Roberts even as he fell back stunned, blood streaming from his nose. Before he could call out, Evan hit him with the pistol butt. He then took hold of his feet and dragged him inside.

After a few minutes Sir Clifford regained his senses sufficiently to ask: 'Who are you? What do you want?' He was in his sixties, tall, well built but not fat, grey-haired with an air of intimidating authority about him. Even lying on the floor, his dressing gown splattered with blood, his hands to his nose, he was damned if he was going to show the peasant before him how much it hurt. He peered up at Evan: 'Good God, I know you,' he exclaimed, recovering his wits now his head had stopped spinning. I'll talk my way out of this, he thought, and have the bastard hung for what he's done. The mess . . . ugh . . . and the oil he was in . . . the stench . . . it was overpowering.

'You're young Griffiths. I was very sorry to hear about your father, oh and your mother too, of course. A tragic accident, tragic,' he shook his head sadly. 'You've obviously heard something that's caused you a . . . a mis . . . eh . . . caused you to be mistaken,' the unwavering gun pointed at his stomach disconcerted Sir Clifford. He tried to move to a more comfortable position, ready to stand, more sure of himself now he knew who he confronted.

'Liar,' Evan snarled. 'Don't move or by God, I promise I'll shoot you in the stomach and leave you to die in agony and knowing it was because you caused the death of my parents.'

'Don't be ridiculous man, of course I did no such

thing. I liked your father. I liked him very much. Why, I even congratulated him on having such a son as you, after your clever negotiating with us.' Sir Clifford hoped flattery would help.

'You're a lying bastard. I know . . . Do you hear? I know you ordered my death, not my father's, but your minions cocked it up.' Evan's voice was low and intense; he was very tempted to pull the trigger and have done with it.

'That's the most . . .'

'I know, I tell you. A youngster in the village was asked the way to the house of the man named Griffiths who was at the meeting. The kid thought it was my father he wanted, not me. I know you sent them, so don't say another word, trying to deny it. Just give me one good reason why I shouldn't pull the trigger.' It was eerie in the light from the moon. Sir Clifford briefly entertained the wild idea of throwing himself into the shadows, perhaps behind the sofa and screaming for help or even overpowering Evan in some way. He dismissed the thought as ludicrous. There was a better way, much better.

'I can give you a thousand pounds.' Aye, and the moment you leave I shall have the dogs and police after you. You'll not get two miles, he thought.

'Trying to buy me off? With a measly thousand? Is that all your life is worth to you? Are my parents only worth five hundred each? They were worth ten times more to me than everything you possess.'

'I'd give you more but I don't keep much more in the house. Maybe a few hundred more but that's all. I don't suppose,' he added sarcastically, 'you'd take a cheque? Oh yes, with a receipt. Shall we say . . . em . . . eh . . . for services rendered? How would that suit you?'

'Shut up,' Evan replied savagely. Christ but you are a cool one and no mistake, he thought. 'I came here to set fire to your house, and by God that's exactly what I'll do. After tying you up. That way you'll see death approaching, the flames eating your flesh, turning it black. If you're lucky you may die from the smoke but I doubt it.'

Sir Clifford blanched. He had been sure the offer of money would have been sufficient to save him. A thousand pounds was a fortune to a man like the one before him. 'All right . . . I . . . I . . . may be able to find some more, say as much as two thousand. I swear it's all I have here. I swear it.'

Two thousand . . . what could Evan do with so much? Why, he would arrive in America with enough money to set them up in a way he had only dreamed of. Two thousand pounds. A thousand for each of them. One for Mam, one for Dad. Blood money that would live with him the rest of his life.

'Get the money and no tricks.'

I've won, thought Sir Clifford. I know people like you. They keep their bargains, the fools. Slowly, Sir Clifford stood up. 'We have to go into my study across the hall,' he led the way towards the door. Next to the suit of armour and partly hidden, which was why Evan had not seen it earlier, was a door. Sir Clifford took a key from a chain he kept around his neck and unlocked the door.

'I'm going to light a lamp,' said Sir Clifford. 'Don't worry, I won't try anything foolish.' He blinked slowly a habit he had when his mind was in a turmoil. A match flared and Sir Clifford lifted the glass of the lamp on his desk, lighting the wick.

Evan looked at the walls lined with leather bound books, the paintings on the walls, the deep armchairs and thick, wine red carpet. He felt such an over powering sense of jealousy he nearly pulled the trigger.

'Get the money,' Evan said harshly, jerking the gun.

Sir Clifford went to one of the pictures, swung it to one side to expose the safe. He turned with a bundle of money in his hands and said: 'If you'd like to look you'll find this is all there is. The rest is just papers. Nothing important,' he added.

'Put it on the desk. Now turn around.'

'But this was . . .'

'Turn around or by God I swear I'll shoot.'

Something in Evan's voice convinced Sir Clifford there was no use in arguing. He turned. 'Look man, just tie me up or . . .' he was turning his head when the blow fell and he dropped to the floor, half stunned. He pretended to be unconscious but his head still hurt like hell and made him giddy. He smelt burning and involuntarily opened his eyes. Evan held the money in his fist and was carefully setting it alight. When Evan turned Sir Clifford closed his eyes again, thunderstruck by what he had seen. He sensed Evan approaching, felt a little heat and just as he thought Evan was going to drop the money on him the heat was gone. A few moments later, through slitted eyes, Sir Clifford watched Evan place the gun on the desk and walk towards the door. At the same time the smell of smoke jerked him into a sitting position and looking over his shoulder he saw the contents of his safe burning. With a strangled cry which brought Evan spinning around, Sir Clifford jumped to his feet. Though the room spun, Sir Clifford had enough presence of mind to grab the gun, aim and fire. Evan threw himself to one side and managed to get out of the door.

Sir Clifford was besides himself with rage. In the safe had been half a million pounds worth of bearer bonds and shares, apart from important contracts he was working on. Now they were lost. Months of negotiation down the drain . . . up in smoke because of a peasant. Sir Clifford walked slowly towards the door, fearing another ambush. Hell but he felt giddy. I'm sure I hit him he thought, quite sure. Where's the rest of the household? Surely somebody heard the shot. Come on Pritchard you lazy sod of a butler, get up and come and help me. The feel of the breeze from the front door told him the hall was empty and when he saw the door was wide open he began to yell: 'Pritchard. Help somebody. Murder.'

Pritchard appeared carrying a lamp, anxious looking, his hair tousled from sleep and his eyes only half open.

'Rouse the men and tell them I want the dogs,' ordered Sir Clifford. 'Then go for the police. We've had a burglar. Give me that light.' He grabbed the lamp from his butler who was rapidly coming to his senses.

'I'll just get dressed your Lordship,' he said with as much dignity as he could muster, determined not to be ruffled.

'Hurry, man, before the bastard gets away. You don't need to be dressed to go for the men. Do it afterwards.' Sir Clifford knelt by the doorway to his study and grinned evilly. 'Got you, you bastard,' he said softly, examining the pool of blood and the trail leading to the door.

'Pritchard,' he shouted, 'also send for the doctor to be here when I get back. I want him to look at my nose.' Sir Clifford darted up the stairs to dress. He was going to enjoy the next few hours.

The bullet caught Evan in the fleshy part of the inner thigh of the right leg; the pain was crippling. It took all his willpower to get to his feet, his hands clutched around the wound to try and staunch the blood. He had got down the front steps and onto the lawn when he heard Sir Clifford shouting for help. Finally, Evan reached the oak tree. He leaned against the trunk to regain his breath and pulled out a handkerchief to tie around the wound. The bullet had passed three inches below his crotch and he shuddered to think what might have happened if it had been higher. The wound would not be dangerous if he could stop the blood. But before he could do that he had to get away, before the hounds were released.

He grabbed hold of the rope and pulled himself up

the trunk. The pain in his leg was worse than ever, something he would have thought impossible when he had been crossing the lawn. Somehow he got on to the branch and clung there for a few seconds, waiting for the waves of giddiness and pain to subside. He straddled the branch, remembered in time that he would need the rope and untied it. Carefully, wincing as each movement jarred his leg, he shuffled towards the oak and slowly and painfully climbed over the wall all the time his mind racing with the options he now had.

The train would come down the valley and stop for about an hour while more coal was loaded and then continue to Cardiff. Could he climb into one of the trucks? Could he even get there and not be found? There were still two hours before the train departed, more than enough time for Sir Clifford and his dogs to get him. He needed help. He had to have help. He could not get away on his own. Who? William? But that would put him in jeopardy. If the positions were reversed would he help? Without question. But what could William do for him? Perhaps he could dress his wound properly and carry him down to the river. This would help put the dogs off his scent. If he could achieve that, Evan thought, he might have a chance. Over two miles away? Could he do it? Gritting his teeth, one hand on his leg, the other using the wall as a prop Evan hobbled towards the mine. He lost count of the number of times he fell but each time he managed to stand again. Christ! he told himself, he had been a bloody fool. To have done what he did had been the work of a madman. It had been an obsession with him and now he stood to lose everything he held dear, everything that really mattered for the sake of stupid, bloody revenge. And what had he done? Burnt a measly two thousand pounds. If he had kept the money it would have made more sense but just to burn it? Why had he not gone to the authorities with what he had known? He knew the answer. They would never have believed him;

he knew he would never have been able to make the charges stick. Evan's mind wandered but his body kept moving in the right direction. He became aware of the mine gates with a sense of shock.

He staggered on. The gates were far behind now and he was in village streets. Llanbeddas was not much further. He fell, tried to get up and drifted into unconsciousness. How long did he lay there? He had no way of knowing. He only knew it took all his will power to bring himself back to consciousness. The pain is unimportant, he hold himself . . . It is only pain. He was tired from lack of blood but he could sleep for a week in a few hours' time. What was the effort needed compared to giving up, feeling the everlasting pain of not having Meg, of rotting in a stinking, rat infested jail? Move you idiot, move, he screamed at himself. A groan escaped his lips.

He got to his feet . . . somehow he got to his feet. Forget the pain. Bring out your reserves, use your bloody strength . . . think only of Meg. He hobbled on, fighting to stay on his feet with every fibre of his being. Ignore the pain he told himself for the thousandth time, think of Meg . . . Meg . . . Meg.

When did he recognise the baying of the hounds? Evan was unsure. All he knew was they were there. He shuddered, the thought of being torn apart sent adrenaline pounding through him and that in turn gave him the strength to continue, pain or no pain.

At last he was in Llanbeddas. William's house was at the far end and up two or was it three streets? Evan shook his head to clear his thoughts. He stopped. He could not remember but it no longer mattered. He could not make it.

But he would not, could not, give in. He never knew how he reached Uncle James' house, but that was where he found himself. He leaned against the door and lifted his hand wearily to the knocker. No Answer. He knocked again. The dogs were much louder now and Evan was surprised no lamps were being lit in the houses nearby. But that was not the way of the valley. The dogs meant Sir Clifford, therefore it was better not to take an interest in what went on. He raised his arm to try again and fell through the door as it swung open. Uncle James stepped back startled, nearly dropping his lamp.

'What the hell . . . Evan . . . My God.' Evan leaned against the wall unable to speak. 'What happened? Where are the others? You're hurt. Come on, let me help you. What's that noise?' Uncle James put his head outside to listen. 'Dogs? After you, Evan?' he asked, incredulous.

Uncle James had been lying on his bed, unable to sleep, thinking about Sion and Dai and America. Had he done the right thing in not going? Yes, he was sure he had. They had not needed him, not really. He would have been a hindrance no matter how hard he had tried not to be. No, it was better this way. He had never told them he had not spoken to his son in six years. After the children, after the warmth, his loneliness was harder than ever. Complete and utter loneliness was a terrible thing. Just one more sunrise he had promised himself, stroking the barrel of his old shotgun. It was not much of a gun as guns went, but packed with powder and rammed tight with buckshot it would blow him in half. At thirty paces it scattered so much it covered an area of yards. This was the best way. Before, he had been able to live with himself, but not now. The Griffiths' family had awakened too many senses he had long thought dead.

The knocking had startled him but curiously he had felt no fear. Perhaps, he thought, having decided to die, there was nothing further to be frightened of. He had lit a lamp and hurried downstairs.

'Lean here.' Uncle James helped Evan to his feet and quickly slammed the door and slipped the bolts home.

'Sorry . . . sorry,' Evan gasped, tiredness and nausea sweeping through him in waves. 'After me . . . Sir Clifford and . . . and his hounds.'

'Never mind. Come on. I'll get you into the other room. Sit here. I'll get some water and see to your leg.' He rushed into the kitchen, poured cold water into a bowl and grabbed a towel. He washed the wound as best he could and bound it tightly. Evan was unconscious.

The dogs were in the street. Uncle James looked down at Evan with a smile. Providence, he was sure, had sent Evan to him. Especially tonight, oh yes, especially tonight.

He went upstairs and opened his bedroom window. In the clear night he could see the pack of six hounds, less than a hundred yards away. They were following Evan's path unerringly. Behind followed half a dozen of Sir Clifford's men, armed with staves and one or two with guns. Sir Clifford rode bareback, along the centre of the road. Uncle James saw curtains on the other side of the road move and had no doubt the whole street watched. The baying of the hounds would have woken the dead.

Uncle James knew there was only one chance. To get Evan away he had to get rid of the man directing the others. It never entered his head to ask why they were after Evan, nor did he care. The dogs turned into his doorway, howling their frustration, pawing at the wood. The men stopped and waited for Sir Clifford's orders. Nobody looked up at Uncle James standing in the shadows with barely two inches of gun barrel protruding, aimed at Sir Clifford.

'Break down . . .' Sir Clifford was starting to issue an order when the gun went off. He was blown nearly in two and was dead before he hit the ground. The horse, also wounded, reared up and bolted, the body of his master lying in an ever widening pool of blood. The other men took to their heels and ran back the way they had come, afraid for their own lives. Uncle James quickly reloaded and fired a parting shot to discourage an early return. The dogs, used to the sound of shooting had paid no heed but continued to paw at the door so Uncle James reloaded with only a little powder and fired into their midst. None were killed but they were frightened and hurt and ran home yelping. Sir Clifford lay still and, sure he was dead, Uncle James spat into the street: 'Good riddance,' he muttered.

He hurried downstairs knowing that it would take the men some time to get organised and come back. Rabble like those Sir Clifford employed were useless without a leader. He also knew none of the villagers would leave their homes to go to Sir Clifford's aid. They would rather pretend they had seen nothing. By the time somebody came from the manor he and Evan had to be a long way away.

He wiped Evan's face with a damp cloth and eased the tight bandage. He lit the fire and put the kettle on before rushing upstairs to dress. He hid what was left of his savings in a money belt next to his skin and took a spare pair of trousers and pullover for Evan. Evan did not stir even when Uncle James undressed him and dressed him in the other clothes. The trousers were a little tight but would do.

He made a strong pot of tea and turned his attention back to Evan. He put a glass of rum to Evan's lips and managed to force some into his mouth. Evan coughed and feebly pushed Uncle James' hand away. Uncle James forced more rum into Evan and at last Evan opened his eyes.

He sat forward suddenly, knocking the glass to the floor: 'The dogs. I must get away. Down to the train. To Meg.' Evan tried to stand but Uncle James put his hand on Evan's shoulder and calmed him down.

'It's all right Evan bach . . . I've, eh, taken care of it. We have at least until dawn. Probably later than that.' He ladled sugar into a cup of tea and added some rum. 'Here, drink this. You'll feel better and then we can leave.'

Still dazed, Evan took the cup, his mind unable to comprehend what was happening. 'How have you taken care of it?' He gradually remembered what had happened and said, 'It's impossible. I'll finish this and go. I'm sorry Uncle James, but now you're involved. God knows what they'll do if they find out you've helped me.'

'Evan bach, concentrate. We'll get away. I told you I've taken care of things. I . . .' he faltered, 'I shot Sir Clifford. He's lying in the street, dead I think. So now we both've got to go.' He saw the shocked expression on Evan's face. 'Don't worry – my mind isn't wandering and I'm not senile. It was the only way to stop them. We've gained a few hours. If we don't make it,' he shrugged, 'I'll die trying. Where are you going?' he asked alarmed when Evan pulled himself up, swaying on his feet. Uncle James grabbed his arm to steady him.

'I must see,' Evan gasped out. 'The body, Uncle James. I must see the body.' Helped by Uncle James he staggered into the passage to the front door. Cautiously Uncle James opened the door, his gun ready, and relaxed when nothing happened. He stepped to one side to let Evan look out. The body lay where it had fallen, an untidy heap in the middle of the street, the blood a black pool in the white moonlight.

'Thanks,' Evan said automatically. 'Uncle James, I don't mean why . . . sort of . . . of . . . I mean, why did you do it? Look at the trouble you're in. Christ, it's a hanging offence. Why did you do that for me?' His voice was full of anguish for the trouble he had caused his friend – aye, and his children's friend too.

'I can't explain. Leave me some dignity and accept I had nothing in this world to lose and everything to gain.'

'What'll you gain? My life isn't worth it, Uncle James. You're not that old. You've got years ahead of you yet. Now there's nothing.'

'Not true,' Uncle James' voice was harsh. 'I had nothing ahead of me, nothing except loneliness. Now, Evan,' his voice softened just as suddenly, 'there's every-thing. Especially if I can get you back to Meg and the children. That'll be reward enough. Just to see them when I thought I never would again.'

'You really love those kids don't you?' Evan said softly, emotion making his voice gruff.

'Aye and I'm glad I'm able to help tonight. You've given me a reason to live a little longer.'

'Uncle James, you're wrong,' Evan startled the old man. 'It's for a lot longer. If we get to Cardiff you're definitely coming with us. You can't stay. There's nothing for you here. We'd meant it earlier on when we asked you to come with us. Well, now you can't refuse,' he paused. 'What do you say?'

'I'd hoped you might say something like that. Now the question is, where do we go from here?'

14

FROM SOMEWHERE EVAN found the strength to grin.
'The coal train leaves at five-thirty, and will be in Cardiff
an hour later. What's the time now?' They both looked at
the ornate clock on the mantelpiece which showed twenty
minutes to five.

'Time enough,' said Uncle James. 'Do you think we
could manage to take a few of my things? Not much, just
the clock and one or two bits and pieces. You know.'

'I know,' said Evan, 'and we'll manage somehow.
Another tea and rum should get me down to the mine.
I'll help myself while you get your stuff.'

Five minutes later they were ready. Uncle James had
packed a battered holdall. He grunted: 'Not much to show
for sixty two years is it, bach?'

Evan pulled himself from the chair. 'There'll be a lot
more soon, Uncle James, just you wait and see. America
isn't called the land of opportunity for nothing, you know.
Can we get out the back way?'

'Yes. Here, lean on me.' Uncle James took his bag in
his other hand and supported Evan as well as he could.
He had one last look around, sad but somehow not sad. He
had happy memories of the house but they were all from
the time when his wife had been alive. Since then the
place had been a prison, until the kids came along. The
thought of seeing them again gave him strength. Damn
but there was a life to live now. If, and it was a big if,
they could get away.

Getting through the back gate was easy. Evan had

new-found strength from his rest and the rum tea. His leg ached but the blood had been reduced from a flow to an oozing trickle. They half slid, half stumbled down to the bank of the Taff and stopped. Uncle James undid the bandage on Evan's leg to allow the blood to circulate and replaced it after a few minutes. The movement had aggravated the wound and it bled more profusely, though not as badly as it had done earlier. Slowly they continued. For all his determination Uncle James was old in body if young in spirit and Evan's new found strength was ebbing rapidly. They fell a number of times when Evan's leg gave out and Uncle James did not have the strength to hold him up. Each time it was more difficult to get up again. By the time they arrived at the place where they could ford the river, they were barely shuffling along. Close to exhaustion they sat on the frost-covered grass, badly in need of a rest. For a minute Uncle James looked at his bag and, before Evan could protest, picked it up and threw it into the river. It swirled along the water for a few seconds then disappeared.

'We could have managed, Uncle James. You needn't have done that,' Evan said softly.

'Never mind that rubbish, bach. Apart from the clock there was nothing of real value, just old memories which are probably best forgotten. Come on, it's time to go. We've got to cross and climb up to the railway yet.' Neither mentioned the fact it was already five past five and there was still a long way to go.

The cold water bit into them like a knife. Halfway across Evan fell to his knees but Uncle James managed to stay on his feet. Evan gasped aloud as the water came up to his chest. Groggily he stood up and they carried on, the water helping. In the frost laden air their clothes froze and Evan's leg went numb. The pain lessened and they could make better time, scrambling up the steep bank to the railway track without stopping. To increase their pace they tried to step from sleeper to sleeper but every few steps Evan had to shorten his stride to ease his leg.

Evan's pace grew shorter. The mine was visible, a stark outline suddenly lost when the moon slid out of sight behind the valley.

They could see the train now. The noise and bustle told them it was still being loaded. They had a hundred yards to go but now they moved carefully in case they were seen or heard. They had covered eighty yards when suddenly the train whistled, steam escaping in billowing clouds from underneath the engine as it started to move.

'Oh God, no,' said Evan. 'So near. Uncle James, try and get on. I'll hide around here. Get to Meg in Cardiff. She'll be at the ship. Tell her to go to America and I'll come down on tomorrow's train. I'll see them in America. Go on.' He added harshly.

They both knew that at daylight the dogs would be after Evan again. He would be caught within hours.

The train was abreast of them moving with majestic slowness but still too fast for them to climb aboard.

'We either go together boyo or not at all,' Uncle James said softly. The trucks, heaped with coal, continued past. Half the train was gone when the truck nearest them shunted into the one in front, the movement repeated the length of the train. The momentum carried the heavy trucks along until the last but one was next to them and only then did the pair of would be travellers realise that the train had stopped. Evan found a strength and determination he thought had been used up. A last chance and Evan lunged for the train, teeth gritted, his leg ignored. Between the trucks he kneeled on the connecting device, grabbed the top of the truck and heaved himself up. He fell onto the mound of coal as the train lurched and started again. Uncle James had one leg on the ground, the other on the buffer, too tired to move. His foot dragged.

'Evan,' he gasped.

Evan leaned down took hold of Uncle James' coat

collar and with a swift prayer it would hold lifted at the moment Uncle James slipped, his strength giving out. Years of work in the mines had made Evan enormously strong in spite of his loss of blood, and years of eating frugally, barely having more than a starvation diet, had left Uncle James' big frame little more than skin and bones. Evan plucked him up, pulled him half into the truck and then dragged him in. They lay gasping, unable to move.

'Are you all right?' Evan managed to whisper after a few minutes. He watched Llanbeddas pass behind for a second time and shuddered at the thought how close he had been to capture.

'I'm all right, Evan, just cold, that's all.' Uncle James paused. 'I've an idea. Push some of the coal to one side and let's try and burrow under. We need to hide in case we're seen and it might give us some warmth.'

'Let me just fix this bandage and we'll do that,' Evan said.

'Let me do that, boyo.' Uncle James crawled over to Evan. Deftly he rebandaged the wound, now bleeding again as much as ever. 'How's that?'

'Thanks. I wish the bloody thing didn't hurt so damned much.' Evan shivered. 'Christ, I'm cold.'

'Don't move and I'll shift this coal.' Uncle James scrambled onto the centre of the pile and pushed the coal to one side. Evan crawled after him and tried to help.

They lay down in a shallow hole in the coal and covered themselves with the small lumps. From time to time one or other of them shivered, but at least the interval between spasms lengthened. Evan fell into an uneasy sleep, completely exhausted. Uncle James tried to keep awake but finally the rocking motion, the soothing noise of the wheels on the tracks and his own tiredness was too much.

He jerked awake to silence and wondered where he was. When memory of the night flooded back he groaned and sat up. He ached all over and a lump of coal stuck in his back was agonising. He shook Evan awake.

'What time is it and where are we?' Evan groaned.

'Ten past seven and I guess in Cardiff.'

'Hell,' Evan sat up suddenly and groaned. 'We must have been here over half an hour. We're lucky we haven't been found. We've got to hurry, Uncle James, the ship leaves at eight o'clock.'

'This morning?'

Evan nodded. 'I planned to return ages ago. David was to meet me near the ship with clean clothes and I was going straight on board.'

'Your brother knew what you were going to do?' Surprise showed in Uncle James' voice.

'No, I wouldn't tell him. I just told him to meet me. I hadn't expected to be in this state, though I'd expected to be dirty. He was a bit upset about my secrecy but I knew he would have tried to stop me if he had known. Between him and Meg I doubt I would have had the determination to go. Come on, let's get away from here before it gets much lighter and somebody sees us.' It was well past dawn and the sky was lightening rapidly.

Painfully, they crawled out of the coal and climbed over the side onto the ground. Evan staggered and fell. His leg hurt with a stabbing pain and he felt dizzy. Uncle James helped him to his feet.

'Thanks,' Evan gasped, sweat breaking out all over him. 'Come on, Uncle James, I think it's this way we have to go.'

Slowly they hobbled away from the train, Evan leaning heavily on Uncle James.

The guard waited for them to reach him. 'What's happened here, then? Where's your passes boyos?'

'Get lost,' snarled Uncle James. 'You ask for passes when you can see my friend is injured?'

The guard was shocked at the venom in the old man's voice. 'I'm only doing my job. You got to show your passes in and out now, you know that. It's the new rules, see.'

'Stuff it – just give me a hand with my friend. Isn't it enough he's been injured by one of the trucks hitting him without you wanting to see passes as well?' He changed his tone from disgust to a plea. 'Please friend. I'm all shook up by the accident. Just give me a hand through the gate, will you?'

The guard responded to the change of tone and helped to carry Evan a few hundred yards up the road. 'I must go back now. I'm sorry about your leg mate. I hope it's better soon.'

Evan and Uncle James nodded their thanks and the guard hurried away.

'That was close,' said Evan. 'But I don't think we'll make it.'

They had a mile to travel to the other side of the docks and not enough time to walk it even if they were fit. The gods were still on their side: a moment later a hansom cab came along the street and Uncle James flagged it down.

'I'll pay you double fare if you get us to the ship for America in ten minutes or less,' Uncle James said, helping Evan in.

The driver eyed their dirty, ragged clothes dubiously but before he could say anything Uncle James reached into his picket and held two shillings in front of the man. 'Five minutes and this is yours.'

'Say no more.' The driver turned on his seat and whipped the horse into a trot. His passengers leaned back with a sigh. It was a quarter to eight. Neither dared tempt the fates by asking whether they would make it or not.

The cabbie turned through a gate a few hundred yards along, ignored the guards and took a short cut across the docks. He knew the place well and within minutes they turned the corner of a large warehouse and saw the ship, only a short distance away.

The place was teeming with people laughing, crying,

waving. A band played and streamers were thrown down
from the ship by the hundreds lining the rails of the decks.
The route to the ship was blocked by a high fence and the
way in was through a low building. The hansom drew up
at the door, Uncle James jumped down, threw the cabbie
his fare and helped Evan. David rushed over to them.

'Where on earth have you been? We've been going
frantic. Meg's about to come ashore again because they
want to remove the gangway. Good God, you're hurt.
And what a state. What have you been doing?' For the
first time he recognised Uncle James. 'Good God,' was
all he found to say.

'Give me a hand, David. I'll write you one day and tell
you all about it, look you.' Evan grinned through his pain
and exhaustion, elated they had arrived in time. 'Come on
Uncle James, the ship won't wait.'

He hobbled between them into the building. As they
passed the ticket collector David waved his hand. 'The
passenger we were waiting for, my brother. He was . . .
eh . . . involved in an accident, that's why he's late and
em . . . in such a state.'

They were beckoned through. The ticket collector
assumed Uncle James was only helping. At the bottom
of the gangway Evan looked up to see Meg. She had
not noticed their arrival, staring fixedly at the main gate
where she expected to see Evan arrive. The ship's whistle
sounded and Meg made up her mind to disembark.

'Mam, it's Da,' yelled Dai, pointing down the gangway. 'And look . . . look . . .'

Meg turned, the relief that surged through her changing
to anxiety when she saw him.

Evan grinned at her, all his love welling up within
him as their eyes met. Never again, he said to himself,
never again. The risk was too great. The Captain on the
bridge leaned down and shouted. All eyes followed as
Evan pulled his way up the gangway with Uncle James
to one side and David behind him. So much for my

inconspicuous arrival, thought Evan. Still, David's idea about an accident was a good one and I'll stick to it. Near the top Evan stopped and turned to his brother.

'Thanks for everything, Dave. I'll write, like I said, but I suspect you'll hear soon enough.' He held out his hand. 'Good luck with the business and all.'

'Here's your parcel before I forget,' David handed it to Evan. They shook hands.

'Where's Maud?' Evan asked.

'At home with a cab ready in case you turned up there, somehow. Take care, Evan and I hope all goes well in America. Come home and see us sometime.'

They smiled wanly at each other, aware of the inadequacy of saying goodbye. The Captain's yells jerked them apart and David turned back down the gangway while Evan and Uncle James staggered onto the deck of the ship. Immediately the gangway was taken away and the seamen began casting off the berthing hawsers. None of the Griffiths' saw any of this, because they were all talking at once, Meg in Evan's arms crying, coal dust spoiling her new coat.

'Evan . . . Evan . . . we were so worried. What happened? Uncle James, what are you doing here?' She asked over Evan's shoulder. Dai and Sion were trying to hug Evan and Uncle James at the same time.

'Are you coming too?' Sion asked. 'To America? To live with us?'

Uncle James smiled tiredly. 'It looks like it. What did you say, Evan?'

'Let's get below. Meg says we have a cabin. Mind my leg, Sion,' he whispered, wincing.

'We're going early,' said Uncle James looking at his watch. 'It's only five to eight.'

'No, we're late,' said Meg pointing at a tower clock in the distance. It showed ten past eight.

'Dear God,' said Uncle James, blanching.

The stir their arrival had caused was lost in the greater

excitement of the ship's departure. There were louder shouts and screams from the passengers, and everyone was frantically waving at relations and friends. Dai and Sion stood at the rails to wave goodbye to their Uncle David while the other three made their way down to the cabin.

It was tiny, with just enough room for four bunks and their hand luggage. Wearily the two men sank onto the lower bunks. Meg sat next to Evan, holding his hand tightly.

'I was so worried, Evan, I didn't know what to do. I had just made up my mind to leave when Dai saw you. What's wrong with your leg? Uncle James . . . one of you tell me. Damn it I don't know whether to cry or laugh now that you're here.' She smiled and at the same time wiped away her tears. 'And just look at my coat. Oh, Evan,' she put her arms around his neck, her face smudged with coal dust.

'Meg, I need a bath and so does Uncle James. Then we need some sleep. Will you arrange another bunk somewhere for Uncle James? It doesn't matter what it costs. We'll just have to pay the price because there's no going back for either of us now.' Evan lay back and closed his eyes, exhaustion and pain sweeping over him. 'Can you . . . fix it?' he mumbled, asleep within seconds.

Meg tenderly straightened his legs out on the bunk. Uncle James also lay back but was not asleep.

'What happened? Will you tell me? What happened to Evan's leg?'

'I guess I'll have to leave the story to Evan. Where can I wash? I don't want to dirty the sheets. Then if I could just sleep for a while here . . .'

Meg nodded. 'If there's a bunk available you can move later. If not, I don't know what we'll do. There's a place to shower just along the corridor. I went to have a look earlier. Separate ones for men and women.' She added as an afterthought, 'I've never seen a shower before. And these electric lights,' Meg flicked the switch on and off, 'are truly wonderful.'

She left to find the purser's office. When she returned half an hour later she found the boys sitting outside the door waiting for her.

'They're both sleeping,' said Dai. 'Uncle James is in bed but Da's lying on the bed still dirty.'

Meg nodded absently. There was a bunk available in a two berth, second class cabin. The ship's officer had rudely told her that unless they paid for the cabin the passenger would be put ashore. It was over sixty pounds. She had argued and pleaded but to no avail.

'Dai, go and find me a bowl of warm water. Sion, come and help me undress Da. I want to wash him and put him into the bed. And listen boys,' she lowered her voice to a whisper, 'not a word to anyone about anything. Da's hurt his leg. If anybody asks, say you don't know what happened, understand? Not that you're likely to be asked, but just in case. I must be getting paranoid,' she mumbled.

'What was that, Mam?' asked Sion.

'Nothing. Come on.' In the cabin she began to undress her husband and gasped when she saw how bad the wound was. 'Sion put these clothes with Uncle James' in the corner.' She washed Evan as best she could and, using clean handkerchiefs she dressed his leg. Finally, she covered him with blankets from an upper bunk.

Meg listened to her sons talking about the ship. She was tired, not having slept all night, worrying about Evan. 'Boys,' she said, 'go and wander around the ship, but take care mind and don't go anywhere you're not supposed to. I'm going to sleep for a few hours. If you come back and we're still sleeping, please be quiet and don't call us for dinner.'

'Is Uncle James going to live with us now, Mam? I mean forever, like?' Sion's questions burst out of him.

'Like he said Sion, it looks like it. That's if you want

him to, of course.' She knew the answer and smiled at
the serious manner in which her son answered.

'Of course we want him to Mam. It's just I thought
he wasn't coming. Is that why Da went back? To fetch
Uncle James?'

'I don't know Sion, I suppose so.'

'What happened to Da's leg, Mam?' asked Dai with
a frown.

'I don't know that either. He hasn't told me yet. We'll
find out soon enough. Now off you go and remember what
I told you. If anybody asks you don't know anything.'

She climbed the ladder to the top bunk and lay down.
The gentle motion of the ship and the throb from the pro-
pellers lulled her and she slowly dropped off to sleep.

15

EVAN SLEPT SOLIDLY for thirty six hours. When he finally woke he lay still for a few moments to recollect his thoughts. With his returning memory, the ache in his leg seemed to get worse. When he tried to move Meg was right there beside him.

She smiled. 'Hullo, Evan bach, how're you feeling?' She held his hand tightly.

With an effort he smiled back. 'Fine,' he croaked, his voice a whisper. He cleared his throat and tried again. 'Fine love, but thirsty and hungry. What time is it?'

'Just after half past eight on Tuesday. I'll fetch some water and then go for some tea and something light to eat.' She suggested. 'I won't be a minute.'

She slipped out of the cabin and Evan eased himself on the bunk. He felt light headed and weak. He tried flexing his leg but it had stiffened and hurt badly. Meg returned with a jug of water. Greedily he drank three cups and then sank back. 'Ahhh, that's better, thanks love. I had a mouth like a chicken coop.' As Meg left the cabin he lay back, a sudden feeling of nausea sweeping through him. He was weaker than he had thought. He gave himself up to the gentle rolling of the ship. He dozed off. The next thing he was aware of was Meg seated on the edge of the bunk, a bowl and spoon in her hands.

'Sit up bach, if you can manage. I've got a bit of broth here for you and a nice omelette to follow. Can you manage?' she asked, concerned when Evan winced.

'Aye, I'll be all right in a couple of days. I just need some rest, that's all. Where's Uncle James?'

'I had to take a cabin for him in second class because that's all there was. He insists that as soon as you can move we're to have it and he'll come down here with the boys. I argued but he was adamant. Oh yes . . . you know that present he gave Sion for us and which we weren't to open until we got to sea?' She waited for Evan to nod. 'Well, it was fifty pounds.'

'What . . .' Evan spluttered, half choking on a mouthful of soup.

While he coughed, his eyes started watering and Meg ineffectively tried to thump his back. 'I thought that might surprise you,' she said with gleeful understatement. 'It shocked me too, I can tell you. It was nearly the cost of his cabin, so I suppose it's just as well.'

Evan had his breath back. 'Meg, could you promise me in future when you tell me something like that you'll at least wait until I've finished eating my soup?'

'Drinking soup . . . and does that apply to anything else, like tea?' She teased him.

'Anything I happen to be putting into my mouth at the time. But good Lord Meg, just think if he hadn't been with us. That must have been a hell of a lot of his savings. Why did he do such a thing?'

'He said something about not having much use for it for much longer. Oh, and he still has another little nest egg to live on.' She handed Evan the omelette. 'Now, tell me what happened,' she said anxiously. 'Uncle James wouldn't tell me; he said I had to wait for you.'

'I guess you've got a right to know,' he said quietly. In a voice devoid of expression he told her the whole story. Afterwards they sat in silence for a few seconds.

'Meg, when I thought I wasn't going to come back I knew none of it was worth the risk. Nothing is worth the worry I caused you nor the risk of never being able to hold you again.' He took her hand, 'I'm sorry.'

She smiled wanly, leaned forward and kissed him. 'I'm glad it was Uncle James and not you who killed Sir Clifford and I'll thank him for saving your life. I'm also glad Sir Clifford is dead. And, most importantly, I'm glad you're back with me because I was going frantic.' She saw his eyelids drooping and the effort he was making to stay awake. 'Go to sleep, Evan,' she said softly, and within seconds he was.

For most of the remainder of the week Evan stayed in his bunk. He found the shower room, and as it had been for Meg, it was the first time he had taken a shower. He was regaining his strength by leaps and bounds and by the Sunday he was fit enough to attend the service, taken by the Captain. Dai still refused to attend.

After the service Uncle James detained Meg and Evan in the saloon over a cup of tea while the boys slipped away.

'My God,' said Evan. 'Sorry,' he added, catching Meg's baleful stare, 'I forgot it was Sunday. I was going to say before I was interrupted by that look that just this voyage makes it all worth while. Who'd have thought it? All this, nice weather,' he waved his hand towards the blue sky outside, 'and a peace that I guess comes from . . . What does it come from?'

Meg laughed, 'You're impossible.'

Evan relaxed and stretched his legs out. The pain had subsided to a throb and irritating itch which he scratched absent mindedly.

Meg put her hand in his. She had not seen him looking so well in ages. Wales and the dangers of that last night were behind them, forgotten. At least, if not forgotten, then put aside, ignored and when they intruded pushed away again by a touch of the hand, a gentle squeeze.

'Have you decided what you're going to do when we get to America?' Uncle James asked. 'I'm not prying,' he added hastily, 'I just wondered.'

'Uncle James, ask as much as you like, you have every

right to,' answered Evan, 'and the answer is yes and no. I have an idea but I'm not too sure about it yet. David and Maud gave me the clue. In fact two clues. Would you like to hear what I have in mind?'

'Of course we would,' said Meg in some exasperation, pouring another cup of tea. 'We've been talking about it for months.'

'Well, the first thing is that business about borrowing money.' Seeing Uncle James' quizzical look he explained. 'It's simple. David dressed like a well-to-do merchant and persuaded the banks to lend him enough money to open a decent shop instead of the smaller one he would have ended up with if he didn't get a loan. The second point was what he said about warehouses and shipping stuff in and out – you know Meg, buying direct from the docks. He showed me his books and explained what he thought was going to happen. Of course, he hasn't been open long enough to know if his plans will work. But I think they will.' He paused to sip some tea. 'Meg, remember the book on America you brought home, all about the frontier towns? And how they're crying out for goods? . . . Well, that's the answer. If we can find a suitable place, I think preferably with a railroad, we set up a large shop or even . . . say a distribution centre sort of place. I guess it'll be a kind of warehouse to supply shops . . .'

'Hang on a minute, Evan bach,' interrupted Uncle James, 'don't get carried away. That takes a lot more money than we have at the moment or are even likely to have for a long time. Come out of the clouds boy,' he said not unkindly, 'and let's start with a shop.'

'Yes, Evan,' Meg added, 'we can start with a shop and see how it goes from there.' She frowned. She knew once Evan got an idea it took a lot to dislodge it.

'No, listen, both of you,' Evan continued. 'What if I go to more than one bank and get a lot of short term loans? Wasn't that what David called them?' Meg nodded. 'Right. I go to one and deposit some money . . .' he talked on for a while but could not persuade them it was worth trying.

Finally, though, Uncle James admitted: 'The decision has to be yours and yours alone,' which made Evan nod soberly.

Dai and Sion returned, both nodding to Uncle James and grinning hugely.

'Ah, well,' said Uncle James, stretching and faking a yawn, 'time for a nap I think. How about you two boys? Feeling tired?' Much to their parents surprise they both yawned and stretched too, aping Uncle James unconvincingly and said they were.

The three were about to leave when Uncle James stopped and reached into his pocket. 'By the way, you'd better take the key to your cabin. Dai, have you got ours?' He walked after the boys, grinning.

Meg and Evan were so taken off balance they had no time to protest. The key on the table was for Uncle James' second class cabin. The boys had been busy exchanging their parents belongings with Uncle James'.

'I forgot he said we were to change with him,' said Evan, thoughtfully fingering the key.

She laughed. 'You, Mr Griffiths are so transparent. Shall we go?'

Later they lay in each others arms, contented. Meg said softly: 'I love you, bach, do you know that?'

'Ah, I was beginning to suspect something but I suppose it's just as well because I happen to love you too.'

Evan fell into a doze; Meg was happy just to lie there, holding him.

Captain John Buchanan, master of the SS Cardiff, was sitting in his chair on the bridge. They were eleven days out from Cardiff and until a few moments earlier he had been a happy man. The voyage had gone well so far.

There were the usual ups and downs with the first class passengers – but that was only to be expected.

The ship was fitted with the latest Morse receiving and transmitting equipment and sometimes, like now when the weather report threatened storms, he wished he did not have it. All it did was add to his problems. Furthermore, the reports were often wrong. How could those on land a thousand miles away predict what the weather was going to do here, he thought? All right, so a front had passed over New York a few hours previously, heading in this direction. Anything could happen to it in the meantime. The glass was steady and the cloud of nimbo stratus was about what he would expect for the time of year. The breeze was freshening from the north west and backing slightly, but nothing to worry about, not yet at any rate. Still, it was better to be safe than sorry.

'Officer of the Watch, tell Mr Beddows to prepare the ship for bad weather. Nothing serious but batten down all hatches not in use and check all compartments.'

'Aye, aye, sir,' the young third officer replied.

What Captain John Buchanan did not know and had no way of knowing was the warm front the signal referred to had joined with an earlier cold one to give an occluded front. A depression was forming to the north west, twelve hours steaming ahead.

During the late afternoon the wind backed further and began blowing whitecaps, gusting to a wind strength of four to five on the Beaufort scale. It was far from dangerous but caused a beam sea. The ship began to roll in a manner which was exhilarating for those who were not seasick and downright unpleasant for those who were.

Evan and Sion took to their bunks after an early dinner. Meg, with a few words of sympathy placed a useful bucket in their cabins and went up on deck to watch the waves with Uncle James and Dai.

Shortly after sunset the upper deck was placed out of bounds to all passengers by the captain's orders. Less than ten percent of the passengers were not in their bunks and Meg was the only one of her family not feeling ill.

John Buchanan knocked the glass again. The pressure had fallen from 1010 millibars at 1200 midday to 981 at 2100 that evening. He had no need of a weather forecast to tell him they were in for a rough night. He had been at sea since he was fifteen and had served on everything from a trawler to a scabby coaster to this, the ultimate ship. He had run away as a lad to make a life of his own but had ended back in the family business with the only offer that could have attracted him – captain of the most luxurious liner in the world. He was not particularly worried because his senses told him the eye of the storm would pass far to the north and within twelve hours at most it would be behind them. He disliked bad weather because it upset the passengers, some acting as though he was to blame for their discomfort. Sod them all, he thought.

He stood at the front of the bridge peering into the black, rain-swept night, praying they would not meet another ship. He had doubled the lookouts and had one man in the forepeak who was changed every half an hour. The ship rolled heavily and he braced himself. She veered a point to starboard.

'Steady on the helm,' the captain said quietly. The greater the pressure the quieter he spoke. His crew had known him long enough to beware when he was in such a mood.

'Aye, aye, sir,' replied the helmsman, steadying the ship on her course of two five zero degrees. Another roll and the ship paid off half a point but the helmsman was ready for it this time and corrected quickly.

By 2230 hours there was a gale force eight on the beam and the ship was rolling heavily, though she was in no danger. It would be very uncomfortable, especially

for those in steerage, poor sods, thought Buchanan. But
if he turned to port to put the sea on the quarter he would
be late in New York, especially if the storm pushed him
a long way south. He would have to steam back north to
get to Boston . . . time, speed and distances went through
his head. The gale would make him late, and he hated the
thought but some things could not be helped.

'Come two points to port. Officer of the watch: plot
a new course and let me know our distance to go as of
eight o'clock in the morning. Call me in my cabin in a
little while. I'm going to do rounds myself. Also pass on
to your relief I want to be called if the glass drops more
than another two millibars.' It had been steady for nearly
an hour at 978. It looked as though the storm was already
abeam, sooner than he had expected.

He put on a sou'wester and went out onto the platform
on the port side of the bridge, known as the bridge wing.
There was no need for him to do rounds but he liked to
at times like this. It let the crew know he was about. Not
like some captains, he thought sourly.

He gripped hold of a stanchion as a wave crashed
over the deck, the spray adding its wetness to the rain
washing over him. If the truth were known he was
actually enjoying himself. He watched the waves for
a few minutes, gauging how his ship behaved and was
pleased with what he saw. There was not a break in
the clouds and the rain lashed down on his handsome,
upturned face. A streak of lightning lit the world for a
split second, showing the towering seas, now on their
starboard quarter.

He steadied himself climbing down from the bridge to
the deck below. Carefully he made his way forward, the
occasional wave which swept over the deck making the
wooden planks underfoot slippery and treacherous. Once
or twice he almost fell.

'Hullo, Jones,' he startled the lookout standing right in
the bow of the ship. 'It is Jones, isn't it?'

'Yes, sir,' cor'blimey, the ole man hisself. I'd heard he did things like this but I never would have believed it.

'Keep a good look out,' Buchanan yelled, the wind whipping his voice away and making it hard to be heard. 'Remember, you could save the lives of everybody on board and the ship too, by seeing if there's anything out there a few seconds before the bridge. Have you checked your voice pipe with the bridge recently?'

'Every time we change, sir,' yelled Jones.

'Good. Goodnight Jones,' Buchanan turned back, glad to duck from the stinging spray and sea.

Meg had been unable to sleep as the ship's motion became more exaggerated. She returned to the saloon, kneeling on one of the seats and peering into the darkness to enjoy watching the waves crash over the ship's side. There was something so raw and harsh about it, something frightening and exciting at the same time.

She felt the ship turn to port and immediately the rolling reduced. All in all it was a much more pleasant motion. A few minutes later she was about to leave the saloon when she saw a figure coming towards her. Suddenly the ship yawed unexpectedly and rolled heavily. Meg saw the man thrown off balance and fall against the saloon's bulkhead. She did not hear the crack of his head hitting the handrail nor did she see him get up again. She turned to run for help but the ship rolled again, throwing her back against the seat. She saw a wave sweep over the deck and the body washed into view. In horror she saw him slide towards the guard rails and just when she thought he would be lost overboard he jammed against one of the uprights supporting the rail. Instinctively, she knew the next wave would sweep him away before she could find help. For a few seconds she hesitated and then hurried to the door. She knocked her shins on tables and chairs, bumped her thigh painfully on something but at last reached the exit. She unlatched it to have it blown violently from her grasp. The rain and wind swept in and

Meg gasped at the sudden cold. Her heavy skirt, blouse and sweater were no protection against the weather.

She shuddered and stepped through the door onto the deck. The wind whipped at her clothes and legs, the deck so slippery she half fell a number of times, only saved from being hurt by grasping the handrail. With relief she saw the body only a matter of a few yards away. She gripped the railing tightly and stretched out her foot but could not touch him. She yelled at the inert form at the top of her voice but there was no response. She was terrified to let go of the handrail and frantically she thought what to do. The ship pitched again and the body slid six inches so the upright now held him at his chest and not his middle. Once more and he would be over the side. The movement decided her. When the ship steadied briefly she let go, dropped to her knees and crawled across the space. She grabbed him and tried to drag him away from the rail. She pulled with all her strength but it was no good. He was a big man and too heavy for her. Desperately, Meg tried again but achieved nothing. She was close to panic. The ship pitched and he moved another few inches. Panic welled up in her. She had no idea what to do. If she left to fetch help he would be gone before she could return. Oh, why hadn't she gone for help in the first place? She asked herself in anguish. She wanted to go now but it would be too much like running away. She had to try again.

Her hair was plastered to her face, she was soaked through and the cold was biting into her, sapping her strength. Suddenly the ship rolled to port, she grabbed him by the waist and heaved with all her might. Together they slid across the deck to the saloon bulkhead. Meg stretched up and grabbed the handrail above her head as the ship rolled heavily to starboard. The body underneath and the jerk of the movement was too much for her and the rail slipped from her grasp. Inexorably they slid towards the railing, Meg frantically trying to push the body back. Her foot was over the edge and still the ship was not coming out of the roll. She fell across the body, her knees slipping out from under her and together they slid under the guard rail.

Then hands. They grabbed her, held her hanging half over the side. The ship's roll stopped, started back the other way and she was lifted inboard. The three men helped drag the body to safety.

'It's all right now, miss,' First Mate Beddows yelled. 'You're safe now.'

When she realised the meaning of his words, Meg fainted.

She came to, surrounded by strange faces but in warm and pleasant surroundings. The seamen had carried the Captain into his bunk and Meg to the sofa in his day cabin. Somebody had wrapped a blanket around her and the First Mate held her propped up, administering brandy to her. She choked on the fiery spirit and pushed his hand away.

'Thank you,' she whispered and then found her voice. 'Thank you, but I'm all right now.' She sat up, cold, wet and feeling vulnerable beneath the stares of her rescuers. 'I must go and find my husband. How is the man I was trying to hold?'

'You don't know who it was?' asked one of the sailors, surprised; surly everybody knew the Captain?

'Eh, no,' Meg shook her head. 'I just saw him fall and eh . . . went to see if I could help. I didn't really get a good look at him.'

'I think, Madam,' the mate said solemnly, 'you should know that you saved the life of the ship's captain. We got to you just in time, thank God, but if you hadn't been there it's more than likely he would have been swept over the side.'

'Oh no,' Meg began to protest, 'he was so heavy. I hardly helped at all. I . . . .'

'It didn't look that way to us Madam,' said one of the men. 'It surely didn't'.

Meg shrugged. 'Will he be all right?'

'He'll be fine in the morning.' said the mate. 'He was knocked out and is still a bit groggy but he'll be all right after a night's sleep. Is there anything we can get you?'

'No,' Meg replied, throwing off the blanket and standing up. A wave of giddiness swept through her. 'I must go down to my husband.' The ship rolled and she fell against one of the men.

'Easy, Madam,' said the mate, taking her arm. 'Here, let me help you. Which cabin are you in?'

'I can manage, really I can, thank you. Please don't trouble.' The ship rolled again and Meg stumbled, admitting to herself she felt very unsteady.

'It's no trouble at all. Come on, now, which cabin is it?'

They had reached the cabin door when it flew open and Evan stepped out. He stopped in amazement when he saw Meg, white as chalk and soaking wet, being helped by one of the ship's officers.

16

EVAN TOOK HOLD of Meg, bracing himself against the bulkhead when the ship yawed. Meg was shivering uncontrollably. 'Meg, what on earth's happened? Are you all right?'

'Sir,' the First Mate answered, 'your wife saved the Captain's life a short while ago and very nearly lost her own while doing so.' He touched his cap in a half salute, amused at the amazement on Evan's face. 'I'll leave your wife to tell you all about it. If her story is as modest as the one I suspect she'll tell, then no doubt the rumours my crew are spreading will add a few more facts. Goodnight, sir. Goodnight, Madam and thank you once again.' He walked away, rolling easily with the ship's motion.

Evan came to his senses and quickly got Meg inside and onto her bunk. He undressed her, throwing her wet clothes into a corner.

He said almost brusquely, trying to hide the worry he had felt when he had woken and found her missing. 'Well, what happened?' He regretted it as soon as he spoke when he saw her eyes cloud with hurt. 'I'm sorry, love,' he leaned over and kissed her. 'I was getting worried, that's all. What are you smiling at?'

'You. Watching the concentration on your face as you undress me. Let me help.' A few seconds later she was under the blankets. Her body, Evan felt, was like marble and she had started to shiver again. He threw his own clothes on the other bunk and squeezed in beside her. The cabin had two bunks, one on either side of the door, two easy chairs, a small table, plenty of cupboard and drawer space and a wash hand basin.

They lay silently for a while, Meg's body gradually becoming warmer, her shivering stopping, her head nestled on Evan's shoulder.

'What happened?' he whispered.

She told him simply without really conveying the horror of the event, particularly the feeling she had had when she thought she was going to be swept overboard. She trembled at the memory. Evan squeezed her tighter and kissed her. He realised how close he had been to losing her.

'I don't know whether to . . . to,' he cleared his throat, his eyes misty, 'to tell you off for being so stupid for trying something like that or kiss you and tell you how brave you were. Which you were, incredibly so.'

'No, Cariad'- Meg lapsed into Welsh, 'I wasn't brave. I was terrified. But kiss me anyway.' She felt him stir against her thigh. 'I love you,' she whispered. 'Make me warm.'

He did. More poignantly, tenderly and at the climax with more urgency than either of them could remember.

They slept late and when they finally awoke were stiff and aching from having nowhere to turn, no room to stretch.

'We're getting too old for this,' Meg giggled to Evan who groaned when he moved his leg.

He smiled. 'I think you're right. Still, I've no complaints.'

Meg was about to reply when there was a knock on the door. Evan fell out of the bunk in his haste, wrapped a towel around himself and called: 'Come in.'

A steward stood in the doorway, a tray in his hands. 'Captain's compliments. I've been ordered to serve you breakfast.' He smiled at their surprise. 'I eh, took the liberty of asking your children what you'd like and they suggested this.' He raised the cover a few inches. 'If it's not to your satisfaction then I can change it.' He placed the tray on the table. There were fried eggs, bacon and kidneys, freshly squeezed orange juice, toast a pot of tea and one of coffee. 'Also the captain would be pleased if you could join him at twelve noon for a drink. Will that be satisfactory?'

'Eh? Yes, thank you,' Evan found his tongue. 'Tell the Captain we'll be eh . . . most happy em, to . . . .yes, thank you.'

'Thank you, sir,' the steward nodded his head and left.

Meg and Evan were too stunned to speak and before either could say anything the door burst open and Dai and Sion ran in. Uncle James stood in the doorway, a helpless expression on his face.

'Sorry, I couldn't keep them out,' he said.

'Calm down, boys,' Evan said, as both of them spoke at once. When they took no notice he said loudly: 'Quiet.' There was a sudden silence. 'Good, now I know you both want to know what's happened and you'll be told all in good time . . .'

'A sailor said Mam saved the Captain's life,' interrupted Sion.

'Yes and all the passengers keep looking at us and pointing,' added Dai.

'Both of you . . .' said Evan in a warning voice.

'Sorry,' they chorused.

'First of all what have I told you about barging into our room like that?'

'Sorry Da,' said Dai, eyes cast to the deck.

'Sorry Da,' mumbled Sion, doing likewise.

'All right, now if you'll both leave for a few minutes and give us time to dress then come back later – and this time knock.' They went meekly out the door, Evan winking at Uncle James over their heads.

Meg and Evan were half way through breakfast when there was a gentle knock at the door. 'Come in,' called

Evan, grinning at the demure look the boys had adopted, when he saw them.

Within seconds the look was gone and they talked nineteen to the dozen, finding out what happened. Around the ship the story made no mention of the fact Meg herself had been rescued just in time. The story being told was Meg had single handedly pulled the Captain from the edge of death back to the saloon. There were a few variations on the same theme, all adding to the confusion.

'Is it true we're going to the Captain's cabin?' Sion asked excitedly.

'Eh, no,' replied Evan. 'Sorry but it's just for me, Mam and Uncle James.'

'Awww, that's not fair. We never get to do things like grownups do,' Sion wailed. 'Why can't we come too?'

'Because the invitation was for drinks,' said Meg. 'But I'll tell you what. I'll ask if you can see the top of the ship. The . . . eh . . . what's it called?'

'Bridge,' her sons answered together.

With that they had to be content. When they had left, Evan noticed how much calmer the sea was now than it had been during the night. 'The storm must have passed us,' he said.

Meg frowned at him; she had not heard what he had said. She was holding her two best dresses. 'Which shall I wear?'

Evan shrugged and sat heavily on the arm of a chair. 'I don't want to go, Meg,' he said quietly.

Meg threw her dresses onto one of the bunks and knelt beside him. 'I know how you feel.' She took his hand and gently stroked the back of it. 'Are you thinking about all those people we've seen? . . . The way they dress? . . . And . . .' she trailed off.

Evan nodded. 'Aye, love. It's no good kidding ourselves is it? We come from a mining village up the valleys. In a few days we'll be in America, trying very hard to make a living. All this has been the sort of holiday we never dreamed we could have. We've had a nice cabin to ourselves instead of being down below where we belong. Hell,' he hated admitting what he believed . . . 'I'm a rough miner. What manners I've got are thanks to you. And I'm supposed to go up there and drink with the Captain? I like a pint of beer. What'll he say to that eh? Look at my hands. They're hard, rough and ingrained with coal. It'll take a lifetime to remove the black. For the first time in my life I'm ashamed of what I am and where I come from. Do you understand Meg? Aye, and frightened too, now we've left the village.' He reached out and caressed her hair. 'Don't cry, I'm sorry. I didn't mean to upset you . . . I'm sorry.'

Meg fought back her tears, her heart going out to him. 'I understand, Evan,' she took his hand and lifted it to her lips. 'But you shouldn't even think it. You're as good as any man on this ship and one day you'll be sitting down to dine with the best of them. You'll see. And in the meantime tell me what's more important. The boys and I and our lives together or what those people think? How many of them, for all their money, have our happiness? Our love?' She leaned forward and kissed his lips. 'I wouldn't change places with any of them for all the wealth in the world. Please believe that.'

He smiled wanly. 'Really Meg? Hearing you say it makes me realise I wouldn't change with any of them either.' He pulled her tightly into his arms and held her until his depressed mood lifted.

'Wear the black and white one,' he said unexpectedly.

It took Meg a few seconds to realise he was talking about her dress. 'Fine and you wear your grey suit, the new one.' She did not need to specify because it was the only one Evan owned.

The ship's bell was sounding twelve o'clock when they were shown into the Captain's day cabin by a smartly dressed, white-uniformed steward. 'Mr and Mrs Griffiths and Mr Price,' he announced and stepped to one side to allow them to pass.

Much to their surprise the Captain was alone in the cabin. As he came forward to shake Meg's hand she thought how distinguished he looked, with his brown wavy hair going grey at the temples and the cut and fit of his reefer jacket with the gold stripes on the sleeves. His smile was broad and friendly.

'I hope you don't mind me asking you here like this but it seemed the easiest way to say thank you.' He had a pleasant voice with no trace of an accent. Buchanan turned to Evan and shook his hand, his grip firm and dry.

'Mr Price, I'm pleased to meet you, too. My name's John Buchanan. Please call me John. I can't stand it when people call me Captain, especially over drinks. Now what can I get you? I'm going to have a beer. I drink enough of that other rubbish when I have to make conversation with the first class passengers.' He poured the drinks himself, guessing that the presence of a steward would probably have made them ill at ease; he was nothing if not considerate. Evan and Uncle James also took beers, Meg a sherry.

Buchanan raised his glass. 'I don't know how to say thank you to someone for saving my life, especially a lovely lady . . . eh . . . Damn me if I can't remember the speech I'd planned.'

'Just thank you is fine, if you must say something,' said Meg with a smile, 'and please forget it. I didn't really do that much. In fact if it hadn't been for your crew . . .'

'Oh, I know. The first mate told me. It still doesn't detract one iota from what you did. You saw me fall, I understand? And came directly out for me? Which means as close as we can tell you were out there over ten minutes holding on to me. That was quite some-thing.' He emptied his pot in one long draught. 'Ahh, that's better. That was for my thirst, the next is for me to enjoy. Drink up, there's plenty more where that came from.'

'How do you know how long it was?' asked Meg. 'It didn't seem that long to me.'

'Well, we know what time I left the bridge and went forward. I was there only a few minutes. The lookout in the bows used the voice pipe to tell the aft lookout that I was on the prowl. The officer of the watch had something to tell me and when I didn't return to my cabin he tried to find out where I was. He quickly established I had been forward but not aft and started a search. Luckily for us it was the second mate on watch who knew what to do. Someone junior might have been too nervous.'

Much to John Buchanan's surprise he enjoyed himself. When he had first learned where they were from he had expected a painful half hour trying to say thank you. Meg he found to be intelligent and well educated, Evan as intelligent and down to earth, and Uncle James very witty.

For their part they too were pleasantly surprised. Captain John Buchanan was an expert raconteur with a fund of personal experiences to relate and the one or two indelicate stories Meg chose not to understand, which fooled nobody.

Since he was enjoying the occasion, Buchanan had food sent in and when the planned emergency – to let him escape his guests if they proved as dull as he had expected – requiring his presence on the bridge came he told the mate to take care of it.

Meg asked if the children could be shown the bridge and Buchanan arranged for a midshipman to show them the whole ship, including the engine room and the steering compartment.

Sensing that the adults too would like to see around he said: 'Could you come up to the bridge at ten hundred tomorrow and if I'm not able to show you the ship then one of my other officers will?' They accepted with delight.

Just before they left Buchanan said unexpectedly, 'Can I ask a favour?'

They nodded.

'Please, I beg you not to take offence.' He hoped he was not about to hurt their feelings. 'In the first class dining room where I have to make an appearance, though by God if there's any excuse possible I try to stay away, we have to wear a black tie for dinner. Now, I know you proud Welshmen . . . but . . . well . . . I'd be honoured if you'd have dinner with me tonight.' They looked at him in surprise. 'The trouble is, even though I'm the Captain, I can't change that rule. Of course, we could eat early, like those who don't wish to change for dinner do, but that would defeat the object of my invitation. Now, please bear with me – I know I'm making a mess of this and for God's sake don't storm out in a dudgeon . . . But if I borrow suitable clothes for you to wear will you consider it?' He waited, unsure what their reaction would be. There was silence for a few moments. 'I'm sorry, I guess that was impertinent of me. I'd hoped I could've done something practical by way of saying thank you. I listened to your plans with interest and there's a man on board I would have liked you to meet. An American. I thought he could have done you some good.'

The three of them had seen the finery worn by the passengers in the first class dining room and it over-awed them.

'I'm not offended,' Evan said, 'and furthermore I'd be delighted. So would the others, wouldn't you?' His smile froze when he saw Meg's face. 'What's wrong Meg?'

She shook her head. 'You two go,' then she shrugged her shoulders. 'Captain Buchanan, I'm not ashamed to say I've nothing suitable to wear. And if you borrowed a dress for me from one of the lady passengers I guarantee the whole saloon will know before I've eaten the first course.'

John Buchanan laughed. 'I couldn't agree with you

more. If I promise you on all that I hold sacred, like my wallet and my ship that it won't happen, will you agree to come?'

Meg hesitated, about to say no, but then she changed her mind. 'If you can guarantee nobody will talk about me, then I'll come.'

'My dear Meg the whole blasted ship's talking about you. And by the end of the evening it'll be talking more. Evan, could you refill the glasses, please? I won't be a moment.' Buchanan went into his sleeping quarters.

'What do you think?' asked Evan. 'This could be the sort of opportunity . . .' he trailed off. 'On the other hand it may all be for nothing.'

'Let's do it,' said Meg. 'Just think of it. Eating with the Captain. And writing home to tell everyone . . . Why, they'll never believe it.'

'That's not like you, Meg,' said Uncle James.

'I know, but then I've never eaten with posh people before either. It'll be something to tell our grandchildren.'

The Captain returned, carrying a large box. 'Evan, with your permission I'd like to give this wee gift to Meg in . . . eh . . . appreciation for saving my life. Furthermore, provided Evan agrees, there's no returning it. It isn't a loan. All right, Evan?'

Evan nodded, as intrigued as the other two. With a slight bow Buchanan placed the box on Meg's knees.

She undid the large bow and lifted the lid, pushed the tissue paper aside and gasped. She saw the dress, held it by the top of the bodice and stood up, the box falling to the deck and the dress extending to its full length.

The dress was pale green, low cut, tight at the waist and trimmed at the neck with a deep green velvet ribbon which matched the sash at the waist. It was full from the waist down, sweeping to the ground.

'I . . . I don't know what to say,' she stammered, looking at Evan, worried how he would react. His face showed no emotion. Meg was sure he disliked the thought of a virtual stranger giving her such a gift.

'You'll look beautiful, my dear,' said Uncle James. 'Won't she, Evan?'

Evan suddenly smiled. 'The prettiest there.'

'Something else Meg, but this is only a loan,' said Buchanan. 'It belonged to my Grandmother. She left it to me to give to the woman I would someday marry.' He held up a pearl droplet on the end of a fine gold chain.

Meg gasped.

'It'll set the dress off beautifully,' said Buchanan, 'and with your black hair you'll look stunning.'

'I couldn't possibly . . .'

'Tch, tch of course you can. There's no point in going half dressed, and you will be without some suitable jewellery. By the way, don't think I always have a dress available to give to the first woman who saves my life. It was a gift for a woman in New York but it doesn't matter. She can wait until the next voyage.'

'Are you really going to eat with the Captain?' Sion asked, watching Uncle James pull on a pair of black trousers. The boys had spent all afternoon being shown around the ship and had returned in time to go for supper, alone. After the meal when they returned to the cabin they had found Uncle James putting on a funny black suit, one they had not seen before.

There was a knock on the door.

'Excuse me, sir,' said the steward, 'Captain's compliments but I've come to help you dress.' He took the bow tie Uncle James was fumbling with and deftly knotted it.

'Thank you,' said Uncle James with dignity, 'and thank the Captain for me as well . . . Sion, where do you think you're going?'

'I was just going to see Mam and Da, that's all,' the little boy frowned.

'I've told you to wait here. They'll be along in a minute,

look you.' He turned to the steward. I'll manage now.
Could you go and help Mr Griffiths, please?'

'He didn't need me sir. Mrs Griffiths looked after him.
If that will be all, sir?' he left with a wink at the boys.

Uncle James was admiring himself in the mirror and
regretting it wasn't full length when the door opened and
Meg and Evan stepped in.

The boys looked at them with their mouths open. Meg
was beautiful, the dress complementing her black hair
and full figure as though it had been made for her. Evan
was very dashing in his dinner jacket, borrowed from the
first mate.

'Gosh, Mam,' said Sion, jumping up from the bunk
and hugging her. 'You look . . . you look . . . gosh . . .
Mam . . .'

They laughed. 'I know exactly what you mean son,'
said Evan, 'I couldn't have put it better myself. Although
perhaps beautiful would have been a suitable word.'

'You'll be the most beautiful lady there,' said Dai.
'Gosh, I wish I was going too.'

'You will one day, Dai,' said Evan, tousling his hair.
'When you're a bit older. 'Ready, Uncle James?'

'As ready as I'll ever be. I hope I don't disgrace you,'
he said nervously.

'You won't,' replied Meg with an assurance she did
not feel. It wasn't that she thought Uncle James would
disgrace them any more than she or Evan; no, certainly not.

They met the captain in his cabin and after he had com-
plimented them on their appearance, he poured whiskies
for the men, a sherry for Meg.

John Buchanan was a master at putting people at their
ease. In his lavish quarters he soon had them laughing
and joking, banishing their nervousness for the moment.
He drained his glass: 'Shall we go? It's time to eat.'
Nervously the three of them nodded.

The captain led the way into the saloon. It was

brilliantly lit with a low slung chandelier, more appropriate in a ball room than on a ship. Inside the talk was
muted, the chink of cutlery and glasses a pleasant sound
against the background throb of the ship. The sea was
calm and the ship's movement barely perceptible. The
saloon was richly carpeted and the scattered round tables
were covered by starched white cloths. Everyone wore
evening dress and every diner cast more than one glance
in their direction. The passengers realised who they were
but none had expected to see such an attractive couple as
Meg and Evan.

'Meg,' said John Buchanan as they arrived at his
table, 'this is Senator George Hughes, a Welshman from
way back.'

The Senator shook Meg's hand. 'Pleased to meet you
ma'am. I've been visiting the old country for a couple
of weeks. My grandpappy was born near Cardiff there
somewheres, though I never did rightly place where
exactly.'

Meg tried not to recoil at the touch of his soft, sweaty
hand, and instead smiled sweetly at the short, fat man.
He was in his sixties and nearly bald; he had developed
a habit of rubbing his hand across his head, as though
to assure himself his hair was really gone or maybe, by
some miracle, had returned.

There were smiles and handshakes all round. The
Senator's wife, Mabel, was as fat as her husband, tall,
with half her bosom showing. She wore a ring on the
four fingers of each hand and a diamond pendant nestled
between her breasts like a winking eye in a sea of flesh.
For all her gaudiness she was a warm-hearted, friendly
person who, throughout the dinner, did her best to put
Meg at her ease.

Among the other passengers was Miss Gloria Johnson,
twenty, pretty in a brittle sort of way with sharp features
and a mouth showing only scorn or distaste. Her elegant
clothes made her appear more attractive than she really

was. Her father was Eric Johnson, a hard faced, distinguished looking and shrewd man. He was a successful
banker whose wife had committed suicide when Gloria
was twelve.

Another guest, sitting between Gloria and the Senator was Mrs Annette Brandon. She was thirty eight
but let it slip she was thirty two, divorced from a
multi-millionaire twenty years older, who had settled a
generous alimony on her.

Captain Buchanan smiled inwardly as he eyed his
guests, knowing what to expect. He wondered how Meg
and Evan would make out. Uncle James did not count
under the circumstances. No, if they did well then there
was a possibility Eric Johnson might be of some help
to Evan. Evan might have only been a miner, thought
Buchanan, but if I'm any judge of character he's a clever
son of a bitch. Especially with Meg beside him, he'll go
far . . . and a nudge from me won't hurt, he told himself.
I like them and I'll enjoy trying to help; Goddam it, they
are the sort of people I'd like to call friends. He kept his
face bland, not showing his feelings. He signalled for the
steward to commence serving the soup and sighed.

'That's a very pretty dress,' said Gloria to Meg. 'I'm
sorry my dear, I forget your name.' Her tone was con-
descending.

'It's Meg . . . so sorry but what's yours again?'

'Gloria,' she smiled sweetly. 'Surely it isn't possible
to buy a creation like that in Cardiff, never mind the
backwater you come from – is it? I always get mine from
Paris,' she added haughtily, ignoring her father who was
glaring across the table at her.

Meg was flustered for a moment, but then understood
what the evening was going to be about. Suddenly she was
enjoying herself. She no longer felt she was an outsider
from a lower level, but an outsider to give as good as she
got and damn the consequences. She hoped she would
never see these people again, so she prepared herself for

a battle of words. Meg smiled dazzlingly. 'Actually, it's the creation of a London couturier, Lord's to be precise.' The label had told her that much.

John Buchanan bent his head to hide a smile while Evan was trying hard to keep a straight face.

'I wouldn't have thought it possible, would you, Annette?' Gloria turned to her left. 'Only Paris surely could have made such a divine dress.'

Before Annette Brandon could answer Mabel Hughes broke in, angered that this chit of a girl could be so rude as almost to call Meg a liar. 'Oh, but it's more than possible. England still produces some of the finest clothes in the world.' God this is ridiculous, she thought, and went on the attack. 'Obviously your dress isn't from Paris my dear. No self respecting fashion house would have produced it.' She turned to Annette Brandon. 'What were you doing in Wales?' Although they had seen each other in the saloon and at various social events they had not met before except to exchange pleasantries.

'Oh, one doesn't do anything in such a country,' Annette replied sweetly, 'one just passes through. In my case I'd heard so much about this divine ship I travelled down from London to catch it.'

While the women bickered the men tried to ignore them and talk together. Senator Johnson, sitting on Evan's left, turned to Evan and said: 'Are you emigrating to America, Mr Griffiths or visiting?'

'Emigrating. We hope to make our home there, though where exactly . . .' Evan shrugged. 'I'm still open to suggestions.'

'You were a miner in Wales, weren't you?' The Senator leaned across the table. Before Evan could reply he went on: 'Do you intend to do the same work in the States, Mr Griffiths?'

Evan smiled coldly. John Buchanan had warned him they would ask him about his past and his ambitions. Now he was going to try out the Captain's advice. 'No,

I'm not. I have an inheritance I intend investing in a business.'

Uncle James was sitting between Johnson and Mabel Hughes, a picture of misery. His collar was too tight, the wine was not to his liking and at that moment he would have given anything to have a large plate of fish and chips and a pint of best bitter.

'Let me tell you,' said the banker, 'that if you're open to suggestions then New York is the place to make money. Yes sirree! The stock exchange there is surely booming. Why in twenty years time we'll be the most powerful nation on earth. We have the resources, the room and the people.'

They plunged into a political and economic discussion which lasted the remainder of the meal. Evan thanked God that Meg had taught him so much. He smiled across at her and she smiled warmly back. Who would have thought this possible? he said to himself, allowing his attention to wander for a few seconds. Here we are in luxury and only thirteen days ago I had been cold, hurt and on the back of a coal truck. He concentrated on what the Senator was saying.

If Meg, Evan or Uncle James made any faux pas while eating nobody noticed. Evan copied John Buchanan, noting what knife and fork he used and drinking the same wine with each course.

On land, the ladies would have left the table before the port was passed, but at sea this convention was relaxed and the ladies remained. The table was cleared and the port was going round for the second time when the steward handed a sealed message to Buchanan. Opening it he read quickly, looked at Evan for a moment and excused himself, promising to return as soon as possible. In his cabin he poured a large whisky and took a mouthful. Then he re-read the message again.

*HOLD THE GRIFFITHS FAMILY AND
ANYONE TRAVELLING WITH THEM STOP
POLICE WILL MEET IN BOSTON STOP THEY
WILL PROBABLY REMAIN ON BOARD AND
RETURN WITH YOU TO CARDIFF STOP
HILLSOME*

17

THE FIRST THING John Buchanan did was go to the radio room, a small cubby-hole situated behind the bridge. The equipment was the latest in communications a basic Morse transmitting and receiving set. He tried to ignore the pungent atmosphere from too many cigarettes smoked in the confined space.

'I want you to send the following,' he said to the operator. 'To Captain Hillsome at head office. Regret nobody of that name on board stop confirm the name is Griffiths stop signed Buchanan.' He stepped out onto the open deck, grateful for the fresh air. He was taking a gamble. Not with Evan and Meg, oh no. He owed his life to Meg and he was damned aware of it. He was going to help her and the others as much as he could. No, the gamble was the radioman. If he told him to say nothing Buchanan was sure the message would be around the crew in less than twenty four hours.

The biggest problem was the purser, but he also knew how to handle him. He knocked on the purser's cabin door. After a few moments a sleepy, grumbling voice answered. 'All right, all right, I'm coming.'

Whatever else the man said was indistinguishable but Buchanan had no doubt as to its contents. The door flew open, the purser started and began apologising.

'I thought it was one of the stewards come to fetch me to sort out a complaining passenger. Come in, please.' He stepped back, to let the captain past. His mind was working frantically. Whatever it was had to be important.

In fact, very important to bring the captain down to him.
Normally he was summoned to the captain, wherever he
happened to be. He pulled his dressing gown tighter and
indicated a chair for his uninvited guest to sit on.

'I'll stand, thank you Mr. Green. Would you like to
start dressing while we talk? You and I have some work
to do.' He saw the man's surprise. 'Don't worry, it's
not difficult nor particularly time consuming.' Buchanan
paused, studying the man before him. 'I've come for a
favour. I'm asking it politely, but if I need to I can enforce
it.' The purser became wary. He was always happy to do
the captain a favour. The more the merrier, provided it
cost nothing.

'There's no need to enforce anything, sir. I'll be happy
to do it,' he said, reaching for his trousers.

'Clive, what I'm asking for is very unusual. I want
your promise,' which is worthless, he thought, 'not to
say anything to anyone about this. All right?'

'About what?' The purser was both intrigued and
wary.

'Just give me your word that you'll help and I'll tell
you what we need to do. I'll explain the reason later.'

Green nodded and smiled. What the devil was the
captain up to? 'I give you my word,' he said, holding
out his hand.

Without hesitating John Buchanan shook it, not allowing the distaste he felt show on his face or in his actions.
'I want all record of the Griffiths family having been on
board removed immediately.'

The Purser looked at his Captain open mouthed.
'But . . . but that's impossible,' he spluttered. 'How on
earth am I to do that? And anyway, what's the point?'

'You'll do it in the same way you always do when you
pocket the excess fares,' he was gratified to see the man
blanch. 'Furthermore, you'll repay that cabin fare the old
man paid. Make any excuse you like.'

Sixty pounds was sixty pounds and the purser did not

intend giving it up without a fight. 'I can't do that, sir. It's already gone on the books. I can't see how . . .'

'I can.' After years of dealing with sailors Buchanan knew how to deal with Green. 'Now listen to me. I've to get back to my dinner guests soon, they'll be wondering where I am. In fact I won't come and help you – you just do as I tell you.' He took out his note book. 'Let me give you a run down of what you did last voyage. You threw overboard three hundredweight of fruit which was fresh and nowhere near as rotten as you claimed. You removed three passengers from your ledger . . .' as he read the man shrank away, and Buchanan knew he had him. 'I won't go on, Clive.' He snapped the book closed. 'I'll tell you what I want done and why. In that way you'll be ready. If you don't back me up one hundred percent, by God I promise you I'll have you put away for ten years. Now listen carefully.'

Five minutes later, completely satisfied, Buchanan left the purser's office and returned to the saloon. His guests were waiting, still apparently enjoying themselves.

'Sorry I was so long, ship's business. You know how it is.' They chorused they did. He smiled at Evan and Meg. He was not going to ruin the rest of their time on board. He would talk to them the night before they docked.

The rest of the voyage passed uneventfully, and on the last night the captain invited Meg and Evan to his cabin. On this occasion Uncle James had stayed with the boys. 'Take a seat while I pour some drinks. I asked you to come here because I've got something important to tell you.' He handed a beer to Evan and a sherry to Meg. 'I've eh, got a wee bit of news, bad news, I'm afraid.' He saw them exchange worried looks and wondered if they had been expecting something. I suppose if the police want you badly enough then you always know it, he mused. Meg's hand gripped Evan's tightly.

'I can see you know what I'm talking about. Now listen, you don't have to tell me what happened if you don't want to. I'd like to know, but it's up to you. Before you say anything I'll tell you what I've arranged so far and what I propose.' He explained his ideas.

When he was finished Meg leaped to her feet and threw her arms around Buchanan, hugging him. 'John, we can't thank you enough,' she felt her eyes misting. 'Damn,' she said and reached for a handkerchief.

'That's all right. Don't give it another thought. I'm glad to do it,' he tried to keep his thoughts on the business at hand, not dwell on the feeling of Meg's body against him.

'Will you tell me what happened?' He looked from one to the other. There was a few moments silence. 'Okay, if you don't want to,' he said, disappointed. He had hoped they would trust him enough.

'Hold on, bach. I was just collecting my thoughts. After what you've done for us and what you still intend doing the least I can do is tell you what happened. It's a long story and all started with the death of our daughter. She was Sion's twin. A lovely girl . . .' Evan told the story, allowing his emotions to show.

'That's when we arrived at the ship.'

'Good Lord, I hadn't realised it was you and James on the gangway. Of course, I can see that now. So much happened after we left the wharf that I didn't have time to find out what it had been about. Well, well, well,' he thought for a moment. 'We'll be in the New York Roads tonight,' seeing their puzzled expressions he explained. 'The Roads are where we wait to enter harbour. Sometimes we anchor, sometimes the delay is so short there's no need. I normally eat in my cabin then as I frequently get called to the bridge. How would it be if you both came with James for a bite to eat and we'll go over my ideas to get you off the ship?'

'Tell me, John,' Evan said quietly, 'why are you

doing all this? Don't get me wrong, look you, we both appreciate it. Its just that I just can't help wondering. After all, we've only just met and, no matter how I look at us, I still see a Welsh peasant family.' The last was said with a touch of bitterness. Evan had heard what some of the first class passengers had to say about them and it angered him. It was thanks to Mabel Hughes he had not been rude to some of them, and more than once. Using the first class lounge and saloon had become a regular part of their lives since their first dinner; the captain had invited them to do so.

John Buchanan shrugged. 'You mean apart from the fact that I owe my life to Meg? I also happen to like you . . . and James and the kids. If ever I'd married they would have been the sort of kids I'd have liked. Especially that Sion,' he chuckled. 'He's a little son of a gun and no mistake. I consider you my friends, I hope you consider me likewise. And what are friends for if not to help one another? Hey? Now enough of this talk. I'm going to get you off the ship and safely into America or my name isn't John Buchanan.'

'Thanks. It sounds inadequate . . .' Evan trailed off.

'John, how is it we're going to New York first and not to Boston?' asked Meg.

'Hmm, it's to get you away without the police getting to you.'

'But surely you can't do that sort of thing,' Evan protested.

'Oh, I can. You'd be surprised how much freedom I've got. It's meant I've had to take my purser into my confidence but he'll do what I tell him. And the storm gave me a good excuse to make for New York. It did blow us further south than normal but we had enough time in hand to keep to the schedule. In future I can claim that if I am going to maintain sailing dates, I need to miss out Boston. I delayed sending a message until tonight; that way the police won't have time to get here. I'll stop over an extra two days to give passengers plenty of time to arrive by train and arrive back in Cardiff on time. We've had to do it before, though not with this ship.'

'In that case . . .' began Meg.

'In that case nothing,' the captain interrupted her. 'This way, we take no chances. Right?'

They docked just before noon. There had been great excitement when, in the dawning light, they had stood on the upper deck, with many of the other passengers, and saw the lights of America for the first time. Meg had put her arms around Evan and said: 'What are you thinking, boyo? You look too serious for such an important day in our lives.'

He grinned down at her, her head nestled against his shoulder.

'I was just thinking that there's the land of the free and pretty soon we might not be . . . free that is.'

'Don't worry, as John said, he knows the routines here inside out and backwards. He's confident he can get us through.'

'What about us then being illegally in the country? Oh, I know what he said about it not mattering, especially as we don't wish to leave for many a year, but you never know when we'll be asked to show our papers. I guess I'm just being a pessimist, which is all wrong on such a beautiful day.' There was a warmth to the gentle breeze, the sun now a diameter above the horizon.

'Gosh, Mam, look,' pointed Sion. 'Aren't those buildings tall? Are they the biggest in the world Mam, do you think?'

'I don't think,' she smiled, 'I know. They are among the biggest and no mistake.'

'Well, Dai,' said his father, turning to his older son, 'how does it feel to have part of your dream come true, eh? I bet you never thought a year ago you'd actually make it, did you?'

Dai's grin was so wide it threatened to split his face in two.

'I wish Sian could have been here now,' said Sion sadly. Meg knelt by his side, her arm around his shoulders.

'We all do, Sion. She probably is here you know, looking down at us, making sure all is well, just like Mr. Thomas, the minister said.'

He nodded and smiled again. 'I guess that's right Mam. Otherwise he wouldn't have said it, would he?'

'No, he wouldn't have, and that's a fact,' Uncle James chipped in. 'Come on, let's try and spot the highest building.'

Sion and Dai followed him further towards the bow of the ship.

'Thank God for Uncle James,' Evan said with feeling.

The labels on their luggage had been changed to show John Buchanan's name and addressed to the Chelsea Hotel on 23rd Street. 'It's eight years old and in the centre of the city's theatrical life. Anybody who's anybody ends up there,' John Buchanan had said. 'I'll be there for the night. Now you both know what to do? I have to get about my duties. I'll leave the rest to you and we'll meet at the foot of the gangway.'

Uncle James and the boys wandered back.

'Now listen carefully,' said Evan. 'We can't go ashore like the other passengers, we have to go on our own. Understand?'

They didn't, but they nodded anyway.

'Now, we want you both to be brave. When all the passengers are in the shed I want you to follow and just play around. You know, cowboys and Indians or something. Just run around. Don't dash straight through the door on the other side, just make your way through the crowd and past the eh . . . men in uniforms who will be behind the counters. If anybody asks who you are point behind you as though we're following.'

'But why, Da?' asked Dai

Evan tousled his hair. 'I'll tell you one day son.'

'But where will you and Mam be?' Sion asked, putting his arms around Meg's legs, panic in his voice. 'Aren't you coming too?'

'Of course we are,' Meg knelt by his side. 'Of course we are. We'll be coming through a different entrance with John.'

'The Captain?' asked Sion.

'Yes,' replied Evan. 'Now listen, you don't have to be worried. When you get through the gate, wait there and Mam will come and get you.' Evan had a thought. 'We'll be about fifteen minutes after you so here, Dai,' he handed his watch to his son. 'If we aren't there after a quarter of an hour, wait another quarter. After that come back to the ship.' Because we won't be going anywhere, he thought.

Dai was speechless and Sion looked at the watch with big eyes. Dai clicked open the solid gold cover and gazed at the Roman numerals. Evan had inherited it from his grandfather some ten years earlier, complete with its gold chain. Seeing it now was all Evan's sons needed to have their confidence restored.

'Come on, let's go for a last cup of tea before we go ashore,' suggested Meg.

Uncle James was already in the saloon. 'I always drink tea when I'm nervous,' he said, 'and this morning I've had eight cups already.'

An hour later the passengers began to disembark.

'Away you go, boys,' said Evan. 'And don't forget what I told you, right, Dai? Sion, you do as Dai tells you , there's a good boy. And we'll see you shortly.'

They both nodded, hesitant about leaving the ship.

'You've got my watch safe?' Reassured they went down the gangway quickly and onto American soil, disappearing through the doorway into the customs shed.

Evan slipped a Steward's white coat on over his grey suit. Meg went below to change.

Evan helped Uncle James to walk down the gangway

as though each step would be the old man's last. He helped Uncle James to stand and lean against the rail; he returned on board for the wheelchair Buchanan had supplied; took it down to the end of the gangplank and settled Uncle James in it, a blanket over his legs. The chair had belonged to an elderly man coming to visit his son in America with his wife. He had died the day before they had landed.

Meg returned, wearing an ill fitting nurse's uniform, one of many uniforms kept for the fancy dress parties sometimes held on board.

They all waited nervously at the foot of the gangway for the captain. It was a few minutes before he arrived; they kept their heads bent and backs to the ship in case they were recognised.

'Sorry. I had a wee problem to sort out. It's okay now so follow me.' Instead of going the way the rest of the passengers had gone, Buchanan led them to a side door, the door the ship's personnel went through, down a short corridor and through a screened-off part of the hall. Here, only a customs officer and no immigration personnel waited.

The customs officer looked up inquiringly as they appeared, Meg pushing the chair and Evan walking by Uncle James' side. Buchanan was recognised and the custom's officer got to his feet, more out of politeness than for any official reason.

Meg's heart missed a beat.

'Hullo,' said Buchanan with a beaming smile, 'Dick isn't it?' He shook the official's hand and waved the others past him.

'Michael, sir,' replied the man woodenly.

'Oh, silly of me, of course, I remember now. I'm just taking one of my older Stewards into the hospital,' he lowered his voice. 'Poor fellow collapsed this morning.' He turned to Evan, hesitating near the door. 'Come on, doctor, what are you waiting for?' he asked irritably.

'Yes, sir,' replied Evan, hurrying through the door, following Meg.

'The trouble with the doctors on any ship,' said Buchanan in a conspiratorial tone, 'is that they're so damned inefficient. I wouldn't trust this blighter further than I could throw him, that's why I have to go with them. That blasted nurse isn't much better either. Know what I mean?'

'I sure do, sir. Mind you, with a face like that who wants efficiency? I bet she looks after the doctor all right.'

Buchanan smiled and hurried away. Outside Meg had already gone to find the boys and would take a cab to the hotel. The three men trundled down the road for a few minutes, waved down an American type hansom and the three of them climbed inside. They tied the chair on the back and set off for nearest hospital where they paid off the cabbie.

'A contribution to the place,' said Buchanan, 'provided nobody steals it first.' He put the chair neatly against the wall next to the entrance.

A few minutes later they were on their way again. This time Evan was able to relax and take in his surroundings. The buildings were bigger than he had imagined, the streets wider and full of horse-drawn carriages, and everywhere was bustle. The excitement of the place took hold of him and doubts he had about the wisdom of pulling up roots and coming to America suddenly left him.

It was said to be the land of opportunity, and by God he was going to look for his. Everything was looking good, and would stay that way if they managed to get out of New York without being stopped by the police. He had finally made up his mind where they were going and what they were going to do.

'You know it's just as well we came ashore the way we did,' said Uncle James suddenly. 'I never had a passport.'

18

THEY TOOK THE train from New York that evening. John Buchanan saw them off; the farewell was a sad one. He extracted a promise from Meg that as soon as they were settled she would write. The money repaid by the purser enabled them to take seats in the second class section instead of in the rear in third where it was packed and the aisles were jammed with families en route for Pittsburgh and the mines. They settled down as well as they could on the hard seats for the two day journey; the first stage to their destination.

They spent a fitful night, the train stopping and starting at various stations along the line. Newark and Reading were behind them when dawn broke. The day, like the land, stretched interminably before them. They played word games, even Uncle James joining in, watched the scenery unfold and often commented on how few towns or villages they saw.

At long last Pittsburgh came into view. Evan was disappointed though not surprised that the capital of American mining was as smoke ridden, dirty and ugly as the towns back in South Wales.

The station was big and crowded, people bustled back and forth, loads of goods were pulled and pushed around the platforms. The noise of talking, laughing and weeping, intermingled with the sounds of the trains made it another Bedlam. With relief they found their train, transferred their trunks, and an hour later were on the way to St. Louis, four days away – if all went well.

After the mountains of Pittsburgh they were on a plain that seemed never-ending. Meg had replenished her stock of food at Pittsburgh; hot water boiled on the stove situated at one end of each carriage ensured they could drink plenty of tea and coffee, a drink Evan in particular had come to like. They passed mile after mile of wheat growing areas and occasionally large herds of cattle.

Meg noticed that the further west they went the more men she saw wearing guns, and soon the exception was the man without one. Evan was beginning to wish that he too, was armed. Then he grinned ruefully and thought he was more likely to shoot his foot off than hit anybody else with it; unless he threw it at them.

After Indianapolis they passed through Terre Haute and a day later they were at their final destination – St Louis – the gateway to the West. Their fatigue fell from them like a discarded coat when they stepped down from the train.

'First, we need a boarding house and a bath,' announced Meg, watching the boys anxiously as they wandered off to look at a group of cowboys sitting astride their horses half way along the train.

Evan felt excitement course through him. Much of the journey had been taken up with making plans. Buchanan had given Evan the name of a local banker and when he was asked if he knew all the bankers in America, Buchanan had grinned and replied: 'Only the useful ones, Evan, only the useful ones.'

'Remember,' he had said, 'shit baffles brains every time. You have to have the correct approach. If he thinks he's dealing with a poor man then you won't get anywhere. If he thinks you're rich then he'll fall over himself to give you money. And whatever interest he asks for argue until you get it down to six percent per annum on a loan of three years and one percent per month on a short loan.'

They had talked a great deal about finance during the

latter part of the voyage. All Evan had learned had excited him more than he cared to admit.

Meg called the boys and they ran back to help with the luggage. Evan eventually managed to hire a buckboard and soon they were entering the sprawling town. The roads were just dirt tracks, rutted and packed by wagon wheels and horses' hooves. The buildings were mostly wooden, but important places like the banks, some hotels, the opera house and an occasional private house were built of brick. All the old wooden houses were being torn down and new brick buildings erected in their place. There were people everywhere, the men armed with low slung guns, the women wearing gay bonnets or carrying gaudy parasols.

It was the beginning of April. The sky was cloudless and blue, the slight breeze refreshing. The boys sat on the back of the buckboard, their legs dangling over the end, while the other three walked, glad of the exercise.

Behind the main street they found what they were looking for. A small boarding house, clean and willing to take a family for as long as they wanted. The rent was ten dollars a week paid in advance.

For the next few days they wandered round the town, getting their bearings and familiarising themselves with the place. The boys went their own way. Meg had worried about them at first but, as Evan pointed out, she could not keep them tied to her apron strings.

The town was situated where the Mississippi and Missouri rivers met. From there the boats and barges went north to Minneapolis on the Mississippi and west to Kansas City on the Missouri. The main stream of the Mississippi ran south to New Orleans in the state of Louisiana, fed by dozens of main tributaries and hundreds of smaller ones. Trade, up and down the rivers, was booming and Evan intended to have a part of that trade soon – very soon.

A week after they had arrived Evan and Meg were

sitting on the back porch after supper enjoying the cool, cloudless, star bright night. The bamboo seats were uncomfortable and worn but neither of them noticed.

'I think the day after tomorrow I'd better start,' Evan broke the peaceful silence between them.

Meg looked at him sharply. 'I suppose so,' she leaned back with a sigh. 'I only hope you know what you're doing.' Before he could protest she continued. 'Sorry, I didn't mean it like that. No, it's a good idea. It's a huge gamble but, with just a little luck it might pay off.' Suddenly she chuckled. 'I've got faith in you, boyo,' she leaned over and kissed him, her voice dropping to a whisper. 'All the faith in the world. But I can't help being nervous about it. That's only natural, after all.'

'I know how you feel love, believe me. Beneath this calm exterior is a stomach that's churning like a bag of butterflies and a heart that's beating like . . . like . . . I don't know what,' he finished lamely.

The door onto the porch swung open and the landlord came out. Without a glance in their direction he made his way through the back yard and out through the gate. He was on his way to the local saloon, where he went every night.

Evan chuckled. 'No wonder he drinks so much. With a wife like his I'd be surprised if they even consummated the marriage.'

'Oh, Evan,' Meg laughed. 'that's very unkind. Shall we go to bed? I know it squeaks but I have an idea. Come on.'

The boys had gone to bed much earlier and Uncle James was out, looking at the night life of the town. When Meg had protested, worried about the danger, he had replied, 'Meg, I'm an old man. I've hardly been out of the valleys all my life and now here I am on the biggest adventure . . . no . . . A bigger adventure than I ever imagined, even in my wildest dreams. I'm grateful to you and Evan. The trouble is I'm not likely to be here long enough to enjoy it all. So I'm going to make the most of it. Don't worry, I'll only be looking. When you've had as much practice as I have it becomes easy to make a beer last all evening. I won't be late,' had been his parting words.

Meg and Evan were glad of their early night.

Evan waited for the train to stop, saw some of the passengers disembarking and walked out of the front of the station as though he had just arrived. He wore his best suit, a leather holdall in his hand and a western style hat on his head. The clothes he wore helped to establish him as a businessman, a successful businessman at that. He walked down the main street to the Lucky River, the best hotel in town.

He went through the large double doors, crossed the carpeted hall to the reception desk and waited nervously for the clerk to finish dealing with some new arrivals. The place was opulent in every sense of the word. Evan had eleven hundred dollars in his pocket, most of the money they had left. John Buchanan had told him that he must create the right impression; from the hotel room to the leather bag.

With sweating palms and hammering heart he said to the clerk, 'My name's Griffiths. I sent a telegram two days ago reserving a room for two nights,' he lied.

The clerk checked his register. 'I'm sorry sir, we don't seem to have your booking. However, we've just had a cancellation and can give you a single room. Unfortunately, it's in the back. All our best rooms are taken. Will that be suitable, sir?'

'That's a nuisance, but I suppose it'll have to do,' Evan resumed his role. 'Have my bag sent up and tell me where the First Bank of Mississippi is situated, please.'

Walking towards the town centre Evan thought that it

had been easy enough to fool a hotel clerk, but what about a bank manager?

He nodded to the armed guard standing just inside the door. Along the left, running most of the length of the building was the counter behind which, protected by iron bars, were the tellers. At the far end of the room to the right was a partitioned off area in which sat an assistant manager. Behind him were two doors. The one on the left was to the manager in charge of loans, the other to the bank's general manager. Evan wanted to get through the door on the left.

There was nobody with the assistant manager and when Evan reached the thigh high swing door he removed his hat and waited politely for the man to look up. He did so a moment or two later and seeing the prosperous looking Evan, got to his feet, stepped around his desk and opened the gate for him, holding out his hand.

Evan never did catch the man's name, though he made sure the assistant manager got his own correct. He sat in the chair indicated. Over a month had passed since Evan had been working down the mine and by now his hands were clean and Meg had filed his nails neatly. Though they were still hard they no longer looked like the hands of a labourer.

'Can I help you, sir?'

Perhaps it was the words or the way in which the man spoke but immediately Evan was put at ease.

'I hope so. My name is Evan Matthew Griffiths and I recently arrived from Wales on the S S Cardiff.' The man clearly did not recognise his name and with a sinking feeling Evan thought he could not have received John Buchanan's letter. 'A friend of mine, Captain John Buchanan, wrote to Mr Andrew Fforest on my behalf. He suggested in the letter that it might be of mutual benefit if we met and discuss a few things . . . Ideas, look you,' Evan cursed himself for letting the 'look you' slip out. 'It seems you haven't . . .'

'Excuse me, sir. When is the letter likely to have arrived?'

The question took Evan by surprise. 'Oh, let me see. Sometime last week I should think. I left New York then and I've spent the last week or so checking other towns between here and there.'

'That'll explain it, sir. I was off last week with a severe chill. I'll just check and see if anything did arrive.' The assistant manager skimmed through the correspondence files and said, 'Yes, I think this is it. Evan Matthew Griffiths. Right?'

Evan nodded. Good old John, he thought. We owe him so much.

The man opened the file and sat at his desk. Evan could see it contained only a single letter on the bottom of which somebody had scribbled in green ink. The man quickly read it through and looked up with a broad smile.

'Welcome to the First Bank, sir. I'm afraid Mr Fforest is busy at the moment but will see you as soon as possible. In the meantime sir, would you like a cup of coffee?'

Evan controlled his elation with difficulty. It was as John said it would be if all had gone well. Evan managed to nod casually and in a controlled voice replied, 'Yes. Thank you.'

The assistant manager beckoned to one of the tellers and asked for two coffees. Now it was the assistant manager who was nervous, convinced that Evan was going to be an important customer.

Their coffee came and they sipped in silence for a few moments until a faint but distinct buzzer sounded.

'Would you excuse me, sir, for just a moment?' he went through the door on the left.

Evan smiled at the sir.

The assistant manager returned, saying, 'Mr Griffiths, if you would step this way please.'

Evan followed him into an office dominated by a desk next to the window. A chair stood in front of the desk, another against the wall, an ornate cabinet filled the furthest corner and in the opposite wall was Fforest's private entrance.

Fforest, the manager Evan now faced, was a squat, broad shouldered man in his early fifties. His hair was thinning and his waistcoat strained across his big belly.

'I'm right pleased to meet you, Mr Griffiths. And how is my old friend John Buchanan? Thank you Fred, that will be all.'

'Yes sir.'

'Grab a seat, Mr Griffiths, and tell me what I can do for you.'

Evan came straight to the point, just as John had instructed. 'I don't know what John told you in his letter . . .'Evan began, nodding at the folder on Fforest's desk.

'Very little. Only that you were a friend, had travelled in the first class section of the S S Cardiff, that you're an astute businessman, prosperous and interested in starting a business over here.'

'Not one business,' Evan corrected him, 'several.' Evan looked across the desk into the shrewd eyes that seemed to be able to see him for what he was. 'To come to the point, I would like a short term loan of twenty-five thousand dollars, say for three months with an option to extend to six months.'

'That's a fair amount of money. Do you mind telling me what you propose to do with it?' A fair amount, not a lot, not too much. Fair.

'Of course not. I intend buying fifty thousand dollars' worth of general merchandise and shipping it here to St Louis.'

'Ah, fifty thousand dollars' worth, I see. And where will the rest of the money come from? If you don't mind me asking.'

'From me. I'd intended putting up the total myself but other, what appear to be lucrative ventures, caught

my eye and I find myself a little short of ready capital.
John Buchanan was aware of the situation and suggested
I see you.'

'What exactly do you have in mind?' Fforest continued.

The crunch question, thought Evan. Here goes. 'I've
carried out a study of your fair city,' Evan boyo, you're
full of it and it comes from the back end of bulls, 'and
I've come to the conclusion that there is an opening
for a general merchandise warehouse. Oh, I know what
you're going to say,' he forestalled Fforest's protest.
'You were going to say that you already have warehouses down on the wharves which deal in all kinds
of goods.'

'Yes, that's exactly what I had in mind.'

'Look at what's there. Warehouses dealing in cotton,
sugar, wheat, meat, wood, furniture,' he reached into an
inner pocket and extracted a notebook. 'Need I go on?' he
looked up at Fforest. 'I'm proposing a general warehouse
under one roof, dealing with all sorts of goods from meat
and vegetables to furniture and imported silks and spices.
My customers will be the small shop owners and only
people who intend to retail the goods will be allowed in
my place.

'How will you able to tell who is who?'

'Easy. They'll be issued with a card which they'll have
to present to the cashier. To get the card they'll need a
letter from their local bank managers stating that they
own a business.'

'Hmmm, it's an idea that's certainly worth examining,'
Fforest mused aloud.

Evan smiled. 'I'm sorry I can't give you more time to
examine it but I must be on my way tomorrow.'

'Couldn't you extend your stay, even by a day? That'll
give me time to think about what you've said. After all
twenty thousand . . .'

'Twenty-five,' Evan corrected him.

'Ah yes, twenty-five thousand is a lot of money. Surely it's worth twenty-four hours of your time?'

'It's not such a lot. Only a fair amount, I seem to remember you saying. I'm sorry but I have to get back. I have a dinner engagement with Senator George Hughes and his wife. Oh yes, I think Eric Johnson will be there too. Do you know him? He's a banker in New York.'

Fforest appeared to be impressed. 'I met him once.' He thought for a few moments. 'If you come back – say at four this afternoon – I can have the necessary papers ready to sign.'

Evan, delighted and surprised at the speed of events, stood, shook hands with Fforest and left. The manager re-read the letter from John Buchanan, noted again the guarantee of any loan to Evan, along with the instruction not to mention it, and called for his assistant.

19

EVAN RUSHED INTO the boarding house and found Meg in their room. Looking at his happy face she knew that he had been successful and flung her arms around him.

'What happened? What did you say and what did the manager reply. Oh, tell me every word . . .'

Evan put his hand lightly to her mouth and said, 'One question at a time. Let me sit down and I'll explain exactly what happened.' It didn't take long. 'Meg, I couldn't believe it. Just like that . . . Twenty five thousand dollars borrowed on the strength of a letter of introduction from a mutual friend and the dropping of a few names. No check on me, nothing. Where's the catch? I keep asking myself.'

'The catch is, my love, that you have to take this money and turn it into a profit within three months. That isn't exactly easy, you know,' Meg said seriously, a frown on her brow now that the first flush of exhilaration had passed and the enormity of their undertaking hit home.

Evan smiled. 'I know it isn't easy but I think I can do it. Along with your help of course and that of Uncle James.'

The next morning Evan was at the station in plenty of time to catch the train for New York. Further along the platform stood Uncle James, a suitcase at his feet. In his pocket Evan had the draft for twenty five thousand dollars, two hundred in cash and had left nearly eight hundred with Meg for her side of the deal. Uncle James still had money though Evan was unsure how much.

While they were away Meg would conclude the deal on a warehouse they had already found, hire local help to whitewash the walls and build shelves. She would also start running adverts in the local newspaper before he returned from New York. For the twentieth time Evan read the draft. Pay the Bearer, Evan Matthew Griffiths the sum of twenty five thousand dollars, signed Andrew Z Fforest. He wondered briefly what the Z stood for. He looked again and again at the magic words – twenty five thousand. He knew he was going to succeed.

Evan's holdall contained list after list of the items the various store owners had said that they needed. There were hundreds of items, many of which had to be imported, such as spices, clothes and certain foods. Wines, carpets and furniture were wanted. Italian shoes and Swiss watches were in demand – the list went on and on.

Evan had a second class ticket in his pocked but climbed into the first class section when the train arrived. When it departed he went back along the carriages to find Uncle James. Both men were beginning to feel as if they had spent half their lives on a train. This time though, without having to keep the children amused, they could take a greater interest in the scenery they travelled through.

When they changed trains at Pittsburgh, Evan was no longer depressed by the place with its reminder of Wales. On the contrary he felt slightly exhilarated. I've beaten you, he thought. I've beaten every lousy, stinking mine in the world. You'll no longer have me inside you, on my hands and knees, digging, hauling and living in fear, taking my health and leaving me to rot on a pittance. He looked at the whisky glass in his hand, downed it and said, 'One more and we'd better get on the train, Uncle James. We don't want to miss it. I couldn't stand the thought of spending a night here.'

The train pulled into New York at ten o'clock in the

morning. Carriage doors flew open, shrill voices yelled greetings, people jostled and shoved, all trying to go in different directions at the same time. The noise of other trains, the passengers, the hissing of escaping steam; that was the background of the high-vaulted, pigeon-infested building of New York Central Station.

Outside, Evan ordered a hansom to take them to Times Square. They enjoyed the sights of the city, no longer awed by the height of the buildings but still impressed.

Suddenly Evan leaned forward and spoke to the driver. 'If we pass that building a third time I'll stop this cab, take your horse whip and use it on you. Do you understand?'

The man visibly started. 'Yes sirree, sorry sir. We're almost there.'

A few moments later he cut down a side street and entered Times Square. He pulled up at the sidewalk and said, 'That'll be two dollars, gents.'

Evan took out a single dollar bill and handed it over 'Next time you try and take somebody for a ride I suggest you find someone closer to your own size.'

The driver, in his early forties, a once muscular body turned to fat, looked at Evan, paused, spat at Evan's feet carefully missing them and drove off. He was not too upset; he had received a dollar for a seventy five cents' ride.

Evan and Uncle James walked along the street looking at the banks, hotels and shops. They passed Wall Street and reached Broadway. The theatre signs attracted their attention and with time to spare they ambled along, reading the advertisements for plays, musicals and shows. They found a restaurant and had dinner before they returned to Times Square, to a smart hotel where they took two rooms.

Evan lay on his bed for hours, unable to still his racing brain, knowing he needed rest but resenting the lost time. Eventually he fell into a deep, dreamless sleep that lasted through the night and into the middle of the next morning. When he awoke he lay still for a few moments gathering his wits and as the noise of the city penetrated, he threw back the bedclothes with a surge of joy, eager to go and exercise those same wits in his quest for a fortune.

He was in the dining room enjoying a cup of coffee, dressed in his grey suit and looking every inch a business-man when Uncle James joined him. They went over their plans for the day and then Evan left to find a bank.

'How would you like the money sir, in thousands, five hundreds or smaller?' asked the teller, Evan's bank draft in front of him.

Evan hid his disappointment at the lack of reaction from the man at the size of the encashment. 'Give me a mixture, please, right down to ones.'

Outside Evan hurried to the next bank, the National Bank of America and went in through its imposing doors. It was a large room, high ceilinged with a long counter down one side. There were four guarded entrances and at the far end six facing doors. There were four enclosed areas with desks, each with a man sitting at it. Three were busy with clients. Evan approached the fourth and stood at the low gate waiting for the man to acknowledge his presence. After a few moments, when it was obvious that he had been noticed but was being ignored, Evan leaned forward and spoke.

'Listen you,' he said in a soft voice that carried no further than the man in front of him. 'I haven't got all day so don't keep me waiting and wasting my time.'

The man was startled. He had not been spoken to in that way for a very long time.

'I . . . I'm terribly sorry, sir, I didn't see you standing there.' The man pushed his glasses up his nose, stood up and opened the gate for Evan. He was in his sixties, grey haired with a bald patch in the middle of his crown. He had a flabby, soft handshake.

'How may I be of service?' he asked, pulling his lips back in a caricature of a smile.

'I would like to see your manager in charge of loans, please,' Evan saw the man's whole demeanour change. His voice was no longer so deferential. 'Would you mind giving me your name, address and a few other particulars and if you give me the details of what you want the loan for I shall pass on your request and you shall receive a reply in the near future.'

Evan leaned forward, smiling pleasantly. 'Are you the man to authorise a large loan?'

'Eh, no, sir,' he was disconcerted by Evan's steady stare. 'I would have to pass your request on.'

'That's what I expected. Now, go and tell the man who can authorise such a loan that Evan Matthew Griffiths is out here and would like to talk to him about a large loan over a short term. Also tell him I don't have an account here but am willing to open one with an initial deposit of twenty thousand dollars.'

The man gulped, at a loss what to do for a few moments. It's those eyes he thought, they seem to pierce right through me. 'Fine sir, fine,' he tried to sound affable once more. 'I need certain particulars anyway so that I can pass them to Mr O'Brian. As soon as he's free I'm sure he'll see you.'

Evan nodded and sat back.

BOOK 3

Uncle James's Story

1891

20

I WAS SIXTY-TWO when we arrived in America and I
have never wished more that I was twenty again. The
opportunities were greater than I had expected and I was
gratified to see Evan and my newly adopted family reach
out for them. That is, I always told the boys I'd adopted
them but they always said: 'No, Uncle James, we adopted
you,' with cheeky grins plastered across their faces. I
didn't do so much around the place as I used to, getting
too old I guess. But I remember back in 1891 when we
first started and Evan and me, we were in New York,
working non-stop. No, working is the wrong word to
describe it for either of us. We put in as many as eighteen
hours a day some days and enjoyed every minute of it.
I have to admit I sometimes found the going tough and
had to leave some of it to Evan but most of the time I
was with him.

He did tell me what happened at his meeting with
the bankers but I don't recollect all the facts. The one
thing that does stick in my mind is him chuckling in his
characteristically throaty way and saying: 'From somewhere he got the impression I owned similar places in
Europe. But I'm sure I didn't come right out and say
so.' He shook his head at me. 'Uncle James, look you,
we've got to make this work. Now what luck did you
have around the docks and shipping agents?'

At the time we were in a small restaurant on Broadway
and I was eating something called spaghetti, with a meat
sauce and a salad covered with some sort of oil. It was

my first of many meals in an Italian restaurant and I was
enjoying it more than any meal I could remember. Since
leaving Wales I had been eating the richest and tastiest
food in my life. The people back home just had no idea
what they were missing, which is just as well, I guess, as
they'd all want to come over. I remember I was making
a right mess of trying to eat them long thin spaghettis
with my knife and fork. The place was quite small with
about a dozen tables scattered around, all with the same
red and white chequered tablecloths. There was a heavy,
warm atmosphere made up of food smells and old wine.
It was run by a fat Italian woman and her short though
equally fat husband who did all the cooking. She was
always laughing and joking with the customers though I
seldom understood what they were saying. When she saw
the mess I was making she came over, took the knife and
fork out of my hands and showed me how to use a fork
and spoon instead. Evan almost cried with laughter and
gave her a glass of wine in appreciation of the lesson.

I told Evan what I'd arranged. 'Tomorrow we've got
appointments with six importers of different types of
goods and the day after with the general manager of
the railroad to St Louis.'

'In that case we're going to be pretty busy. What time
is the first one?'

'Nine o'clock, the second an hour later. The thing is
they're all in the same area so we can walk from one to
the next in just a few minutes. Two are even next door
to each other; the carpet place and a food place.'

We talked until nearly midnight when the previous
week's lack of sleep caught up with me in spite of
the long rest the night before. That night I slept like
the dead.

We were bowling along in our hansom or whatever
the Americans called it when Evan said to me, 'You
know, Uncle James, I would never have thought this
possible even a month ago. So much has happened

and is happening . . . And do you realise it's only the beginning?' He paused. 'You know I used to hate getting up at five to go down the mine. Now when I get up I find it exciting . . . I look forward to whatever the day brings, the challenge. Do you know what I mean?'

I grinned. 'If you think that way, then how do you think I feel after more years than I care to remember down that stinking black hole?' I shuddered. 'I saw too many deaths, too many injuries not to enjoy this – more than you can possibly know. When I think back on a life time wasted, I tell you boyo live today like there's no tomorrow and you'll probably have the best life imaginable.'

'Aye, I guess you're right. Mind you, when I get back I'll never go anywhere else again without Meg. I miss her too much.'

I nodded. There was nothing to say to that. It had been obvious to me from the time I first got to know them that they had a marriage and a relationship that was one in a million. I envied him that. In fact, many people he met during the following years envied him more for his marriage than for his success.

The cabby pulled up. We were on the outskirts of dockland, a desolate area of rundown buildings some occupied, many empty. There were two heavy wagons parked further down the street, one of which was stacked high with goods. A couple of men in coveralls lounged against a wall but apart from that there was no activity that I could see.

'They don't use this place much,' I explained to Evan. 'They prefer to pass the goods to the customer as soon as they clear customs. That way they keep their overheads down. That's what more than one man told me yesterday. Did I tell you one reckoned he couldn't get enough goods to satisfy all his customers?'

Evan nodded.

'I thought I did. An old man's mind wandering.'

'You aren't old yet, Uncle James, not by a long way,'

Evan kidded me, and though I didn't believe him it was nice to hear anyway. I coughed harshly, catching the phlegm in my handkerchief. Evan thought I was being polite, but I was doing it so he wouldn't see the streaks of red.

I led the way up a rickety stair, uncarpeted, our footsteps a hollow tramping on the wood. The first door led to a sparsely furnished secretary's office, a battered desk along one wall, filing cabinets stretching the length of the other and a stove in the corner next to the door. A connecting door on our right led to the boss's office. The woman behind the desk was sixty, grey haired and as skinny as a starved ferret.

'My name is Griffiths; we have an appointment with, eh, Mr Grundy for nine o'clock.' The clock on the wall showed it was two minutes to the hour.

'Yes, sir, Mr Grundy is expecting you. Just knock and go right in.'

If Evan was surprised at the informality he didn't show it. A few moments later, the introductions over, we were seated opposite a florid faced gentleman who was somewhere between Evan's age and mine. His office was as sparse as his secretary's except for the fact that he had only one filing cabinet and the walls were decorated with horse racing prints.

'Mr Grundy, I'm sure my associate here Un . . . eh . . . Mr Price, has told you more or less what I want. I've examined your price list and I feel there is room for negotiation.'

Grundy frowned. 'Negotiation? I don't think so, Mr Griffiths. That's my price, take it or leave it.' He spread his hands in a magnanimous gesture.

'Maybe so, but I want to buy three thousand dollars' worth of different food stuffs. Cash. Surely for so much money you can take something off the price?'

He laughed. 'Mr Griffiths, I deal in sums as large if not larger every other hour, and so does every other importer and exporter in New York. By all means shop around if you like and compare my prices, but I don't think you'll find many offering my quality that are cheaper.'

'I already have and I know there's room for a little improvement.' Evan leant forward and spoke earnestly; I was mesmerised by his tongue. After forty minutes of dickering back and forth Evan had got three percent off the price and a free delivery to anywhere in the city as well.

The day passed in a blur of similar offices and similar meetings. Even the men looked familiar to me, in their shabby suits and sitting behind shabby desks. Each time it was the same. Evan never once paid their asking price though he never managed to get more than three or four percent off. Each time, though, he got free delivery.

When we finally returned to the hotel I was exhausted, but after a hot bath I found the energy to go back to the Italian restaurant where we were greeted like long lost relatives and treated to a glass of wine. For the remainder of our stay in New York we ate dinner there.

Over an early breakfast a few days later Evan handed me lists of goods, split up into their warehouses with the prices alongside.

'When did you do these?' I asked incredulously.

'Last night,' he replied. 'Read through them and tell me what you think. We reckon we can buy about forty thousand dollars worth of goods. We'll know how much it will cost to get them to St. Louis later today, look you, and if there's any money left we can buy some more.'

The railway manager's office was the opposite of the importers and exporters. It was big, carpeted, well furnished and the walls lined with wood panelling. The man behind the desk looked almost funny enough to laugh at. Almost.

He had a large head in proportion to his small body and piercing yellow brown eyes that I found most disconcerting. He leaned across his desk to shake hands.

'Mr Griffiths, what can I do for you?' his voice was deep and hoarse, surprising in the man.

'Mr Stevanti, it's good of you to see us at such short notice. I did tell your secretary what I wanted to see you about. I assume she passed the message on to you?' Evan paused and waited for an answer.

After a pause Stevanti cleared his throat. 'Eh, yes. She said something about you wanting to hire a train, though she gave no details.'

I had the impression that by making Stevanti speak first Evan had won some sort of silent contest.

'That's because I didn't give her any, though I did tell her I wanted it to go to St Louis. First of all can we establish whether or not I can take a train from here straight through or will I have to change trains?'

'I see no problem. It'll take at least a week to arrange, fitting the train in with all the other schedules that are in operation. Now, what sort of train did you have in mind? By that I mean whether it's for use by passengers or for goods?'

'Goods, with one carriage for us.'

'I see. How many trucks do you think you'll need?'

Evan shrugged. 'If you tell me the maximum weight one of your trains can pull and also give me details of the size of the trucks I should be able to let you know in about a week. Before we go any further how do you make up the costs?'

'Ah, that's simple. You pay for the use of the track over the distance involved, the hire of the engine and of each truck you required. The personnel, relief along the way and so on are part of the engine costs.'

'Excellent. Now, if we can talk price – in general, anyway . . . Oh yes, paid cash in advance of course. I just want to get some idea of the cost.'

'May I ask what you're shipping to St Louis, Mr Griffiths?'

'General goods for a new warehouse. If we can come

to a satisfactory arrangement, Mr Stevanti, then I can see
the possibility of a long term contract, provided the price
is right.'

'Of course,' Stevanti's grin was like that of a shark,
toothy wide and just as false. Evan's grin wasn't exactly
friendly either.

The meeting went on for over two hours. When we
finally left the first thing Evan said was, 'Jeez, I need a
drink, Uncle James.'

We stopped in the first hotel we came to. Evan ordered
a whisky and a beer chaser.

'I hadn't expected such a good deal,' he said softly
and suddenly grinned. 'If we pack it right and use every
bit of space, it's going to cost us under eight thousand
dollars. That's two thousand less than I'd expected.' He
paused. 'I thought I would never get that son of a bitch
down that last percentage point. You know something?
If I do sign a long term contract with them, I'm going
to get another five percent off. Just you wait and see.'

I nodded. I was sure he'd get what he wanted.

During the next two days we saw more shipping agents
and importers. We promised orders would be in by the
following Tuesday and wanted confirmation they could
be filled and delivered within six days. We would start
loading on the following Monday and leave, hopefully,
on the Wednesday, provided all went well.

We sent a telegram to Meg with our expected arrival
date. By now she should have taken out a year's lease on
the warehouse, with an option to purchase after twelve
months, and with luck would be well started on repainting
the place.

We worked all weekend on our orders, checking
weights, quantities and prices. We worked late into the
night and when I left to return to my room Evan would
still be hard at it.

One afternoon we took a break and hired a cab to ride
around the city and its suburbs. What was immediately

apparent was the incredible wealth of some and the appalling poverty of others.

'Perhaps this country isn't such a land of opportunity after all,' Evan commented dryly.

'Only for those who have the guts to take it,' I said, looking at him. I could see the anger beneath the surface when we went through the tenement areas of brown stone buildings, crumbling and depressing. Often he gave a few cents to some of the children playing in the streets who would come clustering after us, begging.

We bought forty one thousand, six hundred and thirty four dollars worth of goods give or take a dollar or two. The railway allocated us a siding with a large, partly used shed into which we could move the merchandise, provided we moved it out again within two days. On Monday morning we were there at eight o'clock and during the next half hour twenty men arrived to help with the humping of the goods. As they arrived I directed them to a corner where we had a stove with a large tea pot, mugs, sugar and milk waiting. When all were there, Evan got their attention. 'My name is Griffiths. The goods we're waiting for should be arriving pretty soon. We'll bring the buckboards in here and get the goods as close to that door there as we can,' he nodded to his left, 'before we take the stuff off. It's important that each truck is filled to capacity with no empty space, before being sealed. He broke off as we heard the sound of a horse. 'That sounds like the first buckboard now.'

We loaded dried meats into one truck and carpets into another. Into yet another we put furniture. There were twenty trucks and our coach, which was next to the engine. It had three bedrooms, a lounge area and a separate place for heating water and cooking food. It was the sort of railway coach I never knew existed.

The wagons came non-stop. At twelve we paused for sandwiches and cold chicken, delivered by the Italian restaurant we frequented. The men couldn't believe it, being unused to generous behaviour by other employers. When we restarted half an hour later they worked with a greater will, if that was possible. At eight o'clock we paid them, gave them a bonus, and told them to keep what was left of the food.

'I'm worn out,' said Evan, stretching and yawning. 'It went better than I'd hoped, look you.'

I nodded. 'With the money we were paying and the added food and tea it wasn't surprising it went well,' I rubbed my eyes wearily.

'The food didn't cost much and I was sure they'd appreciate it. I know I would have, back in the mines. It's the sort of thing that makes hard working men loyal. If we ever make it big, Uncle James, don't let me forget what it was like in the mines. That way I shan't forget how to treat the men properly.' He never did need reminding as far as I know, not ever. 'Why don't you take a cab back to the hotel, Uncle James and I'll wait for the watchmen to arrive.'

'No, I'll wait with you, bach.' I paused. 'Do you realise how fast we've been moving since we arrived here in America? It's not been two months and look at us.'

'I know, Uncle James, but we had to move fast.' He grinned. 'If I had stopped to think about what I was doing I would have frightened myself so much I couldn't have gone on with it. I get frightened now. We still have a long way to go. If we can't sell this stuff then I could end up in jail, especially if Fforest looks into my references too closely.'

I reassured him. 'He won't, as long as we can pay him back in time and I've got faith bach, I've got faith.'

On Wednesday we were at the train by seven o'clock, ready for our departure at eight. The previous afternoon we had sent another telegram to Meg confirming our time of arrival and hoping she would be ready for us.

Our carriage was no longer as comfortable as it had

first appeared. It was filled with sacks of coffee grains.
The only space left was a narrow passage from one end
to the other, the two beds and a small area near the store
where we also had two armchairs. The rest of the carriage
was packed high. Neither of us objected to the smell, in
fact I liked it.

There was no fanfare, no hooting whistles, no loud
goodbyes when we left. We just slipped out of the siding
and headed west. It seemed an anticlimax after our efforts
of the previous week.

The journey back was as long as ever. Evan had
bought a pile of books to read which, though I tried
I could not have understood if it had meant my life.
They were all about finance, economics, monopolies
and trusts. One book was about company law which
even after Evan explained some of what it meant was
still double Dutch to me. I did read some of the local
newspapers and a magazine or two I had bought but
most of the time I played solitaire or watched the scenery
unfold. I remember that, though the journey seemed to
take forever, it was one of the most tranquil periods of
my life. I enjoyed just sitting and watching.

I did the cooking and made the coffee or tea but Evan
never seemed to notice what was put in front of him he
was so immersed in his reading. I sat often and looked at
him as he concentrated on his books – he had two going at
once most of the time – and I knew I loved him more than
I did my own son, who was and, I feared always would
be, a waster.

Our arrival a week later was a lot less quiet than our
departure from New York. True, there were no bands or
cheering crowds, but there were Meg and the boys and
about fifteen wagons and a few buckboards with their
drivers.

I stood to one side as Meg dashed into Evan's arms,
hugging and kissing him as though he had been away
for a year. I contented myself with a hug from the

boys, though I couldn't help wishing I too had a good woman to meet me. The boys were jumping up and down with excitement, hugging me, their father and then their mother in turn.

Though perhaps I did have a good woman as Meg turned her attention to me and gave me a hug and a kiss on the cheek. She introduced us to Sonny McCabe, whom she had hired. He had arranged the wagons, hired the help to do the warehouse and had generally proved indispensable. He was a likeable young man in his early twenties, short, stocky, with a friendly smile and, I soon learned, was a willing and hard worker. Meg's judgement, as usual, was correct.

We began unloading within minutes of our arrival. When we realised that Sonny was more than capable of supervising the work, Meg led Evan and I to the warehouse. It was well placed, midway between the railway and the river wharves. It was two stories high and had a long frontage. The main entrance was a double door through which a wagon could drive easily. Inside, the floor was concrete and there were racks upon racks of shelves. At the far end, up a narrow set of steps, were three offices.

'What do you think, Uncle James?' Meg asked, waving her free hand at the warehouse below, the other tucked under my arm.

'I can't believe you managed to do so much in such a short time,' I replied.

'Oh, most of the shelving was already here. It belonged to a sugar and tobacco distributor, of all things. It's been empty for months. All I did was . . . at least, all Sonny did was get the place whitewashed and some rotten shelving replaced. We had ten men working in here at one stage. I was really lucky to find Sonny, otherwise I'd never have managed.'

Evan said, 'Did you move away from the boarding house?'

'Yes, into the Lucky River as soon as I started advertising. I let it be known I was available to answer questions from any of the traders.' She smiled suddenly. 'You should have seen their faces when they found they were dealing with a woman. I could see some of them didn't like it.' She smiled then added, 'Here's the first wagon.'

By evening we had more than half the trucks unloaded. The warehouse had been fitted with electric light a year earlier and therefore we could work late into the night. So far only the major cities of America had electric power, each run as a separate enterprise but it was spreading rapidly throughout the country.

After the boys were sent to bed the three of us sat in the hotel's dining room.

'I think it'll take us about a week to get everything on the shelves and to get properly organised,' said Meg during dinner.

Evan disagreed. 'What I propose is that we get as much done as we can by Monday. Then ready or not we open.'

'Five days,' said Meg musingly. 'I suppose we can be almost ready, though it won't be quite as I'd like it.'

I half choked on a piece of meat and hastily drank some water.

'Something wrong, Uncle James?' Meg asked sweetly.

I shook my head. I think it was Meg's way of telling Evan that she was as much a decision maker as he was, and though ultimately he may be the boss, it was after all a partnership.

A man approached our table, his cap in his hands. 'Excuse me. Are you Mr Griffiths? The man who came in with the train load today?'

Evan nodded. 'I am.' He tried not to show it but I could see he was displeased at the interruption.

'I am sorry to trouble you over dinner. My name is Reisenbach, Hans Reisenbach. I represent a number of the farmers in the area. Do you mind if I sit down? I have a business proposition you may be interested in.'

Evan's attitude changed immediately. He got to his feet. 'My dear fellow, please do. Here let me pull this chair over. Waiter . . . another glass please and another bottle of that . . . what is it, Meg?'

'Burgundy.'

'Aye, another bottle.'

21

'WHAT EXACTLY IS this proposition, Mr Reisenbach?'
Meg asked, surprising him. He was obviously not expecting a woman to say anything during a business meeting
or even to be present. A lot of people during those years
were going to be similarly surprised.

'There should have been a train through tomorrow from
Kansas. A goods train. There would have been enough
room on there for us to send our crops to Pittsburgh.
It isn't coming. These blasted railroads . . . Ach, they
do as they please,' Reisenbach's voice was guttural and
harsh. 'Ve vondered if ve could hire your train to send
our crops . . . if that is you are not sending anything to
Pittsburgh.' He paused to drink some wine, half a glass
disappearing in one swallow.

Evan looked across at us and shrugged.

'How much goods, I mean crops do you intend sending,
Mr Reisenbach?' Meg asked.

'I vould say ve could fill about half of your trucks. It
is mostly early vegetables. Peas for the canning factories,
sprouts and svedes that have been stored from the vinter in
our barns. Ve have also early lettuces, spring onions . . .'
He shrugged. 'There is quite a lot and the market in
Pittsburgh is ripe for it now. That is vhy ve vant to send
the produce.'

Again, much to my amusement, it was Meg who spoke.
'We shall finish unloading by tomorrow late afternoon.
How quickly can you be ready to begin loading?'

Reisenbach frowned and spoke directly to Evan. 'I am

not used to dealing mit frauen,' in his agitation not only did his accent worsen but he lapsed into German. 'Wer ist die Boss hier? You or your vife?'

I was unsure whether Evan would get angry or not at the man's bad manners. Luckily he laughed it off.

'My wife is also my partner. She has as much say . . . almost as much say, as I do. If she asks you a question it's because we require the answer. If you would be so kind as to tell her what she wants to know then perhaps you'll be good enough to answer a few questions from me.' His voice was honey reasonableness and immediately the German was contrite.

'Please excuse me,' he turned to Meg. He had drained his glass. Evan refilled it and Reisenbach absent mindedly drank it again in a few mouthfuls. 'Ve can be ready vhen you are. It vill take us at most a day to bring the crops from our farms. I can spread the void in hours and they vill load up during the night and be on their vay before dawn.'

'Thank you,' said Meg, picking up her own glass and sipping the red wine.

'Mr Reisenbach, vat . . . I mean,' Evan coughed and took a drink to hide his confusion while I nearly burst trying not to laugh. I saw that Meg was having similar difficulties. 'Eh what do you normally pay the railroads for transporting your produce?'

'On average it is betveen four t'ousand and five t'ousand dollars, depending upon the number of trucks ve use. I have here,' he removed a worn envelope from his coat pocket, 'the exact amount. Of course ve expect to pay the same to you.'

'Where do you unload in Pittsburgh?' Evan asked, looking up from the paper.

'There is a siding, it is quite close to the markets and vithin,' the way Reisenbach sometimes pronounced words correctly and other times spoke with a thick accent confused me, 'a short distance of the canneries. It is very convenient.'

'How eager are you to get the stuff away on my train?'
Evan asked.

'Vat do you mean? Are you t'inking of putting up ze
preise? Gott in Himmel . . .'

'Hold it, Mr Reisenbach,' Evan held up his hand to
calm the German. 'Nothing is further from my mind –
quite the reverse. You see my train has to return directly
to New York. It's in my contract. If I sent it some other
way all sorts of complications could arise, like a law suit
for subcontracting when I have no right to do so. You get
my meaning?'

'Ja, I get your meaning,' Reisenbach was crestfallen.
'Den you cannot help us?'

'My husband didn't say that. What he's saying is that
we can't deliver to your usual place. We need to stop on
the outskirts of town on some pretext and unload there,'
Meg smiled at Evan.

That was the first of many times I saw Meg and Evan
act together during a business deal, each seeming to
know what the other was meaning. People often found
it off-putting, as Reisenbach now did. He looked at Evan
for confirmation.

'That is exactly the point I was about to make. Also,
because of the inconvenience this will cause you and the
arranging you'll have to do I suggest twen . . .'

'Ten percent off the price,' Meg swept in blithely.
'There'll also be other conditions as well. We'll tell you
where we can unload and if your people aren't there on
time the train will have to go on to New York. After that,
what happens to your produce . . . I guess the railroad
will keep it and sell it.'

Reisenbach pulled a face, clearly not liking this too
much. 'It vill take a lot of doing. The added expense at
the other end. Perhaps twenty percent reduction vill be
better, nein?'

They settled on fifteen.

Reisenbach suddenly smiled and shook hands all round.

'Listen, my friends, I think ve make a good deal for all of us, especially if you have trains travelling back empty in the future as vell. Ach, I have had enough of this vine. Vould you like to come to a German bar for some good German beer, brewed in St Louis? You can meet some of the others.'

Evan hesitated. 'Mr Reisenbach . . .'

'Please, call me Hans.'

'Hans . . . I'm Evan, this is Meg and this is James. We only arrived back today from New York and would like to have an early night. Perhaps some other time?'

'I see,' he got to his feet, for some reason taking offence. 'Ve are good enough to do business mit aber nicht gut genug . . .'

Evan also stood and placed a hand on his shoulder. 'Sit down man and don't be so daft. Saturday night we'll go out for a meal . . . A German meal at your expense,' Evan grinned, 'and then you can see if we only want your money.'

Reisenbach's temper vanished as quickly as it had appeared. 'Ach, I'm sorry. I am alvays on the defensive about that. Stupid I know but ve . . .' he shrugged. 'I look forward to Saturday very much. Ve vill see you tomorrow, my friends and I, and arrange things. I shall have to get somebody on the early train to Pittsburgh tomorrow to make the other arrangements. Good night and t'ank you.' He bowed his head to Meg, 'Gnadige Frau,' he said and left.

'All we need do now is to bribe the train driver,' said Meg.

'And ask him the best place to stop. We'll have to let the man Reisenbach sends to Pittsburgh know too. Still, the morning will take care of that.'

Although we were back in the warehouse as dawn was breaking, Sonny McCabe was already there and as the men turned up he put them to work unloading the train. Evan and I worked in the warehouse directing the wagons for unloading while Meg and three of the hired help began stacking the boxes and bags on shelves. Even Dai and Sion helped wherever they could.

It was hard work and we drove ourselves all day. By four o'clock the train was unloaded and we were left with a mountain of goods on the floor of the warehouse, a small percentage already on the shelves.

After we paid off the men we sat around drinking coffee, Sonny McCabe with us.

'May I make a suggestion?' he ventured after a few minutes. 'Mr Griffiths, you and Mrs Griffiths will be busy from now until we open working out prices, so you said.' Evan nodded. 'We're going to keep four men on full time and they'll be starting tomorrow. I don't think we're going to be anywhere near ready for the opening next week. We need to get more men temporarily, on the same basis as we've had them for the last two days. That way we just might make it in time. Otherwise . . .' he trailed off.

'Otherwise what?' prompted Meg.

'Otherwise when we do open we'll look . . . well . . . like amateurs . . . I don't know. I guess I should keep my big mouth shut,' his craggy features looked glum.

'First rule here, Sonny,' said Evan, 'is if you've got something to say then say it.' He sighed. 'And actually, look you, I don't disagree. I hadn't expected it to be so much work. I guess it is because we are amateurs.'

'All right,' said Meg decisively, 'that's what we'll do.'

The deal with the farmers recovered half the costs of the train and made us some good friends. That Saturday night, along with Sonny, we met the Germans for a night of sauerkraut, sausage, lager and schnapps. The next morning I felt like death warmed up after too many prosts the night before. A few hours sweating in the warehouse soon removed the alcohol from my blood but that night I found my bed more welcome than ever.

We opened on Monday as planned. Business started by being brisk and remained that way from seven in the morning until seven in the evening. The variety of goods we stocked was mentioned by every customer and though we were no cheaper than other warehouses with such stuff as sugar and tobacco, they still bought from us because of the other merchandise. Glassware, leather goods and our tinned foodstuffs were very popular. We were also selling German cheeses and smoked meats supplied by the farmers, a little deal Evan set up on Saturday evening.

Two weeks later Meg and Evan left for New York. We needed to replenish our stocks before they got too low. Our responsibilities had sorted themselves out by then. Sonny took charge of the men, stocking shelves and helping customers, Meg had two girls under her taking the money while I kept a general eye on things, noting the most popular brands and items and planning with Evan a better layout of the merchandise.

Evan was out of the warehouse as often as he was in. He found and bargained for different sources of tobacco, sugar and planting grain, all of which arrived by boat from the south and west. He visited the farmers and worked out deals with them for more of their produce and with the local breweries for their beer and whisky.

The sign over the door read "GRIFFITHS & Co. CASH AND CARRY".

It took Evan five months to repay the bank loans though it left us with no cash except for the goods in the warehouse – fifty thousand dollars' worth. Already we were thinking that the premises were too small.

Autumn, or as the Americans call it, the fall, was nearly over and winter was fast approaching. The wind coming in over the prairies was sharp and blustery, bringing heavy showers and the occasional thunder storm. We had rented a house soon after we had opened but at the end of September Meg found a house on the outskirts of town. It was in about two acres of lawn and vegetable garden, close enough to town to have electricity and with water from its own well plumbed into the house.

There were a couple of outhouses and a dilapidated barn. The house was two stories high with a veranda running all the way round the outside. There were five bedrooms upstairs, one with a bathroom adjoining. This was to be Meg and Evan's room. The boys had a room each at the back of the house and I was alongside them with a view out of the side towards town and out of the back towards the Mississippi, about half a mile away.

Downstairs there was a dining room, a large lounge, a big comfortable kitchen and a study. The house also had the latest in plumbing and toilets. It was a lovely place, better than most of the houses in the area but nothing like the large mansions that dotted the outskirts of St Louis.

'I don't want a mansion,' said Meg. 'I prefer this. I'm going to get a cleaning woman in every day but I'll run the place myself. I don't want servants cluttering us up.'

I felt a stab of pain. That was exactly how I thought of myself, cluttering up the place. Perhaps it was time I found somewhere of my own to live. I dreaded the thought.

'I just want there to be the five of us to enjoy it,' Meg said, and I immediately felt better. After all, I rationalised to myself, when they go away I'm there to look after the boys.

'Where did you get the money?' asked Evan as we prowled the empty rooms.

'Well, I put a little of the takings by for the house-keeping and borrowed some from the bank,' Meg confessed.

'How much is some?'

'Two thousand,' she put her arm through his. 'Do you like it?' she asked anxiously.

He grinned. 'When can we move in?'

'As soon as we get the furniture after the next New

York trip. Let me tell you what I thought . . .' They walked away while I stood looking out the back at the vegetable garden. I liked the place. I was going to be happy there until the end of my days. I coughed harshly, opened the window and phlegmed into a cabbage patch.

The boys started school about then. They were put into classes according to their ages, but within a month they both complained that they were bored and Meg had to go and see about them being put up a grade. They were doing so well there was the possibility they would be shifted up a second grade after Christmas. Meg ensured that this was a certainty.

Sion continued with his interest in kites and sometimes on weekends I would go with him to a hill not far away to try out a new design. Though we were open from seven in the morning until seven in the evening Meg never came in before the boys left for school and rarely missed being at home when they returned. In fact, about the only time she was not there was when she went to New York with Evan. It was an exciting, happy time. Wales was a lifetime ago, remembered only when Meg and Evan wrote home.

Two weeks before Christmas we received a letter from John Buchanan asking if he could come and stay with us for the festivities. We were delighted, for in all the times Meg and Evan had been to New York they had never been there during one of his visits. Meg used it as an excuse to throw a party, though I think the real reason for doing so was her desire to show off her beautiful home.

She had furnished it tastefully, with dark oak furniture, which contrasted with the white walls in the lounge. The carpet was rich wine-red wool which had been imported from England in spite of the exorbitant import tariffs. In one corner stood a tall grandfather clock that chimed the hour in muted tones and along one wall stretched a sideboard in which Meg kept her best china and the liquor. Evan was talking about building a bar one day but Meg was adamant that it would have to be in the study and not her room. Evan teased her about this, but I had no doubt where it would end up.

By the time Christmas came the warehouse was practically empty. We closed on Christmas Eve at noon, paying the staff a bonus and giving them the perishables to share out. We invited Sonny to the party on Boxing Day, much to his pleasure, and told him to bring a girl friend. Who, at that time, would have thought such a simple invitation would lead to so much?

We stood in the snow waiting for the train from Cincinnati, which was late. We were freezing and stamping around when it eventually pulled in. John Buchanan was one of the first passengers to alight. He gave Meg a hug and each of us a warm handshake.

'I thought I'd never get here. I see from the way you all look that your letter understated your prosperity.'

'Nonsense,' said Evan, smiling. 'We're as poor as church mice.'

'In that case I look forward to some of the cheese they serve around this part of the world.'

Evan took his bag, Meg his arm and I followed behind. I was looking forward to this Christmas and though I told myself I was daft and in my second childhood it did no good. I was still excited.

We had a gig outside, a light, two-wheeled, one-horse carriage into which we piled. The horse was a big, steady animal and trotted sedately to our home.The boys were waiting for us when we arrived. They took the horse to the new stable that we had just had built to give it a rub down and a feed of oats.

'What's life like on the S S Cardiff nowadays?' Meg asked. 'Still fighting the ladies off?'

'They aren't ladies,' John replied solemnly. 'More like bitches in heat.'

We laughed. That first evening was like that. Remarks that were made were sometimes funny, often not, but it was a wonderful time for us all. The boys stayed up longer than usual and when they finally went to bed it was only under much duress.

'I know them,' said Meg, 'they'll be up at the crack of dawn to see what Father Christmas has left them. I've given them strict instructions not to disturb us before seven o'clock.'

'So early?' Evan wailed in mock dismay.

Downstairs was decorated with Christmas trimmings and in a corner of the lounge stood a large fir tree with lighted candles. It promised to be a good time.

I missed their initial excitement because the two scally-wags were up at five o'clock but just back of six I heard them and, putting on my dressing gown, went downstairs. They were sitting on the floor around the tree, presents and paper scattered around them. I really felt a part of the family for the first time. Sion saw me first. 'Uncle James, Uncle James,' he called in a loud and excited voice while I tried to shush him. 'Look,' he said in a loud whisper. 'We've both got saddles and bits and reins. And look at these boots,' he held up a pair of ornate, high heeled boots for me to see, though I didn't let on that I'd picked them for him. 'And a hat, and look . . .'

So it went on. Neither boy had ever been given so much, for their parents had never been able to afford it. I thought Meg and Evan had gone overboard but seeing the youngsters I thought it was worth it. They kept pestering me where the ponies were. They had checked the stable and found nothing.

'You'll have to ask your Mam and Da and you can't do that before seven. While I light a fire why don't you two think of names to call a horse?'

It kept them amused until almost seven o'clock. By then they couldn't stand it any longer. I let them wake their parents for a Christmas the like of which none of us had ever seen before.

22

IT WAS THE EVENING of Boxing Day and we were waiting for the guests to arrive. The boys, needless to say, were almost exhausted from a day with their horses. Each had a pinto pony, two years old and ideal for boys aged ten and twelve. Dai called his King because in his opinion he looked regal. To me it was just another cantankerous horse but I was assured I was wrong. Sion called his Thunderbolt, because the drumming of his hooves sounded like thunder through the earth. I was careful not to laugh in case I spoiled his day. They had also received books on how to care for horses, some of the first published on the subject, and Meg insisted that they read them, though they didn't need much persuasion.

We were having a pre-party drink in the study. I reflected on our changing wealth. A trestle table in the dining room groaned under the weight of the food which had been prepared by Meg, Marie the cleaning lady and some of Marie's friends eager to earn extra money even if it meant working over Christmas. There was cold chicken, trifles and things I had never seen before. Meg had been busy all day but seeing her looking so beautiful you would have thought she had spent the day pampering herself. She wore a new black dress with a pearl necklace, her Christmas gift from Evan. Although she looked elegant she was dressed simply. She was a little concerned in case she was too well dressed for the farmers' wives.

'Tell me something, Evan,' said John, 'what do you think of the current economic situation in the country?'

'Huh?' Evan's reaction was similar to Meg's and mine. We had been talking banalities for the past twenty minutes while we relaxed over our drinks. 'You've taken me a little by surprise,' said Evan cautiously. 'In what way exactly?'

John laughed. 'Evan, one day you'll go into politics. In what way exactly I don't know.' His laugh was deep and infectious. 'I've noticed the books you have lying around. Have you read them all?' Evan nodded and John gave a low whistle whether in surprise or respect I wasn't sure. John went on, 'Let me ask you something else and I hope you don't take umbrage.'

Evan shook his head. 'I don't suppose I will.'

'Did you understand all you've read? I mean, I don't mean just the words, but the meaning behind them. All that stuff about trusts, corporations, tariffs, growth rate real and imagined – all that stuff.'

Evan thought a moment. 'I haven't always understood after the first reading,' he paused. 'But I keep at it until I do understand. Sometimes, I have to ponder on it for a while but, yes, I think I get there eventually.' He took a sip of beer.

'I see you also get the New York Times and Tribune Herald. Do you follow stocks and shares?'

'Not really follow them. I keep a close eye on prices, especially of raw materials, but that's all.'

'What do you think is going to happen in the next year or two?' John held up his hand before Evan could reply. 'The reason I'm asking is because I've heard a few things and after what you said about expanding I was . . . I mean I am, going to pass on what I know. I just wondered what you thought, that's all.'

'What I told you about expansion is in the future. I don't think I'll do anything in this coming year except consolidate what we've got and put some money in the bank. The warehouse may be getting a little small for us but we'll wait another year and see what happens.

Though we may buy some more land around here.' He paused, finished his drink and busied himself replenishing everyone's glass, talking at the same time. 'Since eighteen seventy the price paid for farm products has dropped while the general price of other commodities and raw materials has risen. Look you, whatever we do, whatever we make, there is really only one vital factor. Can we feed ourselves? Against that everything else is trivial. What good is a railroad if we're starving to death? Also, and I think it's going to be important, is the fact that a hell of a lot of farms are mortgaged to banks back east who don't give a damn about the farmers, only their money.' As he warmed to his theme Evan became more eloquent, using his hands to gesture when he wanted to emphasise a point. 'The farmers' alliances are coming to the fore now but I think it's too late and there's too much opposition. The McKinley tariff, the highest ever with its inflexible banking and credit systems, will make it more and more difficult for the farmer to pay the interest on his loans – never mind paying back any of the capital. We've had a few years of drought. It's not been too bad around here maybe, but taken over the country as a whole then I think there's going to be even more problems with farms just closing. I've read Henry George's Progress and Poverty and Edward Bellamy's Looking Backward and they all make sense if the farming world is to be able to do its job properly, which is feed the nation. Coupled with that is the Government's determination to keep gold as the standard for our currency and with all the silver buying they're doing in an effort to ensure that inflation doesn't get out of hand then I think we're in for a bad time. Silverites will fight the Populists in the election next year and if they win, then God alone knows what will happen. A few years of prosperity possibly, but then rampant inflation which will be harder than ever to control. If the conservatives win then we're going to have a few years of real hardship just around the corner.'

He suddenly stopped and looked embarrassed. He took a long drink of beer and said, 'Sorry, I didn't mean to go on like that. But you did ask . . .'

John nodded. 'I was spellbound. You painted a very clear picture of what's happening, as you see it,' he paused. 'Evan, don't take offence, though I think I know you well enough now to know you won't. For a Welsh miner recently down from the hills – or should I say valleys – you show an understanding I never expected. Look, I may as well tell you this but I don't often broadcast it around even amongst my friends. My father owns a controlling share of the stock of the shipping line that owns the Cardiff and her sister the Bristol. There are over fifty ships in the line though most are tramps doing coastal work.' I was astonished and judging by their faces, so were Evan and Meg. 'The point is that I come from a wealthy family and we were intending to invest heavily here in the States later next year. I was going to leave the Cardiff and come and do all the donkey work.' He took a mouthful of beer before continuing. 'However, the company's Board of Directors of which my father is chairman, are a very canny, if you'll excuse the Scottish term, and careful bunch. They had an analysis made of the current and future financial situation of this here United States. And what it all came down to was what Evan so eloquently said a few minutes ago.'

'So what does it mean,' asked Meg, 'as far as we're concerned?'

'Let me just say that in view of what we discovered we aren't moving in here so soon. We see a depression on the way and shipping will certainly be affected. Because of that may I make a suggestion about the business?'

'Of course, go ahead,' said Evan, 'but it'll have to be quick. I think I hear the first guests arriving.'

'I know about your plans, you've told me. I agree about you not expanding yet and I suggest that during the next few months you reduce your merchandise to essentials and foodstuffs only. People have to eat but they don't have to sit on furniture to do so. Also buy gold as well as land and if you can't afford both then buy the yellow stuff. It's going to go up faster than land values over the next few years.' He drained his glass as Meg got to her feet and we followed.

'What a sombre note to start a party on,' she said. She took Evan's arm to go to the front door and to greet her guests.

The evening started well. The drink flowed – there was beer, whisky, schnapps or wine and the food table, by eleven thirty looked as though a swarm of locusts had been through it. A four piece Negro band played music varying from the magic of the deep south to the barn dance of America to special adaptations of Strauss and Beethoven. I learned later that they had heard a performance of a visiting orchestra playing classical music and could accurately reproduce the sound in spite of hearing it only once.

Evan, John, Hans Reisenbach, his brother Joachim and I, as well as one or two others were standing on the back porch enjoying a few minutes of fresh air and smoking our cigars; we weren't allowed to smoke indoors. It was a star-filled night, and a waning three quarter moon lit the snow covered countryside.

We watched a group of four horsemen ride into view along the road from town and stop by our gate. After a moments hesitation, one of them rode along our track and a few seconds later the others followed. At first I thought they were late guests, very late in fact, but when the leader cut across the lawn I was not so sure. I didn't recognise him. He was of medium height and build, wore a six gun tied low on his thigh and a scowl on his face. He was the worse for drink and when he mounted the porch steps Evan stepped into his path.

'Can I help you, boyo?' Evan asked softly.

'Get out of my way,' he tried to push past.

'Hold it, you aren't going in there, look you. It's a private party and I don't remember inviting you. Now back to your horse and get out of here.'

'I've come for my girl. Now get out of my way before you get hurt.' Again he tried to push past. His three cronies were sitting on their horses watching. I don't think they had expected seven or eight able-bodied men to be there to greet them.

Evan grabbed the man's shoulder. 'Listen, young man,' he was about twenty years old, 'you'll be the only one to get hurt if you don't go away, and go now.' The quietness of his voice was more chilling than if a wind had blown up in the still air.

'I'm telling you my girl is in there and I want her. Do you know who I am?' he asked unexpectedly, a nasty grin on his face.

'No and I don't care. If you don't turn around immediately and go then I'll throw you off my land.'

'Huh, you wouldn't dare. My father . . .'

That was as far as he got. Evan's fist, so unexpected, slammed into his stomach and sent him sprawling with a sickening whoosh of air from his lungs. Two things happened at once. The other three on their horses moved as though to pull out their guns and found themselves looking down the barrels of four pistols that appeared in the Germans' hands. The horsemen stopped all movement and very slowly brought their hands back into sight.

Evan stepped down to help the man to his feet and onto his horse. The prone figure, holding his belly suddenly drew his gun. Whether from the pain or his awkward position he moved too slowly. Luckily for him the others were watching the horsemen otherwise the foolhardy young man might have been shot. Instead Evan was close enough to kick his hand hard and send the gun spinning into the snow. Evan bent down, grabbed the man by his jacket and gun belt and lifted him into the air. It was the most amazing display of strength I had seen in a long time. He carried the man clean over his head across to the horse trough.

The man was kicking and yelling. 'My wrist, my wrist. It's broken. You've broken it,' he suddenly sobbed.

Evan dropped him into the trough, or should I say onto it? The ice held for a second and then collapsed under him. Evan calmly walked away, the youth tried to sit up, coughing and spluttering water but went still when Evan returned. Evan dropped the man's gun into the trough.

'Now get off my property,' Evan said still speaking softly.

The man was crying openly now. 'I'll get you. Just you wait until my father hears about this. You'll be sorry.' He clambered awkwardly out of the trough, his teeth chattering. 'You'll live to regret this. I know you Griffiths and I know your kids. I'll . . .' he had been about to climb onto his horse. The last sentence was the worst he could have uttered. Evan was on him like a tiger.

Evan pulled him around, held him with his left hand and hit him as hard as he could three times with his right, all in the stomach. The first caused the man to gurgle for breath, the next two almost knocked him unconscious. Evan then changed his grip, grabbed the man by his hair and brought his right arm back in a blow which if it had connected would probably have caused serious injury. John stepped down and grasped Evan's hand just in time.

'Hold it, Evan. He's had enough. You'll regret it later if you hurt him too much. Let him go home. You can press charges against him tomorrow if you like, for attempted murder. We all saw what happened. But don't do something you'll regret.'

'You're right,' Evan dropped his arm and let the man collapse to the ground. 'John, use his lariat and tie him over his saddle.' He turned to the man. 'If you so much as mention my kids again I'll kill you.' He walked back to the porch and seeing the guns held by the Germans said, 'Thank you. I guess I'd better learn to use one too. Let's go in, I could use a drink.'

'Ja, that is a good idea,' said Hans Reisenbach, though whether he was agreeing about the drink or learning to use a gun I was not sure. Both, probably.

John and three of the Germans took care of our unwanted visitors. Evan went upstairs to wash his hands where the skin on the back of his knuckles was missing while Hans and I waited for him to return, a couple of beers in our hands.

Evan returned, drank deeply of a mug of beer and sighed. 'I needed that. Who was the kid, Hans? Who's his father he threatened me with? Is he some kind of an outlaw or something?'

Hans laughed but then stopped abruptly. 'Sorry Evan. I vas laughing at the idea of Duke Roybal being an outlaw. He owns a big ranch about twenty miles south of here. He's also got interests in the railroad and I t'ink the hotel too. He's a powerful man. I vould say, Evan, that he is a hard man and by his own ideas a just man. At least I have heard nothing otherwise and I've been here tventy years. He has one serious fault and that's Duke Junior, the boy you just sent home. He can do no wrong in the old man's eyes. The trouble is he's a bad one and no mistake. The story goes that Duke has, vhat's the vord? Doted on him? Ah yes, doted. The boy's mother died at an early age and Duke raised him alone. Vhatever young Duke vanted, young Duke got. I t'ink he has taken this idea into his eh, adulthood.'

I nodded. 'Do you think Roybal will come riding to his son's defence?' I asked as John and the others came in.

'I vould say that you can be almost sure of it,' Hans said soberly.

The incident was dismissed for the remainder of the party. It was not until two o'clock that the first guests began to leave, each with a cup of soup to help them on their way. Some of them had as much as twenty miles to go and on the slippery roads the journey could take anything up to four hours.

Hans and his family were among the last to leave. It was then that I noticed that Dai was still up. He was talking to Hans' daughter, a pretty blonde girl still with a little puppy fat but displaying the signs of being a real beauty one day.

'Goodnight, Gunhild,' said Dai. 'I enjoyed talking to you. I guess I'll see you in school next term, now that I'm moving up to your class.'

'Goodnight, David, I shall look forward to it,' she said in a soft and somehow breathless voice.

As he turned away Meg said, 'Dai . . .'

In the light of the setting moon I saw the pain flick across his face. I didn't understand it but Meg did. 'David walk your guest to the wagon.'

Dai was pleased, surprised and flustered all at once, but he followed the girl. Meg looked at me. 'I was going to tell him he should have been in bed ages ago,' she sighed. 'He's only twelve but I suppose he's growing up. He's also big for his age. I think Gunhild is fourteen.' She tucked her arm in mine as we waved goodbye to the Reisenbachs. 'Were you ever interested in girls at that age, Uncle James?'

'I can't rightly remember, Meg, and that's a fact. I might have been, on the other hand . . .'

'You might not have been,' she finished with a laugh. 'Come on Dai . . . David, time for bed.'

From then on he was David though Sion called him Dai whenever he wanted to annoy him.

We left for the warehouse late the next morning. John came with us but Meg stayed behind to supervise the cleaning. On the way we stopped at a gunsmith's shop. The bell over the door jangled merrily when we walked in but with my head, even after the cold brisk drive in the buckboard, I could have done without it.

The shop was small, every available inch of space filled with guns, rifles, pistols, shotguns and boxes of ammunition. The man behind the glass-topped counter was also small, wore a woollen cardigan with the elbows worn away and had a pair of spectacles perched on the end of his nose.

'I'll be with you in just a moment, gentlemen,' he focused his attention on the parts of a pistol scattered in front of him. He did something with a small file for a few seconds and then looked up, placing the file and a piece of gun down. 'Sorry to keep you waiting, but I needed to finish that small, delicate operation. Now, can I help?'

'I hope so,' said Evan. 'I would like to buy some guns.'

'Some guns? What for? I mean what do you want to use them for? Hunting? Bird shooting? . . .'

'Ah, there's a difference?' Evan asked.

The little man and John laughed. Evan looked self conscious. 'Look you, I know nothing about guns, never owned one and never used one. You guide me as to what I need,' he suggested reasonably. 'I want the gun for self-defence. I don't want it for sport or hunting. Just to protect me and my family.'

'I take it the protection required is from other men, not from wild animals,' the gunsmith said dryly.

'There, sir, you're quite correct. So what do you suggest?'

'There are all sorts of weapons to choose from. Let's start with pistols and then move on to rifles.' He lifted a tray from under the counter. 'Here is an example of the standard guns I sell. As you can see they vary in size from this small two shot Derringer to the Colt 45, probably the most popular hand gun in the States at the moment.'

For half an hour Evan examined guns and talked with

the old man . . . I call him old because he looked at
least ten years older than me. It was interesting to hear
an expert talk about a subject he loved but after a while
John and I became restless and left for the warehouse
while Evan remained behind. It was just on noon and
Sonny already had the doors open.

I guess after the Christmas rush and all the over eating,
people were not too keen to spend more money because
though we had customers non-stop we were not as busy as
usual. Evan came in nearly two hours later with a number
of packages.

He put them on his desk and opened them. 'Here you
are, Uncle James, something for you,' he threw me a gun
and holster.

I eyed it dubiously. It was not very big and the holster
had a funny compactness to it which I couldn't see how
to fit on my leg.

'Like this,' Evan took a similar one for himself and
put it around his waist. The holster fitted snugly to his
left side, the handle pointing forward. Under his coat it
was difficult to detect. 'We're businessmen and I figured
that's how we should look, not like a couple of cowboys.
I've tried them out behind the gunsmith's shop, in his
testing range. He persuaded me to buy this rifle,' he
unwrapped a Winchester. 'When I learn to ride I can
put it in my saddle. In the meantime I'll keep it in the
buckboard, just in case.'

'What's in the last package?' asked John.

'Oh, this.' Evan tore off the paper. 'It's a sawn-off
shotgun. The 'smith reckoned that until I learn to fire a
pistol properly, my best chance of hitting anybody would
be with this. He's even making me a special holder.' Evan
pushed a box of shells towards me. 'I'll show you how to
load it Uncle James. Then I want you to call Sonny up
here – for a little chat.'

'Anything up?' asked John.

'I'm not sure,' replied Evan opening the cylinder of the

pistol to load it. 'I had a talk with the gunsmith and he told me Roybal is pretty vindictive. If Roybal comes into town he'll have to go past the gunsmith's shop. It he does, the gunsmith said he'll try and send word. Ah, here's Sonny.' Evan told Sonny what had happened with Junior and as he spoke Sonny became more and more agitated.

'Gee, I'm sorry, Mr Griffiths. I didn't mean to cause you so much trouble. I guess you want me to go, eh?'

'What on earth are you talking about, Sonny?' asked John.

'Well, sir, I eh, I figured you know Marylou was with me and that's who Junior was after. So it was my fault. If I go then old man Roybal won't do too much to Mr Griffiths here.'

Evan grinned. 'How serious is it between you and Marylou? She struck me as a pretty girl with a nice way about her.'

'Well, sir, it's pretty serious, I guess. We've been walking out now for a few months. As soon as I can save enough money I was planning to ask her to . . .' he trailed off.

'So where does Junior fit in to all this?' John asked.

'He'd been walking out with her before me. But after he got into some pretty close scrapes with the law she gave him up. He don't seem to think she's got the right to do that, somehow.' He sighed. 'Well I guess I'd better get my gear. It's sure . . .'

'You'll do no such thing,' said Evan sharply. 'For one thing, what happened last night was my affair and not yours. And for another nobody pushes me or my staff around. Now listen, Sonny, this is what I want you to do if we have to.' Evan outlined his idea and when he had finished Sonny's sombre face creased with a big grin.

'Hot diggerty dog,' he said. 'I'm sure going to enjoy this.' We went downstairs.

I only wished I had the same feeling.

23

I TRIED TO SETTLE down to work but found it impossible. I hoped Roybal would turn up soon and we could clear the air and get it all over with. Finally I gave up and threw down a half completed stock list in disgust. For some time, I sat and thought of the long way we had come in such a short period. And I was not thinking in terms of distance either. A lot had happened and a lot more was going to happen. Provided we survived the day. We? No, that was wrong. Evan was the driving force and Meg the main support. Without either of them, there was no future. I hoped Evan knew what he was doing. I went down below to the stove and got myself a cup of coffee from the staff room.

It was late afternoon when we received the message.

I stood by the door to Evan's office, Evan sat behind his desk. John sat on an upright chair against the wall, his right hand out of sight by his side. From where I stood I could see the main door. The minutes dragged by. More than once I thought I saw somebody outside but then I realised it was my eyes playing tricks. I decided if we got through the day all right I was going to an optician.

I thought I saw something and screwed my eyes up to see better. I was not mistaken: some men had just entered. They went behind a high centre rack of shelves and were approaching the steps next time I saw them. I spoke quietly to John and Evan.

'I don't know for sure, but I guess this is it. There's three of them. The one in front is about fifty, well built and about as tall as you, Evan. The two behind are both wearing guns tied low on their legs. I guess it's like Sonny said. They're his gunslingers and mean looking swine.' I trailed off as they reached the top of the stairs and marched into the office. The front man's eyes swept past John and me and rested on Evan.

'You Griffiths?' he asked with a growl.

'Yes, I am,' said Evan, smiling politely, standing and coming round his desk, his hand outstretched, a smile on his face. 'And who are you, sir?' Evan asked, taking the man's hand, even though it hadn't been offered. Roybal was so surprised he allowed Evan to sit him in a chair placed directly in front of his desk. The thumb of Evan's right hand was casually hooked into his belt close to where I knew the butt of his gun lay. It had all happened smoothly and quickly.

Roybal came to his wits and lurched to his feet. 'Cut out this horseshit,' he leaned on the desk, his face a foot or so from Evan's.

'I've come here to give you the same hiding you gave my son. Now get on your feet before I drag you across your desk.'

Evan sat still and looked calmly at the enraged face before him. Roybal had worked himself into such a state that his face was mottled red.

'What on earth are you talking about?' Evan asked softly.

'Huh? It was you, wasn't it, that beat my son up last night?'

'Are you talking about that drunk who tried to . . .' before Evan got any further Roybal, with a snarl of range went to draw his gun. His two men behind him were doing the same thing when Evan's voice came across like a whiplash. 'Don't.' As he said it he pulled out the sawed off shotgun from beneath his desk. 'Now look behind you and to the side.'

In the doorway and lined up along the glass partition

were five of our men, each pointing rifles into the office. John had lifted his gun from besides his chair and I now pulled mine from its holster.

'If you make a move of any description you'll be dead,' Evan's quiet voice was like ice, his face carved from wood. 'Now tell me exactly why you've come here.'

'For you, for what you did to my son. You're making a bad mistake, Griffiths. I'm not a man to cross easily. One of the hands I left at the door will see the guns and go for the rest of my men.'

'Sonny?' Evan kept his eyes on Roybal.

'Just like you said Mr Griffiths. Mac and Frank got their rifles right up the man's nose now. In fact, I'd say Frank is just itching to pull the trigger.'

'Did you suggest that you're not a man to cross easily, Roybal? If I were you, I'd think twice about issuing stupid threats. At the moment your chances of leaving alive are looking pretty thin. Now, nice and easy like, drop your gun. Sonny, get the guns. Now sit in that chair, Roybal . . . Good. Is your son a man or a mouse that his father has to come to fight his battles?'

'He's little more than a boy. He told me how he come to your place and asked all polite like to see his girl and how you got the drop on him and then gave him a hiding. With,' Roybal spat the words at Evan, 'two of them no good German farmers holding onto him. Well, today I've come to even that score and this time nobody will be holding my hands.' The man was trembling and in such a rage he seemed oblivious to our guns.

'Mr Roybal, it will be with delight that you and I shall meet outside and I shall enjoy teaching you some manners. You are nothing but a common, loutish bully. Your son rode up to my place last night while my guests and I were enjoying my party and tried to force an entrance. He was drunk and abusive. It was only by luck on my part that he didn't shoot me. I was unarmed at the time, incidentally. After disarming him,' the contempt in

Evan's voice was as thick as butter, 'I threw him into my horse trough. At that point he threatened my children. I have two boys aged ten and twelve, Mr Roybal,' while Evan spoke the anger was draining from Roybal at about the same rate as the blood from his face, which by now was chalk white.

'I don't take kindly to threats against them. Mr Buchanan here saved your son from the biggest hiding of his life which is very lucky for him as I would have probably maimed the . . .' Evan took a deep breath, and went on. 'Calling him names won't get me anywhere. At the moment I am seriously considering pressing charges against him for assault, disturbing the peace and attempted murder. I have enough witnesses to prove what I have just told you and there's more than a good chance he'd be convicted. Can you imagine what, say, five years in the state penitentiary will do to him? I can. What's this Mr Roybal? No more bluster? No more threats?'

'I don't believe you,' said the man but with no conviction. 'I don't believe you. My son wouldn't lie to me.'

'From what I've heard about your son he'd do a lot worse than that. He's a no good . . .' Again Evan stopped. 'I have no need to tell you what he's like, do I? Because you already know. Let me tell you something else. I am also tempted right this minute to send for the Marshal and have him arrest you for threatening me. I'm very tempted indeed . . .' Evan mused aloud.

'You wouldn't dare,' said Roybal heatedly. 'I'd close this place in a month if you tried something like that. You'll learn out here, Griffiths, that men don't run to the law, they settle their problems themselves.'

'Oh, I've noticed,' said Evan. 'Which is why until you stop acting like children and use your laws you'll be a second rate country.' Evan pulled back the two hammers on the shotgun. The slightest pressure on his finger would blow Roybal to Kingdom come. 'I've already told you not to make idle threats, Mr Roybal.'

Nobody moved a muscle. The tension in the silence reached breaking point. Roybal knew death was close and was sweating profusely. He was the first to break the silence.

'What do you want?' he croaked.

'Nothing. You and I are going downstairs and out to the back where I am going to give you the hiding of your life. When you return home I suggest you do something similar to your son, before it's too late. Though I suspect it is already. The reason I'm going to do this Roybal is so you'll realise that I am not a man to be trifled with. I don't trust you not to leave here, get your men and return. I think you're that sort of coward. Like father like son. And I know what the son is like. Afterwards, you'll see I do mean business and if you ever cross me again I'll come after you, shooting. Now, on your feet.'

On the way downstairs I caught Evan's arm. 'Are you crazy, bach? He'll beat you easily. What the hell are you achieving by doing this?' I was so angry I felt like hitting Evan myself.

'Just as I said, Uncle James. Though that's only part of it. If I win then the word will spread and they'll leave me and the family alone. You know what this place is like. They seem to think it necessary to find out how tough a man is before they'll leave him in peace.'

I did not, could not and never would agree with him but when it came to Meg and the kids Evan was almost irrational. I believed his real fear was that if Roybal did not control his son then there was a possibility his son would do something stupid. If Evan won the fight, then perhaps the humiliation would force Roybal to do something about Junior. Maybe Evan was right, maybe he was wrong. But as I said, Evan was irrational when it came to Meg and the kids.

'I'm going to enjoy this,' said Roybal with a sneer as he shucked off his jacket and rolled up his shirt sleeves. Evan did the same, though without bothering to reply.

We formed a loose circle around them but were careful to keep an eye on Roybal's man.

'Are you ready you English pig?' challenged Roybal, stepping forward.

'Welsh I am, boyo and I'll thank you to remember it.'

A half dozen or so of our customers joined us and as soon as the first punch was thrown it was obvious which side they were on. Roybal was far from popular with the local people, that much was clear.

Roybal came in fast in spite of his age and the gut he carried. He threw a heavy fist at Evan's head which if it had landed would have finished the fight there and then. Evan ducked, skipped to one side and punched Roybal in the kidneys. It was not very hard, but hard enough to make Roybal gasp.

This time Roybal closed more cautiously. Evan stood in the centre of the circle his feet planted firmly, waiting. Roybal held a loose guard position with his right fist across his chest, his left slightly forward and lower. Evan had his chin well protected with his right, his left further forward, his right arm protecting his body. Evan waited patiently. Suddenly Roybal stepped in and swung at Evan's stomach. This time, instead of avoiding the blow, Evan blocked it and jabbed two fast left hooks at Roybal's chin. Both connected and Roybal's head jerked back each time. Again, I was sure Evan had not hit him as hard as he could.

The yells of encouragement from the small crowd had brought more people, many of whom appeared to be cheering for Evan.

Roybal rushed in again, trying to get close, throwing punches at Evan's face and body. Evan blocked or ducked them all. The wildness of his movements left Roybal exposed and Evan landed seven or eight blows to the man's face and stomach. Roybal ignored the punishment and went on trying to land one good punch, but finally he staggered back. He reeled slightly, while Evan stood there as calmly as ever, a mocking smile on his face. Roybal gulped in air, looked about him at the grinning crowd and lost his temper. He threw caution to the wind and went lumbering in. He took a hell of a battering trying to land his wild punches. One or two got through Evan's defence, but they did not seem to bother Evan in the least.

Roybal now went down for the first time, blood pouring from his nose and cut lips. He was gasping for breath. Evan stood poised, and then relaxed.

'Come on, Roybal, that's enough. There's nothing to be won by beating you anymore and there's nothing for you to prove by taking any more punishment. You're a brave man, nobody will deny that, but I'm twenty years younger and a lot fitter.'

Evan offered his hand, bending towards the prone figure laying in the dust. Roybal accepted the hand and Evan pulled him to his feet. As Evan did so, Roybal's right hand picked up a load of dust and he threw it into Evan's eyes, blinding him.

Evan staggered back, Roybal closed in, not as quickly as when the fight started maybe, but still fast enough. Evan groped to clear his eyes. Roybal landed three or four heavy blows to Evan's stomach. Evan grunted, gasping for air and then he lost his temper.

Evan gave a roar which startled the crowd and startled Roybal too. With his eyes nearly shut, Evan stepped in and took hold of Roybal by the left shoulder, ignoring the two punches Roybal landed on his side, and went berserk. He hit, kicked, kneed so fast that Roybal was probably only half conscious when Evan took hold of his hair and lifted the man's face up, landing a piledriver of a blow which hit Roybal on his chin and threw him half a dozen feet backwards where he sprawled in the dust. He was an inert bloody mass, though he was still breathing. The crowd, silent during that final onslaught gave a whoop and a yell. Sonny, John, myself and the others forgot about Roybal's men as we rushed forward to congratulate Evan.

One of the gunslingers with Roybal pushed one of the crowd forward and grabbed the man's pistol.

'Griffiths,' the gunslinger screamed. We all turned to look, the gun was pointing at Evan's stomach. It was all so clear, time seeming to stand still. There was a shot, the gunman clutched his stomach, shock written on his face, blood oozing between his fingers. The gun slipped from his hand just as he collapsed. We were too stunned to move for a second and then Hans Reisenbach stepped out of the crowd, a pistol in his hand.

'I know these men,' he said in his guttural accent. 'And I do not trust them. It is just as vell, Evan, ja?' He came forward to shake Evan's hand. 'That vas some fight, my friend. I t'ink now ve go for a beer and a schnapps. Vat do you say, James?'

'I agree,' I smiled with relief. 'I thought you said Roybal was a just man, Hans? He's just as bad as his son.'

'Ja, it seems that way. But then I have never seen Roybal in any other position than that of vinner. It is easy to be nice when one always vins. Is that not so?'

The crowd was beginning to break up now the excitement was over. Evan walked over to the two Roybal men who now had guns trained on them.

'You two pick up that hoodlum and your boss and get out of here.' When the men stood still for a second too long, he shouted, 'Move,' and they jumped to pick up their dead comrade. 'Sonny, do you think you can hold the fort for a while? I sure could use that drink Mr Reisenbach just offered me.'

'No problem, Mr Griffiths,' Sonny was pleased at the trust Evan was putting in him. 'And Mr Griffiths, that sure was some fight,' he spoke with admiration. The rest of the men chorused an agreement.

'Thanks, it's nice of you to say so and I won't forget

what you all did for me today. I really appreciated it.'

We went to the nearest saloon where the tale of the fight had already been told a dozen times and had been exaggerated by the same amount. We never did get back to work that afternoon. The Marshal tried to make something of it but there were too many witnesses for him to do much and finally he was forced to make sure Roybal and his men left town quietly.

Meg was angry when we got home, though I suspected the anger was to hide her worry at how close Evan had been to being killed. Within the community Evan's standing was higher after the fight and this became reflected in the business. John had returned to New York shortly afterwards, promising to return as soon as he could. He intended to let us know in good time when the Cardiff was back in New York so that Evan and Meg could visit him.

Over the next month we re-examined our buying policy and the sales of non-food items. Those things that were selling well, like dinner and tea services, glassware and cutlery, we kept on. Other things, like furniture and cheap jewellery, we stopped.

Meg and Evan went to New York on another buying trip and returned with the familiar train load. It was the middle of February and though there was still snow on the ground it had never been really bad. They had been back for three days when Evan was at the bank seeing Fforest and Meg was in town doing a bit of shopping. (Though you'd have thought we had enough stuff of our own, but I guess there is no satisfying a woman . . . any woman). She went under the guise of comparing prices. It was a quiet afternoon, normal for a Tuesday when we had the hold-up.

I was upstairs at the warehouse talking to Sonny when we heard the commotion down below. I rushed out to see what was going on. Three men with guns were lining up the customers and our staff against the wall. Sonny stood at the door watching what was happening while I picked up Evan's sawn-off shot gun and hefted it in my hands.

Although I was now the proud owner of a pair of gold rimmed spectacles through which I saw the world in a much clearer light, I still wasn't much of a shot with the pistol Evan had given me. With the scatter gun, though, it was a different proposition altogether. I walked over to the window and threw it open. As I cocked my leg over the sill to get onto the fire escape Sonny stopped me.

'This is for me to do, Mr Price, not you.' He took the gun out of my hands.

'Wrong, Sonny. You're just the hired help and not paid to risk your life. You know what Evan said if anything like this happened. Just give them the money and let them go. Well that applies to you, not me. Nobody takes from me or mine and the Griffiths' are more family than I've ever known. So give me the gun, quick; before they get away.'

'I ain't arguing with you, Mr Price,' he said taking hold of my shoulders and pulling me back into the room. I sat ignominiously on the floor as Sonny slipped through the window and down the steps.

I got up, dusted myself down and went to the door to take another look. Two of the gunmen covered the people who were lined up against the wall and the third was making one of the girls stuff money into a sack. I knew there was not much cash there because Evan had taken it to the bank. That being the case I expected their attention to be directed up to me at any moment. Nor was I disappointed. Frightened I was, disappointed I wasn't – though I wished it had been the other way around.

I don't know what would have happened if a fourth man had not put his head in and yelled, 'Junior, it's the Marshal, with Griffiths.' The masked man at the tills whirled around. Up until that moment I would not have

recognised any of them but now I knew who it was . . .
Duke Roybal's son, Junior.

'You're Junior Roybal,' one of the women customers
called, pointing a finger at him. What possessed the damn
fool of a woman I don't know. At that second Sion ran in
from a side entrance, and I knew Meg would not be far
behind him. Sonny came in from the back and a number
of things happened at once. Junior must have panicked
when the door burst open and Sion appeared because he
whirled and fired, shooting Sion in the head. A woman
screamed and the three robbers turned to run for the
door. Sonny stepped forward and fired both barrels into
the backs of the fleeing men. Roybal was in front and was
screened by his two friends. He escaped unharmed while
the other two were cut down, almost blown in half by the
force of that scatter gun. All this I saw without really
looking because I was stumbling and running down the
steps to get to Sion.

I was never more scared in my life. He was lying in a
pool of blood but when I knelt beside him I saw he was
still breathing. The bullet had caught him on the side of
the head and though it had furrowed quite deeply there
was still a chance. Meg came in, dropped her parcels and
ran forward. Typically, she neither screamed nor went
into hysterics but instead reached for a roll of cotton, and
tried to rip it. I took it from her and used my pocket knife
to cut it up. She ordered somebody to go for the doctor.

I tried to stop the bleeding and make Sion more
comfortable. I wrapped my coat around him to keep him
warm and Sonny got some more cotton to use as a cover
for him. Sion was ashen white and though his pulse was
feeble at least it was still beating. Evan and the Marshal
ran in. Evan knelt by his son, looking at the inert body.
Tears were in his eyes when he looked at me.

'Who did it?' he asked.

'Junior Roybal,' I replied quietly. 'Meg's sent for
the doctor. He shouldn't be long. We heard Junior's

accomplice yelling that you were coming. Didn't you see them?'

'Yes, but they were away before we knew what was happening.'

'Sonny's killed the other two,' said the marshal.

Meg and Evan held hands, kneeling alongside Sion. 'How is he, do you think?' she asked softly.

'He's still breathing but that's about all.' Evan got abruptly to his feet. 'Aren't you going after them, marshal?' he asked harshly.

'I'm doing all I can Mr Griffiths. One of my deputies is rounding up a posse right now. We'll go and see if we can trail them but I don't have much hope.' He was a slow-witted man in his fifties, ponderous in his movements and never far from the nearest saloon.

'You don't need to trail them. If you hurry you'll probably get Roybal at his father's ranch. If he's left there already then you need to send wires to all the towns along the line to look out for him. That way he won't get far.' Evan had already thought everything through, in spite of his anxiety about Sion.

'Now we ain't exactly sure it was Junior, Mr Griffiths. After all he was wearing a mask. No one can be sure about him.'

'Bullshit, marshal and you know it,' Sonny said angrily. 'Mr Griffiths let me tell you something about our good marshal here. He has always looked after the interests of the ranchers above those of anyone else because he's in their pay. He won't make a move against Roybal until he's had time to contact him and let him come up with an alibi.'

'Now Sonny, that ain't fair,' the marshal said angrily. 'I look after everyone's interests . . .'

'Shit, marshal, and you know it. Mr Griffiths, remember when you had the fight with Roybal? Who did the marshal try and make trouble for? It was only because there were so many witnesses he wasn't able to do anything. If he can cover up for Junior I bet anything you like his bank balance will receive a nice little gift over the next few months. It's a fact, Mr Griffiths, I ain't joshing you.'

Evan turned his piercing blue eyes, like chips of ice, onto the marshal.

'That ain't true and I'm going to arrest you for saying them things without proof. We'll soon see whose side I'm on and that's the fact.' I thought he was lying. Evan must have felt so too.

He stepped over to the marshal, grabbed hold of his vest and when the man squawked Evan drew his gun, cocked it and shoved the barrel into the marshal's face. 'I don't believe you. Say the words and deputise me, you bastard, before I pull the trigger.'

'Listen,' the marshal's voice was a high pitched squeal. 'Listen, you can't do this to me. I'm the marshal. You wait with the . . .' he suddenly stopped as Evan ground the barrel of the gun into his cheek, saying, 'I swear by all that I hold holy that if you don't deputise me right now I'll shoot you and hang the consequences.'

The marshal mumbled some words. 'All right, you're deputised,' he said in a strained voice. 'But I don't have a badge for you to wear and you gotta have a badge.' There was satisfaction in his voice which quickly changed to a meek protest when Evan ripped the marshal's own badge off his vest.

'Now I've got one.' Evan turned to Sonny. 'Is the buckboard outside and ready to go?' Sonny nodded. 'Meg love, will you be all right with the little one? I'll be as quick as I can,' he knelt by her side, the harshness gone from his voice.

She nodded. 'You'd better hurry before he gets away.'

He stood up. Meg looked up at him, tears in her eyes. 'Take care, Evan, and . . . and kill the swine if you have to.'

'Mac, you and Frank stay with the marshal until I get

back. If he tries to send word to Roybal . . .' Evan trailed off. After all he could not, nor would he suggest they did something illegal. He didn't need to.

'Don't worry, Mr Griffiths, he won't,' Mac assured Evan with a grin.

I had helped myself to a jacket from the warehouses rack and when Evan ran outside I was with him. He didn't notice me until he had the reigns in his hands and I clambered alongside him.

'You aren't coming, Uncle James. Stay and help Meg.'

'Nope. I'm coming all right. Meg's got enough help. Now drive on before we lose any more time.'

'No, I . . .' before he could say any more I leaned past him, picked up the whip and flicked it across the rumps of the two horses. They jerked into life and Evan had to concentrate on guiding them. He couldn't argue at the same time.

Sonny galloped past us and yelled, 'I'll show you a short cut, Mr Griffiths. Follow me.'

'Sonny, come back here,' Evan yelled, but to no avail. 'Damn, I'd wondered where he'd got to.'

We kept the pace down until we reached the edge of town. Sonny stayed a hundred yards ahead. Once we were on the country road Evan whipped up the horses and we began racing at a dangerous speed. I hung on grimly for dear life as we bounced over potholes and rocks, but I managed to find time to think about the reception we could expect at the Roybal ranch.

24

WE WERE FIVE miles out of town when Sonny pointed to his right and turned onto a narrow track. We slowed down and followed carefully. We had been going as fast as the horses could manage and now they were badly winded. Mind you, so was I from trying to hold onto that bucking, jumping, swaying, rattling buckboard. Sonny dropped back to ride by our side.

'This road is much rougher than the other way, Mr Griffiths, but it's half the distance. I figure we got a better chance of getting there faster this way because otherwise you're just going to run them horses clear into the ground and they'll be dead affore we gets there.'

'Fine, Sonny,' Evan was concentrating on guiding us past a big pot hole in the snow covered road. The road we had left had been virtually snow free but this one was mostly covered, though here and there patches of ground and bare rocks showed through.

I was glad of the jacket I had picked up. If I hadn't had it I'd have been freezing to death by now. I reached inside the coat and checked my gun was still there.

'It don't look like they came this way, Mr Griffiths. The few tracks I can see look too old to me. Maybe they went the other road.'

'Or maybe they aren't headed this way at all. Perhaps he's not going home to his Pa,' Evan said with bitterness.

'I don't know about that, sir, but I do know Junior. Knowed him most of my life, I reckon. If he's gone anywhere it's home, cause he knows his Pa will do the best he can to look after him. Junior'd know that without his Pa's help he ain't going to get away.'

'Do you think he'll try and run for it?' asked Evan.

'I dunno and that's a fact. I'd say that would be Junior's idea but the old man would cross examine him, find out the chances of bluffing it out and maybe try for that.'

'Have you been out to the ranch before, Sonny?' I enquired.

'Sure, Mr Price. Why do you ask?'

'I want you to describe it to me. Because in spite of what Evan thinks, we aren't just going to bust in hoping for the best. In a couple of hours it'll be dark and we're going in there nice and slow and careful.' Evan looked at me in surprise. 'I'm here to make sure you get back to Meg in one piece,' I said.

That road was certainly rough but when we rejoined onto the main road we had saved about nine miles. It was now fast approaching sunset.

We still had a fair way to go and Evan whipped up the horses again, but this time kept them to a speed they could cope with.

The moon was rising when we finally pulled up at the gates leading to the house. In the silver light I could just make out the house, the big barn, some other buildings and the hands' bunkhouse.

We left the buckboard and Sonny's horse hidden in a copse of trees fifty yards from the gate. Evan had the rifle we kept in the buckboard, Sonny took his from his saddle and handed me the sawn-off shotgun along with a handful of ammunition. I felt better, holding that gun in my hands.

The snow crunched under our feet though mostly the track was mud with deep ruts made by wagons and horses' hooves. Our breath turned opaque in the cold as we made our way silently towards the buildings. Evan had the Marshal's badge pinned prominently to his coat.

I was not altogether convinced that walking straight in like this was a good idea; I would have preferred to sneak by the back entrance. But Evan argued that if Roybal was going to bluff it out he would be acting as normal as possible. If he was going to get his son away then the chances were that he had already done so. The only problem was that Roybal would be expecting the marshal who, no doubt, would have played along with him.

We reached the first of the outbuildings and if we had been seen nobody was giving the game away. We continued to the main house. It was a one-storey rambling building with a veranda running along the front. Sonny went around to the back while we counted fifty to give him time to get into position. Evan and I stood by the front door straining to hear what was being said inside. There was an argument going on and it sounded like father and son. With a last look around Evan took hold of the door handle and turned it silently.

The door opened with a low squeak. We stepped straight into their main room just as Sonny had described it. It was well lit with oil-filled lamps and a fire burning brightly in the grate. The two men spun round and when he saw us, Junior, with an oath, went for his gun. Which was very stupid because Evan had his rifle trained on him. Luckily for Junior the old man stopped him in time. I closed the door behind us just as Sonny came in from the kitchen.

'What's the meaning of this outrage?' blustered Roybal. 'I demand you leave this house immediately.'

'You know something?' said Evan in a low voice. 'You really are the limit, Roybal. Here I am again within an inch of killing you and you're making demands.' Evan shook his head mockingly. 'I've come to take your son in for murder. At least, God willing, it might be attempted murder. If my son is dead when I get back then I shall kill Junior with my own hands and that's a promise.'

'What are you talking about?' Junior said angrily. 'Tell

him pa. Tell him I've been here all afternoon. Go on pa, tell him.' Junior coaxed his father as Evan slowly closed the gap between them. I stepped to one side and kept my scattergun pointed at Junior's middle. The old man was unarmed, but even so, Sonny kept him covered. Sonny moved away from the door and stood with his back to the wall. I did the same thing in case we were interrupted.

'Stay away from me. I tell you I was here all afternoon. Tell him Pa, please tell him.' He was begging now, bending slightly as though he had a pain in his stomach.

'What did you say, Griffiths, about your son?' asked Roybal in a voice so strained I thought he was about to collapse.

'Your son tried to rob my warehouse today. When my youngest son accidentally came rushing in he was shot in the head.' Evan turned his blue, contempt filled eyes onto Roybal. 'Junior fired the shot. I understand that you protect your son, it's a natural reaction, but this time not even you can lie for him. A small ten year old boy lying in a pool of blood, gunned down by this animal.' Evan was now no more than the barrel length of his rifle from Junior and without warning smashed the gun across Junior's right wrist. We heard the unmistakable crunch of bone breaking. Junior gave a scream and dropped sobbing to the floor. Roybal looked as though he was about to jump Evan, but Evan swung the rifle to point at him.

'I assure you, I just want the excuse.' Evan tapped his own chest. 'This badge makes it legal and I don't mind shooting you while you're aiding your son to resist arrest.'

'You'd never get away with it. It'll be murder,' said Roybal hoarsely.

'Sonny, do you think I'd get away with it?' Evan asked in a calm voice.

'Sure, no problem, Mr Griffiths. In fact I'll be right glad to do it myself, now.' Sonny aimed his rifle at Junior's head. 'Just say the word, Mr Griffiths.'

'How,' Roybal's voice croaked and he cleared his throat. 'How do you know it was my son, Griffiths?'

'He was recognised by a lot of people. Furthermore,' I said, answering for Evan, 'the lookout he had stationed outside the warehouse called him by his name, see. Mr Roybal, it isn't an easy thing to admit but your son might be a child killer. At best he's hurt that little boy real bad.'

'It's not true Pa, it's not true.' Junior was holding his wrist, tears running down his face. 'I didn't do nothing like that Pa, I swear it. I lied earlier on Pa,' Junior said desperately, seeing the contempt on his father's face. 'I did try to rob his place Pa, but it was only to get our own back on him for what he did to you Pa. But I didn't shoot the boy, Pa, honest I didn't. It was one of the others. Buck did it, Pa. It was Buck. Don't look at me like that. I only went there for you. For what he did to you Pa, honest, Pa.'

There were tears in old man Roybal's eyes as he looked at his son. 'All these years I ignored it all. I helped you all I could, made excuses because your Ma was dead. I knowed you was no good. Never have been since you was a little un. But I always put it down to high spirits, sure you'd grow up and be able to take over this ranch one day. I did all I could to teach you what I know but you were always more interested in being in town, boasting to your so-called friends, getting drunk rather than be earning a living out here with me. You cost me a fortune one way an' another, getting you out of scrape after scrape – putting me in hock with favours to my friends when I persuaded them you were only joshing. Growing up was the excuse, always. Well, boy, you are growed up now and you got to take what's coming to you.' He looked at Evan. 'I hate you Griffiths but I hope your boy lives and I hope he turns out as bad as my own. So you'll know what it's like.'

'Pa, you can't do this, Pa. Pa I'll be good from

now on. Please Pa, don't let them take me,' Junior sobbed.

'You stupid fool,' said his father angrily. 'What do you expect me to do? There's three guns pointing at me. I'm not immune to lead. Even if I did want to help you there's nothing I can do. Now be a man, damn you, just for once. Try and walk out of here without disgracing me in front of the hands. Just for this once be a man, son. I beg you.' It was pitiful to hear the distress in his voice.

'No, Pa. You can't. Please do something.'

'I'll get you the best lawyer I can find Junior, but that's all. Now get up and go with these men.'

'I won't . . . I . . .' Junior gasped in pain, Evan's boot in his ribs cutting off the flow of words.

'Get up or I'll break your other wrist. And after that I'll start on your legs. With both of them broken I'll carry you to the buckboard. Get up, you little swine.'

Awkwardly, Junior scrambled to his feet. 'They're going to kill me on the way Pa. I can see they are. Don't let them Pa. Don't let them kill me.'

'I don't intend killing him yet, Mr Roybal. I shall if I have to. And I'll have to if my son is dead. If my son still lives, the law will deal with Junior.' Evan prodded Junior in the back and reluctantly he walked towards the door.

If he hadn't turned to beg his father one more time Roybal would have saved him.

'Please Pa . . .' was as far as he got but it made me look back at Roybal. Evan stayed facing Junior, prodding him towards the door. Sonny too, had his eyes on Junior.

I turned in time to see Roybal lift a shotgun down from over the mantelpiece and point it at us. I lifted my scattergun, aimed it in the general direction and fired. Roybal went over backwards, guts and blood spilling everywhere. Evan whirled and crouched. Sonny threw himself down flat while Junior gave a low moan.

There was a commotion outside, made by the hands, but suddenly it all went quiet.

'Sonny, check if he's dead,' ordered Evan. 'Are you okay, Uncle James?' I nodded. 'Fine,' I croaked. 'He had a gun and was going to use it, Evan.' I felt I had to explain.

'I know. It's okay. Thanks. You probably saved our lives. Sonny?'

'He's deader than a skinned rabbit, Mr Griffiths.'

'I guess in the long run he couldn't let his boy go,' said Evan sadly.

Junior just stood still not saying a word.

'You outside,' Evan yelled through the door.

'Who is that? Where's Mr Roybal?'

'I'm a deputy marshal sent here to take in Junior for . . . for possible child m . . . m . . . murder,' Evan stumbled over the words, 'a little boy. Roybal is dead. I'm coming out alone and unarmed. Will one of you men come and meet me, so we can talk?'

'All right, but no tricks now. Come out nice and slow.'

'If there's any shooting kill Junior and try and hold then off until help gets here. The marshal will have to send a posse sooner or later.'

'Let me go, Evan,' I said. 'If something does happen you and Sonny have a better chance of getting away than me.'

'No. It's my . . .,' Evan said and turned to the door. He fell as I stunned him with the butt of the scattergun, careful not to hit him too hard, dropped the gun and opened the door.

I grinned in spite of myself when I heard Evan. 'Son of a bitch. That crazy old man.'

It was not heroics that sent me out there but common sense. If I got killed it wouldn't matter too much. If Evan died then what would happen to the family? Nope, I loved them all and this was the best way. On top of all that I was nearing seventy and Evan wasn't thirty two yet. He still had his whole life ahead of him while mine was almost over.

There were no bullets. No hail of deadly lead, just a hazy figure in the shadow of the bunkhouse who came forward hesitantly.

'Who are you?' he called from the safety of the darkness.

'My name is Price,' I walked off the veranda and into the open. 'I work for the Griffiths warehouse. Remember the trouble between Roybal and Griffiths?'

'I remember.'

'Junior held us up earlier today and shot a ten year old boy – Griffiths' son. We were sent ahead of a posse to arrest him. We're taking him back to town to stand trial. Roybal tried to stop us and I shot him. He's dead. You come up and have a look if you want. I'm not armed as you can see.' I held my hands away from my sides.

Slowly the man came forward. He turned out to be the foreman of the ranch. He took it all calmly. He could see what had happened and I guessed that from his knowledge of Junior and his father stopped him being surprised by it.

'Thirty years I've been here . . .' he shook his head, sadly. 'You never were any good, Junior. But I reckon I owe it to your father to see you get safely to jail. I'm sending three of the men with you.'

We didn't object. The foreman seemed a straight enough man. He was a cowpuncher and not a gunslinger.

On the way Junior begged the men to set him free. He kept at them until one of the riders finally threatened to shoot him if he didn't shut up. 'I don't help no child killer,' were his words.

I saw Evan tense. Now that it was all over we could let our thoughts turn to Sion. I felt a sickness in my stomach. We could not move very fast – the light was bad and the horses tired. We went back the long way round and arrived at the outskirts of town not long before dawn.

We found out later that though our men had stopped the

marshal sending a message to Roybal they had not been
able to stop him cancelling the posse. He was shocked
when we arrived at his office. We turned Junior over to
him and told him about Roybal.

'If,' said Evan, 'you try and make anything of Roybal's
death I'll have you hounded out of office so fast you'll
wonder what happened. And if you think I can't do it,
just try me.'

We rushed home, Sonny with us. The closer we got to
the house the sicker I felt. I found I was praying harder
than I had in a long time. By now Evan was getting every
ounce of effort out of the horses and they gamely tried to
run. At the house we jumped down and ran inside. Meg
must have heard us on the stairs as she came out of Sion's
room and threw her arms around Evan, tears streaming
down her cheeks. For a moment my heart stood still, so
sure was I that he was dead. David came out of the room
his eyes red rimmed and watery.

'How is he?' Evan asked quietly.

'He's still unconscious, but he seems a little better. The
doctor thinks he'll live. But,' her voice faltered, 'he can't
be sure if there won't be brain damage of some kind.' Her
tears were drying up and she wiped her face with the back
of her hand. 'God, it seems an eternity you were gone.
What happened? Oh, hullo Sonny. Let's go down and
I'll make some coffee.'

'I just came to see if Sion was all right, Mrs Griffiths.
I'd better get on back now, but thanks all the same.'

'Nonsense. Come and have some coffee with us. I
know I could use some and I'm sure you can as well,'
said Evan gruffly. 'I'll just go in and see if . . . see
he's okay.'

I followed him. Sion was deathly white, his head
swathed in bandages. He was not moving and scarcely
breathing. I sat by his bedside and took hold of his hand.
It was icy cold. Gently I tucked it under the blankets and
sat back in the chair. Evan touched my shoulder.

'Coffee?' he asked.

I shook my head. 'Later. I'll just sit here for a wee while.' I sat there I don't know how long but well past sunrise. If I could have changed places with that little boy I would have done so gladly. I loved him just a little bit more than the rest of the family. He was . . . special. I thought about the kite flying we'd done and his ideas for a bigger kite. How excited he had been only the evening before about a new design he wanted to try out. He was a clever little lad, there was no getting away from it. I vowed if he died I would kill Junior, not Evan. The thought of Sion having brain damage preyed on my mind until I felt I was going mad trying to imagine how it would affect him.

None of us went to the warehouse for the next three days; I don't think it entered our heads. We thought only of Sion; nothing else mattered.

It was five o'clock on the third morning and Evan was sitting beside him when Sion finally regained consciousness. After that his recovery was rapid. Soon, he was taking a light broth, his hours of wakefulness grew longer and his interest in what was going on increased. As far as we could tell there was no difference in Sion but it was an anxious time.

I stopped working at the warehouse and stayed at home to look after him. Meg stayed for the first couple of weeks too, but gradually the warehouse claimed more of her time. She did some of her paperwork at home, but with me there, there was no reason for her to stay away from the warehouse.

In fact, if the truth were known, I had been finding it more and more tiring going in every day and after we went after Junior I was exhausted for a week.

Sonny had coped admirably by himself during the first few days when none of us went into the warehouse and he easily took over from me. He was given the title of Warehouse Manager and Frank, one of our more able staff, was made up into Sonny's old job. Evan gave everybody on the payroll a ten percent pay rise, in appreciation for all they had done.

Evan wrote to John Buchanan telling him what had happened and John sent Sion a fisherman's knife from Scotland, which became his pride and joy second only possibly to Thunderbolt.

Not being able to ride his horse was Sion's hardest cross to bear and he was forever nagging me to let him have a short ride. But it was out of the question and would remain so for some time yet.

Evan and Meg also began a lively correspondence with the folks back in Wales. I use the term lively in a jocular sense because it took anything up to two months to send a letter and another two to receive a reply. Although Meg wrote to her mother regularly she never received a reply, not once, something that upset her a lot.

Evan constructed a small safe in the floor of the study and we took to keeping the takings there instead of in the bank. He used what remained in the bank account to buy more merchandise but after that kept only a token amount with the bank. It was just as well.

That year, in 1893, Grover Cleveland was returned to the White House as President for his second term in office. No sooner had he taken the oath when a major panic burst across the country. Even before that things had been tough. The Populist revolt that had been sweeping the country had taken hold like a religious revival. The party embraced all the Alliances that had grown up between the various farming groups and the many other minority groups such as the remnants of the Knights of Labour, of the Greenback and Union parties, advocates of woman suffrage, Socialists, single-taxers, silverites and professional reformers. They all came together to help the common people, the small businessmen and farmers. One of their most popular speakers was a woman, Mary Ellen Lease who came to St. Louis one day in Spring.

I remembered some of her impassioned speech which was quoted at length in the newspapers. She said: 'Wall Street owns the country. It is no longer a government of the people, for the people, but a government of Wall Street, by Wall Street and for Wall street. Our laws are the output of a system that clothes rascals in robes and honesty in rags.'

Her speech had a profound effect on Evan and he began to take a more active interest in local politics. That does not mean to say he did anything more than read and keep abreast of the situation across the country. Business houses crashed, banks closed their doors, railroads went into the hands of the receivers, factories shut down, trade languished and creditors foreclosed their mortgages. In the cities, long lines of unemployed men waited outside soup kitchens, and in the country thousands added to the army of tramps. It was all as Evan had expected, though he often said, expecting it and seeing it were monstrously different. Before things got really bad we built up a large stock of non-perishable food, and reduced our stocks of the other, non-food, items. People would always have to eat, said Evan. I agreed with him, except, as I pointed out, when they couldn't afford to. By the autumn an awful lot couldn't.

Only three good things happened that year. Sion made a complete recovery by the late Spring. Junior Roybal was convicted and sentenced to the state penitentiary for fifteen years, lucky not to have been hung. However, he only served two years and three months before he was killed when trying to escape. And we built up a library in the study. While the boys bought and read such books as "Huckleberry Finn" and "Tom Sawyer" by Mark Twain, Meg took to reading "The Portrait of a Lady", "The American", "The Ambassadors", and "The Wings of a Dove" by Henry James. Evan stayed with law and economics. We all read "Uncle Tom's Cabin" by Harriet Beecher Stowe and I then started on all Twain's books like "Life on the Mississippi", "Roughing It" and "Innocents Abroad". These were the first complete books I had ever read, and I took great pleasure from them.

Business, of course, dropped right off but did not stop altogether. There were plenty of wealthy people in the area who found the depression no more than a hindrance. Because of Evan's foresight and John Buchanan's advice we possessed the best stocked warehouse in the area. At the worst period of the depression we were still making enough on our turnover to pay the bills and wages. We also never had to sack anybody or reduce their wages as so many other employers did. The only change was that the work altered slightly. There was not enough to do for all of them to be kept even moderately busy during the day so we started a system of having two men on guard during the night. It was a wise precaution because in the next year alone there were sixteen attempted burglaries, none of which came near to success. Evan occasionally did a spell of guard duty, though not as often as he would have liked because of the pressure of his own work.

In the house it was easy to forget there was a depression. It was only in town that the real meaning of it came home. More and more men were out of work and more and more businesses failed. The papers were filled with gloomy prophecies and slated the President for not doing something about the situation. I noticed there were few suggestions as to what he should do. Unfortunately, the President was convinced the whole thing would blow over and his prevalent philosophy became what the papers called laissez faire. I agreed with them when Meg explained what it meant.

From time to time Evan and Meg went to New York to buy more merchandise, and each time they came back with the most fearful tales of riots, strikes, fighting in the streets between workers and soldiers, the huge soup queues which, luckily, we didn't see in St Louis. And of course prices rocketed. Bank after bank closed and the depression got worse and worse as time went on.

25

THE NEXT FEW years saw a backlash against the government and the moneyed few who were held to be responsible. There was the Homestead strike, resulting in a pitched battle and the great Pullman strike of '94 which tied up the railroads of half the nation and became known as the strike that best exemplified the situation in America. When the representatives of the workers had appealed to Pullman to talk about their wage problem they were summarily dismissed. The workers promptly went on strike and the newly organised American Railway Union sided with the Pullman workers and directed its men not to handle Pullman cars. With that, war broke out between the railroads and workers and it covered half the nation. The North and West became paralysed. One newspaper called it a war against the government and society. An employers' organisation, called the General Managers Association, demanded the Federal Government intervene to maintain the railway service.

An injunction was brought against the workers and suddenly all hell broke loose. The Governor of Illinois was ready, with his state militia, to act, but before he could, Cleveland sent in Federal troops to Chicago. The injunction broke the strike and the troops almost broke the labour movement. The Governor protested that the Constitution had been violated with the sending in of the troops but for his pains all he received was a rebuke from the President and a repudiation by the courts. The bosses had won all along the line and it seemed to me that they always won. We had come from Wales to escape this sort of tyranny but here we found it as great as ever. It was true to say we were making money and had a way of life far better than we'd had in the old country but that was not everything. Evan used to burn with the injustice of it, screwing the newspaper up in disgust when he read what was happening.

Just after the Pullman strike was over, I was making one of my rare appearances at the warehouse. I sat across the desk from Evan, drinking coffee.

'How long do you think all this will go on for?' I asked him.

Evan shrugged. 'I honestly don't know Uncle James and I have no ideas. It's the same all over. There's no work and the queues for soup are lengthening. It'll end, of that I have no doubt, but God knows when,' he paused and sipped his coffee. 'One thing I'm glad of, though, and that's John came to see us a couple of Christmases back. I never told you this but, though I'd had the feeling things were going to go sour I couldn't admit them to myself. Know what I mean?'

'Seemed too far-fetched, did they, bach?'

'Yes. But it was more than that. Hell, I didn't really know much about economics and the like, and still don't really, in spite of all I've read. I just couldn't believe I was right. After all, nobody else seemed to think the way I did. If John hadn't come and confirmed what I was thinking I wouldn't have made the arrangements I did. In fact we could well have gone bust, like some of the others. Oh well, we'll get a bigger place one day but not until things improve.'

'Hmmm. Let's hope they do – soon. When are you planning on another trip to New York? I see the stock is getting low.'

Evan nodded gloomily. 'I didn't want to risk going in case the strike had escalated. But now the railroads are

nearly back to normal I'd better go next week. I'll talk to
Meg about it and see what she says. Mind you, haven't
the boys got something on at their school next week; the
parents go along for a visit or something?'

I nodded. Come hell, high water or business, the family
was first with Evan and always would be. I was about to
reply when Hans Reisenbach appeared at the door. I had
not seen him for months and though Evan had told me
how worn and tired he looked I was still unprepared for
the defeated looking man before us.

'Ach, am I interrupting something?' he said with a
ghost of his former smile. He ambled into the room.

'Nothing at all, Hans,' said Evan. 'Grab a seat while I
go and get some coffee.'

'Ja, thank you. That will be nice. And how are you
keeping, James? You are looking good.'

'I've no complaints Hans. What about you and the
family?'

Hans shook his head and I had the impression he was
trying not to cry. He cleared his throat. 'It is all over, my
friend. I have come to say goodbye to Evan and I had
hoped Meg too, but I see she is not here.'

'She'll be back shortly,' I replied. 'But what do you
mean it's over? Why are you saying goodbye?'

Evan had come back in time to hear my question.

'What's happening Hans?' he asked, handing him
a coffee.

'It is quite simple Evan. I am pulling out. Me and the
family and one or two others are going. Ve are finished,'
he shrugged helplessly.

'I don't understand. How can you be finished? And
where are you going to? Hell, I've seen your place. It's
a thriving farm,' said Evan.

'Evan, Evan, Evan,' Hans spoke with all the weariness
in the world. 'You know I have a mortgage on my
property. There are very few farms in the territory that
don't. Ve have made a good living, eaten well, vorked

hard and enjoyed ourselves. But to stay in the farming business ve have had to keep investing in new equipment, borrow to get us over bad times, like the drought three years back.' He gave a helpless gesture with his hand. 'You know farm prices have steadily dropped during the last . . . God Almighty . . . twenty years and look at them now. I've always managed to get enough cash to pay the interest on my loan but not the capital. Now the bank has foreclosed. In tventy minutes,' he looked at the wall clock, 'tventy-two to be precise, I vill no longer own my farm. After all these years . . .'

Hurriedly he took a sip of coffee, half choking on it. 'Ach, I must go. Ingrid is vaiting for me to help her pack. I believe they give us a veek to get out of our own home. So, goodbye my friend,' he leaned across the desk, his hand outstretched.

Evan ignored it.

'Sit down Hans. Why the hell – Good God . . . I seem to be saying that every other sentence nowadays. Why didn't you come to me sooner and tell me? Do you think so little of me as a friend you couldn't have asked me to lend you some money? And what about the others? Has Wilhelm and Erwin the same problem? What about Heinz?' Evan was angry.

'Evan, don't go on. They vill all be following soon. And it is because you are my friend that I didn't come to you. How soon vould you stop calling me friend if I owed you money? How do you think I could have faced you? Or how could the others face you if the money we owed vas to you and not an impersonal bank?'

Evan's anger evaporated. 'Don't you see, that's what the banks want? They'll get your land for a song and in a few years when all this is over they'll be able to sell it back to you or somebody very much like you for a vast profit. Their hold on this country will be strengthened even further and I believe they already have us in a stranglehold.'

'Ja, that is true but vat are ve to do? I vill not take money from you and I am sure the others vill not either. So they vill vin, yet again.'

'Don't be so bloodymindedly Germanic and pig headed. Before we go any further tell me how much you need to pay.'

'I vill do no such . . .'

'Hans we're talking about money, a small amount when you remember I owe you me life.'

'I vould never trade on such a thing. You owe me nothing, Evan, nothing.'

'I know you wouldn't trade on it but that's immaterial. Just tell me how much you owe.'

Hans shrugged. 'I . . . I owe eight hundred dollars to the bank, and have done so now for . . . for the last ten years, at six percent.'

'Good God Almighty. You're uprooting your family, giving up all you've worked for, for a pittance in interest? Hans, you're a fool and I never thought you were that,' Evan said in a thin voice.

'There is nothing I can do. I know families who have been thrown out for a lot less. The banks have taken over thousands and thousands of acres of good land at less than ten cents in the dollar, the dirty bastards . . .' Hans spoke with understandable venom and a flash of anger. 'I also did not come here to be insulted by you Evan, only to say goodbye to a friend. I had hoped ve could part the same vay . . .'

'That's more like it,' Evan smiled. 'That's more like the fighter of old. Now will you listen to some common sense? Look you, man, we haven't got much time. If I know the bank they really want to foreclose, so you have to get there before noon. Hans, just do one thing. I'll give you a cheque for the forty eight dollars interest. Go and pay the bank before it's too late and then come back here so we can discuss what is to be done for the others.' Hans hesitated. 'Hans, think of the family. Where

are you going? What are you going to do? Don't you owe
it to Ingrid to accept this? You're what? Almost fifty and
too old to be travelling across the country looking for
somewhere to live. How will you support yourselves? By
doing odd jobs for handouts? Hans, there are thousands of
young men doing that right now. How will you compete
with them? You'll have to work to keep the family alive.'
Evan took out his cheque book and began writing. 'This
is not the time nor the place to argue. Hurry now, Hans,
before it's too late.' Evan glanced at the clock and held
out the cheque.

Hans hesitated and reluctantly closed his fingers on the
piece of paper. He smiled sadly. 'I don't like what I'm
doing, Evan, even though I know you're right.'

'You don't have to like it, just hurry, before it's too
late. Just think how pleased Ingrid will be.'

'I vill accept it and I thank you from the bottom of my
heart. I go now.' Hans clapped his hat on his head and
rushed from the office.

Evan shrugged at me, 'I couldn't let him go. David
would never have forgiven me if Gunhild had got away.'

Evan took out his little black book, a gift he received
every Christmas from John Buchanan and began adding
and subtracting figures. I knew that was where he kept a
running account of what he was worth and so I kept quiet
while he did his sums. After a few minutes he closed the
book with a snap.

'We have no debts, right, Uncle James?'

I nodded. I knew that.

'We also have about eighteen thousand dollars worth
of goods in the warehouse. That's below the amount we
usually hold and I need to get to New York soon. At
the present prices I'll need to spend about thirty eight
thousand to restock. That leaves us with twenty two
thousand in cash, in the safe back home. There's also
a hundred or so now left in the bank but that's not worth
bothering about. I think we'll take the whole damned lot

and set up a fund to help the farmers. We'll have to charge interest, but how much? Less than the banks charge, that's for sure. At the moment we're accumulating money which is growing mildew in our safe because we aren't prepared to risk it in a bank. We aren't going to use it until the situation has improved and we've more than enough to run the business. What if we charged five percent? Is that fair?'

'You want to charge interest because otherwise they won't borrow it from us. Try them at four percent. Though altogether, with what they're paying the banks it'll come out at a lot of money. Why, that'll mean Hans needing to find eh, eighty dollars next year. That's a lot.'

Evan nodded. 'Except I only want the interest on what they'll owe. In the case of Hans that will be less than two dollars.'

'Will you want any collateral? Their deeds will be with the bank.'

'I've thought of that. I'll take any farm produce that they have left to reduce their loans. So it's only a matter of finding two dollars or so every year.' He broke off as we heard footsteps on the stairs. 'Ah, if I'm not mistaken that'll be Hans.'

Hans came in panting, and with a smile on his lips. 'That . . . that was . . . vorth it . . . You should . . . have seen . . . Fforest's face . . . He did . . . did not like it . . . one little bit.'

'Good,' said Evan. 'James and I have been discussing things and we've got a proposition to make, above board and legal and it'll allow me to make some money. It'll also allow you and the others to keep your farms. Look, I've got a lot of work to do. Why don't you and James go and have a beer and he'll tell you all about it.'

'Ja, and thank you again. I vould like you to come to a house varming party on Saturday.'

'A house warming?' I asked.

'Ja. That is vat I said. Vhen a man t'inks he has lost

his house and suddenly he still has it, it is like going to a new place,' he chuckled.

We left for the nearest saloon.

I was given the task of administering the fund. Thanks to Hans we had over a hundred farmers using it within a few months, much to the chagrin of the bank. From the day we started until we ended it in the summer of 1899, it was a success.

Whether it was luck or design but when the First Bank of Mississippi failed towards the end of that year we only had a hundred and eight dollars and sixty one cents deposited there. The farmers were jubilant at first. They had paid their interest, so the bank could not foreclose on them. Surely this would mean the banks would have to return their mortgages to the farmers? Or if the banks went into the hands of a receiver, would the farmers be allowed to buy them back at say ten or twenty cents on the dollar? The money could be borrowed from the farmers' fund. Anything was possible, and the farmers looked on the situation with hope which turned out to be short-lived. Within a month the bank reopened under the same name and with only two differences. The bank expanded and the shareholders were now big bankers from back east. Eric Johnson, our fellow passenger from the SS Cardiff was on the board of directors.

Andrew Z Fforest was promoted from loans to General Manager and the bank became harsher in its dealings. No leeway was allowed for repayment of loans, not even extensions of a few days. Small businessmen and one or two farmers who had not used our scheme went out of business for pitiful sums. Suicide was not uncommon and more than one man killed his family before killing himself, rather than face the future and having to start all over again with nothing.

We were sitting in the study after dinner. I can't say we were enjoying our coffee, because Evan was pacing the floor, angrily denouncing the Government and capitalists in equal measure.

'Can't the fools see what they're doing to the country? Doesn't any of them care?'

'Evan,' said Meg, 'I suggest you sit down and calm down. It's no good getting yourself all worked up. If you carry on like this you'll have a heart attack.'

Evan stopped in front of her chair, leaned over and kissed her cheek. 'I'll worry about the country and you worry about me. How will that be?'

Meg turned to me. 'Honestly, Uncle James, what am I to do with him? He's incorrigible,' Meg took his hand in hers.

I sipped thoughtfully at my whisky and interrupted Evan as he was about to start on again. 'You could go and do something about it if you really cared.'

'What do you mean? What could I do?'

'Well for one thing you could go and join the Democrats and give them your active support instead of ranting and raving at home,' said Meg.

After a few seconds of thought, Evan said, 'All right. You find out what happens around town and we'll go and see what we can do.' He took a satisfied drink of whisky. 'I rather like that idea after all. Though,' he added with a touch of alarm, 'there's nothing going to induce me to get up and make a speech in front of a lot of people.'

'I'm sure no inducement will be necessary,' replied Meg with a straight face.

In November Meg received a letter from Wales. She and I were in the kitchen enjoying a cup of coffee when the mail arrived. Meg was nagging me to give up smoking at the time, I seem to remember.

She propped her chin on her hands and said, 'I think I'll have to start doing something about that wee pot Evan is developing. I was reading in a new magazine the other day that some doctor in Europe says if we eat less starchy foods like bread and potatoes we'd be healthier and fitter.'

I looked at her, aghast. 'Meg, that's daft. Bread is the staff of life, it says so in the Good Book and without potatoes on your plate, why it would be almost empty. The man's an idiot, there's no other word for him,' I said in judgement of such stupidity.

Meg sighed. 'I suppose you're right as usual, Uncle James. And anyway, I don't suppose I'll get Evan to change his ways. He can be so pig-headed sometimes.'

I almost choked on my coffee. 'Meg you must think me daft. He'd do anything for you and you know it. You've got him wrapped around your little finger. Oh, I know,' I said cutting off her protest, 'that you're too clever by half to let him know or even guess it, but you and I know it's true. He thinks he's the boss but you and I know who really is. Not that that's a bad thing.'

'Rubbish, Uncle James and you know it,' she said. The twinkle in her eye belied her words.

When the letter arrived I was standing behind her and recognised the stamp from Wales. It was addressed to her, so I politely returned to the table. She would tell me soon enough what was in it because she'd know I was burning up with curiosity. Her cry startled me and I turned around to see her with her hand to her mouth. The letter was shaking in her hand. I got quickly to my feet and put my arm across her shoulders.

'What is it girl, bad news?' She let me lead her to a chair. When she sat down the tears slowly formed. She gulped as she tried to talk.

'Take it easy. Is it from your mother?'

She shook her head. 'From . . . from Aunt Olive. You know, my mother's sister? Mother died about six weeks ago. Oh damn, and she never once wrote in all this time. Why didn't she write, Uncle James?' she asked me plaintively.

I shrugged. 'It's hard to say. She was a strange woman and no mistake. You asked her often enough to come and live here. She had – what do you call it – a fixation, with your father's grave.' I suspected my words were not comforting but I could think of nothing else to say.

'Even though she never replied I kept writing, didn't I, Uncle James?' Meg paused. 'What else was I supposed to have done? Give all this up to go back?'

'Don't be daft my girl. Now you're talking nonsense,' I said brusquely. 'She never liked Evan and she showed it often enough. She was never prepared to even try to like him or to get to know him. She took every opportunity to poison you against him . . . I suspect the success you were having here which you wrote to her about stuck in her throat like a fish bone. That was probably the reason she never came out here. She'd have hated to see you and Evan doing so well, especially after all she had said about him. It's natural for you to be upset, because, when all is said and done, she was your mother. So have a good cry. I'll send for Evan.'

I went and found David, explained what had happened and sent him to the warehouse to fetch his father. I went back to the kitchen and made a fresh pot of coffee. Meg was still sitting there, the crumpled letter in her hands, her tears dried up.

'It's a pity,' she said, 'because one day I'd hoped to return to Wales with Evan. I always knew she would never come here. I think, and I know it's not a nice thing to say, but I think I wanted to rub in the fact of how well Evan had done. I wanted her to know how wrong she'd been about my man. Can you understand that, Uncle James? Can you?'

I nodded, turning to look at her, the coffee grinder in my hands, the aroma of fresh coffee beans wafting through the air. 'Aye, I can understand that, Meg. I don't know what made your mother like she was . . .' I trailed off, changing my mind about saying she was better off dead. 'Does the letter say what she died of?'

'Not really. Aunt Olive,' said Meg with bitterness, 'suggests if I had been at home it wouldn't have happened. She also suggests it was a broken heart she died of. Oh yes, somewhat aided and abetted by a bout of influenza she picked up from somewhere,' Meg said dryly.

'I read about it. It's called Asian flu and they reckon a lot of people are dying from it, especially in the crowded continental cities and towns. Remember I showed you that piece in the newspaper a couple of months back?'

'I remember. You know, Aunt Olive was like my mother, only more so. She finishes with the cry of what is to become of her now mother is dead? That's typical of her. Why she never married I don't know.' She broke off to take the coffee and thanked me for it. 'I should have stopped David. It would have been soon enough to have told Evan when he got home this evening.'

We sat in silence broken only by the rattle of cups and an occasional sigh from Meg.

'Here's Evan now,' I said, looking through the window as Evan's buggy drew up. He jumped down and reached into the back. I saw him lift out an enormous bunch of flowers. At that point I left and went upstairs to my bedroom. I had a good book I wanted to finish.

I sat at the window, looking out the back. The river was a silver gleam in the distance. I could see a couple of barges making their way with the stream, probably headed for New Orleans. One of the big, luxury boats that plied between St Louis and New Orleans was steaming up the river. The passengers changed here, some going further north on the Mississippi and others heading west towards Kansas City on the Missouri. Though trains had mostly taken over from the boats there were still those who preferred to travel by boat. It was my intention to go down river on one of them one day.

26

IN DECEMBER WE had another letter, this time from
John Buchanan. Meg and Evan had seen John a number
of times in New York and they had also kept up a regular
correspondence. He was writing to wish us the season's
greetings and to inform us he was leaving the sea for good
in the following spring. He would let us know the date
of his last voyage and wondered if we could meet him
in New York for a final party. He was 'celebrating' the
end of twenty five years at sea. We were all invited.

Three days later our fourth Christmas in America was
upon us. It rained all day on the twenty-fifth and for
most of the next day too. In spite of the death of Meg's
mother, which did not affect Evan nor the boys except
as they tried to comfort Meg, we had a good time.
Boxing Day parties at the Griffiths' place had become
an established routine, and many old and some new
friends came on this occasion. I was helping myself
to some turkey, when I saw Dai, as I thought of him
but David as I now called him, looking forlornly at the
spread before us.

'Not hungry?' I asked.

'Oh, hullo, Uncle James. No, not very. I think I'll just
go and sneak a glass of punch.'

'Don't let your mother see you. Where's Gunhild? I
see Hans and the others are here.'

'She isn't coming,' he said shortly, which explained
the reason for his sadness.

'Ahhh, I see. Any particular reason, do you think?' I

took a mouthful of beer, trying not to appear amused in front of him.

'No . . . well, I suppose so.' He looked round to make sure nobody was listening and then moved closer just in case, and lowered his voice. The room was quite full of laughing, talking groups of people and nobody was taking the slightest notice of us. 'See, Uncle James, she's a year and eight months older than me,' again I had to suppress a smile at his exactness. 'Well, because I moved up two grades like I did nobody knew how old I really was. They all thought I was older.' He frowned. 'I kept it a secret for so long I almost believed it myself. Anyway, she found out how old I really am and wouldn't talk to me anymore.'

'When was this?'

'Last week. I'd hoped she'd come tonight so I could have a talk with her and explain that I'm no different now than I was last week. But I guess I won't have the chance now.'

Although David had filled out and was a big boy he was, after all, only fourteen. Gunhild at nearly sixteen was more mature and had developed nicely. I guessed it was more than a difference in age that separated them but I did not say so.

'I wouldn't bet on it. Come on, let's you and me find some punch and I'll tell you about women.' I got two glasses and he and I went to sit on the stairs. He took a mouthful of the warm, bitter brew and coughed.

'Take it easy, David. If Mam sees you with that glass and me alongside you, she'll have both our guts for garters. You know, it wouldn't have mattered an iota what you'd said to Gunhild tonight. She wouldn't have listened.'

'How can you be so sure of that, Uncle James? We were good friends . . .'

'That don't matter bach, believe me. She'd caught you out in a lie and no way could you have got back to your old footing. Women may be the nicest, sweetest things imaginable and may look like butter won't melt in their mouths but, Davey bach, underneath they're as tough as old leather, as scheming as the devil and as pernickety as a young colt.'

He thought about this for a few moments. 'Mmm. Gosh, when I think how often I carried her books from the schoolhouse to her buggy and showed her how to swim and even let her ride King . . . and now she won't even talk to me.'

'That's women, son. Everything has to go their way or no way at all. And if it don't – well – you got to look out. There's a saying that hell hath no fury like a woman scorned. I reckon that's one saying that can be expanded in meaning and cut down in words. Hell hath no fury like a woman, full stop!'

He sighed. 'I suppose so. Are all women like that? I mean,' he looked around though there was nobody in ear shot, 'is Mam like that too?'

I laughed. 'Sometimes son but there's another saying about the exception proving the rule. Well, that's your Mam.'

'I see,' said David, reflectively.

'So don't give Gunhild another thought, David. There's plenty more fish in the sea and you're too young to be thinking about any one of them. Heck when I was your age I preferred to go and do other things with my spare time, rather than chase women.' I did not add I was down a mine fourteen hours a day and by the time I was his age I had been doing so for nearly three years.

David took another drink of his punch and pulled a face. 'I don't think I like this stuff,' he handed the glass to me. 'Do you want it, Uncle James?'

I took the glass and got to my feet. 'Tell you the truth, David, I don't neither.' And with that I poured what was left of both glasses into the large potted plant that was just at the foot of the stairs. 'I hope it doesn't die,' I added with a grin and David laughed.

We returned to the living room. There was some sort of dancing going on, a reel I think it was called. I stood by the wall, a beer in my hand watching them. I kept my eyes skinned too, but a woman sneaked up on me before I saw her.

'Why, James, fancy standing here and not dancing,' she said with a giggle that rasped on my nerves. From anybody else, somebody about forty years younger, it might not have been so bad.

'Hullo, Doris. I wondered where you were,' I said, though I did not add – so I could keep out of your way. I guess that was too much to ask in a party of two hundred and fifty people. After all there were only so many rooms to hide in and only so may groups to lose myself among. Of course, I could have hidden in my bedroom but damn it, it was my party too and I wanted to enjoy it. Besides, I would not have put it past her not to have come there looking for me. She'd been a widow for some five or six years, and had let it 'slip' she was only fifty five. I reckoned she looked sixty five. She was a nice enough person, homely and I knew she was a good cook but her conversation always repelled me. Notice I don't describe her. After all, what can a man say about a woman of that age, who'd had five children in her time and liked to cook? Suffice it to say I could not have imagined her in my bed. Though she obviously could.

'Are you enjoying yourself?' I asked politely, clearing my throat and wishing like hell she would go away.

'Yes, thank you, now I've found you.' She gave a little smile, her plump cheeks dimpling in a way that might have been appealing half a life time earlier. I let the compliment go unheeded, waiting for what I was sure was coming next. I was not disappointed.

'I see you are still living with Meg and Evan,' she began right on cue.

'Yep,' was all I said.

'Don't you get fed up with it? I know I would.'

'No, I like it here. I've got myself a nice room, a good stock of books and I like having the kids and Meg and Evan around me.'

'Aha,' she said, as though this was the first time she'd spotted the flaw in my argument, though she had heard it before and reacted in the same way each time. 'You might like it but have you thought if they like it? Don't you think they might be just a little fed up with you falling over their feet all day? Always around to hear their most secret family arguments? Now ask yourself, is that fair, now is it?'

I had asked myself that many times in the past and I was still asking it. Soon after we'd arrived and the business was doing well I had suggested I found my own place to live. I was sure that Meg and Evan's reaction had been neither false nor motivated by anything other than the fact that they did not want me to go. Doris mentioning it raised my old doubts.

'You may be right at that,' I said heavily, admitting it to her for the first time. I think my answer was so different to what I usually said that she was on into her next attack before it dawned on her.

'James Price, what did you say?' She asked, astonished and full of glee at the same time.

'I said . . .' I began but did not get any further. That was another thing about the blasted woman, she could talk the hind leg off a donkey.

'Of course I'm right. Now my place is much too big for me on my own. I'm not suggesting you move in as a lodger mind . . .'

Like a beautiful and serene angel Meg came to my rescue. She did look beautiful that night, even more so than usual if that was possible. She had her hair piled on the top of her head, and was wearing a blue dress that bunched up under her bosom and flowed down to the floor.

'What are you looking so serious about, Uncle James?'

Naturally it was Doris who answered. 'I'd just been saying how annoying it must be for you all to have him under your feet all day and he was agreeing. We were discussing how soon he could come and move in with me – not as a lodger,' she added hastily.

I was so surprised I did not know what to say. Christ but she had jumped to some conclusions I would never have thought possible from the few words I had said.

'He will do no such thing,' Meg said with some austerity. 'This is his home as much as it is ours and we wouldn't dream of him living anywhere else.' She tucked her arm through mine. 'You don't really want to leave us, Uncle James, do you?' She asked, giving my arm a squeeze.

I cleared my throat as something seemed to have jammed itself in there. 'No, Meg, I'd hate it,' I said with all honesty. A year with that bloody woman and she would have talked me into an early grave. Talked? Nagged would have been more like it. I had never known a home like the one I was living in now, nor a family I had cared for more. When I was honest with myself I remembered life had not been as good with my wife as my memory sometimes suggested. I lived for the joy of seeing Meg and Evan and the kids and for being a part of their lives. I had just turned sixty six and I wanted to end my days in the company of the people I had grown to love.

'Good, then that's settled. This is where you live and this is where you're going to stay. Gosh, Uncle James, we need you more than ever and don't you forget it. Now come on, let's go and dance.' She dragged me away, leaving Doris glowering after us. Her words had bucked me up more than I can say. After that I enjoyed the rest of the evening.

*　　*　　*

1895 was no better and no worse than the previous year. That in itself was an improvement because the last few years during the depression had all been downhill. The tide, hopefully, was turning, at last.

We had been to New York for John Buchanan's farewell to the sea party. We renewed our acquaintance with a number of people, including Senator George Hughes and his wife Mabel, and the banker Eric Johnson. His daughter was there too, as scornful as ever with an insipid husband who seemed to spend his life running around answering her every beck and call. The only noteworthy event was the interesting discussion we had about politics – and a further suggestion by John that Evan take a more active role. This time Evan did not dismiss it so lightly.

27

MEG CAME TO find me one day soon after my escape from Doris. She looked desperately worried.

'Uncle James,' she said, 'we went out for a walk and Evan insisted we should go into the casino and watch. He said that we've lived here for four years and have never even put a foot inside. I was reluctant but he made it clear he was going to see what was happening there, so I gave in.'

'Did you find it interesting?' I asked.

'It was intriguing at first, watching the roulette and some of the card games but then I got bored and suggested we should leave. Evan was watching a poker game and though he'd played a bit at home it was different there. The men were all so, I don't know, intense, I guess. Anyway, it wasn't the same and Evan was fascinated. He bought ten dollars worth of chips, which are used instead of money. Evan won at first. I told him we should leave, but he wouldn't come. And now . . . oh, Uncle James, I don't know what to do. He's losing and I'm afraid he's losing quite a lot of money. He's still there. I'm sure he thinks he can win it all back.'

I went with Meg to the casino, where I stood behind Evan and watched what was going on. There were five men around the table including Evan. He must have had a few hundred dollars worth of chips in front of him. I was in time to see the others drop out of the hand and Evan call the unsavoury character opposite him. Evan lost.

Meg bent down to talk to him. 'Evan, let's go, please?

I have a headache and . . .' Evan looked at her with an irritation I had never seen before and Meg stepped back startled.

I watched the character opposite enjoy their exchange then he said: 'Yes, why don't you go, Griffiths? We all know how tied you are to her apron strings. It's well known around St Louis,' he sneered.

'He is not tied . . .' began Meg but got no further.

'Shut up, Meg,' said Evan savagely, 'and go away.' He turned his back to her and faced the man again. 'It's your deal, Thorgood.'

I saw Meg's face crease with pain as she fought back her tears. Thorgood sneered at her and started to deal. I put my hand on her shoulder and pulled her away. She came unresistingly but not willingly either, like a horse being led by its bridle. I bought us a couple of large brandies and we sat at a quiet table. Her hand was shaking when she lifted the glass. She choked and coughed on the fiery spirit and tears came to her eyes, brimming and threatening to flood over.

'How did it happen?' I asked. 'I mean, how did he come to get into a game like that?' I paused to sip my own drink. My hand was none too steady either. 'It's so out of character for Evan to do something so bloody, bloody stupid.'

'I know,' her lip trembled and then she couldn't help herself but buried her head on my shoulder to cry.

After a few moments she pulled herself together and sat up. 'I'm sorry, Uncle James. I must look a mess . . . oh damn. I think I'm going to cry again.' She took a gulp of her drink and held back the tears.

'Do you know how he got into the game?' I asked again.

She shook her head. 'I don't know. I went to . . . to the wash room, and by the time I'd returned he was playing. I . . . I stood and watched for a while and saw him win a little and then he began to lose. I guess he'd lost about a hundred dollars when I came to fetch you. Could you get me another brandy, please?' She held out her empty glass.

I took it and went to the bar. I was worried, very worried. I had never seen Evan like that. I had noticed the whiteness of his pallor, the way he couldn't keep his hands still when he picked up the cards. I had never heard him talk to Meg like that, either. Oh, they had their arguments but they were never real rows. And they always made up afterwards, no matter how ungracefully the loser gave in. After all they were both strong minded people. But this? I had read about gambling fever. It was often compared to gold fever and had ruined many a good man. I prayed it did not have a hold on Evan. The old man looked at me from across the bar, appearing older than I cared to remember him, mirroring my frown. I returned to Meg.

'What shall we do?' she asked in a quiet voice, taking the drink with a nod of thanks.

'I'm not sure. How much money does Evan have?'

'Not that much. A few hundred dollars. Huh, hark at me, not that much. That's more than the insurance money we got when Evan's parents died. Funny how one's money values change, isn't it? Oh my God . . .'

'What's the matter?' My heart lurched at the further anguish in her voice.

'Remember a year or so back when we were returning from New York and we saw that advertisement for an auction of bankrupt stock? Evan was annoyed because we didn't have enough money with us to attend. Remember after that he said he was going to carry an emergency fund with him at all times?'

I nodded, I remembered only too well. I also remembered the amount without Meg having to remind me.

'It was ten thousand dollars, Uncle James. It's in that special pouch he had made. He used it once, not all that long ago. Remember that deal? All those cans of

food at ten cents in the dollar? The profit was incredible.'

'I suppose he has the money on him now?'

Meg nodded. 'What if he uses that? What'll we do
then?'

I shook my head slowly. I was out of my depth. I did
not know what to suggest. If Meg couldn't get him away
then there was little chance of me doing so.

'I know one thing,' Meg suddenly said with fierce
determination, 'sitting here doesn't help,' She stood up,
leaving the rest of her drink. 'Come on, Uncle James.
Let's go and see what's happening. I'll get him away
from that game come hell or high water. And damn that
pig sitting opposite him.' She tossed her head and walked
away. I hurriedly finished my brandy and followed.

Evan now had a stack of chips in front of him that
must have been worth a few thousand dollars at least.
There was a pile of chips in the middle of the table and
I caught my breath when I heard Thorgood say: 'I see
your five hundred and raise you seven hundred.'

The man next to him threw his cards down with disgust.
'Too rich for me, I'm out.'

'Me too,' said another. One of the players had already
quit and that left just Evan and Thorgood.

'Well, Griffiths,' Thorgood said with a sneer, which
seemed to be his perpetual way of talking. 'Are you going
to go along or fold?'

'Don't, Evan,' said Meg. 'Throw it in. Come away,
please.' She was standing just behind him and to one
side. 'It isn't worth it, Evan,' the anguish in her voice
fell on deaf ears.

Thorgood looked at Evan and said, 'This isn't an open
game where advice is given Griffiths. Either play or jack
it. And tell this bitch to stop bothering the game.'

I waited for the explosion from Evan which I was sure
would break the spell. Nobody spoke about Meg like that
in Evan's presence. There was no explosion. No lurching

across the table and giving the man the good hiding he deserved. I could not believe it. I shook my head for suddenly I couldn't seem to think straight.

'Go away,' was all Evan said, not looking around. She did not move and he turned his head. His eyes were like chips of blue flint and when he looked at her there was a contempt I had never imagined possible. Meg shrank back. 'Go away,' he repeated.

Thorgood was smiling hugely, enjoying the drama. If I'd had my gun with me I am sure I would have shot the man and damned the consequences.

Meg made as though to protest, but with a short cry she turned and rushed from the room. She knocked over a waiter who was approaching with a tray of drinks but did not stop. I was torn between running after her and staying. I decided on the latter. The only man who could comfort her now was sitting at the table, his cards already in his hands, a frown of concentration on his brow.

Evan hesitated. I could see the cards he held. Three queens. I knew it was not a bad hand. Don't do it you fool, I willed him. He picked up the chips and threw them into the pile. 'See you,' he said in a voice I hardly recognised.

Thorgood threw down three tens and two fours and won the hand. Evan slumped further into his chair. When the waiter returned with another load of drinks Evan tossed his off and ordered another. It looked like bourbon, barely lightened with water.

'I've had enough for one night,' said one of the players, a big fat man who had been drinking glass after glass of beer. For a moment I hoped they would all pack it in but that hope was short lived.

'I'm game for some more if you fellows are,' said the man on Evan's left and the man next to him agreed. So did Thorgood. Evan said nothing.

'What about you, Griffiths?' Thorgood taunted.

'Whose deal is it?' Evan asked by way of an answer.

'Yours,' said Thorgood. I had never seen Evan in such a state. It was the weirdest thing, watching him go slowly to pieces.

One of the men asked if I wanted to join and I declined, saying I did not understand the game too well.

God knows how long I stood there. All I do know is that my feet and back ached atrociously and in spite of all the coffee I could hardly stay awake. Something about the game began to puzzle me and it took ages to see what. Now, I've admitted I knew little about the mechanics of poker but that was not important. I realised that though Evan and the others won they did not win as often as Thorgood. And when they did their pile of chips was not as high either. Thorgood won most of the hands he served, carefully raising the bidding each time. Perhaps if there had been other spectators he might not have been so casual about it but with just me – and I had admitted a lack of understanding of the game – and the waiter who was there only fleetingly, Thorgood must have felt safe.

Perhaps it was because I disliked the man so much I wanted to believe he was cheating. So I looked for it. It was not even clever stuff like dealing off the bottom. Or, at least, if he was doing that I couldn't see it. No, he just kept a card up his sleeve and when the time was right he would play it. I turned away to think about the problem and get another cup of coffee when with a shock I saw the sun coming over the horizon. The night had gone and with it at least five thousand dollars of Evan's money.

I thought about what Thorgood was doing and thought back to some of the games I could remember. Thorgood's most consistent winning hands were full houses and four of a kind.

I wandered to one side where I could see Thorgood's hands. It was difficult to watch him without being too obvious but I was lucky. He fumbled his palming act and I saw the two cards up his sleeve not one.

'I vote this the last hand of the game,' said the man

on Evan's left. He was florid faced, about sixty and from his conversation I gathered he was a rancher. The other man agreed.

'What do you say Griffiths?' I had to restrain myself from denouncing the bastard there and then. If I had done I knew Thorgood would shoot me. It would be the lesser of two evils for him to pretend not to know I was unarmed rather than to be proven a cheat. I reckoned he was a professional gambler and if he was he would be finished.

'I don't care,' Evan shrugged. 'Just play as long as you like.'

I wanted to hit him, the stupid sod. My anger flashed between Thorgood and Evan. It was Thorgood's deal.

As soon as the first three cards were dealt I could sense it was a special hand. Evan perked up and I thought what a poor fool he was. A man like Thorgood would be able to read Evan like a book.

Straightaway the betting became heavy and after only three rounds there was only Evan and Thorgood left. There was only one thing that I could do.

Quickly I refilled my cup with fresh coffee and contrary to my usual practice I did not cool it with milk or cream. I stood by the table between Thorgood and the rancher. I could see that Evan would have to call Thorgood soon or else he would run out of money. Thorgood's right hand was sliding to his left sleeve and I knew he was about to make the substitution while all eyes were on Evan.

I stumbled and as I did so I prayed my slightly rheumatic hands would not let me down. The hot coffee fell on Thorgood's shirt front, staining it brown. He jumped up with a startled oath and yell of pain. As he did so I fell into him pushing him back into his seat, slipping my fingers into his sleeve and coming away with the cards. I landed on the floor and in the confusion pushed the cards down the front of my trousers.

Thorgood was dabbing at his shirt front and cursing

me roundly. Evan knelt by my side to help me. There was concern on his face and when he asked if I was all right it was in his normal voice.

I whispered, 'Play Evan before he cancels the game. Go on, call him, you bloody fool.'

Evan was startled for a second but stepped up to the table. 'Shut up, Thorgood,' he said more like his old self. 'I call.' He threw his cards on the table.

The look of pure hatred Thorgood gave me was sufficient to tell me he knew what I had done and why. His face was mottled pink with rage and for a second I thought he was going to go for his gun.

Instead Evan thundered at him, 'Thorgood, make up you mind. Show me your cards or throw them in.'

Thorgood jerked around to face him and with a snarl said, 'Three aces, Griffiths.' He threw them on the table.

Evan had three tens and two twos. He began pulling the stack of chips towards him. 'Thank you for the game,' he said to no one in particular.

I climbed to my feet rather shakily as the fall had rattled me somewhat. With another snarl of rage Thorgood stalked out of the room. The other two men, not understanding what had happened, just shrugged their shoulders and left with unanswered goodnights. Evan sat at the table, his head in his hands.

'God . . . I . . . I where's Meg?' Evan asked in a quiet voice.

'Either sleeping or still crying on her bed I suspect. Evan,' I exploded, 'what the bloody hell happened? What made you do such a god damned stupid, thing? How could you talk to Meg like that?' I was so angry I still wanted to hit him.

He shook his head. 'I don't know, Uncle James. Once I started playing I just didn't want to stop. I couldn't stop. I was determined to beat that bastard Thorgood. I wanted the thrill of raking that money in, of winning. It

was unbelievable. I . . . I can't explain it. I just had to
win. That was all there was to it. And I couldn't leave
until I did so. Seeing you collapse like that was such a
shock I sort of . . . sort of came round. Hell, I don't know
how to explain it. It was like having a veil lifted from my
mind. I thought you'd had a heart attack or something. I
thought all sorts of things. But suddenly . . . I just don't
know, look you. It was so strange. It was as if my brain
started working again. What happened anyway? Are you
all right?'

I nodded. 'I am now.'

'And what was all that about? Telling me to bet?'

'Thorgood was cheating you,' I put my hand down the
front of my trousers and felt for the cards. They were
caught in a fold of my shirt. I pulled them out. I held
two sevens in my hand. I explained it all to Evan.

'The lousy cheating . . .' Evan began but I interrupted
him.

'Never mind Thorgood. You'd better go to Meg and
beg her forgiveness or whatever it takes. She's very
upset, Evan.'

He nodded. 'You're right, Uncle James. God what
a fool I was! You'd better be careful. Not only did
Thorgood give me a lot of my money back but he also
knows that you know he was cheating. Come on, if you
give me a hand with these chips I'll cash them later. I'll
walk back with you, just in case.'

I slept until sunset. When I woke I had an aching head
and a mouth like the bottom of a parrot's cage. I couldn't
understand it, after all, I hadn't drunk much in the way
of alcohol. Remembering the night before, I felt better,
trusting that everything was all right with Meg and Evan. I
crawled out of bed with a groan and went over to the wash
stand. There did not appear to be any more lines on the
seamed face that looked back at me I worked up a lather
and scratched at my grey stubble with my silver handled
cut-throat Meg had given me a couple of Christmas'

earlier. Everything I cherished came from the family, even the penknife the boys had given me. I grinned at my reflection when I remembered Sion pointing to one of the blades and telling me it was to remove stones from horses' feet. He hoped King or Thunderbolt would oblige by picking one up, but so far they hadn't.

My memory often flashed back to that day when the twins and Dai had called. It had been a turning point in my life. No, more than that. An awakening. A return to the joy of living which I had not felt for a long time.

Even the present threat of Thorgood, if there was one, could not dampen my spirits. I decided to leave Meg and Evan alone and went out for a walk as far as the nearest bar. Standing at the bar I still had my feeling of well being having enjoyed the night sounds and smells. I ordered another beer, this time not minding so much the old man looking back at me between the bottles. I pondered about going home and finally decided to drain my glass and order a third drink. I had the glass to my lips when I was shoved hard in the back. I jerked forward, spilled half my beer which somehow missed my shirt and splashed onto the bar and turned around to protest.

Before I could say a word though, the angry voice of Thorgood started; 'You clumsy fool, why don't you look where you're going? For two pins I'd give you the hiding of your life. You stupid old goat.' He showed me his empty whisky glass. 'Look what you did. You made me spill my drink all over the floor.'

A few people at the bar turned to look, taking notice, amused. I became angry.

'I did no such thing. You,' I pointed my finger at him, 'purposely bumped into me, making me,' I touched my chest, 'spill my beer.'

'Why, you stupid old man,' said Thorgood, through his familiar sneer, 'I did no such thing. You're so senile you don't even know when you do something stupid.'

Perhaps he was right because my next words showed just how stupid I could be.

'Not so stupid or senile,' I was nearly shouting now, 'so I couldn't catch you cheating last night at poker.'

I was aware of the gasps of the men nearby but my eyes were on Thorgood. Theatrically he pushed his coat to one side, showing the gun strapped there.

'I don't care how old you are, no man calls me a cheat and gets away with it. You all heard,' he said to the saloon in general, stepping back a pace.

I did not move. I couldn't. Christ, I was about to die, stupidly. 'I'm unarmed,' I said in a loud and I hoped, steady voice.

'Then go and get a gun. I'll give you ten minutes. If you don't come back by then I'll shoot you down like the cowardly dog you are.'

It was all so silly, so theatrical and corny I wondered if it was for real. I shook my head, partly to clear it and partly to refuse Thorgood. 'No, I'm not going for a gun. If I do, you'll kill me. If I don't and you kill me it'll be murder and they hang murderers.' I turned my back on him, trying to stop my hand from shaking when I picked up my glass again. If I had been ten years younger I would have gone for him. Oh, not with a gun, but with my hands. Win or lose I could have taken the punishment then, but not now.

The hand that dropped onto my shoulder made me stagger. I was pushed around and Thorgood grabbed my shirt.

'If you won't go for a gun, you coward, then try this.' He brought his arm back and as he did two things happened. Firstly, I threw my beer into his face prior to hitting him with the glass and secondly a hand took hold of his and Evan's voice broke in.

'Okay, Uncle James, leave him to me.'

Thorgood's hold on my shirt was broken by Evan. My fear was gone and I felt a surge of joy. Believe me, I'm not cold-blooded or bloodthirsty. I dislike violence but after the situation I had been in a saint would have enjoyed it. Thorgood's jaw dropped in surprise and the startled 'What?' was suddenly a scream of anguish as Evan hit him as hard as he could in the stomach. The blow doubled Thorgood over, gasping, his face a sickly white. Thorgood would have collapsed if Evan hadn't held him up by his hair. 'Ladies and Gentlemen,' Evan said to the people in the saloon, 'this man did indeed cheat last night when I was playing poker with him. My friend here saw him and foiled his attempt to steal the rest of my money from me.' Evan saw two of the other players from his game. 'O'Grady, Samuels, he cheated you, as well. You saw him pick on this old man,' I wasn't sure I liked that reference to my age or not, but then like they say, only the truth hurts, 'for calling him a cheat. Well I call him a lousy, cheating, cowardly dog of the lowest kind. A . . .' Evan ran out of things to call him. Thorgood was recovering a little from the blow.

'What did you say?' Evan pretended Thorgood had spoken. 'He just challenged me. Did you hear that, O'Grady?' Evan glared at the man.

'Well I . . . I . . . eh . . .'

'Did you, O'Grady?' There was no mistaking the menace in Evan's voice.

O'Grady nodded.

As he did so Evan lifted Thorgood by the hair, almost raising him off the floor and hit him three times, each blow as hard as the first. Thorgood was hardly conscious by the third blow. The agony ripping through his guts must have been unbearable. Evan kept his grip on Thorgood's hair and lifted his face back. This time there was no John Buchanan to stop the blow as there had been the night of the party when Junior Roybal had received a similar beating. The blow to Thorgood's nose spread it across his face, blood gushing down his clothes. Evan let go and he collapsed. Evan took hold of his feet and dragged Thorgood across the saloon.

'Open the door,' he said to no one in particular and a man jumped to obey. Evan walked out, down the two steps and into the street, Thorgood's head bumping hard on the steps as he did. Evan took him to the rails and stood him up carefully so as not to get any blood on his coat.

'Get me some water,' Evan said. Somebody handed him a glass of beer. 'That'll do.' Evan thanked the man and poured the beer over Thorgood's face, talking to him coaxingly. Slowly Thorgood came round. Out of the corner of my eye I noticed a slight commotion and somebody pushed through the crowd. It was the marshal.

'What's going on here?' he asked. 'What are you doing with that man?'

Evan looked at him with feigned innocence. 'Me? Why nothing. I was just trying to bring him round. How are you, Thorgood, old chap?' Thorgood was beginning to groan, slowly recovering.

'What happened to him?' asked the marshal with some asperity.

Evan shrugged. 'You know how it is marshal. He walked straight into my fist.'

'Are you okay?' Evan asked Thorgood again.

Thorgood now appeared to be able to stand without help. He could not have realised who he was talking to for he gave a half groan, half nod. Evan grabbed him by his belt and before anybody knew what was happening he had lifted Thorgood over his head, dashed the few paces across the street to the bank of the river, and thrown him in. Evan ignored the gasp from the crowd and watched as Thorgood splashed in the water.

Evan started to go back into the saloon. I followed, the marshal right behind.

'I demand an explanation,' the marshal was spluttering.

'You're entitled to one at that, Marshal. The people here will bear witness that the man is a cowardly cheat and tried to fight Mr Price. I just happened along in time to stop it. He cheated me at cards last night. If you care to join me for a beer I'll tell you all about it,' he smiled, at his most affable. 'Ahh, Uncle James, the marshal is just about to join us for a drink.'

28

WE WERE SITTING in a restaurant in town having finished dinner when a man I recognised but couldn't place came over to greet us. 'Ah, Meg, Evan and . . . Mr Price, isn't it?' He held out his hand to me.

I said: 'I'm sorry, you have me at a disadvantage. I recognise you but can't remember your name.'

'Charles DeFort. We met once some time back when I called into the warehouse to see Evan. Oh, it must be a year or so ago.' He was a pleasant man, about Evan's age, brown hair and brown eyes with a friendly smile and a firm hand shake. 'Please call me Charlie, everybody else does.'

'Call me James. Mr Price makes me feel about seventy,' I replied.

'If you've finished your meal perhaps you'll join me at my hotel for a drink?' suggested DeFort. 'We've set a bar up in a private room and afterwards we're going to the theatre to listen to Bryan.'

The private room was the banqueting suite and held about a hundred or so people but the room was far from full.

We stood for a while, drinks in hand, greeting people some of whom we knew and many we didn't. I was beginning to get bored with the conversation, which was mostly about William Jennings Bryan and his proposal that silver should be the basis of our currency. I did not mind politics, far from it – I quite enjoyed a good argument. But this was neither. It was an eulogy of what a wonderful leader they had found.

An hour later we left for the theatre which had only
opened the previous month. We were to meet DeFort
and his wife Susanne and another couple whose name
I had forgotten. That'll teach me to pay more attention,
I thought. I asked Meg their names.

'Red McCauley and Evelyn,' Meg said, then added,
'I think.'

'That's right,' said Evan. 'He's got a number of business interests in New York and a hefty interest in a silver
mine out west.'

There was a throng of people around the doors pressing
to get in. 'How're we going to get through that lot?' I
asked, aghast.

'We aren't,' replied Meg. 'Uncle James, you weren't
listening back there, were you?' Meg nudged me. 'And
don't skirt around the answer.'

'Not really. It's just that they went on and on about
our new Moses, leading the country into world politics
and all that. I just stopped listening after a while,' I
confessed.

'Me too,' said Meg 'But I did catch the bit about us
going around to a side entrance. Evan says he knows the
way. Don't you, darling?'

'Sure. Just down here and along the alleyway.'

We edged around the crowd who seemed to be in a
good mood.

We showed our cards at the door and went up a few
rickety steps and along a badly lit corridor. Through
another door and we were in the main theatre. It was an
imposing building with three tiers of plush velvet seats
and ornate walls decorated with large paintings.

Some of the private boxes next to the stage were
already occupied though the general public had not yet
been allowed in. I thought it was an unusual place to
hold a political rally, but then American politics were
unusual at the best of times, what with their bands and

cheer leaders and what I felt amounted to a childishness in the whole business. I never thought they had the same dignity as British politics.

We had seats near the front. A few minutes later the doors opened and the crowd flooded in. A swarm of humanity, talking, laughing, pushing, waving and finally finding seats and sitting. For the next half an hour or so they thronged in, the noise level gradually increasing.

The newfangled electric lights went out one by one until the theatre was in gloom and a hush gradually descended.

There was a movement behind the curtain and a man stepped onto the stage. 'Ladies and Gentlemen. I won't bore you with a long introduction. It's not me you've come to listen to, but the man I believe will return the American government to the people, for the people. He is the man to lead us from the depression we find ourselves in. Indeed, he is the next President of these here United States – that is with God's help and a little encouragement from the voters,' his voice was building up to the final words. 'William Jennings Bryan.'

As Bryan came onto the stage the applause grew and grew until it was thunderous. I had to admit that he had a certain presence as he strode across the stage, head high, hand waving, a smile fixed in place. I swear that for the first time in my life I knew what charisma meant. He held up his hands until the noise died down.

I don't remember all he said but two passages from his speech stuck in my mind for a long time.

He said: 'We do not come as aggressors. Our war is not a war of conquest; we are fighting in the defence of our homes, our families, our posterity. We have petitioned, and our petitions have been scorned, we have entreated, and our entreaties have been disregarded; we have begged and they have mocked when our calamity came. We beg no longer; we entreat no more;' his voice rose, rising to the rafters, 'we petition no more. We defy them.'

At his words the people broke into a frenzy of clapping and cheering. The theatre shook with the applause and yells and screams and whistles and feet stamping. It was many minutes before it was quiet enough for him to continue with any chance of being heard.

'If they dare to come out in the open field and defend the gold standard as a good thing, we will fight them to the utmost. Having behind us the producing masses of the nation and the world, supported by the commercial interests and the toilers everywhere, we will answer their demand for a gold standard by saying to them: You shall not press down upon the brow of labour this crown of thorns, you shall not crucify mankind upon a cross of gold.'

The people went crazy. Was it possible for the cheering and yelling to get louder? I wouldn't have thought so a few minutes earlier, but I swear it did. They went wild and screamed for him to come back when he bowed and walked off the stage. He returned, like a performer taking his bows, five, six times while the crowd screamed itself hoarse. Meg, Evan and I screamed right along with them.

I will never understand what happened though there were many theories for why it did. The one that I favoured the most was the need for wide coverage in the newspapers. Who was going to write about a political speech no matter how good it was when there was a riot to report instead?

First a number of hecklers started and then before we knew it punches were thrown. The fight spread like wild fire. It was a localised incident one minute and the next everybody was taking a swing at his neighbour. It was so utterly, stupidly senseless. Quickly we edged our way to the exit. Who ever had organised it had done their job well. We were in the middle of the centre aisle of seats and though a number of people around us were also only interested in getting out we ended up having to hit, push, kick and claw like the rest of them.

Evan was leading, Meg following and me behind. Evan was pushing men and women left and right to make way for us but as he pushed through others came between climbing over the seats knocking people over and screaming at the tops of their voices. Meg was further separated from me. She looked back and I gave her an encouraging smile. We were halfway to the exit when I either tripped or fell.

Meg had been looking back again and the last thing I saw was her look of horror as I went down. Feet trampled over me bruising my back and legs and when I tried to get up as soon as I reached my knees I was pushed down again. It was very frightening. The others told me later what happened next.

Meg turned and fought the tide of the crowd trying to get to me. She was kicking, screaming and punching for all she was worth, and giving a good impression of a woman gone mad. She lost her purse when she swung it at somebody's head and all she had to use were her hands . . . and her nails. She reached me and managed to fight for enough space so I could stand. I stood there, leaning on Meg, regaining my breath. All over the theatre people were suddenly coming to their senses and the fighting and panic was subsiding. Clothes were torn, faces were bleeding and women were crying.

There were still one or two isolated fights going on but most of it had ceased now. We got to the door to find Evan waiting for us. He had been on his way back but seeing us approaching he stood where he was.

Evan said to Meg, 'Are you all right?'

She nodded. Evan took out his handkerchief and wiped a smudge of blood from her cheek. She winced. 'Ouch,' she tried to smile and put her hand to her face. 'That hurts a little but my eye hurts even more.'

Evan nodded, looking closely at her right eye. 'It's possible it'll be black by morning.'

'Oh no, Evan, no. A black eye? I'll have to stay indoors until it's better.'

'Or buy a veil,' I suggested. 'Shall we go?'

I turned to the door; the theatre was over half empty now. I held back a groan. My back was as painful as hell.

'Are you all right, Uncle James?' Meg asked, taking my arm. 'We're a right pair aren't we? Are we going back to the hotel or what?'

'I, more than anything, could use a large whisky,' I replied. 'And after that, do you know what's better than a large whisky?'

'At a guess,' Meg said with a smile, 'a second large whisky.'

'That's right, my girl. Have I told you that before?'

'Many times, Uncle James, many times. Evan,' she looked over her shoulder, 'what are we going to do? Go for a drink?'

Evan decided we should go to the Grapevine. It had a beautiful lounge area and was now accepted by many of the ladies of the community. 'It's just the place for a post-political meeting,' he said, 'and it's around the corner from here. We'd better hurry, otherwise it'll be packed.'

When we got there the place was almost full but we managed to find a table.

Evan went for the drinks. Meg asked me, 'How're you feeling, Uncle James?'

I shrugged. 'A bit sore, but otherwise . . .'

Meg interrupted me with a little scream. 'Look,' she waved her left hand under my nose, 'the nail is broken. And what's that under my nails?' She picked at her nails with her thumb.

I looked closer. 'I'd better not tell you until you've got your drink.'

'Why not?' Meg put her hand closer to her eyes. 'Is . . . is that . . .'

'Afraid so. It's skin – no doubt clawed from some deserving fellow's face,' I laughed at the look of horror on her face. 'You . . . you women. You fight tooth and nail and then can't stand the gore afterwards.'

I took out my pocket knife. Among its many features was a file which I opened for her. Wordlessly she took it. Evan returned with the drinks and we had a laugh at Meg's expense as I explained what she had found.

The evening passed quickly. People joined and left our table, very excited and highly charged, as the events at the theatre and Bryan's speech were analysed in detail.

The next day Meg had to buy a veil to cover her face because, much to her anguish and our amusement, she had a shiner of a black eye.

The speech by Bryan was not reported in the newspapers though it became one of his most famous. Bryan was now well established in his attempt to get to the White House.

The boys and I went to New Orleans that summer. Our journey was everything I hoped it would be. We hired a buggy for a few days and explored along the coast, staying at small hotels and inns. There were beautiful beaches, warm sun, long walks and the deep, deep blue of the Gulf of Mexico. The three of us tried various sea foods though I did tend to stay with the more traditional type of fish but the boys ate everything from prawns to lobster. I, and I think the boys too, regretted having to leave and return to St Louis. We arrived back thirty two days after we had left.

Business was picking up again and Evan decided it was now time to find bigger premises. We were in the study discussing the problem after dinner on a rain-filled night in October.

'We've established the fact we can't extend,' said Meg, 'because there's not enough room behind the present warehouse. We haven't been able to find other premises big enough for what we want, so that leaves only one thing to do.'

'Two,' I said. 'The first is to build a warehouse to our specifications and the other is to open a second place.'

'The trouble with opening a second place,' said Meg, 'is that we offer a large variety of goods all in one warehouse, and that's one of the reasons we're so popular. If we have two premises, say food in one and other stocks in the other, it'll lessen our attraction.'

'I think you're right,' said Evan. 'We'll also need a larger staff to run separate places instead of one big one and then there's the cost of heating, electricity, transportation and so on.'

I got up to refill my glass. 'To build a place would be expensive, wouldn't it?' I asked.

'Yes, particularly with so many empty buildings around. It's just a case of finding the right one,' said Evan. 'I suppose we'd better go on looking. Here, Uncle James, catch.' He threw his cut glass whisky goblet to me. I managed to catch it as Meg gave a gasp of horror. They were her best glasses, her pride and joy.

'Evan,' she leaned over and poked him in the ribs. 'I'll kill you if you break one of them.' All she got for her pains was a big grin.

'It's a pity that place on the corner isn't next door to us,' I said, handing the glass back to Evan. 'I know it's a bit of a hole but we could have used it.'

'I've had an idea . . .' began Meg. 'We're separated from that corner building by one building. Now, the place next to us bricked up their rear windows a couple of years back because of the break-ins they were having. And they don't use that strip of land anymore. Well then, why don't we buy the empty building and connect it to our place by a corridor? I'm sure it would work if we could buy enough of the land from next door at a reasonable price.'

'I like that,' said Evan. 'It'll still be two places so overheads will be high but the customers will have the illusion that it's all one place. Do either of you know the new man that has next door?'

Meg and I shook our heads. 'I only know he's an importer and exporter and moved in from another part of town. What is it? Two months ago?' I said.

'The building strikes me as being a bit seedy though,' said Meg. 'It's been empty for about two years now.'

'True. But as long as no major repairs are required it should only need internal alterations and a paint job,' said Evan. 'I've also been thinking we'll need another manager, subordinate to Sonny of course, but in charge of his own departments.'

'You aren't thinking of Frank, are you?' asked Meg.

Evan shook his head. 'No, he's a good man but not suitable for something like that. In fact, I don't think we have anybody who is. Not at the moment. It'll mean hiring somebody new. Anyway, it's something to think about,' he drained his glass and stood up. 'I'm for bed.'

I went into town with Meg on Monday morning after the boys had left for school. David was now in his last year and was trying for a place in university, a thought that pleased Meg.

When we arrived at the warehouse Meg was busy with some paperwork for a few hours so I wandered around chewing the fat with Frank, Mac and the others. Although it wasn't much past nine o'clock, there were already quite a few customers, pulling or pushing the little flat cars Evan and Sonny had designed. Afterwards, I got myself a coffee and went to sit in Evan's empty office.

I was lost in nostalgic thoughts of Wales and Sian and that dreadful day when the slag heap buried the school when Evan came in for his coat. I joined him and Meg and together we went to look at the empty building. Evan had located the owners and sent Sonny for a key earlier

in the morning. Apparently they had been eager to give
it to him.

Although it was a windy day with bits of rubbish
swirling along the road at least it was not raining, for
which I was grateful. The rain always brought on my
rheumatics which seemed to get worse every winter.

Evan unlocked a small door, inset in a large double
door and we entered. Inside it was gloomy and dank,
smelling of disuse. I lit the oil lamp I had brought with us.
The windows were boarded over and light only penetrated
in thin strips of white across the dusty floor. Meg started
when three or four rats ran straight across the concrete
floor. The building was a shell of four walls and a roof,
about half the floor area of our present place but about
one and a half times higher.

'This is a waste of space,' said Evan. 'We can't stack
goods that high. I think we ought to consider building a
second floor.'

'Good idea,' said Meg. 'Now can we go and discuss
this over coffee somewhere? It's not exactly warm standing here.'

'You mean,' said Evan, 'there are too many rats here
for your liking.'

Over coffee we decided that we would try and buy
the place. There was now only one thing to take care
of. We needed to persuade the company next door to
sell us some of their land at the back, so that we could
build our corridor. None of us envisaged any problems,
as they no longer had access to the back having bricked
up the doors as well as the windows.

Behind the empty warehouse was an area of waste
ground where buckboards and wagons could load and
unload. It was about one hundred feet long and about
seventy feet wide and surrounded by a brick wall. Access
to the area was through two gateways in opposite corners
where the buildings and wall met.

I went with Evan next door. The offices were on the

ground floor, just inside the entrance. A secretary asked us to wait while she saw if Mr Boothroyd, the owner, was free.

'He won't keep you waiting long,' she came back with a smile. 'In the meantime can I get you some coffee?' She was a nice homely person of about forty.

We declined the offer with thanks. The office was small with a desk near a corner oil heater which threw out insufficient heat to keep the place warm. A filing cabinet stood in another corner and a threadbare strip of carpet in front of the desk. There were two hard backed chairs for visitors. If business was profitable then Boothroyd was not investing his profits in the decor nor for the comfort of his staff. I wriggled on the chair, not trying to be comfortable only trying to stop being uncomfortable. After about ten minutes a florid faced gentleman, big and running to fat, in a large checked suit, threw open the door opposite us.

'Ah . . . Mr Griffiths, I believe,' he walked towards me, his hand outstretched, a beaming smile on his double chinned face.

'I'm Griffiths,' said Evan, intercepting the hand.

'Oh, well, do come in, do come in,' he repeated as he ushered us into his office. I thought for a second I had strayed into another company and looked back at the mean little office we had just left. The room we were now in was large, one wall lined with leather bound books, another with an open fire place. A couple of over stuffed armchairs and a mammoth desk dominated the room. My initial impression, that I was not going to like Boothroyd, was confirmed.

'Get us some coffee will you, Gladys?' Boothroyd said to the woman.

'Not for me,' said Evan.

'Nor me,' I added.

'Of course you will,' said Boothroyd. 'It's specially imported from the Indies and I tell you it's delicious.

Just wait until you try it. Sit down, sit down.' He waved
at the leather chairs in front of his desk while he went
behind. 'Now gentlemen, to what do I owe the pleasure
of this visit?'

'I'd like to buy the land you have out the back,' said
Evan without preamble.

'Oh, I see,' Boothroyd paused. 'For what purpose?'

'Surely that's immaterial?' said Evan. 'Either you sell
it or you don't. I'll give you a fair price.'

'I can't do that, Mr Griffiths,' Boothroyd shook his
head sadly. 'You never know when I might want the
land for myself one day.'

He broke off when his secretary reappeared carrying
a tray bearing coffee. 'Put it here, put it here,' he said
fussily, sweeping some papers to one side. 'Gladys,' he
chuckled, 'these gentlemen want to buy the land out back,
have you ever heard of such a thing? After what I was
saying about expanding out there?'

'But . . .' she abruptly stopped. Boothroyd was glowering
at her and she hurriedly turned and rushed out. Evan and
I pretended not to have noticed her little error, but it was
interesting. Very interesting.

Boothroyd fussed further, pouring the coffee, adding
cream and four heaped spoonfuls of sugar to his own. I
took mine with cream, Evan ignored his.

'Tell me, Mr Boothroyd, is that your final word? There
is no possibility of negotiating?'

'Hmmm? Oh, there's always that, always that. Are
you Irish, Mr Griffiths? I've been trying to place your
accent.'

'No, I'm Welsh. I'm prepared to pay the current market
price for the land,' said Evan, folding his arms and leaning
back in his chair. I think he realised this was going to be a
long session.

'Welsh, are you? I would never have thought so, well,
well, well. The current market price? I don't think so,
Mr Griffiths. I believe the market will be on the way

up shortly – so I'd be stupid to sell now, wouldn't I? Also of course, the area I have is small and wouldn't be worth much at the price per square foot. Are you Welsh too, Mr Price? It is Price, isn't it?'

I nodded, so he had known who we were all the time. Then why the charade of offering me his hand and calling me Mr. Griffiths. I had the feeling that Boothroyd liked playing silly games. I was aware of Evan's attempt to control his temper, though I could not blame him for getting angry. I would have been angry too if I had been younger. I had just learned a degree more tolerance now I was one of the older generation, though I don't know that I was any the wiser.

'Mr Boothroyd, for you to be able to sell that bit of land you need a buyer. I'm the only one in the market so no matter to what height the value of land rises it's no good to you without me. How much do you own out there?'

'All that's along my wall naturally, and extending to the wall. The city records have the exact amount, as do my accountants, oh, and I think the bank as well. Yes, the bank as well. But it's about that much.'

The land he had described covered the area we were interested in; we needed a strip fifteen feet wide running the whole length of the wall. Boothroyd was quick to point out the fact that if that was all we took then the rest would be valueless to him. Evan conceded that point as the argument went back and forth but in reality we were getting nowhere fast.

'I'll tell you what,' said Boothroyd, 'five thousand dollars for a twenty five year lease.' He smiled at the favour he would be doing us.

'Don't be ridiculous, man! That's far too much. It would be too much even if I bought it outright at that price.'

'That's the best I can give it to you for,' said Boothroyd. 'As I said, I intended to expand that way but if the price is right, well . . .' he shrugged. 'A little profit goes a long way I always say. Yes, a long way.'

'What if I bought the land outright for the same . . .' began Evan but I interrupted him.

'Hold it, Evan. I think we should go away and think about it.' I got to my feet as did Evan, showing none of the surprise he must have been feeling.

Not so Boothroyd who sat with his mouth agape. Evan leaned across the desk, shook Boothroyd's hand while I just nodded goodbye. We left him sitting there, too surprised to try and stop us.

'What was that all about?' Evan asked when we reached the street.

'It's simple. His secretary nearly blundered by saying the wrong thing when Boothroyd suggested he was thinking of expanding. Secondly, there was no activity about the place. I mean, none whatsoever. There was no noise, no interruptions, just nothing. At our place there's always a sort of hum of activity, not loud but always present. Well, I'd expect there to have been something, don't you think? Let's just leave him alone for a day or two and in the meantime I'll try and talk to the secretary. Perhaps I'll be able to find something out from her.'

'You think she'll tell you? That would be pretty disloyal,' Evan said, with a frown.

'Evan bach, you saw his office; just compare it to hers. Also,' I paused, and said what I was thinking, 'you're too impatient. Once you start something you want to get it over with. You've got to learn to go slower. Argue more. You'll do all right your way but you'll do better if you slow down just a little.'

'You're right, and I know it. I seem to remember you told me that before,' he chuckled. 'Which is why I like to have you along. You're my patience.'

'Yes, well, I won't always be here, so you'd better learn in the meantime,' I said gruffly.

Later that day, carrying a lot more money in my

wallet than I was comfortable with, I waited in a cab across the road from Boothroyd's place. After about half an hour when the driver was becoming impatient and grumbling, Boothroyd's secretary appeared. She was wearing a scruffy coat against the chill of the evening and hurrying along the road. I waited until she had turned a corner out of sight and told the cabby to follow. We pulled up alongside her.

'Ma'am. Excuse me, ma'am,' I called.

She looked up at me, hesitated and then came over to the buggy.

'My name is Price. I was in to see Mr Boothroyd today with Mr Griffiths.'

'Yes, I remember you.'

'Can I give you a lift?' She hesitated. 'I need to talk to you and I think you'll find it beneficial to listen.'

'I don't know. My husband will be home soon . . .'

'I'll take you straight there. Give the driver your address and climb in.' I moved across the seat to make room for her.

'Well, all right.' After she settled into her seat she said, 'What do you want?'

'I want to ask you about Boothroyd's business.'

'I expected as much. You want to know if you can make a better deal with old Skinflint over that land out the back.'

I nodded.

'I've been thinking about it. I can tell you what you want to know and it'll save you a lot of money.'

'How much?'

'How much will it save you?'

'No. How much will it cost to be told.' I had been prepared to offer her fifty dollars but I had a lot more, just in case.

'Two hundred dollars,' she said serenely.

I gasped. 'You're joking. Good God, that's . . . that's robbery.'

'No it isn't, Mr Price. Me and my family don't have much. I can assure you that what I tell you will save your Mr Griffiths a lot more. Boothroyd told me he was going to get five thousand for a lease.'

'No, he's not, I can assure you of that. But all right, tell me what you have and let me decide what it's worth.'

She laughed. 'No sirree. I'm doing no such thing. I tell you what, you give me the money first and then I'll tell you.'

'Two hundred is too much. I'll give you seventy five dollars and that's the lot.'

'No you won't, Mr Price. Even if it is a lot of money. I know full well what I've got to tell you and it's worth a lot more than that.'

'A hundred?' I offered, intrigued now by the sureness of the bloody woman.

'One eighty and you've got a deal.'

'One fifty,' I countered.

'One seventy five and not a penny less. That's my final offer.'

'You drive a hard bargain,' I sighed, 'but all right.' I reached into my coat pocket for my wallet. 'But tell me your information first,' I said.

'Nope. Give me one hundred dollars now and put the other seventy five where I can see it.'

I counted out the money and handed her the hundred. The other seventy five I put on the seat between us. We both put a finger on the fluttering notes.

'Boothroyd will be bust flat within three weeks at the most. We moved here from another part of town one step ahead of the bailiffs. He'd hoped to keep things going long enough to pay his debts but the bank ain't supporting him no more. He's hurting real bad right now. Unless he pays the bank at least a thousand he can't borrow no more and if he don't borrow he's not going to be doing any more importing and exporting. Well anyway, the upshot is he can't keep going. He was cock-a-hoop after you left because he reckons Mr Griffiths wants that land real bad.'

'Interesting,' I said thoughtfully.

'You can knock him down to two thousand and buy the land by the end of the week. After all, that land's no good to him.'

The cabby drew up and I looked around at the narrow street and mean houses. 'It's useful information,' I looked at her narrowly for a few seconds. 'Why are you doing this?'

She spoke with such bitterness I was startled. 'This money is payment for back services to the bastard. I actually love my husband Mr Price. He's not much good but I love him. When I think of the things that bastard Boothroyd made me do my flesh crawls. This is a lot of money to me. You'll bail out Boothroyd for now, but what happens in a few months time? He's a waster and a fool. I'd be out of a job then, with nothing.' She picked up the money and climbed down. 'Just screw the son of a whore for every penny. I won't finish working for him until the deal goes through but when it does you'll hear him scream clear across the Mississippi.'

The next morning I was at the warehouse with Evan when Boothroyd called. The outcome of their short meeting was Evan offered Boothroyd fifteen hundred dollars for an outright sale, take it or leave it. Boothroyd stalked out of the office.

'I sure hope that woman knew what she was talking about,' Evan said echoing my thoughts. 'What were you saying earlier, Meg, about more staff?'

'I said we'll need to have check out counters there too, or we'll have to alter the present set up to cover both warehouses. That'll mean at least eight counters over here.'

'Or over there,' I said. 'The ones here need changing, you've said so almost every day since we've opened. Why not build exactly what you want on the other side?

The customers will have to go through at least the ground floor over there to get out. It might help sales a bit.'

Three days later Boothroyd was back to say he would accept two and a half thousand. Evan got him down to eighteen hundred and the deal was closed. The money and papers were exchanged in five days.

Boothroyd went bankrupt a week later and in fact we cancelled our plans to make a corridor. There was now no need because Evan bought Boothroyd's place from the bank for five thousand dollars.

29

WE STARTED THE alterations to the warehouse immediately. Meg and Evan took another trip to New York and
set up new contacts for even more stores, buying as much
as possible while prices were depressed.

Although the economy of the country as a whole had
not improved a great deal, at least it had stabilised, and
the forecasts were optimistic. It was a good time to buy
and we were in the fortuitous position of being cash rich
which enabled us to build up our stock.

By the middle of November everything was finished.
The main warehouse was completely filled with foodstuffs, the checkout counters were done away with and
more store rooms were added. The offices upstairs had
been extended and improved, but were still used only by
Sonny, Meg and Evan. A large archway now connected
the two places. The floor area of the new warehouse was
a little smaller than ours but it had two floors. We kept all
our non-food merchandise in the new warehouse, ranging
from household utensils and attractive small items on the
second floor to furniture and clothes on the ground floor.
We had nine checkouts and there were storerooms in the
back corner near three more offices, one of which was for
the man we intended hiring to be in charge of the second
section.

That autumn Sonny married Marylou as he reckoned
now that Evan had given him another pay rise he couldn't
put her off any longer.

Business went well and built up as we approached

Christmas. We heard from Evan's brothers in Wales, learning that Albert and Huw's hotel was doing well as was David's shop in Cardiff.

The last letter arrived about the fifteenth of December and so thoughts of the old country were very much in our minds. It made the newspaper reports of the eighteenth all the more shocking. At first I thought it was a gigantic hoax but realised it was no such thing.

United States about to declare war on Great Britain, were the headlines in thick black, inch high type across the St Louis Star.

The more I read the more I worried about it.

Over Christmas we feared the worst but luckily the British people and their government showed restraint and, with the aid of powerful American newspapers like the New York Word, who condemned the actions by President Cleveland in no uncertain terms, the matter gradually died down. All in all it was a fraught few months but once it had settled down we could breathe more easily. After all, where would we have stood as the citizens of a foreign country at war with the country we now lived in?

Evan and Meg continued their interest in politics and it came as a complete a surprise when later in 1896 McKinley, leader of the Republicans came to power by more than half a million votes over Bryan, though Bryan and his campaign was the most talked and written about of our time. Vachel Lindsay wrote:

Prairie avenger, mountain lion.
Bryan, Bryan, Bryan.
Gigantic troubadour, speaking like a siege gun,
Smashing Plymouth Rock with his shoulders from
  the West.

One of the most important days of David's life took place in September 1896. He was leaving to go to

university. Evan, Meg, Sion and I accompanied him to
Church Hill, Ohio. We got off the train at Columbus
and hired a buggy to take us the rest of the way. Ohio
state university was set on a plateau and was one of
the oldest and most prestigious universities in America.
David had chosen it for that reason. That September it was
lovely, the buildings imposing in the bright sunlight. The
mellow stone and brick walls with Corinthian colonnades
dominated the town, which existed for the purpose of
serving the university.

After David had registered and been assigned to
Lincoln dormitory, we followed him past the lawns and
towering trees to the door of his room. The university was
the most tranquil place I had ever been to and I envied
David his chance to study there. He, naturally, took it all
in his stride.

Evan held his hand out. 'Good luck, son. Work hard
and make us proud of you,' he said in a voice that was
gruffer than usual.

David nodded, not trusting himself to speak. Tears
were forming at the corners of his eyes. This was, after
all, the first time he would have been away from home
for any length of time.

Meg's eyes, needless to say, were brimming over. She
pulled David to her and gave him a hug and kiss. 'Don't
forget, if there's anything you need just write and let
us know.'

'I will, Mam.' David said hoarsely, 'And thanks. I eh,'
he cleared his throat. 'I eh, never did get around to really
saying thanks. I appreciate all you've done in the past
and all the time you took coaching me . . .' he stopped
and gave her another hug.

All I managed was a shake of the hand, a wink and a
smile. I reckon getting old makes you more sentimental.

Sion frowned. 'Is this where I'll be coming in a few
years time? It looks pretty good. What do you think,
Dave?' Because of the shooting incident Sion had lost

a lot of schooling. He was now three years behind David instead of two.

'Aye, it does that. I guess I'd better be going in and unpack. Have a nice trip back.' He gulped, picked up his suitcases and darted through the doors. He was quickly lost in the gloom of the building and somewhat sadly we turned and made our way back to the buggy.

'I think my boy's grown up,' said Meg with a sigh.

The next three years passed quickly. John Buchanan settled down in New York and was soon trying to persuade Evan to go and live there. He reckoned, and no doubt he was right, New York was where the big money was to be made. Evan, however, was not interested. Business was booming and he and Meg had a life they both enjoyed to the utmost. From time to time we talked of expansion but never did anything more about it. One sad event happened during the period and that was King, David's horse, broke a leg and had to be shot.

David came home during his breaks between semesters and each time he was more of a man. He took up smoking at one stage, and had developed a worldliness about him of which Evan was justly proud. He talked a lot about pledging his fraternity in the Phi Gams. I never did understand what he meant but I nodded and pretended, happy to hear him talk.

Sion was filling out too. He would be going to university just as David was leaving for Harvard Law School. Harvard was even further from home, all the way to New Haven, Connecticut but not far from New York. At least it meant Meg and Evan could visit him when they went there on business. David intended making his career in Business Law and Harvard had the best reputation in the subject.

It was June 1899 when I called in to see the doctor for one of my regular check ups.

I waited impatiently in the outer office for the receptionist to send me through. I didn't like the smell of
doctor's places, the ether and soap reminded me of illness
and usually my rheumatism gave a few extra twinges.
Mind you, it had been worse than usual. The previous
winter my hands had been so bad I couldn't hold a glass
properly, at least not on wet days. There was no getting
away from it, I was getting old.

'Mr Price, you can go in now,' said the pretty young
girl, looking full of life, health and vigour. She made me
feel older still if that was possible

'Hullo, James,' Doctor Sims greeted me, 'and how are
we this fine morning?' He rose and offered his hand.

It was a long-standing joke with us and I replied as
usual. 'I'm not too bad but I don't know about you.'

He chuckled. He was a short balding man in his early
fifties, with a stomach as prosperous looking as his office.
I thought for the umpteenth time that one of the boys
ought to become a doctor. The room was large, with
a high ceiling, and the floor was covered with a deep
pile red carpet. One wall was lined with leather bound
medical books, his desk had a deep green leather cover
which matched the couch in one corner. In the other
corner a stove stood, complete with coffee pot, always
warm. He was becoming what was known as a society
doctor but he was still a good one.

'How's the rheumatism?' he asked, cupping his hands
and placing his fingertips together in an arch through
which he peered at me.

'Playing me up a little, in spite of the warm weather.'

'Are you sleeping all right?'

'Not too badly when I take them pills you gave me.
I'm just about out of them at the moment.'

'I'll give you a prescription to take to the drug store.
Don't forget to watch how many you take, they're pretty
powerful. They've only been on the market a short while,
from Switzerland.'

I nodded. He told me the same thing every time.

'Okay. No other aches and pains you didn't have last time?'

I shook my head, 'Nope. I've got enough as it is, thanks!'

'I wish more of my patients were like you, James, instead of complaining of all the diseases and ailments under the sun – and a few more besides. I don't know but I think we'll end up a nation of pill takers. Soon there'll be pills to wake you up, pills to put you to sleep – we've already got them – pills to cure . . . Oh well, like I said, it'll be all pills soon. Come on, let me examine you. Just go behind the screen and strip down to your long john's please.'

Behind the screen his voice followed me. 'How's the cough?'

'Same as always,' I replied, knowing what was coming next.

'It's like I've told you before. You cough so hard you break one or two of the alveoli in the lungs and a spot of blood is discharged. Nothing to worry about there. Even your silicosis isn't as bad as some I've seen.'

He pushed, prodded, listened, tickled, looked and finally told me to get dressed.

'You'll still be alive when you come for your next examination,' he said, handing me a prescription for the sleeping pills.

He had started giving them to me a year previously and they were, without a doubt, a godsend when my rheumatics were bad, and kept me from sleeping. I usually called in every month or two to renew the prescription with the receptionist, not bothering the doctor at all.

'Thanks. See you in six months,' I said. I paid the receptionist and went out into the warm sunshine. At least, it was warm in the shade, in the sunlight it was hot enough to make a man think of a long, cool beer. I got the pills from the drug store and stood at the cross-roads for a moment debating whether to go for a beer or to the new coffee house for a coffee.

'Pardon me, sir . . . Pardon me,' said a voice behind me.

I looked around, not sure if I was being addressed.

'Are you Mr James Price, formerly of Llanbedas, Wales?'

'My name is Price yes, but not from where you said.'

'You are from Wales, aren't you? South Wales?' He was a dapper, little man, dressed in a black coat and tight trousers. He wore a gun at his side from which his right hand didn't stray too far. His black hair was sleeked down with oil too sweetly smelling for my taste. His moustache drooped down either side of the corners of his mouth and he had a habit of continually stroking it with his left thumb and fore finger.

'I am from there but not the place you said.'

He took out a note book. 'L.L.A.N.B.E.D.D.A.S . . . Lanbedas.'

'No man, it's pronounced . . .' I sighed. 'Never mind. Yes, that's where I'm from.'

'Yes, I was sure you was. My name is Brown and I'm a detective with the New York Smithson Agency. I'd like you to come with me to the Marshal's office. You're under arrest for the murder of Sir Clifford Roberts.'

I gasped. I could not believe my ears. It can't be true my brain told me but my eyes and ears told me different. I felt slightly dizzy for a moment and then the situation became crystal clear and I could think straight once more. 'I haven't a clue as to what you're talking about,' I replied haughtily. 'Now, if you'll excuse me, sir, I shall bid you good day.' I turned to go but he grabbed my arm. I was on the point of yelling for help but thought better of it. I suddenly realised I needed to talk to this man, to find out what he knew and if he wanted only me or Evan as well.

'Please unhand me, it's most unseemly,' I said. 'There's

a coffee house over there, shall we go and discuss this?' I started towards the place I'd indicated but Brown stood still, his hand on my coat. For some time now I'd been using a steel topped cane to help me around when my rheumatism was especially bad and before Brown could stop me I swung the cane and brought it down sharply across his forearm. With a scream of rage and pain he let me go, his hand holding his right arm.

'Don't attempt to draw your gun, Mr Brown. You'll be too slow and next time it'll be your head I'll crack open. Now, shall we go for that coffee?' Without waiting for a reply I stalked off, leaving him to follow. In the coffee house I selected a table at the back, next to the rear entrance. I was unsure what I was going to do yet, but I wanted a quick exit just in case. I smiled humourlessly to myself. Quick . . . that was a laugh. I couldn't move quickly if my life depended on it. Which it probably does, I told myself.

It was a long, low place, wide enough for two tables abreast and space to walk between. There were twelve or fifteen tables each side, with white cloths and comfortable seats. The special, tantalising aroma of coffee beans permeated the air, reminding me as always of that first trip from New York with Evan. Brown sat opposite me.

'Don't do something like that again old man or I'll kill you,' he growled.

'Really! An unarmed, old man?' I had stopped wearing the gun Evan had bought for me because of the problem I had with the arthritis in my hands. 'I don't think the marshal will be too pleased with that, do you?'

He scowled. 'Hurry up with your coffee and we'll go down to the marshal's office where I'll get you locked up.'

'Before we do I want to know what this is all about,' though I knew full well. I just wanted time to think.

'All I know is that you killed a man in Wales about

eight or nine years ago and I've got a warrant for your arrest.'

'This isn't Wales. What jurisdiction do you have here? Not you personally but the warrant.'

'Mr Price, a number of very influential people in Wales have had my agency looking for you for years. You'll be deported back to Wales as an undesirable alien and there no doubt you'll be arrested. The warrant I have is for your deportation, granted by a New York judge on the understanding that federal officers would not be called in to search for you, only a private agency like ours. What I said about you being under arrest for the murder of Sir Clifford Roberts was to put you off balance so you'd come more easily. It doesn't matter because you'll still come easily, or else.'

'But . . . but Good God, surely that isn't constitutional? I'm not an undesirable alien as far as the States are concerned. I've done nothing wrong, caused no harm, not committed any crime. So what grounds can they possibly have for deporting me?'

'Mr Price, surely you aren't as naïve as that? These people in Wales have many interests in America. I know some of their names and believe me they can wield as much power as the President himself if they want to. They can have you deported like that,' he snapped his fingers. 'Where's the waiter in this place? I could use a coffee too,' he rubbed his right arm. 'You sure gave me a clout with that blasted stick.'

'I wish it had been your head,' I said bitterly, seething at the injustice of it. There was no getting away from them. The bastards at home had so much power they could wield it in the land of the democratically free. Some joke that was.

'I'll get the coffee,' I made to get up.

'No, you don't. I don't trust you not to run away.'

I looked at him with disgust. 'Mr Brown I'm near enough seventy. I have rheumatic problems. I carry a cane not as an affectation but because I need it, look you. So don't be such a stupid son of a bitch.' I said the last sentence with a bitterness that took him by surprise and he sat back to watch as I went to the counter to order coffee.

I kept my back to him and slipped my hand into my waistcoat pocket. I brought out my sleeping pills and dropped three into his cup while waiting for my change. I prayed they would dissolve quickly as I returned to the table.

'Here you are, the best coffee in St Louis,' I said then cursed myself. I sounded jolly, which was far from the truth. I pushed the sugar and cream bowls on the table towards him. To my relief he put in three heaped spoons of sugar.

I added cream and sipped. It tasted more bitter than usual. 'What's meant to happen afterwards?'

'It's not what's meant to happen as to what will happen,' he said, sipping his coffee. 'Hmmm, good. And what's going to happen is that I'll arrange for the marshal to lock you up until I arrange two seats on the train back to New York tomorrow or the day after.'

'It's just me they want then?' I asked hopefully.

He smirked at the eagerness in my voice. 'Nope, they want Griffiths as well,' he replied, dashing my hopes to powder.

'Are you going to arrest Evan too?'

'Nope.' He was playing me like a cat plays a mouse and enjoying the game.

'Why not, if you want him?'

'Because for all their influence they couldn't persuade no judge to say he's an undesirable alien because he helped an old man escape his country. No sirree, there's no way they can touch him.' What a load of ridiculous contradictions, I thought. First he was telling me these people who wanted me had as much power as the President and now he was saying this. His next words startled me. 'They can't get him legally, but there's another way.'

My blood ran cold. Surely he did not mean they were going to have Evan murdered?

'What are you going to do, then?' I asked in a harsh tone. I watched him drain his cup.

'Nothing,' he chuckled again. 'Mr Price, we've known of your whereabouts for a few months now and I've been studying you and the family. It's mighty clear how high a regard they have for you. If you're taken back to Wales what do you think Griffiths will do about it?'

I knew, and from the way Brown chuckled again I could see he read the answer on my face.

'Exactly, Mr Price. He'll move heaven and earth on your behalf. I don't know all the details of the case but it seems he was at this Sir Clifford Roberts' manor house or castle, whatever these people live in over there and he attacked the old man before getting away. Didn't they chase him with hounds or something? Anyway, you killed the old man outside your house. You was seen doing it by a woman opposite and she reported you hoping for a reward. You then got away on the S S Cardiff. Griffiths' conscience more than anything will take him back to help defend you. Not that there's much chance of him doing you any good.' He put his hands to his face and rubbed his eyes. 'I don't feel too good,' he grimaced, closing and opening his eyes slowly.

I knew he was right. It was the sort of thing Evan would do. 'How much is it worth for you to go back to New York and say you made a mistake about finding us?'

'Are you trying to . . . to bribe me?' He was squinting at me, trying to focus on my face.

'Yes, why not? Presumably you're only here because somebody is paying you? I'll pay you more.'

'Mr . . . Mr Price, Jeez, I feel odd. Mr Price if it ain't me it'll be somebody else. I've already sent in a report categorically stating you're here. To . . . to deny

it will . . . will seem strange. Mr. Price, what . . . I . . .
I.' He fell forward over the table, stirred feebly and then
started snoring. I heaved a sigh of relief. Those pills of
the doctor's were certainly strong.

I slumped back in my seat and wearily rubbed my
eyes. My glasses were hurting my nose and I rubbed
the tender spot. I knew what it would mean if I did go
back. Evan had some influence here in St. Louis through
his political friends but not in New York. What could he
do there? Very little, I feared. And if there was one thing
I did know about American politics it was that there was
little love lost between the courts and the parties, whether
Democrat or Republican. If Brown had a warrant then
there was little chance of getting it quashed. And I
was sure, as night follows day, that Evan would come
with me.

And I was too old to run. Where could I go? My life,
or what I had left of it was here with Meg and Evan and
Sion and David. I'd had a good nine years with them. I
thought back, lost in the memory of it all. Little Sian and
Sion. And Dai. They had started it all. I chuckled when I
thought of some of the tea parties we'd had. And the doll's
house I'd made for Sian. Her death had greatly upset me.
I continued lost in my memories for a while, forgetting
where I was and who I was with. I'd had so little for so
long before the kids came into my life – and then I'd had
an awakening. That was all I could call it. An awakening.
My mind went from one incident to the next. The kite
flying which Sion was still interested in, now more so in
fact than ever. Indeed, I no longer really understood what
he was talking about half the time with these new fangled
inventions, like that man flying. I shook my head. That
was an incredible thought. Perhaps I had misunderstood.
Oh well, it no longer mattered. I got to my feet. I had
to see them all once more. Just once. Though David was
away at the university of course.

I got a cab down to the warehouse and went up to

Meg's office. She was at her desk writing but stopped when I entered.

'How'd it go? Everything all right? Did the doctor say you're going to live to the next time?'

From somewhere I managed a smile. 'As usual, Meg, as usual. Mind if I sit here for a while? You go on with what you're doing.'

'How about a coffee? I'll go and get us some,' she said brightly.

'Not for me, thanks. I'm swimming in the stuff. You just go on with what you're doing,' I sat next to the door; Meg picked up her pen and went on writing. She held her head slightly on one side in her concentration. At thirty-seven she had matured into a great beauty. She wore a dark grey business suit, with a skirt to just below her knees, and a short coat reaching her waist. After a while I got up. Time was marching on and I had a lot to do.

'Going so soon, Uncle James? Why not have a coffee and come home with me in an hour?' Her smile lightened my heart and nearly made me tell her what had happened. I couldn't talk because of the frog in my throat so I shook my head, managed a smile again and left. For a moment I thought she was going to come after me and I knew that if she did I'd have told her. I wasn't strong enough. I cursed myself for my weakness.

Evan was down on the floor by the dairy produce counter. I stood and watched him for a while talking to Sonny, oblivious of my presence, half hidden by a rack of shelves. At thirty-nine he was a fine figure of a man who had a commanding presence about him but somehow managed to seem approachable as well. The men were never too slow to tell him their problems. He was a born leader and for some time I had hoped to see him as one of the State Congressmen and perhaps even a Senator one day.

I wanted to hear him talk. I wanted very much to

see his smile and hear his voice, not just the mumble coming my way. With a sigh I turned away and left the building. It took me a while to find a cab but finally I got one. I knew if I hurried I could see Sion before he went out after school. He had been talking about a new kite or something. I shook my head, my memory was getting worse.

I was too late. I could see he had been and gone. It was a bitter blow. I sat in the study to write my letters. I addressed them both to Evan. The second I marked 'TO BE OPENED FIRST.'

I wrote: *My dearest Evan Meg, Sion and David, This will no doubt come as a great shock to you but when you read this I'll be dead. Evan bach, don't go running upstairs or upsetting everyone, just sit down and finish reading. I'm now with the angels and I've no doubt our lovely Sian is the loveliest of them all. I'll tell her how much you all miss her and think of her. Believe me, my mind isn't wandering. I really do think there's life after death. Upstairs is my body with not a spark of anything in it. My soul will have gone to another place and that's what matters.*

I had a man from a detective agency come up to me today. He had papers to have me sent back to Wales as an undesirable alien. All to do with that night when we escaped from Llanbeddas. I don't think you ever did understand when I said that I'd nothing before me except loneliness and now I had a reason for living. Remember, Evan? You see Bach, I was going to shoot myself which was why I had the gun handy. Instead I put it to better use. So you see every day since then has been a bonus and every day has meant more to me than the day before. It's been so exciting hasn't it? All the things we've done. I hope I've been able to contribute a little bit towards it. I've loved you more than I can say on paper. You know me, I never was all that good with words. Evan, my son – that's the way I think of you and that's the way I like it, like Meg is my daughter and the boys my grandsons. See how lucky I've been? No man has had such a family like mine. Evan, with me gone there's no way they can get you back to Wales. That was their idea. They knew if I was taken back you'd come and try to help me. That way they would have got both of us and I would have been hanged and you'd have ended in jail which wouldn't have done any good for Meg or the boys. The other letter by the way says that I did everything that night. I don't know whether it'll help if there is any question of them trying to get you as well but I have stated that it was me at the mansion, not you. I also state that . . . well, you can read it and give it to the detective. I left him in a coffee house on Pennsylvania Avenue fast asleep. Those pills the doctor gave me are pretty powerful. A box of them and I won't wake up but die nice and quiet in my own bed. Don't grieve for me I beg you. I want you to have a real good wake. In fact a great wake. Hans and the others will come, I know. I'm sure they know how to send a man to his grave properly. Well, my dears, there's nothing more to say. I want to write all night but if I go on much further you and Meg will be home and I won't have the courage anymore. I love you all dearly, God Bless and tell David it's time he started back to church.

    Goodbye, my dears,

                  Uncle James.

BOOK 4

The Story of Sion

1899

30

'EVAN, DINNER WON'T be long,' Meg called. 'Sion, go and see where Uncle James is.'

Sion called upstairs and then went out back. Evan went into his study to leave some papers and saw the two letters sitting on his desk. He picked them up, recognising Uncle James' hand writing. For some reason he was struck with foreboding. He tore open the letter marked 'TO BE OPENED FIRST', the first sentence made him sit down in shock. For a moment he could not, would not, believe it. When he finished the letter he knew it was true and that Uncle James was dead. In a daze he stood up. Over and over in his mind was why? Why? Why? They could have fought it. And if they could not have beaten it they could have gone elsewhere. It was a big country. There must have been another answer. Walking towards the door, he heard Sion call something but it took a few seconds to realise what he had said.

Sion was bounding up the stairs when Evan shouted for Sion at the top of his voice, but he was too late. Evan saw his son come to the banister, a sickly white look on his face. At his shout Meg had hurried in from the kitchen.

'What on earth . . .' she began and stopped, seeing the look on her husband's face as he stared up at Sion. Evan suddenly ran up the stairs and into Uncle James' room. The old man was laying on his bed, looking as though he was asleep. For a second Evan hoped but even as the spark flared it died within him. Meg was right behind him.

'Oh my God, Uncle James!' she ran to the bed just as Evan finished checking for his pulse.

'It's no good love,' he said softly, 'he's dead.'

Meg put her arms around Evan, crying, as Evan led her from the room. Sion was standing on the landing, white faced and also on the verge of tears.

'Go and tell the marshal, son, and tell him Uncle James is dead. Ask him who we have to notify, will you? Oh, and . . . and,' Evan cleared his throat, 'ask him if it makes any difference that it was suicide.'

Meg and Sion gasped. 'Suicide?' Sion asked. 'But it can't have been, Dad. What would Uncle James want to commit suicide for?'

'To save me going to prison, that's why. Now hurry up, Sion,' Evan said more harshly than he intended.

Meg looked at Evan in horror. 'What on earth do you mean? Why should you go to prison? You haven't done anything,' she paused. 'Evan, what on earth's going on?'

'Let's go down to the study and I'll tell you. There's a letter there from Uncle James which explains it all. Damnation,' he cried, 'why didn't he come and talk to me? Why didn't he come and say something?'

They slowly walked to the study. 'Here, read this,' he thrust the letter into Meg's hands.

Shakily he went across to the drinks cupboard and got them both a large whisky.

Meg's hand was trembling as she took the glass, though her tears had stopped. 'Poor Uncle James,' she said softly.

Evan nodded. 'It's all my fault . . .' he began.

'Don't be silly Evan. If you hadn't gone back in the first place Uncle James would have been long dead and we wouldn't have had his company for so long. It's not your fault. Goodness, he was a wonderful old man. I wondered why he'd been so strange this afternoon. I almost stopped him leaving. God, why didn't I stop him?' Meg began to cry again.

They talked for a while, waiting for Sion to return. Finally they heard him galloping back. It wasn't long before he arrived breathless in the study.

'The marshal says he'll tell the coroner and he'll come out tomorrow if we're sure he died of either natural causes or by his own hand. That's how the fat slob put it.' There were no more tears with Sion now, just an undirected anger. 'What did you mean, Dad, about saving you from going to prison? Thanks.' Sion took the proffered glass of whisky and gulped at it. Unused to strong liquor he was left half choking and gasping. He found a bottle of his mother's lemonade and poured it into the glass until the whisky colour had turned a bright yellow.

'Do you remember about nine years ago, when we left Wales?' Evan asked.

'Some, but not all. I seem to remember we went to Uncle David's place before leaving for the ship the next day. You and Uncle James turned up at the last minute. You were in a bit of a state I seem to remember. Hadn't you hurt your leg or something?'

'Yes, I had. I'd been shot.'

'Good grief,' Sion looked at his father with wide eyes.

'Do you remember Grandad and Grandma dying in a fire?' He waited for Sion to nod. 'That fire was meant for me . . . to kill me. The murder – as it would have been – was ordered by a man named Sir Clifford Roberts . . .' Talking steadily, Evan relived that night and told Sion exactly what had happened. When he finished he handed Sion Uncle James' letter. Evan reached behind him and picked up the other letter, which was still unopened. He held it as though weighing it in his hands and then tore it open.

Dear Evan,
This isn't going to be very long. I'm sorry if I've caused you any inconvenience but you remem-
ber what I told you I'd done that night back in

Llanbeddas when I got away to you in Cardiff? I told you about me going up to the manor house that night and how I was going to set the place on fire. What I hadn't told you was I killed Sir Clifford that night too. I have no regrets as I shall curse his memory from my grave, the black hearted son of a bitch. I won't go into the details here about why I did it and all that happened. Today a detective was going to arrest me and send me back to Wales. He talked some rubbish about getting you too because you'd go back to help defend me. I didn't really understand what he was talking about but it doesn't matter now because I'm dead. It's the best way. I couldn't stand the thought of going back to stand some sort of trial. We know what justice means over there – under British tyranny it's a matter of wealth is right. I want to thank you all for what you've done in the last ten years that have made my life so enjoyable. I'm sorry again if my actions that night cause you any trouble now. Evan, I swear here and now you had nothing to do with it.

I shall take fond memories away with me, to keep me happy through all eternity. I love you all.

My last will and testament is with my lawyer, John Driscole.

Uncle James.

Evan handed the latter to Meg who read it and passed it to Sion. Sion handed it back to Evan and grimaced. 'Could they really have done it Dad? I mean send him back as an undesirable alien?'

'It seems like it. Or else why did they spend so long looking for him? And me too come to that. There's another point which I don't know whether they're aware of or not. We entered the country illegally. I don't know whether the relevant authorities know about that, but if they ever found out,' Evan shrugged. 'Who knows what it could mean. And I know what you're going to say. There's tens of thousands of immigrants coming in every year illegally and nothing is done about it.' He sighed. 'We had better make the funeral arrangements tomorrow and send a telegram to David. Thank God he's finished his exams. It would have been very hard on him to have this on his mind when he was taking his finals. He should be able to come home in a few days.' Evan looked sadly at his glass and then drained it. 'I don't think I'll bother with any food tonight,' he said getting up and refilling his glass. He refreshed Meg's as well.

'You?' he offered the bottle to his son who shook his head.

'No thanks, Dad. I think I'll go for a walk. I won't be long.' Sion wandered over to the stable and went in to stroke his horse. He gave him a rub down with a fist full of straw. 'Well boy, he's gone,' Sion spoke to the animal, the horse's ears pricking up at the sound of his voice. 'He never did get around to taking a stone from your shoes, eh?' Sion patted his rump. 'I'm going to miss him. It was special between us, somehow.' Sion looked over his shoulder, to the corner of the house he could just see through the open door. 'Uncle James you shouldn't have done it. Me and you could have gotten away,' he spoke softly, the horse whinnied and turned his head to nuzzle Sion's hand. 'Mam and Dad would have understood and helped. We had the whole of the States to choose from, Uncle James.' The tears started filling his eyes and then he was sobbing, leaning on the back of the horse. Sion was nearly seventeen, well built, his shoulders filling out. He was of medium height, not as tall as David, but stockier. He had a winning way with him, full of charm.

Sion had not heard the buggy pulling up nor saw the two men climbing down. Nor did he hear them knock loudly on the door or see Evan answer. The little man in front of the marshal said something and then Evan was on him. He had him by the throat, shaking him like a terrier shakes a rat, the marshal trying ineffectively to pull him away. Sion heard the commotion and ran to the door. He recognised the marshal, a man he detested, ran back to his saddle and drew out his rifle. Meg appeared and screamed at Evan to put the man down. Sion had never seen his father in such a blind rage. The marshal pulled out his gun and raised it to hit Evan over the head with. Sion pointed his rifle in the sky and fired. The marshal stood still, his gun raised, hesitating. Evan stopped shaking the man and Meg fell silent.

'Put the gun down, marshal, nice and easy like. That's it. Now please just drop it to the ground. Dad, I don't know what's going on but are you aiming to kill him or just frighten him out of his wits? If it's the latter I think he's frightened already and if it's the other you haven't got far to go.'

'Please, Evan,' Meg begged, 'put him down.' She stood by Evan. 'Who is he? The detective?'

'Yes. He identified himself and then demanded to see Uncle James' body.' The man was stirring, beginning to groan. Evan let him go and the detective collapsed onto the earth.

'Pick him up and get him off my property, marshal. If I ever see him again I'll kill him. And that's a promise.'

'So will I, marshal,' added Sion. 'You can tell him if he's still here tomorrow I'll be coming looking for him.'

'Sion, don't be so stupid,' Meg said, half in anger and half in fear. 'This man is a gunslinger. What would you do to him?' She had never seen her son like this before. In the mood he was in he was capable of anything.'

'I'm not talking stupidly, Mam. This man killed Uncle James and when the men at the warehouse know about it I reckon we'll have a little hanging.'

'Rubbish, boy,' exploded the marshal, angry because he had been made to drop his gun and look foolish.

'There'll be no necktie party in my town. All this man was doing was his job. Nothing more, nothing less.'

'Shit, marshal and you know it. He was paid by some rich swine to find and hound an old man to death, which he did. To death,' said Sion bitterly.

The object of their discussion groaned, moved and then sat up, groggy and holding his throat. He tried to talk but could not manage more than a painful croak. Sion pushed the man hard in his back and he sprawled on the ground again.

'All right, son,' said Evan softly. 'Marshal, it won't be my son and my men coming for him, but me. I just changed my mind about what'll happen if I see him. I'll come into town looking for him. There are at least three trains before noon. He'd better be on one. Now take him out of here.' With that Evan spun on his heel put his arm around Meg and beckoning to Sion, led them indoors.

'Thanks, son. It was a bit melodramatic I suppose but you were right. He caused Uncle James' death and as far as I'm concerned he ought to pay for it.'

'Listen to you two,' said Meg bitterly. 'Are you both out of your minds? It's almost nineteen hundred and you talk like it was thirty years ago. I've never heard such nonsense. Do you think I want my husband and son killed, or arrested because of your blasted male stupidity? Evan, you should act your age. You know as well as I do that if it hadn't been him it would have been somebody else. The marshal was right. He was just doing his job. Nothing you two do will bring Uncle James back. Instead it might take you from me as well. And where's the sense in that? Men. You're so busy being masculine you can't see the more important things around you. Tell me, what will I do if either of you are killed? Eh? Tell me.'

'We aren't going to get killed, Mam,' said Sion.

'Oh, you aren't, are you?' Meg turned her scorn on her son. 'Have you got a special contract with God to look after you? Do you think that because you believe you're right you'll live? I thought you had more intelligence than that, Sion. Damn you both. I'm going to get a drink.' She stalked back to the study and, more than a little shamefaced Evan and Sion followed.

'I'm sorry, Mam. You're right,' Sion said heavily.

'Yes, I'm sorry too, Meg. And I'll have a whisky. Here's my glass.'

Sion sighed. 'I wish Uncle James was here to enjoy his dram as he used to say. This was his favourite time of day.'

They sat talking in a desultory fashion for a while but there was nothing really to say, each aware of the others' heartache. Sion soon sensed his parents wanted to be alone and excused himself.

He lay on his bed for hours, unable to sleep, thinking, remembering. A noise from downstairs brought him out of his reverie. Carefully he opened his door and listened. The scuffling footsteps were peculiar somehow and he wished he had his gun. He opened the door further and looked over the banister.

Evan was trying to walk up the stairs with Meg over his shoulder. Sion hurried down to meet him. Evan was half way up when he teetered.

Sion steadied his father and asked in alarm, 'What's wrong?'

'Nut . . . nothing,' said Evan, the words slurred. 'Chust me and your Mam going to bed. Sh . . . she tried to drink . . . drink me one for one in whish . . . ky, but . . . but didn't. Now I gottergetertobed,' he said in one concentrated rush.

Sion didn't know whether to laugh with relief or feel disgusted with his mother for getting into such a state. In the end he felt only pity and helped his father get her upstairs.

'Thanksh shon,' Evan said and fell backwards across Meg's thighs. Sion pulled him around until he was laying straight and went back to his own bed.

Meg suffered in silence the next day very ashamed of herself, while Evan suffered loudly. The marshal returned with a doctor from the Coroner's Office and issued Evan with a death certificate. The marshal also informed them that the detective had left first thing that morning.

Evan made the funeral arrangements, Sion sent a telegram to David and John Buchanan and in accordance with Uncle James' wishes, Meg arranged a wake.

Uncle James was buried in the local cemetery, and over three hundred people turned up to pay their last respects. John Buchanan had cancelled a trip to Europe to be there, because like he said, Europe could wait. There were the German farmers for whom Uncle James had run the fund Evan had set up, businessmen he had known over the years and the Griffiths' political friends from all walks of life.

The wake later that afternoon was a huge success. Evan and Meg intended it to be an occasion to remember, just as Uncle James would have wanted. A cow, two sheep and a pig were spit roasted. The whisky and beer never ran out and an enormous barrel of punch had been prepared for the ladies and children. Uncle James was toasted so often that it caused one of the farmers to remark, 'His spirit must be drunk by now.'

By nine o'clock Sion was quite merry, sitting beside David on the grass. 'How are you big brother?' he asked affectionately.

'Not bad, not bad at all. Christ, I don't know why I'm smiling. Too much drink, I suppose. I'm going to miss having Uncle James around.'

'Me too,' said Sion, his voice barely more than a whisper. 'I'm going to miss him something terrible. You know, he'd become so much a part of the family it was as though he'd be around forever and now he's gone.'

David signed. 'Aye, that's so. But life must go on. Or it will go on I should say. There's no must about it. Cigarette?'

'No thanks. I might drink a bit now and then but I don't smoke. I'm surprised you do.'

'Everybody smokes at the University. I just followed the rest so as not to be the odd one out. You'll see what I mean when you go next month. It's a pity I won't be there. I'd have liked to have shown you the ropes for the first year. You know, helped you get settled in, like. Oh well, it can't be helped I suppose. Pity you lost a year after you got shot.'

'Are you pleased about Harvard?'

'I am and I'm not really. I'd have liked a longer break. I've been studying since I can remember and I get a bit fed up sometimes. Still, two more years isn't so much, I suppose.' David stared moodily into his beer.

'I know what you mean. I feel like that now. If it wasn't for Mam and Dad I don't think I'd go. I'd just push off for a bit, see some of the country, maybe the world.'

'You know what they'll say if you suggest something like that. There's plenty of time when you've finished your education.' David tried to copy Evan's voice and nearly succeeded. 'And I guess they're right. I'll be twenty one with a qualification that'll allow me to practise law. A year or two in practice and then I'll come and sort out Dad's business for him. Or at least I'll turn us from being a well off family into a rich one.' He smiled at his brother. 'What do you plan to do?'

Sion laughed. 'Not that, that's for sure. I was reading about this bloke S P Langley and his flying machine. It rather interests me and I thought I'd look a bit further into it. With the new type of gasoline engine I think there might be something in it.'

'Hmmm, I dunno. There could be, I suppose, but it's pretty farfetched. I mean, getting something heavier than air to fly.'

'But Langley did it,' Sion protested.

'So it said in the newspapers but I don't think you

can believe all that's written in them. Mind you, the rate they're inventing new things nowadays I suppose anything's possible. Oh well, we'll see what we shall see.' He paused to drink some beer. 'What're the girls like around town? Anything good?'

'Not really. You know Peggy-Sue McAlister? She's being used by just about everybody in the class. Man, I'm not kidding but if you're feeling horny about lunch time she'll go with you down to the bottom of the field and, well, you know.'

'You're kidding? You mean that pretty blonde girl with the big boobs?'

'That's the one. I guess there's something wrong with her or something because she just can't get enough. She's always wanting to feel it, you know. There's one or two others who, if you go out for a couple of walks with them and be nice, they'll let you touch them up but they won't do much for you. At least, I haven't found one yet that will. But I keep looking,' Sion said with a grin. 'What about you?'

'Oh, we don't do so badly. Of course, being an all male Uni like it is, there ain't much to spare around the town but . . . I'm not complaining about my time there,' David said with a smirk.

'Trust you. Who is she?'

'Oh, nobody who matters. Just a local girl. Good for a relaxing evening. Not too bright and likes quiet moonlight walks, if you see what I mean.'

'I see all right. What's her name and how do I contact her when I get there?'

'Cathy. But her folks took her out West with them a week ago and they aren't coming back.'

'That's a shame. There's Gunhild over there,' Sion nodded towards the blonde figure near the food table but watched for David's reaction. Sion was not disappointed. David reacted like an electric wire had touched him. He jerked around, saw her and got to his feet.

'I'm going to talk to her. Has she got a boyfriend, do you know?'

'Oh, she's had plenty on a string but at the moment I think she's between men.'

'Thanks. See you later,' David wandered nonchalantly away. It was not obvious to look at him but his heart was pounding and his ears buzzing.

Sion sighed and drained his glass. I think he's in love with her he thought. Either that or he's really itching to get into her knickers. He got up and went to refill his glass of beer. He drank half of it and topped it up again. There was still the best part of three hundred guests scattered around the lawns and throughout the house. Tables groaned beneath the weight of food and drink. The men and women were in groups, some large and some small, milling, talking, laughing and toasting Uncle James.

'Are we wrong, Uncle James?' asked Sion, in a soft whisper. 'Is this what you really wanted? I guess, knowing you, it is. Wherever you are, I hope you're enjoying it as well. Is Sian with you? Have you told her how I'm always thinking of her? It was always different for me, us being twins and all. I was closer to her than the others can imagine. Oh well, Uncle James, here's to you.' He raised his glass in silent salute and took a few mouthfuls.

He wandered about for ten minutes and finally stopped next to a group of farmers.

'Hullo, Mr Reisenbach,' he greeted the man. 'How are you?'

'Sad at the departure of my dear friend James,' Hans replied. 'But apart from that all is vell. And you Sion? Are you not off to the university soon?'

'In a few weeks time. I'm looking forward to it.'

'Ach, I am sure you are. You are lucky boys to have such a fine education. I sometimes vish my Gunhild had done the same. Of course the boys vant to stay vith the farm as it should be and anyway they vere never so bright at school.'

'Gunhild'll meet the right man, settle down and give you grandchildren. That's what you really want, isn't it Mr Reisenbach?' Sion teased.

'It could very vell be so, young man. And who do you have in mind, eh? Your brother?' he chuckled. 'Mind you I vould like that very much, yes. But I vant for more than that. I vant my Gunhild to be happy. If she picked David as vell then I vould be twice as happy. Oh vell, ve must see vat happens, eh?'

Sion nodded. 'Yep, we must see what happens. How's the farm now?'

'Good. Very good now that prices are vat they should be. You know, Sion if it had not been for your father I and a lot of others vould have lost our farms. Ve vould have lost everything ve'd vorked for all our lives. I tell him – Evan, you should stand for Congress and ve vould vote for you. But he says no. I have heard him make some very good speeches and vat he says makes a lot of sense. Perhaps one day he vill do it, eh?'

Sion grinned. 'Mam reckons he will, and in the not too distant future. He's just itching to get some things done. You know he's always on about the labour laws and the agricultural laws and stuff like that. Who knows? We'll see what happens, eh?'

The farmer laughed. 'You are right. Tell me Sion I read that letter from James but I cannot believe it somehow. He was such a peace loving man.'

'Oh, it's true all right. I remember when it happened. I wish Uncle James had told us about the detective though. We could have done something, I'm sure.'

'Ja, I'm sure, too. Vell it's been nice talking to you Sion, but if you'll excuse me I must go and talk to your father.' Reisenbach walked away.

31

SION WANDERED BACK to the party and helped himself to another beer. He had a raging thirst. Some of the guests began to leave and he went around saying polite goodbyes, swapping small talk, his mind on Uncle James. He met up with David.

'What are you looking so happy about?' Sion asked.

'Oh, nothing much,' David assumed a nonchalance he did not feel. 'I'm meeting Gunhild tomorrow for a drive in the country.' His grin widened if that was possible.

'Well, well, well. So you two are getting together at last, are you?'

'Don't be daft man, of course not. Just going for a ride, that's all.'

'Sure, sure. I reckon she's more than a bit sweet on you, you know.'

'Rubbish. I hardly know her anymore.'

'You've only been friends with her for about the last seven years,' Sion replied.

'Not really. Oh, at one time sure but not now. I don't really know her. But I'm going to enjoy finding out. She's a nice girl. She might not have been to university but she's read a lot. Stuff like Voltaire, Dickens, all of Twain. She really is fun to talk to. And that voice of hers, with just a twinge of accent even after all this time in the States.'

'Like yours, you mean.'

'Only German not Welsh, fool,' he joked.

Many of the guests had left by this time, only a few

stragglers remaining. At last even they had gone and Meg and Evan came across to join their sons.

'Did you enjoy yourselves?' Evan asked them. They both nodded.

'It was easy to forget why they were all here,' Meg said sadly. 'I kept looking around expecting Uncle James to appear and say something funny or . . . or . . . Oh hell. He'd really have enjoyed himself tonight.'

'True,' Evan put his arm around her. 'Dave, pour me a beer will you?'

'We'll all miss him,' David said softly, filling a glass for his father. 'He was a really great person. He was always so happy. Even when his rheumatism was playing him up he rarely grumbled.'

'I'm going to miss having him around the house,' said Meg. 'He was always helping with something, or suddenly getting out the buggy and going into town to buy a book or two.'

'Don't forget boys we have to attend the will reading tomorrow at John Driscole's office,' said Evan.

Driscole was both the family and business lawyer, though frequently Evan could tell Driscole more about corporation and company law than the lawyer could tell Evan. It wasn't that Driscole was not a good lawyer, it was just that the laws were so complex and specialised that it was impossible for him to know it all.

'I suppose we must,' said Sion, not wanting to go.

'We're all asked for specifically, though that's hardly surprising under the circumstances,' said Evan. 'It's at ten o'clock and as that's only,' he looked at his watch, 'five and a half hours away I suggest we go to bed.' They nodded in agreement and the boys followed their parents across the grass to the backdoor.

The next morning Evan went in to wake up Sion, having had only limited success with Meg and David.

'Come on, bach,' Evan shook his shoulder. 'It's time to get up.'

Sion groaned and turned over. A second later he was asleep again.

'Okay, boyo, if that's the way you want it.' Evan bent down and took hold of the mattress. He heaved Sion, sheets, blankets and mattress onto the floor. Sion sat up, looking about him. Then seeing his father grinning down at him he groaned, ran his hand through his hair and lay down where he had landed, looking as though he intended going back to sleep.

'Sion, if you don't get up I'll get some water to throw over you,' Evan threatened.

Sion mumbled something and settled himself. Evan stalked out of the room and came back a couple of minutes later with a bucket of cold water. He pulled the bedclothes away and grinned when Sion curled into a foetal position for warmth. Evan slowly poured the water over Sion's head. Sion shot awake, spluttering and gasping.

Evan toyed with the idea of trying it on Meg but then disregarded the notion; it was more than his life was worth. After ejecting David from his bed he did not have to resort to using the water. The threat was enough to get David hurriedly up off the floor.

'Coffee's ready downstairs,' was all Evan said.

Back in their room Evan sat on the edge of their bed and looked tenderly at his wife as though he was trying to memorise each feature, something he had done so often in the past. He thought her so beautiful and constantly thought how lucky he was. He kissed her cheek, and then gently let his tongue play across her lips. She stirred, her nose and lips twitching slightly at his touch and then she came awake. Without opening her eyes she smiled and put her arms around his neck. Evan took hold of the bedclothes and pulled them off, the sudden cold made her protest.

'Come on. Time to get up. Coffee's ready downstairs.'

Meg sat up and squinted at the sunshine streaming

through the window. She sighed. 'Okay bully, I'm getting up, though I'd rather stay here.'

They arrived at the lawyer's fifteen minutes late. His secretary showed them into Driscole's well furnished, wood-panelled and book-lined office. Driscole was a dapper little man, in his early sixties, with a head of grey hair and thick glassed spectacles perched on the end of his nose.

'Ah, Evan, you're late,' he said standing and shaking Evan's hand. 'Hullo, Meg,' he took her hand and shook it before greeting the boys.

'Believe me, I had the devil's own job getting them here at this time, after last night,' Evan said.

'Had a good time? Sorry we couldn't make it, but Deidre has her usual summer cold and keeps sneezing all the time. Supposed to be something to do with the pollen in the air but I reckon she's been in a draught again. Probably too early into her summer frocks, I reckon. Sit down, sit down.' He pushed the pile of papers on his desk to one side and then remembered the will was amongst them. He went through each paper one by one. The others sat, patient and quiet, subdued by the occasion.

Driscole gave a satisfied grunt and pulled out the relevant document. He cleared his throat and said: 'I'll ignore all the technical jargon about sound mind and all that. Ah, here we are. I give to Sion my penknife, the one for getting stones out of horses hooves,' Driscole looked up and peered at Sion short sightedly in spite of his thick glasses. 'He insisted on that, said it would mean something to you.'

Sion nodded, too choked to say anything.

'And he leaves you half of his collection of books. To you David he leaves the other half of his books and his pocket watch.'

David nodded in acknowledgement. He too found it difficult to talk.

'He says here, Evan, that the rest of his belongings are left to you though there is very little of value. He asks that you give his clothes to the Salvation Army to do with as they please. And that leaves his shares.'

'What shares?' asked Evan.

Driscole smiled. 'He said when I was preparing this will for him that you'd say that. As you are fully aware he didn't really have anything to spend his money on and the income he was getting from the business was, in his words, too much for him. I, in fact, recommended that he invest in some stocks and shares. He did so, successfully. The bulk of them are left to you Evan and to you Meg. He says here, 'I don't want to make it too easy for the boys, it'll do them good to have to earn their money and though I love them as if they were my own I leave them only ten percent each of whatever the shares are worth, for them to keep or sell as they wish.

'That's about it, you can take this away with you and read it later. There are a few personal messages which are better read in private. The shares, by the way, are in rail, coal and gold mining. The value as of yesterday is,' he paused to rummage around his desk for a writing pad, 'let me see. Yes, here we are. Eh, a hundred and thirty five thousand, four hundred and seventy six dollars, and some cents.'

They all gasped. 'So much?' Evan asked incredulously. 'But that's impossible.'

'Under normal circumstances I'd agree with you, and in fact most of the value is in some of the coal shares. He took a gamble about a year ago and bought into a new company who reckoned there was coal out Nevada way. They were right, and are doing very well. They've got their offices in San Francisco I believe. The bank here has a stake in it as well and know more about them. You can check with them if you want further details. Anyway, that's about it, Evan. I know it's barely a quarter past eleven but can I offer you a sherry or a coffee? I usually do after such an occasion.'

'No, neither thanks, John,' replied Evan, still bemused. They shook hands with Driscole and left.

'I'm nearly a millionaire already,' said Sion as Evan turned the buggy and started home. 'That's over thirteen thousand dollars. What am I going to do with it?'

'You could spend it,' David suggested, still trying to come to terms with such sudden wealth.

'You'll do no such thing,' Meg replied sharply. 'You can either invest it further or leave it alone. Neither of you are to touch it until you finish your education.'

'Sorry, Mam,' David said unexpectedly. 'But Uncle James said I could do what I liked with the money. And I've got one or two ideas I just might try out.'

'He's right, Meg,' said Evan. 'It's their money and they can do with it as they please. I don't think Uncle James realised how much there was, otherwise he wouldn't have left them so much. Listen, you two, all I'll say is don't waste it. Sure, go and spend some of it and enjoy yourselves but . . . well, don't waste it. If you decide to go into business for yourselves one day you've got just the start you'll need.'

After they arrived home Evan went with Meg into the study to read the will while the two brothers went to help the women cleaning up after the party.

'What time are you meeting Gunhild?' Sion asked.

'Half past three. Can I borrow Thunderbolt? She's meeting me half way in her father's buggy, so I don't really want to take a buggy as well. And Dad will be using it anyway, along with his two nags. I don't suppose he's learnt to ride yet?'

Sion chuckled. 'Not since he fell off that time. Do you remember?'

'Do I ever. Mam was going frantic until she found he hadn't hurt himself and then she collapsed with laughter.'

'Mind you, she can't talk. She refuses to even try. I suppose,' said Sion standing with his hands on his hips, surveying the seven women and Marie their cleaning lady, carrying glasses and bottles back to the house, 'we'd better take the tables and put them in the big shed. After that I think I'm going to bed for a few hours.'

'What are you going to do with all that money?' David asked Sion.

'I don't know, and that's a fact. I guess I'll finish my education and then go and see a bit of the world. I'd like to see about this flying business. I might get into that,' he paused. 'What about you?'

'I'm definitely going to visit Wales sometime, just to see how everybody is getting on. That'd be something, hey? Arriving like royalty? Pretending to be really rich. God, think what that'd do to them all at Llanbeddas.' He gave a half laugh, half snort. 'Well perhaps not. I'd just go and see the family. Come on, give me a hand.'

Sion said unexpectedly, 'Tell me something. Do you ever think about Sian and what it would be like if she was alive?'

'Sometimes, but not all that often. I find it impossible to remember what she was really like. I can remember odd incidents and things but I can't see her somehow. Do you know what I mean?'

'Only too well. I think of her from time to time but I have the same problem. I just can't picture her properly. I feel I ought to be able to, but I can't. I bet she'd be beautiful if she was here now.'

'Heck, we'd be going frantic trying to keep all the boys away. This is morbid. I'm going to saddle Thunderbolt. See you later.'

'Are you going to do some of that school work I gave you?' Meg asked Sion.

'No, Mam. I'm going to read that last book Uncle gave me – Herman Melville's Moby Dick. One boys at school's read it and said it's very good.'

And anyway he thought, I'm not going to do anymore of those lessons Mam. I've had enough. I've just got to put it off a bit longer and I'll be away to university. Not that I didn't appreciate your help, I did. It's just there's no need now, but I won't hurt you by telling you.

The summer went past in a rush, until it was time for Sion to leave. David had already left for Harvard to study for his master's degree. Now it was Sion's turn. He would study for a general degree for the next three years. After that, he hoped to follow his brother to Harvard, although in what subject he was unsure as yet.

Early in the morning of his last day, Sion wandered over to the stable and saddled Thunderbolt. He rode down to the river and sat for a while watching the water rushing past, lost in his childhood memories.

He had enjoyed his childhood and youth, of that there was no doubt. The swimming in the pool above St Louis, making the rafts to ride way down to the south and then the long walk home, usually wet. He was the only one from his class going to Church Hill, two others were going elsewhere but the remainder were going to work for their fathers or look for jobs, disdaining the thought of further education.

'I wish Uncle James was coming with us tomorrow,' he said to Thunderbolt, the horse's ears flicking at the sound of Sion's voice.

'What about you my beauty? Who's going to run you; to stop you getting fat and lazy? Not that you aren't lazy enough as it is. Perhaps Dad can arrange with Sonny or one of the men to use you while I'm away, eh?' He heard the hoot of a river boat and looked up to see it sweeping majestically into view. He could never see one without feeling a stirring of longing for travel and adventure, for exotic lands and wild places.

One day, he promised himself, one day. Reluctantly, the sun already hot on his back, he turned the horse and broke into a gallop for home and breakfast.

Meg heard him coming and, alarmed at the speed at which he was riding, rushed out to see what was wrong. Sion pulled up by the back porch, in a flurry of dust, smiling and swept off his hat.

'Nice day, ma'am,' he said.

Meg returned his beaming smile. 'Flapjacks, eggs and beans are ready,' she said, her hands on her hips. She thought to herself, young man you're going to break a few hearts in your time. David, she had a sneaking feeling, was going to marry Gunhild and settle down. Maybe he'd take over the business from Evan and let Evan concentrate more on politics like he wanted to. Life was as perfect as it could be.

Sion pottered around the house all day. Meg stayed at home, helping him to pack. Meg also packed an overnight bag for herself and Evan.

That evening the three of them were in the study when Evan said to Sion, 'You've left your dinner jacket out, haven't you?'

'Ready on my bed. I'm looking forward to this. It'll be nice to have a decent meal,' Sion said straight-faced.

'I agree, son,' Evan said, neither of them looking in Meg's direction. She stared from one to the other, open-mouthed. Neither of them could keep a straight face and both burst out laughing. When she realised they were teasing her she smiled too, though not quite as broadly.

They left for the hotel a little after eight o'clock.

'What you ought to buy, Dad,' said Sion flicking the reigns and getting the horses moving, 'is one of the new type of motorised horseless carriages made by that fellow Ford. He's making quite a few of them nowadays.'

'That's all very well but I hear they frighten the horses and there are too many problems with them at present,' said Evan. 'You've got to get gasoline and there's none around this area. They're always breaking down and they're dirty, oily and smelly. Mind you, I'm not saying they won't catch on though I doubt if they'll ever replace the horse and buggy entirely. But you never know. You just never know,' he repeated.

They pulled up at the Lucky River Hotel where Evan had stayed when he first borrowed the twenty five thousand dollars from Andrew Z. Fforest. The hotel had recently been taken over by new management and was reputed to now serve the best food in St Louis.

With the last drink of the evening before them Sion asked: 'Are you going to stand in the next election, Dad?'

Evan shrugged. 'I'm going to become an American citizen first. After that I'll think about it.'

Meg nodded sagely at her son. 'Oh, he'll definitely end up in politics. He's as bad as the Irish for his talk. If you and David come and run the business for us, then that's exactly what he'll do.'

Sion nodded non-committally.

'What are you planning to do?' Meg asked with more austerity than she had intended.

Sion shrugged. 'It's too early to say yet. I've still got five years of university to finish . . . Assuming that I get to Harvard.'

'Of course you will,' Meg had no doubt whatsoever.

'Yeah, I suppose you're right,' said Sion. 'What do you fancy then, Dad?' He changed the subject. 'Congress or the Senate?'

'I'd have to try for Congress first,' Evan said seriously. 'Providing I receive the nomination. If I got that far I could then go on to try for the Senate. But that's a long way away yet,' he drained his glass. 'Come on, drink up and let's go home. We've an early start in the morning.'

Exactly on time the next morning the train pulled out of St. Louis.

Over a lunch of cold meats and salad Sion asked, 'What

are you going to do with the business, Dad? Do you have any expansion plans?'

'No. I'm quite happy as we are. We have enough on our plates so I think we'll leave things as they are for a while.'

Sion had half expected him to say that and was slightly disappointed because he would have liked to see his father make a fortune. One day, he said to himself, I'll do it. I'll make the biggest damned fortune in the US.

They got off the train at Columbus and spent the night in an hotel. The next morning they hired a buggy for the two hour drive to the university.

At the main entrance Sion found an office with the sign "New Students" on the door. He knocked timidly and then harder. He heard a loud yell for him to enter. The room was bare except for the young man sitting behind a battered desk, smoking a smelly pipe with type-written lists in front of him.

'Name,' he barked, glancing up.

'Griffiths, Sion Griffiths,' Sion replied, a little intimidated.

The man puffed furiously for a few moments while he scanned his lists. 'You're in Lincoln dormitory. Out of the door, turn right and it's straight ahead at the end of the quadrangle.'

Sion turned to go but the man called him back.

'Hang on. Are you any relation to David Griffiths who left last term?'

Sion nodded. 'He's my brother.'

The man smiled and stood up, hand outstretched. 'Well, well, well, fancy that now. My name's Callaghan, Colin Callaghan. Welcome to the university. Say, if you aren't too busy later drop around to Seymore for a beer. But don't advertise the fact? We aren't exactly allowed beer in our rooms but everybody knows it goes on and it's okay as long as we keep quiet.'

'Sure, thanks. I will,' said Sion, gratefully.

Meg and Evan said goodbye to him at the door to Lincoln. He had tears in his eyes now that the time for parting had come. With a final farewell he entered the building.

32

INSIDE, SION FOUND the porter's lodge just as David had described it. 'My name is Griffiths. I . . . I'm new,' he added superfluously.

'I can tell that, sir, but don't you worry none, you'll soon know your way round like an old'un. Griffiths, you say? Ah, here it is. Second floor, room two eleven. The two means second floor and eleven that it's the eleventh from the stairs. We had a Griffiths here last year. Played football,' the old man mused.

'My brother. Thanks,' said Sion, picking up his bags and going through the swing doors and into a long corridor. He was going to have to get used to telling people he was David's brother. So long as they don't start comparing us, he said to himself. He was surprised to find somebody was already in the room when he reached it. Then he remembered David telling him that some had to share a room while a few lucky ones had a room to themselves. David had been amongst the lucky ones.

'Eh, hullo,' said Sion from the doorway. 'I'm sharing this room with you.'

The man who was there looked up from his unpacking and waved his hand. 'Come on in, come on in. You can have any bed except that one,' he pointed to the bed on Sion's left. As there was only one other, on the right of the door it seemed a strange thing to say but Sion surmised he was joking and smiled. There were two beds, two chests of drawers, two closets, two desks and two hard backed chairs. On either side of the unlit fireplace were two arm chairs and between them a low table. The walls were cream in colour, the furniture a drab and battered brown. Sion walked across to the window to look down at the quadrangle, a large area of grass surrounded by the high, three-storied building.

He turned to his new roommate who was still unpacking. 'Eh, my name is Sion Griffiths.'

The man grunted but made no other reply. If this was all he was going to get from the man he expected to share a room with for the next year Sion was not looking forward to it. He was quite a big fellow too, about half a head taller than Sion, broader and heavier. After a few seconds Sion asked: 'What's your name?'

The man paused, his folded clothes in his hands and then carefully replaced them in his suitcase. He went over to the door, closed it and came back to Sion who was beginning to feel slightly alarmed at his odd behaviour.

'Can you keep a secret?' he whispered.

Sion nodded warily. 'Eh, sure,' he said hesitatingly.

'My Father sent me here . . .' he began, looking piercingly at Sion.

'So did mine,' said Sion, thinking if he humoured the man he might act a little more sanely.

'No, no, no, you don't understand.' He drew himself up to his full height from the slouch he had assumed when he began whispering, pointing his finger at Sion. 'I have been sent by the Father of Mankind, to save Mankind from itself. Do you understand me?'

Sion nodded, suddenly dry mouthed. He managed to croak. 'Sure, I understand that. I . . . I'm honoured to meet you, real honoured.'

'You lie. You speak with the voice of Satan.' The man screamed the name Satan. Sion sidled to one side and said, 'No, I'm not lying. You can read my thoughts, being who you are, and so you know I'm not lying.'

This disconcerted the man for a moment and then he slowly smiled. 'Exactly. You can keep nothing from me.'

'Then you know I'm not lying,' said Sion desperately, trying to see something he could use as a weapon.

The logic seemed to get through to the man. 'That's right. You can't lie to me because I will know it. Therefore you will always tell the truth.'

Sion nodded frantically. 'That's right. That's exactly right. How can I possibly lie to you? You have the all seeing eye of . . . of our Father with you.' Jesus Christ, he thought, is this for real? I must be dreaming.

'Kneel,' the man suddenly ordered, pointing his finger at him. He himself got down on his knees and said in a thunderous voice, 'Kneel. I shall pray for your forgiveness. Yours will be the first of the souls I have come to save.'

Sion gulped and thought about dashing for the door while the maniac was on his knees but then decided not to. It was too risky, so he kneeled.

'My Father,' the man held his hands up high, wide apart. 'This is the first soul I ask you to forgive for all the blasphemies he has committed whilst he has been here, on this hell called earth. I ask you with . . .' he looked balefully at Sion, who was looking at the man, fascinated. 'Bend your head,' he shrieked. 'You are in the presence of God Almighty who has visited us here, so that I can save your miserable soul. Show the correct obeisance before our Lord and Master.'

Hastily Sion dropped his head, his heart pounding. How did one deal with a nut?

The prayer droned on, Sion's knees ached and tears formed in his eyes. How could he live here with a lunatic like this? How was he supposed to work with the fear that he could be attacked at any time of the day or night? He would never be able to sleep knowing this maniac was in the same room. Suddenly the man screamed: 'O Lord,' and bowed low until his forehead touched the floor. Sion scrambled to his feet, staggered while the circulation started flowing again but reached the door.

He threw it open when, with a bellow of rage the man jumped to his feet.

'Satan has you,' he screamed. 'You are in the hands of Satan. I shall sacrifice you to the one true God. The just God can have his will with you.'

Sion ran blindly along the corridor, going away from the stairs. There was no way out; a blank wall faced him.

'Help, help,' he yelled. 'For Christ's sake, help me.'

'Blasphemer,' screamed the maniac, stopping in front of Sion.

Sion yelled again and doors all along the corridor opened and heads appeared. The man came slowly towards Sion, hands outstretched, held like claws. He had a glazed look in his eyes, staring at Sion.

'Help me,' Sion yelled again at the doubtful faces. Then the man was on him, his hands around Sion's neck and he was squeezing tighter and tighter. Sion grabbed the hands and tried to pry them loose. The man's face leered down at him, saliva dribbling from the corner of his mouth. Sion's head was swimming, his lungs starved for air. He felt unconsciousness clouding over him and then blackness.

When he came to he found the maniac lying out cold beside him and four or five faces peering down at him. One of the men held a baseball bat in his hands. He was asked if he was all right and somebody helped him to his feet. Sion tried to say thanks but all he managed was a painful croak.

'What do we do with this fellow?' somebody asked.

'I dunno,' said another. 'One of us had better see the porter and get the man from admissions. He'll know what to do.'

'I'll go,' volunteered a third. 'Are you all right?' he asked Sion, who was leaning weakly against the wall, massaging his throat and trying to get his voice back. Sion nodded.

'Okay, you fellows. Watch this guy and I guess bop

him on the head again if he tries anything. I won't be long. You sure are handy with that thing,' he said to the man holding the bat who so far had said nothing. The man smiled and nodded.

Sion held out his hand. 'Griffiths,' he said in a hoarse and painful whisper. 'Sion Griffiths.' The man, around Sion's own age, shook hands, nodded, smiled and pointed at his own throat.

'Sore throat, eh?' Sion said, 'Me too.' He lapsed into silence again because talking was so painful. The minutes dragged by. Finally, Colin Callaghan appeared with the porter.

'What have you been up to, young Griffiths?' he greeted Sion. The others looked at Sion wonderingly. That a third year man knew the name of a freshman was unusual to say the least. 'And who's this?' he nodded at the inert form on the floor.

'He . . . he attacked me,' Sion croaked, his hand still around his neck. 'Tried to kill me. To strangle me,' he added, seeing the look of disbelief on the other man's face.

'It's true. I just told you,' said the man who had gone to fetch him. 'If it hadn't been for this fellow here,' he jerked his thumb at the man with the bat, 'he'd most likely be dead now. Look at his neck if you don't believe us.'

Callaghan said to Sion, 'Pull your collar down . . . Jesus Nelly,' he whistled when Sion showed him the big black and blue bruises already forming. 'What the hell did you do to antagonise him like that?'

Sion shrugged. How could he tell him the man was a nut? 'He said he . . . he was from God and had come to save mankind. He was . . .' Sion broke off, his throat protesting. 'He said he was here to . . . to save mankind. He was wailing and talking to God and . . . and it's true, I tell you,' he said with a fierce, very painful whisper. Callaghan looked more doubtful than ever.

'I heard him yelling something about Satan,' one of the others said.

'And I heard him calling to God, as well,' said another voice. 'My name's Green. I'm in number twelve. Are you in eleven?' Sion nodded. 'Yeah, well I heard some of it. I didn't know what to think of it. It sounded terrible. I guessed some nut had got loose or maybe,' he gulped, 'maybe . . .' but he could not bring himself to say it so Callaghan said it for him.

'Or maybe that's the way they always act around here, is that it?' Callaghan grinned. 'Well, funny things do happen I guess, but we draw the line at calling down God on us. Okay you guys, pick this jerk up and help me get him to the Dean's office. I reckon he's more than a mite crazy. You'd better come too Griffiths, to show your throat and you too, Whalley,' he said to the man with the bat. 'You can tell what you know. I mean in your case, write down what happened if the Dean wants you to. Okay, take it easy with him now,' he told the others as they grabbed an arm and leg each.

'Hell, he weighs a ton,' one of them complained. 'Did you have to hit him so hard?'

Whalley shrugged.

'I . . . I'm glad,' Sion croaked, 'that you did. I'd rather have him like this than conscious.'

They staggered across the quadrangle and into the building opposite. They found themselves in a wide corridor, with four or five doors leading off on either side. Callaghan knocked on the first door, marked "Dean's Secretary".

He opened the door without waiting for an answer and led the way in. Behind a desk was an attractive redhead in her early twenties. She was annoyed at the intrusion but her annoyance quickly turned to alarm when she saw the body carried by the sweating and puffing freshmen. The mad man groaned when they dropped him on the carpet.

'Is the Dean in?' asked Callaghan, nodding towards the door to the adjoining office.

'Ah, em, yes,' she answered, dragging her eyes from the body on the floor. 'But he's pretty busy at the moment, with the heads of departments.'

'It's very important he's disturbed,' said Callaghan. 'This nut on the floor here tried to kill this fellow,' he jerked his thumb at Sion. 'Show her your neck.'

Sion craned his neck painfully, by now curious about what he was showing.

'Good Lord,' she gasped, 'that's terrible. I . . . I'll go and get him immediately. Wait here,' she said, superfluously. She opened the door and went inside. A few moments later the door opened and a small, neat man, completely bald, came out. Sion had a glimpse of two or three faces peering out at them, 'What's all this about, Callaghan?' he asked annoyed.

'I'm sorry to disturb you, sir,' replied Callaghan. 'But this fellow on the floor here attacked this man. He's David Griffiths' brother, sir.'

'Ah, indeed. What happened, Griffiths?'

With difficulty Sion told him. The others added their part and when it came to Whalley's wielding of the bat the freshmen had a surprise.

'Bill Whalley knocked him out, sir. He can write down what happened for you,' said Callaghan.

'Why can't he tell me himself?' The Dean glared at Whalley who looked uncomfortable, shuffling his feet, still holding on to the bat.

'Sir,' Callaghan sounded embarrassed. 'Bill Whalley . . .'

'Yes, yes, yes, I know his name. You've told me already. What of it?'

Callaghan shrugged helplessly at Whalley who smiled back. 'Sir, Whalley can't talk. You were told about his accident before he got here.'

'Oh yes, of course. How could I have forgotten? Call the deputy's office and have him deal with this man.

Arrange it so his admittance is withdrawn and let the local authorities deal with it all. Yes, they can deal with him,' he said again. 'See to it, Callaghan.' With that he turned and went back into his office.

'You fellows stay and watch him while I go and get some rope to tie him up with. Do any of you know where the deputy sheriff's office is in town?'

One of them admitted he did and was promptly sent to fetch the deputy. Callaghan left to fetch some clothes line from the kitchen scullery.

Callaghan returned only just in time to tie up the prisoner before he groaned and sat up. His hands – tied in front of him – held his head. The man suddenly puked all over the floor. The secretary screamed and the sight and smell turned some of the others green. The Dean rushed out and sent them into the quadrangle with their prisoner.

'Let me go,' said the prisoner holding his hands to them. 'Gee, come on. I ain't done nothing. Come on, fellows.'

They looked at him and then at Sion.

'Not much you ain't – I mean haven't,' said Green. 'You only attacked Griffiths here and tried to strangle him to death.'

'I did?' he looked at Sion, puzzled. 'I've never seen him before in my life. What is this? I was unpacking my gear and the next thing you got me tied up here.' He put his hand to his head. 'And with a big lump too. Did one of you guys hit me?' he asked plaintively and then noticed the bat in Whalley's hands. 'You, you hit me,' he struggled to his knees but because his legs were tied could get no further.

He pointed at Whalley. 'The Lord shall damn you for this heresy,' he said in a ponderous voice, rising to a scream on the last word. 'I have come here to save Mankind from the follies and you do this? I command you by God the Almighty and His Holy Spirit to undo these ropes so I may then pray for your miserable, misbegotten soul.'

The freshmen looked with open-mouthed astonishment, while the man ranted and raved in the same vein until the deputy sheriff arrived. By this time quite a crowd had gathered and the Dean had been out of his office more than once demanding quiet.

The last Sion saw of the man he was locked in a wagon, still screaming at them, calling down the wrath of God upon their heads.

Later Sion sat in his room, his throat sore, appalled by the size of the bruises around his neck, feeling lonely and still shaken. He did not know whether to unpack his case or find a buggy and go and find his parents in Columbus. He thought about giving up the University and going to work for his father. He could learn the business and take over in a few years, or even just become Sonny's assistant . . . The longer he sat there wrapped in his misery the more attractive the prospect became. He did not hear the knock on the door but out of the corner of his eye he saw it opening and was surprised to see Bill Whalley. Bill smiled and gestured with his hand that said clearly, can I come in? With a feeling of relief at no longer being alone, Sion nodded.

Bill sat beside Sion on the bed, a slate and chalk in his hands. He wrote "Bill Whalley" – ?

'I'm Sion Griffiths. By the way, thanks again for saving me. I reckon you came in the nick of time.'

Bill wrote – Nothing. I came in because I thought you might be feeling a bit fed up. Hope you don't mind.

'Far from it,' said Sion. 'I was feeling more than fed up. I was thinking of going home.'

Bill wrote – Mustn't do that. Never give up. I almost did once but I learnt to keep fighting.

'Can I ask what happened to your throat? Your voice?' Sion pointed at the scarf Bill wore around his neck.

He wrote – Glad you asked. Prefer to tell you. But it takes a long time to write it all down.

'That's okay. I'm not going anywhere. And I reckon if we're going to be friends I'd better know because I'll only wonder,' Sion smiled at Bill who nodded vigorously.

Bill cleaned the slate with a rag and began writing. Although he told it cryptically the story was as follows:-

I was down in El Paso on the Mexican border just over four years ago. On the other side of the border is the town of Ciudad Juarez. I visited there with my parents, brother and sister. Mexico must be the most unhappy land in the world. They have a Dictator named Porfirio Diaz who has made his people virtual slaves. Well, there's a lot of unrest caused by the peons and some of the middle classes. A man named Francisco Madero is leading them but if you ask me I'd say he's no better than Diaz. He just wants power and money.

There is a lot of shooting all the time and people are always being killed for one reason and another. The peons shoot them while the Government hangs them. And when I say that I mean they hang whole villages if one man has been found to be on Madero's side.

'Women and children as well?' Sion asked in horror.

Yes, wrote Bill. They are always robbing banks to pay for their revolution. My family and I were in a bank in Juarez when it was robbed. Some army men appeared and started shooting at the robbers. All my family were mistakenly gunned down by both sides as were most of the other customers. I was shot through the neck.

Bill took off his scarf to show Sion the puckered red and white scars either side of his throat.

By a miracle I lived. Even the doctor thought I should have died. For a long time afterwards I wished I had. All my family were gone and I had nobody to turn to. Although I'm not religious, a priest helped me a lot and while I was getting better he taught me quite a lot and taught me how to speak with my hands.

'How do you mean, speak with your hands?'

Bill put the chalk down and moved his fingers and hands quickly, then wrote – That means you're a good bloke. Another person who can't speak or is deaf could possibly understand me, though the hand language isn't that well known. We copied the idea from the Red Indians I think, though I'm not too sure about that. It meant, after a while, I could talk to Father Mendez. He was a great man. It was he who persuaded me to try for college and to use the money I inherited from my father to get an education. Just before I left he was hanged by the Government troops in Juarez and that was when I came here. I was in Columbus for about three months waiting to learn whether or not they would accept me as a pupil. I'm cynical perhaps but I think my money finally persuaded them. I've been told, though, if I'm too much of a nuisance I'll have to leave.

It had taken nearly an hour for Bill to write the full story and by that time Sion realised his sore throat and the minor incident was nothing by comparison to what had happened to Bill. And he had been thinking of running home to Mam. He felt disgusted with himself and suitably humbled.

He noticed the time and exclaimed: 'I'm going over to meet Colin Callaghan for a beer. Why don't you come too? I'm sure he won't mind.'

Bill nodded, then wrote – Will there be many there, do you think?

'I shouldn't think so. Come on, if he objects I'll leave too. Heck it's not every day a guy owes his life to someone.'

They found Seymour block without difficulty and a few minutes later Sion knocked on the door behind which they could hear loud voices and laughter. It was opened by a stranger who scowled at the intrusion.

'Eh, my name is Sion Griffiths and Colin asked me over.'

'Hey, Colin,' the man called over his shoulder, keeping his foot to the door, 'a chap named Griffiths is here. Says you said to come over.'

Sion heard a mumble in the background and the foot was removed. Bill followed Sion into the room. There were about a dozen students lolling about the room, glasses of beer in their hands, all staring at the two newcomers in a most disconcerting way.

'Eh, Colin,' said Sion, 'I brought Whalley. I reckoned after he saved my life like that he deserved a drink. Well, if you want, we'll go,' Sion cleared his throat nervously.

'Naw, it's all right. Hey, fellows, this is the man I was telling you about. His first introduction to uni was sure a unique one.' They laughed and somebody thrust a glass of beer into Sion's hand. Names were exchanged but Sion did not catch any of them. Sion realised one or two were looking strangely at Bill.

'This is Bill Whalley. He can't talk due to an accident a few years back.'

'A real strong, silent type,' one of the men said.

'That's not a nice thing to say,' Sion flared up. 'You ought to apologise to Bill or . . .'

'Hey, take it easy,' Colin Callaghan intervened. 'Nobody meant anything by it. Bill here is going to have to learn to take a lot more cracks than that and if you leap to his defence everytime, well you're going to be doing a lot of fighting – an awful lot in fact, and all for nothing. Know why?'

Sion shook his head.

'Cause nobody'll mean anything by it, that's why. They'll only be joking. It's the only way to treat something like that. You ask Bill here. Right Bill?'

Bill nodded and squeezed Sion's shoulder.

'See what I mean?' Callaghan waved them to sit on

the floor. 'I was telling you fellows what happened this afternoon. Anyway, the maniac was taken away still screaming and hollering something terrible. Isn't that right?' Callaghan turned to Sion and Bill and they nodded. 'And to top it all off, guys, don't you see the family resemblance between Sion and David Griffiths? They're brothers.'

'Well, I'll be,' said one of the men on the floor. 'I've been sitting here wondering who he reminded me of. Now you've said it, it's obvious.' He turned to Sion. 'Do you play football as well?'

'Eh, no. That is, I haven't really learned how to play. Dave told me about it but back where I come from there isn't much of that in school. But I guess I can always learn.'

'Sure, you can always learn,' said one of the men sitting by the desk. 'You've got the build for a fastish runner. I guess we can try you out sometime. What do you say, John?'

'Sure, why not,' said John Greenboro, a big man with brown hair, broad shoulders and a broad grin.

'John's captain of the team,' said Callaghan. 'How's them beers coming along, boys? Ready for another one yet?'

Sion and Bill shook their heads.

'Don't forget what I told you, young Griffiths. No letting on you've been over here, okay? If you're caught and they prove you've been drinking, then tell them you brought it with you. If you keep quiet then there's no reason why you don't come back again.'

Sion nodded, pleased at the honour.

'I invited you to meet these guys because I figured you might prove to be as good a footballer as Dave. And the sooner we try you and find out, the better. If you do all right it'll mean plenty of trips away and cutting lectures to practise,' said Callaghan.

Sion nodded doubtfully. He was not that interested in

sport and he did not like the idea of cutting lectures. He was not about to tell the occupants of the room however, that he thought it senseless for grown men to go chasing an odd shaped lump of leather around a bit of grass.

It was getting late when Bill and Sion left to return to their own rooms. Sion had learned that his brother had been a very good player during his time at the university and was surprised David had said so little about it. Or maybe he had and Sion had not appreciated the significance of being on the varsity team.

They had also learned that Bill's room mate was not due to arrive until the next day so Sion moved his stuff in with Bill.

33

ALTHOUGH HE TRIED hard, Sion never did make it as a footballer. Somehow he could not co-ordinate properly and would drop easy catches or slice his kicks. After a month of trying he finally decided to give up. 'That's my last game Bill. I'm not playing any more.' He looked around to make sure nobody was within hearing distance and mouthed the heresy. 'I used to think it all pointless, well I no longer think so.' He smiled at his friend's puzzled look. 'Nope, now I know it is,' and Sion burst out laughing. Bill's shoulders heaved though he made no sound.

On the whole Sion and Bill attended the same classes although Bill was working towards becoming a doctor whilst Sion still didn't know what he wanted to do. So far there had been no social scene apart from the occasional beer drinking party but that evening Bill and Sion decided to go into the town. According to Callaghan and the other third year students there was very little to see or do.

Not only had Bill and Sion become good friends now but Sion was also trying to learn Bill's sign language so that communication would be quicker. When they walked through the main gate they were warned by the gate-keeper to be back before ten o'clock because the gates were locked promptly.

They followed the road into town, about half a mile away. Along the main street were a number of general stores, numerous book shops catering for the university, and a hotchpotch of shops. There were a number of bars

and hotels. They quickly learned the bars were out of
bounds to university students, although they were allowed
to eat in the hotels.

Not being hungry and with little else to do they were
ready to return to the university when Sion suggested
they went up one of the side streets, where they came
across a restaurant. They wandered into the dim but
pleasant atmosphere to find a small bar and a dozen
tables scattered around the room. In a corner three men
were eating, the rest of the place was empty.

'This looks interesting,' said Sion and Bill nodded in
agreement. 'Shall we get something to eat here?' Sniffing
the air he said, 'Whatever's cooking back there smells
good.' From behind a beaded curtain a young girl came
out, picked up a menu from the bar and walked across
the room.

Sion handed the menu back to the girl with an order
for two plates of sauerkraut and sausage. 'And can we
have two beers, please?'

She frowned but said nothing and went back into the
kitchen. A few moments later a big bellied man came
from the kitchen to their table. 'Can't serve you. You
must leave please.' He crossed his arms and looked
sternly at them.

'But why?' Sion protested. 'We haven't done anything
wrong. Why can't you serve us?'

'You're from the university. I can tell. You're new
boys. You're not allowed to eat here.'

'Look, we won't have the beer, how's that? Surely we
can have something to eat?'

'No. It was decided that it's not good for young
gentlemen,' he spat on the floor, 'to eat in a Polack's
place and to eat Polack's food. So you've got to go. Or
else I'm in trouble.'

'Wait a moment. Surely it's us that'll be in trouble?
We're the ones breaking the rules, not you.'

'If you don't go the law will come and close us down.

They say that this place is a bad influence on young Americans.' He grimaced as though he had a bad taste in his mouth.

'That's no problem then,' said Sion with a smile. I'm not American. I'm Welsh. So you can serve me, can't you?'

'No, I cannot. Now please go before I throw you out.'

Sion shrugged helplessly at Bill, who signalled that they should leave.

Sion looked up at the man and said, 'Before we go will you tell us what it's all about? Why are you a eh, bad influence on us?'

'Because we are Polacks, as you people call us. They say we are trouble makers. Now go before I get mad.' He scowled even more and the boys got to their feet. As they did so, one of the customers said something in Polish and Joseph shrugged and spoke to them again.

'Sit down a minute. You're going to have a beer before you go. I'm going to tell you something. We're from Poland. We came over here to escape from the persecution that exists in our motherland; we came to the country of the so called free. Most of the immigrants ended up in the mining area of Pittsburgh. Do you know where I mean?'

Both boys nodded.

'There I started a school and we got on fine for a couple of years. I made about what the men in the mines were making, charging them for English lessons. We found that if the miners – and I mean only the new immigrant miners like we Poles – did not give a backhander to the manager of the mine they would have no job.'

'That's terrible. What happened? Did you do anything about it?' asked Sion.

'We tried to complain but it didn't get us anywhere. In fact it made matters worse. So some of us left Pittsburgh and we came here.'

'My Dad told me a lot about what it was like when he was a miner.' Sion went on to tell them about the disaster with the slag heap and Sian's death and in particular the hatred felt by the miners for the bosses and owners. 'I get really angry when I think about the injustice of it all. I wish I could do something about it. I guess that's why Dad is so interested in politics. He figures it's the only way to get things done. One day he might even run for Congress. But that still doesn't explain why we can't come in here.'

'It's simple. Because we're Polish. Because there are rumours around the town about what happened in Pittsburgh. Because we are called anarchists and anti-American. So there's a ban on all students visiting the place.'

'That's unfair,' Sion said, aghast.

'Its maybe unfair but it's true. Bigotry rules, even here. So, now please, you must go.'

They stood, said goodnight and left. They returned to the university feeling despondent.

'How about us going across to Colin's and seeing if he's got a spare beer?' They swerved towards Seymore block. 'You know I'd like to do something for the Poles. Show them that we support them.'

Bill squeezed Sion's shoulder in agreement.

They sat in Colin's room sipping beer and telling him what had happened.

'I knew about it,' said Colin, 'but didn't know all the details. You guys want to remember something, it's big business that runs this country and not justice and fair play like it says in the books.'

Sion frowned for a moment and then said: 'Why not fight power with power? Listen. How many guys would like to use that place? It's cheap and has a pleasant atmosphere. Right?' Colin and Bill nodded. 'Okay. Say we got enough of the men interested and we all just went. Told the Dean that we don't agree with the ban and that he had no right to stop us going. What would happen then? After all, if he took any action against any of us and we all stuck together what could he do? Send us all down?'

'How about shutting the place down?' suggested Colin, Bill nodding in agreement.

'Same thing. We stick together and threaten to leave en masse if he does that. I reckon we could get away with it, you know. If there's any problems we use our influence, perhaps get our fathers to help, threaten to leave, anything like that,' Sion finished lamely.

Colin and Bill continued with their head shaking and Colin explained, 'I agree with the sentiment Sion but I don't think there's much we can do about it.'

On that note the two left for their own room. He lay awake well into the night and from time to time a boiling rage flared up in him at the injustice of it all.

Sion did not bring up the subject again and so it came as a surprise when Colin said to him and Bill, 'By the way, I talked things over with some of the others and forcing the Dean into something he doesn't like rather appeals to them.'

They looked at him puzzled. 'What are you talking about?' asked Sion, while Bill's fingers and hands flashed the same question at Sion.

'About the restaurant. They reckon it might not be a bad gag to . . .'

'It's not a gag, Colin,' interrupted Sion. 'If they only think of it as a gag then I don't want them to do anything.'

'Gag was maybe the wrong word. The others feel badly about it too. Especially Jonas McCarthy and do you know why?'

Sion shrugged and then read Bill's signals.

'Because according to Bill, Jonas' father owns some of the mines around Pittsburgh.'

'Could you read all that from Bill's fingers?'

'Not really. He said father had mines and I guessed the rest.'

'You know that when his grandfather died he was left twenty five percent of the shares in his father's companies and at the ripe old age of twenty one he'll be on the board? So he'll have a lot of influence. If he learns enough about what happened in Pittsburgh he may be able to help the miners there in the future. So this is not just about a small restaurant owner in a small town.'

They talked football for a while. Although Sion was no longer playing he and Bill now helped to manage the team – arranging games and transport whenever necessary.

It was the last Friday of November when twenty or more students left the university and made their way into town. The restaurant was empty when they went in and grabbed tables close together. A few seconds later, hearing the noise of scraping chairs the girl came from the kitchen and called her father.

'What's wrong n . . .' he stopped in astonishment, took a pace forward and then halted when Colin and another half dozen came in.

Sion suddenly took heart. 'Beers all round please, Joseph.'

Joseph hesitated and then shrugged his shoulders. When one of them asked for a menu the others quickly followed. Joseph was unsure whether to laugh or be worried. He chose the former.

The conversation was brittle, the laughter forced and the attempts at joking a strain to begin with. But the more beer they drank the more relaxed they became.

Joseph said to Sion, 'I suppose this was your idea, eh?'

Sion shrugged and looked embarrassed. Joseph also shrugged, smiled and went to serve at another table. When he returned he said to Sion and Bill, 'You know that this will not last. That they will give in?' Joseph waved his hand indicating the others in the restaurant.

'They won't,' said Sion. 'We've got the football team here and they're pretty tough guys. They'll stick it out.'

Joseph was not to be stopped. 'Football is a game which bears no relation to real life. After a hard game you can leave the field and forget about it, or talk about it over a beer. You can't do that in real life. There's nowhere to hide. Do you understand?'

'Yes,' said Sion, doubtfully.

'Sion,' said Joseph, 'for myself and my family I want to thank you for trying but give it up. It won't do any good.'

'We've done nothing to deserve your thanks,' Sion said.

Joseph shrugged. 'It's nice to know that at least there's one person outside our little community who, shall we say, sees our point of view?'

Sion did not remember the walk home. Later he laid wide awake worrying about Joseph and his friends. If he had been in his third year he might have been able to wield more influence. Influence . . . That was an important word for what he was trying to do. He needed more authority, needed to be more powerful. Yes, that was what it took. If he had an important position, like captain of the football team, then he could possibly influence the men more. There it was again. The same word. It was all intermingled. If he was rich and powerful . . . He eventually fell asleep.

In December Sion realised that Bill had nowhere to go for Christmas and wrote a note to his parents informing them he would be bringing a guest.

In reply Sion received a letter from Evan telling him to be careful in his dealings in connection with Joseph and not to antagonise the Dean unduly. Evan went on to say that although he agreed with what Sion was trying to do he felt Sion should wait until he had graduated before he took on the establishment.

After he read it Sion showed the letter to Bill. 'It annoys me that my father agrees with what I'm doing and in the next sentence tells me to stop. I can believe in things as strongly as he does. Why wait until I'm older?'

Bill interrupted him and wrote:- Wait Sion. Your father agrees. He did not say stop only be careful. He's right. What good will it do if you're expelled? None what-soever. We have our victory. We use the place as we please. Nothing is said. What are you aiming for now? A public apology to Joseph for the way he has been treated?

Sheepishly Sion shook his head and then his mood lifted. 'I guess not. Roll on the holidays. It won't be long now and we'll have three whole weeks of freedom and fun.'

Except for the homework we're being set, Bill sig-nalled.

With constant practice Sion was now becoming adept at reading Bill's signals though he often had to guess the full meaning.

The next two weeks brought snow and freezing nights. They both studied hard and were pleasantly surprised with their end of semester test results. On the last day before their holiday the countryside gleamed white under the bright sun and clear blue sky. There was much excite-ment and boisterous laughter while the undergraduates prepared to leave. Sion and Bill arrived at Columbus far too early for their train and spent the afternoon in a local hotel drinking coffee. The time dragged, but finally it was time to catch their train.

Meg and Evan met them in St Louis the next day and for the first time in his life Sion was embarrassed when Meg kissed him.

'This place hasn't changed much,' said Sion, half disgustedly, looking around while they drove through the town.

'What did you expect after only a few months?' asked

Evan, smiling. 'Is this your first time in this part of the country?' he asked Bill. Bill nodded and signalled to Sion.

'He says it's very nice. More picturesque than he had expected.'

Meg looked at her son in astonishment. 'How on earth do you know he said picturesque?'

'I didn't really. Bill said it was like a picture and I just put it differently, that's all. Did you mean what I said, Bill?'

Bill nodded and signalled – as always. They both laughed.

'What's so funny?' asked Evan.

'Nothing, really,' replied Sion. 'It's just that I've got into the habit of changing the words he signals to me into . . . sort of better prose, I guess that's the only way to describe it. Anyway, Bill tells me I put what he wants to say more eloquently than if he could still speak.'

His parents smiled tentatively at one another, unsure whether they should bring more attention to Bill's injury or ignore it. Bill signalled.

'Bill says not to worry about talking about what happened. He says it doesn't bother or embarrass him. He says I can tell you if I wish but I reckon you know everything from the letters I wrote you.'

They drove on in silence for a while. The weather was a few degrees warmer than is had been in Ohio and it was a pleasant journey.

'We'll be having our usual party on Boxing Day,' said Meg. 'It'll give you a chance to introduce Bill to everybody.'

'Is Dave coming home for Christmas?' Sion asked.

'He's arriving tomorrow,' his father replied. 'You don't think anything will keep him away from Gunhild, do you?' Evan winked at him.

'Oh, it's serious is it?'

'It looks like it. I'm sure he spends more time writing to her than he does on his studies,' Evan said and then sighed. 'Another good man gone.'

'Dad, Dad,' Sion said with mock sadness, 'it's not too late, is it? I mean, isn't there anything we can do to save him from this fate worse than death? I know,' Sion snapped his fingers, 'we can send him to join the French Foreign Legion. That would be much better than, ugh, marrying.'

'All right, all right you clowns, that'll do,' said Meg with a touch of faked austerity. 'I think she's a very nice girl and will be just right for David. In a few years time, of course,' she added.

'Thank goodness for that,' said Sion, 'I thought you were already helping to plan the wedding. How many bridesmaids will there be?'

'I haven't talked to Gunhild about any wedding yet, so don't try and be clever young man,' said Meg. 'Furthermore, I'm sure they don't have any firm plans just yet, and won't have any for a few years, at least. Gunhild is very sensible and knows David has to finish at Harvard and will need at least a year or even longer to get himself established in business. In the meantime they enjoy each other's company, write to each other and leave the future to take care of itself.'

They lapsed into silence as the buggy turned into the drive.

'How's Thunderbolt?' asked Sion jumping down for the buggy.

'Just fine, son,' said Evan. 'Marie's brother Juan is now working full time here looking after the grounds and horses. Here he comes.' Evan nodded towards the short, stocky figure. 'Juan, I'd like you to meet my son Sion and his friend Bill.' They shook hands.

'I'll take care of the horses,' said Juan, taking the reigns and leading them towards the stable.

'I'll come with you and see Thunderbolt. Want to

come?' Sion asked Bill and together they followed the buggy towards the stable.

That evening they were in the study having a pre-dinner drink, a ritual Evan and Meg rarely missed, when Evan asked: 'What's happened about that restaurant business you wrote about?'

Bill and Sion shrugged. 'Nothing much,' said Sion, and explained what was going on and how it had mostly faded.

'Just as well,' said Meg. 'The last thing we want is for you to be expelled.'

'There are plenty of other good universities,' said Sion.

'That's not the point and you know it,' Meg replied, annoyed.

'I know, I know. But there was a principle at stake. Why should Joseph and his family be punished the way they were when they'd done nothing wrong?' Sion's voice rose as he began to get angry.

'Simmer down,' said Evan. 'We aren't questioning your motives or your ideals. I think your principles are sound and if more people felt like you do, then there would be hope for the working man in this country. And, I want to add, there are plenty who do feel as you do. All we're saying is that you should take it easy for now. Okay, do what you can, but don't get so involved that the only recourse for the Dean is to expel you. All right? If we're asking too much then say so now and we can argue about it.'

Sion looked sheepishly from his father to his mother. 'I'm sorry. It's just I get so mad when I see what goes on and read about what happens with the unions in the coal fields and steel works and hear stories like the one about Joseph.'

'I know, and so do I,' said Evan. 'I hope you always feel like that but remember; patience and hard work is far more effective than all the anger and harsh words in

the world. And it's even more effective when you're in
a position to do something about it.'

'I guess that's true. Bill keeps telling me the same
thing.'

'Bill's got more sense than you, then,' said Meg.

'Dad, I agree with what you said. You believe it. So
why don't you do something about it?'

'Like what?'

'Like you said in the summer. Run for Congress or
something. Why wait any longer?'

'I agree. I'm not waiting. I'm running.'

'Exac . . . what did you say?'

'I'll be a citizen of the United states of America
in a month's time. Some members of the party are
rushing it through for me. The present incumbent is
unwell and wishes to retire by the end of the year. I'm
being nominated as a candidate,' Evan paused. 'Though
whether or not I even get the nomination remains to be
seen. And as for winning . . .' Evan shook his head

'Good grief!' was all Sion could manage.

34

CHRISTMAS PASSED IN a whirl of laughter, fun and parties. David was always with Gunhild, while Sion and Bill met two sisters who, pretty in an insipid way, were free with their favours.

All too soon it was time to return to the university and, in a freshly falling snow storm they left St Louis for Columbus. As soon as they arrived Bill wrote a thank you letter to Meg and Evan.

'You don't need to do that,' said Sion, looking over Bill's shoulder as he wrote.

Sure I do, Bill wrote on a piece of scrap paper. If I didn't then I wouldn't get invited back. And boy, that Carol was surely something.

Sion laughed. 'So was Beryl. And don't worry about not being invited back. Like Mam said, they really do hope to see you next holiday. Can you think of a reason why they won't?'

Bill shook his head vigorously and Sion clapped him on the shoulder. 'Right then. That takes care of that. How about us going down to Joseph's and wishing them all a Happy New Year? Perhaps have a beer? Even something to eat?'

Bill shook his head and wrote: Not tonight. Maybe tomorrow. I feel I can't eat for a month. I had so much at your parents' place.

'Me too. Sheer gluttony made me suggest having a meal. Boy, am I glad you came home with me. Only your hard-working nature kept me on the straight and narrow path which leads to a degree.'

Bill signalled: Your laziness is an example to me of what might happen if I stop trying. He grinned.

The next evening they did go into town. When they arrived at Joseph's and saw the shuttered windows and barred door they thought the place was closed for the day, which was unusual as Joseph boasted he never closed.

'Still, everybody's entitled to a day off. And he had said he was going to stay open for Christmas day. We can come back tomorrow.'

Sion turned away but after a few paces realised Bill was not following and turned back. Bill was standing in the doorway reading a paper pinned to the door.

It was a Sheriff's notice closing the restaurant as an undesirable influence in the area and that the closure would be enforced pending an appeal to the courts.

'They can't do this,' said Sion in anguish. He put out his hand to tear the notice down but was stopped in time by Bill grabbing his wrist.

'Who ordered this? Why?'

Bill shrugged and made their special, rude signal denoting the Dean.

Sion nodded. 'This is all my fault,' he said bitterly. 'If I hadn't interfered this wouldn't have happened. What can Joseph do? Where could they have gone? Do you realise, Bill, that while we were enjoying our holiday Joseph and his family were being evicted? I wonder when it happened? Before or after Christmas? Not that it matters. It's happened, and that's that. Oh Christ, what have I done?' Sion rubbed his eyes wearily. 'What should we do?'

Bill put his hand on his friend's shoulder and slowly they walked away. Sion was desolate. They walked with heads bowed, their thoughts in a turmoil.

'Sorry,' Sion mumbled when he bumped into some-body and looked up into Joseph's furious face

'I suppose you've been to the restaurant? That's a

stupid question, of course you have,' he paused. 'I am trying very hard to control myself. If you hadn't interfered then I and my family would still have a roof over our heads. Still have a place to call home, instead of being thrown out like animals, with no rights. And what about you two? You'll go back to your warm cosy rooms and plan the next act you can do for us little people. Well, let me tell you something, both of you. We don't want help, certainly not from the likes of you. We knew we shouldn't have let you in. Now look what you've done. Now go away. If I ever see you again then I might do something stupid which I'll regret.' Joseph was shaking with anger and both boys looked at him with fear.

'But Joseph . . . please . . .' Sion began.

'Shut up and go.' Abruptly Joseph turned on his heels and walked away.

Sion and Bill looked at each other in dismay. 'Is he right? Is that all it meant to us? Was it just a game?' Sion voiced his doubts. They discussed what had happened.

Finally Sion burst out, saying, 'No, it's not like that. It's not. I really do believe in what we tried to do. Damn the Dean. We'll never get the men to protest this. Well I'm not stopping now. Bill, listen,' he grabbed his friend's arm in excitement. 'I've got quite a lot of the money I inherited from my Uncle James. I could use it to hire the best lawyer available to fight the case in court on Joseph's behalf.'

Bill suddenly smiled but a second later the smile died. He shook his head and signalled beneath the dim light of a street gas lamp: No good. The court will take place here. I read it on the warrant. The best lawyer in the world couldn't win here.

Sion nodded. 'You're right. Tell you what though, we could get the court's location changed. I remember reading somewhere that if it was deemed that a fair trial could not take place in a particular court then the court's location could be changed.'

Bill nodded: And afterwards? What then? Where do

they live? Here? In peace? Bill shook his head.

'God, Bill, I must do something! This is all my fault,' Sion shivered. 'We'd better go back, it's freezing. We must think of something to help them.'

They trundled back to the university the few inches of snow crunching underfoot. Neither spoke while Sion made a cup of coffee but finally, handing the cup to Bill, he said: 'Did you see Joseph's face? His hate? . . . It was terrible. Well, I've made up my mind. Tomorrow I'll see the Dean, ask for an explanation and tell him I intend hiring the best lawyer to fight the case.'

Bill shook his head and picked up his slate and chalk: Don't do that. It will achieve nothing. Get you expelled. Better idea. Write your father.

'Ask my father for help? You must be joking. I caused this mess and . . .' he stopped because Bill was shaking his head.

Bill wrote: Not help, advice.

Sion shook his head. 'I can't do that. I can't run to the old man whenever I get into trouble or . . .'

Bill, showing his vexation with Sion, waved him to silence and wrote: Now I know your father I'm sure he'll help. He has the contacts and knowledge to know what to do. Look Sion we've already messed it up for Joseph and his family. It makes sense to call for help.

They argued back and forth. Bill disregarded his slate for paper and a pencil so that he could write faster and for longer without having to keep rubbing out what he had just written.

Finally, Sion saw the sense of Bill's suggestion and although it was late they composed a letter to Evan. Sion posted it the following morning.

They spent a miserable week waiting for a reply though they knew it would take up to ten days before Evan could send a letter back. The reply when it arrived was a surprise to them both.

They were in their room working when there was a

knock on the door. It opened and Evan said, 'May I come in?' He grinned at their open mouthed astonishment. 'Well, don't look so surprised. Is that a kettle I see over by the fire?'

'Dad,' Sion jumped to his feet to shake his father's hand. 'What on earth are you doing here?'

'I came to sort out this mess,' Evan said heavily. 'I can't say I'm happy to be here. I'm upset and angry that because of you an innocent family has been so badly treated. I do appreciate what you were trying to achieve. I'm sure at the time Joseph did too but now it's all gone wrong. Whichever way you look at it, you're to blame. Don't look so glum. I haven't come here to admonish you but to give you some advice and to do something for Joseph and his family.' Evan broke off to accept a cup of coffee from Bill.

'Thanks. Your idea to go to a lawyer and fight it in court was a good one but it wouldn't have got you anywhere. And what about you two? How would the Dean have treated you if you did something like that? You told me, Bill, that if you were to cause a nuisance – because of your throat – he'd expel you. This would be all the reason he needs and I'm sure he'd also get rid of Sion quickly enough.'

They both looked glumly at Evan.

'But Dad, how can anybody do such a thing to an innocent family? How can they throw them out of their home, into the snow, for Christ sake? Why didn't the law protect them?'

'Sion, I'm sure the men responsible believe that they did the right thing. I've no doubt that the Dean and any-body else involved are God-fearing, law-abiding citizens who feel threatened by those they see as anarchists. They see their whole way of life threatened by people who, in their opinion, want everything for nothing and who aren't prepared to do a proper day's work.'

'That's rubbish, Dad . . .' Sion began.

'I know it's rubbish. But these men have the wealth and influence to enforce their beliefs. They have the law do their bidding and still feel righteous at the end of the day. I feel like you do. You know where we come from, Sion, and I don't ever want you to forget it. But to fight these people you need to be up there with them, with the power they have. One day it'll happen, but it'll be a long while yet.' Evan drained the cup. 'That's enough of a lecture for now. We'll talk some more over dinner tomorrow evening in the hotel. In the meantime I want to go and see Joseph.'

'But we don't know where to look for him,' Sion pointed out.

'Don't worry, I've got Sonny with me. He's waiting at the hotel. We'll find him all right. See you tomorrow, and cheer up, boys, things'll work out.' Evan buttoned up his overcoat, put on his hat and left.

Sion looked at Bill, a smile beginning to spread across his lips. 'Was I dreaming or was my father really here?'

Bill pointed at the third cup.

'I guess he must have been. Yahoo,' Sion shouted. 'Ain't he the greatest? Coming all this way just for us?'

The following evening they found Evan and Sonny sitting at a table in the dining room of their hotel.

'What have you done, Dad?' Sion asked eagerly.

Evan sipped his whisky before replying. 'Well, we found them. Joseph was unforthcoming at first. But after a while we persuaded him that what we were proposing was for the best.'

'Yes, but what exactly were you proposing?' his son asked impatiently.

'Let's just say that . . . No, that's the wrong way to put it. Sonny?'

Sonny smiled. 'I guess we can say we've just gone into a new line of business with a new partner. At least your father has.'

'What I've done, Sion, is persuade Joseph to open

a restaurant in St Louis in partnership with a wealthy businessman. It'll be a fifty-fifty share of bottom line profits but ownership will be fifty one percent mine. Never mind the details now. If it works out it'll be a good deal for me and for Joseph. All that matters now is whether his cooking is any good.'

'Dad, it's like I told you. He's a better cook than Mrs Reisenbach and you know what her food is like.'

'I hope you're right. Anyway, let's order dinner. I've often thought about branching out but I never expected it would be into the restaurant business. Mind you, since I supply stores to most of the hotels and restaurants in town I guess it makes sense.'

'If you had a ranch you could even supply a lot of your own meat and things,' said Sion.

'Sonny and I have discussed that but we decided against it.' Evan dismissed the subject and beckoned for a waiter.

When Bill and Sion returned to the university they were happier than they had been since the start of the semester.

A week later they were in town when they saw Joseph again. The three of them awkwardly faced each other, clearing their throats and shuffling their feet. Then Sion and Joseph spoke together.

'Joseph, I . . .'

'Sion, I . . .'

Bill smiled and held out his hand. Joseph shook it and then shook Sion's.

'I'm sorry for what I said. I didn't mean it. It was just that I was going through a real bad time. I guess I just blamed you for all our troubles because . . . because it was easier that way. Please forgive me.'

'Honestly, Joseph there's nothing to forgive. It was our fault for starting it all in the first place. We should have minded our own business. At least, I should have. And then I dragged Bill into it.'

Bill shook his head and signalled.

'Bill says he was dragged in only because he wanted to be. He said . . . At least if he just said what I think he said about me, he's a cheeky blighter.'

'Thank you for what you got your father to do. I must admit that I was angry when I first spoke to him. Shall we go in here for coffee?' He nodded at the doorway of the hotel they were standing next to.

Over coffee Joseph said, 'When I was talking to your father and Sonny I told them it was a typical rich man's trick to get his son out of trouble. How could I trust them? Oh, and a whole lot more besides. Your father took me by surprise when he agreed. He said that was only true as far as it went. He told me that if he didn't think it was a sound business venture then he wouldn't do it to get any son out of anything. He has a way of talking and looking at you that leaves you with the distinct impression that he means what he says.'

'That's my old man.'

'Your father did say he had been thinking about starting some other business in St Louis for some time and this was an opportunity to do himself and me a bit of good.' With a shake of his head he continued, 'You know, he managed to convince me that I was doing him as big a favour as he was doing me.'

They finished their coffee in silence and, almost reluctantly, shook hands and said goodbye.

The remainder of the year passed quickly. Sion worked hard, enthralled in his studies. For their summer vacation they went to St Louis where Evan gave them a job in the warehouse, though not quite in the capacity Sion had in mind.

'Damn it, Bill,' Sion said on their first day, 'I hadn't expected to be shifting cases of goods from the store rooms to the sales area, nor,' he kicked the offending article, 'sides of beef. I wanted something better than this.'

What? Bill signalled.

'Anything. As the boss's son I just expected a position more in line with my status.'

What status?

'Well, you know. My father is . . .'

The owner. You don't know enough to do anything except shift goods. Neither do I. I'm not complaining. I'm earning some money which I need and I'm also learning about business.

'Shifting all this stuff is giving you ideas? Don't be daft, man. How can that teach you anything?'

Bill gestured around him and Sion looked.

'I don't see anything.'

Bill took out his note pad and pencil. Wasted manpower. There's a store room here where all the food is put. There's enough room over there to build another storeroom so when we unloaded the train we could sort out the merchandise and store it where it should be. That way we wouldn't have to waste effort carrying the stuff all the way to the shelves from here. See?

'Not a bad idea I suppose. If nobody else has suggested it you may have made a ten bucks.'

Bill looked puzzled.

'Didn't you know that Dad gives ten bucks to anybody who comes up with a labour-saving or money-saving idea? I know Sonny has won it a few times. Ah, I shouldn't say won. Dad says it's earned, not won and I guess he's right. I tell you what, how about us going and talking to him now?'

They started for Evan's office.

'Where in hell do you two think you're going?' the storeman yelled at them.

'To see my father,' Sion replied haughtily.

'I don't give a damn. Your father told me to treat you

guys like any other members of the staff. If you want to
see him you go through me first. Okay?'

'But that's ridiculous. He is my father, after all.'

'I don't give a double damn who he is or who you are.
You'll do as you're told while you're here, just like your
brother had to. Now get those boxes over to the other side
and be quick about it. They should have been there half
an hour ago.'

Sion was about to protest but Bill dug him in the ribs
and bent to pick up one of the boxes. Seething with anger
Sion gave him a hand, wisely not saying anything. As
they trundled away the storeman's face split into a wide,
toothless grin. That'll teach him, he thought. A good kid
but with a lot to learn, he chuckled to himself.

It was not until Sion and Bill arrived home that they
could speak to Evan and tell him about Bill's idea. By
that time Sion had calmed down and wisely decided not
to say anything about his run in with the storeman.

After Sion explained Bill's idea Evan said, 'It could
work. I'll go over it with Sonny in the morning and see
what he says. If he agrees, well, we'll see.'

'Dad,' said David, 'when are you going to stand for
Congress?'

'I'm not sure yet. There's a lot of talk and things keep
being changed. Old Riley says he definitely isn't going
to stand again and wants to nominate me. The election
is due in December so we'll see.'

'Surely, if the election is due so soon then it ought to
have been decided by now and you should be campaign-
ing,' said Sion.

'It's not as simple as that,' Meg joined the conversation, smiling at her sons. 'There's a lot of internal
bickering going on at the moment and they can't decide
between your father and Francis Hick. Charles DeFort is
on our side and so is Wesley Riley. But Hick has plenty of
support too. Your father refuses to make an issue of it and
has asked the party to decide once and for all what they

want to do. He's also told them that if Hick is nominated he'll give his support.'

'Well, I hope you get it, Dad. I reckon you'll do a great job,' said Sion loyally. 'Fancy a father who's a Democratic Congressman? How about that, Dave?'

'It won't do me much good. Most of the guys I know in Harvard are Republicans. So I'll have to keep it a secret until I finish.'

'Any ideas yet as to what you intend doing once you qualify?' Evan asked him.

'Not yet but once I've finally made up my mind, I'll tell you.'

'We're going to New York in November,' said Meg, 'to see John Buchanan. We had a letter from him the other day, and he says he's finally given up the fight and getting married, though he doesn't say who the girl is. He's also suggested, David, that you meet us there for the weekend.'

'Sounds great. Can I let you know nearer the time because I don't know what my program is going to be until the semester starts. I wonder if Gunhild can come too?'

'I don't see why not,' said Evan. 'Ask her, and if she wants me to, I'll have a word with Hans. She can come with us.'

'I got a letter, too,' said Sion. 'From Uncle William. I meant to show you earlier. It's all about unions and things. I wrote to him before last Christmas and since then we've sort of kept up a regular . . . sort of exchange of views. It's really interesting what's happening over there. The unions are much more advanced there than they are here. A lot of his problems are similar to the ones here, though. At least the government there seems to be on the people's side.'

'That's not true, Sion,' said Evan. 'The government pretends to be on their side because it can see the way things are going. The concessions that are made are only the merest start, and are designed to keep the union leaders happy. Until the workers get a government that really looks after their interests nothing really significant will change. Mark my words, there's going to be a lot of strife and hardship before the working man gets what's rightfully his.'

35

DURING THE NEXT two years Sion and Bill spent their holidays in St Louis working for Evan. Meg was beginning to adjust to Evan's frequent absences, now that Evan was elected to Congress. Sonny more or less ran the business on his own and was doing a good job. To Sion's excitement and Meg's disappointment Sion proved to be both a mathematician and something of a scientist. Not only did he excel at the pure sciences of physics, chemistry and mathematics but was proving to be very adept at the new science of aero-dynamics. Flying was a craze that had swept France and was already enthusiastically embraced by some Americans. To date flying had been mainly confined to lighter than air craft but a great deal of work was now going into flying machines which did not rely on any form of gas to lift them.

Sion avidly read the works of James Means whose three volumes titled Aeronautical Annual became of great importance in making known the work of past and present pioneers especially that of Lilienthal. Sion joined the Boston Aeronautical Society. This was the first of it's kind and he submitted a number of papers to them on his ideas about flight. Sion's mania for kite flying was paying off in undreamed of dividends. Meg, however, had always harboured the hope that Sion, like David, would enter into one of the professions. Wilbur and Orville Wright had already flown their warping kite, the first aircraft to have helical twisting of the wings for control in a roll which they had invented. During 1901 the first petrol driven aeroplane flies and the Aero Club of Great Britain is founded. All of it fired Sion's imagination and enthusiasm and he spent much of his spare time working on aerodynamic designs which, on the whole, failed to fly.

Joseph's restaurant was doing very well and was proving to be one of the most popular places in the city. It was patronised by businessmen, farmers and ranchers. Counting the head waiter, the waiters, barmen, cooks and dish washers there were thirty-two people working for Joseph and Evan by 1902.

David had finished his LLb at Harvard and was working for a small company of lawyers in St Louis. He had been hired primarily in the expectation that Evan would transfer his business to them from John Driscole but Evan had no intention of doing so. David accepted this although his new bosses were not happy. As a consequence, coupled with the fact that he was bored with his job, after less than a year David began to look for something else to do.

After their graduation Sion and Bill worked for five weeks at the warehouse and then decided to take a holiday. After a lot of argument where to go the decision was made for them when two friends from the university arrived. Paddy McCormick and Stephen Anderson had been class mates with Sion and Bill and were on their way up the Missouri to Sioux City, a small frontier town. From there they were taking horses into South Dakota and heading for the mountains. They hoped to do some hunting, a bit of fishing, perhaps some trapping. Paddy McCormick, a tall, wide shouldered youth, was the expert on the outback, having been brought up on a large ranch in Texas.

Stephen Anderson in contrast to Paddy was neat and small. His slow speech hid a sharp brain, a testimony to which was the fact he had graduated top of their year. He

was going to Harvard with Sion and Bill whilst Paddy
was returning to Texas, maintaining that he'd had enough
learning for one lifetime.

'Why don't you two come with us?' Paddy asked, as
they stood on the porch of the Griffiths' house.

So it was settled. They spent a few days getting their
gear together and left by boat for Sioux City. It was an
uneventful eight day journey but finally they arrived at
Sioux. It was not much of a place: a single main street
on either side of which were houses, a few stores, a hotel
and a couple of saloons. Nearest the wharf was the livery
stable with a large sign offering horses and buckboards
for hire.

'I don't think I've ever been to such a wild west type
place before,' said Sion with some awe.

'Me neither,' said Steve.

Bill and Paddy laughed. They had both seen a lot worse
in New Mexico and Texas.

'At least it's not a one horse town,' said Paddy.

'What is it then?' asked Sion innocently.

'Two horse,' and Paddy whooped with laughter. 'Come
on, let's go and find us four horses.' He led the way
towards the livery. 'If that's possible in this town.'

Outside the double doors sat a wizened old man,
chewing tobacco and spitting into the dust.

'My name's McCormick. Are you the owner?'

'Yep,' said the old man, emphasising the word with a
brown jet of tobacco juice out the side of his mouth.

'I sent you a wire. Did you receive it?'

'Yep,' he did not offer any further comment.

Paddy took a grip on his patience and smiled. 'Have
you got the horses and mule available?'

'Nope.'

'Jesus. Why not?'

The old man played with the wad of tobacco for a
few seconds, shifting it from one side of his mouth to
the other. 'Don't rush me young fellow and I'll tell you.'

A few more seconds of chewing then: 'I kin get em by tomorrer. Not before.'

'With saddles, bags . . .'

'Ever'thing you want,' the old man said.

'What time tomorrow?' asked Steve.

'Noon,' was the reply.

'Thanks. Come on, let's find a room for the night and come back tomorrer . . . I mean tomorrow,' said Sion.

'Thank you, sir,' said Paddy with exaggerated courtesy, touching his hat.

'What a crow ball,' said Steve with feeling. They wandered up the wooden side walk towards the largest building with a peeling sign saying "hotel".

They took the last two rooms, each with a double bed, a chest of drawers with a water jug and bowl sitting on top. They discovered there was a bath house out the back where for fifteen cents they could have a hot bath. If one followed the other then it only cost the second five cents for the same water. They each paid fifteen cents. The building was wooden, had a low ceiling, six baths barely big enough to sit in and at one end a large stove to boil water on. The water was carried in by bucket from a well outside.

'Who would have thought it would be so primitive so close to home?' Sion asked in wonder, sponging hot water over his head.

'Heck Sion, it gets a lot worse than this I can tell you. You remember all the stories I told you about down my way . . . Didn't you believe me?' Paddy asked in some surprise.

Sion winced. 'It wasn't that I disbelieved you, just that I thought you could have been, shall we say . . . using poetic licence?' He ducked as Paddy threw the soap at him and missed.

'Poetic licence my foot; like the poetic licence you used to write when you got a story into that useless university paper? Huh, at least I always told the exact truth, not like some of the excuses you made when the football team lost.'

Steve laughed loudly while Bill smiled broadly.

After a meal of black-eye beans and cremated steak they returned to the hotel. In both rooms a similar scene was being enacted.

Sion and Bill looked dubiously at the bed and then at each other. Although they had been sharing a room for three years and seen each other naked many times they had never actually slept in the same bed, even a double one. They both shuffled around it, sat down tentatively and slowly undressed. Once he got his night shirt on Sion quickly slid under the blankets, his back to Bill, almost off the edge. Bill did likewise. They both spent a rough night half hanging out of the bed, their backs carefully to each other. Paddy and Steve spent a similar night. The next morning they were up with the dawn, stiff, tired and short tempered. By eleven o'clock they had bought fresh provisions and were back at the livery stable pestering the old man for the horses.

From the monosyllabic replies it appeared that the horses were still not available and so they hung around for the next hour. At precisely noon the old man got up and went into the stable then reappeared leading four horses and a mule. Biting back their anger they paid for six weeks hire plus a deposit of fifty dollars per horse and thirty for the mule. After packing the mule with their stores Paddy led them slowly out of town.

'At least they seem to be pretty good mounts,' said Sion.

'Aye, not bad,' said Paddy, running a practised eye over them. 'I guess they'll do for what we want.'

'Where are we going from here?' asked Steve.

'Like we discussed,' said Paddy. 'Up to Yankton and then along the side of the James river.'

'No, I mean right now. I know where we're headed.

Are we just going to follow this path or are we going to
follow the river?'

'I was told in town this path cuts out a few miles of
bends and joins up again with the Missouri. So we'll just
follow and see where it gets us.'

They lapsed into silence. Sion gave himself up to the
feel of the horse, the sound of the woods and the beauty
of the flowers and trees. A sense of well being stole over
him. When they stopped on the bank of the river it was
nearly sundown. Slowly and achingly they climbed down
from their horses.

'God, I didn't expect to be so stiff,' said Paddy. 'Heck,
I could ride before I could walk. That's what three years
at a desk does for you.'

Bill signalled Sion and Sion said: 'And holidays in
New York City.'

Bill was referring to the fact that Paddy had spent his
time between semesters at Steve's home in New York.
There had been few opportunities to go horse riding.
Steve's father was a banker and though he owned an
imposing mansion with plenty of grounds somehow they
never got around to doing anything more than taking a
buggy from restaurant to theatre to party.

Paddy grinned at the recollection. 'Boy, what a place
that was. I learned so much. Oh, my blasted back. It's
killing me. Hell, I hope this doesn't last too long.'

'I hope you're right,' said Sion, stretching. 'I ache all
over. I'll go and find some fire wood.'

'Hang on, Sion,' said Paddy. 'Before you do that we
need to take care of the horses. They need to be unsaddled,
rubbed down and hobbled or tied on a long rope. After that
we can think about ourselves.'

'Okay, point taken. Sorry.'

'That's okay. I'll take care of the mule. After that I
think a swim will go down well.'

They were camped on the river's bank, in a glade. It
was quiet, no wind, the only sound was the murmuring

of the water brushing the river's bank and the droning of insects.

After taking care of the horses and gathering firewood, Paddy set three fishing lines twenty yards upstream and then they went swimming. They splashed and fooled around until the sun dipped down behind a far away peak and with the chill getting to them they climbed out, dried and dressed. Paddy went to inspect the lines but found only one three inch trout which he threw back. They lit a fire, cooked beans and bacon, and soon afterwards were rolled up in their blankets. In spite of the hard ground they quickly fell asleep.

Sion woke shivering in the dark, just before the dawn. He lay still for a few moments collecting his thoughts and then stretched his aching body. Awkwardly he rubbed the small of his back where a stone had been digging into him during the night. He felt worse than after a hard football game in his early days at university. He clambered to his feet still half asleep, pulled on his boots and wandered down to the river to wash. The cold water revived him and he set about lighting the fire. To the east the sky was turning a pearl grey colour, there was no wind and it promised to be a very hot day.

With the fire burning brightly he went to check the fishing lines and found two fat, twelve inch trout. They kicked feebly when Sion removed the hooks but he quickly poked his finger into their gills and with a flick of his wrist killed them. He cleaned them on a large flat stone and returned to camp. The others were up by this time and had a pot of coffee going. They all agreed that the fish was the best they had ever eaten in spite of the smoky flavour.

They struck camp and continued along the river bank, heading almost due north. For two days they followed the river, found a place to ford, crossed over and headed west. They were now riding a large plateau, just over fourteen hundred feet above see level, the land undulating with many hills rising another thousand feet. There was plenty of game and they enjoyed the hunt for rabbit, and occasional pheasant and once, a deer. They could see the general lay of the land and the way it sloped gently but persistently upwards. The days were hot and sunny, the skies cloudless. Night times had an edge to them, not cold, just refreshingly cool.

At the Missouri, they found an old man living in a tumble down shack. He made a precarious living by doing some trapping, selling appalling liquor he distilled himself and taking people across the river. He charged ten cents a person and fifty for each animal. Here, luckily, although deep the water was not too fast. They crossed one horse and rider at a time on a dilapidated wooden raft, with rotten rails against which they were warned not to lean. It rocked alarmingly as the old man pulled them over using a rope they were sure would part any second. Sion went first. He had never been so glad to reach dry land. The others followed and finally Paddy went back for the mule.

Paddy led the animal to the water's edge, stepped onto the raft and was jerked half off his feet by the reins draped over his right shoulder when the mule dug its feet in. Paddy pulled with all his might but the mule would not budge.

On the other side of the river they could hear Paddy cursing fluently and monotonously. It was Bill who grinned first, then Steve and then Sion. Then Sion chuckled and soon the three of them were laughing so hard it hurt. Bill, who had tears running down his cheeks, was bent over, his chest heaving with silent laughter. The other two screeched and yelled encouragement at Paddy who by this time was behind the mule pushing.

After a few minutes the old man shrugged, walked behind his shack and reappeared carrying two carrots. He fed the mule one and then dangled the other in front of it. Greedily the mule stretched its neck but would not move its feet. After a minute or two of straining it took a reluctant pace forward and the old man stepped back. The mule followed, its fear of the raft forgotten in its greed for the carrot. Once on the raft the old man allowed the mule the reach the carrot while Paddy shoved off and began pulling them across the river. Sion and Steve cheered while Bill jumped up and down with joy. The mule stood there, contentedly munching on the carrot as though to say, who's the fool?

It walked serenely off the other side and Paddy paid the ferryman.

'Another two bits for the carrots.'

Paddy was about to protest but Steve handed over the money. 'It was worth it for the laugh we had,' he said, sending the other two into gales of merriment They dragged themselves onto their horses, still chuckling, and slowly headed west. The next few hours were spent in reminiscing the incident of the ferry and the mule.

They cut down towards the south west until they reached a river Paddy said was called the Niobrara, though none of the others had heard of it. They topped a low hill and stopped to rest when in the distance a movement caught their attention.

'Look, buffalo,' said Sion, pointing. Sure enough, less than a mile away what appeared to be a family of buffaloes were grazing, though always with one of them looking suspiciously around them.

'Do you fancy trying to kill one?' Paddy asked.

Sion squirmed, Steve looked down at his saddle horn but Bill savagely shook his head.

'Good,' said Paddy, with a grin. 'I don't either. I just thought I'd better ask. After all we are on a hunting trip.'

'Hmmm,' said Sion. 'I don't really want to kill anything more than we need to eat. I was sorry we killed that deer, because we couldn't eat it all. I don't like the idea of killing for say, skins, or the fun of it.' The others agreed with him.

'I remember reading the story about the plainsmen,' said Paddy. 'About men like Bridger and Crocket. They said that sometimes a herd could take as long as five or six days to walk past them, not stopping, just heading God only knew where and for what purpose. Now if there's half a hundred in a herd it's considered a large one.'

Sombrely they looked down at the peaceful, grazing, shaggy headed buffalo.

'There's eight I think,' said Steve.

'Nine,' said Paddy. 'See the calf over there,' he pointed to the right of the group. 'Just under the tree.'

'Oh yes. Wait. Look, something's disturbing them,' said Sion.

The buffalo were looking around, pacing nervously. Suddenly one of the smaller cows broke into an ungainly trot, the others followed and then they started to gallop, in a mad, mindless panic that would bring them closer to the boys and upwind of them.

'I wonder what caused that?' asked Steve.

'Look at the small calf. The one that was by the tree. He's changing direction. He's coming straight towards us, not following the others,' Paddy said. 'I wonder what's making him do that?'

Bill pointed and signalled Sion. Sion said: 'A cat. A cougar? Bill thinks it's a cougar.'

'What the hell is a cougar doing down here? It isn't mountainous enough for them, nor are there enough trees for them to hide in,' said Paddy, thoughtfully.

'I can see it,' said Steve. The calf was now only about five hundred yards away. They could see the animal's fear, it was in the calf's movements, in it's frantic darting. Heading it off was a sleek, black animal that at first looked like a cougar. As it drew nearer they could see it was a large, wild dog.

Without thinking Sion shucked his rifle from his saddle and broke his horse into a gallop. The others followed, a few seconds behind. The calf, seeing further danger, panicked, staggered and fell heavily onto its shoulder. It scrambled to its feet but now the dog was in position and launched itself into the air, going for the buffalo's throat.

It was luck when Sion's snap shot, taken at the gallop, hit the flying dog in the shank and bowled it over. It lay stunned for a second or two and then tried to get up. Sion closed to within fifty yards, fired again and missed. Now the others, still closing, also fired and at least one other shot found its mark. The dog was whimpering pitifully, trying to get to its feet, trying to escape. Sion pulled up in a flurry of dust and steadied his aim. The dog snarled, baring his fangs. Sion fired into the dog's head, killing it instantly.

They drew around the long haired, inert form. In a sad voice, Steve said, 'He only wanted to eat.'

'I bet he was once somebody's pet,' said Sion. 'Probably just got lost and was trying to stay alive. I bet if we had called him he would have come to us knowing we'd have food for him.'

'You don't know that, Sion,' said Paddy. 'He'd probably reverted right back to his wild state, as though he had never known people.'

Without saying another word they wheeled their horses and started west once more, heading back to the river.

After a couple of miles their spirits returned and Sion said, 'You know, I don't think I could ever kill anybody. I hate killing animals, think how I'd feel if I had to kill another human. I don't think I could ever do that.'

'You could if the circumstances were right,' said Paddy sagely.

'How can the circumstances ever be right, to take another life?' Sion asked.

'If it's your life or theirs for one. Or if somebody near and dear to you was threatened, or had been hurt in some way,' said Paddy.

About to deny it Sion suddenly remembered the night

Uncle James had died and how he had been ready to shoot the detective and the Marshal, if necessary. 'I guess you could be right at that.'

Eventually they reached a marsh stretching back a few miles from the river's edge. They followed it around, keeping to the firm ground. There were large clumps of a hardy type of bamboo growing and Sion found two lengths, about eight and six feet long which he cut and cleaned of leaves.

'What do you want with those?' Steve asked, watching him tie them to the back of the mule.

'Just an idea I've got for a kite. If we find a high enough place I'm going to try something out,' he said vaguely.

Whenever the opportunity arose, using a spare cotton sheet, Sion worked on his kite. It was one of the most ambitious he had ever fashioned.

36

FOR A MONTH they wandered towards the state of Wyoming and the distant Rocky Mountains, still three hundred miles away. Once the aches and soreness had gone they were developing into hard young men, losing excess weight and toughening up their muscles. As their height above sea level increased so the nights got colder, though the days continued warm and dry.

Once there was a heavy thunderstorm but they found a large overhang of rock under which they could light a fire, keep dry and even shelter the horses.

They had given themselves two weeks to return to St Louis and the day dawned when, reluctantly, they decided that after one more day they needed to start retracing their path.

Disaster struck shortly after they made their camp that night. They had been swimming in the river and had just finished eating a rabbit stew. None of them heard the approach of the intruders. Suddenly they found themselves surrounded by ten men, pointing rifles at them. There was something about these men that chilled the boys' hearts. It was not merely the silence, nor the odd way they were dressed. It was possibly the lack of emotion; the way they held themselves. They seemed to be ready to kill for any reason. It might have been all these things or none of them.

Sion was lying on his bedroll and suddenly sat up. 'What do you . . .' he got no further as a rifle butt smashed into his jaw and sent him sprawling. For a few seconds he lay unmoving and gave a low groan, trying to clear his head. His jaw was not broken but badly bruised. Tentatively he touched his chin and tried flexing it back and forth. It was too painful to move. Nobody else risked saying a word. Paddy realised that they were surrounded by half-breeds, men of mixed white and Indian parents – outcasts from both societies. Two of them saddled the boys' horses and packed the mule. One of them indicated that the boys should get up, get their bed rolls and climb onto their horses.

In the confusion of movement and blankets Sion slipped his Bowie knife from its sheath where it had been hidden under his saddle and pushed it down the top of his boot. He kicked the sheath into some long grass out of sight. The knife chafed uncomfortably against his leg at every pace he took. Their captors collected their guns and their knives but did not search the boys.

All night they rode west. When Sion was convinced he could no longer stay awake a halt was called, and a frugal camp set. Wearily the boys stripped their tired horses, led them to water and then tied them amongst long, lush grass. After that they unfurled their bed rolls and dropped on to them.

At all times two of their captors kept them covered with rifles. At no time did any of them speak; it was more and more uncanny. In spite of his exhaustion Sion was unable to sleep. What did these men want? If they were being kidnapped for ransom surely they would not go further west away from their families. But surely there was no other reason for taking them? What possible use were they to these men? These and other thoughts whirled through Sion's mind until he finally fell asleep.

They were woken by hearty kicks which brought them instantly to their feet in spite of their weariness. From the position of the sun they could only have slept for about three hours. Their captors had taken their watches, all their money and even their hats.

All day they went west. The sun seemed hotter than ever, especially since they had no cover for their necks and heads. They were not given water or food even though their captors drank and ate.

By the second day they were desperate for a drink and finally, towards evening, they were given some. Greedily they drank their fill. They were also given a piece of jerky, tough and unpalatable. Somehow Bill managed to keep the rancid stuff in his stomach. Sion was not so lucky. Unable to chew properly because of his aching jaw, he puked when he tried to swallow chunks which were too large, much to the amusement of their captors.

Sion and Bill exchanged views using their sign language. Why did the gang say nothing? Where were they going? What was their captors intentions? Slavery? It had taken a long time to pass their signals as they would make part of a gesture and often have to complete it when the guards looked away. Bill and Sion rode side by side, Steve and Paddy in front, the half breeds surrounding them. One man rode a few hundred yards ahead and two trailed behind.

The way they back tracked, the frequency with which they changed direction, though continuing generally westward, and the pains they took to hide their tracks suggested the gang was frightened of being followed.

About mid-morning on the fourth day they approached a high butte, rising sheer for seven or eight hundred feet and sticking out like a thumb into the clear blue sky, surrounded by low lying undulating hills. All day they rode directly towards it, with no meandering off course. It was evening when they got to the foot of the butte and rode around it to the other side.

The sun set and night was falling fast when they camped. Dawn had just broken when they were again roused by the now regular kicks. They were given water and more jerky to chew on and were taken towards the path up the butte.

Sion noted that one of the gang stayed below. The path was easy to follow until they reached the first bend. Then it narrowed and became steeper. Rocks were dislodged and dropped out of sight. The horses became more and more nervous. Finally, the group came to a natural chimney; a fissure in the rock that wound round like a spiral stairway. They went round and round as well as up, the light alternating from deep gloom to brilliant sunshine. The going got harder and towards the top they were almost dragging their reluctant mounts behind them. The gang's horses seemed to take it in their stride and were obviously used to the route. Sion did not like the idea of leading his horse down again. The mule, after being cantankerous at the river crossing took the climb surprisingly calmly; it was loaded with all their gear including the cane Sion had cut for his kite. At the top the view was incredible. In the crystal clear air they could see for forty miles in any direction.

The top of the butte was flat and dotted with boulders. In the middle were a couple of scrubby trees and patches of lush grass. The four of them were taken to a catchment area where water bubbled gently out of a rock. They could see six, round, bee-hive tents each about four feet high, near the trees. There was nobody else present.

After drinking their fill, still wondering what was going to happen, the boys were taken to within a few yards of the butte edge and made to sit down. Pegs were hammered into the ground and the boys were spread eagled, their wrists and ankles tied to the pegs. When their captors left them there was silence for a few minutes.

'What's this all about?' Steve asked in a pained whisper. 'What in God's name do they want with us?' His voice came out as a rasp in his fright.

'I don't know,' said Paddy. 'I just don't know,' he paused. 'But I don't mind admitting to you guys that I'm scared clear through. I've never seen people act like this before. I guess they're probably from a reservation, perhaps outcasts. But what do they want with us?'

The loneliness, the fear, the uncertainty swept through Sion and suddenly tears trickled down his face. He was overwhelmed by his feelings. He knew, with a clarity, with a flash of understanding, that they had been brought here to die.

The sun was beating down on them unmercifully and their last drink seemed to have been ages ago. From the sun's position it was just past noon, though on what day none of them could have said.

By straining his head Sion was able to catch glimpses of their captors as they prepared a meal and argued over the gear they had stolen from the boys. He watched them throw his kite sticks to one side along with the sheet he had cut and sewn to cover the frame. The afternoon was never ending. The sun was a burning, yellow ball, dehydrating them and leaving them with parched throats and aching heads. Throughout the afternoon there was no sign of their captors but towards sundown they heard the gang yelling and laughing.

Paddy said: 'They're drunk. Right out of their rotten skulls, the lot of them. Look at the fools dancing around. The pigs. I hope they stagger over to the edge and fall off.' He hid his fear behind hate and disgust.

The sun had just set when three of the gang staggered over, laughing and giggling like children and cut the ropes holding Steve. They hauled him roughly to his feet but because Steve had long lost any feeling in his hands and feet and he collapsed. The breeds laughed and began kicking Steve in the head and side. They were so drunk their efforts did not hurt him much but did get him awkwardly to his knees and finally to his feet. They pushed him roughly and each time he stumbled it sent the breeds into fits of laughter. In the rapidly falling light the boys saw him thrown down and staked out again.

'I wonder what those devils are going to do?' asked

Sion, his voice sticking in his throat, fear like bile in his mouth.

'I don't know, but I sure as hell don't like it,' rasped Paddy. 'Those bastards are capable of anything,' he lapsed into silence.

The moon was up and still the sound of revelry went on. The silence that descended took them by surprise. Suddenly into the night came the most awful, blood curdling scream of terror and pain they had ever thought possible, even in their darkest nightmares. It seemed to go on and on and on. The boys went into a frenzy trying to get loose from their bounds, trying to block out the noise of Steve's agony.

After what seemed like an eternity the sound dropped to a whimper in the still air, though from time to time, unexpectedly, it would rent the air apart again.

'What have they done to him?' Sion was nearly whimpering. 'It's the unknown that I hate the most, this not knowing. Oh God . . . God . . . God.'

Soon afterwards the night fell silent. Their captors had fallen asleep in a drunken stupor and Steve made no more sound. Now they were cold, shivering in the bright moonlight. Nervous exhaustion sometimes let them dose off fitfully but on two occasions during that long night Steve's ugly scream, dying to a sob, brought them alert and trembling. Dawn broke in a radiance of colour and clear skies. It was going to be another hot and beautiful day. Was Steve still alive?

None of the gang was in evidence and nobody disturbed the tranquillity of the camp until the guard from below appeared without his horse. He went and roused one of the others who made his way in a staggering gait towards the pathway.

It was late afternoon when the others started to emerge from their bee-hive tents. They could hardly walk straight and spent ages at the water hole drinking. After another day in the sun without water the boys were half crazed for a drink and the three of them had blood around their wrists where they had fought against their bonds.

'What did they do to him?' Sion screamed the last word and then struggled against the ropes in a frenzy but to no avail.

A few seconds later one of the gang whom they had identified as the leader, loomed over them and looked down with contempt and hate on his face. It was the first time any of them had shown emotion to the boys except when they had been laughing at their discomfort. It was also the first time one of them had spoken to them.

'I shall tell you white boy what we did. You will think about it until your turn comes to die.'

'For God's sake why are you doing this?' Paddy asked in anguish. 'We haven't done anything to you.'

The steady, blue expressionless eyes looked from one to the other. The man's nose was hooked like a beak, his hair jet black and tied at the nape of his neck. Although he wore buckskin trousers and moccasins he had on an old army jacket and battered hat with a feather stuck in the band. 'Never mind why. Only know what. Your friend died sooner than we had expected. A slip of the knife. I cut open his belly and pulled out his innards. After a while I poured molasses over him. It's a type the red ants love. He was tied over an ant hill. He should have lived until tomorrow at the earliest. It was a pity he didn't. Our enjoyment has been shortened by one day.'

'You swine,' Sion yelled at him. 'You filthy bastard. I hope you rot in hell.'

'You will be there a long time before me,' said the man calmly.

'For God's sake, why?' Paddy was almost pleading. 'Tell us that, man. What have we done to deserve this? If you must kill us, if you want our scalps, at least kill us quickly.' His voice changed and the last word was begging. 'Please.'

Suddenly the man towering over them became animated. 'I'll tell you why,' he said fiercely. 'I'll tell you why. My grandfather was white. The rest of my ancestors have been Indian. We,' he waved his hand to indicate the other men with him, 'are from similar backgrounds. We have been outcasts in our tribes, given the dirtiest jobs and been treated like dung beneath the feet of the other braves. The white men treated us worse. What they have done to me and my friends would take longer to tell than you have to live. We left our tribes and banded together. We settled on unused land, raised a few cattle, started our own village. Then, a few years ago white men wanted it. One day while out hunting we returned to our village to find it burnt, the women and children killed and our horses gone. Some of the women had been raped and then burnt alive at the stake. One of the women was my wife. She had been lovely, gentle and kind. Our two sons had been made to watch before they were killed. Now we have nothing to live for except revenge. Our revenge is to kill as many white people as possible in the most painful way until we die or are killed. With you three I shall be more careful than I was last night, I promise you. You shall die in mad agony, eaten alive by the ants. You will be aware of them crawling into your eyes and brains until you go mad.' Abruptly he walked away.

The boys lay in silence for a few seconds and then Sion spoke. 'Oh my God,' was all he managed to whisper because he was then sobbing, his body heaving.

The evening was a replay of the night before, starting with the heavy drinking, the laughing and the giggling.

'Who is it to be?' Paddy asked when they saw the figures looming out of the moon lit night.

One of the men was the leader. 'Listen,' said Sion desperately, 'why don't you ransom us? My father would pay much gold to have us back.'

Taking no notice of him, as though he had not spoken, one of the men drunkenly bent down to cut Paddy's ropes.

Paddy gave a low moan. They pulled him to his feet but he collapsed almost immediately. The breeds giggled inanely, kicked him for a few minutes and then pulled him up again.

The two men holding Paddy's arms staggered back a couple of paces and from somewhere Paddy found the strength he needed. He barged one of them in the chest, wrapped his arms around the second, a small man barely up to Paddy's shoulders, and rushed for the butte edge. Before they could be stopped Paddy and the breed went over in a long drawn out duet of screams. Then silence.

The remainder of the gang rushed to the edge, screaming and cursing. Yells were exchanged with the guard at the foot of the butte and then one of them bent down to cut Sion's bonds. The leader stopped him and indicated Bill.

They hauled him to his feet and Bill collapsed, held up under the arms by two of the gang. The two friends looked at each other for a long moment, tears in their eyes.

'Let him go you bastards, let him go,' Sion screamed, struggling against the ropes. A kick sent his head reeling and the word please was only spoken inside his mind.

Bill fought like a madman. He kicked, bit, punched, and scratched. From the yells and curses in a mixture of English and Indian he was hurting some of them. Finally a rifle butt in the back of the head dropped him. They took an arm each, one grabbed his hair and they dragged him away.

After Steve had died they had thrown his body over the edge of the butte, leaving it to the coyotes and buzzards. Now Bill was tied down in the same place as Steve. The shock of one of their number being killed, Paddy's suicide and Bill's struggle seemed to have sobered the men a little. Now there was no laughter and dancing, just a business like preparation of the staked area and Bill's inert form.

Sion went frantic with rage and anguish. He struggled

and fought against the ropes. He no longer felt the pain in his wrists where the skin, layer after layer, had been chafed away. He only felt that somehow he had to get to Bill before it was too late. He stopped to regain his breath and think. Finally he bent his wrist back and gripped the stake. Concentrating his mind and body on his arm he exerted all his strength.

Sion's head throbbed and his body ached and after an age of effort he stopped, panting, his arm aching as though a red hot poker had been shoved through it. Again, he braced himself to try. His ears buzzed, his arm was on fire but he thought for a second there was some movement in the stake. Suddenly the night was split asunder with a cry that was to haunt him for years. Bill had made a noise that defied human description. The remaining part of his larynx had been made to work one last time. It was the only sound he made, the only sound he was capable of.

Sion gagged and retched until his stomach ached. Fear swept through him and once more he took hold of the stake and heaved upwards. He kept on . . . and on . . . and on. Waves of pain swept through his arm and down into his body. Red and black mists floated across his eyes . . . and on . . . He passed out.

When he came to Sion was first aware of the pain in his arm, then the stillness of the night. The moon impinged on his consciousness, and then the fact that his arm was out straight by his side. Awkwardly he moved it, lifting the stake to his eyes unable to believe what he saw. Pain swept across his shoulder and along his arm and he dropped it, his fingers too numb to let go the stake.

A while later he sat up and groped for his boot. With difficulty, because his fingers would still not do what his brain told them, he reached his knife. He slashed at the rope holding his left wrist until the rope parted and he could sit up properly. His fingers were beginning to tingle and his wrists throbbed painfully. After freeing his feet he tried to stand but no matter how hard he tried he couldn't make it.

Eventually, the numbness in his feet gave way to pins and needles that drove him frantic as he exercised his toes trying to get the feeling back more quickly. Finally, he could move but he sat immobile for a while, terrified to move. While he regained the use of his feet Sion looked round for a guard but could see nobody. Carefully Sion skirted the beehives and crept towards Bill. He stepped down into a hollow and nearly screamed in shock to see Bill laying at his feet. It took all his will power not to retch at the sight.

Bill was wriggling in nameless agonies, the yellow and red of his bloodied intestines barely recognisable under the mass of seething ants, black in the moonlight. Bill was covered with them from his hair to his feet. Sion stood over him for a second, the knife clenched in his fist and looked down into the mad, staring eyes of his friend. For an instant, as he sunk to his knees, Sion could have sworn there was recognition in the eyes and then he had the knife in his two hands, above the body and he drove it with all his might into Bill's heart.

Again and again Sion stabbed in a frenzy of horror, dislodging the ants, which rushed about in panic, trying to get away but not wanting to leave the food. Finally, Sion staggered away, the bloodied knife dangling from his hand, his mind in a stupor. He walked to the edge of the butte and was only a pace away when he heard something.

The sound penetrated the haze surrounding his mind and Sion looked back. The sight of the man crawling out of his beehive and going to urinate over the butte edge saved Sion's life.

The fear evaporated. In its place was a hatred so all consuming he wanted to scream at them. He was about to rush stupidly at the man when Sion's brain turned cold and sharp as ice. The hatred was there but so was cunning and intelligence. Silently, Sion crept to the side of the beehive he had seen the man crawl out of and waited. He wanted to escape, that thought was firmly embedded in him. He did not wish to die. On the other hand he knew he could never get safely down the path in the darkness leading a horse, even with the aid of a full moon. Also he did not think he could kill all of them. Counting the one down below there were nine of them. Coldly and analytically Sion came to the conclusion he could not escape. As much as he wanted to he could not get away. And that left only one thing to do. To kill as many of them as possible until he too, was killed. Unless . . . unless he got an escape route ready. A last ditch attempt and if it failed he would die anyway.

The man was returning. Sion stayed hidden until the half breed bent to crawl into his hovel and then Sion stepped out and, more by luck than judgement, drove the knife as hard as he could through the man's neck, severing the spinal cord. The man died without a sound. Taking hold of his feet Sion dragged him out of sight behind some rocks. Overcome with weariness he went to the water hole and drank his fill.

After a few minutes rest Sion went to find his poles and cotton sheet. Slowly, because his hands were still not responding properly, he tied the bamboo in a cross and fitted the sheet over it. He now had a diamond shape some eight feet by six. To the cross arm he tied two pieces of rope and to the main length he tied one piece a third of the way from the front. He knotted them together and from that he hung two loops, through which he intended placing his arms. From his years of experience playing and making kites, he hoped he would hang along the centreline and slightly back of the cross piece. Sion had made smaller kites in the past, hanging stones on them, experimenting with size and weight, hoping one day to launch himself into the air and float to the earth. The day had arrived.

Looking towards the east Sion felt the wind rising
from the cooling rock below and coming in a gentle
breeze directly into his face. That was the direction he
had to take.

His knife in hand, he walked over to where the horses
were tethered and hesitated. He had had a vague notion
of killing all of them but realised it was impossible. There
were thirteen horses as well as the mule and besides which
he did not have the stomach for it.

In the centre of the scruffy camp were piled all the
weapons and ammunition. Gathering up the guns he took
them to the western edge of the butte and threw them over.
He kept two of the six guns as well as a rifle which he
slung across his back. Next he stoked up the fire until it
was blazing, the flames reaching three or four feet into
the air. By now his hands were almost back to normal
although his wrists were throbbing with pain. Flexing his
fingers he noticed a little blood seeping out at his right
wrist so he went to the water hole, washed both wrists
and bound them with pieces of cloth. He took another
drink and as an after thought filled a water bottle and tied
that to the kite. If there was too much weight that would
be too bad. There was nothing he could do about it. He
got six fire brands ready and he made up six bundles of
ammunition in bits of rag. He tied the ammunition to the
brands and took a deep breath. He was now ready to kill
the men.

He threw each flaming brand into a beehive. He let go
the last one when the first scream rent the air and one of
the men, his shirt on fire, crawled into the open. Coolly
Sion swung the rifle he had dangling from his neck and
in the bright light from the moon and the fire, shot the
man through the head. More screams started and then
the bullets in the bundles began exploding. The six men
still alive came tumbling out, yelling, panic stricken, their
beehives blazing up in flames. One of them was crawling,
hit in the stomach from an exploding bullet, another was

on fire from head to toe but the other four darted for cover. Sion aimed at the back of the furthest, held his breath and gently squeezed the trigger. He was gratified to see the man throw his arms out and fall face downwards. Switching targets smoothly he shot another in the side as he crossed from right to left but the other two dropped from sight before he could pull the trigger again.

The man on fire was rolling in agony across the ground and the one with the stomach wound was curled up in a foetal position, moaning. He fired a snap shot at the burning man, missed and slipped away towards the eastern end of the butte. A sense of foreboding swept over him and bone weary tiredness made him stumble.

For fifteen minutes Sion sat hidden, watching the scene at the camp. The man holding his stomach tried to crawl out of the light but stopped after a few yards, the effort plainly too much. The man who had been on fire lay still, the flames now out.

There were two left and at each shadow Sion jumped, sitting in indecision as to what to do. They could stay hidden for as long as they wished, sleeping and probably doing without food and water a lot longer than he could. They could yell down to the guard below and tell him to come up, though after so much noise he was probably on his way. The more he thought about it the more Sion realised there was only one thing to do.

Slinging the rifle behind his back he picked up the kite, got underneath and put his arms through the loops. He was hesitating at the edge of the drop, fear like bile in his throat, when he heard the scuffle. Turning his head he saw one of the breeds running towards him, less than five yards away.

Without another thought Sion threw himself forward and went over the edge.

37

He never did remember what it was like. He knew he was not hurtling to the ground. He was aware of the screams and shots behind him but somehow the actual flight was lost. He travelled out nearly three quarters of a mile, swooping down towards the earth. In the moonlight he saw his shadow, like a huge bat, following him across the grey plain of rock which turned to grass as he travelled further away from the butte. He saw the horseman and knew it was the guard coming after him. He remembered feeling surprised that the man was not hidden in a funk at the sight of him sailing through the air. And then the earth was rushing up to meet him and he was going to land harder than he had expected. He braced his legs, by now the ropes under his arms paining him badly. He was down to within fifteen feet of the ground when the cotton sheet started tearing. As soon as the corner ripped the rest tore apart and he fell in a heap, rolling over and over down a grassy slope, the sheet and poles tangling him in knots. He lay still, badly winded, not seeing the horseman pull up, swing off his horse and rifle ready, advance towards him.

Sion was so tightly wrapped in the sheet he could not move. Somehow the rifle that had been dangling from the rope on the kite was laying alongside his leg, his hand over the trigger guard. Sion's head was spinning and his breath came in heavy gasps. Remembering the horseman he started to struggle but when the shadow suddenly loomed over him he stopped. The man's rifle was pointed at Sion's stomach but seeing how tangled he was the guard lowered the gun. With a superhuman effort Sion swung his feet up and pulled the trigger. The guard doubled over, hit in the belly, surprise and shock written all over his face. Sion's feet dropped and he knew he did not have the strength to repeat the movement. If the guard had raised his gun he could have shot Sion, and he would have been unable to prevent it.

With difficulty Sion untangled himself from the wreckage of the kite and stood up. His legs felt wobbly and his breathing was painful. His rifle ready he went over to the moaning figure laying on his side, holding his belly. He looked at Sion with hate filled eyes, no thought of asking for mercy. Gently Sion turned him over. The bullet had hit one side and passed clean through. It was painful but Sion thought the man would live. He took the man's knife and rifle to prevent him committing suicide and then drew his hand gun. He smiled at the breed and put the muzzle on the man's balls. For the first time fear showed in the man and then Sion pulled the trigger. The shock waves of pain sent the man unconscious and for a moment Sion thought that he had killed him. Then he saw the man was breathing. Sion hoped he would live many hours. Gathering up his weapons he walked slowly towards the horse, so used to gunfire it was contentedly chewing the grass.

The horse started when Sion approached but allowed Sion to pat his nose, stroke his neck and swing into the saddle. Sion now had two rifles across his shoulders, two six guns, a knife and water bottle. He turned the horse towards the east and set it at a gentle canter. Shortly afterwards the guard he had shot began screaming, a long drawn out wail that ended in a sob that followed Sion for miles in to the night. Sion smiled to himself all the way.

When he could no longer hear the screams Sion climbed painfully to the ground. Breathing was still painful. He guessed he had probably broken or at least cracked a

couple of ribs. Taking strips of the sheet from the kite
he bound his chest tightly and immediately his breathing
became easier. Back in the saddle and the horse once
more at a canter, he gave himself up to thinking what
to do and where to go. He was sure the remaining men
would be after him. As sure as day followed night. How
long would it take them to bring their horses down the
butte? Would they risk doing it in the darkness? Two
hours? Not much less. Sion was honest with himself and
recognised his limitations when it came to tracking and
woodsmanship. So he could never hide his trail, of that
he was sure. Therefore he had to outrun them. But how
far? All the way to the Missouri and the crossing? All the
way to Sioux City? He was aware that the men after him
were tough, able to go days and nights without food and
water, and more importantly, sleep. The only way Sion
could think of to cover his tracks was to cross water. That
could possibly delay his pursuers for a while.

The moon dipped out of sight, bathing the landscape
in blackness like the extinguishing of a faint but huge
lamp. Sion turned the horse further south and broke into
a gallop, panic spurring him recklessly on.

An hour later the dawn was breaking, a pearl and
yellow hue far to the east. At last he saw the glitter of
water and in his eagerness to get to the river spurred the
horse on again.

For a while he sat looking at the rushing water, as the
sun chiselled open the sky, dazzling him when he looked
towards the east. The water was fast and turbulent, four
feet below the bank, clear and deep.

Sion walked the horse along the edge, searching for a
way down. After a couple of miles the bank began to
lessen perceptibly and soon it spread out in a large area,
obviously flooded by heavy rains. He let the horse drink
and filled his water bottle. Wearily he climbed back into
the saddle a sharp needle of pain stabbing his chest. He
sat still, indecision tearing through him.

What to do? His mind screamed at him. Come on you idiot, decide! With that thought he suddenly spurred the horse hard in the flanks and headed for the centre of the river. Almost immediately the current caught them and began sweeping them along, faster than the horse could move its feet. The horse panicked for a second, put its nose under water and came up spluttering while Sion tried to calm him, talking and stroking his neck. The horse tried to swim but after a few seconds sank and started the spluttering routine again. Sion slipped off the saddle, held the saddle horn and swam alongside. The horse settled down and now swam steadily back for the bank they had just left. Sion pulled on the reigns and got the horse to go towards the further bank, a good thirty yards away. They were being swept downstream by the strong current and only occasionally did the horse's feet ever touch bottom. Whenever they got too close to one bank or the other Sion pulled the horse's head around and got him back into the middle. Somehow, for three hours, Sion kept the horse swimming. By then Sion was bone weary, shivering continuously and aching all over. When he felt he couldn't manage another minute in the water Sion let the horse have its head and steer towards the furthest bank. Now the bank was steeper than ever and even at the edge the water was too deep for the horse to stand. Sion became desperate, aware he could not hold on for much longer. With a superhuman effort he took the lariat and wound it tightly around his wrist, ignoring the pain, and tied it to the saddle horn. After that he couldn't remember what happened. He kept passing in and out of awareness like opening and closing a door. He lost track of time and was not sure how long he stood on dry land, hanging from the saddle, the pain in his wrist finally brining him to his senses.

He was shivering violently although the sun was burning down and, tired beyond endurance, pulled himself once more into the saddle and turned towards the east.

He knew he dared not stop. He thought of his friends and tears came to his eyes. He cursed himself for not having pulled out the stake earlier, before it had all begun. But how was he or the others to have known what the men had intended? There had been no way of knowing, but still he cursed himself. After that first night, surely then would have been the time? The other two might now be alive, he told himself, if only . . . If . . . only . . . If . . . If. He wandered into a nightmare not knowing how he stayed on the horse, only sure he was still heading away, putting distance between himself and the devils he was sure were following. Sometime in the late afternoon the earth moved up to hit him and he fell unconscious.

When Sion came to the first thing he was aware of was the cold and the second, his raging thirst. With a sense of shock he saw it was night and the moon had risen. He sat up quickly, trying to ignore the pain in his chest and the wave of giddiness that swept over him. He sat still for a few seconds and then staggered to his feet. Fearfully he looked around for the horse and with an overpowering wave of relief saw it standing in the shadow of a tree less than a hundred yards away. Calling softly he approached the animal and patted his neck. He climbed stiffly into the saddle and set off at a canter. The cloths around his chest had slipped and were no longer effective. The pain finally forced him to stop to replace them. His clothes had dried whilst he had been unconscious and he had stopped shivering. A drink of water from his canteen refreshed him and he felt a little less tired. The rest had done the horse some good but Sion desperately wished he knew how long he had lain there.

Sion continuously looked around him imagining all sorts of things, convinced half the time that the men chasing him were about to pounce. He tried to find solace in the thought that they would want him alive but it failed to be of any comfort. All night he rode. If he kept going he estimated he would reach the Missouri in about ten days. If he could keep going. Both he and the horse needed sleep and rest, regularly too, if he did not want the horse to collapse under him or for him not to fall from the saddle again. The next time he fell he could hurt himself badly, last time he had been lucky, very lucky.

By the time another dawn lit the sky he and the horse were all in and Sion knew he had to stop. He sat on a rise overlooking the confluence of a stream and the river. He went further downstream, paused, looked at the rushing water and then spurred the horse in. With difficulty he persuaded the horse to swim upstream and after a few minutes it got its feet on the bottom and surged towards the confluence of the river and stream. He walked the horse into the middle of the stream and with the water barely up to the horse's knees he headed upstream.

Sion kept moving for hours while he looked for somewhere to hide. The land gave way to thin brush and then woods which got thicker the further Sion travelled. And then he found what he wanted. From the stream's edge was a large flat rock leading up to a jumble of boulders and an isolated mass of rock about thirty feet high. All around was thick undergrowth and tall trees, impassable except along the stream. Getting off the horse, Sion led him out of the water and over the rock. Around the back was a patch of tall grass, well hidden from view, with enough fodder to keep the horse happy for a week. Sion tied the horse so that it couldn't wander, removed the saddle, tied the end of the lariat to the saddle horn, and with his guns over his shoulder, scrambled up the rock face. He pulled the saddle up after him, found shade behind a large boulder and thankfully lay down. Within moments he was asleep.

He awoke in the middle of night. He was shivering cold and had an empty, gnawing belly. His back and chest ached, his wrists pained him and his memories filled him with anguish. Eventually, he dropped into an uneasy, dream filled doze. He woke well before the dawn and lay listening to the sounds of the night; to the whispering of the wind rustled leaves, to the hoot of an owl and the burbling of the stream. He took a drink of water from his canteen and tried to sleep again. Whether it was from the cold or his hunger or both but after a few minutes he gave up, stood and stretched. Cautiously, he crept to the edge of the rock and looked down, studying the land in the moonlight. The moon was so far down the sky the deep shadows could have concealed an army. He listened but could hear nothing out of the ordinary. He unsnaked his lariat, made it fast around a large boulder and threw it over the edge. With a rifle slung over his shoulders and a six gun strapped to his side he climbed down to the ground. He stood for over twenty minutes studying the area while the moon vanished from sight. In the dark, just before the dawn, he crept deeper into the woods.

The sun had risen when he found what he thought was a rabbit's run and settled down to see if one came his way. Luck was with him and after less than an hour a big, fat buck came into sight. He took aim. His mouth was watering when he took up the slack on the trigger. Common sense suddenly prevailed. Any shot would be heard for miles. Slowly he lowered the gun and sat for some time, his head slumped between his shoulders, tears of frustration in his eyes. Finally, with a sigh, he rose and started back to the horse. Before blundering into the camp he examined the area until he was as sure as he could be that all was clear. He derided himself for his excessive caution because he knew in his heart of hearts, if they wanted to, the men could hide a few feet from him and he would never know they were there.

By now it was the middle of the morning and his stomach was rumbling in protest. He cut two feet off the lariat and tied a whipping in the end to stop it unravelling. He made his way back to the rabbit's run and, untwisting the rope into three strands, made a trap with the aid of a small, springy sapling. Now, thought Sion, as long as a stupid and blind rabbit blunders into it, he might get something to eat.

He returned to the stream and after a few minutes saw a number of trout swimming under a rock in a pool about four feet deep. For some time he sat and thought, occasional prods from his stomach stimulating his brain. He had nothing with which to make a hook, and the only line he had was the lariat. He thought about tickling trout but knew from past experience that he was hopeless at it. Damnation, he cursed himself for not having brought some of the fishing gear they'd had. There had been gut and hooks to spare. And he only wanted one hook and a short length of gut. He forced himself to think of a solution and not waste time cursing his stupidity. He thought of the stories of Bridger, Crocket, Bowie and the other plainsmen. It was in the back of his mind. There was something one of them had done. And then he remembered.

Back in the woods he down cut as many thin straight saplings as he could carry. He then followed the stream for about an hour until it widened out and was only about six inches deep. He started at one side and pushed a length of stick firmly into the stream bed every inch or so. He made numerous journeys into the woods to find more saplings. The sun was setting by the time he was finished. His back ached, and his feet were a cold, wrinkled, sore mess from being immersed in water for so long.

Sion lay down on the bank watching the water. He was so tired that after a few minutes he closed his eyes and the last thing he remembered was the sound of the water and the rustling of the trees.

Sion awoke with a start and lay for a few seconds recollecting his wits. He sat up, still groggy, to look into the trap and in the moonlight he thought his eyes were playing tricks on him. The pool was packed solid with fish. Eagerly, he got to his feet and waded in. Even with so many to grab they somehow had the knack of wriggling out of his hands and after a few minutes he still had nothing to show for his pains. He knelt down absolutely still, one hand in the water, palm up. A trout came and sat virtually in the middle of his hand. Sion closed his hand tightly, picked up the fish and broke its neck. He went through a similar routine twice more and clambered onto dry land.

He was considering returning to his camp when he changed his mind. Instead he went deeply into the woods and built a fire. He skewered the fish through their gills with a green stick and set them to roasting. The aroma made his mouth water and it took a superhuman effort not to eat them before they were cooked. When he could stand it no longer he took one of the half cooked trout and began stuffing his mouth with it. He finished the meal, was about to put out the fire and return to where he had tethered the horse when he paused. Why go back? He was safe here. Or as safe as he was anywhere. He banked the fire, lay down staring into the flames and was thinking about what he should do next when he fell asleep.

The sun, hidden from him by the trees and under-growth, was high in the sky when he finally woke up, feeling refreshed for the first time. Going down to the trap he saw there were so many fish they looked in danger of smothering one another. He caught another three, threw them onto the bank and then pulled out a few of the stakes. The fish streamed through the opening and he waited until it was almost empty before he replaced the stakes. He stoked the dying fire and grilled the trout on a hot stone. After two fish he could eat no more, so wrapped the third in large leaves and headed back for the horse.

Although feeling better he was still a long way short of being well. His ribs hurt like hell, his wrists were swollen and aching and he tired quickly. What should he do? He needed to rest, to regain his strength. He took the horse deeply into the woods and tied it up. He climbed a tree and then painstakingly clambered from tree to tree until the horse was no longer in sight. He tied himself to the branch of a high cottonwood and fell asleep.

After two days in the area of his trap Sion pulled up the sticks and headed further upstream. He had enough fish to last him at least three days although he was already getting sick and tired of speckled trout.

His breathing was becoming easier and the pain in his chest had reduced to an ache, turning to a sharp reminder only when he exerted himself. He was also getting used to sleeping in a tree with his lariat around his waist to prevent him falling. Although he saw no sign of being chased his fear made him continue with his precautions. For a few days rainstorms left him feeling like a drowned rat but also gave him hope that any sign he left was being washed away.

For over two weeks he wandered alongside the stream. When he came to the end of the woods he set his horse towards the east once more. It had been so long since he had escaped he now felt it was safe to use his rifle and one afternoon he shot a deer. His meal that evening was a feast of smoky, burnt and raw meat. He skinned the animal the next morning, scraped the skin as best he could and wrapped the best pieces of meat in it. Three days later he acknowledged the fact that the stink was more than he could stand and he buried what was left. From then on he shot only small animals like a rabbit and sometimes a wood pigeon or two.

Time became meaningless until with a shock he saw he was back on the plain. He was on a hillock, looking down on the vast expanse of grass he knew stretched to the Missouri. Somewhere up on his left was the Niobrara, though it occurred to him he might have passed the point where it joined the great Missouri. That night, under his bed of leaves and grass, he looked up at the myriad of stars and admitted to himself he was scared to leave the shelter of the woods. Would they still be looking for him? The thought haunted him to sleep.

He was awake before dawn, shivering, the light covering of leaves and grass not sufficient to keep out the heavy dew. He drank some water, wishing it was coffee, saddled the horse, carefully strapped one of the rifles across the back of the saddle and then climbed up himself. He checked his two six guns, his knife was at his side, and the other rifle was tied over his back, ready to be swung around, up to his shoulder and fired all in one fluid movement. An action he had practised ceaselessly. He sat the horse for a few minutes looking for any movement over the plains but could see nothing. It was so still not even the long grass was stirring.

He dug his spurs in and set off at a mad gallop, the only sound the pounding of the horse's hooves.

38

HE KEPT UP a breakneck speed for as long as possible. Finally, Sion was forced to slow to a canter and then a walk. He twisted his lips wryly, so far so good. He looked about him continuously, paying particular attention to the left and rear. Were they still searching? How long had it been? Sion couldn't tell. The nights were drawing in steadily and getting colder so it had to be either the end of September or the beginning of October. He wondered what his parents were doing. Was there anybody out looking for him? And if there was, what chance did they have of finding him? To his way of thinking, none. Therefore, he had to get to Sioux City on his own. How much further did he have to go? He had not travelled far in an easterly direction, which meant he still had most of his journey ahead of him. On the other hand his wrists had healed to ugly red scars, his ribs no longer hurt, and he was as lean as whipcord and just as tough. It surprised him how thin he was and now he could only keep his trousers up with his belt two notches tighter. He also had a scruffy thin beard, well past the itching stage of growth.

For three days he headed a few points north of east, his vigilance never relaxed, his fear alive within him. At nights he slept a couple of hours, woke, moved a few miles and settled down again. He thought of travelling at night and sleeping by day but decided against it. The anonymity of darkness was safer than daylight.

It was the middle of the morning when he saw the

ribbon of silver. Turning further to the north he broke the
horse into a canter, eager to get to the water. He needed
to refill his almost empty canteen and he wanted to wash
away the accumulated sweat and dirt. It was further than
he thought, an elusive glimpse from the top of a hillock,
but each time clearer and nearer. An hour before sunset
he arrived at the river. He stopped a few hundred yards
short and examined the area. He saw no sign of either
man or animal. But still he hesitated. So far Sion had
seen no sign of being followed but guessed that if they
were still looking for him it would be along the banks of
the river. They would need to ride back and forth over a
large distance until they cut his track.

He stayed where he was until the moonless night
wrapped him in a feeling of security and then cautiously
he made his way to the water's edge. It was so dark he
could see no further than a yard or two, but his ears were
strained for the slightest sound. He stopped at the bank
and waited a little longer. The water masked any small
noise he made, whether it was the creaking of the saddle
or the snorting of the horse. Sion walked the horse down
the bank and a couple of paces to the water, where the
horse eagerly drank. Sion sat there a while until he was
satisfied there was nobody about then he climbed down,
filled his canteen and only then took a drink. With the
sun gone, the night was cold and Sion changed his mind
about washing.

The next afternoon it happened. He was riding up the
brow of a low hill when he stopped to look back. He
saw nothing at first until a movement out of the corner
of his eye caught his attention. He thought it was back by
the copse he had passed half an hour earlier and had just
put it down to his imagination when he saw it again. His
heart missed a beat and then started hammering wildly.
Within a couple of minutes he saw three horsemen. Sick
with anticipation and fear he started the horse again,
fighting back the urge to gallop until he was out of

sight. As soon as he was over the skyline he broke into a mad, fast gallop. He kept looking back for signs of his followers and ten minutes later they came over the brow of a hill. It was almost a relief that they had found him. No more wondering, no more fear of a surprise attack. The worse thought that had haunted him was to have been taken alive.

The horse kept up the mad pace for sometime. The men behind him neither came closer nor dropped further back. Darkness fell rapidly and Sion was forced to bring his flagging mount to a walk. In the pitch black night it was foolhardy to try to go too fast. Sion took consolation in the fact that the men would be forced to slow down for the same reason. On the spur of the moment he turned the horse and headed back for the river. There were very few places to take cover where he was and if he did end up having to stop and fight, he wanted somewhere he could protect his back.

Sion kept the horse to a walk throughout the night, but with the first streaks of grey in the east and as the ground beneath took shape, Sion coaxed him into a gallop. The sun had risen when Sion saw the three horsemen again. With a shock he saw that they were barely three miles away and coming as fast as ever. With the river in sight Sion spurred the last ounce of effort out of his mount. He needed a place to stop and fight.

The distance closed between them. They were less than a mile away and Sion knew it was time to make a stand. Ahead, near the river bank, was a copse of trees. Griffiths' last stand, he said to himself. He now recognised the horsemen. The leader was in the middle, the one on his right seemed unharmed but the other was riding awkwardly.

Sion rode around the low hillock and the copse until he was out of sight on the other side. Pulling up the horse he tore off his rifles, some smoked meat he had prepared and his canteen. He slapped the horse's rump hard and with a pang of regret watched it canter on along the river's bank. Picking up his gear he ran back to the shelter of the trees and up the shallow incline. Carefully, he crawled the last few yards to the top. If they saw him now then his strategy would have been for nothing. The grass and bushes gave him shelter, the four tall elms shade, and a fallen trunk protection. They were now less than half a mile away and closing steadily.

It was cool in the shade after the heat of the plains and the gentle breeze was refreshing. After travelling all night Sion felt bone weary and his legs trembled slightly from the effort of gripping the horse for so long. He was nervous too, which was probably why the rifle was not quite steady in his hands.

He waited until they reached the foot of the hillock, less than a hundred yards away. Sion took aim at the leader, held his breath, took up the slack on the trigger and squeezed. Sion had concentrated so much on the man in the middle that he had not noticed the nearer man spur his horse and as Sion fired the other rider crossed into his sights and took the shot through the neck. Before he could get a second shot off there was nothing to aim at. Except the horses which, still surprised by the sudden lack of riders, kept on galloping. The man he had hit was lying, unmoving, half hidden by the grass. No movement betrayed the whereabouts of the other two. Sion strained his eyes but could see nothing. After about ten minutes he had the uneasy feeling they could be approaching from any direction and with a start he sat up to look about him. It was nearly the last thing he ever did as a bullet chipped a chunk out of the tree about his head. He ducked, lifted his rifle but could see nothing to fire back at.

It was a long day. Sion moved behind the fallen log from time to time and though occasionally a shot rang out making him duck he saw nothing to shoot at. They were playing on his nerves. He wanted to jump up and go screaming down at them, his gun blazing to get it over with once and for all. The quiet, the flowing river, the buzzing of insects was so soporific that, more than once, Sion caught himself nodding off. He would come awake with a jerk and look around frantically in case one of them had closed in on him. With his heart hammering and the adrenaline flowing he would be alert for a couple of minutes and then sink into a semi-stupor. By evening Sion realised he had to move. His biggest fear was falling asleep and being taken alive. He thought of suicide but now he had come so far he was determined to go down fighting. If he could stay awake long enough.

After leaving he had to make them think that he was still there. How was he to do that? Think fool, think, he told himself. If they couldn't see him they had to hear him. But hear him doing what? Coughing? Sneezing? Ridiculous. So what was left? A gun shot? But how? He looked at his rifles laid out at his feet, the two six guns on his thighs. He had his lariat, water, the canteen.

As part of his plan Sion began firing one shot at approximately fifteen minute intervals, not aiming at anything, just setting a pattern. In the hour before sunset he firmly fastened one of the rifles to the log and ran a strand of rope from the trigger to a bush. Next he tied his boot to the rope so that it dangled above the ground. He poured water from his canteen into the boot and when the canteen was half empty the weight in the boot caused the rope to tighten and the rifle to fire. He fixed the second rifle alongside the first and ran another strand of rope from the trigger to the bush. This time, it wasn't as tight. When he finished pouring the water from the canteen into the boot the second rifle fired. By now it was dark. He used the water from the boot to refill the canteen and hung the canteen over his boot. Next he dug a small hole in the bottom of the canteen and tried to gauge how fast the water seeped out. It didn't seem fast enough and so he enlarged it a little. As he finished, he heard a sound and panic-stricken he pulled out his two six shooters and blazed away in the direction he thought the noise had come from. There was no response and with shaking hands he refilled the guns. The wind freshened and caused the leaves above him to rustle and the grass to sway, fear of the unknown bringing him close to panic again.

Sion slipped silently down to the river's edge. The cold water made him gasp as he swam slowly out to the middle. He could feel the current sweeping him along. A shot rang out and he realised it was the first of his rifles firing. He began to swim the breast stroke to increase his speed away from the copse. Too soon, the second shot rang out.

Now he was fighting to keep his head above water. The guns on his hips were dragging him down. For some reason he had kept on the right boot and, full of water, it too was making swimming difficult. Holding his breath he struggled to remove the boot, gasping and spluttering as he did. Once it was off he found it easier to stay afloat. Ten minutes later he began to tire, the guns still weighing him down. Awkwardly, his fingers going numb with the cold, he untied the thongs around his legs, undid each buckle and with a sigh of regret let them fall. Now he felt he could stay afloat and let the current wash him downstream at least for the remainder of the night. But soon afterwards tiredness and cold crept through him and he knew he had to land.

Sion swam towards the other bank. He had been in the water over two hours and the cold was sapping his strength. With despair, in the faint light from the sliver of moon, Sion saw that the bank was a good three feet above his head and that there was no way he could reach it. He kept going but there was no change to the bank. Sion could feel his strength ebbing and thought he was going to drown. Kicking became harder, his feet dropped and he held his breath. It was a shock when his feet hit the river bed and his head stayed above the water. His tired brain got the message and he stood in about four feet of water, his legs like rubber, shivering hard. He waded in closer to the bank and found the water down to his waist but the top of the bank was still out of reach. He waded further downstream and eventually the bank dipped a little closer and he decided to try and climb out. He scrabbled at the bank, grabbing at roots and tufts of grass his feet dislodging stones and earth behind him. With the last of his strength he dragged the upper half of his body onto the bank. He stayed still for some minutes, too exhausted to move and in danger of falling back. He gathered his strength and rolled onto the bank, gasping and shivering, unable to move. He drifted into a half sleep, half unconscious state, haunted by nightmares and what would happen when the men caught up with him. He was still there when the sun rose, warming his body and drying his clothes.

When he awoke Sion had a muggy headache and a dry mouth. It took a few seconds to remember what had happened but as memory flooded back he sat up quickly to look around. He saw nobody and with a sigh of relief sank back down. He had to move from where he was, but how? No horse, no boots, and no guns. Only a knife with which to protect himself. Move he told himself, move. Stifling a groan, he got to his feet and began walking from the river. Once they discovered the trick he had played on them they would be after him again. On foot it would not take them long to catch up. They would see where he had gone ashore and have him before the day was over. His walking faltered and then he stopped altogether. This was not the way. It had to be by river, but how? More swimming? Find a place to hide? At least if he hid he wouldn't be leaving any tracks.

Reluctantly he returned to the bank and for a few seconds stood looking down at the swirling water, cold and uninviting. He jumped in, the shock making him gasp. He swam to the centre and let the current take him again. Soon the cold began to take a toll of his strength. When he could go no further he headed towards the southern bank. He hoped that if they rode both sides of the river they would find where he had gone ashore. The other would cross and thinking Sion was armed would surely follow carefully. Sion's tracks would lead them in a semi-circle back to the river and there would be a further delay while one of them crossed again. Then there was the difficulty they would have in climbing the banks on either side, especially with horses. In fact, the more Sion thought about it the better it looked if he could just find the energy to go back and forth a few more times. There was even a chance he could survive until night fall. He did not try and think further ahead than that.

He needed to get out of the water but the bank was too high. Then around a bend he saw the tops of trees near the waters edge and he made for them, hoping to find a way out. When he got there he found a tumbled down mess of nature, with two trees collapsed and in the water. They were prevented from being swept downstream by an old and withered root embedded in the bank. The bank was washed away from underneath and it looked to Sion that the third tree was on the verge of falling in. The idea flooded into his mind when he heard the horse's hooves. He quickly pushed his way through the rotten roots and climbed under the bank.

On the other bank he saw one of the men galloping past. He heard another horseman riding overhead. The earth trembled and for a fearful moment Sion thought the bank was going to collapse on top of him as earth and small stones rained down. Then they were past and Sion breathed easily again.

The squeaking made him look over his shoulder to the ledge about two feet further back and he had to suppress a shudder and a yell of horror when he saw the grey sleek bodies of water rats. There were over a dozen of them, running back and forth, stopping and staring at Sion's white face. Taking solace in the fact that they

were probably more frightened of him than he was of
them he turned away, to keep an eye out for his pursuers.
The water was up to his waist and the warmth drained
out of his legs taking his strength with it.

The day passed slowly. When it was dark Sion left his
bolt hole and crawled back through the roots of the trees.
Outside, he climbed onto one of the fallen trees and felt
his way around. He found the root that appeared to be
holding the trees in position and began hacking at it with
his knife. Either the root was tougher than he thought
or his knife was blunter, because it took him a good hour
to get through the wood, but finally it parted. Nothing
happened.

Sion sat still for a few minutes, expecting the tree to
move. When it did not he placed his feet against the bank
and pushed with all his strength but to no avail. He could
have cried with frustration. He got off the trunk and this
time put his back to the bank and his feet on the tree.
He strained as hard as he could and just as he was about
to give up he felt the trunk move. He rested for a few
minutes and tried again, this time he pushed until the
blood pounded in his temples and his head span. Then
it shifted. At first an inch, then two, then Sion's feet shot
out in front of him and the two tree trunks were picked
up by the current, slowly at first, but as they drifted out
towards the centre of the river they picked up speed.

Sion rested for a few moments then slid into the
water. He swam quickly, reached his makeshift raft, and
pulled himself on. For a while he lay still, too exhausted
to move.

The trees were well and truly interlocked and quite
steady. The biggest of them, close to two feet in diameter
had a clump of roots at one end. Sion crawled along to the
roots and settled down in the small cradle they fashioned
and quickly fell asleep.

He awoke with the sun in his eyes and a gentle rocking
motion which caused him to smile with self satisfaction.

Lifting his head he looked to right and left but could see no movement on the banks, the nearest to the south only fifteen yards away. He was laying on earth and mud that had come away with the roots and now he began digging with his hands and placing the earth on either side of him. When he had finished he had hollowed out his cradle so he was hidden from the banks when laying out flat. Satisfied, he settled down to sleep again, ignoring the pangs of hunger from his protesting stomach.

This time when he awoke it was late afternoon and he was still near the middle of the river. He carefully looked about him and when he was satisfied no-one was watching he drank some water. He guessed he was doing between two and three miles an hour which over a day made for steady progress in the right direction. His clothes had dried on him and he had stopped shivering. Night fell with no change to his gentle movement and under the stars, in spite of the cold, he drifted into an uneasy sleep.

It was only after the sun came up and he was warm once more that he could sleep properly for a few hours. He did not feel the different movement of the trees, the slight jerk as he came to a stop on the end of a rope. Nor was he aware of the change of direction as he was pulled inexorably to the southern bank.

Something woke him, though he did not know what and he sat up to look across ten yards of water and a length of lariat to see the breeds sitting on their horses, one with the end of the rope around his pommel. Both men were looking directly at Sion, no expression on their faces, their guns laying casually across their laps. Sion felt a bitter frustration having come so far. If he was captured it had been his intention to plunge his knife into his neck rather than be taken alive. He did not have the courage. Instead, Sion prepared to fight.

'Your death will last forever,' the leader said, throwing down his rifle and pulling out a knife.

The trees hit the bottom and Sion jumped into the shallow water. He waded ashore and stood with his knife held awkwardly in his hand, his body leaning forward. His opponent suddenly darted forward, his knife sliced through Sion's forearm and blood oozed through the three inch gash. For the next fifteen minutes that was the way of it. Sion was unable to touch the man whilst cut after cut went into Sion. He was getting dizzy, and his vision was blurring when he stumbled and fell to his hands and knees. The breed moved in slowly and Sion knew it was all over. He found the courage from somewhere and lifted the knife to plunge it into his neck when it was torn from his grasp.

Sion looked up at the man and said: 'Please . . . kill me.'

A shot rang out and the man's head disintegrated in blood, skull and gore. Another shot knocked the other man off his horse. Sion turned his head and saw three more bullets pluck at the inert body. He looked back, wiped the sweat from his eyes and could have sworn he saw his father and David running towards him. He thought he saw an Indian walking sedately behind them when he passed out.

BOOK 5

David's Story

39

SION SAID LATER he thought he had been hallucinating. He also apologised for his tears but we could understand his reaction. Clive Fleetfoot had some sort of herbal, foul smelling stuff to put on Sion's cuts which Sion said made him feel cool. We stayed where we had found him for a couple of days telling each other our stories.

We explained to Sion that it was not a fluke we had arrived when we did, though luck got us there in time to save his life.

We knew most of Sion's story thanks to the incredible powers of Clive. With few errors Clive had told us what had happened by reading the sign, as he called it, both up on the butte and later when we tried to find Sion. Sion was surprised to learn that it was the second week of October, but he did say he thought the leaves on the trees were losing some of their green and he had wondered.

A week before he had been due to leave for Harvard we began to keep a watch for them. By the middle of the week Dad had been cursing them and Mam getting worried. On the weekend Dad had sent a telegram to Harvard explaining that Sion, Bill and Steve would be late. He sent another to Steve's parents informing them of the situation and that if the boys didn't appear by Monday he was going to go looking for them.

'That was when I told those idiots I was working for that I was going with Dad,' I grinned at Sion. 'They were glad to see me go and told me that under the circumstances, as they had no idea when I'd be back it was only fair I gave in my notice. I did so, gladly.' I reached over to the coffee pot and refilled all the cups.

'I've been dreaming about having coffee to drink instead of water,' said Sion, looking at his mug, 'but now I've got some, I don't see what I was missing,' he grimaced. 'Or is it just the way you make it?' he asked me.

'That's it exactly. Anyway, on the Tuesday we caught the train for Sioux. It didn't take us long to get from the livery man that you hadn't returned. We asked around town and, who was it Dad? The girl in the eating house?' Dad nodded. 'She had overheard you talking and she told us you were going up the river and crossing at O'Toole's Ferry.'

'Where?' Sion asked.

'Where one of you pushed the mule onto that rickety ferry.' Sion nodded. 'The old man told us about it. He also said that it had been so long ago he only remembered you because of the mule. It was while we were there that we met Clive Fleetfoot.' At the mention of his name Clive gave a big toothless grin, nodded and went back to shredding his chicken, the only way he could eat it.

'Luckily,' said Dad, 'I had the forethought to bring enough gold with me to bribe an army to look for you.'

'We decided to stay the night at the crossing and leave first thing in the morning.'

'You forgot to tell him about Pinker,' Dad reminded me.

'Oh yes, him. In Sioux we hired a so-called scout who claimed all sorts of tracking powers and woodcraft knowledge. He turned out to be worse than useless and when Clive came on the scene we told him to get lost. In fact, meeting Clive was the best, single bit of luck you can imagine. See, Clive had seen your sign a few weeks back near the Niobrara River. He also knew where the half breeds had taken you. He knew all about them and told us what they wanted you for. You can imagine our

reaction. We had a choice to make; either to go back to
town and get enough men to get vengeance, or rush like
mad after you in the faint hope we would be in time
to help. Dad decided on rushing after you. He gave old
Clive here a hundred dollars in gold and a promise of
another two hundred if we were in time to save any or
all of you. Boy, did we ride hard. Clive says the gang are
well known amongst the tribes and the outlaws that live
further west. We must have been about half way to the
butte when we detoured north to a ranch Clive knows and
there we changed horses and bought another three. That
way we could change mounts when they were beginning
to tire . . .'

'Hang on a minute,' Sion interrupted. 'Since when
could you ride, Dad?'

'I needed to ride to help with my electioneering for
Congress. Just as well under the circumstances.'

'Unfortunately, the ranch owner was in the middle of
branding and couldn't spare any men to come with us
though he did say if we were too late then he and his
men would help to wipe the gang out once and for all.
When we got to the butte we went in slow like, spread
out and real quiet. It was Clive who saw the buzzards
first, flapping around the top. You wouldn't believe his
eye sight Sion, it's remarkable. Anyway, seeing them
we rode straight in. We left the horses at the bottom
and climbed the pathway.' I paused, the horror of what
we found washing freshly through my memory. 'Clive
worked out what had happened and what you've told us
coincides with what he said. Except he couldn't figure
where you had gone. He was adamant that you had gone
over the edge. The trouble was we couldn't see your body
from up there. We buried what the buzzards had left of
Bill but . . .'

'But I wouldn't let him bury the breeds,' Dad said.
'They deserve to be picked clean by the buzzards. I
only wish I could have got my hands on them before

they died.' Dad's voice was steady but intense. I knew how he felt. Having been with Dad all the time I hadn't noticed any change in him, but Sion said he seemed to have aged ten years. Sion pointed out the grey in Dad's sideburns which I hadn't noticed before. The going had been rough on both of us but especially for Dad. Though like I told Sion, if anybody had changed, it was him. There was now a hardness, a toughness to him. And I didn't mean physical toughness either. It was a mental toughness that showed itself in small ways. From the way Dad sometimes looked at him I guessed he saw it too. Even then I knew there was no question of him going to Harvard.

'We went back down the butte, searched around the bottom, found Paddy and Steve and buried them. We found the man you'd killed. Clive couldn't see how you had got there but after he explained what he read in the sign it was Dad who suggested you had somehow flown down on a kite. Clive clearly thought Dad was mad and, I must admit, I was pretty sceptical myself. That must have been something. Weren't you scared?'

Sion thought for a few seconds. 'I dunno really. I am now I think about it. But I was more scared of being caught. When death is the best solution anything else fades into insignificance. Know what I mean?'

I shook my head. 'Most importantly though, we knew you were alive.'

'What about the horses?' asked Sion. 'The ones up on the butte?'

'The gang had brought them down, hobbled them and left them in the long grass. We cut them loose and scattered them,' said Dad. 'One of the men had stayed on the butte for a couple of weeks, injured according to Clive, and then went to find the other two. In fact we found his body where you shot him. He had some bad burns on his hands and body.'

Sion nodded. 'I did that when I fired their tents.'

'Just as well,' said Dad, 'otherwise we would never have found you.'

'That's right Sion,' I said. 'See, it had rained a short while after we left the butte. But then we cut the tracks of the man who'd stayed behind and presumably he was going to a prearranged meeting place with the other two. We realised, or I should say Clive told us, that they couldn't find you and were still looking.' I broke off the story to exclaim, 'You should see him working Sion, he's incredible! Honestly, I wouldn't even be able to tell a herd of buffalo had passed while Clive can tell where an ant has peed!' Clive obviously liked the analogy because he gave a wide grin.

'We, or again I should say Dad, decided we would keep on their trail in case they led us to you. Trouble was we had more rain and the sign was washed out again. So then Dad decided to search for them and kill them before they got to you.'

'You know,' said Sion, 'I can't help wondering why they tried so hard and so long. It doesn't make sense, I could have been anywhere.'

'We wondered about that too,' said Dad. 'Not even Clive could give us a proper answer. We think that you had become an obsession with them.'

I continued, 'By accident we came across their sign near the river and then yours. We came hell for leather after you. We saw where you ambushed them and then we followed their tracks. We could see the knife fight but if we had just charged straight in then they might have killed you before we got close enough. Clive told us that the man was only playing with you.'

'Sorry, son. Perhaps I could have saved you a few of those cuts but Clive was adamant they would not be killing you so easily. It was he who shot the one through the head. He's got some sort of hollowed ammunition that blows anything apart. David and I shot the other one. And that's the story. Now all we've got to do is get you home to your mother. She's probably out of her mind with worry. We need a telegraph office as soon as possible.'

There was a pause and then Dad said, 'Son, I'm sorry about Bill and the others. It must have been a hell of a thing to go through.'

Sion nodded slowly. About the only part of Sion that wasn't cut was his face. His arms, hands, chest and back had been sliced. The cuts were not very deep nor long but there were so many of them he had lost a lot of blood. When we moved Sion complained that they were beginning to itch like buggery. A good sign according to Clive. He accompanied us back to O'Toole's Ferry but left us there before we crossed.

'With three hundred dollars gold I rich man,' he said. 'I go live with my wives and have plenty kids. No more have to work.'

'Just make sure no robbing white man comes and steals it from you,' Dad warned with a grin.

We sent a telegram from Sioux City and arrived back in St Louis on the 22 October. There were tears from Mam when we got off the train and a wooden smile from Sion. He left it to me and Dad to tell her what had happened. He had been okay while we were in the outback and even in the hotel in Sioux City. But now the nightmares started and he would wake up in the middle of the night screaming, or yelling Bill's name and sometimes Paddy's or Steve's. It was Mam who helped him the most. She understood that he should not keep it all bottled up. It was only when he woke in the nights that he would open up and then she would sit with him for as long as he wanted, talking. Afterwards he would go back to sleep and then get up at all times of the day. He spent a lot of time with the horse he had escaped on which we had found further along the river bank after we found Sion. He would talk to that damned horse for hours.

One day Mam told me to get rid of the horse before Sion came down. I sold it to a farmer I met in town and returned to the house worried how Sion would react. Mam and he were in the middle of a yelling match in which she screamed as loud as he did. Finally he accepted that the horse had to go. After that his nightmares became less and less frequent until they all but disappeared.

One thing Dad had insisted upon, no mention was to be made of the others being tortured. When their families came, Sion had a story to tell of how their sons had died killing some of the gang. It was no consolation to Steve's parents but it seemed to help Paddy's a little. They wanted to know how Sion had survived and their boys had not. Sion just shrugged and said it was luck. With Dad's assurances that the boys had received a Christian burial they returned home. Once that ordeal was over there was more chance for Sion to recover, but for all that he stayed changed. He had a restlessness about him which Dad and Sonny began channelling into the business.

I was also working for Dad now, giving legal advice when he wanted it, though I suspected he had already spoken to John Driscole. Dad was more and more involved with matters of state and was having to leave the business to Sonny. Sion began to work all sorts of crazy hours, reading old files, pouring over figures and making financial calculations. One day he rode out of town leaving a note to say he would be back in a week. In fact he was away ten days. When he returned he brought completed plans to expand into three other towns simultaneously. Realising work was the best therapy for him, Dad gave his approval provided Sion and I entered into the partnership using the money we still had from our inheritance from Uncle James. Sonny was given a ten percent stake and we had fifteen percent each, leaving control with Dad. As soon as the partnership was formalised Sion was off again. It was that spring when I became thoroughly discontented. The year was 1904.

*　　*　　*

I couldn't settle down and I couldn't get enthusiastic about work. I knew that both my family and Gunhild's were waiting for me to make an honest woman of her but I didn't want to. It was not that I did not love her, because I did, madly. It was not that we had any rows or anything like that, in fact, far from it. Oh, we used to argue about religion and a bit of politics but really we were as happy together as any two people can be. I just had to get away and do my own thing for a while. That was all there was to it. Since I could remember, I had worked hard to pass exams and get on. I had done all the right things, now I wanted to do what I wanted to do.

It was only fair that I told Gunhild first. It was a Saturday when I went over to her parent's house for dinner. Usually, I stayed the night, because it was such a long ride home, sharing a room with one of her brothers. After dinner, as we often did, we went for a walk along the lane. It was cold on that last day of March and she had a shawl around her shoulders.

'Gunhild, I eh, I want to tell you something.'

'And what might that be? Let me guess. It can only be one of two things. The first is to ask me to marry you, the second is that you're going away for a while. And if it was the former, knowing you, you would have taken me to Joseph's, and dined me royally and then proposed. Therefore, I suppose you want to tell me that you're going away.'

I put my arms around her shoulders and drew her to me. 'It won't be for long. Six months at the most. I just need to go and do something before I settle down.'

She nodded. The moon shone down on her upturned face and I could see the tears glistening in the corners of her eyes. I kissed her gently and then more passionately. After a few moments she broke away, took my hand and led me back to the barn. We made love. It was a while afterwards she said in a matter of fact voice: 'I think you'd better go now. When are you leaving?'

'Soon. I'm taking a boat to New Orleans. After that I don't know where I'll go. South America perhaps.'

We stood close together and she suddenly clutched me tightly. After a few seconds she pushed me away from her and ran to the house. I stood there like an idiot, not knowing what to do. When the door closed behind her I got my horse and started home. Women, I thought. Christ, anybody would think I was going for good. I shook my head and kicked the horse into a gallop. I would never understand women.

Telling Mam and Dad was just as bad.

'Dave,' said Dad, 'with all my work in Government I have less and less time to devote to the business. With the expansion you're needed here more than ever. Sion is young and headstrong. You're needed to keep him on the straight and narrow. And with your training and knowledge you'll be invaluable.'

I shook my head obstinately.

'Please, Dave, reconsider,' said Mam. 'What about Gunhild? What about all the education you've had? All the . . .' she trailed off.

'Look, Mam don't tell me about the sacrifices you and Dad made in Wales. We know, we remember and we're grateful. But that doesn't leave us in your debt for life does it? Or does it? Is that what you think?' I asked more harshly than I intended.

'Of course it doesn't,' said Dad, equally harsh, 'and nobody has ever suggested it. You've both been brought up to be your own men without any obligation to us.'

'Christ, Dad, anybody would think I was going forever or something. All I want is to go and do what I want to do, as I keep saying, for six months or so. Is that so unreasonable?' When they hesitated I continued. 'I remember Wales vividly. I remember what it was like and I know how far you've brought us from those days. But did you do it so that Sion and I would have to be slaves to work and money? Or was it in part because it would give us a freedom of choice? Please, it's important to me to go away for a while.'

'Yes and do what? Tell me that,' Mam said in a more reasonable voice.

'Anything that isn't academic. Anything that doesn't involve books and the law and writing and clients. Just anything I feel like, okay?' I said more belligerently than I intended.

'What will you do about money? I thought you put every penny into the business,' Dad said.

'I put in all I had left from Uncle James' legacy. The same as Sion, in fact. But I've been working long enough and I've saved some of what I've earned. Altogether I have just over a thousand dollars. More than enough to live on, in fact live very well. Which is why I'm taking tomorrow's ferry for New Orleans.'

That night I pulled out my old atlas. Battered and torn I remembered the many hours I'd spent in Llanbeddas day dreaming about America and travelling the world. I thought of Sian and wondered what she would be like if she were alive today. One day I'd go back.

There was no more argument and they all came to see me off the next day. Gunhild didn't appear and when the hooter sounded and we cast off I had a heavy heart, standing alone at the rail, waving goodbye. It was irrational because I did not intend being away for very long.

I had a few drinks in the saloon followed by a tough steak which I helped down with a bottle of red, vinegary wine, supposedly all the way from France. After a few more large brandies, more than a little drunk, I went to find my cabin.

It was one deck down, decorated with a floral wallpaper, and had room for a single bed, a wardrobe and behind a curtain, a tub. The tub was filled and emptied by an old and wizened black man, who said his name was Moses. He told me he looked after a dozen cabins on the deck and his duties included cleaning, making the beds, putting away clothes, seeing to the bath, shining shoes, pressing clothes and a few more jobs I did not quite catch. I was sitting on the edge of the bed and when I leaned back was almost instantly asleep. I guess another of his jobs was to remove boots.

I felt more than a bit lonely to start with. The Mississippi is a big, wide and muddy river, and also a busy one. There were always boats and barges moving up and down, though they kept clear of the deep draught, paddle-wheel boats which sailed like Queen Dowagers along the deeper water channels, imperiously clearing the lesser fry away from their path. It took two weeks to get to New Orleans where I walked disconsolately down the gangplank and on to the wharf. There was so much happening, so much excitement in the air, that I optimistically went to look for a quiet hotel not too far from the waterfront.

I found a place, a kind of poor carpetbagger's hotel, as I described it in a letter to Gunhild. It had two floors with six bedrooms, a communal bathroom at one end and served food which was renowned for its mediocrity. After two dinners there I had learned my lesson, and from then on I went to different taverns and inns around the town, mostly down by the water front. I was advised by the hotel owner that I was going to a rough area. I told him I would rather take my chances with the unknown of the waterfront, than risk the certainty of food poisoning. After that he never spoke to me except to coldly say good-day when he gave me my room key. He was right of course. Some of the places were not suitable for me to enter and it might have been bravado that made me visit them. Looking back I think it was more akin to stupidity. Smooth talk and a generous buying of drinks usually calmed any potential antagonists. Some of the stories those men had to tell were incredible. Most of them were seamen sailing to Africa, Britain, or the Far East. From one week to the next nobody knew who was going to be in any bar. They came and they went, and the ones who replaced them were like the ones who had gone and so the same people seemed to stay forever.

The truth was that apart from sitting in those foul-smelling, smoke filled rooms for an evening and often staying there until the dawn I did nothing. In spite of missing Gunhild I was not tempted by the painted prostitutes who solicited me for my trade and they soon learned to leave me alone. I had been there for two months when, very drunk one night, I made up my mind to take a ship to Africa, working my passage and returning six months later. The next day I changed my mind when I learned more about how much I would be paid and the sort of conditions I would have to live and work under. It scared me silly.

I was in one particular den called the 'Gut to Throaters' when I met Jake Kirkpatrick. He was a big, scrawny man with huge hands like shovels and a lopsided grin. He looked as though he found the human race an object of derision. Only when I met him he was not smiling. What happened was that I, minding my own business as usual, got to the bar and ordered a dark rum and a beer. The Gut to Throaters was a long, low room in the basement of a whore house. One wall was taken up with a bar running the whole length with three sweat stained men behind trying to cure the thirst of half a hundred or so seamen. If there was any decor it could not be seen through the smoke and gloom of the hanging lamps. Tables, chairs and men packed the place, with about a dozen women, who from the frequency with which they were going through the back door were doing a brisk trade. It fascinated me the time they took. So far the quickest had been a young lad who was out and back in three and a half minutes. From his smirk when he returned he had not been disappointed, though I did wonder what she had done in such a short time. I never did find out.

I was minding my own business and looking the place

over, sipping my drinks, one in each hand, when this
drunken oaf knocked into me and sent the glasses flying
to the floor.

'Careful,' I yelled over the din, putting a steadying
hand out to him. I had lost many a drink that way and
I expected to lose a lot more. It was the price paid for
being in such a dump.

The man turned to face me. He was about six inches
taller, broad and had a huge fat gut hanging over his
belt like a roll of whale's blubber. 'Whar yer say?' he
scowled at me.

'Nothing,' I yelled back. 'Let me get you a drink,' I
offered. I could see that he was spoiling for a fight.
I turned and yelled for a barman. It was inevitable that I
would meet a man who could not be bought off with a
drink, or turned easily from his purpose, which, in this
case, was to murder me, or at least cripple me. So it
was not totally unexpected when he caught hold of my
shoulder and swung me around. His arm was back and
his fist clenched to knock me into next week, which
he would have done if he had connected. Not only
did I duck but as the momentum of his swing brought
him staggering closer I hit him with all my strength in
his fat belly. I could not believe it. I had spent years
playing football, was still pretty fit and I knew I had
muscle when I needed it. My fist sank in like it was
dough and he hardly blinked. Perhaps he had taken
on so much alcohol he was immune to pain. I only
knew I suddenly wished one of two things. The first
that I was somewhere else, or the second that I too,
was immune.

I followed up my first blow with a second, aimed
roughly at the same spot. The effect was the same. I
stepped back hastily, realising he had recovered from his
first swipe at me and was steadying himself for another.
I then encountered a further problem. It was so packed
there was not room to step back anywhere. His left hand

was about to close over my shirt front and haul me to meet his swinging fist when I caught his wrist, swung him around and pushed him as hard as I could, my foot up his backside.

40

HE WENT SPRAWLING into a group of equally drunk
men and for the first time others began to take notice
of what was happening. I wish they had not bothered,
because all it meant was they yelled, pushed each other
into a rough circle with me and fatso in the middle and
screamed for blood – my blood. I had hoped to be able to
push my way through the crowd before fatso recovered
but now there was no chance.

There were cries of 'Gut him Eric,' 'Slice his balls
off,' 'Cut his throat,' and other similar expressions, all
of which scared me to death.

One thing I had learned from football, in which my
speciality had been place kicking, was the follow through.
We had been taught to kick as though what mattered
was the top of the trajectory of the foot, and the fact
we contacted a ball mid-way was incidental. I couldn't
beat this oaf with my fists, of that I had no doubt. If he
was as impervious to a kick as he was to a blow in the
guts then I could say goodbye to life. I did not wait for
him to come to me. I moved in to get the range right. I
put more behind that kick than I ever did at university,
even when going for a match kick.

He did not scream. I don't think he could. He went
a sort of puce and green colour and collapsed in a
heap on the ground, his hands clutched in front of
him. There was a sort of stunned silence while the
knowledge that their champion had been defeated sunk
into their pickled brains. Then the clamour started and,

contrary to my expectation, they did not acclaim me but
howled for my blood. Before I could do more than blink,
a swarthy fellow, a bit shorter than me, with bow legs
and an earring, stepped into the circle and faced me. The
crowd clapped and cheered.

While they dragged the fat man unceremoniously out
of the way the man said: 'Mo'sieur, he was my friend. I
shall take his place.'

'I don't have any quarrel with you,' I replied and turned
my back on him. The trouble was there was nowhere to
go. The sea of faces before me was not going to let me out.
Resignedly I turned back. That was when he produced a
wicked looking knife and held it in front of him in a way
that convinced me he knew how to use it.

'That's it Frenchy, give the ponce what for,' said a
voice. More yelled similar lines of encouragement. None
were directed at me.

Now I was really scared. Frenchy looked sober whereas
the fat man had been so drunk he could hardly stand.
Frenchy also knew I could use my feet to good effect,
so I would not have much chance to do that again. I did
the only thing I could think of. I backed away. Those
behind gave a little and a few more paces I realised why.
I stopped at the bar.

I had made up my mind to jump the bar and make for
the back door, the one the whores used, when another
man intervened.

'That'll do Frenchy,' he said in a quiet voice. 'Leave
him be. He ain't done you no harm. So leave it.'

'Aww, c'mon Jake,' Frenchy whined. 'Just let's us
have a bit of fun, that's all. He ain't not'ing but a dude
what got no rite in zis bar.'

'Maybe, but leave it. If you don't, you can try taking
me on.'

There were a number of loud protests but no one person
was heard above the rest.

'None of you liked Fat Hugh. He's had that coming

for a long time and you all know it. You,' he pointed at me, 'come here.'

Fearing another trick I didn't move but braced myself for my play.

'Don't jump the bar sonny,' he said. 'You won't stand a chance. But you will if you come here and follow me out.' He suddenly clamped his hand over Frenchy's wrist and effortlessly squeezed. Frenchy's eyes popped and the knife clattered to the floor.

I had no choice: I went with him. Following him, a path opened up like the Red Sea rolling back for Moses, and in an atmosphere of hostility, expecting a knife in my back any second, we climbed the stone steps and into the fog laden night.

We walked a few yards in silence and then my rescuer said, 'I leave you here. I go this way. If I was you I wouldn't go down there again. The Gut to Throaters isn't a place for the likes of you.'

'Hey look, let my buy you a drink and say thank you. That's the least I can do. Come on man, I probably owe you my life,' I took hold of his arm. 'Come on. It isn't every day a man gets to thank somebody for his life. You pick the spot and I'll buy the best drink money can buy.'

He hesitated a moment and then gave his lop-sided grin. 'Hell, why not? It's an offer to drown my sorrows in and I won't have another chance.'

'Good. Where shall we go?'

'You did mean it about the best money could buy?'

'Sure,' I said in an expansive frame of mind.

'Okay, let's go to the Carlton.'

'Eh, eh . . . okay. Except we aren't exactly dressed right for the Carlton.' It was the smartest, best and most expensive place in New Orleans and that was saying some.

'Don't worry about that,' he replied. 'There's a back bar where no mind is paid to the way you look, only to the colour of your money.'

I followed him in silence. We went past the imposing entrance to the best known hotel in the Southern States and through a side door. We descended a short flight of steps, Jake knocked on a door, an eye appeared at a spy hole, Jake murmured something and we entered. It was a cellar, I presumed part of the hotel, with a small bar, a few tables and chairs and not too many patrons.

'Smiley, give us a bottle of best French and two Champagne,' said my companion to the dour faced man behind the bar. The man looked at me quizzically. 'He's all right – have I ever let you down before?' With a shrug Smiley turned to get our drinks. Twenty dollars was expensive but under the circumstances I didn't mind.

'My name is David Griffiths,' I held out my hand.

'Jake Kirkpatrick,' he replied, shaking my hand. 'Let's grab a table.' He led me to a corner and we sat down.

'What is this place?' I asked.

'It's a part of the Carlton, like I told you. Here the drinks are exactly what you can buy upstairs, a lot cheaper and with no fancy frills,' he paused. 'Also it's run by the management but the owners don't see the profits, if you get my meaning.'

I got his meaning.

Smiley thumped the bottles and cut glass tumblers in front of us with a frown in response to my thanks.

Jake mixed brandy and Champagne in equal amounts, filling the glasses to the brim. 'Cheers,' he said, lifted the glass and drained it. I tentatively sipped mine and looked at him in awe. 'I intend getting blind, legless drunk and when they sweep me out I shall wake up in the gutter sometime tomorrow and remember you made it possible,' he grinned humourlessly.

I shrugged and tried a mouthful. I half choked, much to his amusement. After a few more tries it seemed to slip down easier, though I can't claim to have kept pace with Jake. At some stage I passed out.

When I did come to a hundred little men were inside my

head trying to get out. The world about me was creaking and moving in a most peculiar manner and I felt sicker than I could remember. I think I groaned.

'You're alive,' somebody said in a cheerful tone. I opened my eyes the smallest fraction and tried to identify the person. It took a few moments. Jake somebody or other. It took a few more seconds to recollect the night before but no matter how I tried I could not remember anything after we arrived at the Carlton. The secret bar I told myself, pleased I could remember that much. I croaked and then tried again. 'Where am I?' I managed with some effort. 'Christ, I feel sick.'

'Feel free. I no longer own her so puke to your hearts content.' He spoke with a great deal of bitterness.

Somehow I sat up, holding my head tightly to prevent it falling off. I looked about me and then closed my eyes quickly.

'Is this a boat?' I asked with what I thought was inordinate intelligence considering my condition.

'Yep, that's right. The Lucky Lady. Registered New Orleans and stolen from me by legal shenanigans. The bastards.'

'If it was legal then it wasn't stealing,' I defended the law.

'It was stolen – but I don't know how, by a fast, smart talking lawyer,' he paused. 'I'll make you a coffee. You'll have time to drink it before the Sheriff gets here and throws us off.'

The coffee was strong and bitter but not destined to stay in my stomach. I just made it up top when I vomited. Another coffee and the room stopped spinning, a third and I could think, after a fashion. 'Why are you having the boat taken off you?' I asked, finally.

He shrugged. 'All I know was that after I thought I'd made my last payment the deputy came here, said I had to appear in court and gave me a paper. I didn't know what was going on so I went thinking there was a mistake. When I got there I was told I still owed another payment and as I hadn't paid the boat was forfeited. I kicked up hell and asked for more time but it didn't get me anywhere. So now I lose her.'

'Didn't you get a lawyer to help?'

'What good is a smart-arsed lawyer? All it would have meant was more bills. And anyway I had to pay the money to one of the biggest lawyers in town – so I supposed he knew the law all right.'

'Didn't it occur to you he might have been using the law to his own ends?' I asked, irritated with such stupidity.

He shrugged. 'I guess it did occur to me but I didn't have a brass nickel to do anything about it. Anyway, there wouldn't be anybody in this town that would buck him.'

'What's his name?'

'Neil Guinn.'

I nodded in understanding. I had seen and heard his name around; it seemed that he was one of the biggest and sharpest lawyers in the State, if not in a lot of states.

'Didn't anybody tell you that you had another instalment to make?'

'A what?' Jake asked, sipping his scalding hot and hair curling strong coffee.

'Didn't anybody tell you there was another payment to make?'

'No, they didn't,' he thought for a moment. 'I only heard, when I got to court.'

'Hmm, I see. Look, something isn't right about all this. I don't deny you may owe money but the way things have happened it seems to me you're being taken for a ride.'

'What would you know about it?'

'I, em, I'm a lawyer myself.'

I did not see what was so funny. I think it must have been my indignant look that stopped him sufficiently to ask, 'Are you joking?'

'No, I'm damned well not,' I retorted with some heat.

He picked up my hands and looked at them critically. 'I saw last night you weren't used to hard work.'

'Believe me it's just as hard to work with your brains as it is with your brawn,' I replied acidly.

'I'm not arguing. Still. Are you going to help me? Oh hell. There isn't anything you can do, so what's the point of thinking about it?'

'There might be something. Get me all your papers and let me read them.'

'What papers?' he asked with a frown.

'The record of loan repayments, the court order. The loan agreement. And while you're at it, if I'm going to try and focus to read I'd better have another cup of coffee.' I handed him my cup.

He rummaged around in a drawer for a while and then handed me some badly creased, official looking documents. The loan he had arranged was simple. Fifteen percent interest plus capital to be repaid in one year.

'Why did you take the loan with Guinn and not a bank? This interest is exorbitant.'

'If you mean it's high, you're right. But no bank would lend me the money, Guinn would.'

'Could you make the payments easily enough?' I asked him.

He shrugged. 'There wasn't much over but I did all right.'

'It seems a lucrative sort of market, whatever you were shipping,' I replied but he did not expand.

He had borrowed a straight two thousand dollars to be repaid in thirteen instalments at four week intervals. I scanned his repayment receipts. Guinn had not been too particular at the regularity of the payments because it was certainly not every four weeks. The contract said within three days of the due date payment had to be made or else the loan could be foreclosed and the remainder of the loan plus interest would have to be found, and if it wasn't the boat would be seized in forfeiture. It seemed clear enough until I added the number of repayments made.

'Why did you only pay twelve times instead of thirteen?'

'What sort of lawyer are you? Everyone knows there's twelve months in a year,' he frowned. 'Though come to think about it the court said something about that but I didn't understand the blasted problem. All I knew was I had lost my blasted boat. And after paying for it, too.' His lopsided grin, now in a downward position, gave him a ferocious scowl.

'That's calendar months but this contract is for four weekly periods. Hence thirteen payments.' I guess I was being a bit thick or it might have been the drink from the night before but it was only then it dawned on me. I rechecked the payment dates. I should have spotted it earlier but every payment had been made within the first three days of each month. 'Tell me something. When you were in court did Guinn say that he had been patient letting you pay late and finally given you an extra month to pay in?'

'Something like that. I didn't know what he was talking about. I even got a paper there that said I had paid it all. Underneath that lot,' he added.

'Is this it?' I asked, he nodded. I read the letter warning him he was in default and that unless he paid up within one week he would be taken to court. 'How did you get this?'

'I think it was one of Guinn's men who gave it to me.'

'And when he did he said it was your final receipt, finishing the debt?' He nodded. 'And did you show this to the court?'

'They had the same letter there. I compared them and saw they were the same.'

'What exactly does it say?' I asked softly.

He took the paper out of my hand, looked at it and said:

'Hell, I don't need to tell you, you just read it,' his voice became louder and he thrust it back at me.

'You dumb cluck,' I said. 'And I don't mean that because you can't read, but because you didn't hire a lawyer to do it for you.'

He looked embarrassed for a moment and then grinned. 'I was going to get angry and chuck you off but I reckon that'd be pretty stupid. Okay, so I can't read.'

'And I don't suppose you asked anybody to read it to you?'

'What do you take me for? And let all the waterfront know how stupid I am? I'm well known as a smart man amongst the sailors, a man not to be tangled with, too. How else do you think I got you out last night? You know what they'd think of me if they knew I couldn't read?'

'What do they say now you're going to lose your boat?'

'That I had some bad luck but I'll be back again soon, making my fortune.'

'Bad luck my Aunt Fanny. You were taken for a ride. You paid most of the money and now you've lost it all. Weren't you told you had to pay every four weeks?' But I knew the answer to that one. 'One thing I don't understand and that is what the judge was doing. Any half-arsed judge worth a nickel would immediately have seen what had happened. Hang on, tell me something. That paper about you still owing money, was it read out or did the judge ask you if you understood and agreed with it?'

'He asked if I understood and agreed with it.'

'That figures, and you said yes. All nice and legal and I bet if the court records were examined they could prove to be straight as well.' I paused and managed a few more mouthfuls of his foul coffee. 'So who was the judge?'

'Name of Masters.'

'Not his name but what's his reputation like? Is he known as a fair man? A crook? Or what?'

'I don't know much about him. All I can tell you is he's Guinn's wife's cousin.'

'God Almighty,' I said with a groan. 'Knowing that and you still didn't get a lawyer?' That fact still rankled with me.

'I've already told you. I got no money and I couldn't see any lawyer bucking Guinn in this town.'

'From your payments you appear to have made good money. Why didn't you go and make some more?'

'I was going to. I made my last payment, or so I thought, and was enjoying a few weeks here, spending what I had until I was broke before going on another job.'

'And just before you went they slapped a court order on you forbidding you from sailing until after the hearing which was another few weeks later when you were really skint.'

'How do you know?'

I didn't bother replying. 'If I go and see Guinn I reckon I won't get anywhere. Also, it'll take a judge's order to change things anyway, or even to order a retrial. And of course you would still be liable to make the payment though I could possibly get that deferred for a month,' I paused while the idea took root. 'If I can get your boat back and if I pay the outstanding amount, will you let me be your partner? Owning say one fifth of the boat and receiving half the profits for the next six months? After that the ownership and all the profits revert to you?'

He looked at me as though I had suddenly grown a second head and then his grin really blossomed out. 'You mean it, don't you? You think you can get my boat back for me?'

'I think so. In fact I'm pretty sure about it. Is it a deal?'

'It's a deal,' he held out his hand and we shook. 'That's the only sort of deal I know and that's the one we stick to. No papers, just my hand.'

It offended my lawyer's sense but I agreed.

'Does that mean I don't have to leave today?'

'No, I'm afraid not. If you stay you'll be breaking the law. But we'll be back. Let's not waste any more time. I need to find out a few things, like the names of the important politicians in the state. And a town this size surely has more than one judge.'

The court house was an imposing building near the centre of town. There were two judges for New Orleans and the area. They were both in session when we arrived and we went in to listen to a Judge Hogg. From where I sat he appeared the usual bigoted, small minded man who aspired to the office, particularly in the southern states. I guessed no Negro ever won a case under him – even if they managed to get to court. I stayed for the rest of the afternoon, listening to him hand out judgements on drunk and disorderly cases, shooting-up-the-town cases and other petty misdemeanours. No defence lawyer was listened to and each was often interrupted, reducing the proceedings to a farce. I sighed. It was going to be tougher than I had thought, especially if he and Masters were friends – more than likely under the circumstances.

When the court was finally adjourned for the day I said to Jake, 'Let's go and see him in his rooms. We might get somewhere, though I doubt it. I expect that as soon as we talk to him, he'll be around to tell Masters as fast as he can get there.'

Jake grinned. 'You couldn't be more wrong. I hear those two haven't spoken to each other in five years.'

'Why not?'

'It was something to do with Masters' wanting to marry Hogg's widowed sister and she being stopped by Hogg or something stupid like that. It seemed Hogg wanted her to look after him, him not being married and all. So they aren't what you'd call friendly, not by a long chalk.'

'Good. That's about the best news I've heard all day.'

I knocked on the door and when a gruff and imperious voice told us to enter, we did just that. The judge was sitting at his desk, shoes off, feet propped before him, the dubious value of his sister's housework shown through the holes in his socks. The room had one wall lined with books, a fire place, a window overlooking the main square, a threadbare carpet and one seat for a visitor. He neither greeted us nor offered his hand, but just sat there, with a scowl on his unpleasant face. He was a little, wizened man, skinny, grey haired and had the biggest ears I'd ever seen.

'My name is Griffiths, David Griffiths and I'm an attorney at law, representing my client here, Jake . . .'

'I know Kirkpatrick,' he interrupted me. 'He's been before me enough times. What's he done this time?' he asked with a sneer.

'Nothing yet. But through me he's going to. I've written the facts of the situation here,' I offered him the few sheets of paper I had prepared while I was sitting in the court. He waved them away.

'I can't be bothered with them. I'm a busy man. State what you want and make it snappy. I want to go home.'

'I don't think you'll be in such a hurry when I've finished,' I replied and then wished I had kept my mouth shut after he shot me a look of pure venom. Before he could say anything I launched into Jake's story. When I was finished I was surprised by his reaction.

'So? If that's all you've got to tell me, then good day, sir,' he sat forward in his chair and dropped his feet to the floor.

'Aren't you interested? There's been a blatant miscarriage of justice. More, it's plain crooked. I want the case reopened and if Guinn doesn't agree to settle properly I want a retrial. And if I can't get an honest one here I want it in another state.'

At this he lurched to his feet, all five feet nothing of

him, finger pointing to the door, shaking with indignation and wrath. 'Get out, before I have you thrown out.'

'You aren't having anybody thrown out,' I said softly. 'In a similar case of Merrick versus Abernathy, when illiteracy was proven, the court ruled in favour of the defendant. It was in this state less than five years ago,' I added. If I was going to lie, I thought, I might as well make it a good one.

'What do you know about state law for this territory?' he scoffed.

'Judge,' I said with resigned patience in my voice, 'at Harvard we dealt with many interesting cases, especially those that set a precedent for future ruling as long as they were within the Constitution. Those cases that aren't within the Constitution are naturally illegal and an incorrect ruling can lead to investigation of the trial and its running by certain senior state officials.'

'Fine young man. Then I suggest you get somebody else to deal with it for you. I will do nothing to besmirch the name of my colleague. And what's more, I'll have nothing to do with a lawyer who suggests the law is less than perfect.'

'Less than perfect?' I repeated incredulously, knowing full well that whoever had suggested the law was an ass knew what he was talking about. But I realised that to have said so would have made matters worse. The trouble was, if I could not get the old sod to act for us, God alone knew how long it would take to get matters resolved and there was no way I wanted to get involved with a long drawn out legal battle.

'In that case I would like you, please, to sign that you have read the notes I have here and that you refuse to help.'

'What for?' he asked suspiciously, with a good deal less bluster this time.

'My name probably didn't mean anything to you. My father is a Congressman in Missouri. A telegram to him

with all the facts will ensure that I get an interview with
Chas Littlefield pretty quickly. I'm sure he'll arrange for
Neil Smears or Freddy Hall to be there, at least. The
Governor and a Congressman can order and supervise
an investigation into corrupt court dealings, as I'm sure
you know.' I didn't know if they could, but it sounded
good to me.

'Ah yes, but this is not my case. I have done nothing
corrupt. It's nothing to do with me,' he said smugly.

'True, but there's possible collusion when you won't
act without . . . I don't have to spell it out to you. You
can imagine what the papers would do with it all. And let
me assure you these men are friends of my father's. I'm
sure I'll get what I want in the end. On the other hand,
strictly within the law, you can rule that there should be a
new hearing and get the confiscation order squashed. You
can tell Guinn that my client is even prepared to pay the
final instalment now, without delay. If he doesn't wish to
settle, would you remind him about what could happen if
we win the case? I doubt he'll be able to practise in this
State again. He could even be disbarred altogether.'

'How do I know you're who you say you are?' he
asked with a scowl.

'Please telegraph my father. Give a description of
me, tell him what I'm doing and he'll acknowledge
me all right.'

'Hmm, supposing I do what you say? What's in it
for me?'

I was a little taken aback by the question because I had
not expected such blatant corruption. But at least I had
the little worm hooked.

'What's in it for you?' I paused to think. 'Well, I'll
certainly tell my father of your help and ask him to pass
onto Chas and the others what a sterling fellow you are,'
somehow I kept the sarcasm from my voice. 'Oh, and of
course you'll have the satisfaction of knowing that justice
has been seen to be done,' I smiled.

'Hmm,' his fingers drummed the desk top for a few moments. 'I need to think about it.'

'I'm sorry, Judge, there's no time. I shall make a statement here and now saying you won't help and that I'm turning to the State for aid.' I reached for paper and pen.

'Hold it, young man, hold it. Don't rush me. I have to think about it. Do you realise what you're asking me to do? Never mind Masters, but you also want me to go against Guinn. And that's something I don't do lightly. Nobody does in this state if they're in their right senses.'

'Guinn doesn't frighten me, judge.'

'You don't have to live here,' he replied.

For a fleeting second I was sorry for him, but I quickly squashed the feeling. 'Are you prepared to act on our behalf or not?' I asked. 'If not I've got a lot of things to arrange.' Like a return ticket to St Louis, I thought.

He opened a drawer in his desk and rummaged around for a cigar. He took his time lighting it, the frown on his face deepening each second. 'What exactly do you want me to do?' he asked finally with a sigh.

I told him and not long afterwards we left.

'So what happens now?' Jake asked when we were outside and walking towards the waterfront.

'That all depends on how Guinn reacts and how the judge presents his case. Legally we have a good chance of winning and in the process I think I can throw enough horse manure around to damage a few reputations. Like Guinn's and probably Master's. It'd be a hard fight but I've got plenty of time and enough money to take care of it. And, as a by-product I'll enjoy it. I hate men like the judges down here and that crook Guinn. There's plenty of money to be made without cheating the law.'

'Are you really the son of a Congressman?'

'Yep, but I tell you what. If you don't tell anybody, I won't either, okay?'

'Sure, I just wondered. I guess it was my lucky day meeting you last night,' he gave his grin.

'Maybe. I may save you a boat, but you saved my life.'

'I suppose you're right,' he said with due lack of modesty, 'but it wasn't anything. Mind you why the hell did you go into the Gut to Throaters?'

'The what?'

'The Gut to Throaters. It's called that because of the fights when men get slit from their guts to their throats. At least, that's what they say, though I haven't seen any of that for, oh, at least a year. Except last night. I thought it was about to happen again.'

I gulped. 'I did wonder about the name,' I said with feigned nonchalance.

41

THE BOAT WAS a gaff-rigged ketch, fifty five feet long, thirteen feet wide, drew eight and a half feet and was built of pitch pine on oak. In spite of my hangover I had noticed the oak panelled interior and the general lavishness of the fittings. When we stopped for a drink in one of the more reputable bars around the area I asked what he used it for.

After Jake had hedged for a few sentences, talking about this and that and anything that came along, I pinned him down.

'Jake, I'm coming with you on the next trip, so I want to know precisely what this and that is.'

He looked a bit startled, his grin slipping. 'Coming with me? You got to be joking. I thought I'd pay you a proportion of the profits and if you're worried about me cheating forget it. I'll play it square, I promise that. Hell, I've shaken on it, haven't I?'

'I've no doubt Brutus shook Caesar's hand often but that didn't stop him stabbing him in the back,' I replied dryly.

'What the hell are you talking about?'

'Nothing, forget it. I'm coming not because I don't trust you but because I want to.'

'But you told me that you don't know anything about sailing,' he protested.

'True. But I will soon because you're going to teach me,' I said smoothly.

He shook his head. 'Impossible. I'm sorry, I like you and all that but I can't take you with me.'

I drained my beer and stood up. 'Fine, I'll go and tell Hogg that there's no case,' and walked out.

'Hey,' he called after me. I was in the street by the time he caught up with me and began protesting. 'Slow down for Christ's sake will you and let me talk?'

'Nothing to talk about, Jake. If I hurry I may get to him while he's still in his office. I'm sure he'll be relieved to hear that I've withdrawn from it all.'

He caught hold of my arm. 'Listen a minute, Dave. You at least owe me that.'

So I stopped.

He looked about him to ensure nobody was listening and lowered his voice. 'That boat is about the fastest thing around these parts and a few more parts as well. You saw she ain't exactly a trader. I told you about her general lines and build. With full sail she goes like a racing horse and don't never need to stop,' he paused. 'Listen Dave, you're the son of a Congressman and a lawyer. You don't want to get mixed up in nothing I do. Just take the money and don't ask any questions.'

'So it's illegal, whatever it is you do.'

'Not against no United States law that I know of,' he said haughtily. 'Mexico isn't that far away. And there's a revolution brewing down there, though you wouldn't know it to see the place. One day the people are going to overthrow Porfirio Diaz and to do so they need arms. It's a social need I'm taking care of,' he said with his grin.

'Great. I'll enjoy helping you help those oppressed people.'

'Listen, you don't know what you're saying. So far I've been lucky. But there'll come a day when the troops of that pig Diaz will see me and what happens then?'

'You set sail for the open seas, leaving the peasants to fight,' I half joked.

'True,' he said resignedly and then shrugged. 'So why do you want to come along?' He finally got round to the question.

'Simple. I'm bored out of my mind. I want to go and do something different for a while before going home to marry and settle down to a life of making money.'

'Hell, you're out of your mind,' he gave apparently considered judgement. 'Okay, you can come. But I want you to know something. On the boat the captain's word is law, you do exactly what I tell you, okay?'

'Fine by me. I wouldn't presume to usurp your authority. There's only one catch to the whole business though, and that is we haven't actually got the boat yet.'

The thought took his mind off me and back to his own problems. 'Let's go and see if them bastards have been there yet,' he said gloomily. 'I thought it was all over bar the celebrating.'

'It could be if Guinn sees sense. If he doesn't then it's just starting. I'll have to prepare a better case than any I've done so far. I'll need to contact my father for a bit of influence, which'll probably mean a trip home. Though I don't know what he can do,' I added thoughtfully.

'Hey, you said he was friends with the Governor and everything.'

'To the best of my knowledge he hasn't even met the man,' I corrected him.

'Jesus, now you tell me. All them dreams about my boat and it was all for nothing.'

'You're wrong there. We'll win the case, though if they prove awkward, it'll take a bit longer than I first thought.'

'How much longer?' he asked suspiciously.

'A few months,' I replied with a grin.

'Jeesuuus,' was all he managed to say.

When we got back to the boat there was a deputy waiting to see Jake and tried to hand him the seizure notice. Before Jake could take it I stepped in and received it. I cut off the startled 'Hey,' of the deputy by saying, 'I'm Mr Kirkpatrick's lawyer. I'll take this. Mr Kirkpatrick is going on board to remove his personal belongings. He will be returning to the boat to live once the Judge has ruled for a new hearing. I suggest you inform the Sheriff.'

The deputy was fat, round and stupid. His gun was slung low on his right hip and his hand hovered near it all the time. I wondered if he practised fast draws while playing at being Jesse James.

'What's this? You can't go on there. It's now the property of Mr Guinn and he said that nobody, especially him,' he jerked a thumb at Jake, 'can go onboard again.'

'Listen, deputy, I happen to know the law as well as Mr Guinn and he's talking rubbish. This man is entitled to remove his personal gear.' I scanned the warrant and smiled, Guinn had got it wrong. 'Also, all other contents in the boat from sails to . . . to . . .'

'Halyards?' Jake supplied.

'Yes. Because this warrant only mentions the boat, not the contents. So you go and tell Mr Guinn that if he wants an empty shell he had just better hold fire with preventing Mr Kirkpatrick from going onboard.'

'Well now – I don't know about that,' the deputy scratched his ear with a sausage like finger. 'I just don't know.'

'That's fine, deputy, you don't know. I think you'd better go and find somebody who does know, like the sheriff.' I spun away and clambered awkwardly down onto the deck.

Jake shrugged at the deputy, gave his grin and agilely leapt down after me. The deputy stood there, indecisive, and then walked away.

The problem only took a week before it was resolved. In that time we were threatened with all kinds of dire consequences if we did not obey the law as already stated in the first hearing. Judge Hogg came close to caving in under pressure but luckily when I drew the local newspaper's attention to the case they wrote strongly in our favour and praised Hogg highly. It was enough to boost the little man's ego sufficiently to order a retrial but before it came to that Guinn agreed to our demands. I paid what Jake owed for the final instalment and the boat was his again. The evening we got the boat back we went out to celebrate. I was stupid. I should have realised a man like Guinn wouldn't take this laying down.

This time I drank the Champagne without the brandy and remained relatively sober. We were back in the bar of the Carlton and we had company. Jake had insisted on calling two girls over from the bar. They were both pretty in a brittle sort of way and both whores. Jake intended that we take them back to the boat with us, with me footing the bill.

While having a pee in the gutter outside I told him he could have them both. When he asked me if I was funny or not I didn't know whether to laugh or hit him. Luckily for our future partnership and my immediate health, I laughed and told him about Gunhild.

I almost changed my mind when the blonde, sitting next to me, ran her hand up my leg. She was the prettier of the two, wore too much lipstick and rouge but had on a low cut blouse that showed off her breasts to the nipples. I felt myself reacting to her insistent hand.

'Listen, Jake,' my voice had taken on an odd croak, 'why don't you and the, eh ladies, go on back to the boat. I'll join you later, after I see about that business.'

'Aw c'mon honey, you come with us too,' she whispered in my ear, blowing softly and warmly, her hand and breath eroding my will power like a gale-lashed sea eroding a sand dune. Jake saw my discomfort and grinned wider, the louse.

After a few more minutes I was about to give up when Jake said, 'Okay girls, let's go. Dave can follow later.'

'I'll stay with Davey,' said the blonde in a sickeningly sweet voice. I cringed.

'Eh no, you go with Jake. I've eh, got some business

to attend to. I may eh, be a long time. A few hours at least.' I stood up.

'Hell, look at the time. I'm late for my appointment already. You eh, finish the wine and I'll eh, see you later.' I hurried towards the door, drunk enough to be weaving and bumping into the tables in my path.

The air was hot and oppressive, hardly any different from the heat of the day. There were heavy clouds, pregnant with rain and it was pitch dark. I bumped into the first man and mumbled an apology. He pushed me hard and I staggered back into the arms of another man.

'That's him,' said a voice I thought I recognised.

Before I could say or do anything a fist hit me in the stomach, knocking the breath out and pain in. Something connected with the back of my head and through a mist of pain and nausea I felt another knock somewhere around my left ear. The world spun so fast I dropped off the end into a dark pit.

When I came to I felt worse than I had after the drinking bout with Jake on that first day. For a second or two I thought it was still night and then with a shock I knew it was too dark and that I was blind. I tried to put my hand to my face.

'Take it easy,' said Jake, taking my hand. 'Don't disturb the bandage.'

'My eyes, Jake,' I cried out but it came in a whisper, 'my eyes,'

'It's the bandages. Your eyes are okay, I promise you. You've got a busted nose, some cuts around the eyes, a lump like an egg on the back of your head and an ear half torn off. Apart from that,' he said dryly, 'there's only a couple of cracked ribs and some nasty bruises. The doctor said you're lucky to have such a thick skull or you could be dead.'

'The doctor?' I asked stupidly.

'Yeah, there was a bit more wrong than I thought I could deal with. Your eyes are all right, so don't worry.'

'What happened?'

'You were beaten up by experts. I'm sure one of the men I saw was the deputy who was here the other day, but I can't be sure.'

The voice, I knew it now. Anger made me clench my teeth and pain made me force myself to relax.

'It was the deputy. I recognised his voice.' My voice was stronger now and my throat as dry as hell. 'Can I have some water, please?'

I heard him at the pump and took the mug of water he put into my hand. I drank greedily before I asked, 'So what happened then?'

'Because it was dark and had just started to rain I didn't dare fire at them so I yelled at the top of my voice and let a shot off into the air. They ran like hell and I stopped to look after you. I gave one of the girls twenty dollars to get a doctor I know; I promised her the same for herself when she returned.'

Jake was generous to a fault. The fault being it was not his money to be generous with. Not that I minded under the circumstances. 'This is Guinn's work,' I said bitterly.

'Sure it is,' Jake's voice sounded cheerful to me, 'and forget about any sort of revenge. Take it from me you wouldn't get near enough to shoot him with a rifle, never mind trying anything else.'

'I wasn't thinking about that. I was thinking about the law. I could have him arrested for . . .' I did not get any further.

'What you mean is you ain't thinking at all. We know the deputy was there which means the other man was more than likely the sheriff. Look, I know this town and I know what I'm talking about. Guinn didn't do it himself and he'll have as many witnesses as the court will require to prove he had nothing to do with beating you up. And you won't get near enough to hurt him. So just accept the beating and put it down to one of life's experiences, okay?'

I grunted in my hurt and anger.

I slept a lot for the next three days. The pain was always there nagging at me, but by degrees it was lessening. The doctor came a few times, removed the bandages from around my head and localised them more on my nose. The back of my head gave me hell when I moved and I had a persistent headache for days. The doctor was very apologetic but he could not straighten my nose because it was too badly broken. All he could do was let the bones knit together as best they could. I could see in a mirror that under the scabs and dried blood it was going to be slightly to one side, flatter and broader. I wondered briefly what Gunhild would think of it.

After a week we sailed out of New Orleans. I could move without pain, my ribs were okay, the bruises were turning yellow and my ear was healing.

Down river, near the sea, I saw dozens of men handling large floating rafts and asked Jake about it.

'They're clearing away the rocks. Prisoners from the pen, I heard they were.'

'What are they doing that for?'

'It's something to do with stopping a build-up of silt in the river mouth. The banks here do change a lot and there's not as many exits to the sea as there used to be.'

'But what are they using those big raft things for?'

'At low tide they tie rocks to them. Then as the tide comes in it lifts the rafts and picks up the rocks. They tow them into the shallows and when it touches bottom they wait for the next low tide and tighten up the ropes. They keep doing that until they're in close to shore.'

'Very interesting. The wonders of modern science.'

'It ain't modern. They was using it thousands of years ago in other countries,' he grinned. 'The engineer in charge of the work said so.'

Jake showed me the rudiments of sailing and told me some of the more common nautical terms. He explained what a forestay was, shrouds, reefs, cringles, clews, leaches, luffs, hoops and a million other terms, most of which passed straight over my head. But slowly I was beginning to remember them.

'Just about everything is connected to or with a piece of rope,' explained Jake. 'Forget the term rope, it's too general. You need to be more explicit so that I know what bit of rope you're talking about. Okay, what's that bit of wood sticking out of the bow?'

That bit of wood was a three foot long mast, almost horizontal to the water, on which the foot of the jib sail was attached. 'The bowsprit,' I finally came out with after searching my memory.

'Right. So what's that bit of rope called?'

'A bow stay,' I hazarded a guess.

'No, no, no, for Christ's sake. It's the bowsprit shroud,' he screamed the last word, at the same time throwing his peaked cap on the deck. For a second I thought he was going to jump on it, but he disappointed me; he only kicked it. Watching it sail over board was unfair because the pain caused by my laughter was almost unendurable.

He did not tell me where we were headed until after we had reached the sea. It was a fine day, with a steady breeze from the north west. We were running before the wind and soon after we cleared the Mississippi delta the muddy water turned a deep sea blue. We were using two working jibs, the main sail and an after mizzen. We flew along as the bow bit into the water, the spray thrown out either side. It was mid morning and the sun shone out of a blue, cloudless sky. At that instant ships, sailing and the sea seeped into my blood. I felt both exhilarated and excited.

'Good, eh?' asked Jake.

'Incredible,' I replied, my grin matching his.

Below decks there were two cabins forward, each with two bunks. A main saloon had two wood burning stoves, one for heating the boat and the other for cooking on; it was situated in the area known as the galley. Then came the office area as I called it, much to Jake's chagrin, where he kept a few charts and books all connected with the art of seamanship and navigation, none of which he could read. But then his knowledge of the sea and the area made charts and books superfluous. Next to the office was the sunken steering position with the compass, wind indicator and close to hand most of the running rigging on the boat. Aft of that was the master cabin in which was a large double bed, neatly fitting cupboards and wardrobe, and a private sink with pump. The only other sink was in the cooking area, or galley as Jake insisted I call it. The Lucky Lady was fitted out to a degree of luxury I would not have associated with a work boat. It even had a water closet, or head, and one of my jobs was to empty the bucket. After the first time I always made sure I threw it well downwind.

I commented about the luxury onboard and he said, 'True, but most of my customers expect it.'

'What sort of customers are they?'

'Rich ones who don't like their native country no more. Or maybe the country don't like them. Not that it matters either way. The end result is the same. They come for a ride to some other place.'

'Where are we going now?'

'Cuba.'

'What for?' I asked excitedly. I had always wanted to see Cuba and I said so to Jake. I did not think I was being funny but evidently he thought so.

'We aren't stopping and all you'll see is a dark coastline with an occasional twinkling light. At least, that's all I hope we see. Before you ask what we'll be doing there I'll tell you. We're picking up two men, some crates of ammunition and rifles and getting the hell out of there. And don't ask me where we'll be going because I don't know. And I won't know 'til the men get on board.'

'How on earth do you arrange all that sort of thing?'

'Contacts,' was his only reply.

'How long will it take to get there?'

'It all depends,' he replied looking around the horizon. 'From the look of the weather and wind I'd guess about four days. We're heading straight across the Gulf for Cape San Antonio. Once past there we've got another six or eight hours to sail. We're going to a little beach I know which has deep water almost to the shore and a steep cliff at the back which is awkward to climb whether you go up or down. We can be pretty sure that if we get the right signal it'll be our passengers and not the bloody soldiery. It's all that any smuggler could ask for, minimum effort by us, maximum for them. Haul down on the shroud there,' he pointed. 'Get it good and tight.'

So my introduction to life at sea began. The more I saw the more I liked it. Jake was very patient during those first few days, explaining time and again what each piece of gear was used for, giving it it's proper name and how to maintain it all. The thing that impressed me most was the eternal vigilance required, watching the compass, gauging the wind, getting the fastest speed from the boat. The first time we jibed I made a hash of things but soon got the hang of it.

I was mending by leaps and bounds and put it down to the fresh air, the sun and the good food. When it came to provisioning the boat Jake had left nothing out. He was proving more and more adept at spending my money as time went on. I insisted on keeping a proper record – somewhat to his chagrin – and told him the operating expenses would be deducted from the profits before the share out. I seemed to remember he called me something along the lines of a skinflint, but I let it wash over my head.

That first evening was something to remember for the rest of my life. Running with the wind as we were, there was little breeze across the deck, the sun was setting in a shimmer of gold and orange, the clouds a halo in the sky and that brandy the best I could recollect drinking. We sat in the cockpit swapping tales about our lives, though to me Jake's was far more interesting. Mine seemed mundane and boring by comparison. He was interested in the university and Harvard while he regaled me with stories of foreign countries and unusual customs. I told him he ought to write a book.

'I will one day,' he replied dryly, 'if I ever learn to read and write.'

I apologised, wishing I had kept my big mouth shut. I realised how embarrassed he was and suggested I taught him. 'After all, you're teaching me a lot more than I could teach you. And this would mean that I wouldn't feel it was all a one-way affair.'

'Well, I don't know . . .' he stroked his chin.

He didn't put up much resistance especially when I got one of his books and read some of the interesting facts to be found there. We would start the next day.

The night that fell was like none I had seen on land. There was no moon, the air was clear and the stars appeared brighter and closer. At first I could not understand why it was so different but slowly it all made sense. The emptiness was something I had never experienced before; it was only to be found at sea. The wind whistled gently through the rigging and the water lapped, and slapped the side of the boat as we sped along. There was a luminosity in the water that I had never seen before, little sparks of green and blue which according to Jake were plankton, the food of the fish. Whatever it was, it added to my sense of well-being, sitting in the cockpit, my hand on the wheel, attempting to steer south, south east. A feeling of peace stole over me. I wished with all my heart Gunhild was there to share it with me, it was the sort of thing I knew she would understand and appreciate. I could never imagine somebody like Jake understanding how it felt.

'It's unbelievable, isn't it?' he broke a long silence.

'The feeling of being alone in the world, the peace and contentment of it. I still feel it after all these years but I can't describe it, not even to myself,' he added.

I felt ashamed. He understood only too well.

We got into a habit in those first few days of sharing the night. He would take the first half, usually until about one o'clock, and then I would have it until dawn. Jake was adamant that I call him if the wind changed by more than two points of the compass or if I had difficulty holding the course. It was the evening of the fourth day when Jake sniffed the night.

'Do you smell it?'

I sniffed too, but was unsure what I was supposed to smell. 'What?' I asked with a frown.

'It's a mustiness . . . no, that's the wrong word. It's rotting jungle, it's the smell of fresh earth, perhaps flowers. It's the smell of Cuba after four days at sea,' he shrugged, unable to suggest any other description.

Now I too could smell it. Two hours later there was a darker smudge on the horizon which persisted and hardened in the light from the stars and the first sliver of a new moon. Cuba. My heart began to pound at the thought of adventure.

We passed about two miles off shore and rounded the cape. I had no appreciation of the feat of navigation and seamanship shown by Jake in getting us there so accurately.

We followed the coast until I saw the headland directly in our path. Jake lowered the main sail while I held the tiller and we crept in close. We changed places and I stood ready to hoist the sail as fast as I could heave on the tackle and to duck as we went about if we had to get the hell out of there.

We were now moving slowly. Jake took a lantern and flashed two long, three short and another long flash at the shore. Two short flashes, three long and one short came back. Jake grunted in satisfaction.

'We'll stop about a hundred yards off, perhaps more if there's too much of a lee and the wind can't get to us. Keep her moving with just a little headway, and if there's any trouble get the hell out of here. Come back at midnight every night for the next week to get me,' he said softly.

'Hang on,' I whispered back. 'I can't handle the boat that well. You stay here and let me go,' Jake hesitated. 'Don't be stupid Jake. If there's any trouble I'll try and swim back. If I don't make it don't bother coming for me another night because I won't be returning.'

He nodded slowly in agreement. 'When you get close, say to the men there "Jesus Christ" and they will say "The only one". Have you got that?'

I looked at him as if he'd gone daft.

'I didn't make it up. I was told to use it.'

We launched the small dinghy and awkwardly, with stifled curses and ineptitude, I rowed towards the shore. I could see nobody nor hear anything above the noise of the surf.

When I was close in three shadow detached themselves from the towering cliff face and approached.

'Jesus Christ,' I called out, and received the reply, which did nothing for my hammering heart.

I landed on the beach, my senses alert. At the slightest untoward sound or movement I was going to dive into the sea and swim for the Lucky Lady. Nothing happened.

We greeted each other with suspicious handshakes. The three men put down their rifles and returned to the foot of the cliff. When they returned they were carrying a long box each. Three of these and the boat was full, with just enough room for me. One of them gave me a shove off and I made my way back to the Lucky Lady. I made the trip eight tines, the last time with two of the men.

Within moments of returning to the Lucky Lady we had the dinghy on board, I was hauling up the main mast and we were headed for the open sea.

Later I wondered at what point during the proceedings I had stopped being nervous. I suspected it was when I caught a crab for the third time. My elbow had hurt too much to be nervous.

42

AN HOUR LATER, after showing our two guests to the forward cabins, I sat in the cockpit with Jake.

'Aren't you wondering where we're going?' he asked.

'Naturally. I figure you'll tell me soon enough. We're headed west and from what I already know of your other, eh, operations, I guess we're going to Mexico. If my memory serves me right we'll be in the Yucatan Strait shortly and if we carry on we'll get to Yucatan itself.'

He nodded. 'That's exactly where we're going – to a little cove south of Cozumel Island. We'll land these jokers there with their guns and head on out to Jamaica, I reckon.'

'Why? What are we going there for?'

'We're about half way already. With the money we get from this trip we'll buy some of that nectar known as Jamaican Rum. We sell it back in New Orleans for half again what we pay for it. Hell, having that stuff is better than money.'

I grinned. 'Sounds good. Eh . . . how much are we getting for this trip?'

'A thousand,' he said laconically.

'Not bad for such easy work,' I felt pleased with myself.

'Don't be fooled and don't get careless, Dave. We get paid so much because the risks are there. Tonight could happen for the next ten, twenty times. And then somebody talks. Then they're waiting for you. And before you know it you're dead or worse. So believe me we earn our money.'

It took a day and a half to cross the Strait and past Cozumel. We kept out to sea and out of sight of land until just before midnight. Then we sailed directly to the cove we wanted. The signal and password were the same again. I rowed the men ashore and followed with the guns. This time we were in closer and so I did not have so far to go, and furthermore I was becoming more adept at rowing. There was a welcoming committee of a dozen or more men who appeared for one heart stopping moment just as I beached the dinghy the first time. Relief flooded through me when I saw the manner in which they greeted my passengers. When I had the last box ashore I was given a bag of coins.

'Here's your blood money. One thousand dollars,' hissed the swarthy and heavily moustached individual. 'I hope you do not enjoy it,' he spat at the pebbles beneath my feet. To say I was startled was an understatement. 'We will contact you in the same way. Tell that to the Gringo, Jake. And tell him I hope we meet in hell one day.' With that he spun on his heels, barked commands at his men in Spanish and stalked up the beach, the pebbles crunching underfoot.

I climbed back into the boat and returned to the Lucky Lady. Once more with a fair wind and a heel to starboard, we headed east. I told Jake what the man had said.

He laughed. 'That's Miguel for you. As ungrateful as hell and twice as bad.'

'What was he on about?'

'He, like a lot of them, believe we should help their cause for nothing, or shall we say for the betterment of mankind? Mind you, it's only their ideas about mankind they care about. The things they do in the name of their revolution is terrible and I mean terrible. Do you know what was in that sack?'

'Gold,' I guessed.

'Right, gold. And where do you think they got it from?' Before I could answer he continued. 'From robbing the poor, that's where. They can't get it from the government and seldom from banks or places like that. It's too difficult and dangerous. So they do what the government does, and that's take it from the poor and defenceless. If they don't get given it willingly, which is rare, they take it. They rob, murder and rape like the rest of the bastards and the people in the middle, as usual, suffer.'

It gave me food for thought for a while. 'Why do you do it, then?'

'Because if I didn't somebody else will. And anyway, I told you, I enjoy this work.'

'Knowing that you're causing misery to untold numbers of people?' I did not try to hide the disgust in my voice.

'Get this straight. I didn't ask you to come, and if you remember I didn't want you to. Well, now you're here and it's too late to back out. You could have thought through all I've told you for yourself, you aren't stupid. And who's to say what difference another government will make. There are plenty of people who do believe in their revolution and are praying it'll happen one day. And, I want to tell you something, there's another side to the coin,' he paused and hawked over the side. 'Some of those men on the beach have been fighting for years and they know they'll be fighting for many more. Can you imagine what that does to you? Knowing no peace, nowhere to rest for fear of being caught? They all started with good intentions. Can you imagine what it does to you when they ask for gold and jewellery to help them fight, and don't get it? Don't you think they get bitter when they go to a village where life may be hard and taxes a burden but at least the men there have a roof over their heads and a woman in their beds. The people want freedom without giving anything towards it. So the bandits force them to help whether they want to or not.

And to do so their methods are as bad as those of the soldiers.' His voice lost its intensity. 'It's sad but true. Then most of what I've seen of life is,' he ended on a philosophical note.

After a while, during which we sped through the black night, the hiss of water along the hull and the wind in the rigging the only sound, I said, 'I'm sorry Jake, I shouldn't have moralised,' and held out my hand.

He took it. 'That's okay, lad. You're still young yet and for all your education and knowing ways you don't know much about life. But you'll learn different.' I grinned; he wasn't much over thirty himself. 'It's a dog eat dog world and you know something? I wouldn't have it no other way.'

The next day the weather changed and we had a few rain showers. The wind backed a couple of points and increased and we had to reef in some sail. We were flying along, the sea spraying back into the cockpit, intermixed with the rain. I had the most incredible feeling of freedom; the rougher the weather the stronger the feeling became. I wanted to pit myself against the elements, against nature herself. Later that afternoon the feeling slowly died as the pitching boat kept ploughing through the green seas and white topped waves. I think it was the coffee that did it. I hardly got it down when I heaved it up again and there followed a sickness that left me wishing I could die.

'Don't worry David, it'll pass. It had to happen some-time, it gets to everybody. You'll soon get over it and be as fit as ever.'

I knew he was only trying to cheer me up but in my mind I could see him preparing to bury me at sea. Much to my surprise I survived and two days later could actually keep my watch without heaving. I felt hungry but just the thought of food would suddenly turn my stomach.

The next day, though the wind abated a few knots, the sea was still as rough and I followed the dictates of my rumbling belly and eat. The stew was delicious and I kept it down. In fact, two hours later, I had some more. After that I recovered quickly.

To watch the sun rise behind the green jewel of Jamaica in a blue, mirror calm sea was one of the most beautiful sights in the world. Jamaica. The word conjured up all sorts of exciting things in my mind. And this time we were going to land, in Kingston no less, the haven of the old-world pirates, of Captain Bluebeard and his murderous crew, of Morgan who later became Governor, of Kidd and the rest of them. The pirates were a part of the history of the island . . . a corrupt, killing, raping, looting, burning history.

The harbour was crowded with boats of all kinds. There were sturdily built fishing craft, fast sloops, ketches and yet another just like the Lucky Lady. There were one or two large trading boats which ploughed the oceans to the Far East and Australia, taking rum and sugar and returning with exotic goods.

We made fast alongside another boat, stepped over it and onto the shore. To have a steady platform beneath my feet after so long at sea was odd and both Jake and I rolled slightly as we made our way through the throng of people towards the nearest inn. I noticed the black men and women were tall and handsome and the girls caught my eye, in their light, flowery clothing, with their flashing eyes and quick smiles. There were street vendors all over the place, selling everything from small casks of rum and sticky sweets to knives and swords. Away from the sea it was hot and humid and I was soon sweating, pushing our way through the bustling crowd.

We came to a whitewashed building, went up a couple of steps and ducked through a doorway. Inside was a long, cool room, the walls white and the ceiling lined with black beams. There were a dozen or more men sitting at the heavy round tables scattered about; few of them bothered looking up when we entered. There was sawdust on the floor and a long bar facing us. My eye was caught by the row of bottles behind, all containing a different sort of rum.

We sat for an hour or two, sipping rum and talking, but finally we went back into the sunlight. It was now well into the afternoon and there were far fewer people on the streets.

'They've gone for a siesta,' Jake said. 'Tonight there'll be even more people out and about, the taverns and bars will be jammed and there'll be fun all over the place. Careful with your money when we come back ashore because there's as many pickpockets as there are honest people. More, I suspect. Come on, let's get some sleep.'

The sun had set when we went back onshore again. We found a waterfront restaurant that served a delicious lobster and a good bottle of white wine. Afterwards we shoved our way through the jostling crowd looking for a bar which, according to Jake, served the best rum in town, if not in all Jamaica.

We were past the waterfront and walking up an ill lit, badly smelling, narrow alley when we heard a muffled scream. It came from ahead of us and, drawing our guns, we hurried forward. We came to another alley on our right and heard scuffling. Jake darted across the opening and we kneeled on either side of the alley, cautiously looking around the corner. From the light of a half moon we saw three men with a girl stretched out on the ground. One of the men was holding her hands over her head, another held her legs and the third was kneeling between them, groping for his fly.

I looked across the narrow gap to Jake. 'Rape?' I barely whispered.

He nodded. 'If one of you move so help me I'll shoot,' he said loudly. In the silence his voice was startling. The men froze. 'Get up and leave her alone,' he continued, in a conversational manner. 'Don't try it, mister,' Jake added when one of them sneaked a hand to his holster, 'because I'll enjoy shooting.' The click as he cocked his gun was loud in my ears.

At that moment the moon vanished behind a cloud and the light went out like a lamp being extinguished. They were stupid, that was the only explanation. Two shots were fired in our direction, both passing well over our heads. Jake and I both opened fire, shooting low and rapidly. I heard one man drop and a gun clatter on the paving stone. We waited, hardly breathing, listening intently. There was a scuffle but I could see nothing. After a few minutes the girl called softly.

'Don't go,' said Jake. 'It may be a trap. With a knife at her throat she'll say anything. We'll wait for the moon to reappear, it won't be long now.'

In the moonlight we saw the girl but nobody else. Her attackers had gone and slowly we crept forward.

'See if she's all right and I'll look further up,' said Jake.

I nodded and knelt by her side. She looked up at me, her eyes wide with fear. Even in that poor light I could see she was a beautiful Negress. She was breathing hard and fast, and I could not help but notice the rise and fall of her breasts beneath her thin cotton dress.

'It's all right, we aren't going to hurt you. Can you get up?' I asked gently.

She nodded and I helped her to her feet. She leant against a wall for a few seconds. 'Th . . . thank you,' she said in a husky voice.

Before I could reply Jake called to me. I dashed down the alley and found him standing over a body. I stood beside him looking at the widening pool of blood, black in the moonlight.

'He's dead,' said Jake. 'Stupid bastard. There's so much to be had here that not even white trash need rape a woman. I'll never understand men like them.'

'White trash?'

'Yep, poorer even than the blacks and won't do no

work. Look at his clothes. Even I would have thrown them away a long time ago. Come on, let's go. How's the girl?'

'Seems all right. What about him?'

'Leave him. If his friends want him they can come back. If they don't we sure as hell don't either.'

The girl was where I had left her. I dragged my eyes away from her full breasts and tried to wipe away the thoughts I was having.

'Where do you live?' Jake asked kindly, taking her arm and leading her from the alley.

She gestured to the way we had been going. One on either side of her we went up the steep, cobbled alley.

'We'll see you home and leave you,' I said. 'Did you recognise any of the men who . . . em . . . did you recognise any of them?'

The bottom of her dress had been torn almost to her waist and she held it together with one hand.

'No . . . at least . . . I'm not sure.' Her voice was naturally husky and not from fear, as I had first supposed. It sent tingles up my spine. 'I see so many people in my work . . . men that is . . . that it's difficult to be sure.'

I thought – damnation, a whore. We had saved a whore from being raped? It was ludicrous. How many times had she been on her back making money? We'd killed a man because she would not give what she usually charged for. I was angry and we continued in silence. Abruptly she stopped.

'I live here. I work in the Blue Pelican. If you call perhaps I can thank you over a drink or something.' Her smile was dazzling. She had high cheek bones, wide brown eyes, a straight nose and though her lips were full they were more delicate than those usually found in Negroes. I was sure there was white blood in her somewhere, probably French or Spanish.

Jake said good night but I turned away and went on up the alley, walking faster than I intended.

'For God's sake, slow down,' he said after a few minutes. 'We aren't in that much of a hurry.'

I grunted and slackened my pace.

'A very nice girl,' he ventured.

'Yeah, great. A whore,' I replied.

Jake led me down a few steps and I had to duck through a low doorway. We entered a quiet room, with lanterns lit in small nooks casting a yellow light, there was no bar, but tables lined the walls with comfortable looking benches either side. The walls were festooned with old cutlasses and knives. I recognised a Claymore and an old type epee, the sharp pointed duelling sword which had been a favourite with the nobility of years ago. The room was quiet and steeped in nostalgia of a bygone age.

A black man materialised at my elbow and bowed. 'Can I be of service to you, gentlemen?' he asked in a deep voice with an English accent.

'Yeah, we'd like to see the rum list and bring us a bottle of white wine while you're at it,' Jake ordered.

The man nodded in acknowledgement and glided away. His black tail coat was stretched tight across his broad back and I had noticed the gleam of his starched shirt and the impeccable knot in his bow tie.

'I don't believe it,' I said in a hushed tone that seemed to be called for in the atmosphere and gentility of the place.

'Oh, it's real enough. Don't be fooled by Casper, though. He isn't as soft as his manner might imply, as many have found out to their cost in the past. Ahh, here's the wine now. Thank you, Casper,' Jake said with a grin.

'My pleasure, Mr Kirkpatrick. Allow me to say that it's nice to see you again. We had heard there had been a spot of bother with the Lucky Lady. We trust it is now sorted out satisfactorily.'

'Yes, thank you, Casper. This is Mr Griffiths, my friend and partner.'

'Indeed we thought as much, sir,' he inclined his head again, this time at me. 'We have heard of your success with the law courts in New Orleans, without having to revert to the use of the court,' he said with a straight face, while Jake burst out laughing. 'It is indeed a pleasure to welcome you,' he withdrew.

'Casper runs the best spy network in the Caribbean,' said Jake. 'In fact, David lad, you may as well know that this is where I get most of my business from. Casper makes all the arrangements.

I was impressed. 'Was that how the last job was arranged?'

Jake nodded.

'Kind of him,' I said.

Jake grinned. 'Hardly that. We have to pay ten percent of the take.'

'I guessed as much. And how much does the other party pay?'

'Sharp, David, sharp. That's what I like about you. They pay the same.'

'Who owns this place?'

'I've no idea,' he surprised me. 'And nobody I know has a clue. I'll tell you one thing though. So far it's always been a black man who has brought me any messages. So I've often wondered if it's Casper himself who's the brains and organiser behind it.'

'A Negro?' I asked astonished.

Jake shrugged. 'Why not? Drink up while I order a few glasses of rum from this list.'

'Eh?'

'I know, but I can pretend to read the list and anyway, I know what I want.'

I nodded, understanding his need to put on a show of being able to read. We tried five different rums, from a very rough to an oily smooth. The ones in between were shades of difference I couldn't tell apart, though Jake said he could. I bet him a ten dollars he couldn't. I lost.

When we left Jake put a small bag next to the dirty glasses which contained Caper's commission for the last job. From there we headed for the more boisterous dives near the water front. The thought of the girl from the Blue Pelican kept coming to mind and I was sorely tempted.

Somewhere along the way we staggered into a low ceilinged, dimly lit, smoke filled inn and ordered large rums and lime juice. We sat at a corner table. The place was packed to the gunnels with men and dozens of women, all black, all whores. Two of the women who to my bleary eyes looked quite pretty, came and sat next to us. One of them had dark brown eyes, full lips and a deep cleavage. I could not ask for more. I had never thought of a black woman in a sexual way before and now I was curious. She had a musky scent I found arousing and the feel of her breast through her thin cotton dress against my arm made my imagination run riot.

'You buy us a drink, yes?' she whispered in my ear, her warm breath completing my arousal. I was uncomfortable and wriggled to ease the pressure of my trousers.

She slid her hand along my thigh, 'I take good care of him later, you see. And it only cost three dollars, all right mister?'

I looked down at her heavy breasts, her dress as low as the top of her nipples, the start of a deep purple colour just noticeable. I wanted to get my hands on them. She leant forward and turned her back slightly to the room, took my hand and cupped it under her left breast as though weighing it.

'You like? I can show you wonderful time with these.' She let go of my hand but I kept it there, fascinated by the weight and firmness of her breast. Her hand gave me another squeeze and then she sat back, pushing my hand away. 'If you want more you pay for it,' she said abruptly. Then she picked up our bottle, poured more rum into my glass and took a mouthful on which I would have choked. She offered me the glass and licked her lips slowly and suggestively. 'My name is Bonny.'

When we staggered outside the air was fresh after the fog in the inn, but it was still hot and humid. I recalled reeling along with my arm around Bonny, my hand cupping her breast. Back on the boat I paid her three dollars and she told me I could use her anyway I wanted.

I sat on the edge of my bunk and more roughly than I intended, pulled her dress off her shoulders. I got my mouth around a nipple, which was in proportion to her large breasts and I felt it rising hard in my mouth. I lay back on the bunk, the rum took hold on the last of my senses and I passed out.

When I awoke or, rather, regained consciousness, I felt like death warmed up. My mouth and throat were dry and felt as if they were filled with cotton wool, my eyes ached, the cabin was spinning and I cursed Jake for leading me astray. Memory of the previous night forced its way into my brain and I wondered where the girl was. I lay back with a groan, trying to remember what had happened. I did not feel as though I had been through a night of satiating sex. Quite the reverse in fact.

I felt sick and fumbled my way to the upper deck. The blazing sun intensified my headache tenfold and I hung over the guard rail trying to vomit, to no avail. I got a bucket, filled it with sea water, sat next to the rail and forced myself to drink as quickly as I could. My stomach contracted in protest, I heaved and then puked until I thought my insides were coming out. I can't say it left me in my prime or even a degree better. I made my way back down to my bunk and collapsed onto it with a groan of relief, happy not to have to hold my head up any longer.

It was dark when Jake woke me. My head was throbbing but apart from that I felt reasonably normal. 'What time is it?' I asked.

'Going on for midnight. Do you fancy a drink? A rum or something?' I saw him grinning in the darkness.

'Coffee will do fine, thanks. I think I'll give up rum for Lent.'

'Until the next time,' he said knowingly. 'Come on, let's go and get something to eat. We'll have coffee then. How did the night go?'

'It didn't. At least I don't remember it going. I think I passed out,' I admitted sheepishly.

'What a waste. If I'd known that was going to happen I would have had her as well, especially as she was all paid for.' Then he added as an after thought, 'Nothing gone, is there?'

'Gone? Why should there be?' I asked dopily. But I knew the answer and so I checked under the mattress. I checked again and sank back with a groan.

'All of it,' I said.

'Christ Almighty, all of it? How much was there?'

'Seeing as you already gave me back our expenses and my share of the job, em, about eleven hundred.'

'Jeesus. What a little bitch. We needed your share for the rum. Come on we'll go and find her. Either she's one hell of a stupid woman or else she's got a lot of protection here.'

'Why do you say that?'

'She took too much. If she had taken fifty, then we probably wouldn't bother looking for her and that's why their pimps tell them to keep the amounts small. They don't want any trouble either. But with so much missing we have to find her. If she's got any sense she'll be half way across the island by now. On the other hand she just might have gone back to her protector, hoping for the best. Come on, let's go.'

Despondently I followed Jake onto the Quay. Each step fired my anger, which swamped my headache and by the time we got back to the bar where we had met her I was ready to kill.

It was as packed as the night before and it took us about fifteen minutes to check all the corners and make sure neither girl was there.

We went to a few more places asking the bartenders if they knew Bonny and Lulu. Some of them knew the girls but could not tell us where to find them. Then in the sixth or seventh place we had some luck.

'Yeah, I know who you mean,' said the bartender. 'Their pimp is Cat Ball.'

'Do you know where we can find him?' asked Jake, slipping him a five dollar bill.

He palmed it like a magician and said, 'Sure, at the end of town. He's got a big house there with nine or ten girls. It's painted pink with a white roof.' He suddenly leaned forward and dropped his voice. 'He's a mean son of a bitch, real mean. Got a couple of hands there to help protect the place and take care of any suckers who create too much fuss over the prices.'

'Yeah,' said Jake. 'I know something about him.'

'Okay, thanks,' I said. 'Come on, Jake.'

'Hang on, David lad. Let's go and get some coffee and something to eat first and maybe in a few hours we'll go down there and see what we can find out.'

'Why wait?'

'Because we need to repair our wits, that's why. And food and coffee is the only way. Believe me, I know what I'm doing.'

I believed him and we went to find one of the lousiest steaks I could remember eating. It was nearly four in the morning when we finally returned to the Lucky Lady and then went on to Cat Ball's house. Like most of the houses, it was next to the road. A balcony ran around the house at the second floor where most of the windows were open. The door looked stout, and from the sounds of laughter and screeching going on inside I guessed there was a party going on. Jake suggested an orgy and I didn't disagree.

'I've been trying to think what I've heard about Ball,'

said Jake. 'He carries a knife between his shoulder blades and pretends to yawn and stretch when he goes for it. I'm sure I saw him kill a man with it a few years back. He's got a hell of a reputation. He's mostly white but part black and never goes into the sun so his skin doesn't tan. Still want to go in?'

'You're damned right I do. If he so much as blinks I'll blow him in two with this,' I waved the shotgun. The sawn off barrel would cut down two men easily at four yards.

'All right. We'll go in over the balcony and look for his room. If he ain't there we'll wait for him to come up and take him nice and quiet. Then we'll have a little talk with him.'

43

JAKE CUPPED HIS hands, I stepped into them, straightened my leg and at the same time he lifted. I grabbed the top of the balcony and climbed over. I reached down; Jake jumped for my hands and within seconds he was alongside me, the noise minimal.

I looked through one of the windows but could see nothing in the darkness. I climbed over the sill. From the smell of perfume and the clothes I found in the closet it belonged on one of the ladies of the house. The bed was huge, one of the biggest I had ever seen. The sheets were silk and I could feel the thickness of the carpet beneath my feet. Ball ran a rich place.

I opened the door and looked out onto an internal balcony, six feet wide, which surrounded a large lounge. The room was crowded with men and women in various stages of undress.

Opposite this room there were four doors and to the left, near the stairs, another three. There was only one door in the wall to the right. I crept out of the bedroom on all fours, keeping close to the wall. Jake followed, closing the door behind him. I opened the door in the right hand wall.

We were in a lamp-lit room that ran the width of the house. The walls were hung with rich velvet curtains and the floor was covered with the deepest pile carpet I could imagine. The bed must have been eight feet wide and ten long.

'God in heaven,' was Jake's response. 'I think we're in the wrong line of work.'

'Watch the door while I search the room. If we find the money we can leave without Ball ever knowing we were here.'

'Aye, aye, sir,' Jake saluted sarcastically.

I grinned. 'Fair's fair. You're always captain. Now it's my turn.'

He grinned back and went over to the door. I started on the drawers and cupboards all of which were filled with the frilliest of shirts and the softest of linen; Cat Ball liked to do himself well. I did not, however, find a single dollar bill or piece of gold. Apart from a few pieces of jewellery there was nothing of value. In the back of one of the wardrobes I found a loose board and for a moment thought I had found where he kept his money. But there was nothing except leather clothing, some nasty looking whips and lengths of rope.

When I showed it to Jake he shrugged disdainfully and said, 'Bloody pervert.'

I was standing in the middle of the room thinking where to look next when Jake suddenly left the door.

'Somebody coming,' he whispered.

Quickly we crammed into the largest cupboard and closed the door just as somebody walked into the room. I knelt down and through a crack in the door saw two men enter. I realised the big fat man, dressed in bright red trousers and a black, frilly shirt, must be Cat Ball. The short, skinny man with him looked silly with nothing on except his shirt. They spent some time on their own until three girls, two black and one white, joined in the fun. One of the girls was Bonny. Loath though I was to break up their party, I pushed open the door and stepped out. The room was so opulent and they were making so much noise they did not hear us until we stood on either side of the bed and Jake drew their attention by cocking his pistol. I aimed my scattergun in the general direction of the bed and they froze. Ball looked from one gun to the next, his calmness unnerving me a little. I was gratified to see the fear in Bonny's rolling eyes.

'I want my money, Ball,' I said, lifting the gun to point at his head.

'What money?' he asked and at the sound of his voice they began to move.

'Hold still, all of you,' said Jake. 'I like you the way you are.'

They stopped wriggling. 'What the hell goes on?' asked Ball, showing indignant anger. 'I suggest for your own good you get out of here and we'll forget this little intrusion. One word from me and I can have a dozen men in here.'

'That would be very, very stupid, because long before then you'd be very, very dead. Bonny, my dear,' I looked down at her, 'what did you do with the money you stole from under my bunk last night?'

There was silence. 'Crawl out from there slowly, honey,' I said. 'Jake is going to tie you up.'

Using the rope from the wardrobe Jake quickly tied all three girls and left them lying on the floor. He then tied up the little man whose reaction to the events was startling. The man began to get excited again.

That left Ball, unmoving, his shirt still on but with no pants.

'You men are a bore. You don't think you're going to get away with this, do you?' He yawned and stretched to prove his boredom but even as his hand was reaching behind his back I rammed the barrel of the shotgun as hard as I could into his stomach. There was an explosion of air from his lungs and he curled up, his face distorted with pain. He was in bad condition, like most fat men, and had difficulty breathing. I leant down, reached behind him and removed a small, two barrelled Derringer.

When I showed it to Jake he shrugged. 'Can't be right all the time,' he said.

I looked at the others, their astonishment clear. The

little man was wriggling and I thought he was in pain until I realised he was enjoying himself.

Jake roughly spread-eagled Ball and tied his hands and feet to each corner of the bed, the knots digging into his flesh.

'Do you still say you know nothing about my money? Because if you don't tell me where it is I'll extract eleven hundred dollars worth of pain from you.' I saw the look of malevolence he cast at Bonny. 'Oh, oh, so she didn't give it all to you? Now wasn't that silly of her?'

Bonny cringed. 'I did, Cat. Honest I did. He's lying . . .'

'Shut up, you little fool,' he said, through clenched teeth.

I smiled mirthlessly, while Bonny sank back and seemed to shrink into herself. Her pallor had turned a sort of grey under her brown complexion.

'Thank you, Bonny. That was exactly what I wanted to know. I don't care how much she gave you Ball, I want my eleven hundred from you and I want it fast.' In the light from the lamps I saw he was going to make a move. A move? That was impossible. He was about to yell. I was holding the shotgun across my chest and when I swung it into his guts it was with more force than I had intended.

Ball gasped horribly and gave a weird grunt but said nothing. His hands and legs convulsed as he tried to cradle the ache. His mouth opened and closed like a fish out of water but he did not seem to be taking in any air. I wondered for a second whether he would die somehow, but slowly he recovered.

He whispered painfully, 'I'll kill you for that.'

'You stupid bastard. At the moment there is very little between your life and your death. Your woman took what was mine and I want it back. I'll hit you again, in the same way, if you so much as think of yelling. Now where's the money?'

'It . . . it's downstairs in my office. In a safe. You can't get to it because I have four men down below looking after my interests,' he spoke slowly and with difficulty.

I did not believe him. What would he want an office for? He would not be keeping books in order to pay taxes. I looked at Jake who shrugged.

'Give me a hand, Jake.' I pulled the pillows from the end of the bed and with Jake's help shoved them under Ball's back. From the cupboard I took a leather whip with a long handle, the thong tapering to a single strand.

'I don't believe you, Ball, and I'm going to gamble on you being a liar.' I took one of his frilly shirts, ripped a sleeve off and stuffed it into his mouth. He had difficulty breathing through his nose but that was his problem. I put the handle of the whip just outside his anus.

'I'm going to ram this about twelve inches in if you don't nod to tell me you'll show me where your money really is. After that, if you still don't talk it's going all the way in.' The sweat was standing out on Ball's forehead, his face ashen.

I gripped the end of the whip more firmly and suddenly rammed the knobbed end into him. His body bent up into the air, straining, trying to get away from the pain. I turned away, trying hard not to vomit.

I was disgusted with myself and I grabbed hold of Ball by the throat, tore the gag from his mouth and squeezed. 'That was a warning. Now if you don't talk I'm going to throttle you.' I squeezed harder, the folds of his chins almost covering my fingers. 'Talk, damn you, talk!' I said harshly.

Ball couldn't breathe and I felt the slight nod of his head rather than saw it. I relaxed my grip. He sucked air into his lungs and after a few moments managed to gasp out. 'Corner of room . . . lift carpet . . . under boards. Please . . . please . . . take the whip out . . . please . . .' tears rolled down his cheeks. I ignored them and left the whip where it was.

Jake continued watching, as impassive as though he

was carved out of stone. I hated what I was doing but nobody was going to steal from me and get away with it. Nobody. I tore the carpet up and saw the outline of a flap about twelve inches long by twelve inches wide. I inserted my knife in one corner and levered it open. Inside it was packed with bank notes. I pulled them out and scattered them around the room. Underneath these were bags of gold which I also took out and emptied. Ball appeared to be in worse agony from the way I was treating his money than he was from the whip.

I counted out eleven hundred dollars in gold. I guessed there was over fifteen thousand there all together but I ignored it. The little man and the three girls were staring in wonder at such wealth. Jake was not nonchalant about it either and bent down to pick up a handful.

'It's not ours, Jake,' I told him.

'I know. I can kill him,' he gestured at Ball with his gun, 'and pay a thousand to each of these others. Nobody will ever know.'

'We will. Can you shoot him in cold blood?'

By way of answer Jake walked over to the bed, pointed the gun at Ball's head and cocked the hammer. Ball lost control of his muscles and was urinating even as Jake lowered the gun again.

'I guess not. However, I'll keep one sovereign as a memento of the night's work,' he slipped one of the gold coins into his pocket. 'Shall we go, before somebody comes looking for them?'

'Wait a moment.' I counted out a thousand dollars in bills, fanned them before Ball's eyes and struck a match. Seeing the money burning, Ball was beside himself with anguish and horror. The other four were speechless.

'Ball, I care nothing for money,' I lied. 'If we have any trouble at all I promise you that you'll die and this place will be burned to the ground. Understand?'

His hate-filled eyes glared back at me; he didn't answer. I shrugged and walked over to the girls. 'Bonny,

I'm sorry. He'll blame you for this but you did steal my money. I suggest you get away from here.' I cut the rope and helped her to her feet. She stood there dazed for a few seconds and then nodded dumbly. The sweat was glistening on her naked body and running down between her breasts. She looked so vulnerable that I toyed with the idea of taking her with us. But only for as long as it took the thought to flash through my mind and be instantly dismissed.

'Come on, Dave, for Christ's sake,' said Jake. 'Hurry up.'

We retraced our steps and dropped down from the balcony into the lane just as dawn was breaking. The sky was clear and it promised to be a beautiful day. I wondered if I had done the right thing in leaving Ball alive

'I would never have thought you had it in you,' said Jake. 'It's nice to find out I've got a partner who's a hard bastard.'

I nodded, tucked the shotgun under my arm and thrust my hands into my pockets. It was the only way to stop them shaking.

Two days passed with Jake and I constantly on edge. We took it in turns to sit on deck with our guns ready certain that Cat Ball and his men would be coming for us. We rushed through our preparations for leaving wanting to get as far away as possible before anything happened. Late on the second day I went to the Blue Pelican. It was not as bad as some places, a bit cleaner and tidier, and the clientele seemed a little better heeled than usual. We were glad to be leaving the next day now that we had our cargo of rum. Neither of us felt able to relax wondering what Cat Ball might be up to.

The place was half full with about fifty men and a few women. Within the hour the bar had filled up, the air was blue with smoke and heavy with the smell of rum and cheap perfume from the whores.

Somebody turned off some of the lamps making it even murkier and a ring of candles were lit around a big table. A hush descended as a girl stepped into the circle of light and a band started playing at her feet. It took me a few seconds to realise it was the girl we had rescued. She had on a shimmering dress in gold and green, cut to her navel but with her breasts covered. Her voice was low, yet it carried. It caressed each man there, leaving us with a promise of love and wild nights. At the end there was silence for a few seconds and then the room erupted into applause.

Somebody threw a coin onto the table, which was quickly followed by another and then a shower fell around her feet. She nodded her head graciously and the band started to play again. The rhythm changed, the tempo increased and her song was one of joy and laughter. At the end of her performance there was more money throwing, wild clapping and loud cheers. Disdainfully she stepped off the table and walked away from the money and out through a side door. I was on my feet and following her before I knew what I was doing. At the door a burly fellow with a low slung gun barred my way.

'I'd like to see the lady,' I said politely.

'Sure mister, so would every other guy here. Only she ain't seeing nobody. Get lost.'

He was big, black and mean looking. I knew better than to argue. As I turned away, she came back out and I looked into her eyes. It took her a moment or two to place me but when she did her smile stirred my loins. I knew I was not in love with her but I wanted her – God, how I wanted her.

'It's all right Samuel,' she said to the guard. 'He's a friend of mine.'

'Yes, ma'am,' the man said sullenly, throwing me a look of pure vitriol.

'Would, eh,' I cleared my throat. 'Would you like to join Jake and me for a glass of wine?'

I escorted her to our table and ordered Champagne.

'I had no idea you were a singer,' I said.

She shrugged. 'What else could I do here?' I didn't answer.

'We, eh, hope you're fully recovered after the other night,' I said.

'Thank you,' she smiled across her glass at me, 'but I'm fine. It really was very kind of you to rescue me. I hear you've been quite busy in other ways too.'

'Eh?' She surprised us both for a second. 'We've done little. In fact,' Jake said, 'we were waiting for a job offer. Unfortunately, as none has come our way, we're returning to New Orleans tomorrow.'

'Oh, I wouldn't call what happened with Cat Ball little,' she smiled impishly while Jake and I started and looked to see if anybody was listening. 'Don't worry, nobody else knows about it.'

'How the hell do you know?' I asked more harshly than I had intended.

She shrugged. 'My sister was one of the girls in the room. She told me what happened. Of course, you left. But you must have heard what happened after you'd gone?'

We both shook our heads. We had spent the last two days covering our backs and keeping a low profile.

'You freed Bonny, right? Bonny freed my sister and then went to free Ball. He was bleeding quite badly. He didn't yell out or anything but according to my sister, before Bonny could cut him free, he said to her that she would live to regret that day and never have a man again. Bonny had a knife in her hand and instead of cutting the ropes she stabbed Ball through the heart. The other man there was the Governor's secretary, a renowned little pervert but has too little money to indulge his whims too often. They all saw a chance and shared Ball's money between them. They hid his body in the cupboard and escaped. My sister and the other two girls left for South

America yesterday. With their money they intend starting
new lives, finding husbands and having children. Whether
they will or not I don't know. Unfortunately, my sister
enjoyed her work a great deal and I don't think she'll
change. I pray I'm wrong about her.' When she saw the
incredulous looks on our faces she said, 'You really didn't
know Ball was dead?'

'No,' I said. 'Eh, what happened to the secretary?'

'This morning he took a boat to Cuba. It's said to be
even wilder there than it is here.'

'Good God,' I said, pouring some more wine. Whether
I meant at the thought of Cuba being wilder or the story
she had told us I was unsure. I was shaken, and so was
Jake, but for a different reason.

'Damn and blast them. And all we got was a lousy
gold piece. Shit.'

The whole situation for some reason struck me as
funny and I started to chuckle which upset Jake. The
more annoyed he became the more I laughed.

'What's your name?' I asked bluntly. 'Mine's David
Griffiths and this is Jake Kirkpatrick.'

'So I gathered. Mine's Elizabeth,' she replied in her
husky voice that sent shivers along my spine.

I cannot remember what we talked about after that.
From time to time she sung and while she was away I
kept on at Jake to move out and get drunk elsewhere.

When she walked away from the money thrown at her
feet for the third time I asked when she was paid it. She
and Jake burst out laughing though I could not see what
was so funny.

Elizabeth explained. 'I don't receive any of it. The
louse who owns the place often starts it all by throwing
a coin or two and the suckers follow. They think it
wonderful I leave the money for a minion to pick up.
The trouble is he's not my minion. I never get a nickel.'
There was no bitterness in her voice.

'If you know about it, Jake, surely they all do as well?'

'Some do, sure. Maybe most of them. But in their state they feel good and so throw their money away. Christ man, it happens all over the place,' Jake was now beginning to look a little owlishly at me. He was drinking brandy and Champagne cocktails while I stuck to wine and drank sparingly at that. Elizabeth did too, in spite of the fact I tried to get her to drink more.

It was three in the morning when Jake announced he was going back to the boat. Unsteadily he got to his feet and weaved towards the door.

'Shouldn't you go with him?' Elizabeth suggested. 'He looks as though he won't make it.'

'Don't worry about Jake,' I assured her. 'He can find his way without any help from me. Besides, I'd rather ensure you got home safely.'

'Oh? I don't suppose I'll be attacked again. I should be quite safe thank you, and it is rather a long walk.'

'I don't mind. The fresh air will do me good. When can you leave this place?'

'Now. I'm finished for the night.'

I followed her out of the door. I was in a nervous sweat all the way to her house which turned out to be a small, white bricked place at the back of the town. We stopped outside her door and she turned to say goodnight. I put my arms around her waist and drew her to me. Her lips were soft, her breasts thrust hard against me and it took all my willpower not to try and get my hand inside her dress.

We broke apart after a long time. 'Goodnight, David,' she said, looking into my eyes. The moon shone down on her upturned face and she looked even more beautiful.

'Goodnight,' I croaked back. 'Would you like to come for a picnic or something tomorrow?' It was all I could think of.

'I thought you were sailing tomorrow?'

'We can stay here a little longer yet and Jake can see about another job. We're not so desperate to get away now we know that Ball's dead. Would you like to come?'

'Yes, if you don't sail. What time?'

'It's too hot at midday. What if I meet you at three o'clock and we'll go along the coast in a buggy?'

'Lovely. Goodnight,' she turned to go and then looked back, 'and thank you for a lovely evening. I haven't been treated like a lady for so long I'd forgotten what it was like.' With that she whirled and rushed indoors.

Damn, I thought. Damn and double damn. I did not want to treat her like a lady. I wanted her body with no complications and that was all. Okay, I liked her . . . liked her very much, but that was all. I loved Gunhild, of that I had no doubt. The thought haunted me to sleep.

44

IT TOOK A week. During that time Jake ranted and raved about being led by what hung between my legs but I ignored him. He thought my efforts to get into Elizabeth's bed were hilarious and spent hours and hours telling me what a great night he had with one or even two whores. I dined Elizabeth, wined her and talked to her. I flattered her, gave her a couple of sentimental presents, not too expensive and treated her like a lady. In the end it worked. For seven days I escorted her home and each time she said goodnight on the doorstep. I was becoming demented with longing for her.

Then on the eighth night it happened: she asked me in. I hardly noticed the house but I remember the place was small, clean and neat. There were icons and Jesus on crosses all over the place, proof of how religious I had already discovered her to be. I sat on a sofa with my arm around her, kissing her gently and then with more passion. She responded and I slipped my hand to her breast, the thin cloth of her blouse not hiding the hardening of her nipple.

Slowly I undid the buttons, savouring each moment until I put my hand inside her blouse.

'You have been very patient,' she said softly. 'Now I shall reward you. I was frightened of becoming pregnant but it's safe now.'

From somewhere, God only knows where, my common decency lifted its head and I found myself withdrawing from her, pulling her blouse shut.

I explained. 'I want you very much. But you see, Jake and I must go tomorrow. We've got a job on. I don't know whether or not I'll be back. If we make love now and I leave then what will you think? That I've had my way and now I've left. I know it sounds stupid but I want to leave with you thinking better of me than that.'

'I know,' she said, taking my hand and putting it on her breast. 'Jake has already told me that you are leaving tomorrow. But it doesn't alter a thing. I want you,' she smiled and undid my trousers.

I left late the following afternoon with a promise to return soon.

We were now into July and God alone knew where the time had gone. I had left St Louis in the second week of March but it seemed a life time away. I would have had to return to St Louis in a month or two to marry Gunhild. I had sent her a letter shortly after we arrived in Jamaica, but at the time I had no way of knowing that she never received it.

Onboard the Lucky Lady, Jake was in a foul mood, berating me for not being there in time to catch the early tide. The next tide was still a couple of hours away so I went below to sleep.

We left for Puerto Rico. The island was no longer controlled by the United States, ever since the Spanish-American war that had started on 1st May 1898, and been over within ten weeks. General Miles' army had marched through the island as though on a holiday parade. At the time there were many rich Spaniards living on the island and some of them had elected to stay in the hope that they would be able to keep their land and wealth. With the democratic freedom now available to the people and the courts it was a short lived hope. Many Spaniards were tried for theft, corruption and the abuse of privileged power. Some were deported penniless, others were murdered, but some managed to hide upon the island in the hope that life would improve or more importantly, that they would be able to escape with the gold and other wealth they had amassed. We were on our way to pick up one such family and then take them to Bermuda – a distance close to a thousand miles. All the arrangements had been made by Casper. It was a long journey to undertake but for seven thousand dollars it was more than worth it.

We sailed south of Haiti with the island barely discernible on the horizon. After passing Santo Domingo in the Dominican Republic we put into a small village on the easternmost tip of the Antilles to take on water and replenish our food supplies.

Because of the adverse winds, it was two o'clock in the morning of the eleventh day when we approached a small, deserted bay, twenty miles west of San Juan, on the north side of the island.

The night was pitch black, the moon hidden behind heavy clouds, the air oppressive with a feeling of impending rain. The coastline here was straight and the bay barely more than an indentation. The water was deep until close inshore, so Jake took us to within fifty yards. We exchanged lamp signals and all seemed safe. It had been arranged for the four passengers to have their own boat to save time.

Now and again an unsteady squall rocked the Lucky Lady and caused the sail to flap, the sound like that of a gun shot. Jake kept the boat as steady as he could, with the wind blowing sometimes over the port and then the starboard bow. We would drift out fifty yards before closing on the shore again, waiting impatiently. What the hell was keeping them? We stood in the cockpit, ears strained for the sound of oars. I could see no further than the bow and the first indication someone was coming was the sound of a faint creak of a rowlock. Then there was a yell from further away, whistles rent the air, yells

and orders were screamed and shots were fired. All hell
was breaking loose. Jake and I stood frozen for a few
moments, our rifles ready.

With a curse Jake thrust the wheel over, the wind
filled the jibs, turning us until the stern faced the island
and the main sail and mizzen took effect. Flashes from
guns ashore were pinpricks of instant yellow and red,
followed by the noise of the shot. It sounded as though a
battle was taking place, but whatever was happening they
were not firing at us. Or if they were, a combination of the
darkness and poor shooting prevented any bullets coming
close. There was a lull in the noise and somebody shouted
to us to stop.

'Jake, somebody asked us to wait, a woman I think.
Shall we just slow and see what happens? We're far
enough away not to be hit by a stray bullet or an aimed
one if it comes to that.'

By way of reply he let the wind out of our sails and
we hove to, trying to penetrate the night with our ears.
Behind the background of the noise ashore, now some
three hundred yards away, we heard a whimper, a curse
and a man's voice telling somebody to row, for the love
of God.

A plaintive voice said, 'Which way? I can't see them.
They're probably out to sea by now.' It sounded like a
youth speaking.

'We cannot go back, so we may as well go on,' the
woman, whoever she was, broke into Spanish which I
did not understand.

I took the lamp, lit it in the shadow of the cockpit and
flashed it briefly, once, towards the shore. There was an
exclamation, a vigorous sound of oars being used and I
called out, 'Who is it? What's your names?'

'Mendoza,' came the reply and the small boat came
into sight a few yards astern of us. Jake was ready to
pick up the wind the instant anything untoward happened
while I was ready to shoot. The boat came alongside and

in the heat of the moment all passwords were forgotten. I helped the passengers aboard, two women, a young man and a wounded older man. The youth passed up two heavy boxes about two feet long, one foot wide and one foot deep which nearly caused me to topple over the railing because of the unexpected weight. Then he passed up two trunks which I assumed held their clothes and other personal effects. If we had used our own dinghy I would have needed a trip for each item.

Once aboard, I let the boat drift free, Jake caught the wind and we turned north once more. I showed the Mendozas into the saloon, helping the wounded man. We had closed and curtained the port holes and with the door shut no light seeped out when I lit the lamps.

The older man, frail looking and with a white, carefully trimmed beard, lay on the seat alongside the table. His breathing was uneasy, his face chalk white and his clothes were stained with blood. The older woman – his wife I assumed, was wringing her hands in useless anguish. The black haired and beautiful daughter did nothing, looking distraught, while the youngster stood with a pistol pointing at the deck.

'Isn't anybody going to help him?' I asked. 'Or are you just going to stand there and watch him die?'

'Signor,' said the older lady, 'I and my children do not know what to do.' Her voice had a dignity that was unexpected under the circumstances.

'You, you do something,' said the youth, waving his gun in my direction. 'It is your fault. If you cowards had waited for us instead of sailing away this would never have happened. If my father dies, so will you.' He could not have been more than seventeen years old, slick black hair showing under a black, Spanish style hat. His clothes were expensive though dishevelled.

He was about four feet from me and I did not give myself much time to think what I was doing. I took a half pace towards the prone figure of his father, backhanded the youth across the face as hard as I could and at the same time clamped my other hand across the hammer of his gun, preventing him from pulling the trigger. There was a shocked silence for a second and then Jake put his head through the door.

'It's all right, everything's under control.' The boy lay on the deck, glaring venomously at me. The girl stepped forward as I put the gun in my belt.

'Hold it. Don't do anything stupid. I don't have any qualms about hitting a woman, believe me, especially if I think they need it.'

She stopped.

'You will die for that insult to my sister,' the boy tried to speak through clenched teeth, sounding absurd.

'Grow up, sonny,' I said, annoyed. 'I could shoot you now and throw you overboard and nobody would be any the wiser. Your family could follow you. So keep the melodrama to your imagination. You,' I said to the girl, 'light the stove and put some water on.' She did not move until her mother spoke to her in Spanish. Sullenly she did as I had ordered.

I found our first aid kit and rummaged around until I had a pair of scissors and some bandages. Carefully I cut away the old man's coat and shirt. His clothes were sodden with blood, right down to his tight-fitting trousers. The wounds in his shoulder and side were worse than I would have thought possible for a man to suffer and still breathe. A bullet had entered his shoulder, smashed the bone, been deflected and exited under his left wing bone. Blood was still seeping steadily through the hole in his back. The other bullet had hit him in the right side of the chest; there was little blood and no exit. If he lasted the night I would be surprised.

'We had better get him into the port cabin. You, give me a hand.' The boy, who was now standing, glared at me and then bent to take his father's legs. Carefully we carried him forward and put him on the bunk. I cleaned up as much blood as I could, not knowing what else to do. His breathing was becoming more laboured and shallow.

'Will he live, Senor?' asked his wife.

I shook my head. 'I don't think so. I can clean the wounds but I can't do anything more. He needs a doctor and even then . . .' I trailed off and shrugged.

'I have seen other wounds like these, Senor and I am sure my husband will not last the night. A doctor could not save him. Please leave, as I wish to pray over him.'

'I'll help you clean him up some more and then bandage him,' I said. The girl appeared with more hot water and we washed most of the blood away. The old lady was more of a hindrance than a help but finally there was nothing further for me to do and I left. In the saloon I poured myself a stiff brandy and another for Jake. I wanted fresh air badly.

'Pour one for me too,' said the girl haughtily, coming to sit at the table, her brother with her.

I was about to tell her to do it herself when I thought what the hell. For seven thousand dollars I could pour her a drink. 'My name's David Griffiths,' I said, handing the brandy to them. Neither bothered to reply. 'Listen you two, we're going to be stuck here for the best part of two weeks. We need to get on together even if that only entails being civil to each other.' Still no reply so I left them to their silence and went up top. I explained the situation to Jake.

'That's all we need. The sooner he's dead the better. If he lingers on life will be hell and it looks as thought it's going to be bad enough as it is. Did you ask them what the shooting was about?'

I shook my head. 'I didn't think of it. I was too busy.'

'It doesn't matter. You take over here and I'll go and find out. I won't be long.'

I could no longer see the island, not even the lights of villages. We continued sailing without navigational lamps, ploughing through the stygian darkness, under heavy cloud, heading due north with the wind fine on our port beam. When Jake reappeared he had the brandy bottle with him and refilled my glass.

'According to the girl they had been at the rendezvous with about twenty armed men to protect them. Some of the men they've known for years while others were just hired for the occasion. After they exchanged signals with us they left the shore and the firing started. They've no idea who attacked them, whether it was soldiers or crooks after their money. The boy then said that they are carrying a fortune in gold and jewels, the stupid bugger.' Jake chuckled. 'You should have heard the girl telling him off when he said that. I know some Spanish but not enough. Eeee, what a tongue she must have. And that body, phew, beautiful isn't the word.'

'No fondling the merchandise,' I warned him. 'It could lead to too much trouble. It would probably besmirch his honour for a gringo to even so much as look at the fine lady his sister.'

'No doubt,' Jake said with a sign. 'Pity.'

The old man never regained consciousness and died a short while later. We wrapped him in a weighted piece of canvas and to my surprise Jake said an appropriate prayer over the body. The dawn was breaking into a dull and grey day when we committed his body to the sea. The women cried while the boy stood silently, white faced. The body floated for a few seconds, a grey blob in the grey looking sea and then sank. The Mendozas went below to the forward cabins – presumably to grieve in private. The two women shared the port cabin, the boy had the starboard one, while I now slept in the saloon.

For the first two days while the weather remained unsettled our passengers remained in their cabins, being ill, refusing all food but taking water. The girl was the first to appear, looking pale and very sorry for herself. She managed to eat some stew, kept it down, and with a few hours in the fresh air got some of the colour back into her cheeks. That evening her brother joined us but their mother did not reappear for another two days.

Senora Mendoza looked terrible and I tried to imagine how Mam would feel under the circumstances. Perhaps I understood something of the anguish the woman was going through which made me very attentive and I helped her as much as possible.

The boy continued to be rude and surly and a number of times I had to resist the temptation to hit him again.

The girl gave Jake seven thousand dollars in gold and we both spent the days wishing the journey away. On the sixth day the weather cleared, the sea calmed and the wind dropped. I was standing by the main mast when I realised the girl was sitting on the starboard side, staring at the water.

'I hope the weather stays like this until we get to Bermuda,' I said. No response. 'For what it's worth, I'm really sorry about your father. I hope you realise there was nothing Jake and I could have done about it. If we had stayed closer then the chances are . . .' I trailed off. The chances are what? I thought. Perhaps the old boy would still be alive, or perhaps Jake or I would be dead instead. She still acted as though I had not spoken. 'Do you have anybody to go to once we get to Bermuda? Any family or friends waiting for you?'

Before she could answer her brother, who was approaching from the cockpit, yelled something in Spanish which startled her. Then he turned to me, a wicked looking stiletto held low down in his right hand.

'I told her not to answer,' his voice was strained. 'I know why you want to know. If there is nobody then you will kill us and take all our money. I know you gringos for the cowards and bullies you are.'

'You take it easy, young fellow,' I tried to soothe him. 'Neither Jake nor I are interested in your money. We've been paid to deliver you to Bermuda and that's what we'll do. I was just being pleasant.'

He must have mistaken the way I spoke, for he suddenly smiled. That is, if the grimace of stretched lips across his teeth could be called a smile. 'So this little knife makes you realise who the master is, does it?' He twisted the knife in his hand, the blade gleaming in the sunlight.

'Don't talk so bloody stupid, and put that thing away before I take it off you and put you across my knee, you silly little boy.' As I expected, I infuriated him, and he even became more angry when his sister smiled.

'I shall kill you for that insult, and for the blow I received when we came on board. Prepare to die, gringo.'

It was so childishly melodramatic that I could not believe my ears. He was standing to windward of the boom and half way along when Jake yelled, 'Jibe oh,' and spun the wheel hard to port, while I ducked. The wind came over the starboard bow, filled the mainsail and pushed the boom hard to port. It took young Mendoza about shoulder height and swept him over the side. The girl screamed and scrambled across the deck to see her brother floundering and yelling for help. Jake was already coming about and I was getting a life belt ready to throw. Their mother rushed on deck to see what was wrong, fear on her face.

'Save him, save him, he cannot swim,' she called, wringing her hands as she had done over her dying husband.

He was waving, sinking, reappearing and spitting out water. Jake aimed to pass close, not attempting to slow down. I threw the life belt as we drew abreast and watched him grab hold of it. We then came about and tacked in closer. He had the lifebelt over his head and watched us with malevolence in his eyes. While this had been going on the girl had been talking to her mother and I could see

Senora Mendoza becoming angrier and angrier. We hove to and I threw the boy a line. I pulled him alongside and helped him aboard. As he lay on the deck his mother tore into him in Spanish and from the way he flushed I guessed he was getting a real earful. He muttered something in a disdainful way. Before I so much as blinked the old woman's hand flashed and struck him across the cheek with a sound like a pistol shot. She said something again and this time he mumbled an apology to me in English. His mother added one of her own.

'I am sorry for the bad manners of my son, Senor,' she said sadly. 'He has not been brought up in the way a mother would like. I only hope he learns better before it is too late. I have told him to go to his room and stay there. My daughter, Estella will bring his meals to him. I hope the rest of the voyage goes quietly.

'Look,' I said, 'there's no need for that. I can appreciate how he feels, with the loss of his father coming on top of everything else. He blames us and I know how easy that is for him. The fact that there was nothing we could have done is besides the point. If he promises to behave then there's no reason why he should not move about as freely as he likes. If he gives his word, that is.'

'Well?' his mother asked him. 'Do you give your word?'

He nodded sullenly and from his glare I was not sure that at the first opportunity he would not put a knife in my back.

An uneasy peace settled once more, except that this time the girl, Estella, was more ready to talk.

She told us they had been a wealthy land-owning family before the US invaded the island. After that, though her father tried to set himself up in business, punitive laws were gradually but surely leading to the loss of all their money in taxes. Some old enemies of her father had tried to have him arrested on a charge of conspiracy, something to do with an attempted coup to re-establish the old regime. It was all nonsense but the courts only wanted an excuse to confiscate his money. Justice and proof were not the order of the day. Learning what was going to happen, the family had attempted to leave openly from port but had been prevented at the eleventh hour. In desperation, they had arranged, through friends, for a boat to pick them up secretly. Jake and I had got the job.

The next day Jake took over from me around dawn and I went into the saloon for a few hours sleep. I was back on deck around midday and stepping into the cockpit I could see black clouds forming on the horizon. Jake cast a worried look over his shoulder and nodded grimly.

'We're in for a bad time. See how the clouds are forming. Does it remind you of anything? That shape?'

I stared and then shook my head. 'Can't say it does.'

'See how straight the sides are and the way if flattens out on top, just like a blacksmith's anvil. See what I mean?'

'Yes. It's plain now you've pointed it out. The top of the anvil is pointing in this direction.'

'Yep. That means it's coming this way. In an hour or two you'll see grey clouds rolling underneath and then a dark, very black area. That's where the rain is. Depending on how high that black area reaches will depend on how bad it's going to be. And from the look of it, I'd say it's going to be a bad son of a bitch.'

'There's nowhere to run to? No land in reasonable distance?'

He shook his head. 'Now that the wind has gone so far round we may as well keep on for Bermuda. In fact, I'd say it's the closest place.'

The wind was almost directly astern and we were running before it. I went below and secured everything I could. Already the wind was chilling and the sea was beginning to run from the south east, from the direction of the storm. All day the cloud kept on building up and soon the day darkened ominously. Our passengers had been up to see what was going on and one look at what was brewing had been enough to send them back to their bunks. When I passed the forward cabins I heard the two Mendoza women praying and I just hoped somebody was listening.

The wind increased steadily. I could see the billowing grey, cauliflower shaped clouds beneath the towering anvil and the blackness where the rain was blotting out the horizon. We put two reefs in the mainsail and took down the other sails. The boom was right out to starboard and we were running before the wind.

The seas began to break against the stern and we were surrounded by whitecaps, four or five feet high. We put on our oilskins and took in another three reefs of sail. The whole of the sky astern of us was a black, tumultuous mountain of cloud while ahead it still showed blue. It was becoming cold in spite of the fact we were only just north of the Tropic of Cancer.

Jake and I stood in the cockpit and watched the black wall of rain sweeping down, cutting off the light as it overtook us. There were a few minutes of light rain and then it became torrential. The wind whistled through the rigging and we had to shout to make ourselves heard. The boat was pitching and turning like a corkscrew, and the day had turned to twilight. We pulled the boom in but still had plenty of headway to keep the stern to the wind. Inexperienced though I was, I could appreciate that if a wave ever turned us broadside to the sea and wind there was every chance we would turn turtle.

The wind whipped the sea and rain across the cockpit so hard it lashed us like buckshot pellets, visibility was as far as the bow, and lightning was splitting the sky every minute. I was scared to death.

'We need to keep running before the wind,' Jake yelled in my ear. 'This storm is going to last for some time and it takes a lot out of you. You go down below and try and get some sleep, or at least rest and come and relieve me in four hours. Okay?'

'Okay,' I yelled back. He helped me to open the hatch to the saloon and close it behind me, gallons of water sweeping in as we did. I threw off my oilskins and sat down heavily at the table, trying to think if there was anything else I could do. The stoves were out and every moveable item tied down.

I did fight my way across the heaving deck forward, scraping my shins only a couple of dozen times and looked through the hatch down to the bilge's. They were bone dry. I looked in on our passengers trying to encourage them. The women were still kneeling by their bunks praying, the boy lay on his, staring at the overhead bulkhead. He ignored me when I told him not to worry. I went back to the saloon and sat at the table. All that was left was for me to worry instead.

45

TWENTY FOUR HOURS later Jake and I were close to exhaustion after spending four-hour watches on, fighting the wheel and weather and the next four off, sleeplessly lying on our bunks. It was impossible to rest, the movement of the boat threatening to throw us out of our bunks onto the deck. We saw nothing of the Mendozas and I did not know whether they were alive or dead; anyway, I was feeling scared enough so that I no longer cared.

The wind did not abate by so much as a knot. The seas were mountainous and often, as I stood at the wheel and we plunged down the side of a wall of water, I wondered if we would come up the other side. Jake kept telling me the Lucky Lady was a highly seaworthy craft, well built and able to take far worse. I sometimes wondered which of us he was trying to convince.

Then disaster struck. Jake and I were changing over and I was looking forward to going below for a drink of water and to wash the salt off my face when there was a loud ripping, rending sound. In the grey afternoon light we saw the mainsail tear in half, flapping wildly, making a noise like a number of pistol shots. The mast creaked ominously under the strain.

'Stay here,' yelled Jake. 'I'm going to get the sail down.'

I watched helplessly while he crawled over the deck, a safety line paying out behind him.

The sail was ripped from the top to the bottom and was now in two almost equal halves. Jake slackened off the halyards, pulled down armfuls of sail and rolled it up under his feet. It was hard, dangerous work, the boat pitching and yawing like a mad thing, and many times Jake had to stop and just hold on for grim life to avoid being swept overboard.

Once it was down, he undid the clew outhaul and pulled the sail clean off the boom. He passed the sail back to me and I shoved it underfoot, out of the way. Jake then tightened down on the main topping lift, pulling the boom tight against the boom jack, a rope which held the end of the boom to the deck. He left the lazy jacks, used to contain the sail while it is being lowered, and fought his way back to the cockpit. It had taken him the best part of an hour to carry out an evolution which we had done in ten minutes on a bad day when we both nursed a hangover.

He stood alongside me in the cockpit, regaining his breath and watching how the boat performed. We now had no way to keep the stern pointed at the waves and though I spun the wheel back and forth as far as it would go it was more luck than judgement that stopped us turning turtle.

'I thought we'd have this problem,' yelled Jake. 'Leave the wheel and help me get the sail to the stern. We'll tie it to the stern cleats and throw it overboard. It may act as a sea anchor and steady the boat.'

I nodded and together we pushed the sail to the stern guard-rail. I was freezing, soaked to the skin and frightened to death. We tied a dozen lengths of manila rope to the canvas and worked it overboard. Immediately the stern steadied into the wind and waves. We hugged each other with delight and returned to the cockpit. Jake lashed the wheel to prevent the rudder damaging itself and we both went below to the saloon. There was nothing further we could do, except pray and I had not done that since I left Llanbeddas.

We had a brandy to warm ourselves and then Jake went back to the after cabin. I lay down and must have dozed off. The next thing I knew we were being thrown about as wildly as ever.

I climbed into my oilskins and went up to the cockpit. Jake was already there. Glumly we stared at the stern where the ropes had parted and were flapping wildly in the wind.

'Do we have enough canvas to do that again?' I yelled at Jake.

He shrugged. 'I don't think so. I can repair a sail but I can't make a complete new one, and so I don't carry that much.'

'Then what the hell do we do?'

'Cut down the main mast,' his reply startled me.

'Don't be daft man, we can't do that.'

'Do you think,' he screamed, 'that we could hoist a mizzen or jib, come about and keep her pointed into the wind?'

'How the hell should I know? You're the seaman.'

'Well I'm telling you, we can't. So far we've been lucky but we could turn over anytime. If that happens we'll probably slide to the bottom and meet Davy Jones. Without the main mast the boat has a good chance of righting herself again. With it there's no chance. Understand?'

I nodded.

'Get the axe out of the locker,' he yelled. 'I'm going to cut the mainstay ropes off above our heads. That way no flying rope can take an eye out or cut our faces open, all right?'

I nodded and suddenly grabbed the wheel to stop from falling. We were now yawing as much as sixty degrees either side; any more and we would turn over. I did not need Jake to tell me that.

Carefully we made our way out of the cockpit and towards the mast. The wind plucked at our oilskins. Sea waves and rain poured down our necks and the lightning flashing across the sky added a further touch of unreality to the scene. In spite of the weather it took only seconds to cut the ropes free and clear the deck. Jake took the axe from me. He loved the Lucky Lady with a passion I would never equal, but even so it hurt me to see the axe bite deeply into the foot of the mast. He cut a chunk out of the downwind side and then attacked the mast behind and above the cut. The mast bent a few degrees, then another swing and it went a little further. Jake was panting heavily but would not let me take over. Instead he swung the axe with greater effort, blow quickly following blow. With a loud crackling noise the mast toppled, still not cut free but now touching the water, dragging the boat to starboard. A few more strikes and it was severed completely. With a heave from both of us it slid over the side and was immediately lost from sight. We crawled back to the cockpit and down into the after cabin. Jake was utterly spent and I helped him into his bunk.

'Go and tell the other three to tie themselves into their bunks and not to get up for any reason. Tell them if we turn turtle we'll still be all right and to wait for us to come upright again,' Jake ordered.

I took some rope from the cockpit locker. Both women had been sick at some stage but had been unable to do anything about it and just lay in the filth, holding on to each other. I told them what the situation was and tied them to their bunks. They accepted it with resignation.

The boy screamed that I wanted to murder him when he was tied down so I threw him the rope in disgust, explained the situation again and left. I went back to the after cabin and tied myself alongside Jake, lay back and wondered if there was a God.

How long it lasted I have no way of knowing. I do know I was hungrier, thirstier and more scared than I had ever been before. At one time, some hours later, the worst happened and we turned upside down. We hung painfully from the ropes across our chests and stomachs, our legs dangling in front of us. For a heart-stopping moment I waited to see the water pouring in as we slid to the bottom of the ocean but then we slowly began to turn upright, the pressure eased and we found ourselves on our backs again.

That never happened again, thank God, though we came close a number of times. Sometime in the night Jake and I got off our bunks and put on our oilskins. We were thrown around like straw men in a hurricane, bruising ourselves badly but we were finally ready to brave the storm. Out in the cockpit we manned the two hand pumps, feeling them bite, pumping water out of the bilges. I skinned the knuckles of my hands before Jake called a halt and we returned to the relative warmth of the cabin.

It seemed never-ending. I was aware of light filtering through the porthole at one stage but I had no idea of the time of day. Darkness followed and another day of greyness, unreality and fear. I was so exhausted I floated in and out of oblivion a number of times.

Suddenly, I was wide awake, listening to an ominous scraping sound along the hull which lasted for a good ten seconds. We were heeled right over. Then the noise stopped. The boat righted itself and remained steady. I looked at Jake in a sudden spasm of deep fear and he must have had the same thought because he shook his head.

'It's impossible, we can't have sunk. Come on, we had better go and see what's happened.'

We undid the ropes and staggered on deck. Through the driving rain, a hundred yards away we saw a beach with palm trees bending before the fury of the storm. Astern of us was a coral reef we had somehow crossed, the waves in the lagoon were only two or three feet high, virtually calm after what we had endured.

'Quickly, help me get the anchor out,' said Jake.

As the anchor dug into the sea bed we came round with our bows facing the storm. We sat in the cock-pit for some time, thankful to be alive and cursing

the ugly stump of the mast. Estella appeared at the
saloon hatch.

'My mother, quickly please. There's something wrong
with her.'

At first glance I thought the old lady was unconscious
but when I felt for her pulse and touched the cold skin I
realised she was dead. There was no mark on her and I
surmised she had died of a heart attack, the strain having
proved too much for her. I remember comforting the girl
while she sobbed bitterly with her head on my shoulder.
The boy came out of the other cabin, saw what was wrong
and threw himself alongside the bunk, sobbing and yelling
'Mama' in a manner that surprised me. I left the brother
and sister to their grief and went back to the cockpit.

Ironically, there was now a lightening of the sky to the
south and the wind felt as if it was beginning to abate. The
rain slackened and we could now see more of the land.

'Is this Bermuda?' I asked Jake.

'I don't think so. Though where the hell we are, I've no
idea. It's possible I suppose that we've travelled further
than I think. No, hell, this can't be it. I thought I knew
every bay in Bermuda and I don't recognise this place.'

'Shall we stay here or go ashore and find out?' I
asked.

'I think we'd better go ashore. We'll take the old
lady. I don't like having a corpse on board for long.
It's bad luck.'

We wrapped her body in a piece of canvas and Dominic
and I took her ashore in the dinghy. I returned for Jake and
the girl and we stood in a silent, irresolute group on the
shore. Finally, Jake and I used the axe and our hands to
dig a shallow grave while the two youngsters stood side
by side, crying. When we were finished Jake and I left
the two of them to pray over their mother's grave.

'It'll stop raining soon' said Jake, looking towards the
patches of blue sky to the south. 'If we are on Bermuda
then we should find a village or something quite close.

We could go and look or return to the boat and start in the morning.'

'Now we're ashore,' I said, 'there's no point in returning and wasting the rest of the daylight. Anyway, it's nice to have solid ground underfoot again, instead of her heaving deck,' I pointed at the Lucky Lady.

We looked through the thinning curtain of rain, at the boat riding at anchor, a dark silhouette, bobbing on the water.

For most of the way the jungle and palm trees stopped about five yards from the water's edge, but here and there it sneaked in clumps to the sea. We had not gone a hundred yards when we came to a shallow stream of fresh water, near where the beach curved out in a spit. Here the reef joined the land and we could see the white coral only a foot or two beneath the surface. On the other side there was no more reef, only a beach. Here the trees were further away from the sea and an expanse of white sand swept unbroken for a half mile or more before curving out of sight. Inland we could see a hill rising above tree top level, its domed top reminding me of pictures I had seen of volcanoes. I was looking for a sign of life, such as rising smoke or a house. I saw nothing.

Jake and I shrugged helplessly at each other and continued along the beach. The rain stopped and a shifting cloud allowed the sun to shine through from the west. A rainbow appeared to start from the end of the beach and curve towards the sky, beautiful beyond words. With the sun came a buoyancy of spirits, an unfounded hope that all would soon be well and we walked more briskly. We removed our oilskins and left them under a palm tree. The sand was soft underfoot and our boots would sink a few inches but it felt good to have solid ground to walk on again.

At the end, the beach curved north and before us stretched a similar beach to the one we had just walked along. That too curved out of sight about half a mile away.

'Do you know what we'll find when we get there?' asked Jake.

'Yeah. The same again, only this time heading west. Then when we get to the end it'll turn south and we'll be back where we started,' I said bitterly.

Jake nodded. 'There's no doubt that this is not Bermuda.'

The other two had been listening and the girl asked, 'Do I understand you don't know where we are, Captain?'

'That about sums it up, Senorita. There may be natives living here but I don't think so. We ain't seen hide nor hair of them so far so why should they be around the other side? Especially with the lagoon back yonder. That's where these people usually make their homes. I guess we night as well go back, get some sleep on the boat and plan what we're going to do tomorrow.'

We didn't hurry. A lassitude was creeping over us and I wanted to sleep more than anything. We picked up the oilskins and reached the sand spit. The sun was shining off the sea on our left when we turned north. Against the barrier of coral the sea broke endlessly in a white spume and here and there clumps of coral rose two or three feet above the sea level.

'Jesus,' Jake screamed, dropping his oilskins and running along the beach.

I was only yards behind, panic and fear bubbling up within me as the Lucky Lady sank fast. Water was slopping over the gunwales and only her remaining mast and superstructure were visible. By the time we reached the dinghy only the mast was showing. Jake stopped irresolute and stared, his fists clenching and unclenching as even that slid further down. I grabbed a paddle, lined myself up on the Lucky Lady and drew a long mark in the sand, pointing at where she was disappearing.

The Mendozas caught up with us and they too stood

and stared. As the top of the mizzen slid from view the girl gave a little sob and sank to the sand. Her brother put his arm around her shoulders trying to comfort her as she began to cry bitterly.

For the next hour Jake cursed himself continuously for not staying with the boat, for not pulling her closer to the shore, for not checking if she was holed, for not noticing she was sinking earlier. We remembered the scraping noise as we reached the lagoon and that sent him into another paroxysm of rage and cursing.

We spent a hungry and miserable night under a cloudless, star-filled sky. In spite of our predicament I managed to sleep and the next morning woke with the sun in my eyes, an ache in my back and hope in my heart. That hope died around midmorning after we walked all the way round the island and saw no sign of human life. We breakfasted on coconuts while walking, and though the milk was refreshing the white flesh was far from filling.

I said, 'It's a deserted island. We need to find shelter or build some, and we need to find food. There's plenty of fresh water and there's always coconut milk. If we can learn to live here for awhile I'm sure a boat will come our way and rescue us.' A sudden thought struck me. 'How deep do you think the water was when we threw the anchor over?'

'I'd say about forty feet,' Jake replied.

'I reckon the mizzen mast can't be far below the surface.'

'Don't be stupid. The boat will be over on her side.'

'Damn, I hadn't thought of that. Okay, say it is. It may still be possible to dive down and get something off, perhaps even empty the cockpit locker.'

'I dunno. It'll be pretty difficult,' Jake said, thoughtfully.

'I didn't say it was going to be easy. But if we can get up some of the rope, the tackle and that spare piece of canvas we'll be in far better shape.'

'I suppose we can go and have a look. Hey, Dominic,' Jake yelled to the youngster. 'Come here. How good are you with a rifle?'

'I am an excellent shot,' he replied with his usual haughtiness.

I tossed the rifle to him. 'Go and find us something to eat,' said Jake. 'We're going to try and see if we can salvage anything off the boat.'

'Estella,' I called her over, 'I want you on the shore looking along the line I drew in the sand. Point left or right to show us which way we need to go, all right? That should make finding the boat much easier.'

'Is that why you drew the line in the first place?' Jake asked.

'Yeah. Our walk this morning only confirmed what we guessed last night. I thought it might be useful – and don't forget something, those kids have a lot of money on board,' Dominic glared at me. 'Take it easy, we don't want your money, but it's all you've got now your parents are dead. Come on, Jake. Don't get lost,' I warned Dominic.

The stiffening of his back was all the sign he gave that he had heard.

I rowed the dinghy out, watching Estella as she pointed first left, then right. We were two thirds of the way to the reef when Jake told me to stop.

His arm was in the water, holding us steady. 'I don't believe it,' he said in a hushed tone,. 'I just don't believe it but the bitch is sitting upright. I'm holding the mizzen.'

I looked over his shoulder and saw the boat through the crystal clear water. She was resting against what I took to be a jumble of rocks.

'Christ, we were lucky,' I said.

'Lucky? To have lost her in the first place I call the worst bloody luck imaginable.'

I yelled to Estella that we had found the boat and she waved back. I slipped off my shirt and trousers, took a number of deep breaths and dived over the side, the dinghy rocking wildly. The water was warm, the salt stung my eyes, and I swam as hard as I could for the bottom. The deck was about thirty feet down, the seabed closer to forty. Whatever the distance, it was a long way. Although I had learnt to dive and swim I was not used to this sort of stuff. I reached the deck, my lungs at bursting point and I headed straight back to the surface again.

I was gasping when Jake helped me into the boat. 'Did you reach her? It looked like you did.'

I gulped air. 'I just got there . . . I needed air . . . and came back . . . before I could reach anything . . . If I'm going to do any good . . . I need to get down faster . . . without wasting energy swimming.'

'What about this?' Jake picked up the dinghy's painter. It was normally only a few feet long, but had broken in Jamaica. I had tied a forty-five foot length of manila in its place, meaning to cut it short and splice the end, like Jake had taught me. 'If we tie a rock or something to the end you can pull yourself down in no time.'

We spent some time on shore searching for a heavy rock until we found one which we could barely lift between us. The dinghy had a mere inch or two of free-board when we rowed slowly back across the lagoon.

'We need to be careful not to drop this bloody thing on top of the Lady,' gasped Jake, helping me to lift the rock, to throw overboard. 'I'd hate to damage her any more, seems sac . . . sac . . . wrong, somehow.'

'I agree, almost sacrilegious,' I grinned. I soon stopped grinning as with an oath we overbalanced, fell into the lagoon and the boat overturned. Spluttering, gasping and spitting water we righted the dinghy and climbed in over the stern. If we had tried to climb in over the side the dingy would have tipped over again. Leaning over the side we saw the rock a foot or two to the side of the Lucky Lady. I stood, took three deep breaths and dived in. The rope was, of course, tied to the dinghy. I grabbed hold of it a few feet below the surface and pulled myself rapidly down to the sea bed. I cut the rope near to the rock, swam to the cockpit and tied it to the wheel. I was gasping for air when I reached the dinghy, my head was dizzy and Jake had to help me into the boat. After a few minutes my breathing returned to near normal and I sat up.

'If you get down Jake, start opening the locker, will you? It shouldn't be too difficult.'

Jake rubbed his chin. 'I've been thinking. We need more rope to tie stuff to and to haul up. I'll go down as far as I can and cut the mizzen stays. I can feel the top of them here. Together they'll easily be long enough.'

He dived over the stern and I watched his progress, his body a shimmering white mass through the ruffled water. After a second dive we had a length of rope some fifty feet long. Next I went down and opened the locker. Jake followed and tied the rope to a roll of spare canvas. As we hauled it inboard it unravelled and we had to drag it behind us to the beach. There was only an hour of sunlight left and we decided to stop. We had just landed when we heard the gun shot.

'I hope he's as good as he says he is,' said Jake. While waiting for Dominic to return we lit a fire and spread the canvas out to dry. It would be enough to make a couple of tents.

Dominic arrived a short while later with the carcass of a half-grown wild pig slung over his shoulder.

By no stretch of the imagination could we be called a happy group as we ate our half burnt, half raw, smoked meat, but at least we were no longer hungry.

The next morning at dawn, after a breakfast of cold pig and coconut, Jake and I went back out to the Lucky Lady. We took it in turns throughout the morning to empty the locker. We removed pieces of tackle, some rigging and some of the tools. By noon we were exhausted, and shivering in spite of the sunshine. If we could possibly empty the boat then life would be more than bearable until help came along.

The next day neither of us felt like diving again, so we spent the time looking for a place to set up a camp. Alongside the stream, about ten yards from the water's edge, there was a flat grassy section surrounded by palm trees. There was some shade and an evening breeze cut through the grass just after sunset. We cut some poles and made two rough tents using the canvas. The grass was coarse, the ground hard and that night I slept worse than I had on the beach. From the looks on the faces of the others the next morning I guessed they hadn't done much better.

'We ought to make some beds,' I suggested.

'How?' Dominic asked, sneering at the suggestion.

All I could do was shrug. It was Jake who supplied the answer.

'Easy. We'll get up the jibs and mizzen sail and make hammocks. It's been some time since I slept in one but once you're used to it they're very comfortable. Heck, it'd be the easiest thing in the world to make.'

'But it's not easy to get the canvas Jake. That stuff is all in the forward locker. There are eight or ten butterfly screws holding the hatch down and each one takes a minute or more to undo. We'll be up and down all day just opening the bloody thing.'

'We haven't much else to do, have we?' he asked dryly.

So we went back on the lagoon. We had an estimated forty five seconds on the bottom, not long but long enough. I did the first dive, reached the cockpit, cut the rope and swam to the bow. I managed to tie it to a deck cleat before returning to the surface, my lungs bursting and stars exploding in my head.

We alternated, slowly undoing each nut. It was long and arduous work, the temptation to stay down too long almost overwhelming but finally we were finished. We started to remove each item and take it ashore. We recovered two coils of one inch manila, each four hundred feet long as well as half a dozen blocks, other lengths of rope and finally the canvas sails. It took us three days but, eventually, the locker was empty.

We resited the tents so that they covered the hammocks when we slung them between palm trees. From the tools we had salvaged Jake took his sailmaker's kit and showed us how to use the palm, a device that fitted into the hand to push against the needle, and taught us the stitches we needed to use to prevent the canvas from tearing. Jake was adept with the thick needle but the rest of us managed only with loud groans and muttered curses, as the needle slipped off the palm and into our hands. The edges of my hammock promised to be a lovely shade of blood red, in irregular blotches, by the time I had finished.

Jake graciously gave his completed hammock to Estella and elected to spend another miserable night on the ground.

46

WHERE DID THE time go? It was more than a week before we started keeping track of the days, and from then on they mounted with frightening speed. We dived often and removed all the loose gear from the Lucky Lady. We had plenty of rope, canvas and tackle. Our tools consisted of two axes, a chisel, two hammers, a bucket full of nails, two more buckets, two brooms, the needles, palms and thread of the sailmaker's kit, a fid – used to worm a way through rope and then thread more rope into the hole created – for splicing, and a dozen hard eyes for certain types of eye splices. We also had a block of pitch used for re-corking the decks and hull. There was nothing else we could salvage without going inside the hull and neither Jake nor I were capable of doing so.

We had now been on the island for ten weeks and had seen no sign of another ship or boat. Dominic had turned out to be a happy, friendly person once we got to know him, though he was still capable of extremely childish moods. Estella was lovely; she never complained and was always willing to work hard. She was friendly to both Jake and me and would often sit and talk to us for hours about religion and politics.

The island, apart from the coast, was covered with jungle. The only way up the hill was to follow the stream which bubbled mysteriously out of the ground about twenty feet short of the summit. Sitting at the fire in the evenings we often discussed such subjects as where did the stream come from? Was there a subterranean, artesian well buried in the coral of the island, or did it come all the way up from the sea bed? How deep was the sea bed away from the coral reef? What plants could we eat? Coconuts and mangoes we knew. But what about the green fruit in the middle of the jungle that Dominic had brought back from a hunting expedition? It looked tempting but none of us dared risk sampling it. We had seen at least half a dozen different types of snakes but which were poisonous and which weren't? Living so close to nature showed us how appallingly ignorant we were and how we took so much for granted living in civilisation.

There was plenty of food to be had from wild pigs, of which there were three or four families scattered across the island, to the fish in the lagoon. There were hundreds of birds which screeched and cackled whenever we passed close, from parrots to whippoorwills. As our hope of rescue faded, our desire for creature comforts increased and we started building a wooden shack to live in.

We built a platform, fifteen feet by ten, four feet above the ground, supported by twelve uprights buried deep in the earth. We left a narrow veranda, two feet wide in front of the door, built walls six feet high of thin bamboo interlaced with palm leaves and left a canvas covered window in the back. We covered the roof with a double thickness of canvas for added protection and covered a frame with another sheet for the door. It took three weeks to complete – in between hunting, fishing and, on some days when the despair got worse, lazing.

We had half completed the first hut when we started on a second for the Mendozas, planning a canvas partition to give Estella some privacy. By this time I realised that Jake and Estella were particularly friendly, often going for walks together, often looking at each other in a private and special way. Dominic too had noticed and began to act petulantly, especially when Estella did any small kindness for Jake, like handing him his food or mending his clothes. Once, when they were away for over three hours Dominic worked himself into a paroxysm of rage, threatening all sorts of consequences to Jake. Nothing came of it of course, except that Dominic and Estella had a blazing argument.

I was shocked when Estelle and Jake announced one day that they would take one of the huts together and Dominic and I could have the other. For a week Dominic sulked, stormed and argued with his sister. He did no work and went for long walks across the island alone. No arguments of religion, marriage, age difference or the lack of noble ancestry could change her mind. She loved him and that was all there was to it.

'What would Mamma say?' wailed Dominic. 'You need to go to a Church, you need to be married properly . . . Estella, it is unthinkable.'

'No it's not,' she replied sweetly. 'Jake was captain of the boat and captains have the right to perform wedding ceremonies.'

'Is that true?' Dominic asked, but before anyone answered he continued, 'But that does not matter. It is a sin to live together without a proper blessing from a priest.'

'We have been here for nearly four months,' Estella said patiently, 'and in that time we have seen no sign of a rescue ship. How long must we be together before we are able to live like husband and wife? Years? And for what? A so-called blessing by a man who has studied the Bible and another man has said to him, you are now a priest.'

'Estella,' Dominic was scandalised, 'how can you talk so? I shall pray to Our Lady and ask her forgiveness.'

'Yes, do that. And while you're at it ask for her blessing too. Dominic I want you to know something I've never told anybody. I have followed the church for our parents sake. I have gone to mass three times a week and spent hours on my knees. I have met many senior men within our church, almost all of whom I have despised. I have seen the suffering in villages, I have seen the starving children and I have seen men and women go hungry to place their money into the hands of the church. The church grows fat and rich on the exploitation of the people it's meant to help. The priests grow fat and rich, they never go hungry, they never suffer. Remember Archbishop Francisco who visited us two years ago; the man you said was so wonderful? I had to threaten to scream one night when he was staying with us, to get him to leave my bedroom. Don't look so shocked, Dominic. He was not the first to have tried. I hated them all and their rotten church, and when we leave here, if ever, I shall become a Protestant. In the meantime Jake is delegating his authority as captain to David who will marry us.'

'Hang on,' I protested. 'Surely that's not possible?'

Jake shrugged. 'Estella wants it that way, so that's the way it'll be.' And that's the way it was.

Curiously enough Dominic began to accept the situation and instead of questioning the right or wrong of their action, began questioning his religion. I was more or less a confirmed atheist and we had many interesting discussions on the subject.

One evening after we had completed the huts and were sitting near the fire enjoying a baked fish, I said, 'I'd give anything for a cup of coffee laced with rum,' I poked a stick into the flames, causing a shower of sparks. 'Or even a tin of beans. Anything to remind me there's civilisation out there.'

'It would be easy if we could breathe under water,' Jake joked, and the others laughed.

'And we could raise our treasure too,' said Dominic, and they laughed again at the preposterousness of the idea. Except I didn't.

I was silent for some minutes as the idea took root and grew. I smiled and then chuckled. 'Sometimes I wonder if my parents wasted their money giving me an education. Do you three want to know something? The Greeks were diving and staying under water for long periods as much as two thousand years ago.' I wrinkled my brow in thought. 'I believe it was Herodotus who wrote about a diver named Scyllis who worked for the Persian King Xerxes, recovering sunken treasure in the fifth century before Christ. I think that's right. Hell, history is full of examples of divers being used for warfare. There's been salvage going on in the Mediterranean for over two thousand years. I know that the ancient Greeks trained from childhood to hold their breath for long periods,' the others groaned at this, 'but in the sixteenth century in Massachusetts, or,' I added as an afterthought, 'more precisely, that's where the inventor came from, they were using diving bells.' I was becoming excited now, my mind racing ahead of my thoughts. 'You know there's plenty of air pumps on the market nowadays, Jake. I've even seen one working in New York harbour.'

'I hate to point out the obvious, Dave lad, but we don't have an air pump.'

'Of course not,' I said impatiently, 'but there's another way. Have any of you heard of Boyle's law?' They shook their heads. 'What it comes down to is that air taken to thirty feet under the sea occupies half its volume it did originally. That's not what the law states but that's what it means to us.'

'So how does that help?' Estella asked.

'We take the dinghy, turn it upside down and haul it to the yacht. We'll use blocks and rope, or even just weight it with stones. We dive down, get under and breathe. From there, with only a few feet to travel we ought to be able to get into the cabins and get some, if not all, the gear out. We don't need to come to the surface but go back into the boat for the next breath. See what I mean?'

The next day we started making a raft. If the boat was to be used, as I suggested, then we would need a platform over the Lucky Lady. We made our raft six feet square, with a double layer of logs, each six inches thick. We added a piece of stave to the Lucky Lady's mizzen mast so it projected out of the water, and then ran a length of rope to the shore. We could now pull ourselves quickly back and forth.

Along the gunwale of the dinghy we fixed two lengths of wood and then surrounded it with a shelf which helped to stabilise it. We tied stones as evenly matched as we could find onto the platform. When in the water it floated and left six inches of keel showing. Underneath, a volume of air was trapped in a space five feet from bow to stern, three feet at the widest part and two feet deep. The preparations took a week, but finally we were ready.

The raft was buoyant enough to take the four of us, so with our home made diving bell towed behind us, we pulled ourselves across the lagoon. Once it was in position we rigged blocks and tackle and Jake and I took it in turns to swim down to the cockpit of the Lucky Lady and to fit the blocks each side of the gunwale. With those in place, we hauled on the ropes roved through the blocks and watched with satisfaction as the boat slowly vanished under the water in a horizontal position. I dived to check it's position after which we lowered it another few feet until we declared ourselves satisfied. The dinghy was now over the centre of the cockpit, directly above the door to the forward cabin.

This time when I went down, pulling myself along the rope, I ducked under the boat and lifted my head into the air space. I wanted to jump and shout, I felt so exultant. All that the Lucky Lady held was now available to us and, most importantly, the one item I wanted above all others.

Taking a deep breath, I closed my eyes against the salt water and felt my way into the main cabin. I reached the further cupboard, tore it open and rummaged under the cloth until my hands closed around the object I was seeking. I also picked up a bottle and swam back to the dinghy. Two deep breaths and I was on my way to the surface. A curious thing happened then. My lungs seemed to inflate as I ascended and, before I reached the surface, I was exhaling continually and even on the surface I found I still had a lung full of air. Later I realised it was Boyle's law working in reverse, with the air doubling in volume as the pressure reduced. It occurred to me there was a possible danger of over-extending our lungs and Jake and I talked about it for some time. We called a halt after that first dive as there was now something I wanted to make. During the weeks we had been diving, Jake and I suffered a lot with salt water in our eyes, and often we carried out the salvaging with our eyes closed. The spare glass port-hole I had recovered was going to prove invaluable and the bottle of rum helped us to celebrate the fact that night.

The next morning, we could not have dived if we had wanted to. After so long without alcohol even the small amount we had imbibed left us with terrible hangovers. The only one not suffering was Estella because she had not drunk anything, and needless to say we got no sympathy from her. In the afternoon I began to fashion a mask. The porthole was six inches in diameter, half an inch thick and weighed about a pound and a half. I used tripled canvas, stiffened with pitch to shape a mask that fitted me snugly from below my nose to the middle of my forehead and reaching almost to my ears. When I tied it in place and put my head under the water of the lagoon, a new world opened out before me. For the first time I could see clearly the myriad of different coloured fish, the shells and rocks on the bottom, the sponges and anemones, the crabs and lobsters hidden under the stones and the pattern of the fine, white sand. I forgot that I was under ten feet of water, seeing the Lucky Lady clearly, just a hundred yards away, when I took a breath. I came very close to drowning. If Jake had not been attentive to my jerking on the line attached to my waist and dragged me ashore, I could well have died. As it was, I coughed and spluttered my way back to normal breathing, but the incident had certainly shaken me.

The next day we started to remove the insides of the Lucky Lady systematically. It was Jake who had the next frightening experience, after he had been down about twenty minutes. He had been in and out of the dinghy, tying various items to the length of rope we were using, when he could no longer get enough breath into his lungs, no matter how hard he breathed. Alarmed, he swam swiftly to the surface and had to be helped, gasping, onto the raft. When he got his breath back he told me what had happened and complained of having a headache.

'God, I'm stupid,' I groaned. 'Bad air, that's what the trouble was. What we need to do is bring the boat to the surface, turn the dinghy over and freshen the air. Hell, that's an elementary problem I should have foreseen. Come on, let's undo these ropes and bring the boat up.'

So it went on, day after day. We brought up the treasure belonging to the Mendozas, all our clothes, tinned food, the mattresses from the bunks, blankets and our extensive stock of liquor. The work occupied us for two months. The mask fell apart regularly and I was forever repairing it. Amongst the most useful items recovered were the pots, pans, cups and other utensils. To eat off a plate and drink out of a glass was a luxury of unimaginable proportions.

By this time we estimated that we had been on the island six months and two weeks. The weather had been mostly sunny and warm throughout, we were eating off a table and sitting on chairs, our hammocks had been exchanged for bunks and Jake and Estella were closer than most husbands and wives. She was also two months pregnant, much to Jake's joy. My thoughts turned more and more to Gunhild and I was beginning to despair of ever escaping. We kept a look out for other vessels but saw only one in all that time, and she had passed on the horizon, hull down, with only her masts showing.

I thought often about what was happening back home. Had they given me up for dead? Had they tried searching for me? Even if they discovered I had been to Jamaica there was no way to learn where I had gone from there. What was Gunhild doing? Was she seeing another man? The thought turned me cold. Like most men I operated under double standards. The thought of her being unfaithful to me and sleeping with another man filled me with abhorrence. Yet I considered it quite natural to use other women. No amount of intelligent persuasion could change my mind and Gunhild and I had often argued the point in the past. She maintained it was as natural for a woman to want to make love as a man, which every man knew was rubbish. Men needed to use women. Civilisations over thousands of years had acknowledged the fact, as indeed had the bible, by the admission that female prostitutes were an accepted part of life. Who had ever heard of male prostitutes available for use by women? I hadn't. Women just did not have the same needs as men, that was all there was to it. It probably accounted, in part, why men thought that they were superior, to women.

During the months we spent on the island I had lost the small amount of excess weight I had picked up since my university sporting days and had never felt so well and healthy. Both Jake and I had grown beards until we had emptied the insides of the Lucky Lady and had both felt a great relief to salvage our razors and shave for the first time in months. Probably the rationing of what we drank also helped. There were even days when not a drop of rum or whisky passed my lips. The cargo of rum we had bought to sell in New Orleans was still in the boat. It was stored in the lower hold, snug amongst the ballast, and to raise it would have been extremely dangerous.

A few times we were lashed by rainstorms and high winds. One night the walls of the hut Dominic and I shared were blown away, but luckily the other hut held tight. On two occasions lightning struck the island, though each time it was on the other side of the hill. We did find one tree that had been split in half, its charred trunk an awesome reminder of the power of nature.

It was in February that I made up my mind to leave the island.

'We're now pretty comfortable. We have nothing to do except eat, sleep and potter around making even more comfortable chairs or something equally inane,' I began, as we sat at the table, shortly after an evening meal of grilled fish, lobster, mango and coconut flakes seeped in rum. 'Tomorrow I propose to start building a raft. I don't intend spending my life rotting on this damned island – in fact I don't intend spending one day more than I have to.'

'I don't know,' said Jake. 'It's not as easy as you may think. How many times did we have to rebuild the raft we use for diving? The rope works itself apart, stretches or breaks. How do we fix that in the middle of the ocean when the nearest land is half a mile away, straight down?'

'By good husbandry,' I answered. 'If every day we examine each section, each knot, each log, then I think we can do it. At least it's worth a try. If we start now we can have it ready in, Christ, I don't know, two months at the most, I reckon. I've made up my mind to try it. We can build a low shelter in the middle, have a single mast not too high but carrying a fairly broad sail, and a long oar for a rudder.'

'Why not build a proper rudder while you're at it? It would be easy,' said Jake. For a second I thought he was being sarcastic. 'The one thing we have plenty of is time. So we'll take our time, work carefully and make us something that stands a good chance of getting us somewhere. All we need do then is point west and keep going until we hit America.'

'Dominic, Estella, what do you think?' I asked.

Estella put her hand on her thickening belly, now four months pregnant. 'I think it's time we got back to civilisation, too. I would like my son to be born in a hospital.'

'I don't know if we can manage that,' I grinned, 'but we can certainly try. There are a lot of problems we need to think about, the most important being how we'll carry enough water to last us. We've got the pitch, of course, and plenty of canvas, so we ought to manage if we make enough barrels.'

'That won't be easy,' said Dominic. 'And we'll need to cook plenty of food too, before we leave. Smoke some pig, maybe smoke some fish as well.'

'I think we should stop eating any of the tinned stuff we have left,' I suggested. 'There's enough there to last us a month or more, if we're careful.'

We got out a bottle of rum to celebrate our new venture. We had lived in hope of a ship passing within hailing or signalling distance and nothing had happened. Therefore it meant we had to get ourselves off. That night, as I lay on my bunk, my mind too active to let me sleep, I once more thought of Gunhild. The first thing I was going to do when I arrived home was marry her, of that I had no doubt.

I was up before dawn, impatiently waiting for daylight, ready to go looking for suitable trees to cut down. We had used those in the immediate vicinity for the huts, but there were plenty more on the island. And also it would be an easy matter to float the wood from any part of the island to our camp; all it would take was time and effort.

While Estella prepared a breakfast of mangoes, coconut and dried meat, we discussed how to build the raft in more detail. For maximum buoyancy we intended to make it double thick, like the small raft. We would make two main cross members of trees at least ten inches thick, and lash the first layer of logs to them. A second layer would be secured in the other direction. The whole would

be big, heavy and clumsy. We wanted a length of fifteen
to twenty feet and a width of at least ten. We would also
build two outriggers, at least, as near as we could get
to proper outriggers, to help stabilise it, ten feet out on
each side, eight feet long, and with two or three logs
as floats.

The main trees we found with no trouble, along the
beach next to the spit where the coral reached the land.
They were side by side, about twenty feet inland from
the beach and with little jungle to hamper us. Each
had a straight trunk, eighteen feet long and a foot in
diameter. We cleared a space and cut a section out of
the trees facing the sea. On the opposite side, above the
first cut, we started to chop in earnest, the axes sharp
and biting deeply. The sweat was soon pouring off me
as the sun crept higher in the sky to produce the fierce
heat of noon.

I had a great deal of satisfaction cutting down that first
tree. We stripped off the branches, cut the top off and
dragged it clear. Dominic was well into the second trunk
and a few minutes later it, too, came crashing down. We
rolled them into the sea and floated them back to camp.
We laboured from dawn to dusk.

On the day we assumed was a Sunday, Dominic
and Estella would go to their mother's grave and pray.
Dominic had spent some time carving a headboard for the
grave, while Estella ensured fresh flowers were always
there.

Sometimes the days flew past and on others time
dragged so slowly I felt I was going insane. One of
us had to spend half a day hunting or fishing, while the
other two worked on the raft. Estella was busy cooking,
cleaning the camp, washing clothes and generally doing
whatever was necessary. She was also swelling at a steady
rate and her pregnancy drove us all on. We assumed it
would take a month to reach the States or to be picked
up by a ship once we got into busier waters. Therefore,

we needed to be away at least six weeks before the baby
was due. If we did not finish our craft in time, Jake and I
thought we would have to wait at least four to six months
for the baby to get strong enough to survive the journey.
It was going to be no picnic on an open, flat raft, even on
the calmest of days. Desperate though I was to get away,
I knew I could never live with my conscience if the baby
died because I was impatient. The extra months would
not make that much difference.

We finished half of the base but we were now floating
the logs from half way along the next beach. To save
time we tied four logs together and hauled them through
the water. We rolled them over the spit one at a time,
and then floated them singly the rest of the way. At the
end of the day we bathed in the stream, which was cold
and refreshing, especially on the days we relaxed with a
glass of rum. At such times I often thought how good it
would be if Gunhild was with me. There was no doubt I
was living in a sort of paradise on earth; a clean, good
life. But it did not satisfy me and the main reason was
because I had no woman. It's also true to say I missed
the bustle of crowds, restaurants, theatres, all the things
that made life enjoyable to civilised man. Soon though,
I told myself each evening . . . soon.

Since we had to bring the wood from further and
further afield we realised after two months that we would
probably not be finished in time. We had enough logs for
the bottom layer and a third of the second, but as yet had
not tied them together. To save the ropes lying in the sun
and rotting we had decided to collect all we needed before
making the other items such as the casks and rudder, and
then commencing the main construction.

By now Estella was six months and three weeks gone.
When I mentioned it to the others Jake gave his lopsided
grin. 'I'm afraid you're right. Still, we tried. We can take
our time and get it built properly now instead.'

'Yes,' said Dominic. 'It would be a bad thing for the

little one to go too soon, especially if the journey takes more than a month.'

'It's a great pity we can't raise the Lady, then we could go anytime,' said Jake sadly.

'Aye, I know,' I agreed. 'Don't talk about it. I've thought a million times if . . . if . . . if . . . But I don't see any way we can do it. She's fifty-five feet long, is fifteen tons dead weight and is a hundred yards out from land. There is no way, believe me,' I said.

I suddenly realised that it was April and that I had been away from home for over a year; and it looked like being another six months before I got back. I often wondered what changes might have taken place back home. The thought of Gunhild and whether she still waited for me, or if she had given me up for dead, haunted me all the time and was hardest to bear when I lay on my bunk, trying to get to sleep at night. I thought of Mam, Dad and Sion and what they must have been thinking. Did they also assume that I was dead?

I had been going through a particularly bad patch for some days. I was bad tempered, morose and churlish to the others. I had thrown down the saw in a fit of temper and walked away, fed up with the raft, the island and despairing of ever leaving. I walked around to the other side of the island alone. I cursed the sea, the weather and God. Jake and Estella had found a peace and contentment together that I could never have without a woman with whom to share it. In spite of the paradise we found ourselves on it was still a prison. I craved to get away more than anything else in the world. I walked all the way around the island and back to the edge of the lagoon. I sat on a rock, out of sight of the camp, alone.

I was there for hours. It was a beautiful day, mid afternoon, with a brilliant sun in a blue sky, a few white cotton ball clouds and a refreshing breeze from the west. An ideal day for sailing, I thought ironically. I don't remember what I thought about as the afternoon wore on. I sat watching a bright red piece of coral about three inches long, embedded in a white surround, being lapped by the blue sea. It was with a sense of shock I saw the sun dipping down over the horizon. I took one last look at the red coral, now some twelve inches above the lapping water and walked back to camp. It wasn't until I was in bed trying to get to sleep when the significance of what I had been looking at struck me.

I sat bolt upright with the thought. I could not believe it. Had I imagined it? Quickly I began to dress.

'What's the matter?' Dominic asked sleepily.

'Come on, there's something I want to show you,' my voice was quivering with excitement, some of which I must have imparted to Dominic.

'What is it? Where are we going?' he asked, also dressing rapidly.

'To the end of the lagoon. Come on.' I led the way. It was a clear, star filled night, a half moon just rising above the horizon. The coral gleamed in the white light, the red piece showing black. I estimated it was five hours since I had left and there it was, close to being lapped by the water again. When I saw it, sure it had not been my imagination, I yelled for joy. I jumped up and down and danced around. Dominic was alarmed, thinking I had gone crazy, or so he said to Estella and Jake when they hurried over.

'I'm not crazy,' I said with a laugh. 'Stupid maybe, but not crazy. How many times have we looked at the sea, sometimes seeing more coral at the reef than others? Okay, I know the difference has not been great and the slope of the beach is so gradual we hardly ever notice a difference in tides. Jake,' I grabbed his arm, 'there's a rise and fall of about a foot, perhaps a little more. Don't you see? We've got the wood for a raft. All we need do is modify the design a little and we can do a – what do you call it? They were doing it in New Orleans when we left, clearing those rocks. Remember you pointed them out to me? They were using large barges.'

'A tidal lift?' Jake suggested softly.

'That's it. A tidal lift.'

To Dominic's and Estella's perplexity Jake and I jumped, danced and laughed together. It was some minutes before we calmed down enough to explain to them.

47

AT DAWN THAT day we began to construct the raft, but this time with a difference. We lashed four logs together to establish its boundaries which would be eighteen feet long and ten feet wide. We then placed the bottom layer, running the whole length of the raft but left the two middle logs off. This was to fit around the mast and to allow it to feed through as the yacht neared the surface.

'How many times will we have to do it, do you think?' Estella asked.

'It's hard to say,' I replied. 'At a foot a time . . . probably forty to fifty. If we work during both tides we can have her on the beach in three or four weeks after the first lift.' I did not add the fear that worried me. Was the lift sufficient? I thought it was, but until we tried I could not be sure. The thought gave me sleepless nights.

Slowly the raft fitted together. Each log was lashed down separately, care being taken to use as little rope as possible, since our supply was not inexhaustible. With no water barrels, rudder, nor housing to make we would be ready to launch the raft as much as a month earlier than expected. What we would have though, would be big, heavy and unwieldy. The problem of the launch had occurred to us, and we hoped we had the solution. We were building on the sloping beach. If we dug away the sand down to the water, a mere six feet away, we hoped to be able to get the raft into the lagoon.

Jake and I dived to the Lucky Lady using our home-made bell. We positioned it near one of the starboard portholes so we could reach out and remove the glass. We used it to fashion a second diving mask. We then spent the best part of a day examining the Lucky Lady and discussing where and how we would pass the lifting ropes. The fact that she was sitting upright on a pile of coral had helped when stripping her and now was going to prove a Godsend when it came to the lift. She was angled slightly to port, lying with her side against a large piece of coral that stretched over three quarters the length of the hull. On her starboard side there were a number of broken segments of coral, some as much as eight feet high, though none were touching the hull.

Now I was doing something definite to get away I no longer suffered the depressions I had previously. Every day we were working by sunrise and did not finish until sunset, stopping only for a light lunch and frequent drinks of water or coconut milk. Even through the heat of the early afternoon we continued, wearing large, floppy sun hats which Estella had made out of palm leaves.

We finished the construction in the third week of May. The days had flown by unnoticed, except for the fact that Estella was fast approaching her time. She accepted it far more stoically than we men. She mentioned the fact, hitherto ignored by us, that one of us would have to deliver the child. We all blanched but Dominic and I agreed entirely on one thing. Jake was responsible for putting it there, he could damned well deliver it. He went into a positive paroxysm of panic at the thought and kept insisting Dominic or I were much better at that sort of thing than he was. What sort of thing he meant he did not expand on. At first it was funny, but as the day got nearer the problem took on gigantic proportions.

'Listen,' I said, 'this has been going on for years. Millions of men have helped deliver babies. It must be as easy as falling off a log.' Estella cast a reproachful glance at me. 'Well, you know what I mean. Surely you know what must be done.'

'Of course I do,' she replied tartly. 'Unfortunately, apart from lying on my back with my legs open there is little I can do to help you. I've told you all a dozen times what you must do, I can't do more than that. And I want to add, you three are a great help to a girl, I must say. You instil me with such confidence, I wish I had never become pregnant,' and she promptly burst into tears.

We looked helplessly at each other and then Dominic and I sneaked quietly away leaving Jake to comfort her. When it came to some matters I was amongst the fifty percent of the cowardly population in the world, all of us male.

The day came to launch the raft. We scraped away the sand from around it, and dug down in front until the sea was lapping at the logs. Behind the raft we built a sturdy tripod, which acted as the fulcrum for a lever made of a fifteen feet long, ten inch diameter tree trunk. With the lever at the centre of the raft, and with two thirds of it behind the fulcrum, we attached a triple sheaved block and rope. When the three of us pulled on the rope the lever came slowly down, the raft tilted and slipped all of six inches over the sand. We repeated this again and again . . . and again . . . until finally the front third was floating, then a half, then two thirds, and then we were standing behind pushing it slowly into the water. That night we men celebrated by getting drunk.

Which was a great shame really, because around mid-morning next day, just as we were surfacing, Jake yelled for help. Dominic and I rushed to their hut to find Estella lying on their bed, her hands over her waist, pain on her face.

'He's early,' she whispered. 'It is time. Don't forget what I told you. Plenty of hot water and use the white sheets I've got ready from that top drawer,' she pointed to the rough chest of drawers Jake had made.

'Oh, Christ,' one of us said.

Dominic and I collided in the doorway as we rushed to

light a fire and put water on to boil. Our haste to get out of there before anything happened was unseemly. We hung around outside, listening to Jake and Estella talking in quiet voices; he seemed to be reassuring her. The morning dragged. We had a half hearted lunch of cold meat and mangoes and sat in the shade waiting for the big event. It was late in the afternoon when Jake yelled to us:

'Come here quick. Bring the water. Heck, it's coming.'

Dominic and I leaped to our feet like frightened rabbits at the first yell from Jake. We bumped into each other going for the water, now simmering on the stones by the side of the fire. We scrambled up the steps and into the hut as the miracle began. Jake was incredible in the calm, proficient way he delivered the boy. It came out head first, covered in blood and a slimy substance. He handed it to me, and without thinking I took him.

'What do I do?' I asked plaintively.

'Hold him by his feet and smack his bottom,' Dominic said, 'like Estella told us.'

The baby was crying gustily, his eyes screwed tight, his fists clenched. Jake had cut the umbilical cord with a pair of scissors and Dominic was putting some sheets into my hands, to cover the baby with. Luckily the placenta had come out with the cord and Jake took the mess and threw it on the fire.

'But he's breathing all right,' I said in awe. 'And Estella said . . .'

'So she did,' said Jake. 'So just hold him you big ape, until Estella can take him.' He was busy cleaning Estella and covering her with a sheet.

'I shall take him now,' she said sweetly. 'Let me see my baby.'

Tentatively I held him out to her. She took the bundle, still crying, from me, opened her night-dress and began to feed him. The noise stopped like a tap being turned off. As she fed him, she reached into the sheet and counted his fingers, toes and looked him over. Finally she was satisfied and lay back with a beaming smile. 'We shall call him David Dominic Rodriquez Mendoza Kirkpatrick.'

'That's a bit of a mouthful for such a little fellow, isn't it?' asked Jake. 'I was thinking more along the lines of Jake Junior.'

'Never,' Estella said with finality.

I was honoured. Dominic thought Dominic David had a better ring to it than David Dominic and Rodriquez had been chosen as it had been their father's name.

We did no work for the next couple of days. Jake wanted to stay close to Estella and the three of us would be needed for the next part of the operation. Estella was soon on her feet, preparing meals for us or fussing over the baby.

Estella assured us he was beautiful, but I confess all I saw was a red, wrinkle faced, sleeping, or crying bundle about eighteen inches long. I could not see any trace of the beauty she talked about. But then I was not alone; neither his father nor uncle could either.

Four days after the birth we were ready to pull the raft into position. We used the rope from the top of the mizzen mast of the Lucky Lady to pull ourselves slowly and sedately along. The raft was a heavy bitch and tended to tilt if we walked from one side to the other. But she floated with the whole of the second layer out of the water. We pulled the bell down over the cockpit and Jake and I dived down. We had two strops to pass round the hull, one near the bows and the other near the stern. We held the strops in place by hammering nails into the hull and bending them around the rope. It was a simple task but having to hold your breath, swim out and back to the bell, and every ten minutes take the bell to the surface to freshen the air, made it a long and tedious process. Each time we took the bell up to the surface wasted about forty minutes, provided all went smoothly and the ropes and tackle did not become tangled, or the blocks tumble.

On each side of the raft we made two sets of reels, each with long handles. We had the tackle roved to advantage, able to haul from the running block fixed to the eyes of the strops around the keel of the Lucky Lady. On the raft we had the standing block tied on a pendant around the reel. We turned up the reels until the ropes were bar taut. Jake and I dived down to see how the boat was laying, and agreed it was as good as we could have hoped for.

While we had been working Estella had been keeping a note of the times of high and low tides and this allowed us to know accurately when they would next occur. A high tide followed a low tide every six hours and twenty minutes, as near as we could tell. Also at one part of the month, the range – the difference between high and low water – was only five or six inches, while two weeks later it was as much as fifteen to eighteen inches.

Low water on that first day was at eight o'clock in the evening. With the last of the rope, we ran a block and tackle from the front of the raft to a tree near the huts.

Nervously we ate a cold meal, sitting on the raft on the lagoon, watching the last of the sun's rays disappearing from sight, and waiting for low water, which would be in another hour and thirty minutes. We kept the lifting tackle tight by means of a ratchet wheel and peg Dominic had made on the reel. When the peg was pushed into place, after the wheel was turned, there was no chance of it unwinding. It was a calm night, with only the gentlest of breezes, little cloud, the sky full of stars, the moon not yet risen. We could see Estella sitting by the fire outside the huts, peering anxiously our way, her face an undistinguished white blob in the poor light.

'I'm sure we moved slightly then,' I whispered, 'What do you think?'

'It's possible. What the hell are we whispering for?' Jake suddenly said in a normal tone. 'We ought to start lifting soon after low water, not before.'

We heaved until the ropes were taut and the sea was lapping over the edge of the raft. Would it lift?

'Shall we haul on the rope and see if we move?' asked Dominic.

'I think we'd better wait,' replied Jake. 'There's a few rocks in the way which we don't want to scrape across. This tide should give us a twelve inch lift at the end of the six hours so we may as well wait another hour at least.' It was then half-past eleven.

I checked the towing tackle and felt the slack in the once taut rope. 'We're floating. Yahoooo,' I screamed at the top of my voice, sending the birds in the jungle into a screeching panic and making the baby cry. 'Sorry, Estella,' I called.

We pulled without having to put in too much effort, and had the satisfaction of seeing the water wash past the edge of the raft. We were careful and hauled on the rope inch by inch. I would have given my eye teeth to see what was happening to the Lucky Lady down below. I don't think we travelled more than a couple of yards when we came to a halt.

'I think,' I said, 'we should only move at high tides, to reduce the number of times we knock against the sea bed or on the coral.'

From them on one of us stayed on the raft all the time to keep the lifting tackle tight, while whenever high tide approached, all three of us went out. As we neared the beach the mast moved up, a permanent and accurate reminder of our progress. When the Lucky Lady struck a piece of coral, or bumped onto the sand, the raft would swing slowly on one side, as though on the end of a pendulum, but always closer to the beach. We used the masks to watch her progress and dived regularly to check the way she sat her cradle of strops. Each day diving to the bottom became easier as the depth was now little more than twenty feet and our distance to the shore halved. It was going so well it was inevitable something would go wrong. The after strop around the hull parted.

The forward strop held, however, and the boat remained upright, helped by the mizzen mast protruding through the raft. It took us a day to rerig the broken strop and, as an added precaution, to replace the forward one too. And so it went on, tide after tide. We erected a canvas cover on the raft to protect us during the day from the sun and the occasional rain shower. Twenty-three days after the first lift we tightened the ropes and the deck and forward superstructure of the Lucky Lady jammed tight against the bottom of the raft.

We knew we had buoyancy to spare, so we removed more of the central logs to allow the boat to come further through the raft until it was as high as the deck. With one more lift we dragged the Lucky Lady as close to shore as we could. With the next low tide she would be sitting on her keel, balanced by the raft, with a foot of hull showing. Would it be enough to keep her afloat when the tide turned, or would the water fill up quicker than we could keep her empty?

Estella brought the baby's cot near to us and while he slept she helped us bail. Slowly the water level in the cockpit went down. Then Jake and Estella were able to man the pumps in the cockpit while Dominic and I used buckets. We went into the saloon, filled the bucket and returned to the cockpit to throw it over the side. We were midway through the tide when I dived to find the Lucky Lady floating an inch above the sandy bottom.

I took the raft apart while the others continued bailing and pumping. The water was going down at a steady rate and made us wonder why the Lucky Lady had sunk in the first place. Where was the leak? It took us some time to find it. We found that three boards had sprung just below her plimsoll line. In the normal way, using the pumps, we could have contained the leak easily, but because we had not been on board on that fateful day she had sunk.

A few minutes work with the hammer and some heated pitch cured the problem and she was as sound as ever.

With all the hatches open, the stoves lit and a pleasant breeze directed into the boat by our cannily erected canvas screens she dried out rapidly. While that was happening, we replaced her rotting rigging, greased everything that needed greasing and slowly checked the whole of the hull for further damage. As our thoughts turned to escaping, Dominic made the discovery that shattered us for days.

He had been out in the dinghy, now once more in its more usual role. When he returned after some hours, he was almost in tears.

'There's no way out, you stupid bastards,' he screamed at us, when Jake asked him what was wrong.

'What do you mean?' I asked stupidly.

'That . . . that coral,' he almost choked on the word. 'It . . . it doesn't end. There's no gap, nothing. I . . . I thought I'd find the channel which we came in by, but there is none . . . God . . . So what good is the stupid boat to us now?' he yelled, on the verge of becoming hysterical.

'Take it easy,' Jake shouted at the top of his voice, and Dominic seemed to calm down a little.

'But what are we to do?' he pleaded, needing an answer.

'Get the masks,' I snapped at him. 'We'll take it in turns to be towed behind the dinghy and find the way out. There must be one because we came in.'

That we hadn't noticed a channel, but always assumed there was one, was not as ridiculous as it may seem. After all, the coral was a hundred and fifty yards away from the beach and stretched for nearly a mile. It showed above the sea in some places, but was mostly covered with spray continually flying over most if its length. Dominic had clearly missed seeing the channel, that was all.

We started at the spit, only needing a small gap a mere four or five feet wide and some eight feet deep. They rowed while I was dragged behind, lifting my head every minute to gulp air.

We took fifteen minute turns to be towed and moved only slowly, determined not to miss anything. By the time I was in the water a second time we were a little under half way and I found where I thought we had entered the lagoon. As the afternoon faded, so did our hopes. Dominic was proved right, there was no channel.

We were sick at heart, dumbfounded. Seeing Estella standing on the shore watching us return, the baby cradled in her arms, was enough to move me to tears of frustration.

'There has to be a way,' I said fiercely. 'There has to be,' I paused. 'I know how we got here,' I added, and the others looked with interest and hope. 'In the rough seas, about there,' I pointed, 'we hit the reef with the bottom of the keel and were pushed over. I guess the side of the Lucky Lady hit a corner of the reef and the boards sprung. With the wind and the waves behind us we slid over easily enough. Remember the scraping we heard at the time, and I thought we were on the bottom?' I asked Jake.

He nodded glumly. 'God, what fools we've been. If we'd noticed earlier we could have built the raft on the other side of the spit and been ready to leave here by now.'

'The baby is still too young,' Estella said quietly.

'True,' Jake put his arm around her, 'but all I'm saying is . . .' he sighed, 'in a couple of months we could have been away.'

'Jake, I'm not sure,' I said. 'You saw how difficult it was to handle that monstrosity in the lagoon. What would it have been like out there? I don't think we'd have survived. We need to get the Lucky Lady out of here, and that's what we ought to be thinking about. I don't give a damn now if I spend the next year digging a channel through the spit, but I'm going to do something. That's for sure.'

I stalked away, only half believing what I had said. The thing was I did care if I spent a year. I regretted spending one day too long on that blasted, gilded prison of an island.

A channel, was it feasible? Feasible yes, but a hell of a lot of work. I walked over to the spit. At its narrowest part there were fifteen yards between the open sea and the lagoon. If we dug out the centre part first, then worked outwards, when the water finally came in it might wash the walls down. That was a possibility. The gap would need to be four to five feet across and seven to eight feet deep. The sand was about three or four feet deep and then came the coral. We would have to chip away chunks of it with our axes and anything else we could use. Then once we got to the edges and the sea swept in? We'd have to dig the edges out from under the dinghy, if it was necessary. Despair hit me like a thunderbolt.

For three days we were incapable of doing anything, except think about our misfortune. And then I had another idea.

'Jake, let's go out in the dinghy.' I took us to the spot over which I guessed we had come into the lagoon. Here, at low tide, was a square cut channel, two feet deep, eighteen wide and only a tantalising fifteen feet to the open sea.

'Even at high tide we've only got three feet of water or so,' said Jake, reasonably, 'and the Lady draws seven feet six inches to be exact.'

'True, and how much was the raft drawing when we were lifting the boat?'

'A little over a foot, I suppose. But don't forget how buoyant the Lucky Lady is when she's sunk. Her dead weight out of the water must be nearly doubled, if not more.'

'I know, but how much more? If we put her on the raft what will it draw then?'

'I don't know but it doesn't matter. It'll weigh too much to even pull through the water.'

'Damnation Jake, it shouldn't be any harder than when she was on the bottom. In fact, it'll be easier because the drag will be that much less. Anyway, do you have a better idea?'

'No, but I can see plenty of difficulties with yours. For instance, how are you going to get the Lady onto the raft? It's much too heavy.'

'A few centuries ago a mathematician said "give me a big enough lever and I can move the world". That same man did very clever things with blocks and tackles. We've only ever used one set, rigged to advantage to get maximum lift. Supposing we rigged one set to another set and then added a third? We'll increase our lifting power a hundred times.'

Jake stroked his chin thoughtfully. 'I suppose,' he said finally, 'it's possible.'

Once more we began to reconstruct the raft. It was lying scattered around the lagoon, some of the logs still tied together. We worked like demons and in three weeks finished the job, this time with no centre logs missing.

To lighten the dead weight of the Lucky Lady, we removed everything from her that we could. We stripped out the bunks, the cupboards and even the after cabin superstructure. We removed the store of rum and tried to dig out some of her ballast, but that proved impossible.

We covered the edge of the raft with all the grease we had left and placed a double layer of canvas across it. Hopefully, when the boat slid onto the raft the canvas would come with it and protect the hull.

Next we lined up the Lucky Lady, broadside to the raft and overlapping on either side by eighteen feet. We attached ropes to the outer side of the raft, led them over the superstructure and secured them to the furthest side of the hull before hauling them taut.

With the raft jammed along the edge of the beach we

fitted three lots of blocks and tackles to the Lady, one to the bow, one to the stern, and one to the top of the mast. It was this last one we were counting on to pull the boat over to the horizontal. The standing blocks we fixed to tree stumps in the vicinity, the trees already part of the raft. The inhauls we secured to another set of running blocks and the standing blocks to more tree trunks. We joined the second in-haul to a further set of blocks and tackle and around midnight, a month after we had first raised the Lucky Lady, we were ready.

In spite of being exhausted when we went to bed that night, I could not sleep. I could see Gunhild's image before me, so real I could have touched her as I dozed in that dream world between wakefulness and sleep. I dreamed I had lost her but how or why I couldn't see. There was a reason but it eluded me. Was she dead? Nobody would tell me. I woke up in a sweat, more tired than when I had gone to bed, the sun creeping over the horizon to a day I was dreading. What if it didn't work?

We did not bother with breakfast but instead went directly to the ropes and tackle. I said to Dominic. 'Grab that end and when I give the word heave like hell on the rope.' I took a deep breath and yelled. 'Heave!' Slowly, the Lady heeled over until we had got her to an angle where the keel was almost out of the water.

'What do you think?' I asked Jake.

'It's possible, I suppose. A little further and we'll be dragging her onto the raft properly.'

'There's no room left between the blocks, they're jammed together. So we'll have to run it out again and reset it,' I said.

We spent the rest of the morning resetting the blocks, and then stopped for a light lunch. The trouble with using a rig like the one we had made was that the blocks travelled a long distance but the length of pull between the boat and the furthest standing block was short. It meant we had to keep resetting the tackle but the arrangement gave us a very high lifting factor.

We started again after lunch, this time pulling on the forward and after ropes alternately. The Lady slid a foot onto the raft and then tilted back, jammed. We changed to the tackle on the mast, took up the slack and pulled the Lady over again. When we hauled on the other two sets of ropes she slid another foot onto the raft and jammed again. So it went on, changing back and forth, first tilting the Lady and then dragging her further onto the raft. It was back breaking, eye popping, muscle straining work but at long last she was sitting firmly on the raft, completely clear of the water and well and truly jammed on the shore. That night I slept soundly with no dreams to haunt me.

We began digging away as much of the sand beneath the raft as we could. At one stage the raft tilted suddenly a few inches towards the water; luckily Jake removed his arm just in time to prevent it being crushed.

'There are two things we can do,' said Jake. 'One is to build a tripod like the last time and the second is to run all these ropes together and fix them to the raft and that stump way over there.' He pointed to a stump close to the water's edge.

'What good will that do?' asked Estella wearily.

'See how the beach curves? A straight pull from here might drag the raft around and further into the water.'

'Anything is worth a try. Come on,' I suggested.

'Oh no,' said Estella. 'I'm worn out. Can't we stop for the night? Please?'

'You stop,' I said, 'but I'm going to try it anyway.'

'I'll help,' said Dominic.

'I'll start on the tripod,' said Jake.

'And I'll make something to eat,' said Estella.

It took us another two days to finish. When we pulled on the long rope the raft swung as though on a pivot. Jake and Dominic pulled down on the rope attached to the lever and the raft slid six inches nearer the water before

the lever toppled over. We reset it and did it again. By
the fifth time, half the raft was being lapped by the water
of the lagoon. On the ninth go she unexpectedly floated
free and we suddenly found we were pulling her parallel
to the beach. She floated with the water washing over the
raft, only drawing about three feet.

We made another dawn start after a sleepless night.
We ran ropes across the lagoon, stood on the coral, either
side of the shallow channel, and heaved. The raft moved
slowly but surely. I ignored the sweat, the backache, the
screaming muscles. As the Lady got to within a few yards
of the coral we moved further across the coral until our
feet were on the outer, almost perpendicular, edge. In the
channel the sea was two and half feet deep. Carefully we
lined up the raft. She nosed in until half way through when
she jammed. No matter how much we rocked and heaved
she would not budge but there were still two hours to go
to high tide.

We waited, not speaking. Every now and again we
pulled on the ropes and she slid a little further . . . and
further. The front edge reached us and we moved the
ropes to the back of the raft. High tide came.

'Come on,' yelled Jake. 'Now. Give it all you've
got.'

We threw ourselves against the ropes. I heaved until
I felt the blood pounding in my temples and the world
was turning dizzy. She moved and stopped.

'Dominic,' panted Jake, 'get on the raft and rock her
like hell. Dave, pull like never before.'

I nodded, too tired to speak.

She moved another foot.

'One last time,' Jake yelled. 'Now.' And we heaved
and heaved. Nothing happened for a few seconds and
then she suddenly shifted. Jake and I fell back into the
open sea and the raft floated through. The Lucky Lady
was in open waters, again.

While working on the hammocks we lazed on the beach

and did a little fishing. We caught more than sufficient for our needs.

'At least we won't starve,' Jake commented as we sat down to a midday meal of fried fish. That is, if squatting outside a ragged tent with a blackened fish on a stick can be called sitting down to a meal.

'That's about all we can say for it,' I said bitterly, thinking for the millionth time about Gunhild and wondering what she would be doing.

48

WE RE-FLOATED THE boat by the simple expedient of cutting out the logs, one by one. The keel touched down to the water and then suddenly the Lucky Lady sprung upright, bobbing in the waves and threatening to be washed down onto the coral. We jumped aboard her, hauled up a jib which we had ready, and with the wind blowing along the length of the coral, slowly edged our way out.

Jake hoisted the mizzen sail, I steered and Dominic held the jib out to starboard to catch the afternoon breeze. The mizzen filled and she heeled over, slowly picking up speed. It was the greatest feeling in the world to stand there, with the wheel in my hands, and feel the Lucky Lady responding.

Around the end of the coral reef we neared the shore and dropped the mizzen again. We kept the sails out until we were within ten yards of the beach and could see the laughing figure of Estella with the baby in her arms. I put the wheel hard to port, we turned into the wind and stopped. Dominic took a rope, jumped into the water and swam ashore. Jake brought the anchor from the camp and we used it to keep the bow pointed seaward, and the keel clear of the bottom.

That night we celebrated with grilled fish, crab, roast pig and copious draughts of coconut milk laced with rum. Our feelings were indescribable. We laughed at every little thing, joked and played the fool. There was still work ahead but now it was plain sailing all the way home. With luck I would soon be in St. Louis and it would be a long time before I left again.

'The Lady will look funny, sailing without a mainsail,' said Jake sadly.

'But she'll definitely sail all right?' I asked, suddenly anxious.

'Yep, slow but sure,' he replied with his lopsided grin.

Another week was spent replacing the interior we had ripped out including the cupboards, bunks and after superstructure. We put the remaining stock of rum back into the bottom hold, still planning on making some money if we had any luck. Finally we provisioned the Lady and filled the water tanks.

Then came the last night on the island. It was a happy, sad occasion. We had been there one year, two months, three weeks and, we thought, four days. We had come to love the place, in spite of our eagerness to get away.

We left well before sunrise, dawn a faint streak of pearl grey in the east, the night inching away. The wind was from the north west and we sailed with it close to the starboard beam. After four days, the wind veered to the east and we ran before it, our speed being close to four knots.

'Dave,' said Jake, six days after we had left the island, 'as soon as we get to civilisation Estella and I are going to get married in a church and have David Dominic christened. Will you stay for that?'

In my eagerness to get home I was about to refuse but hesitated. 'Sure, of course I will. One more day won't make any difference. Where do you think we'll land, anyway?'

'Somewhere on the Florida coast. There are plenty of villages around. As soon as we find out where we are we'll head for a big town. I presume you want to telegraph and tell them you're on your way?'

I grinned at the thought. 'No. I'm going to turn up on

the doorstep and surprise them. Hell, after so long they must have given me up for dead.'

'It'll be a surprise all right. I hope there's nobody with a bad heart back there.' Jake paused, while I took the helm from him and got the feel of the boat and wind. 'By the way,' he added, 'I want you to have the seven thousand we would have made on this trip. The money the old lady paid us.'

'I can't do that. Half of it is yours.'

'I don't need it, Dave lad. You saw what was in those chests. It's more than Estella and me need, far more. We're going to Europe for a while, to, em,' he chuckled 'to let me get some education and decorum. Her words, not mine,' he added hastily. 'She's going to teach me Spanish and get me to appreciate art. Some hope she's got there, though.'

Estella had been teaching him to read and write, succeeding where my earlier attempts had failed, and Jake was now proficient at both. 'Okay, thanks for the money. I still want half the profit from the rum,' I said, and we laughed.

'You'll make your fortune yet,' he said, 'and I agree.' He went below, chuckling.

We had plenty of food and water and the days passed easily. Then, on the fifteenth day, an hour before dawn, I saw a light. Then another and then a dozen. It was a village and I yelled for the others to come up.

It was a fishing village and as we neared the coast we saw boats sailing out of the small harbour. When we got near enough we hailed them to find out where we were. We were off Fort Brunswick, fifty miles north of Jacksonville which was where the nearest railway line was. We decided to follow the coast to the larger town and arrived in the early evening.

It was a bustling place with a well-developed harbour, ships of all sorts, some coastal and others ocean going. There were also fishing boats, just in on the tide, unloading baskets of quivering, jerking fish. The market was raucous with the noise of bidding and the crowds of people. In some respects it was an anti-climax to sneak quietly alongside, unobserved. I wanted to yell at them all to come and listen to our story. Hell, we had lived on an island for over a year, castaways in the best Robinson Crusoe tradition. Seeing these people made me nervous for some reason, and I realised the others felt the same when I heard Estella whisper to Jake. I said it out loud and we were able to laugh at ourselves, stepping boldly ashore to look for the best hotel the town had to offer.

The excitement of being in civilisation again gripped me. I could not keep my eyes off the women and girls passing by, and once more a picture of Gunhild came to my mind. I would last until then, I told myself. We had dressed in our best clothes for our entry into harbour but even they were tatty and threadbare. We had a problem at the hotel until Jake threw a ten dollar gold piece on the counter and told the clerk we wanted the best rooms and to send for a tailor and hairdresser. Money worked as always, and soon I was enjoying a hot bath, a glass of ice cold beer in my hand, and a tailor showing me his wares while I luxuriated in the suds.

I suggested to the others after we ate that we go on a bar crawl to see how many we could get thrown out of. Dominic jumped at the chance, but the light in Jake's eyes died quickly when Estella told him they were going to bed early.

I don't remember too much after that. We definitely made three bars and a hotel. Somehow I awoke in my bed to a hammering on the door. I staggered out of bed and after a lot of fumbling with the lock managed to open it and crawl back to bed. It took a lot of cajoling, threatening, and bullying, but Jake finally got me downstairs and two cups of strong, black coffee inside me. It seemed we had only an hour to get to the church for the wedding and christening. Estella had not given him a chance to change his mind.

'I would have thought after last night you'd have your doubts,' I said. 'You missed a good time.'

He smirked. 'Want to bet?'

'Hmm, perhaps not,' I grinned back. 'How did she manage to arrange things so quickly?'

'She saw the minister this morning. She told him everything. He was very sympathetic and kind. Mind you, I'm not suggesting the two hundred dollars she gave him for the poor box didn't have anything to do with his decision. So it's all fixed.'

The four of us went to the church at noon. We were dressed in new suits, had been to the barber's and bath-house and felt ill at ease as we stood around the font. Estella was radiant in a wedding dress she had conjured up from somewhere. It was to be passed down to her daughter when the day arrived. I acted as best man and handed over the wedding rings and Dominic held the baby. In view of the solemnity of the occasion and the commitment it represented it was all over in a very short time.

We thanked the minister and a short while later we were having a meal in a nearby hotel. We sat there all afternoon, drinking a little and talking a lot, each of us in our own way aware of the passing of time and the separation to follow.

It was nearly eight o'clock that evening when we went to the railway station. A train was about to leave for Charleston and I was catching it.

'Hey,' I said, as the three stood outside the window and I leaned down to talk to them, 'what about the rum?'

Jake chuckled. 'And I thought you were such a good businessman. I tell you what, I'll sell it and you and Gunhild can come and collect the money from me in Europe during your honeymoon. Okay?' He held out his hand, his lopsided grin as wide as ever.

'I'll do that,' I said, suddenly finding I could not see properly through a blur. Jake seemed to have the same problem. We were saved from any further embarrassment when the guard yelled to stand clear, we gave a final wave and the train pulled away.

From Charleston I went through North Carolina and on to Richmond. I changed trains there and went to Washington, although it never occurred to me that one or both of my parents might be there now that Dad was a Congressman. Soon I was en route to Pittsburgh and once more in familiar territory. I ignored the scenery and I was unable to concentrate on any of the books and magazines I had bought to pass the time. I sat for hours staring vacantly, dreaming of my arrival home.

At last I was on the last lap of the journey to St Louis. My excitement mounted to an unbearable pitch. I wondered where I should go first. It would be Thursday when I arrived, four o'clock in the afternoon, if we were on time. I would go straight home. Mam would surely be there? What would they look like? How changed would they be? Hell, I told myself, it's only been what? A year and seven months altogether. What was Sion doing? And how was Dad enjoying politics?

Then it was seven o'clock in the morning on Thursday, and I could no longer sleep. No longer? That was a laugh. I had barely slept all night. I hadn't really slept since catching the train in Jackonsville, in fact. After Washington I'd had a sleeping berth but even so . . . Now it was midday and I just could not sit still. I paced the corridor, pausing to look out of the window to see if I recognised anywhere and looking at my watch every few moments.

It was the longest afternoon of my life but at last the outskirts of the city came into view. I could see the gleaming Mississippi occasionally as we approached and from one angle I caught a glimpse of the Missouri. Then we had stopped and I was leaping out, my bag in my hand. I had returned with eight thousand three hundred dollars mostly in gold, and a small grip holding a change of shirt and underclothes. I was also sporting a trimmed black beard, my hair curled over my collar and I was sun tanned a deep brown.

I hired a buggy and told the driver to hurry. I was disappointed to see the town had not changed, the same buildings, same streets, everything; the only difference was that there were motorcars on the road. Many people still called them horseless carriages and I had read in one of the magazines that back east, the motorcar could already go as fast as twenty miles per hour. It was staggering to think they were already talking of doubling that in a few years. I tried to keep my mind on anything except the slowness of the journey but, at last, I saw the house.

'Faster,' I told the driver, 'up the drive just ahead. No, stop here and I'll walk,' I added as we slowed to take the turn.

'Make up you mind, mister,' he grumbled, but cheered up when I gave him five dollars.

After all the dreams, the heartaches and the travelling, here I was. I walked slowly towards the house, noting again that nothing was different. I hesitated at the corner and on impulse went round to the back door.

It was open and I stepped into the kitchen. Mam was by the sink, her side to me. She must have sensed my presence because she looked up, slightly startled, a pile of dishes in her hands. I couldn't speak all of a sudden and things became hazy. I cleared my throat and said: 'Hullo Mam, I'm home.' It came out sounding rather husky and strained.

The dishes smashed to the floor and with a shout she flew across the room. We hugged and hugged and hugged. She was crying, but then so was I. I only caught some of the words she said, like 'dead' 'couldn't find you,' 'where have you been?'

I looked over her shoulder at Dad, hurrying through the door. He stopped for a second and then gave a kind of roar. Mam let me go long enough for Dad to grab me in a bear hug and waltz me around the kitchen. Somehow, a semblance of order established itself and I could speak. I told them briefly where I'd been but I was more interested in them and Sion and Gunhild.

'Wait a moment,' said Dad, and went to the back door. 'Juan, Juan,' he yelled at the top of his voice. I heard running footsteps and he appeared in the doorway. 'Juan, David's back,' said Dad. 'Grab one of the horses and get into town as fast as possible and tell Sion to come home.'

I went over to shake Juan's hand and he said, 'Nice to have you back David, real nice.'

'Thanks Juan, it's unbelievable to be back.'

'When you get to town,' said Dad, 'don't tell Sion why we want him. Just tell him it's vital he comes home immediately. You know what he's like. He'll have something he'll want to finish. If he does, grab hold of him and tell him he's got to come immediately. Stress the importance, okay, Juan?'

Juan grinned. 'Okay, sir,' he replied and ran back to the stable.

We went into the study where Dad opened his drinks cupboard. 'Malt whisky,' he hefted the green tinted bottle, 'a present from Huw and Mair. I've been keeping it for a special occasion and I don't think there'll ever be one more special than this.'

While he poured I sat on the arm of Mam's chair. It was difficult to do anything else as she kept hold of my hand as if she would never let go.

'So what happened exactly?' she asked. 'Where were you? Oh, I know on an island, but where? And your nose? What happened to it?'

'My nose? Oh, that was so long ago I forgot. It happened in New Orleans just after I met Jake Kirkpatrick.

It got kind of mangled up but no real damage was done.'

'I see,' said Dad. 'Okay, but where exactly were you?'

'We don't know. It was fifteen days sailing off the coast of Florida. We have no way of telling more accurately. But never mind me, what's been happening here? How's politics going? How's Sion?'

Mam laughed. 'It's going to take a week to exchange the news. Sion is working too hard,' she said soberly. 'We're thinking seriously of selling this place and buying a house in Washington. We spend a lot of time there, now your father's in the House of Representatives. What a place it is. The stories we have to tell you are unbelievable, especially when you consider they're all about the so-called leaders of the country.'

'Now, Meg,' said Dad, 'keep off your hobby horse for now. What we thought we might do was buy a ranch out this way, as an investment. It'll be somewhere to call home. I'll find a manager, probably Juan, and Marie said she'll stay as the housekeeper. Having a husband and wife team has it's advantages. I don't know yet. We still have to decide. But enough of us, what about you?'

I began telling them the story of the storm and what we were doing. Then I asked, 'What's this about Sion working too hard?'

'He works all the hours God gave him,' replied Dad. 'You know he's taken over from me entirely now? No, of course you don't know. Let me refill your glass,' he poured a generous three fingers of the amber liquid. 'We're opening a new warehouse in Indianapolis and he has plans for Cleveland and Pittsburgh. Sonny manages to talk him out of his wilder ideas, but all in all I have to admit he's doing better with the business than I ever did. He has a knack and, furthermore, he seems to love it.'

'I wish he'd enjoy life more,' said Mam. 'He's too intense for a young man. I know he's interested in this flying business but I think that's all foolishness. It'll never get further than being a hobby and a very dangerous one at that.'

'Flying?' I asked perplexed, thinking about his kites.

'Some men have built a flying machine of wood that will take off into the air, go in a circle and land again,' said Dad. 'It's interesting to hear him talk about it. I'm not sure I agree with your mother entirely but on the other hand I don't agree with Sion either.'

'Why? What does he say?' I sipped my whisky. There is something special and smooth about a malt which I appreciated.

'Oh, he has ideas that one day there'll be hundreds of machines carrying people and mail across America. It's daft. It'll never happen,' said Mam decisively. 'Listen,' we could hear a horse arriving at the gallop. The front door clattered open and we heard his boots on the wooden floor.

'In the study,' Dad called.

The door flew open. 'What's the . . .' Sion stopped, staring at me.

'How's things?' I asked with a grin.

'David,' he yelled, knocking my glass to the floor when he grabbed me in a bear hug equal to Dad's. 'Christ Almighty, I can't believe it.' He held me at arm's length. 'The beard and tan makes you look older, and you're definitely leaner. That nose makes you look like a tough,' he chuckled. 'But where have you been? Do you know I spent three months looking for you?'

'What?' I was startled. 'You did? Where?'

'Let me grab a drink and I'll tell you. Hell, it's so good to see you. We were sure you were dead. There didn't seem to be any other explanation. Oh, thanks Dad,' he broke off as Dad handed us both drinks. He had changed a little too, looking older than I remembered. Or perhaps it was the air of authority he had about him that made him appear older.

'Yes, I looked all over for you,' he resumed. 'The last we or, em . . . the last we heard,' I did not think anything of his hesitation just then, after all I had written to Gunhild from Jamaica, 'was that you were in New Orleans. By November last year we were so worried I took a train to try and find out where you were. It didn't take long. I must say when you make enemies you make good ones. That creep Guinn. I counted my fingers after shaking his hand.' We laughed. 'I found out about the boat deal and about Jake Kirkpatrick. It took a few hundred dollars but I found somebody who knew somebody who said he had seen you both in Jamaica. So that was where I went next. I must say it wasn't unpleasant seeing these places. In fact, it was quite an adventure. A bit like being a detective. I found your em, friend, the singer in the Blue Pelican. What was her name? Elizabeth?'

I nodded.

'I'd asked around the bars and taverns for nearly two weeks before I found her. She told me all about that business with Cat Ball too. Oh, yes, and it was she who put me on to Casper. Trying to get information from him was like trying to get blood from a stone. He said he needed time to check out me and my story. So I hung around another couple of weeks until he sent for me. He told me about San Juan and what you were going there for. So then I took a boat to Puerto Rico, but learned nothing. I asked all over the damned place but couldn't come up with anything. Everywhere I went I spread the word that there was a thousand dollar reward for information about you, and I put adverts in the local newspapers. But apart from a few cranks there was silence,' he paused to replenish his glass. 'We came to the conclusion the boat must have sunk and you were dead. It took a long time to accept,' he shrugged, 'but when we heard nothing for so long there was no alternative. And here you are,' he laughed again. 'There's so much to tell you, too. The investments we made in the business are going to pay off like you can't imagine. Business is booming. Do you know the banks are falling over themselves to lend us money? They can't do enough. If you take over here I can go to Indianapolis and get things straight there while Sonny . . .'

'Hey, no business,' said Mam with a frown. 'Not tonight, Sion, please. There's plenty of time for that. I want to hear more about what happened to David. How were you rescued? Did another boat come along and pick you up?'

I laughed. 'I wish it had. It would have saved us a hell of a lot of work. No, we salvaged the boat from thirty no, forty feet of water and brought her to the surface.'

'Good Lord,' said Dad. 'How on earth did you do that?'

'With difficulty,' I replied. 'No, that's not true. It wasn't difficult, just time consuming and hard work. We had plenty of problems of course but it was not difficult in a technical or complicated sense.' I told them more of what had happened.

'I'll go and make some sandwiches,' said Mam. 'Just don't say another word until I get back. You can talk business and politics while I'm out.'

'Wait until you come to Washington,' said Dad, 'and I'll show you around. Things are beginning to get better now for the working man, law-wise that is. All we need now is to get the laws obeyed. Roosevelt has worked wonders. We've had the Elkins Act passed which means that shippers and railroads have to publish their rates, and are liable to pay back any rebates they've got if they don't stick to them. That's allowed the government successfully to sue the great Chicago packing houses and the Standard Oil Company, which is quite an achievement, believe me. Soon the Hepburn Act will be passed. It'll extend the jurisdiction of the Interstate Commerce Commission to storage and terminal facilities, sleeping cars, express companies, pipe lines, and also force the roads to surrender their interests in steamship lines and coal. There's a lot more besides. I've got a bill going forward about the working week and long hours. There's plenty happening about the child labour laws, oh yes, and about food purity and drug legislation. It's really an exciting time with one drawback to it all,' he said sadly.

'What's that, if it's like you say?' I asked.

'Because these are just laws, made in Washington. Look at the size of the country. How do we enforce those laws? It'll be years, decades even, before we can make people obey them. You mark my words.'

'Yes, sure, Dad,' I agreed. 'But at least it's a step in the right direction.'

'Oh, there's no doubt about that.' He busied himself opening a bottle of French red wine, last year's Christmas gift from John Buchanan, he said.

Mam reappeared. 'What a mess in the kitchen. All my good crockery,' she said with mock severity. 'Here's some chicken and beef and there's some salad I must bring in. Won't be a second.'

Not long after I stood up. 'I must get one of the horses. I want to go over to the Reisenbach's farm and see Gunhild,' I grinned. 'I can't wait any . . .' I trailed off.

It was funny the effect my words had on them. Silence reigned as they looked at each other.

'What's wrong? What's happened to her?'

It was Sion who told me. Two words that turned the memory of the evening to ashes. That changed my life forever.

'She's married,' he said quietly.

49

THE ONLY THING I noticed about the day, riding along the dusty road, was that the wind was chill and there was a hint of rain in the air. I was going to see Gunhild. I had to. I did not know what I was going to say or achieve by it, but I had to see her. After over a year and a half of thinking and dreaming about her, to find it was all for nothing caused an unendurable ache within me. When Sion had told me I had had the weirdest feeling of being instantly sober and feeling more than a little sick.

They told me what had happened. After I had left, Gunhild had received a few of my letters while I was in New Orleans and had written to me there. If I had received her letter I would never have left with Jake. She had written to tell me she was pregnant. I had been so numbed by the news of her marriage that this second piece of information bounced off me. She had been upset not to hear from me after she had written but as time wore on she became worried that something might have happened to me. By the time Sion had come to look for me she had been convinced something serious had happened. When Sion had returned he had more or less convinced her that I was dead.

Reisenbach had been understanding up to the point when Sion had returned. After that, he had insisted Gunhild should marry the first man who would have her. He had thought her very lucky when Gunther Kallenberg, a farmer from the old country, wanted to marry her. The man had three teenage sons, was a widower and needed a mother for them. She had resisted at first, determined in spite of the stigma, to have the baby but not to marry. Her family had constantly nagged her and pushed her until finally she had given in. They had married two weeks before the baby was born. She had been born on the second of January, a little girl, with blue eyes and black hair. Mam had seen her and cried. She was the spitting image of our dead Sian.

The remainder of that night was spent sleeplessly lying on my bed, in an agony wondering what to do. Dawn had just broken when I could stand it no longer. I wanted Gunhild to come away with me. One thing I had learned while on the boat, was that the world was a bigger place than even I had suspected. We could pass ourselves off as a married couple, and bring the baby up with her true parents. The thought comforted me along the way. We could even buy a boat and return to the island. That was a great idea.

About eleven o'clock I rode over a low hill, now well into the farm lands of smallholdings, each of about two or three hundred acres, and saw what I took to be her place. The house was not very big and from where I sat, looked in need of a coat of paint. Apart from a main one storey building, there was a barn and a few outhouses. I could see chickens roaming the yard and in one corner, a pig sty. In front of the barn was a pump and water trough and I decided to ride up to it and water the horse. I had never felt so uncertain in all my life.

As I approached a few chickens squawked and fussed out of the way, a mangy dog lifted his head and looked at me, deciding that I was not worth the effort of a bark. I had my hat low over my eyes and my coat collar turned up against the wind. I could see the place was running to seed in a general way, with broken slates and rotten timbers in the barn walls. I reached the trough and swung down from the horse, letting him drink. I stood with my back to the house, fifty feet away. My senses were

stretched to breaking point and I had no idea what to do
next. I heard the door open and heard footsteps on the
rough boards around the house. I knew it was Gunhild.
My throat constricted and I turned slowly. She held a
shotgun loosely in her hands. She looked beautiful, the
wind blowing a few stray strands of hair across her face.
She hesitated a moment and then came closer.

'Who are you?' she asked, lifting the gun slightly. The
sound of her voice was as I remembered and suddenly I
couldn't speak.

I thought I said, 'It's me, my darling,' but it came out
in a croak.

I did not know what to expect. I had dreamed of this
moment too often. For it to be different from what I had
expected took me by surprise. Instead of running to me
and throwing her arms around me while I covered her in
kisses, she stood stock still, rooted to the ground. Slowly
her hands dropped and the shotgun fell to the earth. I took
a hesitant step forward and as I did she gave a low groan,
put her hand to her mouth, spun around and fled back
towards the house. I caught her at the door and grabbed
her arm. She turned back to me, tears streaming down
her cheeks, whispering my name over and over, clinging
tightly to me. For the second time in two days I felt my
own tears rising. I knew without doubt, not that there had
been many before that moment, that I loved her more than
anything in the world. Without her, life would become
meaningless.

I don't know how long we stood that way. I think
we were both afraid to let go, to come back to reality
and face the future. Perhaps we both knew, somehow,
there was not going to be one. I only know the feel
of her body against me, the touch of her lips on mine,
caused my dreams to fade into insignificance. Nothing
was important any more except now, right that instant,
which I wanted to go on forever.

She pushed away from me. I tried to pull her back, but

the interlude was gone, as fleeting as it had been intense. I looked down into her blue eyes, seeing the love there, and the despair, and the fear, and the words which she would say. Later, I thought about that moment so often, that I could have persuaded myself into believing anything.

'W . . . what . . . happened?' she asked hesitantly. 'Oh God, David, I can't believe it.' Fresh tears streamed down her face, her shoulders heaving, and she allowed me to pull her back to my shoulder. 'You look so different. You're nose,' she tentatively touched my slightly misshapen nose.

'It's a . . . a long story, my love. I've been living on a deserted island with . . . with a few people. We only got away a short while ago. I . . . I came as quickly as I could.'

We might have stayed there forever, incoherently trying to talk, if the baby had not started crying. Gunhild pushed me away and went inside and I followed. The room was spotlessly clean but shabby. A perverse pleasure seeped through me. If her life was so poor it would be easier to convince her to come away with me. I crossed the small room with its rickety looking table and chairs, to a door opposite. In the gloom of the darkened bedroom I could see the cot and the baby standing there, crying for her mother. A surge of love for them both welled up within me, as I watched Gunhild bend to lift her. In the light I could see there was no doubt she was a Griffiths, with her big beautiful blue eyes, black hair, pert nose and now a cheeky smile, a little hesitant, as I was a stranger to her. I said nothing, sitting at the table, watching Gunhild deftly change a wet diaper, a rag held in place by a safety pin. Gunhild lifted the baby to the floor and with a squeal of delight she crawled towards the open door. Gunhild rushed after her, picked her up and sat on a chair close to me.

'Sion told me what happened,' I said, my voice a croak. I cleared my throat and continued. 'I don't blame you for marrying but I do blame myself for going away. If only I hadn't been such a bloody fool this would never have happened.'

Gunhild gave a little smile. 'If only. Can you imagine how often I said those words? I was still saying them up to the second I said I do to the preacher. If only he would walk through that door, now . . . now . . . now. But it never happened. I hoped, I prayed you were still alive, but I suppose as the days passed the hoping and praying died a little more. Did Sion tell you I did not want to get married? I was so sure you were still alive. I was sure even after your family had given up hope. I felt . . . I felt I would have known somehow. I was sure I would feel it if you were dead. Oh,' she signed, 'I don't know. But my parents . . .' she let the sentence hang between us.

'I know, my love. But does it mean we have to live to regret it? This place is a hovel,' I said with disgust, at which she began to bridle. 'I'm sorry,' I added hastily, 'but I can see what it's like.'

She sank back onto her chair, her shoulders dejected. 'Let's go away, now,' I said earnestly. 'Get whatever you need and let's go. We won't go back to St Louis but down river to one of the stopping stages. We can catch a river boat and head for New Orleans. Once there the world is ours. We can go wherever you say.' I was speaking eagerly, trying to convince her with my enthusiasm and for a few seconds I was winning. Then the light died in her eyes.

She shook her head. 'It's a grand dream, David, but it won't work. I'm married, for better or for worse. The Catholic Church does not allow us to divorce to marry another man without very, very good reasons,' she said sadly.

'There's a good reason,' I said pointing at the baby. 'And anyway, sod the church. If they won't grant you a divorce we can go away and just live together . . .'

I floundered, when she recoiled from me. 'What's the matter?' I asked lamely.

'I . . . I can't do that. It's impossible. I will never do that. I have been forgiven by the mother church for the sin of being with child out of wedlock, I would never be forgiven if I did as you suggested.'

'Gunhild, I know you went to church regularly and all that, but you were never particularly religious. Why should you start now?'

Her words stunned me. 'I have received comfort and understanding during the blackness of the last months and I have grown to love the church in a way I would never have thought possible. It is the bright spot in my life. It is the,' she hesitated and then continued firmly, 'the single sustaining factor in my life which has helped me to retain my sanity. If not for the church and Father Christopher I would have killed myself . . . No, both of us,' she hugged the baby, 'a long time ago. I would have committed a mortal sin but . . . but he helped me over it. I . . . I owe him the salvation of my soul and to go with you now would be unthinkable.'

I could not believe it. Gunhild had never been like this. Religious yes, but not stupidly, fanatically so. I compared her to Estella. Gunhild had been brought up as a moderately religious person, while Estella had been brought up in the cloistered atmosphere of a Spanish family. Estella's stories came to mind. Yet both had gone in the opposite direction to the one I would have expected.

'Gunhild, you can't be serious,' I pleaded. 'I've thought of you every day we've been apart. I . . . I've dreamed of our life together so often that anything else is unbelievable . . . unthinkable. I need you as much as I love you, please.'

Her eyes softened and she put her hand on mine. 'I love you too, David,' she said quietly, 'and always will. Please believe that, but what you ask is impossible. What will she think,' Gunhild stroked the baby's black hair, 'when she's old enough to understand? She'll think me a . . . a harlot,' she choked over the word. 'To learn I am living in sin with a man, against the wishes of God and the church.'

'The church,' I said bitterly, 'has caused more strife and anguish than any other thing in the world. I stopped believing in God a long time ago, when I began to understand that. Look at history. The Spanish Inquisition and what was done in the name of the Pope. How can a man be in a position like that and then be claimed as a direct link to God?' I paused waiting for her reaction. Then when she just stood there looking at me I rattled on, desperately trying to break through her armour of religion. 'It's insane. Look at the men there have been who were Popes. All of those conniving thieves, preying on the ignorance and poverty of the masses and keeping them poor by demanding massive payments to the church. Go out and take a good look, Gunhild, and then tell me what these so called men of God have done for the people. I can't remember seeing a thin Pope,' my voice grew bitter. 'They're all fat, sleek, wine-sipping creeps. And we are a further example of the misery the church causes, you and I. Why shouldn't we get married by asking for a dispensation if that's what you want? All right, it's what I want too. It'll take a little time but we can do it.' The bitterness had left my voice and I was pleading once more. All she did was shake her head.

We sat in silence and I felt myself becoming angrier and angrier. This wasn't how it was supposed to be. The problem was not insurmountable. She loved me for Christ's sake, didn't that count?

'Please, my love,' I begged. 'Come away with me now.'

'I can't,' she whispered. 'Please understand.'

'Damn it,' I said bitterly, getting to my feet, the Griffiths' pride taking over, 'how can you throw away your life for an . . . an ideology that's . . . that's, what's the use?' I strode to the door and paused. 'If there's anything you need for the baby, anything at all, contact Sion or my mother. All right?' She nodded slowly. 'What's our baby's name?' I asked softly.

She looked at me for a few seconds, tears in her eyes, the baby sitting on her lap, looking puzzled and wonderingly at me. 'Susan . . . Susan Sian,' she said in a whisper.

I pulled the door open and glanced back. When I left I took away the picture of her sitting in that squalid room, at the table, her head bowed, her shoulders heaving, the baby with her arms tightly around her mother's neck.

Why didn't I stay longer? Why didn't I try harder? In years to come I was often going to ask that question. Now I was in a towering rage, hating the church and cursing God.

The horse was sweating when I reached home. I left it for Juan to see to, throwing him the reins as I jumped down and stalked into the house. My mind was made up. I had pleaded once, never again. If she wanted me she could come and get me, wherever I might be. I grabbed a bottle of whisky from the study and rushed upstairs, not wanting to speak to anybody. I had a lot to do if I was to catch the night train for New York.

I packed my best clothes in a portmanteau, threw in my gun and holster, and the gold I had brought with me. With a large drink in my hand I bathed and planned some more. I dressed with care in my black travelling suit, white shirt and necktie, and went down to say goodbye to Mam.

'David,' Mam said with a smile which quickly turned to a frown when she saw my face. 'What is it? . . . Oh, of course, Gunhild.'

I nodded miserably and wearily sat at the kitchen table and told her about my conversation.

'Oh, David, I'm so sorry. So terribly sorry.' She put her hand on my shoulder.

I looked up at her, Mam's eyes filled with tears. I knew at that moment that I couldn't leave just yet. Mam needed me to be around for a while. If I left then I would be punishing my family for something they hadn't done.

I stayed for nearly six weeks. Then one day I was in town getting a few things for Mam when I saw Gunhild standing next to a buggy with the baby in her arms. I went to walk across to her, to try again, when I saw an elderly man walk out of a nearby store and without a word climb into the buggy. Gunhild followed and with a flick of a whip the buggy moved down the street. I stood rooted to the spot, my heart leaden. Watching them vanish around a corner I made up my mind.

'I have to go,' I said to Mam, when I found her in the kitchen with Marie. 'She won't leave him because of her damned religion,' I said with renewed bitterness, 'so I can't stay. I'll let you know where I go and what I do. Where's Dad?' I asked, kissing her cheek and hugging her. She was trying hard not to cry. I was forever grateful she understood me well enough not to try and stop me.

'With Sion, in town,' she replied tonelessly.

'Thanks, Mam, and don't worry,' I managed a smile. 'I'll be all right. Jake's gone to Europe and I'll go and meet them in Spain, or somewhere. I'll be okay,' I repeated.

I packed my bag for a second time and took the buggy to town. I found Dad and Sion in what used to be Dad's office, going over some papers together.

I told them my decision and promised that I would write soon.

'Hang on, son,' said Dad. 'Don't you think you're being a bit hasty and overreacting a little? Give it a while longer. Gunhild may change her mind yet you know. You haven't been back with us long. Think of your mother for a moment, can't you?'

'I'm sorry, Dad, I really am. I know Gunhild won't change her mind. She's had weeks to think about it. She could have come to me at any time. I can't stay. I just can't. Sion, if she needs anything, let her have it, will you? I told her to see you or Mam if she wanted anything for the baby.' He nodded. 'And will you continue to look after my investment in the business? Do anything you like with my money.'

He hesitated a second and then nodded again. 'Why not wait until we're ready and then you go and see about the new businesses,' he offered.

I shook my head. 'Thanks, but no thanks. You're the brain behind them and you should run it. Can you give me a few thousand? Say three? It'll save me going to the bank and I assume we can afford it?'

'No problem,' said Sion, opening a safe and counting out the money from a large bundle. 'Is that enough?'

'Sure, thanks. I still have the gold I earned with Jake. I've got my naturalisation papers from the study, Dad. I'll get an American passport in New York. I've also got Uncle John's address which I might use,' though I doubt it, I thought. We shook hands and I left. I bought three bottles of whisky from a local store and went to the railway station. The train arrived on time, departed on time and a berth was available for me. The days dragged and the nights were hell and the whisky was finished by the morning of the second day. After that I paid the car attendant inflated prices to keep me drunk all the way to Grand Central, New York.

There I found a decent hotel and stayed sober long enough to arrange my passport. By coincidence, by the time my passport was ready, the first ship sailing for Europe would be calling at Cardiff. I arranged a first class berth. I had plenty of money and if I ever managed to spend it all I could always send for more. I did not go and see John Buchanan and two weeks after arriving in New York I was aboard the ship. Amid cheering and weeping crowds, paper streamers fluttering in the sharp, snow laden breeze, and the sound of the tugs whistles signalling to each other, we left the dock side. I did not see the event, I was too busy in the bar.

I ate in my cabin, drank in the bar and finished the process into a painless sort of oblivion in my bunk. It was usually in the early morning hours of four and five before I finally fell asleep, and the middle of the afternoon before I got up. I remained meticulous in the way I dressed and even went to the barber's for a haircut and beard trim.

It was late in the evening of the fourth day when it all changed. I was in the bar getting on a warm glow, the room beginning to sway a little, when the old man came in. He was bleary-eyed, scruffy-dressed, in need of a shave and when he stood next to me, stank like an old brewery. I was surprised he was in the first class lounge and even more surprised when the barman served him. He was skinny, about five feet six inches tall, with thinning grey hair and I guessed he was about sixty-five or seventy years old, but I didn't look too closely. The barman half filled a glass with brandy, the old man gripped it in both hands, smiled weakly at me and drained it. He thumped the glass back on the counter and received a second. Two of the waiters caught him as he passed out, a second after he replaced the empty glass on the counter. I watched them carry him carefully through the door.

'Who's he?' I asked the barman who was standing close by, wiping the counter with a towel.

'A rich bum,' he replied with a sneer. 'If he had been a poor bum we'd have thrown him out. He's worth a fortune. He's a year younger than me and all he can do is drink himself to death, the fool,' and with a curled lip of disgust he moved down the bar, to serve another customer.

The barman was short, fat and about fifty. The thought of the way the other man looked by comparison was a shock. I sat and looked at my glass of whisky, a special malt from Scotland. My thoughts were in a whirl but one thing was uppermost. I did not have it within me to drink myself into some sort of everlasting stupor because of a woman. I was young, reasonably well off, a trained lawyer and acting like a fool. I felt better as the thoughts took shape and I realised I had not even enjoyed my drinking bout. With that thought came another one; I was also hungry. It was time I had a meal in the restaurant.

They were still serving, in spite of the fact it was nearly 10.00 p.m. I found a quiet table in a corner of the ornate saloon. The white electric lights artfully surrounding the walls cast a subdued glow over the room. The cutlery gleamed like an array of surgeons' instruments before a delicate operation and the single red rose in the centre of each table completed the effect of richness. There were still twenty to thirty people dining, filling half the tables. I ordered a filet mignon with salad, a bottle of red Burgundy, and while I waited for the order I looked around to see if there were any interesting women. There were but they appeared attached to men.

I noticed one in particular. She had black hair, a pretty but hard face and was wearing a dress cut low enough to prove her breasts were better than adequate. She was sitting two tables away and when I looked she turned her head slightly and smiled. I smiled back.

Later, after I had finished my meal and we had exchanged numerous glances and small smiles, I lingered over my last glass of wine and wondered how to approach her. There were four people at her table, two men and a woman. I guessed the man on her left, with his back to me, was her husband from the way he kept patting her hand. He was running to fat, his hair thinning and greased down to hide a bald patch. I watched them leave and from the way he weaved he was obviously the worse for drink. The woman paused at the entrance, looked back at me and smiled once more. The invitation was unmistakable and I followed them into the bar.

While the other three threw gin down their necks the brunette drank soda water and I sat at the bar drinking coffee. The time dragged and I was thinking about going to bed, regretfully alone, when there was a commotion at the table where they were sitting. The man I thought was her husband had apparently passed out. A couple of waiters helped to carry him out while the others followed. The second man could barely stand and the brunette helped him along. She turned her head and smiled again. I waited, deciding to give her fifteen minutes. If she did nor reappear by then, I told myself, the whole thing had been with no promise at all. I need not have worried because she was back within ten minutes. She slid onto the stool alongside me and ordered a brandy and soda.

'I'm David Griffiths,' I said with a smile.

'Barbara Hunting,' she replied, giving my hand a firm, cool shake. She had wide apart, brown eyes, a pointed chin and thin lips.

We sat in silence for a few moments and then I said, 'Where's your husband?'

'Him,' she said with a curl of her lips. 'The pig has passed out as usual. And as usual I've put him to bed.' She looked steadily in my eyes. 'He won't wake up until morning.'

I nodded. 'Good. Cabin 8A. I'll leave now and you follow in a few minutes.' I did not wait for a reply but left the bar. I was not sure she would follow, but what the hell, I had nothing to lose. I had only just removed my coat and poured a whisky and water when the door opened and she came in. I handed her my drink and poured a second one. We touched glasses and exchanged smiles. I took a mouthful of my drink and stepped close enough to kiss her. She had a nice figure, though a little plump around the waist and backside, but warm and vibrant. Her dress was all frills, cut low on her shoulders. I pushed it lower and her breasts sprung free.

She helped me get her clothes off and then undressed me while we were still standing in the middle of the cabin. The night was one I remembered for a long time.

More nights were spent in a similar way until we reached Cork. There, she and her travelling companions were leaving the ship. I was only partly sorry to see her go. We had spoken very little, neither of us interested in the other in any way except sexually. I did learn her husband was a wealthy land owner in Ireland and that they were returning to their estates. I did not bother to ask where in Ireland and she did not bother to tell me.

On Friday morning at eight o'clock we arrived at Cardiff. I had been in a quandary about what to do when I got there and though I did not want to see any of the family I felt it would be churlish not to do so. Mam and Dad would never forgive me if they ever learnt I had been there and not visited everyone. Reluctantly I came to the conclusion I had to break my journey and stay at least a few days. As I disembarked I had a sudden impulse. Instead of going to Uncle David's shop in Rhiwbina I grabbed a cab at the customs shed and went to Cardiff Central Station. There I bought a first class ticket for Llanbeddas.

As the train pulled out I watched the city unfolding with interest, trying to remember what it had been like when we had left. It seemed to me that the grey squalor, the cramped houses, row after row of them, were unchanged. After America the first thing I noticed was the lack of space and the myriad of people. Even New York, by comparison, had seemed more open somehow.

The train travelled alongside the Taff, winding up the valley, stopping every few miles at small junctions with barely more than a few houses and a church nearby. The depressing air of the valley altered my mood and I began to regret the impulse that had brought me there. After all, what was I going back to see? An old house I had lived in years ago, an uncle and an aunt with whom we exchanged Christmas cards and occasional letters? There was little else apart from one thing. I changed trains in Pontypridd. My mind wandered back and I remembered incidents long forgotten in the excitement of being in America. I remembered the strike and the attack on the militia train. I thought of how we had come to know and love Uncle James but most of all that day intruded and I tried to keep it away. I played back every second of the other times, like when Grandma and Granddad died. I noticed there were no longer any gaps in the houses between the villages. Instead, the rows of houses were endless, boring, box after box of grey slated and grime covered walls.

I left my case at the station and trudged the familiar road towards Llanbeddas. God, how the memories continued washing over me. I passed the old house with hardly a glance and went up to the chapel.

I stood at the graveside and looked sadly at the headstone. Somebody was looking after it, as there were no weeds and a sprig of holly sat in an earthenware pot.

Sian
Dearly beloved
Daughter of
Evan and Megan Griffiths
Born 29th July 1882
Died tragically 14th October 1890
"Suffer the little children to come unto me."

The engraving was still legible. 'You'd have loved America,' I whispered. 'It was meant for you, little sister. You would have had a pony, and lots of boy friends, and gone on picnics like you always wanted to. I wonder what you would be today. Married? With children? Would you have gone to university? What would it have been like to have had a sister with us? I suppose Mam and Dad have often wondered. Especially Mam, now Sion and I have our own lives. Think how much of a friend you could have been to her,' I said sadly. The memories continued, mixed with make believe of what if . . . I heard footsteps coming along the path and looked up guiltily.

It took me a couple of seconds to recognise the old man as Lewis Lewis and I felt a little surprised that he was still alive. I had no wish to stop and talk to him, so I began to walk towards the gate, intending to pass him by. I could see the ruined building of the old school, now clear of sludge but with the roof collapsed and the walls a heap of rubble. I had tried not to think about it but now that day came back to me. The day it had all started for us. If it hadn't been for the terrible accident at the school our lives would have taken a different path entirely.

I stood and looked over the valley. My thoughts now a kaleidoscope of memories. I had noticed Lewis Lewis looking strangely at me but he said nothing and I didn't acknowledge him. As my eyes scanned from the turning gear at the mine, along the river, over the houses towards Pontypridd I realised that the past was a foreign country. Down the valley was the way out. The way of escape. I realised that I had changed not only in appearance but, more significantly, mentally. My horizons had been broadened to a world that few of the people here could comprehend. I felt superior, a greater being than those we had left behind. As I turned to go I looked back at Lewis Lewis. He was kneeling at Sian's grave, picking weeds, tidying it up and immediately I felt a burning sense of shame. I had no right to feel superior or even different. I turned back, a lump of contrition in my throat.

'Mr. Lewis. Sir. It's me . . . David . . . Dai Griffiths,' I walked towards him and he stood and brushed his knees.

'Dai, boy? It's you? Really you?'

I saw him through a blur of tears as I held my hand out to shake his.

At last, I felt a sense of fulfilment at my return.

Epilogue

The reporter surreptitiously wiped his eyes, the picture of David Griffiths at the cemetery alive and fresh in his mind. It had been two weeks but, my God, this was going to be a story and a half. Just then the door opened and the butler entered. 'The Prime Minister is waiting in the drawing room, Sir,' he told Sir David and then withdrew.

Sir David had nodded his thanks, also too emotional to reply for a few minutes. Finally, he cleared his throat and said, 'That was the beginning. You've seen some of the written evidence of it all in the safe,' he waved his hand at the open safe door. 'It began around the day a million tears were shed. It changed everything for all of us. It led us onto the world stage of events and for the last fifty years we have helped to shape the world. I thought it was important for you to know where we came from, how it is that my parents laid the foundations for the family which have guided us, or more specifically, have guided me, all these years. In 1912, thanks to my father, I began . . .,' Sir David stopped. 'No. That can wait.' He heaved himself up out of his chair. 'I mustn't keep the PM waiting any longer. Help yourself to a drink,' he waved his hand in the general direction of a cut glass decanter containing amber liquid, 'and I'll send Sian to entertain you.'

With that Sir David left the room while the young reporter poured himself a stiff malt whisky. He stood at the window and peered into the darkness; night had fallen early with a gathering of low dense clouds as snow was forecast. The door behind him opened and Sir David's granddaughter entered.

'What did you think of his story?' she asked, helping herself to a glass of whisky which she promptly drowned with lemonade and ice.

The reporter hadn't seen much of Sian during the past fortnight, the phrase 'ships that pass in the night' sprang to his mind. He pursed his lips in thought before answering. 'We've only just begun. I think we've reached about, em, 1910, when the old boy returned to Wales.'

Sian nodded. 'I persuaded Gramps that it was time to tell the story properly. After all, there have been loads and loads of rumours over the years and none of them have even come close to the real story. When you think what it was like back then – all that the family had to go through to get us here today – it makes you wonder.' She broke off, tilted her head to one side and looked penetratingly at him. 'Are you going to write the story?'

'Yes, of course. I've decided to call the first book *A Million Tears*. The second book hasn't been named yet,' he suddenly smiled at her. 'Can I take you out to dinner?'

She nodded.

The second book in the series about the Griffiths family is called *The Tears of War and Peace* and is available from Good Read Publishing Limited.

The Tears of War and Peace

by Paul Henke

It is 1911 and David Griffiths is in Wales, bored and lonely. He travels to London at the behest of their family friend, John Buchanan, to start a new business in banking. There he gets caught up in the suffragette movement and falls in love with Emily. Against the backdrop of women's fight for votes and the looming First World War, the Griffiths build a vast, sprawling company encompassing banking, aircraft manufacturing, farming and whisky distilling.

The enmity of a German family follows them tragically throughout this period, leading to murder and revenge. At the end of the war, thanks to a change in the Constitution, Evan is invited to run for President of the United States. The family rally round for the most important battle of Evan's life.

With the Brown-shirts running rampage across Germany, David and Sion are soon involved in a battle for survival.

Sir David Griffiths is a colossus of a figure, striding across the world and through the century, a man of integrity and bravery, passion and dedication. Determined to win, nothing comes before the family.

The story is as compelling as ever. Historical fact woven into the fictional characters makes a breathtaking tale of adventure you will not want to put down.

ISBN 1-902483-03-0

Silent Tears

by Paul Henke

Silent Tears is full of passion and adventure. You will be captivated as three generations of the Griffiths family struggle to meet the challenges of their time.

From the depths of the depression and the rise of fascism to the abdication of Edward VIII and the Spanish Civil War, Henke's meticulous research brings the period and vibrant characters to life.

David, powerful and dynamic, at the centre of political intrigue, his love for the family is put to the ultimate test . . . Meg, his mother, stalwart and determined, guides the family with humour and devotion . . . and Susan, beautiful and tempestuous, fighting for justice. No sacrifice is too great for those she loves.

Packed with excitement, Silent Tears is a masterpiece. A novel that vibrates with sheer narrative power and relentlessly builds the emotional pressure until it explodes in a firestorm of passion and high-octane adventure. A spellbinding epic.

ISBN 1-902483-05-7

Débâcle

TIFAT File I

A Nick Hunter Adventure

Following a summit meeting in Paris an alliance of interested countries form an elite fighting force to combat terrorism throughout the world. Based in Britain and under the command of a British General, the team is made up of Western, Russian and other non-aligned countries' special forces.

Without warning the terrorists strike. A group of bankers, politicians and industrialists are taken prisoner off the coast of Scotland and the new, untried force is sent to search for them.

The Scene of Action Commander is Nick Hunter, Lieutenant Commander, Royal Navy, an underwater mine and bomb clearance expert with experience in clandestine operations.

The enemy is one of the world's most ruthless and wanted terrorists – Aziz Habib! Hunter leads the team against Habib, backed up by two computer experts: Sarah from GCHQ and Isobel, hired by the General to run the IT for the new force.

While stock markets take a pounding and exchange rates go mad, the state sponsoring the terrorism is making a fortune. It has to stop. At all costs.

This is non-stop adventure from beginning to end. A riveting story told by a master story teller. You are guaranteed not to want to put it down!

Débâcle mixes fact with fiction which will cause you to wonder, how true is this story? Did it really happen?

ISBN 1-902483-01-4

Mayhem

TIFAT File II

A Nick Hunter Adventure

Israel faces imminent destruction, nuclear Armageddon. A series of kidnaps, bombings and senseless murders have left her isolated from her allies and threatened by enemies of old. Unknown to all but a few, the situation has been orchestrated by multi-millionaire Zionist, Samuel Dayan. His vision of a Greater Israel will be carved from the charred ruins of the Middle East.

But Dayan is up against the international anti-terrorist organisation, TIFAT, and our hero Nick Hunter. To the age-old struggle of Good against Evil, author Paul Henke adds state-of-the-art communications technology and computerised warfare. In a desperate race against time, Hunter and his team of hand-picked specialists deploy satellite intelligence and high-tech weaponry to track Dayan to his lair.

The plot twists and turns in a series of setbacks, betrayals and mind-blowing developments. Myriad minor characters deserve story-lines of their own.

Relentlessly building the tension, Henke strips his hero Hunter of all resources but those within himself – knowledge born of experience and the inability to give up. Hunter simply must not fail.

ISBN 1-902483-02-2

Chaos

TIFAT File III

A Nick Hunter Adventure

Ambitious Alleysia Raduyev has inherited the family business – the largest crime cartel in Georgia. Operating on the classic theory of supply and demand, she caters for her customers every desire – narcotics, arms, prostitution, forced labour. Her payroll has extended to include lawmakers and law enforcers. No one is safe from her tyranny and oppression.

Power base secured, Alleysia moves on to her next objective – the formation of a super crime cartel, whose actions will result in global chaos. As a deterrent to those who would oppose her, she chooses the ultimate weapon – three nuclear warheads.

Desperate to prevent a new, anarchic world order, the West declares World war III against the cartels and their terror organisations. As violence escalates, the now battle-hardened troops of TIFAT are pitched against their toughest adversary yet.

Spearheading the battle is Lt. Cdr. Nick Hunter, the fearless explosives and diving specialist seconded to The International Force Against Terrorism.

The latest TIFAT novel is a clarion call to the Western world as it comes to grips with the realities of modern terrorism.

ISBN 1-902483-04-9

The Tears of War and Peace

'Henke isn't just talented, but versatile too. His books are very convincing. As good as Stephen King, Wilbur Smith, Tom Clancy and Bernard Cornwell.'

Burton Mail

'Read them and weep.'   *The Stirling Observer*

'He's one of the best new writers we've had in ten years.'   *The Burton Trader*

'A family saga with non-stop adventure from beginning to end.'   Tony Cowell, *PressGroup UK*

Débâcle

Mayhem

'A non-stop action adventure set in Scotland and the Middle East.'   *The Edinburgh Evening News*

'A fast moving tale of terror and destruction set amidst the charred ruins of the Middle East. An international force exists to fight terrorism. Terrific realism.'

The Stirling Observer

'The hero, Nick Hunter, embarks on a non-stop roller-coaster adventure from the Scottish Highlands to the Middle East. Henke is being hailed as the next Wilbur Smith.'   *The Aberdeen Press and Journal*

'Mayhem is a classic airport thriller. It's a veritable page turner and a cracking read.'

The Milngavie & Bearsden Herald

'A cracking good yarn. Non-stop action from beginning to end.'   *Central FM radio*

'Fiction becomes fact in Paul Henke's action thrillers. A superb read.'   *The Northern Echo*